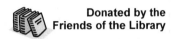

Bard's Oath

Tor Books by Joanne Bertin

The Last Dragonlord
Dragon and Phoenix
Bard's Oath

Bard's Oath

Joanne Bertin

TOR®

A Tom Doherty Associates Book / New York

This is a work of fiction. All of the characters, organizations, and events portrayed in this novel are either products of the author's imagination or are used fictitiously.

BARD'S OATH

Edited by James Frenkel

A Tor Book
Published by Tom Doherty Associates, LLC
175 Fifth Avenue
New York, NY 10010

www.tor-forge.com

Tor® is a registered trademark of Tom Doherty Associates, LLC.

ISBN 978-0-312-87370-7 (hardcover)
ISBN 978-1-4668-0115-8 (e-book)

First Edition: November 2012

Printed in the United States of America

0 9 8 7 6 5 4 3 2 1

For
Matthew Logan
Our own private miracle
Without whom this book would have been finished a lot sooner
but not nearly as joyfully

and to

Sam
Daddy par excellence

Acknowledgments

I would like to thank my editor, Jim Frenkel, for believing in this book and waiting for it. Also, thanks to Tom Doherty, whose vision makes Tor Books the great publishing company it is; my thanks also to Art Director Irene Gallo, who brought Bob Eggleton's beautiful jacket art to my books; and thanks to the many other people at Tor in editorial, production, publicity, advertising and promotion, sales and marketing, who work together to produce and sell my own and so many other wonderful books.

Bard's Oath

The Story So Far

Dragonlord Maurynna Kyrissaean, the youngest of the great weredragons, cannot Change from human to dragon at will. Such a thing has never happened before and the Lady of Dragonskeep wants to keep Maurynna close to ensure her safety.

But Maurynna's childhood friend Raven Redhawkson journeys to Dragonskeep, bringing with him one Taren Olmeins, an escaped slave from the mysterious, isolated kingdom of Jehanglan far to the south. Years before, Taren had been on a northern ship that had dared the forbidden waters of Jehanglan and sunk. Taren had somehow survived the wreck and was taken prisoner. After years as a slave, he escaped to bring the Dragonlords news he had discovered.

The tale that the former slave brings to Dragonskeep horrifies everyone: a dragon is kept prisoner in Jehanglan, its magic used to confine a Phoenix and keep it from its pyre. The Phoenix's magic keeps Jehanglan separate from the rest of the world. No one save one trading House in the island country of Assantik to the north of Jehanglan may enter or leave Jehanglan save by a secret sea route protected by magic.

But the prisoner, whether Dragonlord or truedragon, must be rescued. The truedragons, led by the ancient and powerful Morlen the Seer, fly to Jehanglan in an attempt to free the draconic prisoner. Their invasion fails and many die.

Now it is left to the Dragonlords to free the prisoner if they can. Dragonlord Lleld Kemberaene, nicknamed Lady Mayhem by her fellow weredragons, digs into the archives at Dragonskeep. She discovers that among the few things the Jehangli allow into their kingdom are troupes of entertainers whose memories are magically wiped before they are allowed to return to their home countries.

Before she was a Dragonlord, Lleld had been a performer in a troupe of acrobats. Despite the Lady of Dragonskeep's misgivings, Lleld devises a plan: Some of the Dragonlords will form a troupe of entertainers. And although the Lady would like to forbid it, Maurynna must be one of the Dragonlords. As a result of her inability to Change, no Dragonlord or truedragon can sense her. Only she can approach the mountain where the dragon is held prisoner without alerting the Jehangli priests.

It is decided that the members of the troupe will be Maurynna and her soul-twin Linden Rathan; Lleld and her soultwin Jekkanadar Surael; Raven and his great-uncle Otter Heronson, a bard; and Taren Olmeins, who will guide them.

According to old accounts Lleld has found, the Jehangli hold horses in high esteem. Raven comes up with the idea to use Llysanyins, a magic-touched breed of very long-lived, highly intelligent horses, as part of the show. But they need more than the four Llysanyins that are bonded to the Dragonlords themselves. All save Taren Olmeins visit the herd; Lleld asks if two would be willing to accept the truehumans Otter and Raven. As Llysanyins bond with their riders and live much longer than truehumans, that asked the intelligent animals to face heartbreak when their truehuman riders die.

At first, the herd turns away. Then two Llysanyins come forth, a grandmother and grandson. The elder, named Nightsong by Otter, agrees to carry the bard. Her grandson chooses Raven and is given the name Stormwind. Nightsong bullies two more of her offspring into joining as part of the troupe. Taren, claiming he is unworthy of the honor of riding a Llysanyin, is given an ordinary horse.

The company journeys first to Casna, a city in the realm of Cassori. They stay a few days with Maurynna's Cassorin aunt, uncle, and cousins. At the Dragonlords' request, the regent of Cassori gives them a ship and crew to take them to Thalnia, the island nation where both Maurynna and Raven grew up.

Once there, they spend the winter in a secluded estate belonging to Maurynna's family, to devise a show and rehearse. The high point is to be a performance by the Llysanyins.

When spring comes, the company sails to Jehanglan. Taren warns the Dragonlords not to use any of their magic, not even to mindspeak, because doing so might enable the priestmages of the Phoenix to detect their magic and hunt them down.

Maurynna and Raven are to split off from the others to free the captive dragon from his prison. The plan is hardly to the liking of Linden, Maurynna's soultwin, but it is feared that to do otherwise would risk that the priestmages might "feel" Linden's Dragonlord magic and the quest would fail.

But unknown to the Dragonlords, Taren is leading them into a trap. He is not an escaped slave, but instead is the trusted servant of a Jehangli noble who wants the Phoenix throne for himself. A prophecy made in Jehanglan promises the throne to the one who fulfills it:

One alone—the Hidden One—means the end of the Phoenix. But four will give you the throne.

The Dragonlords and their friends travel through Jehanglan unaware of their danger. But there is one trailing them, someone only Maurynna senses, though she has no idea who or what it is. That someone is a dragon-child named Miune Kihn, a waterdragon, a breed unknown in the north, and the only one of his kind left in the world. When Miune realizes Taren is bringing soldiers to capture them, he warns the Dragonlords and their friends. They break free and as planned, the group splits: Maurynna and Raven depart on their mission, and the others head in a different direction to draw pursuit away.

Linden, Lleld, Jekkanadar, and Otter are taken prisoner by a band of Zharmatians, one of the tribes the Jehangli consider barbarians, and their bitter enemies.

When some soldiers pursue Maurynna and Raven across a river, Miune Kihn comes to their rescue, attacking the soldiers' horses from below. Maurynna and Raven travel for days to reach their goal. They ride hard and the journey is exhausting, especially for Maurynna who is still an indifferent rider.

During a break in riding, Maurynna goes down to a river to bathe, and she meets Miune Kihn for the first time. Kyrissaean, Maurynna's dragon half who should be sleeping for many years yet, resents her human half's speech with the young waterdragon. But when Miune mentally "thumps" her dragon half, Maurynna realizes what has been going on within her divided self: Kyrissaean, only a dragon-child herself, had been awakened too early and was throwing tantrums. At Miune Kihn's urging, Kyrissaean subsides—somewhat.

Later in their journey, Maurynna and Raven meet a young man, a Tah'nehsieh tribesman named Shima, who in turn is the spirit drummer to a shaman named Zhantse. Shima brings them to his home where, to Maurynna and Raven's astonishment, they find his mother, Lark, is a Yerrin who had been shipwrecked on the Jehangli shore years before.

There Maurynna learns of Taren Olmeins's true identity: a kinslayer under a death sentence who had tricked the captain of the ship Lark was on into taking him on board. Lark blames Taren for the madness that came upon the captain and caused him to dare the enchanted waters around Jehanglan. Of all on board that ill-fated ship, only Lark and Taren lived. She is certain that the gods punished the crew for unknowingly aiding a kinslayer.

Because Raven's strawberry blond hair would stand out in a country filled with dark-haired people, it is decided that Shima will go with the black-haired Maurynna for the final stage of her journey. Raven is not happy with this. When he tries to follow, Lark confronts him. She appeals to Raven's Llysanyin, Stormwind, telling him of Zhantse's Seeing that the mission will fail if he goes. Stormwind refuses to go any farther.

But Raven is not balked for very long. With the connivance of Shima's little brother, Tefira, and a fake "Seeing" that they made up, Raven and Tefira convince Stormwind that they need to follow Maurynna and Shima. What neither realizes is that Tefira's Seeing is indeed the truth: They are needed to save the youngest Dragonlord.

By now Maurynna and Shima have figured out what dragon is the prisoner:

Pirakos, a truedragon. Maurynna and Shima reach the place where he is held underground. Maurynna is armed with the sword of the dead Dragonlord Dharm Varleran who had accompanied Pirakos on their ill-fated expedition to Jehanglan. They sneak into the tunnels that lead to the chained Pirakos.

It's only when Maurynna's conjured ball of coldfire disappears that she discovers that Shima has recently suffered from intense attacks of claustrophobia. They find a place in the tunnel system with an opening to the outside and rest there. To their horror, they see Raven and Tefira are prisoners of a Jehangli patrol. Maurynna orders Shima to go help them; she'll continue alone.

Though his senses seem to be going mad, Shima tricks the patrol and rolls a rock down upon them, killing most of the soldiers and allowing Raven and Tefira to escape. Shima runs in one direction, leading the remaining soldiers away. Raven and Tefira go in another direction.

Tefira guesses where his brother is going and leads Raven there. They watch from one ridge as Shima comes over another. Shima falls and rolls down the slope into the "bowl" formed by the ridges. He takes shelter in a small cave as the patrol chasing him clears the ridge.

Just when Shima thinks he's safe, his claustrophobia drives him into the open. His senses reeling, Shima fears he's gone mad, because he feels as if he is melting. The last thing he sees is one of the patrol readying to cast a spear at him.

Only Raven understands what is happening: Shima is Changing. Knowing that if the iron spearhead should touch the red mist forming around Shima, the young Tah'nehsieh will be unmade, Raven throws a rock at the spearman. His aim is true, and Shima, unharmed, safely Changes into a dragon.

Meanwhile, Maurynna goes deeper and deeper into the tunnels to Pirakos. Driven mad by his long confinement, he tries to kill her when she arrives. Using the dead Dragonlord's sword, she weakens each of the chains binding Pirakos's feet. She flees into the tunnels, knowing she has little time before he breaks free. With the insane dragon in pursuit, she runs through the tunnels.

Just as Pirakos corners her, the massive doors leading to the outside open for a procession of Jehangli priests. Distracted by the first touch of fresh air he's felt in centuries, Pirakos forgets Maurynna long enough for her to beg her dragon half to allow her to Change. When Pirakos turns his attention back to her, he finds a dragon. Their battle is brief; the longing for freedom is too much for Pirakos. He runs for the open air, Maurynna right behind him. Both burst into the sunlight. Unexpectedly, Pirakos turns and flies away. Maurynna and Shima, both still in dragon-form, follow as best they can.

Meanwhile, Linden, Lleld, Jekkanadar, and Otter have remained with the Zharmatians. An unknown dragon, Miune Kihn, again mindcalls them and tells them they must destroy the three stones that anchor the circle of enchantment that holds the Phoenix captive. So they Change. Each chooses a point of attack;

Linden, as the fastest and strongest flier, makes for the city where the Phoenix is held after accomplishing his mission.

When the magical shield holding the Phoenix falls, Linden does his best to keep the furious creature from taking revenge upon the humans who kept it imprisoned. But Linden is no match for the Phoenix; only the arrival of Pirakos stops the unequal battle before its inevitable, tragic end.

Pirakos and the Phoenix, each consumed by hatred for the other, close in battle. It ends with both falling to the ground, locked in a fatal embrace.

Yet out of the fiery ending comes a newly risen Phoenix. But this one is not the unthinking animal of previous incarnations. As the new Phoenix rises, it becomes clear that this one is a melding of phoenix and dragon.

Once the young Phoenix is safely away from the city, Linden, Maurynna, and Shima make their way to Shima's home, a part of Jehanglan held by Shima's tribe: Nisayeh, land of the Tah'nehsieh. There they meet again with Otter, Lleld, and Jekkanadar.

Soon it will be time for all to return to the north with the newest Dragonlord, Shima Ilyathan.

Prologue

Raven and Beast Healer Gunnis rode easily on their way to the Beast Healers' chapterhouse of Grey Holt, close to both the Yerrin town of Fern Crossing and the border with Kelneth. The sun shone high overhead in a cloudless sky. In another candlemark, it would begin its journey to the west; but for now it was high enough that it didn't shine in their eyes. And by the time Raven came back this way, it would be behind him. What could be better?

Oh, yes; a good day, this, Raven thought with contentment. The haggling was done with; Gunnis had confirmed all the horses they'd bought were healthy and fit for the journey north. And his aunt Yarrow was well-nigh walking on air, she was so pleased with her new band of broodmares. All that was left now was to get some liniment from Grey Holt's store of medicines to replenish their supply. For the morrow would see them on their way back to Yarrow's holding with their fine new mares.

Raven patted his Llysanyin's neck. Even now he sometimes still couldn't believe that one of the legendary mounts of the Dragonlords had chosen to share his life with him, an ordinary truehuman. Yet Stormwind had.

"I feel bad for Lord Sansy that he had to sell those mares," he said. "But his bad luck at gambling is our good fortune—that and Reed Thornson buying five palfreys from my aunt at just the right time. Those mares of Sansy's are some of the best I've ever seen."

Gunnis nodded. "They're fine animals. It's a pity, really. Rade Welkin, the old Lord Sansy, worked hard to build that herd. And now his son Agon sells the best part of it for a fraction of what it's worth. Agon started out years ago with everything his father had left him—it was a good bit, too!—and let it dribble away from him. All because he can't stay away from the dice."

Gunnis sighed, staring down at his horse's mane as if he saw something else there. The long-legged, shaggy hound that was his familiar—or brother-in-fur, as the Yerrins called the animals that shared a Beast Healer's life—looked up at him as it loped alongside his horse and whined softly. A meadowlark's song drifted sweetly on the warm air.

"Don't worry, Bouncer. It's nothing we can help, old fellow." The Beast Healer shook his head and went on, "I wonder if it would have been different if title and manor had gone to one of the children from the first marriage."

"A younger son inherited? The others all died?" Raven asked. Gods, but that house was plagued by ill luck, he thought.

"No, not all died—one went for a bard. The others were still alive then, you see."

"And a bard can't inherit a title." Raven remembered his great-uncle Otter telling him that when he was young. At the time, Raven hadn't thought it was fair. But his great-uncle had reminded him that a bard had to be neutral, it was part of the oath they took—and you couldn't be neutral if you were tied to a manor or farm or whatever. It made sense to him now.

"Just so. Old Rade married again—he had to or the title would've gone to a cousin he detested. He married a girl from the weaver hall he founded in one of the villages on his lands. Everyone thought him a foolish, besotted old man whose head was turned by a beautiful girl."

The Beast Healer fell silent. Raven waited, wondering if there was more.

After a time, Gunnis went on, "Agon and his sister, Romissa, were the children of Rade's old age. One of the older servants once told me that the old man was fair tickled that he sired a son and daughter so late in life. He doted on them, the boy in particular. Then something happened, I don't know what, and he threatened to disown them. But he died before he could do so. Perhaps this is how Agon is repaying him for trying to cast him and his sister aside. His father must be weeping in his grave over those horses." Gunnis shook his head. "Sad—very sad."

A pall settled over Raven's good mood, but lifted at the Beast Healer's next words.

"Still, I think he'd rather the horses be with someone who'll treasure them as I know your aunt will. Some things are worth more than gold," Gunnis said.

"Don't worry—my aunt already treasures them above the Hoard of Lanresh," Raven said, naming a greedy, long-ago Kelnethi king whose lost treasure hoard was the stuff of legend.

"I know. That will ease the old man's heart wherever he is in the Summerlands. That, and knowing they'll be bred to this fellow," Gunnis said, tilting his head at Stormwind. "The old lord probably would've sold every one of his own offspring for such a chance!" he finished with a chuckle.

Stormwind tossed his head, sending his heavy grey mane flying. He arched his neck and pranced. Bouncer barked gaily at him, wagging his tail.

Raven laughed at the dog. "So tell me—are there any Beast Healers with horses for brothers-in-fur?" he asked, imagining a Llysanyin as one. That's what he'd have wanted if he'd been a Beast Healer. "I've only seen a dog or a cat as a familiar."

"Oh, yes, there are a few. There are also various birds, rabbits, ferrets, a fox or two—all kinds of animals. At my chapterhouse there's even a girl with a woods dog—what you northern Yerrins call a *ghulon*—for her brother-in-fur."

Raven gaped at him. A *ghulon*? The shy, badgerlike creatures were known for their fierce tempers and incredible strength; even a bear would think twice, thrice, and many times more before stealing a *ghulon*'s meal. "Good gods!"

"That," replied Gunnis dryly, "was what a number of us said, too. When it wasn't something much worse, that is. Come to think of it, it was your friend, Dragonlord Linden Rathan, and one of our Beast Healers, Conor, that gave her the name Pod—"

He broke off at the sight that greeted them as they rounded a bend. A fair distance down the road a group of riders circled two small figures huddled in the dust. Raven could hear faint weeping. Now and again one of the riders would dart in and turn aside just short of riding down the youngsters. Jeers greeted each terrified shriek.

Raven's first thought was bandits toying with their victims; he half-drew his sword. Then he saw that they were too well dressed and well mounted. Young nobles bored and looking for amusement at someone else's expense, the sods.

"Bloody little—" Raven snarled in frustration as he slammed his sword back into its sheath. If only they'd been bandits. . . .

"That's Teasel and Speedwell!" Gunnis gasped. "Reed's fosterlings!"

Even as he spoke, a gap opened in the circle. Teasel grabbed her little brother's hand, hauled him to his feet, and dashed toward the opening and safety in the gorse bushes beyond the edge of the road.

But a scarlet-and-blue-clad rider was suddenly before them, cutting them off. One booted foot kicked out and Teasel fell to the ground on top of her brother.

With a scream of rage the Llysanyin broke into a run even before Raven's signal. As they raced down the road, Raven shouted at the attackers. He heard a yelling Gunnis following as fast as his horse could run. But no ordinary horse could keep up with a Llysanyin; the Beast Healer and his baying familiar were soon left behind.

But it seemed the attackers had heard Bouncer. The one who had knocked Teasel down reined his horse around in a tight circle and called to his friends. They lined up across the road, facing the oncoming Raven.

"Such a hero, plowboy!" the scarlet-and-blue-clad man called mockingly through cupped hands. "Are you going to spank us?"

But well before he reached them, one of the men pointed past Raven and cried out. The line broke and they raced off, heading for the crossroads and the road south that led to Kelneth.

Of course; they'd seen the Beast Healer's tunic of brown and green. No, they wouldn't want a witness such as Gunnis testifying against them, the cowards.

Swearing in frustration, Raven pulled Stormwind to a stop by the two children. "Are you hurt?" he asked as he jumped down from the saddle. "Let me see."

Teasel, a thin trickle of blood running down her cheek, shook her head. "Never mind! Get them! Get them before they get into Kelneth!"

Gunnis rode up. "That was Lord Tirael, wasn't it?" he asked in the tired voice of one who already knew the answer.

"It was," Speedwell sniffled as Bouncer nosed him, whining anxiously. "He's a rotter, he is."

Raven turned to Gunnis. "You know him?"

"Unfortunately, yes. Tirael Barans, son of Lord Portis of Cassori and a cousin of Lord Lenslee from just over the border. And he is, as young Speedwell says, a rotter," said Gunnis as he dismounted. "As are his friends."

"They scared off our ponies," Speedwell added as if this was the ultimate proof of villainy.

Raven thought Gunnis was about to say more, but with a look at the shaken children, the Beast Healer pressed his lips together. He knelt in the dusty road before Teasel.

"This," he scolded as he examined the thin cut on Teasel's face, "is what happens when you give your tutors the slip and go riding by yourselves."

"Yes, sir," they said with downcast eyes; Speedwell asked, "How did you know?"

"Hmph!" was the Beast Healer's only answer. He opened his scrip of medicines. Taking a clean cloth and a small flask of herbal wash, he bathed Teasel's cheek. She grimaced against the sting but held still.

When he was done tending to the children, Raven beckoned him aside. "Will Reed seek justice, do you think? I got a fairly good look at most of them. I think I'd be able to recognize them if they were brought before the Shire Mote."

Gunnis shook his head. "They'll be long over the border before anything can be done—they're all Kelnethi or Cassorin. Reed may be the shire reeve but his arm doesn't stretch beyond Yerrih's border.

"Yet if that bunch have half the wits of a sausage amongst the lot of 'em, they'll find somewhere else to play their foul little games for a good long while. Reed won't forget—or forgive—this."

Raven rubbed the back of his neck. "Hmm, yes. Reed has a long memory. But even he can't keep up that kind of watch forever."

"And in time the outrage will fade like Teasel's bruises because it was no worse than that," Gunnis said with a heavy sigh. "Thank the gods," he hastened to add.

Raven didn't want to think about what might have happened if he and Gunnis hadn't come along. "So they've done something like this before?"

"Gods, yes! And worse. How do you think I know so much about them? A bunch of bullies—and pretty Lord Tirael is the worst of 'em all."

And nothing could be done about it. That rankled. Raven caught up Stormwind's reins. "I'll go round up the ponies."

He stood a moment before mounting, looking down the road, remembering the blood trickling down Teasel's cheek. *Done this before, have you? May I be there the day this all catches up with you.* Then he swung back into the saddle and set off pony hunting.

Dunric of Appington urged his horse up alongside Tirael's. "Do you think there'll be trouble over this, Tir?"

"From who?" Tirael scoffed, brushing the hair back from his brow. "Who'd take the word of two brats against ours?"

"What about the Beast Healer? Think he got a good enough look at us?" Dunric persisted uneasily.

Tirael shook his head. "I doubt it; I think that Ulris saw him in time. Besides, the plowboy was between him and us. Stop worrying, Dun."

Dunric tugged at his ear, frowning. "The plow—? Oh, him. Why do you say he was a plowboy? I don't think that horse was—"

"Oh dear gods! Can't you tell a plow horse when you see one, you ignorant oaf? Didn't you see the feathers on its legs? That was just a Shamreen draft horse some fool was riding." Tirael laughed in derision, then drawled, "If you're going to be a nervous granny, Dunric, go somewhere else so you don't bore me."

Dunric fell back, feeling his face burn. "Still," he muttered under his breath, "that 'plow horse' was *damned* fast."

One

The Dragonlords came to the inn after a miserable day of riding in the rain. Water pooled among the cobblestones of the yard between inn and stable; the earth was so sodden it had nowhere to go.

Linden swung down from Shan and stepped right into a puddle. Brown water lapped over his boot toes. He sighed in resignation; it wasn't as if his boots—and Maurynna's and Shima's—weren't already soaked through, but still . . . He heard Maurynna's disgusted "Feh!" and knew she'd done the same.

"Gods, but I'm sick of this rain," she said. "If we don't dry out soon, we're going to turn into fishes."

Shima pushed back the hood of his cloak a little. "I don't think I've seen as much rain in my entire life as we've had in the last tenday. I'm glad we're stopping so early in the day." He looked up at the leaden sky and grimaced. "If this keeps up, I'm going back to my desert in Nisayeh!"

Even the Llysanyins looked disgusted as the little party waited for the grooms. The three stallions stood morosely, water dripping from the ends of their noses.

"Hopefully it will end in the next day or so and we can wait out the rain here," Linden said, eyeing the inn.

It was a large one, and—to him—new, being only about fifty years or so old. Though he'd never had occasion to travel this particular route since the first timbers had gone up for the Gyrfalcon's Nest, other Dragonlords had. "Damned fine ale," Brock Hatussin, another Yerrin like Linden, had reported. "Even better wine and cider. Good food and plenty of it. And best of all, not only are the beds clean, they're long enough for a Yerrin or a Thalnian."

For which I will thank the gods, Linden thought. Both he and Maurynna were fed up. The last few inns where they'd stopped, they'd had to sleep curled up like hedgehogs to keep their feet from hanging over the ends of the beds.

Thinking that the grooms might not have realized that more travelers had arrived, he led the way toward the stable. "I'd really like to get inside and dry out as quickly as possible," he said to his Llysanyin, Shan. "Will you go with the grooms when they come? Brock said that they know their business."

Shan snapped at a raindrop. Linden knew the stallion was as annoyed as he was with the turn the weather had taken a tenday ago. Before that, their journey from the College of Healers' Gift in Pelnar had been pure pleasure. Up in the crispness of dawn, a leisurely ride in the morning coolness, then a long midday halt to avoid the worst of the summer heat, followed by another easy ride and a stop at an inn or a night spent under the stars: a traveler's delight. Everyone had enjoyed it—until the cursed rain started.

As they neared the stable door, it opened and a man bustled out, followed by two smaller figures so swaddled in their cloaks it was impossible to tell their age or sex.

"Sorry, m'lords and lady," the man said cheerfully, peering nearsightedly at them through the curtain of rain. "But a large party arrived a bit ahead of you and we've just finished with their animals. Luckily we've enough room left for your horses." He beamed at each of them in turn.

One potential disaster averted, thank the gods; Linden knew if Shan had to spend another night outdoors, he'd make sure Linden would be in for a bad time the next morning. He tossed the reins to the nearest groom. "Behave yourself," he whispered to Shan.

Shan slapped him with his tail as he passed, then danced out of reach and calmly followed the groom. Boreal and Je'nihahn snorted in amusement as they followed.

"One of these days," Linden muttered as he turned toward the inn. "One of these days . . ."

"Let's get inside and dry off," Maurynna said. "Then I want something hot to eat and drink. I'm starving and I swear the wet has gotten into my bones. Heat spells just aren't enough anymore."

"I just hope this town we're going to is worth it," Shima grumbled.

"Hmm—I'm not so certain the *town* is worth it, but the horse fair certainly is," Linden said.

"Isn't that where the fair is?"

"No. It's close to it, though. There's the Balyaranna Fair outside the royal town of Balyaranna, where Balyaranna Castle sits. The grounds that the fair is held on belong to Lord Sevrynel and are part of his holding, the Honor of Rockfall."

"So why isn't this the Rockfall Fair?" Shima wanted to know.

"Because it takes its name from Balyaranna Spring in the Honor of Rockfall," Linden said with a grin.

Shima threw his hands up in mock exasperation as they turned the corner to the front of the timbered building. Linden pushed open the heavy oaken door.

A swell of warmth and rich, savory aromas washed over them as they paused on the threshold. Linden's stomach growled in anticipation. Stepping inside, his first impression was of wall-to-wall people and a constellation's worth of rushlights. Maurynna and Shima followed, the latter turning to close the door behind them.

Linden took a few steps into the common room and pushed back the hood of his cloak, as did Maurynna. He surveyed the scene before them.

There weren't quite as many people as he'd first thought, but the inn was certainly crowded; there was barely room to turn around. Many looked to be merchants, dressed well but not richly. They sat with their heads close together in conversation. Their clerks sat nearby, some jotting figures on tally boards, most playing dice or other games, a few looking bored unto death. One and all, the well-to-do merchants and their assistants ignored their lesser brethren, the peddlers, as the latter moved among the other patrons.

These were peasants dressed in homespun. Some of them sat in a corner with a peddler as they pored over wares spread upon a cloth on the floor. There was even a red-and-yellow-clad minstrel at one table, listening intently to two men and a woman dressed in hunting leathers. A group of peasant women sat off to one side; judging by the gales of laughter and the knowing looks, Linden guessed their husbands and lovers might not be pleased with the tales making the rounds. A few of the women looked him up and down and smiled a welcome. Then their gazes went to Maurynna standing by him. Next came a good-humored, resigned shrug and they turned back to their friends.

But merchant, peasant, peddler, farmer, or the gods only knew what, they all had one thing in common: All talked at the top of their lungs. The noise in the common room was well-nigh deafening.

Shima joined them now. He still wore his hood pulled low over his face and kept his hands hidden inside his cloak, thank all the gods. Linden and Maurynna had found it was no use trying to pass as truehumans when Shima was with them. One look at his dark, honey-colored skin and long, arrow-straight black hair, and anyone with half his wits knew he wasn't of the Five Kingdoms or even from Assantik. Worse yet, too many folk also knew by now that there was only one such man in the Five Kingdoms—and they well knew that he was a Dragon-lord, one of the great weredragons that held a rank equal with any king or queen.

Linden sighed. *If only Otter hadn't written that song about our mission to Jehanglan. . . .*

Shima muttered, "Is there a quieter room we can go to? It's too hot to stay bundled up like this, but you know what will happen if I drop my hood."

Linden nodded. They knew all too well: instant, uncomfortable silence. But the serving girls were too busy to notice them and he couldn't tell where the two doorways at the far end of the room led; the last place they wanted to wander into was a busy kitchen.

Then the right-hand door swung open; before it shut again, Linden caught a glimpse of the kitchen as a portly woman sailed through. Weaving a path through the crowd, she came up to them.

"Good day, Dragonlords, and welcome to the Gyrfalcon's Nest," she said quietly. "I'm Elidiane Tunly, one of the owners of this inn, and at your service. I'm sure that you'd prefer a bit of privacy, so please follow me if you will." She turned and started off.

Linden blinked. A quick glance told him that Shima was still hidden within the folds of his cloak. He caught up to her. "How did—?"

"My husband. Watkin, my lord. You met him outside." She looked back at them, her brown eyes alight with amusement. "We've had Dragonlords here before, Your Graces, so Wat knows what a Llysanyin looks like. That there were no bits on the bridles clinched it. He sent our son to warn me."

She led them through the other door and into a quiet hallway. As soon as the door closed behind them, Shima tossed back his hood with a sigh of relief. "That's better. I hate the smell of damp wool—too much like having a wet dog in your face."

Four more doors lined this hall, two on each side, and the murmur of voices and muted laughter could be heard behind them. These were the private rooms where travelers who did not care for the hubbub of the common room—and could afford it—might dine and take their ease.

The innkeeper asked, "So—how may I help you, Your Graces?"

"Food, a quiet place to eat, and rooms," Maurynna said. She twitched her cloak, sending drops of water flying. "I can't wait to get dry again."

A tiny frown creased Elidiane's forehead. "Oh, dear—we've only one room left. . . ."

Damnation. Linden had been looking forward to a bit of privacy. For one moment he considered insisting she roust someone, *anyone,* out of their room. But the desperate look in the innkeeper's eyes made him relent. Likely the private rooms were already taken by nobles or wealthy merchants who were the inn's regular custom, while he, Maurynna, and Shima might well never pass this way again in her lifetime. And he knew full well who'd suffer if the unlucky person or persons took offense; it would not be the Dragonlords.

"We're willing to share." He tried to keep the resignation from his voice. By the amused look in Shima's eyes, he didn't do very well.

"And there's only one bed."

"I'll sleep on a pallet on the floor," the Tah'nehsieh Dragonlord said. "I don't even care anymore as long as the roof doesn't leak."

"That it doesn't. Thank you, Your Graces." The relief in her voice said that someone had not been so reasonable. "The rooms are up—"

One of the doors opened and a richly dressed man stepped out. "Ah, there you are, Mistress Tunly! We were wondering if you've heard any news about— By the gods! Linden Rathan! Maurynna Kyrissaean! And you must be Shima Ilyathan, are you not, Your Grace?" He bowed to them.

"I am, my lord," Shima said, nodding. "But I'm afraid I don't recognize you."

Maurynna said, "Shima, this is Lord Tyrian of Cassori. He helped us on the first leg of our journey over the sea to Jehanglan. It's not easy finding a ship and crew on short notice, even if they are the crown's own, but Lord Tyrian did it." To Tyrian she said, "If I'm ever in command of a ship again, I want that crew."

Tyrian smiled broadly. "My lady, I'll be certain to tell them you said that; they'll be prouder than peacocks." He looked more closely at them. "Once you've had a chance to change into dry clothes, the party I'm traveling with would be honored if you'd join us for the midday meal."

Linden quickly consulted the others by mindvoice, then said, "It would be our pleasure, my lord. If you'll excuse us for now?"

Lord Tyrian bowed once more and went back into the private dining room. They followed the innkeeper to their sleeping chamber. As they gingerly removed their dripping cloaks, Mistress Tunly knelt before the wood already laid in the fireplace and expertly set it alight with flint and steel from her belt pouch.

Standing once more, she said briskly, "My son will bring up your saddlebags shortly, Dragonlords, and I'll fetch you towels to dry off with." She made them a courtesy and left.

Towels and saddlebags came a short while later. Not long after, they were on their way back down the stairs, urged on by their rumbling stomachs.

To their dismay, when the Dragonlords reached the private dining room they found Mistress Tunly waiting to announce them. She opened the door, said into the noisy discourse, "My lords and ladies, Their Graces Linden Rathan, Maurynna Kyrissaean, and Shima Ilyathan," then stepped back.

Silence. Then, as they entered the room and the innkeeper closed it once more, everyone scrambled to rise and either bow or make them a courtesy. Lord Tyrian came to meet them.

"Thank you for inviting us to share your meal," Linden said for the three of them. The savory aroma of roast goose with sage tickled his nose; he hoped his stomach didn't pick this moment to rumble again.

He glanced around quickly to see how many of the people present he knew from his time as one of the judges of the regency question in Cassori a couple of years before.

None were from the Cassorin Council, which was a relief beyond words. But nonetheless, many of the faces were familiar; it took him a moment to place where he'd seen them: one of the horse-mad Lord Sevrynel's "little gatherings." Thank the gods; horse talk was just fine with him. Politics were not.

He went on, "As you can see, we're not wearing our formal garb, so there's no need for such ceremony, my lords and ladies. Please—let us dine as friends."

The babble of voices broke out once more, and the Dragonlords found themselves seated at the large trestle table in the center of the room. Then all settled to the serious businesses of eating and horse talk.

After the edge was off his hunger, Linden asked Tyrian where his party was bound for.

"The fair at Balyarannna, of course," Tyrian replied. "And you, Your Grace?"

"The same. We plan to meet our friends Otter Heronson and his grandnephew Raven Redhawkson there, as well as Maurynna's cousins, who will be with the royal party."

Tyrian turned to Maurynna. "Ah! Of course—I remember them. Especially the little girl who wanted to go with you as a tumbler, Kella, Prince Rann's friend. I've been at my own estate much of the past year rather than at court, but from time to time I've had word of their . . . adventures."

"Oh dear. It is indeed that same little girl, my lord. Her sister, Maylin, will be with her—for the regents were kind enough to invite her as well." Maurynna paused. "Though I suspect Duke Beren and Duchess Beryl wanted someone around who'll sit on Kella if she needs it."

"Hmm, yes," Tyrian said with a twinkle in his eye. "I've heard once or twice that she can be, ah, impulsive, Your Grace."

Linden, nearly choking on his wine, thought with amusement, *Now there's an understatement!*

Maurynna laughed. "If by that you mean she has a nose for trouble, my lord—you're absolutely right."

Someone called down the length of the table, "Does Lord Sevrynel know that you're going to the fair, Your Graces?"

"Not as far as I know, my lord," Linden replied.

Whoops of laughter followed his words. "My, won't Sevrynel be surprised!" a few voices chorused. After the laughter ended, another voice said, "I hope you enjoy looking at pedigrees, Linden Rathan."

A fresh burst of laughter greeted this pronouncement.

"Oh?" Linden asked.

"You'll see, my lord," Tyrian said with a grin. "You'll see."

At the end of the meal the party broke up into smaller groups. Shima found himself the center of attention of a circle of the younger lords and ladies. They plied him with questions about life in Jehanglan and what it was like to live at Dragonskeep.

Many of the most intelligent questions and comments, he found, were from two young Kelnethi noblewomen, Lady Karelinn and her sister, Lady Merrilee. They now sat opposite Shima on a bench by one of the windows.

As Karelinn argued a point with one of the young men and Merrilee listened, nodding from time to time, Shima marveled at the difference between the sisters. He would never have guessed they were siblings.

Where Karelinn was plump, rosy, and, to be honest, quite ordinary, Merrilee was pale, slender, and ethereally beautiful. Indeed, she seemed so delicate that Shima wondered if she was really but a waking dream. If he reached across the short distance separating them and touched her, would she vanish like mist?

He noted with amusement that every young man in the party watched her with dog-like devotion, vying for a scrap of her attention, a word from her. Yet she seemed not to notice; Shima wondered if she even realized the effect she had on men.

Lady Merrilee was quieter than her sister and rarely spoke. Instead her wide-eyed gaze went from speaker to speaker, her entire attention on each person in turn; she radiated an almost otherworldly aura of sweetness and innocence. Yet there was also, Shima thought, a touch of sadness in her eyes, as blue as a summer sky in Nisayeh.

But for all Lady Merrilee's beauty, it was Karelinn's smile that attracted him. Ordinary she might be—especially next to her younger sister—but when Karelinn smiled, it was as if she was lit from within. A man might warm himself with that smile, Shima thought, captivated. Nor did she seem to resent her sister's otherworldly beauty; the way their heads bent together to share a joke spoke of true affection with no taint of jealousy. He'd seen his own sisters do the same many times. The sight made him a little homesick and he wandered off into his own thoughts.

He barely noticed when the door opened once more, revealing Mistress Tunly; he ignored whatever the innkeeper said, for in his mind he wandered the stark, beautiful land of his people, smelled the sharp scent of scrub pine and *kaqualla* bush, sat by a river waiting for his friend Miune Kihn, the young waterdragon, to splash up the bank and sit beside him. He could almost smell his mother's cooking. . . .

Sharp cries of dismay brought him back. Startled, Shima looked about. Nearly everyone had jumped up to crowd around the innkeeper. The clamor was deafening. All Shima could make out at first was "But I *must* get to Balyaranna! I've two horses for the big race!" over and over again. Someone else just cursed long, hard, and impressively.

He turned to Karelinn. "Lady, what is it? I wasn't paying attention."

But Karelinn had her own distractions. Whatever the news was, it had upset Merrilee. She looked, Shima thought, like a frightened doe. "Oh gods—Kare?" the younger woman said uncertainly.

Karelinn put her arm around Merrilee's shoulder. "Don't worry, Merri. He wouldn't dare disobey Father. He won't follow us." She spoke so softly that only Shima could overhear in all the tumult.

And what is this all about? Shima wondered, suddenly alert. Had someone threatened the gentle Lady Merrilee?

"Did Mistress Tunly say how long the bridge will be impassable? I couldn't hear," Merrilee whispered before he could offer his protection as a Dragonlord.

Spirits! So *that* was the cause of the uproar. From what Linden had said during their journey, Shima knew that this was the only bridge within a tenday's ride. True, there was a ford; but it was at least three days' ride downriver, and if the Ostra River had flooded enough to wash out the stout stone-and-timber bridge they'd come over a few tendays ago, the ford was a lost cause.

He hoped they got to Balyaranna before the horse fair was over; he looked forward to seeing Raven and his aunt again.

But things would fall out as Shashannu, Lady of the Sky, willed it, Shima thought. Until then, he would see what he might do here. "Lady Merrilee—is there something I or the other Dragonlords might help you with?"

A rosy flush suffused Merrilee's cheeks. A quick look passed between the sisters; after a moment, Merrilee smiled her thanks, but shook her head.

At that moment their father, Lord Romsley, called Merrilee. He looked worried. *What on earth is amiss?* Shima wondered.

As Merrilee stood up to go to her father, Shima rested his fingertips on the back of her wrist, holding her back for a moment. Their eyes met.

"Just remember—if you do need help, any of us will aid you," he said quietly.

"Thank you, Shima Ilyathan. But I fear this is a thing that only time can mend." As she turned away, he caught the glint of tears in her eyes.

Ah; that sounded more like a heart broken than a life in danger. Somewhat relieved, he turned to her sister. "Lady?"

She took a deep breath. "By your courtesy, Your Grace, but . . ." Her eyes begged him to understand.

"I see—telling or not is Lady Merrilee's decision, is that it?"

"Yes, if you please, Your Grace." Her voice trembled.

He knew he could force the issue; he knew how powerful the words "Dragonlord's orders" could be. He had obeyed Maurynna when she'd said them to him back in Jehanglan and he'd had only his mother's stories of Dragonlords. To one raised to obey a Dragonlord, it might as well be a command of the gods. It would be that unthinkable to disobey him.

He was tempted, sorely tempted. But he also knew such power was not for whims. So he said, "Very well, my lady. But if you or your sister need help in the future, I lay this command upon you: You will come to me for aid."

Her smile lit her face; Shima basked in the warmth of it. He found himself thinking, *I hope this rain goes on for a few days yet. . . .*

Leaning forward, he said, "Now—it looks as if we'll be companions here for a while yet, lady, so let us talk to pass the time."

"You're from Kelneth, I heard your father say before. I've had no chance to go there yet, though Linden's spoken of it. He knew one of your long-ago queens. Tell me about your home."

"I will—if you'll tell me more about Jehanglan and Dragonskeep?" Karelinn countered.

"Done," he said. Then, with a grin, "You first."

Two

At the sound of a knock, Otter turned from sorting the sheets of music lying upon the desk in his chamber. Even as he stood up to answer it, the door swung open. Charilon, another of the older bards and a longtime friend, entered.

"What's wrong?" Otter asked in concern as the other sat on the edge of the desk. Charilon's eyes were red and he looked grim and sad. Strands of his grey hair had escaped from the tie that held it back and hung limply around his lined face.

"You'll be wanting to hold off on going to meet your nephew at the horse fair in Balyaranna, I'm thinking," Charilon said.

What on— "Oh?" Otter said, puzzled. Charilon knew how much he was looking forward to meeting Raven there. So what could be important enough to hold him back from the trip? A sudden chill danced up his spine. Something was very wrong. "Why?"

His voice breaking, Charilon went on, "I came to bring you the news. Sether's dead. His journeywoman, Rose, just found him."

Otter's jaw dropped. Whatever he'd expected, it wasn't this. Sether, the master of the wood barn, the man who helped everyone from the newest journeyman to the Guild Master himself find the perfect woods for their treasured harps? For a moment Otter's thoughts froze. Then a torrent of possibilities flooded his mind. Had Sether finally fallen from that rickety old ladder by the woodbins? He finally managed to ask, "How? Did that damned ladder get him finally?"

Charilon shook his head.

Otter couldn't imagine what else might have befallen the master. Then a thought came to him; the Wood Master was getting older. . . . *Aren't we all?* another part of his mind asked sadly. "His heart?"

"No. He, he . . . Sether hanged himself." The master for the older apprentices wiped at his eyes with a sleeve-covered hand.

"What!" Suddenly Otter's legs would not support him. He fell back into his chair. "Dear gods!" was all he could say at first; then, after a moment, "That poor, poor child." He could imagine only too well the scene she'd come upon, and what she'd felt. Too well—

The next thing that burst from his lips was a single, anguished word: *"Why?"*

Charilon shook his head.

"Did—did he leave any kind of a message?"

Once more Charilon shook his head. "Not that anyone's found yet. And before he did it, it seems he built a bonfire out behind the Wood Barn. From the way it's burning, they tell me, he must have poured oil or something on it. That's why Rose found him—she ran to warn him about it. She thought it was a student prank. But one of the first-year apprentices saw him building it. The boy had no idea at the time that it was something untoward."

Otter still couldn't believe it. Why would Sether, the Wood Master for the Bards' School in Bylith, build a bonfire, then take his own life? Yes, his wife, Herala, had died, but that was years ago and their children were grown, with families of their own. As far as he knew, all was well there. Had there been some recent, unspeakable sorrow in his life that Otter hadn't heard about?

He must have asked the question aloud, for Charilon said, "No—not that I know of, at least. And I talk—I mean, *talked*—with him whenever I bring—damn it all, I mean *brought*—one of my 'prentices down to choose the wood for their journeyman's harp.

"Hell—I saw him just last night! He told me he was still courting Widow Theras—Thomelin the luthier's wife's friend, remember Sevrynel told us about her?—though gods know why any man would fall head over heels for such a priggish—"

Charilon stopped with a sob. He bowed his head and wiped his eyes again, then wrapped his arms around himself, rigid as a statue. His harsh breathing filled the room.

He's taking this very hard, Otter thought. *I've* never *known him to babble like this.* Taking a deep breath to calm himself, he said in as soothing a voice as he could manage, "I never understood it either. But he was pleased with his courting?"

Not that Sether had seemed the kind of man to hang himself if a woman turned him away, and certainly not for a woman such as Widow Theras, no man in his right mind would . . .

Otter wrenched his thoughts back to the matter at hand. No, *he* might not kill himself for the love of a woman like Theras, but another man might be so driven. It was not his place to sit in judgment.

Still . . . *Widow Theras?*

Charilon's voice broke into the swirling jumble of thoughts in his mind.

"Yes, curse it—he was pleased! All smiles about it, he was. I was chatting with him about it. We were at the Green Rushes having a pint or four or five with that timber merchant who'd brought in a shipment of cherry and walnut. Beautiful wood it was, and Sether was delighted with it. True, he got upset and left when one of the carters told some idiot tale he'd heard, but nothing unusual in that."

"Oh?" Otter asked, leaning forward. *Could that have—oh, wait; I'll wager it was a—* "Scary story?"

"First shot right in the gold. You know how Sether was. Did the usual; said such tales gave him the cold grues and nightmares, then lit out of the tavern as if Iryniel the Punisher was snapping at his heels," Charilon said, referring to the savage, wolf-headed servant of Auvrian, the patron god of the bards. "Stayed longer than he usually did, I'll admit, but I think that, between ale and accent, he was having trouble understanding what the fellow was saying. But the moment he realized it was a ghost story—*phwwp*! Gone."

No surprise there; it was a well-known foible of Sether's, and one that had often gotten the poor man teased over the years. Otter remembered how poor Sether would be the only one left in the apprentice dormitory when everyone else had sneaked out for the midnight story sessions. All alone, blankets pulled over his head, listening to every creak and rustle, knowing that everyone else was telling those ghost stories that he just couldn't bear to listen to . . .

Otter shook his head, wrenching his thoughts back from the past. He still couldn't believe Sether had taken his own life. "What was the tale about?" he asked.

The question steadied Charilon as Otter had guessed it would. The man was a bard before all else; no matter if the sky was falling, he couldn't resist the lure of telling you a story you hadn't heard before.

"Oh, something about a screaming tree and people gone missing in a 'forest of evil' somewhere up north. Eaten by the tree, I think it went, or something like. Couldn't hear very well, I was up by the kegs talking to the innkeeper just then, but old Burley—the timber merchant—told me the gist of it later.

"Now, I'd never heard this particular foolishness before, but you know the kind of hoary old chestnut I mean. Good for telling around a campfire. Don't even have to really think about it, just play a few eerie chords now and again and sound menacing. Gives everyone the shivers and shakes and makes 'em look over their shoulders into the night. Great fun and all that."

Smiling, Otter nodded. He'd done it many a time himself.

"This tale was nothing more than that, and badly told to boot. The fellow was so drunk, it was a wonder he was still standing. Burley told me later that Sether asked some questions, then turned bone-white and hurried out. Guess that was when he realized what kind of story it was. Funny how such things took him. He never would sit through to the end of that tale of the little run-in you and Linden Rathan had with that hag."

Otter blinked. That encounter had been more than a "little run-in." But a scary story wasn't enough to drive a man, even Sether, to suicide.

"So what could it have been?" Otter asked in despair. Gods help him—were Sether's friends never to know the *why* of a good man's death by his own hand?

Suddenly overwhelmed, he covered his eyes; he'd known Sether for years. They'd entered the Bards' School at the same time. So now there was one less of the friends of his youth—and there were already far too few. All at once he felt as ancient as the huge oak before the main hall.

Slamming his fist down on the desk, he said, "There has to be a reason! A man doesn't kill himself on a whim."

Charilon nodded. "So what was it?" He rubbed the bridge of his nose, his eyes shut. He suddenly looked far older than his years. "Oh gods. The Guild Master has sent word to Sether's children, they live here in Bylith, but his sibs still have to be told. And it will likely fall to me—Sether and I were from the same village. They still live there. This will break their hearts."

"Why not Leet?" Otter asked, naming another bard who had been a fellow student with them—though no friend, especially to him. "His half brother is still the lord there, isn't he? I'd've wagered that Leet would demand the task as his 'duty.'"

Though a bard was supposed to put his past life behind him when he or she took the bard's oath, Leet somehow never let anyone forget that, but for becoming a bard, he would have been Lord Sansy of Sansydale.

Despite his grief, Charilon snorted in wry amusement. "Ah, yes—we must play the noble lord whenever possible, eh, complete with our nobly cleft chin held high in the air and looking down our long, noble nose at the peasants around us, don't we? A pity Leet didn't get his mother's sweet disposition along with her chin. No, he left a few days ago. Didn't you know?"

"No," Otter said dryly. "I try to avoid him when I'm here and he does the same."

"Then I'm thinking you'll be delighted to know that he's on his way to Balyaranna."

Otter grimaced. "How . . . splendid. And how odd; he usually doesn't bother with it unless the Kelnethi royal court is going. And since the Guild Master was at court last night at the queen's request, I know they're not."

"He's bothering this year, gods only know why. Wonder if he'll bring the new harp he commissioned. Took Thomelin the luthier long enough, too, I've heard." A pause. "Won't you two have fun together at Balyaranna."

For a moment Charilon snickered at him; then his face fell once more. "Oh gods, Otter—save that he'd do it in the coldest way possible, I would wish this task upon Leet. I don't want to have to tell Raefus and Timmea that . . ." A tear slid down his cheek. He whispered, "We all played together. . . ."

Otter rose and crossed the room to a small cupboard. He pulled out a flask of wine and two goblets, filled them, and made the ashen-faced Charilon take the chair while he sat on the edge of the bed.

They drank slowly, trading stories and memories of the dead man, trying to understand *"Why?"*

They could find no answer.

The evening after Sether's death, as Otter left the stables where he'd gone to visit his Llysanyin mare, Nightsong, he found Charilon waiting for him. After seeing the other bard's face, Otter asked in surprise, "What's wrong? You look like you've just found some idiot apprentice carving his sweetheart's name into your harp." For there was fire in the other bard's eyes and his face was mottled red with anger.

Otter had *never* seen Charilon like this; he hadn't thought Charilon could get that angry. What on earth . . .

It was a moment or two before Charilon could master himself enough to answer. "Otter, my lad," he finally growled, "all I can say is that in all of my years as a bard, I've never come so close to betraying my oath."

He held up his forefinger and thumb; there was perhaps the width of a hair between them. "This close I was," he said, his voice shaking with rage. "This close to throttling that woman—hell, throttling *both* of them."

Otter stared at him openmouthed. This was no exaggeration for effect. Charilon meant every word—and Charilon was one of the gentlest souls Otter knew. He also knew how sacred the other bard held the oath that all bards shared: that they would do no harm to another except in self-defense or to save a life.

That oath cut them off from family, clan, and country. They forswore all thought of vengeance for wrongs done to themselves or their kin. They could not take up arms in a war. Instead, their task—impossible as it all too often seemed— was to remain impartial and seek a peaceful solution to conflicts.

By all the gods, who had pushed Charilon so close to the edge? One wrong word and he'd explode into violence. Otter jerked a thumb over his shoulder at the bench beneath the old apple tree in the courtyard. "Let's go sit down and watch the last of the sunset," he said. "You're not ready to talk about this yet."

As he led the way, Otter called to one of the first-year apprentices to fetch them two mugs of cider. That should do the trick, he thought; last year's cider had been one of the best in memory. One mug could make an iron bar relax.

He bade Charilon sit. To his consternation, the other bard dug his fingers into the cloth of his breeches, hands clenched in a death grip as he stared straight ahead, seething.

When the boy returned with the cider, he said in an awed voice, "Priestess Kaelwyn's just arrived at the main gate, sirs, to cast the preservation spell for Master Sether."

"Good," Otter said as he took the mugs and handed one off to Charilon, who seemed not to have heard a word. "Thank you, lad." He nodded a dismissal. The boy sketched a rough salute and ran off.

Otter sipped, thinking. They *were* lucky that Kaelwynn was available, for she was skilled at this, and, as a priestess of the Crone—the aspect of the Goddess that dealt with death—she was usually at the small temple-hospice three days' ride away. She must have been in Bylith to consult with the Head Priestess at their temple. Her spell would give more time for the mourners to gather.

Not until the cider was half gone and the dangerous red hue had left Charilon's face did Otter ask, "What happened?"

Charilon took a long pull on his cider. Staring straight ahead once more, he said, "Guild Master Belwynn asked me to break the news to Widow Theras since I know her better than most. I found her at home; unfortunately Thomelin the luthier's wife was visiting."

"Ah." Although he'd never met the woman, Otter had heard a few stories about the luthier's wife. He didn't know what was coming next, but suspected he wasn't going to like it one bit.

As the last edge of the sun sank below the horizon, a few petals from the apple tree drifted down. Otter caught some in his hand. He fancied that he caught a faint hint of their lovely fragrance. So beautiful, so fragile, so quick to pass— like human life.

"Tell me about it," he said. He let the petals fall as Charilon began his tale.

"They were in the garden, brushing some fallen leaves from that little shrine of Sarushun the widow has and scraping the candle wax from the stones. At least Theras was. Romissa—pardon me, *Lady* Romissa—was just standing there, telling her how to do it and preaching the way she always does."

Charilon took another drink. "I swear, Otter, the woman can't open her mouth without preaching at you—how to live your life, how to do this, that, and every little thing, which you and everyone else ought to do according to what *she* believes, of course. Gods help me, she'd probably hector you on whether you should fart facing east, west, north, or south, the sanctimonious bitch. Never lets you forget she's nobly born, either—just like her brother."

Which tallied with everything that Otter had ever heard of her. Poor Thomelin; sometimes it worked out when an impoverished noble married a well-to-do merchant or craftsman. Most times, though, a lord or lady never let the base-born spouse forget the difference in their stations. He suddenly found himself glad he'd never had the displeasure of meeting the good Lady Romissa. Her half brother Leet was quite enough. If Romissa had ever come to visit Leet at the school, it had been when Otter was away, thank the gods. "And?"

Charilon ran a hand through his thinning hair. "Damn it all, Otter—it's hard enough having to tell someone about their suitor's death, but what came next! That's when I saw red. Sether was my friend!"

"At first, when I told her Sether was dead, Theras just stood there. I'll give her this: I think she was honestly shocked and distressed. Maybe not brokenhearted, but distressed. She may not have loved Sether with the passion of youth, but I think she was truly fond of him.

"Then Romissa opened her big mouth. 'How?' she wanted to know. Have you any idea how hard it was to go there in the first place, to tell Theras that Sether was gone? Then to have to tell her it was by his own hand? Otter, that's like telling someone that, no matter what was wrong in his life, your betrothed didn't love you enough to live. Which I don't understand, because Theras was everything to Sether. Everything." Charilon drained his mug. "So I had to tell her that he'd—what he'd done."

He stopped. Otter waited, knowing there was more to come. The twilight deepened and darkness pooled around their feet before Charilon spoke again.

"And do you know what that bitch Romissa said then?" he asked indignantly. He tugged with both hands at his grey-streaked beard.

Otter was suddenly sure he didn't want to know; fanatics of any sort were capable of incredible cruelty. But it was his duty to listen.

Charilon's voice rose in an imperious whine. " 'Stop grieving for the creature this instant, Theras, or I shall tell Priest Amas. You know Sarushun forbids suicide. One who takes his own life is stricken from his holy books and is lower than a worm. Such a one is not worthy of notice from a Believer. Ask that he be left for the dogs to worry and tear apart. It's your duty.' "

Otter closed his eyes for a moment in disbelief at the brutal words. "Why isn't she at home with her family? Surely she has duties there."

"I suspect she fobbed the children off on Thomelin's sister Analiss so that she could play busybody. Ever since Ana's husband died and she went to live with her brother, Romissa has treated her like a servant, Sether once told me. Thomelin usually puts a lid on the worst of Romissa's antics, but he's off on one of his buying trips. He likes to pick the woods and the gems for the harps himself if he can."

Otter nodded. That made sense. He knew that besides making harps for a number of the senior bards, the luthier made instruments for many Kelnethi nobles and even members of the royal house. That's where the gems went, of course; no serious bard tarted up a harp that way.

Not to mention the poor fellow probably seized any excuse to get away from his shrewish wife. The gods knew *he* would if he stood in Thomelin's shoes.

Gazing up at the first star of the evening, Otter said wistfully, "I know she's Kelnethi and Gifnu usually doesn't take Kelnethi, but I truly hope he's holding a very special place in one of his hells for Lady Romissa."

"Either that or that Auvrian tosses her bone by bone to Iryniel the Punisher," Charilon growled. "Though she'd probably poison him even though he's a godling. She'd poison anything she touched.

"But do you want to know what was the worst part? Theras just said, 'Of course, Lady Romissa, you're right as always,' meek as a mouse. Then Romissa began talking about the best place to buy beeswax for the altar candles, as if the news I'd brought them was nothing! And Theras joined right in!"

The outraged bard snapped his fingers and went on, "Just like that she denied Sether. Instead of putting that ironhearted bitch in her place, she trampled on Sether's memory like he was dirt. That was when I had to leave."

"Or dishonor your oath."

"Or dishonor my oath. It was a near thing, let me tell you." Charilon ground his teeth.

"I can well believe it." *And I don't know that any of us would have blamed you,* Otter thought. *Hell, Guild Master Belwynn would toast you in private.* He went on, "Come on, then—let's gather up the others and drink and sing to Sether this night." He stood and offered a hand to the other bard.

Charilon used it to heave himself off the bench. "Feh—these old bones are getting stiff. Not that many of the old crew left now," he said ruefully. "But we'll do what we can, eh?"

"So we shall, old friend," Otter said. "So we shall."

Three

The full moon shone overhead as Bard Leet urged his tired horse on. Where the hell was that carters' shelter, anyway? He'd passed the river what must have been candlemarks ago, and skirted the swamp. It should be *somewhere* near here.

For what seemed the hundredth time in the last candlemark he held the crude map up in the cold white moonlight and squinted at the squiggles and markings upon it. At least he was certain he was back on the right path; between taking the wrong turning and his horse throwing a shoe, he'd lost nearly two days.

A cloaked and hooded figure stepped out of the shadows at the side of the road. Leet's mare squealed in fright and shied, nearly throwing him, and even the stolid packhorse he led jumped to one side.

"I beg your pardon," the figure said. There was not an ounce of remorse in the soft voice. A dark lantern appeared from beneath the cloak; the man slid the shutter back, allowing light to spill forth.

He held it up and pushed his hood back. The glow revealed a tired, lined face framed by a dark beard shot through with grey. Leet stared down at him, hand pressed against his chest, his heart thudding against his ribs.

"Well met, brother-in-law," said Thomelin the luthier. "I was hoping you wouldn't come. So you're still set upon this course?" His voice was tight with anger. But the luthier made no attempt to argue. Leet knew he dared not.

Leet did not deign to answer. Thomelin shrugged as if to say "On your head be this." "This way, then," the luthier said, and led the way to a spacious tent.

Once inside Leet waited impatiently as his brother-in-law pulled back a traveling rug from a large "lump" on the floor of his tent, revealing two identical boxes, each a traveling case for a harp.

He peered more closely. No, not quite identical; one had a small mark burned into a corner of the lid. Leet nodded and smiled. The mark was a V—like the silhouette of a seagull in flight. How very appropriate. . . .

He pushed the lid to one side and beckoned Thomelin to bring the lantern closer. The yellow light fell upon a cloth-wrapped bundle. Frowning, Leet rubbed the heavy fabric between his fingers and looked closely at it. Whatever it was, it wasn't black as he'd first thought, but a deep, deep red. "What's this?"

"Silk. As you value your soul, touch the damned thing as little as possible and keep it wrapped when—"

The bard cut off his brother-in-law with a contemptuous gesture. "I don't need advice from *you*."

Only a soft hiss betrayed Thomelin's anger. He said, "Very well, Leet. I'm sure you know best." The words dripped sarcasm. A long pause, then the luthier went on softly, "Don't say I didn't warn you . . . brother-in-law."

Craven peasant, Leet thought, ignoring Thomelin, though a part of his mind grew uneasy at the luthier's moment of hesitation. Pushing it from his thoughts, Leet eased the fabric back, exposing a section of a harp's pillar. With a touch as light as a butterfly's, he brushed his fingertips along the polished wood. A faint tingle ran up his arm.

Was it just his imagination? Or—or did he feel . . .

Hardly daring to breathe, he jerked at the cloth, revealing part of the harp's soundboard. He laid one palm against the spruce boards.

This time there was no mistaking the prickling sensation. It was real. Dear gods, his idea had worked!

Leet bared his teeth in a wolfish smile. "And now—did you get the information I wanted?"

The luthier spoke reluctantly. "About Lord Lenslee? Yes. Yes, I did."

"Excellent." Leet rubbed a forefinger along the indentation between his lower lip and chin for a satisfied moment. *Perfect so far. Now let us see . . .* Then he pulled the silk aside completely and lifted the harp from its traveling case. Ignoring Thomelin's gasp, the bard cradled the instrument in his arms. It felt right. So, so right.

Thomelin stared at him for a long moment; his face turned pale and ashen. At last he whispered, "You know that you hold Death in your arms." It was not a question.

Leet smiled thinly. "Yes. Yes, I do know it. Now—tell me about Lenslee and that cursed horse. Tell me everything."

After he woke the next morning, Leet sat in Thomelin's tent and emptied his saddlebag. The items he sought were at the bottom; when he had found them, he carefully laid them out on the pallet bed.

He knew *what* he wanted to do; he just wasn't sure of the *how* yet. But as he studied the items before him, he felt certain that it would come to him. It *had* to.

And when it did, he would know that the gods approved his course.

Arrayed before him was the garb of a minstrel, one of those whose talents were above the common run, yet not quite good enough to raise them to the coveted rank of bard: a torc of thin twisted wire, a red and yellow particolored tunic, a yellow cloak with red trim. The tunic was threadbare and shabby, the cloak patched and fraying at the hem. It had been easy to steal them and a pair of well-worn leather riding breeches from a storeroom of the Bards' School.

Next to them was a large packet of the powder that mummers used to turn their hair white. Despite his years, Leet's light brown hair still had little grey in it. Only growing a beard would change his appearance more; a pity he couldn't stand the feel of one.

He smiled and stroked the indentation under his lip. It was time for Leet, Bard of Bylith, to disappear for now, and for one Osric, a somewhat adequate minstrel, to take his place. But first he wanted to talk to Thomelin.

Pleased with himself, Leet pushed aside the canvas door and cautiously poked his head out into the dawn's chill. Garlands of white mist wrapped the large camp; he peered through it. At last he saw Thomelin talking with another man before one of the smaller tents the carters used.

"Thomelin!" he called imperiously.

The luthier looked around. When he saw who called him, his eyes narrowed and his lips pressed together. After a final word to the other man, he walked through the drifting ribbons of mist that wreathed him like ghosts. "Yes, brother-in-law?"

Angry now, Leet glanced around. Good; no one was close enough to have heard. He ground out, "Don't call me that," and withdrew into the tent, holding the door flap aside so that he could still see the luthier.

Thomelin stood very still. After a moment he followed Leet into the tent, letting the canvas fall behind him. He said with quiet sarcasm, "Oh, yes—someone might hear, mightn't they? My apologies, bard. How stupid of me to forget that I'm still not good enough to be part of your family—though my gold was."

The reminder that his brother, Agon, had in all but name sold their sister Romissa in marriage to the common-born luthier soured Leet's mood still further. Nor had the bard tried to stop the union; indeed, it was he who had introduced Agon to Thomelin all those years ago.

Guilt made him short-tempered. He snapped, "Why did you stop lending Agon money, anyway? Because of you he had to sell my father's herd to some yokel from Yerrih."

"You know damn well he had to do *that* because of his own bad judgment and lack of control. Your father, Rade, left Agon well off, Leet. *He* chose to piss it away with gambling and roistering—no one held a knife to his throat to make him throw those dice.

"Nor was I lending money to him, no matter what pretty name he's put on it. He's paid not one copper back and says he never intends to." Thomelin paused and pressed one hand to his chest. "And after the fine example his father set him, too."

Leet stiffened. Was that a hint of . . . irony . . . in Thomelin's voice, mockery in his eyes? *Does he know?* Leet's stomach twisted. If so, his hold on the luthier was as nothing. He dreaded the next words.

But all the luthier said was "No, the money stopped because my lady wife—*your* dear sister, bard—wants to curry more favor with her damned priest, the greedy bastard.

"That's where too bloody much of the coin I work for goes, bard," Thomelin snapped. His eyes blazed. "Or shall I make my wife sell the jewels and fine clothes she demanded of me as the proof of my love when I was still fool enough to think she might ever care for me? Like her brother, she never made good her bargain, either."

The luthier glared, his chest heaving. Leet stared at him in astonishment. Thomelin had never dared speak to him so. No matter what insults Leet had heaped on him before, Thomelin had always bent his head. He'd had no choice. For the first time in many, many years Leet had no scathing rejoinder.

Nor did he wish for one; not this time. For he feared what he might hear if he lashed out at the angry luthier. The man was as tightly wound as one of his own harp strings. Leet began a slow retreat further into the tent.

But Thomelin was not yet done. "Oh, yes," he hissed. "That's where my damned money goes. A greedy brother-in-law, a greedier priest, and to pay for . . . certain goods, bard. *Your* goods."

Thomelin raked his fingers through his grey-streaked hair. "A harp of ash, the wood of war, and that cursed . . . ," he whispered, his voice close to breaking, as he rocked back and forth. "Oh gods, oh gods—what have I . . ."

Then he drew himself up, grim and determined. "Get that hellish thing out of my tent, out of my life—and never let me see it again."

With that, Thomelin turned on his heel and stalked out of the tent.

Once more Leet wondered if Thomelin had guessed *his* secret. If Thomelin did, Leet would never again be able to bend the luthier to his will. But surely Thomelin didn't know; after all, he'd made the harp. . . . Still uneasy, Leet shook his head and made ready to leave.

A short while later as he swung up onto his horse, Thomelin came up.

"Where are you going now?" the luthier demanded.

"Not your damned business." Leet urged his horse on. The packhorse snorted and ambled after. To his dismay, Thomelin walked alongside.

"By all that's holy, Leet, will you please give up this mad plan?" Thomelin begged. "At the very least, there's no honor in it—as head of your family, Agon accepted the wergild for Arnath's death, damn it! And what about your oath as—"

"Don't prate to me about honor, you coward," Leet said coldly. "If you had been a man—if you had given a damn about your son—you would have Challenged that murdering filth then and there."

Thomelin grabbed Leet's reins and dragged his horse to a halt. His lips pulled back in a snarl. Leet shrank from him, suddenly afraid. Had he finally pushed the man too far? The bard looked about for help but they were alone on the road.

"I couldn't have loved that boy any more than if he'd been my own blood, you filthy bastard," Thomelin grated. When Leet sputtered in indignation, the luthier laughed, a cold, harsh laugh. "Oh, don't try to tell me Romissa wasn't already with child when we wed—and that you didn't know it.

"Yes, I was fool enough to believe her when she said she got pregnant on our wedding night. I believed her until Arnath was born nearly two months 'early'— and was as long as my forearm, fat as a suckling pig, and had lungs to rival a herald's. No babe that early is that big and healthy. I've seen my share of newborns—or did you all forget I'm the oldest of seven?

"But from the instant his fingers curled around mine, none of that mattered. I loved Arnath as my own. If my death could have saved him, I would have laid down my life for him as I would for my own blood.

"But to *throw* my life away? No. I would not abandon my other children." He let his hand fall from Leet's reins. "Unlike you, dear brother-in-law, I think of others—not just myself."

Leet kicked his horse so hard it crow-hopped in surprise, jerking the packhorse's line. The packhorse, with its burden of twin harps, squealed in protest and bucked as well. Thomelin jumped back. It was a few moments before the animals settled into a trot, leaving Thomelin behind.

All the damned luthier's fault, Leet fumed. He cursed Thomelin—but there was an edge of fear in it. He'd never dreamed that the luthier would dare speak to him this way! It unnerved him.

But Thomelin wasn't done. Leet heard him shout, "You may think it's for someone else, Leet, but the death that follows you is your own!"

Four

In the private dining room that Lord Tyrian's party had taken over, Shima sat across from Lady Karelinn at a small gaming table. Lady Merrilee sat to one side, watching and offering advice from time to time or applauding moves.

Shima frowned at the board, trying to ignore the noise all around them as the last of the noon meal's dishes were cleared away and everyone broke up into groups once more. This game of draughts was harder than it seemed at first; there were nuances to it he had not appreciated when first shown the board and pieces. They'd looked so simple: a board of dark and light squares and round markers, also dark and light.

This is like diyinesh, he said to himself, thinking of the ancient game of his people that he had introduced to Dragonskeep. It had become all the rage among the Dragonlords. Simple, so very simple—but like this draughts game, harder than it looked.

He had just made a move when the door opened and one of the younger lords—Olliner, it was—entered. "I say, Lord Tyrian, look whom I found walking in the door," the chubby Olliner said cheerfully.

A man followed him in. He looked tired; deep lines etched his face. At first Shima wondered at his odd, halting gait. He understood when someone took the man's sopping fur-trimmed cloak from his shoulders: the newcomer leaned on crutches. As he came forward slowly, Shima noticed that one leg was twisted; the toe of his riding boot barely touched the floor.

Cries of pleasure greeted the man; he was clearly well-known to many of the party.

"Eadain! It's so good to see you again!"

"Welcome, lad, welcome! Are you bound for Balyaranna?"

"I am," he said.

Eadain's voice was younger than Shima had expected. He looked again and saw that what he had taken for lines of age were old lines of pain.

"By the gods, old fellow," another of the young lords called, "you look like a half-drowned marsh rat."

A rueful grin took the years off Eadain's face. He shook his wet brown hair back from his face. "I feel like one, too. But that's nothing to what this poor little fellow feels like, I'll wager."

With that, Lord Eadain carefully slipped one hand into the large embroidered pouch hanging from his belt. When the hand reappeared, it held a tiny kitten, its black fur plastered to its body and its eyes squinched shut. The little mouth opened wide in a plaintive "Mew!" It was a pitiful sight.

"Found him under a hedge not a mile from here," Eadain said. "I'm not even certain how I heard him with all that rain drumming on my head."

"Oh, the poor thing!" Lady Merrilee gasped and sprang up from her chair.

A moment later she bent over Eadain's hand and touched gentle fingers to the kitten's head. "My lord, if you'll let me, I'll see that this poor creature is fed and warmed," she said, looking up at him.

Eadain just goggled at her for a long moment. Then, recovering, he managed to say, "Ah, yes, my lady. If you would be so kind . . ."

His voice trailed off as she scooped up the kitten. When she looked up at him once more and smiled, whatever he'd been about to say ended in a strangled gurgle. As Merrilee bore her charge to one of the benches by the fireplace, calling to her sister to please fetch a bowl of milk and a clean bit of cloth, Lord Eadain gazed after her with something of the look of a poleaxed steer.

As Karelinn rose, she leaned over and whispered impishly to Shima, "There goes another one!"

It was late; few people were left in the common room of the Gyrfalcon's Nest. Shima knelt to lay a small log on the fire. It caught and flared up, popping merrily; sudden heat washed over his face. Shima rose and went to stand by the side of the hearth, where his clothing would be safe from flying embers. He leaned upon the mantel, smiling down at the two young women seated side by side on the bench before the hearth as they gazed dreamily into the flames.

Soon it would be time to let the fire burn down for the night—but not quite yet. For a little while longer, he would enjoy this quiet time with Karelinn and her sister. The rain drummed a never-ending lullaby overhead; over in the corner, burly Lord Ephris and his lady wife, Kiela, talked softly. The soothing murmur of dainty Lady Kiela's voice reminded Shima of the cooing of a rock dove. He fought the urge to yawn.

"Dragonlord, may I ask a favor of you?"

Merrilee's gentle request brought Shima back from the edge of a waking dream. "Of course, my lady. What is it?"

"Ever since a visiting bard sang Bard Otter's song 'Dragon and Phoenix' about the great journey to Jehanglan, I've been fascinated with what I could find out about that land. I know you said your tribe is different from the Jehangli, with a different language, but . . . Do you speak any Jehangli?"

Shima answered, "Yes, I do." Well enough, he almost added, to trick Jehangli soldiers to their deaths when necessary. But he was afraid that the young women would ask for the story behind it and it was not a thing he wanted to talk about. Spirits help him, he could still hear the screams of those soldiers as the avalanche he'd started took them. Even now he sometimes saw their faces in his worst dreams.

"Would you say something in Jehangli for me, then? Part of a song or poem, perhaps?"

Caught off guard—he'd been back on the hot, boulder-strewn hillside with a Jehangli patrol closing in on him—Shima racked his brains for a moment, then recited the first thing that popped into his head. It was a few lines of something that he'd heard from an itinerant Jehangli storyteller. When he'd finished, he asked, "Well? Was it what you expected?"

Merrilee tilted her head. After a moment she said thoughtfully, "No, it's not, Your Grace. For some reason, I'd thought Jehangli would be harsh and guttural, with hard sounds like rocks knocking together.

"But that . . . that was full of the sound of, oh, rushing streams and the wind rustling through leaves. Especially rustling leaves, I think. It was pretty—what was it? It sounded like it might be a poem."

"It's part of what the Jehangli call a *juashen,* a story-poem," Shima said. "I heard it from a traveling Jehangli storyteller. He'd been captured by my people's allies, the Zharmatians, the People of the Horse. His 'ransom' was his stories. I was visiting their camp when the man was brought in, and I stayed to listen. It took many evenings, for he knew a great many tales."

The huge blue eyes filled with worry. "Oh, dear—I hope they didn't hurt him."

Shima smiled. "When they released him, he was richer by two good horses, a little gold, and many furs."

Merrilee smiled back at him. "Good. But what did those lines say, my lord? Can you tell me?"

"Hmm—it's not easy to translate, but I'll try my best."

He closed his eyes, thought for a bit, then said:

> *"You ride to join your men,*
> *while I must stay behind.*
> *The sky weeps bitter tears,*
> *but they are as nothing*
> *to the rain in my heart."*

He smiled at her. "It's much prettier in Jehangli."

"What is the poem about, my lord?" Merrilee asked. "It sounds very sad."

"It is. Are you certain you want to know?"

"Yes, Your Grace," she said firmly.

"Very well, then—I'm no storyteller, but I'll try." He looked up at the ceiling for a moment, putting his thoughts in order, making certain he *did* remember the entire tale.

Satisfied, he said, "It's about a young couple, Amsuro and Lenshi, who must part soon after their wedding. Amsuro, an officer in the army, is summoned to war while Lenshi stays behind, pining for him. Though word soon comes that he's missing in battle and is presumed dead, Lenshi knows in her heart that Amsuro is still alive.

"But when she goes to search for him, her brothers stop her. It's not just because it would be too dangerous. A Jehangli noblewoman would never be allowed to do anything like that. They're very sheltered.

"So for many days and nights Lenshi prays to the Phoenix—the Jehangli worship it—for help. Her prayers are heard—she turns into a swallow and flies off to look for her husband.

"After many years, she finds Amsuro, who is a prisoner of the enemy. But by then she's been a bird for so long that she can't change back. Nor can she tell him who she is, for she's lost the power of speech. All Lenshi can do is sit on her husband's shoulder or flutter around him. He thinks of her as a pet.

"Eventually Amsuro escapes and Lenshi leads him back to their home. Finding their house empty, Amsuro thinks Lenshi has deserted him. He curses her for a faithless jade and takes a new wife. On his wedding day, Lenshi flies one last time to rest in his cupped hands, then dies of a broken heart."

Shima looked at Merrilee; the dying firelight glittered on tears standing in her eyes. "I warned you it was very sad," he said, feeling a little guilty.

"You did, my lord," she said. "You did, and I thank you for telling it to me, Shima Ilyathan. I think I shall go to my room now. Soot"—the name she had bestowed upon the kitten—"must think he's been abandoned." Her voice broke on the last word and she rose unsteadily to her feet.

Karelinn stood up as well. She said "Merri . . . ?" as she slipped an arm around her sister's shoulders.

It was not enough, or perhaps too much. The tears spilled over; Merrilee pulled away and ran sobbing from the room. Lord Ephris and Lady Kiela turned in their chairs to stare after her in surprise.

Spirits! Shima thought, bewildered by Merrilee's reaction. *It wasn't that sad a story—at least not the way I tell it!*

He looked to Lord Ephris and Lady Kiela for understanding. They glared in icy accusation as they rose and left the room as well.

Shima leaned back against the wall. *But I didn't* do *anything!* he wanted to protest. He caught Karelinn's eye as she turned back. She stared at him, her eyes cold and distant.

"Don't look at me like that," he implored. "I did warn her. Should I have refused? I had no idea she was so tenderhearted."

Karelinn blinked; the frozen stare disappeared, to be replaced by a look of contrition. "I'm sorry, Dragonlord; I didn't mean to imply it was your fault at all. I—I wasn't even seeing you—"

She broke off as her father burst through the door. He looked as harried as a fox with a pack of hounds on his tail and no way over the river before it. "Karelinn—what on earth happened to Merri? I saw her just now on her way up to the rooms. She tried to tell me she's not crying, but I *know* she is. Is she still thinking about that worthless scoundrel?" The harried look disappeared, banished by a frown as Lord Romsley snapped, "You're supposed to keep her from—"

Karelinn burst out, "And how am I to do that, Father? I can't tell her what to think!"

Her father glared at her, lips pressed together.

"I—I'm sorry, Father." Her distressed whisper was hardly louder than the rustle of a leaf.

"The gods know I'm not an unreasonable man, but—"

It was, Shima decided, time to end this. Lord Romsley stopped, flustered, as the Tah'nehsieh Dragonlord stepped out of the shadows.

"Oh, er, ah—hello, Shima Ilyathan. I—I'm sorry I didn't see you. I beg your pardon."

"Not at all, Lord Romsley. It is I who should be begging *your* pardon. I'm afraid it's my fault that Lady Merrilee is unhappy."

Romsley's expression shifted to half-indignant, half-astonished. "Eh? What do you mean, Your Grace?"

"Lady Merrilee asked me to recite something in Jehangli. I'm afraid I made a rather poor choice. It was part of a very sad story, and of course she asked me to translate," Shima said, hoping the man would leave it at that.

So, of course, he didn't. "What was so sad about it, Your Grace?" Romsley asked.

Shima looked back as innocently as he could while desperately trying to come up with a plausible fib. He *still* didn't think his telling of the story was anything to weep over—except for a bard. Unfortunately, Lord Romsley's gimlet stare seemed to bore holes in his mind and all his ideas leaked out before he could catch them.

"The little swallow that had been such a faithful companion in the story died," Karelinn said into the growing silence. "You know how she is about animals, Father. I'm sure it made her think of poor little Goldwing. She still misses him so."

"Hrmm, hrmm—yes, that would do it. She's too softhearted sometimes." With a sigh of relief, the now reassured Lord Romsley lumbered from the room.

As the Kelnethi lord disappeared through the door, Shima let out a breath he hadn't realized he'd been holding. Karelinn sank down on the bench and wiped her forehead. They looked at each other and laughed weakly.

"That was close," Karelinn said ruefully. "Too close."

"Indeed." Shima studied her for a moment; he had two questions for her.

She met his eyes, then looked away. "Thank you for taking the blame upon yourself, Shima Ilyathan."

"It was no more than the truth. Who was Goldwing?"

"Merri's pet songbird. He was a darling. Aunt Perrilinia's cat got him—right in front of Merri, too. It was awful and happened just before we left."

"Then I'm surprised she's so concerned for that kitten Lord Eadain found. I would think she'd hate cats."

"Oh, no! Not even Lady Bella, Aunt Perrilinia's cat. It's a cat's nature, after all, to chase birds. If only Aunt Perrilinia's maid hadn't left the door to the room open . . ."

She must have guessed that there was another question lying in wait. Before he could ask it, she jumped up. "I should make certain Merri's well," she said with forced brightness as she sidled toward the door. "And bring Soot some milk. If you'll excuse me, my lord?"

She was away before he could reply. Shima gave her enough time to get up the stairs, then followed. It was late, he was tired—and he could always ask her the next time they were alone.

Five

Near the border between Yerrih and Kelneth, the dawn was breaking over the Kiltren hills to the east. As the first rays of light spread rosy fingers over the thatched roofs of Grey Holt, a door opened in the main hall of the Beast Healers' compound and a slender figure slipped out. A heavy, short-legged animal scrambled out just as the door shut once more.

Yawning and rubbing the sleep from her eyes, Pod hurried to the stable for her morning chores. Close on her heels came her familiar, one of the powerful, bearlike woods dogs of the north.

Shaking her head, Pod grumbled, "Bah! Just can't wake up quite all the way this morning, Kiga."

She slapped at her cheeks. What if the Guild Master looked out his window and saw her like this? He'd think she was just a lazy slugabed and would never consider her fit to go with the Healwort Guild for Wort Hunter training.

"And I really want to go with them before I'm a journeywoman," she told her familiar. "Only the best go while they're still 'prentices—like Conor did. I wonder when they're coming—d'you think I can talk Gunnis into putting in a word for me? Conor will be so proud if I'm chosen to go." She stifled another yawn before it could escape and slapped at her cheeks once more.

It didn't help. Still yawning, she heaved open one of the stout oak doors and slipped inside, Kiga so close, his nose almost touched her boot heels.

Shrill neighs of alarm woke Pod up that last little bit. She jumped, her heart pounding, trying to look everywhere at once in the dimly lit stable for the cause. Was there a fox, a lynx, a wolf—maybe even a snowcat—in here? What *was* it? She couldn't see anything wrong, but the horses were plunging and kicking in their stalls and neighing like battle trumpets.

It was a long, scary moment before she realized that the frightened horses were none that she knew. And if she didn't know them, they didn't know her—or her familiar. She hustled Kiga out of the stable.

"I guess we can't blame them for being afraid of you, boy. You're a bit much first thing in the morning for tired horses. Go back to the house, there's a good woods dog."

Kiga rumbled in annoyance but turned and loped back to the timber-and-wattle guildhouse. He was almost there when he had to dart to one side or be trod upon by a half-dressed man bursting from the house. With one hand the man held up his breeches as he ran; in the other he clutched a stout cudgel.

As he passed the crouching woods dog, the man glanced at him. Then came a second startled look, a stumble, and a muffled curse; Pod held her breath, fearing the man would fall flat on his face. But he caught himself and staggered to a halt.

The woods dog hurtled across the stableyard to place himself between his person and this unseemly stranger. He crouched at Pod's feet, snarling.

The man gestured at Kiga with the cudgel. His heavy black brows met in a fierce frown and his lips were set in a grim line. "*That,*" he said, glaring at Pod as if she played him a trick, "is a wolvering."

For a moment Pod didn't know what he meant; then she remembered "wolvering" was the southern Kelnethi name for a woods dog. She nodded. "That's Kiga, my familiar."

He studied her, looking, she knew, at her hair. "A girl with white hair and a wolvering. . . . You must be Pod."

"I am." She tilted her head, frowning a little. Was he a Beast Healer visiting from another chapterhouse?

Then she realized that the breeches he wore were dark green; a Beast Healer's would be brown. Her breath caught; she thought she knew who—or rather, *what*—he must be. "You—you're from— Am I—" She was so excited she couldn't finish.

"I'm Leeston from the Healwort Guild. I arrived late last night." He smiled, all fierceness gone. "And yes, you're one of those chosen to go on this training journey, Pod."

She whooped with joy and grabbed Kiga's front paws, pulling him up into a clumsy, shuffling dance.

"We're going, we're going, we're going!" she sang. "We're going on a journey!"

A few days later, Pod stared at Leeston's back as he rode ahead of the group of Beast Healer apprentices. She wished they weren't so pressed for time. She would have liked to ask questions about the plants they passed. But time was in short supply; Leeston had been late getting to the chapterhouse, so now each day they rose before the sun and made camp after its setting.

This journey, Pod decided, had stopped being an adventure. Now it was just a thing to be endured. She turned in the saddle to wave at the other 'prentices strung out behind her. Darby and Marisha, riding side by side, waved back. Their familiars, Hazel and Jobbin—a squirrel and a raven—rode on their shoulders. Jeord, lagging behind, didn't see; he was busy talking to the grey wolf loping alongside his horse.

Funny how Conor never talks about how sore his bottom gets when he goes on his journeys, she thought wryly as she turned back. *He always leaves that part out. Or maybe he's just usually not in this much of a hurry. I wonder if he'll come back for a visit once the big horse fair in Balyaranna is over.* She hoped so; she missed him.

Sighing, she kicked off the stirrups and let her legs dangle. Risla, riding along-side her, said, "Good idea." They both groaned. Risla's familiar, a stag named Fleet, snorted at them as if in amusement as he walked beside his person.

"Wonder how much further," Risla said idly. She twirled a long blond curl around a finger. "Any idea?"

"None. I've never been this far from the chapterhouse since I was brought there," Pod answered. "But it had better be soon. The horses are just about done in."

"So's my butt," Risla said. "You?"

"The same. Still, this makes a nice change from training at the chapterhouse."

"True—and we need to learn the wild plants sometime. This is as good a time as any, I suppose," Risla said.

Pod found her stirrups once more and patted Little Brown's neck. The gelding wearily flicked an ear back at her. "Dare you to ask Leeston if we're close."

"Hah! Do I look stupid? You heard him nearly bite Jeord's head off this morn-ing when he asked. But I suspect it'll be another day or two."

"Jeord's worried about Trebla." An accident as a pup had cost the wolf two of the toes on one paw. Pod thought Trebla was keeping up well, but the freckle-faced Jeord was a worrier. At her back, Kiga grumbled and shifted on his riding pad. "Want to run alongside a bit, boy?"

At the woods dog's yip, she pulled out of the double line of riders and halted. She dismounted and helped Kiga down, then shook her head and smiled. She'd wager that a few miles down the road, Kiga would be begging to get back up. So be it; it was a small price to pay for her familiar. The woods dog started off as she hauled herself back into the saddle with a curse.

"I heard that," a grinning Darby sang out as he passed. Hazel, the squirrel perched on his shoulder, scolded her, one paw twined in her person's hair to steady herself.

Marisha, his twin, laughed and shook back her long, brown hair. Jobbin cawed, a raven's laugh.

"And you'll likely hear worse before this is over," Pod retorted with mock se-verity. "So get used to it, Darby-me-lad."

Six

The rising sun had no strength to break through the grey clouds. *A pity—the dawn was always Sether's favorite part of the day,* Otter thought as he looked out the temple door. *All the monsters of the night flee before the sun.*

The little courtyard before the temple of Auvrian seemed even smaller than usual because of the crowd that filled it despite the louring sky.

You'd think with all those different-colored cloaks that it would look cheerful, Otter thought vaguely as he looked out upon the gathered crowd: mostly bards in red, some minstrels in yellow, and a few townsfolk in other colors. It was good that so many had been able to come to honor Sether. Otter reminded himself to thank Priestess Kaelwynn for her well-cast spell of preservation, which had given them these few precious extra days.

Behind him came the sounds of hammering as Cadfa the coffinmaker nailed down the lid of Sether's coffin. *It should look cheerful. Instead with all that red it looks like, like* . . . He refused to give name to the image that came to mind.

The hammering stopped, replaced by a soft rattle. Charilon came up beside him. "They're almost ready," the other bard said quietly.

Otter nodded and turned back into the temple. Before him the plain coffin of pine, now sealed, rested upon its bier. As he approached it, Cadfa slid the second of the carrying poles through the iron loops that were to hold them. At a signal from the Temple of Auvrian's priest, four sturdy young apprentices bent to the poles and, at a whispered "Now," lifted bier and coffin to their shoulders.

For a moment all was still. Then a soft drumbeat broke the silence. *Gone. Gone. Gone. Gone,* it said. On the fourth beat, the pallbearers stepped out. Otter and Charilon fell in behind as the small cortege began Sether's final journey. By unspoken agreement they went to either side of Rose, Sether's apprentice. She wept softly as she walked.

They passed through the silent crowd, which parted before them. Pacing slowly to the steady beat of the drum, the crowd of bards, apprentices, minstrels, and others followed the coffin out of the temple courtyard and up the long, wide path that led to the guild's cemetery. From time to time a soft sprinkle of misty drizzle blew into their faces.

Otter still couldn't believe it wasn't only a bad dream. *Surely I'll wake up any moment now. . . .*

But before him were the strong backs of the pallbearers, and beside him Rose wept for her master.

It was a long walk at any time and always an extra league or two when it was a friend, Otter thought sadly. But at last the sorrowful parade reached the newly dug grave.

The ceremony was simple. Ropes were slipped under the coffin; when it was secure, the coffin was lifted up over the grave. Then Sether's remains were lowered into the dark earth. Many came forward to cast flowers they'd brought into the grave as the priest intoned the words of farewell.

Charilon began singing "Lady of the White Rose," Sether's favorite song, his voice thick with tears. Others joined in, raggedly at first, but growing strong and true, doing honor to their friend.

When the first shovelful of dirt thudded onto the coffin's lid, many of the mourners began drifting away, unable to watch. They left the rest of their flowers by the side of the grave. Most went back down the winding path; others gathered in small groups, talking quietly and shaking their heads. One by one, they eventually wandered off. In the end, even Rose succumbed to the ministrations of her friends and left with them to a warm fire and a hot meal.

At last only two figures stood by the graveside. A fine mist swirled against Otter's face as he and Charilon looked down at the freshly turned dirt of Sether's grave with its simple stone plaque. They began scattering the mass of flowers left behind over the grave.

When they were finally done Otter said tentatively, "I didn't see Widow Theras. Did she . . . ?" He stopped at the sound of Charilon grinding his teeth.

"No," the other snapped. After a moment Charilon managed to say calmly enough, "I went there last night to tell her that we would be burying Sether today. I was hoping she'd come to her senses. Care to take a guess who was there?"

Otter closed his eyes and wearily rubbed the bridge of his nose. "Lady Romissa."

"How ever did you know?" Charilon said with heavy sarcasm. "You never told me you were a Seer, m'bucko."

"There are many things I've never told you, my lad. Let me make another prophecy: Theras wanted to come, but the good Lady Romissa—"

"Opened her cursed big mouth and rode roughshod right over Theras. Threatened to snitch to their priest, the bloody cow." Charilon spat in disgust.

"And that was that," Otter said.

"And that was that," Charilon agreed.

Both men fell silent again. *Poor Theras,* Otter thought. *Not only did she lose Sether, she's had even the small comfort of saying farewell taken from her. Wonder if she'll ever forgive herself for not having the backbone to stand up to that bitch?*

The faint wind tugged at their cloaks. "Gods, what a waste of a good man," Otter murmured as he pulled his cloak a little closer.

"And still we have no idea why. Even the heavens are weeping over it," Charilon said, looking up at the leaden sky.

"So they are." Otter knelt and gently pushed aside the flowers covering the granite stone set in the center of the grave. He ran his fingers over the outlines of the harp chiseled above Sether's name. The edges rasped sharp and new against the calluses on his fingertips. In time wind and weather would soften them, he knew, just as they'd softened the carvings in another stone not far away.

Otter didn't come here often; there were too many hopes, too many memories buried here, and one day soon enough it would be his turn. Was there still enough room, he wondered. . . .

Otter must have turned his head—or Charilon knew him all too well—for the other bard said, "There's still space on her right. The Guild Master's made sure of it."

Otter nodded, then replaced the flowers and stood. He set off, wending his way among the stones marking the graves of his kind, seeking one particular resting place.

She—they, really; the babe that had been both her joy and her bane rested within the circle of her arms—lay near a spreading maple. Which was only fitting, Otter thought, as he gazed down at the weathered stone. Jaida had always favored a harp of maple wood. Its bright sound suited her lilting voice.

The sweet woodruff he'd planted so long ago sprawled now over both grave and stone. Bending over with a slight groan—damn, but this mist was crawling into his bones—Otter pushed aside the exuberant tangle of whorled leaves so that he could make out her name.

His fingers brushed against something hard and smooth, something that rocked, then steadied itself with a soft clink of pottery against stone. Curious, Otter pulled it out from beneath the woodruff.

It was a small, narrow-mouthed jar, its pale blue glaze crackled and crazed. He could see something inside, but it was too dim to make out what it might be. Charilon joined him as he turned the jar upside down into his other hand. The dried remains of some flowers spilled into his palm.

No, not a jar; a vase.

"What is that stuff?" Charilon asked. "Or, rather, what was it? And who . . ."

Though the dried flowers were so withered as to be well-nigh unrecognizable, Otter felt certain he knew what they were. "Bluebells," he said grimly. "Leet."

Charilon leaned closer for a better look. "Are you certain it's bluebells? And does that have to do with—oh, that's right; bluebells are a part of his family's crest." Charilon shook his head. "He still hasn't forgiven you, has he?"

"For what? That Jaida married me instead of him, or that she died bearing my child?"

"Both. Either."

Otter sighed and poured the crumbling flowers back into the jar. "No, he hasn't. For either thing. Although the first was hardly my fault. She couldn't stand the way he sniffed around to find out hurtful things so he could hold them over people's heads, or how he did petty things to get back at those who crossed him." He set the little vessel back down; no matter who left it here, it was Jaida's now. "I've always been surprised that he hasn't tried to 'punish' me somehow for her death."

"It's odd," Charilon said, half to himself. There came a long silence while the other bard stared down at the weathered gravestone; Otter suspected that Charilon saw something quite different in his mind's eye. He waited for the man to gather his thoughts as the grey mist swirled around them.

"Odd," Charilon repeated vaguely. "How it's back to Leet . . ."

Baffled, Otter asked, "What do you mean, 'back to Leet'?"

Shaking his head like a man waking from a doze, Charilon said, "Oh—thinking about Leet made me think of Sether again. He—Sether, that is—he'd seemed happy enough. But I wonder . . ."

"Wonder what? Was there something after all?"

"Sether always denied it. Said I was imagining things. But if I'm right, it started, oh, about two years or so ago, I think. I remember because Leet took a rather long journey. That was odd for him, so it stuck in my mind. He's not that fond of traveling, as we well know. Might miss a call to play for the king and queen at the castle if he's away!

"Anyway, Leet came back, consulted with Sether—you'd've thought they were bosom friends, Leet was at the Wood Barn so often!—and went off again," Charilon said. He rubbed his chin. "He wasn't gone for so long the second time, and when he came back, he looked damned pleased with himself. Never said why, though. And Sether wasn't quite . . . himself . . . at that time."

Leet up north, about two years ago. Why did that—ah, of course! "He was at Dragonskeep," Otter said. "For at least part of that first journey."

Charilon's eyebrows went up. "Dragonskeep? Really? How strange; I always thought he wouldn't go there because you're there so often. And may I say *that's* been a long drink of vinegar for him all these years, you being so close to Linden Rathan and such a favorite there."

"Be that as it may, he'd made an exception that time," Otter answered absently, thinking of something else. Or, rather, *trying* to think of something.

"Odd how he never bragged about going to Dragonskeep," Charilon murmured as if to himself.

Leet, Sether, and . . . ? But the thrice-damned thought continued to elude him.

Charilon went on, "Wasn't that around the time that outcast came back from Jehanglan?"

"That's right." *Wait—stories . . . books?*

Otter held his breath. He almost had it, it was dancing at the edge of his mind, blast it all, thumbing its nose at him. . . .

"Damn—what was the bastard's name again? Taren Something-or-other, wasn't it?" Charilon waved a hand as if he could pull the name out of the air.

The errant thought slipped away. "Taren Olmeins," Otter answered absently, trying to catch the tail end of his idea before it vanished.

But it was gone for good. He sighed. Ah, well; if it was important, it would no doubt come back to him.

Seven

Raven looked up from the steaming kettle as his aunt Yarrow, a slender, wiry woman, came back from her evening inspection of the horse lines. "All well?" he asked, handing her a bowl of stew and a spoon as she sat on the log seat by the fire.

"So far," Yarrow said as she scooped up some of the hot stew and blew across it. She swallowed the first spoonful and gave a contented sigh. The firelight played on her hair, the same red-gold hue as Raven's. He sat down next to her on the log to eat his own meal.

She turned her head to look at him. The movement set the long clan braids on either side of her face swinging. Had she been a man, there would have been but one braid, and that hanging down her back. "I'd like you to do something for me, Raven."

"Whatever it is, consider it done, Aunt Yarrow," Raven said, and he meant it. Yarrow had taken him in when he'd broken with his father back in Thalnia after his return from Jehanglan. Redhawk Robinson had vowed that if his son didn't come to heel and take up the wool trade, he would disown him. He had done so. Even the knowledge that his son had returned a hero from the journey with the Dragonlords to the mysterious empire of Jehanglan had not been enough to turn aside his wrath—or bend his pride.

But not only had Yarrow given him a place in her holding, she'd made him a partner in—and heir to—her horse-breeding business. Of course, that Raven came with a Llysanyin stallion—unheard of outside of Dragonskeep—hadn't hurt.

Still, he knew she would have taken him in even without Stormwind. He would do whatever he could for her.

"I'd like you to go on ahead to save my place," she said. "Having to use White Birch Pass instead of Widow's Rock set us back at least three days. Damn that landslide!"

"At least we hadn't gotten far into Widow's Rock before those other travelers coming back told us about it. They lost much more time than we did since the 'slide was near the end."

"Thank the gods for that much at least. But we're still behind, and I don't want to push the horses so hard that they lose condition. I also don't want to lose my place on the horse lines at Balyaranna—it took a long time to get such a good spot. And I know of more than one greedy bastard that will claim it in a heartbeat if the fair marshals think I'm not coming."

"And to get it back from them next year would be next to impossible, am I right?" Raven said around a mouthful of stew.

"It *would* be impossible. I might even have to start from the bottom again. Stormwind's the only horse that can get there fast enough and not suffer from it," Yarrow said. "It'll mean a few days of hard riding and being alone until we get there. Will you do it?"

"Of course. I'll pack some things tonight, turn in early, and leave at dawn." He scraped up the last of his stew. "Are you finished? Then I'll take those," he said, and set off to wash bowls and spoons in the nearby stream.

He was to have a few extra days at the fair! And alone! It was all he could do not to whoop aloud.

As he was loping off, his aunt called after him, "Stop by my tent before you turn in. I'll give you money and a letter to the fair marshals."

He knew Yarrow would be generous above the fair's fee and money for food and lodging. *This,* he thought, *is going to be a very good fair.* Raven grinned. He couldn't wait to get started in the morning.

A few days later, Raven rode slowly into the little village of Duffenwich, looking for a likely place to rest for a bit. He hadn't ridden this hard and long since his and Maurynna's desperate journey through Jehanglan.

The road meandered to the village green. There it split and circled the green like a mother's arms before continuing on. At the heart of the close-cropped sward was a well with a stone horse trough beside it. Close by, a chestnut tree spread its branches, shading a rough bench.

Three old men sat on the bench. They watched avidly as he rode up and dismounted.

"Well met, grandfathers," Raven said politely as he lowered the bucket into the well. "A good day to you all."

"And a good day to tha, young man," the old man in the center wheezed as Raven filled the trough for Stormwind to drink.

"Where tha bound for, youngling?" the old man on the right asked when Raven was done.

"Balyaranna." Raven sent the bucket down again, this time for himself. When it was full, he brought it up and balanced it carefully on the stone lip before reaching for the long-handled tin dipper that hung on a nail.

"Ah—tha be going to the big horse fair, are tha?" the old man on the left asked with a toothless grin.

"I am." Sitting on the edge of the stone lip and sipping the cold water, Raven listened indulgently as the old men launched into a veritable flood of advice, memories, and debates on the merits of horses past and present. One horse's name and praises came up again and again: Summer Lightning, the prize of Lord Lenslee of Kelneth's stables.

"His dam, Sun Lady, were foaled around here," the old man in the center said with such pride in his quavery voice that he might have given birth to her himself, Raven thought, amused. "I were there when it happened. I were head groom at Lady Fanna's manor, I were."

Raven talked with them awhile longer while Stormwind cropped the nearby grass. When he was certain Stormwind had grazed enough—and he thought his tired legs wouldn't shake when he stood—he bade them good day and swung up into the saddle again. From here he could see where the road resumed on the far side. As he turned Stormwind's head, one of the old men called up to him.

"If tha does see Summer Lightning, lad, mind thaself around him. His dam were a sweet creature, but his sire were brother to a demon and Lightning took after him and then some, I've heard tell."

Raven was about to say that it was highly unlikely he'd ever be allowed with spitting distance of a noble's favorite, but then considered that, riding a Llysanyin, he might well be able to go places another could not. "Thanks for the warning," he said instead. "I'll remember it."

Eight

Linden rose from his chair at the small table and peered out of the window of their room. Behind him Maurynna and Shima still sat studying the carved and painted game board that took up most of the table's surface. Small tiles of ivory, each with a colored pattern carved into its face, lay here and there upon the board in a seemingly random pattern.

But the arrangement was far from haphazard. For this was *diyinesh,* a game Shima had brought from his homeland. So simple to learn that a child could play it, yet its subtle depths could only be mastered after long study.

"I can't believe it's raining again," he said, glancing over his shoulder. "It's been, what? Three days now? Every time I think it's stopped for good and the sun will soon be out, it starts up yet again."

"If it keeps on like this," Shima said, looking up from the game, "the next time we Change, it will be into Jehangli waterdragons. A pity Miune Kihn isn't here; he at least enjoys rain. Whenever we had a storm back home, he'd dance in the village square and the children would dance with him."

Linden smiled at the image Shima's words conjured: an eel-like waterdragon dancing happily in the rain, waving the feelers on either side of his snout in the air, surrounded by prancing children. It was something he wanted to see one day.

Maurynna put onto the board a blue-edged ivory token with a sun eagle carved on its face.

Shima frowned. "Are you certain you want to play your Luck now? I see at least two other moves you can make. . . ."

"Which will both lose," Maurynna replied tartly, "if they're the same I'm thinking of. And perhaps you can see other moves than those, but I can't." She tapped her Luck piece. "This is my only chance. Now give me the wretched dice."

Cupping them in her hands, she shook them hard, her lips moving silently, then cast the dice on the table. Linden watched with amusement as Maurynna and Shima both leaned over the board, counting aloud.

She sighed. "Oh, bloody . . . Still not good enough, even with the Luck doubling it, is it?"

"Ahh, no."

"I swear those dice hate me," she grumbled as she removed the pieces she'd lost from the board and handed them to Shima. "Thank the gods we don't play for gold—I'd be a pauper ten times over. It's your turn, Linden."

She leaned back in her chair and sipped at her mug. "Oh, well—at least the ale is good and so is the company. They're all horse-mad and half the time I can't follow what they're talking about, but I like Tyrian and his friends. They keep forgetting."

Linden nodded; he knew what she meant. Tyrian and his fellow travelers often forgot they were not truehumans and talked to, argued with, and even chaffed the Dragonlords as they did each other.

As he took his seat once more and scooped up the dice, Linden said, "I'm glad you like them—because when I was downstairs a little while ago, Tyrian and Romsley approached me and invited us to join them on the journey to Balyaranna. I told them that I'd discuss it with the two of you."

From the sudden smile that lit Shima's face, it was plain that *he,* at least, would have no objections.

Maurynna's expression, on the other hand, told another tale. She frowned slightly, and Linden was certain she was about to object. But instead she looked over at Shima and hesitated.

To gain a little time, Linden cast the dice. *It will slow us down, but not too badly, love,* Linden said in her mind as he picked up the tokens he'd just won. *We'd been planning to ride at a leisurely pace, after all.*

True, but we've already lost so much time because of this rain, and the gods only know how much more we'll lose keeping to the pace of ordinary horses. I don't want Raven worrying about us. . . .

She glanced at Shima once more. The Tah'nehsieh Dragonlord must have guessed what was afoot, for he smiled wistfully at her. She went on, *Oh, for pity's sakes—I'll feel like an ogre if I say "No!" Ah, well—if we're too delayed, I can always Change and get word to Raven. So let Shima enjoy Karelinn's company as much as he can.*

"I've no objections," Maurynna said aloud. Then, in outrage, she demanded, "Linden—did you just win the last pieces I still had on the board?"

Startled, Linden looked down and studied the remaining ivory tiles. Not one had the blue edging that marked Maurynna's tokens—but the pieces he held in his hand did. "Ah . . . yes, I guess I did. Sorry, but it was the way the dice fell."

"That tears it. No more *diyinesh* for me. I'm off to tell Tyrian that we'll be traveling with him and his party."

With that, Maurynna stood up and went to the door. Pausing, she said sweetly, "Shima, do me a favor. Grind him into the dirt, will you?"

Before Linden could reply, she blew him a kiss and slipped out the door, laughing. As it closed behind her, he heard her greet Lady Merrilee and Lord Eadain and then their cheerful replies.

As he bent over the table once more, Linden remarked, "Does Lady Merrilee seem happier to you? Since Lord Eadain arrived, I mean."

"What do you mean?" asked Shima.

"There always seemed to be a hint of sadness in her eyes before—Maurynna noticed it as well. She remarked last night that the sadness had eased. She said she didn't think it was just the kitten. Quite the wicked little grin when she said it, too," Linden said with a laugh.

Shima rubbed his chin. "I hope you're right," he said at last. "And a good thing it would be, I think—Eadain seems a good man and it appears the others think well of him. I suspect that there may have been someone else who courted Merrilee, with perhaps a less than happy result. I don't know what happened, but if Eadain can make her forget that other, I know that Karelinn will be happy."

"Bard Otter!"

The call came as Otter and Charilon left the dining hall that evening. The meal had been a somber one; the pall of Sether's death still hung over the school.

Otter had eaten very little; a dull headache beat a drum behind his eyes. He wanted nothing more than a goblet of mulled wine and his bed. Instead he sighed and looked around.

As Otter feared, it was Gwenna, a fifth-year apprentice and one of the Guild Master's messengers. A student he could put off; not so the Guild Master.

She trotted up to him. "Guild Master Belwynn would like to see you, sir."

Otter bit back another sigh. "As always, I'm at the Guild Master's disposal. Lead on, fair maiden."

She giggled. "This way, sir—he's in his workroom."

He followed her through the stone-and-timber halls of the school to the Guild Master's workroom. Gwenna opened the carved door, announced "Bard Otter is here as you requested, sir," and stepped back so that Otter could enter.

As he did, Gwenna closed the door behind him. Belwynn looked up from the lap harp he was stringing.

"Find a seat if you can and sit down, old friend," the Guild Master said. "That one'll do—just move that pile of music over there." He pointed at a table already laden with piles of parchment in danger of toppling over. "Wine?"

Thank the gods, this was to be an informal visit, then. "Thank you, yes."

He must have sounded tired, for Belwynn looked sharply at him, bushy salt-and-pepper eyebrows drawn together in a concerned frown.

"You don't look well. I know you were a good friend of Sether's, but you and Charilon shouldn't have stood about in the mist and rain as you did," he chided.

Trust Belwynn to know. "Sether, Charilon, and I entered the School in the same year," Otter said, accepting a goblet of the spiced blackberry wine that Belwynn favored. "And were fast friends within a tenday." He sipped; a little sweet for his taste, but the spices warmed a man something wonderful as it went down.

"I'm sorry. As I'm also sorry for what I'm about to ask of you; I know you're planning to meet your nephew at the big horse fair in Cassori."

The wine suddenly tasted sour. "Ah?"

Belwynn set the harp aside. "You know that Charilon and Sether were from the same village? Fool thing to say—of course you did. This has been so upsetting. . . ." He shook his head. "Charilon will leave tomorrow morning for their home village to break the news to those of Sether's family still there."

Otter nodded, suddenly sure of what was coming next. "And you'll need someone to take over his students while he's gone."

"I do. The only ones I'd trust with Charilon's most advanced students are Bellina or Leet—or you. I'm sorry, Otter, but with Leet gone and Bellina still recovering from the lung sickness, you're the only one. Tarwillith is not quite ready to take on such advanced students. In a couple of years, yes. But she's not ready yet."

I should have seen this coming, Otter thought wearily. *I knew that Charilon would be making this journey. Damnation; I should have left while I had the chance.* But he'd been so wearied by grief. . . . "I understand. Of course I'll do it, Belwynn."

"Thank you."

Otter could almost hear the unsaid *For not arguing.* Not that he would have won, so why bother?

The Guild Master went on, "I'll arrange for a message to be sent to Balyaranna to your nephew so that he won't worry."

"I'd appreciate that," Otter said. *Poor Nightsong—she was looking forward so much to seeing Stormwind again.* Raven's Llysanyin was her favorite grandson; until they'd chosen to accept truehuman riders, the two Llysanyins had been inseparable.

Then Otter realized he'd have to tell Nightsong it was unlikely they'd go to Balyaranna. He remembered how Shan often reacted when Linden delivered unwelcome tidings.

Oh gods—I hope she doesn't have Shan's temper hidden away somewhere.

He took another sip of his wine. A question popped into his head and onto his tongue before he could squelch it. "Charilon said Leet left before Sether . . . before Sether hanged himself. Do you think he knows about it yet?"

"Not unless one of the messengers came across him by chance. Why?"

Tugging thoughtfully at his beard, Otter said, "No reason, I guess. Just that Charilon had mentioned Leet had spent quite a bit of time with Sether."

"So he had, so he had. I'd forgotten that. Gods, I hope whoever tells him breaks the news gently. It's odd, though—I never would have thought they'd become friends after so many years."

"Nor would I," Otter murmured, staring into his wine.

Nine

The rain finally stopped. Everyone in the inn cheered as the sun broke through the smothering grey clouds at last; in twos and threes they wandered outside, blinking in the bright light like owls forced out into the day, peering up at the sky as if they'd forgotten what the sun looked like.

"Thank the gods!" Linden said fervently as he raised his mug of ale in a toast with the other two Dragonlords. "I'd almost forgotten what that yellow thing in the sky was!" he jested.

Better yet, that evening, while everyone gathered in the private room after the meal, word came that the bridge was passable.

"How?" the gathering chorused in astonishment.

"It was a tree, my lords and ladies, a huge tree that had smashed into the bridge and been tossed half onto it by the flood. They were able to finally get it off and repair the damage with the help of Aderis Wellins, the mage at the Pelnaran court. It seems he was in a hurry to get back to court and had no mind to find another way."

As Elidiane Tunly delivered her news, Linden thought he'd never seen anyone look so relieved.

Wonder if the inn's supplies of ale and wine are running low? he thought in amusement as the eager nobles crowded around her for further information.

I'll speak to Lord Romsley about leaving first thing in the morning, he said in the other Dragonlords' minds.

Shima nodded.

Maurynna replied, *Even if they're not ready to leave so soon, I'd like to set off tomorrow—though I wouldn't want them to feel insulted. Perhaps we could split up and you and I ride ahead, Linden. Shima, would you mind?*

Being hostage to their goodwill? the Tah'nesieh Dragonlord said. *Not at all—it will give me a few days more in Karelinn's company.* He smiled, his teeth white against his dark skin.

It seemed, though, that there would be no need to split up. Their fellow travelers were already at the door, calling excitedly to their servants to begin packing. It seemed everyone had the same idea.

As he made his way to the door, Linden caught a last snippet of the conversation with Mistress Tunly:

"What was that, my lord? Oh, yes—let us indeed hope the gods spare us any more such rain for a good long while!"

The party of Dragonlords, Cassorins, and Kelnethi left the Gyrfalcon's Nest the next morning before dawn.

"We'll have to push the horses to make it there in time," Lord Romsley told the group just before they set out. "And some of us won't be able to keep the pace for one reason or another. Others of us have horses entered in the races and *must* get there if at all possible." He met each sober gaze in turn. "Much as I don't want it, the group may have to split up."

"Don't worry, Romsley," Lord Ephris called out. "I think everyone here understands and there'll be no hard feelings."

Nods and murmurs of agreement met his words.

"Thank you," Romsley said. "And now, my good lords, ladies, and Dragonlords—let us ride!"

They set out at a fast walk, bidding farewell to the inn's owners and staff who had come to wish them a safe journey. The plan was that the group would alternate walking and trotting the horses throughout the day, covering as much ground as they could before stopping.

Thank the gods, Linden said in Maurynna and Shima's minds as they fell into place behind the leaders. *Romsley's set the stage for us to leave the group with no ill will or insult taken.*

But we'll ride with them for a few days at least, won't we? Shima asked anxiously.

We shall, Linden replied. *But Tyrian mentioned last night that Sevrynel will likely ask us to be marshals for the Queen's Chase, the big race held on the solstice. It's considered an honor. We should get there early enough that he doesn't have to ask someone else to give up the honor.*

Isn't that cutting it a bit close, waiting until the last moment to ask for marshals? Shima asked.

Don't worry—the man's well known for it. Linden smiled at a memory.

Race? Marshals? Maurynna's eyebrows went up in alarm. *Will we be expected to ride in the race itself? I'm not certain my riding is up to that.*

No, love, Linden answered, amused. *The racecourse is long and winds through forest and fields. Only the start and finish are seen by the spectators. The marshals are posted along the course to make certain that the jockeys stay honest, ride a clean race, and send the messengers for help if anyone is hurt.*

Ah—is that all? That I can do, Maurynna said confidently.

For a candlemark or so the band of riders kept to the order they'd started in. But after a time, they broke up into groups that shifted and changed as some fell back to give their horses a rest or pushed up to talk to someone else.

After a bit of maneuvering, Shima managed to fall in with Karelinn, Merrilee, and Merrilee's smitten young men. They rode together for a time, talking. Then Merrilee, pleading fatigue, fell back in the group. Her faithful swains followed.

But Shima had seen the wink she'd given her sister. He flashed Merrilee a smile. Merrilee smiled back; but the smile faded as she looked over her shoulder, back the way they'd come.

It was just as he had seen her do in the inn; more than once he'd surprised her gazing from the hall window that looked down this same road, looking back into Pelnar. Once, on his way back from taking carrots to the Llysanyins, he'd even seen her walk to the road, her hooded cloak pulled tight against the rain, to look down it for a short time. Then her head had drooped and she walked slowly back. He'd caught a glimpse of her face, and it was the same expression as always: half hope, half fear. He wondered whom she was looking for—or whom she feared.

He looked around for Lord Eadain; Shima had the feeling that if anyone could lift Merrilee from her doldrums, it would be the crippled young lord. But Eadain was caught between Lord Ephris and Lady Casleen as they argued good-naturedly about the merits of various grasses for hay.

Shima and Karelinn had been riding for a while, talking of this and that, when Shima lifted his face to the sun's warmth. "This is much better!" he said. "When I close my eyes, I can almost imagine myself back in Nisayeh."

"I've heard you mention Nisayeh a few times now, Your Grace. At first I thought it was a city, but it sounds more like a country, which I don't understand. I thought you were from Jehanglan."

Shima shook his head with a grin. "Don't ever let a noble Jehangli hear you say that. It would give him apoplexy. No—I'm but a Tah'nehsieh barbarian from Nisayeh." Taking pity on her confusion, he went on, "While you of the Five Kingdoms call that entire land 'Jehanglan,' in truth only part of it is properly called that. Where the Tah'nehsieh—my people—live is called Nisayeh. It can be a harsh land, but it is also a very beautiful one."

"Ah, I see. Bother—this ribbon's coming loose." She slid the rose-colored ribbon from her hair. "You said you could 'almost imagine' yourself back there. What's different? And do you miss it?"

"Oh, yes—I miss it, but not as much as I feared I would. I think part of me always will miss the desert. Yet when I first saw the mountains of Dragonskeep,

I felt I was finally coming home at last. Every other Dragonlord I've asked about it has said the same. It's taken longer for some than others, but now 'home' is Dragonskeep.

"And as for what's different—the scents are wrong, the sun's not quite hot enough for this time of the day in this season, the calls of the birds are different— oh, a dozen little and big things." Shima shook back his long black hair. "But none of it matters. We're no longer cooped up in that inn, fine as it was!"

"A good thing, too," Karelinn said with a laugh. "I overheard the Tunlys worrying about the food running out—another two days and the meals would have been pease porridge morning, noon, and night."

"Had it come to that," Shima vowed, "I would have braved the rain."

They rode past Lady Kiela. She treated Shima to a barely civil glance and hrmphed slightly as she eased her horse to the side.

"Ah," Shima said. "I fear Lady Kiela still hasn't forgiven me."

Karelinn blinked at him. "For what?" she asked in surprise.

"For making Merrilee cry."

"When—oh! But *you* weren't the one, it was because—" She stopped in confusion. Her cheeks flamed.

Shima nodded. "I wish someone would tell Lady Kiela that. As I also wish I knew what had happened. Who were you 'seeing' that night when I told you two the story of Lenshi and Amsuro and your sister ran off? Whoever it was, I could almost feel sorry for him. I was glad when you said it wasn't me," he said, remembering the hard look in Karelinn's eyes. And perhaps he would find out at last why Merrilee had so often looked down the road leading back to Pelnar. He suspected he could guess at least part of it.

For a moment he thought Karelinn would refuse. Then she looked down at the hair ribbon now twisted around her fingers. She smoothed it out and said, "His name's not important, and I'd rather not say it anyway, my lord. You might meet him yourself someday, so it wouldn't be fair to prejudice you against him. Who knows? Perhaps he'll mend his ways. Let us call him—Lord Charming."

But the way her mouth twisted on the last words told him she thought him anything but.

Karelinn went on, "He's a young Cassorin lord we met the year we stayed with our aunt in Pelnar. Wild and reckless he is, ever ready to flirt, handsome, and with an eye for a pretty girl and a fast horse." She smiled wryly at him. "In short, Your Grace, a young lord like nearly a hundred others I could name for you."

"I could throw in a few of my fellow tribesmen and some Zharmatians I know, my lady," Shima offered. "We'd get that hundred and more easily."

Now her smile lit the world. "Ah, you men—just the same no matter where you're from," she teased him. Then, serious once more, she continued. "Then you know exactly the kind of fellow I mean, my lord. He's the apple of his father's eye. His mother thinks the very dirt he treads upon is diamonds and gold.

Whatever T— Whatever Lord Charming wanted, he got—and more. Much more. All his life, too many people have stumbled over themselves to give him whatever he's wanted."

Shima sighed in dismay and shook his head, thinking that he knew where this trail would lead; no doubt Merrilee had fallen in love with this man, and he cared nothing for her, the fool. "My people have a saying: It is neither wise nor kind to spoil a dog, a horse, or a child. Only ill will come of it."

"Ill did—but I'm getting ahead of my tale. The spoiled child became a spoiled adult. In some ways, Your Grace, it got worse. Women throw themselves at Tir—at Lord Charming. He's as handsome as Merrilee is beautiful."

She stopped, frowning at some memory. To encourage her, Shima ventured, "Let me guess: But he's not as good as Merrilee."

Nodding, Karelinn said, "That's it in a golden nutshell, Your Grace. As I said, he's utterly charming—one of the most charming people I've ever met. That's why almost everyone has indulged him. I swear, sometimes I wondered if he had a 'little magic' that blinded many people to his true self."

Shima nodded. While he'd not met anyone with a talent like that, since he'd been in the north he'd met one or two people with a tiny spark of wizardry in their souls that enabled them to do something that their fellows could not. One of the shepherds that lived near Dragonskeep could call his sheep to him and they would stand like statues for shearing, turning this way and that as he bade them and even rolling onto their backs. "You may well be right."

She went on. "And there's, well, not a 'darkness' within him—that would be going too far, I think. At least, I hope it would be. Yet I would never trust him as a friend, my lord. He's the kind who doesn't give a fig for anyone else—or so I would have said.

"But then he met Merrilee. Aunt Perrilinia said she'd never seen anyone fall so hard in love so fast. I think for the first time in his life that spoiled little lordling cared about another person."

That was a surprise. Shima had been certain that the love was one-sided. *Good thing Lleld wasn't here to lay a wager. I'd have lost,* he said to himself, thinking of the smallest Dragonlord. "What happened?"

Twist, twist, twist; now the ribbon cut into Karelinn's fingers. Shima leaned over in his saddle and gently took it from her.

"Thank you. I hadn't even realized . . ." She inhaled deeply, staring down at the red welts on her skin. "Oh, how he courted Merri! How kind and gentle he was! She began to fall in love with him. Then Father came for a visit. We were supposed to stay for another year, you see, but . . . Merri told Father she thought of marrying. He was happy for her—he truly was. Sad to lose her, but glad that she was happy.

"Then he asked who the lucky man was. When he heard the name . . . My lord, it was awful. He turned first red, then white, and raged that no daughter of his would marry such a bullying, sadistic, cowardly cur. I've never seen him like that. He has a temper, yes, that we've seen often enough. But never anything like that. He was terrifying."

Shima could well imagine that the bearlike Lord Romsley would be frightening if angry enough. But to turn such rage on his daughter? "Why does he hate the man so much?"

Karelinn laughed, a light, bitter laugh. "But Father doesn't hate him, Your Grace."

Shima blinked at Karelinn in surprise. "He doesn't?"

"Oh, no, Dragonlord—Father *despises* him. Utterly. It seems that Merri's charming suitor has a cruel streak in him that he'd been careful not to show her. He got into some kind of trouble back home—that was why he was in Pelnar. His father had sent him away to stay with a distant kinsman.

"You see, Lord Charming and his friends often made a game of tormenting those who couldn't fight back. Most of their victims were peasants, particularly peasant children. Quite safe—who would take their word against that of noble young lords?"

Shima snapped out a curse in his native tongue. "That's not just cruel," he said in disgust, "it's the worst form of cowardice."

Now the laugh was real. "Almost my father's exact words, my lord. But one day they made a mistake. The wretches should have looked more closely at the clothes those 'peasant brats' had left on the riverbank when they went swimming. Two or three of the boys will bear whip scars until they die, Father said. One is the son of a friend of his, Lord Dunhallow. That's how Father knew that the tale was true and not just malicious hearsay.

"And," Karelinn went on, frowning slightly, "there might be worse. Father wouldn't tell us, because he didn't know how much was rumor and how much was truth. Merri and I overheard part of it. Whatever happened, it might have been only a tragic accident, or . . . We never knew for certain. It was something about a horse and a young boy—and the boy died.

"When Merri heard all this, she confronted Lord Charming. He tried to make light of it. To him, he'd done nothing wrong. It broke her heart that he was not the person she'd thought him to be. Oh gods—how he raged when she told him that she would no longer hear his suit. He was like a madman. Said that if he couldn't have her, no one would.

"When his kinsman heard why Lord Charming had left Kelneth and that he'd threatened Merri, he turned the craven out. Then Father told Lord Charming that he'd Challenge him if he ever came near Merri again."

Shima asked, "And is your father a good swordsman, Lady Karelinn?"

She smiled. *Like a cat looking at a mouse,* Shima thought with amusement.

"Your Grace, Lord Charming was gone by the next dawn."

Ten

"See that, lad?" Raven said. He pointed to a wooden sign hanging from the branch of a huge old oak at the head of a small lane that branched off the road. It bore the gaily painted image of a brown-and-white cow standing in a patch of sunflowers.

"This is the Spotted Cow. Aunt Yarrow said that it's a day's ride to Balyaranna from here. But it'll be less than that for us, won't it?" He guided the Llysanyin onto the turnoff to the inn.

Stormwind nodded, but turned his head to look back at the road as if to say, *So why are we stopping? It's early yet.*

Raven laughed and patted him. "I know you're still fresh, but I'm about done in, we've been riding that hard. And I'm tired of camping by the wayside to save Aunt Yarrow's coin. A hot meal and an easy night's rest will do us both good. Not to mention a bath for me and a good grooming for you. I want us both to look our best when we reach the fair."

The Llysanyin rumbled deep in his chest as if agreeing. They rode slowly down the lane, baking in the noonday sun.

A short time later, after a meal and a rest, Raven decided to wander out to the stable to see how Stormwind was faring. Before he could get to the door, it opened and some travelers he had passed earlier that day entered. Raven stood to one side.

Three of the travelers, two men and a tired-faced woman, all dressed as servants, hurried past him. They carried bundles in their arms.

They were followed by another group, likely a family, he thought; an older couple, two young men laughing about "the plow horse" in the stable, and a boy of thirteen or so. One of the young men looked familiar to Raven now that he got a good look at him, but he couldn't place the man. The boy chewed his lip like one trying to figure something out.

Judging from both clothing and bearing, they were noble. He bowed as they passed him; he was in Cassori now and the highborn folk expected such as their due. They, in turn, ignored him after the barest glance. *Servant,* their eyes said. *Commoner.*

All save the boy. He looked back at Raven and fell behind the rest. The woman noticed. "Arisyn! Come along now."

"Yes, Lady Venna!" the boy said, and scurried after the others.

Guessed wrong, Raven thought with amusement. *It wasn't his mam after all.*

He continued on. But when he glanced back as he went out the door, he saw Arisyn standing on the bottom step of the stairs to the sleeping rooms, staring after him.

I wonder what that's about! he thought a little uneasily as he crossed the courtyard to the stable. *Maybe I just remind him of someone and he's trying to remember who.*

After all, fair was fair; he was trying to remember one of the boy's companions. He pulled a brush from the saddlebag hanging by Stormwind's stall.

"Move over, lad," he said, slapping Stormwind's rump.

Though the Llysanyin had been well groomed, Raven began brushing out his tail; the ritual was soothing for both of them. He hummed under his breath as he worked.

"Ready for the fair?" he asked after a time.

Stormwind nodded.

"I thought it was you!" a young voice said.

Startled, Raven jumped and looked around. Standing in the aisle was Arisyn.

The boy stared at Stormwind, his face screwed up in thought. After a long moment, he relaxed and shook his head. "You passed us on the road. I know that Coryn and Dunric think your horse is naught but a Shamreen, one of those big draft horses from northern Yerrih, but I don't. Even big as he is and with the feathers, there's something too refined about him. He's not a plow horse, I don't care what they said!"

Arisyn chewed his lower lip in fierce concentration for a moment, then blurted out, "But for the life of me, I can't figure out what he is!"

And you likely wouldn't believe me if I told you, my fine young lord, Raven thought. He hid a smile. So the lad fancied himself an expert on horses? *Hmm— compared to his two kinsmen or friends or whatever, he is an expert,* Raven decided. Stormwind a plow horse, indeed!

Before he could speak, the boy held up one hand imperiously. "No, no—don't tell me! I want to figure it out on my own." Then, after a long moment, "Um—but perhaps you could give me a hint? Just a little one, mind you!" he said in a rush.

Chuckling, Raven bowed with a flourish. "As you wish, my lord. Here's your hint: Those like my lad here are not *commonly* found."

The boy's mouth twitched up in a wry grin. He was a sturdy fellow, with brown hair that fell back from a sharp widow's peak, and a pleasant, snub-nosed face that Raven liked. "As if I hadn't guessed *that* already. Ah, well—it's my own fault, I suppose. I did say a 'little' hint."

"That you did, my lord."

Stormwind snorted in amusement.

Before the boy could say anything else, an irritated voice called, "Arisyn! Where are you, curse it all?"

Arisyn groaned and rolled his eyes. "That's my cousin's friend, Dunric. I have to go."

At the door to the stable he turned suddenly and demanded, "Are you going to the fair?"

"I am."

"Good! I'll find you there. I *will* figure this out, you know."

"I believe you, my lord," Raven answered.

Eleven

It had been a hard ride to the encampment that served as the Wort Hunters' starting place for the teaching treks. Pod groaned and stretched in the saddle; Little Brown's head drooped as he came to a halt. Behind her Kiga shifted on his riding pad and grunted his impatience to set paw to dirt once more.

"Give me a moment, Kiga! There's no need to get your whiskers in a knot," Pod complained as she wiped the sweat from her forehead. "First we need to see where we're supposed to go."

The rest of the apprentices from Grey Holt pulled up alongside her. Knowing that some of the brothers-in-fur might frighten horses that weren't used to such creatures, they kept well back from the picket line of the Wort Hunters' mounts.

Darby's squirrel, Hazel, was not likely to be a problem, Pod thought, nor Marisha's raven, Jobbin. But Jeord's Trebla and her own Kiga almost certainly would be. Even Risla's stag, Fleet, might spook a horse or two. And often that was all the excuse the other horses in a picket line needed to panic.

"Feh," Jeord said in disgust. "My tunic feels like it's glued to me." He tugged at it. "I hope there's a stream to swim in."

"Look," Risla said. "Someone's waving us over to him."

Sure enough, a tall, lean fellow with the weathered look of one who spent his life outside was pointing to a small, shady grove bordering the encampment. They turned their tired horses and rode to meet him.

"Welcome," he called. As they neared him, Pod realized most of his height was in his legs; she thought they were the longest she'd ever seen. "My name is Fiarin," he said.

They returned his greeting in tired voices.

As they cared for their horses, Fiarin went from one to the other lending a hand, learning each 'prentice's name and the name of his or her brother-in-fur, and introducing himself to the animals.

Pod was pleased to see the last; it meant that even if he didn't regard the familiars as "people" the way every Beast Healer did, Fiarin understood the courtesies. And Kiga seemed to like him. The woods dog snuffled the hand held out to
him, then bumped his head against it, asking for a scratch behind the ears. Fiarin
complied with no hesitation.

Points to him, Pod thought. *It's not everyone who'll trust a familiar that's a
wild animal—especially a woods dog!*

When they were done with the horses, Fiarin led them to tents already set up
for them in a line with the Wort Hunters. "And if you like," he said, "there's a pond
beyond those birches for anyone who wants a swim."

He grinned at their whoops of joy. "Mind you, though, it's spring-fed and
cold."

A moment later they'd left him behind. As they raced for the pond, he laughed
at their mad dash.

Refreshed by her swim, Pod sat behind a line of tents and brushed Kiga. The
woods dog made little growls and grunts of satisfaction as she worked.

"Have a seat. Want some wine?" a man's voice asked.

Pod jumped and looked around. There was no one there.

"Don't mind if I do," another man answered, and she realized that the voices
were coming from the tent next to hers. Relieved that she wasn't imagining things,
she continued working on her familiar.

"Thank you kindly, old fellow. So what did you think of *that?*"

She knew she shouldn't eavesdrop, but she was too tired to move. And, she
admitted to herself, too curious. What was the mysterious '*that*'?

"Baylor's news about Currin, and the fire at White River chapterhouse? I
think Currin is a damned lucky dog—can you imagine finding a stand that size
of King's Blood! Fifty plants!" A sigh of pure envy followed.

"I once found three plants and counted myself the most fortunate of men,"
Second Voice said. "Let us hope Master Heron doesn't hear of it before he leaves.
I swear the man's been thinking of looking for the old stand."

"By the gods, you don't think he'd really do that, do you?" First Voice said,
shocked. "He wouldn't! Not with two youngsters in tow—not even he would be
so mad."

"We hope he wouldn't." Second Voice sounded as if he wasn't as certain.

First Voice went on, "Any road, he won't hear of it. I saw Baylor stop to tell
Mistress Helda the news after he told us. She damn near dragged him off his
horse, shaking her head and telling him to shut his mouth. She had that look of
hers that says 'Don't cross me,' and Baylor's not fool enough to do that even for
such a fine bit of news as this. So if we keep our mouths shut as well, Master

Heron won't hear of it before he leaves—" Here First Voice paused as if to take a drink.

Master Heron? Who's that? Pod wondered. She was certain she'd met all of the Wort Hunters and just as certain none was named Heron. She began going over in her mind who it might be.

First Voice continued, "*Or* about the fire. Do you think it was really as bad as Baylor said?"

"If he's right, we're in for a bad time when the lung sickness returns next winter. White River *is* where the most valuable herbs are kept, after all," Second Voice said heavily.

Silence followed the last words. Kiga bumped Pod's hand, reminding her that he was there. She tickled him under his chin and continued brushing.

The conversation in the tent resumed once more. "Then let us hope Baylor is exaggerating—as usual!—and not about Currin. Pass your mug over, lad, and have a bit more wine."

"Thank you. Heh—when he finds out, Master Heron'll be so pissed we'll have to pour him into a bucket! He and Currin have been rivals for years."

"Gods, yes! I'd forgotten, they're both so rarely about the chapterhouse."

"Always out hunting, those two. Old Heron found a patch of twenty or so plants years ago and has lorded it over Currin—and the rest of us—ever since. This will be a sweet payback for Currin when next they meet." There was a long pause, then, "Oh, to be that proverbial fly on the wall . . ."

The voice sounded so wistful that Pod nearly laughed.

From the other side of the camp another voice hallooed something Pod couldn't make out. First Voice yelled back, "What? Oh, very well. We'll be right there."

She heard the two men grumble their way out of the tent. The next moment the whole conversation was driven out of her mind when the solid weight of the woods dog slammed into her and knocked her to the ground. He snarled fiercely, his ivory fangs snapping in her face.

Kiga wanted a wrestling match.

That evening after the meal they gathered around a roaring bonfire, mingling with the Wort Hunters, introducing themselves, learning names, answering questions about their familiars, and asking their own about herbs. Pod found herself talking with Kaeliss, a young journeywoman originally from Pelnar. She seemed entranced by Pod's white hair, for her gaze kept straying to it as they talked.

"Are you one of the Kelnethi royal family?" Kaeliss finally asked. "Though your name sounds Yerrin," she added doubtfully.

It was a question Pod was used to, but that didn't make it any easier to answer. "I don't know," she said.

"Didn't your mother or father ever say anyth—" Kaeliss began.

"I never knew them. I'm an orphan," Pod said shortly. And for all she knew it was true. Her mother at least was dead; that she knew for certain. As for her father, well, only the gods knew. But "orphan" was better than "bastard." People looked at you all sideways if they thought you were a bastard, as if it were somehow your fault. She went on, " 'Pod' is the nickname that Conor and Lin— The two people who found me gave me the name."

She'd almost said "Linden Rathan" but was suddenly afraid that Kaeliss would either not believe her, or worse, think she was bragging. And everyone always wanted to know all about the Dragonlord. But she'd been so young that her memory was simply of a big man with blond hair and a deep, comforting voice, a man who had been kind to her.

She was saved from more questions by a summons from Master Varron, the senior Wort Hunter in charge of the encampment. "Gather together!" he boomed. "All come to the bonfire, all co-ome!"

Pod quickly stood, thankful for the reprieve. Along with her fellow apprentices and the Wort Hunters, she made her way to the circle of logs around the bonfire and took a seat. Kiga plunked himself down on the ground between her feet. Pod scratched his back and stared into the blazing fire that held back the night around them. Kaeliss took the place next to her.

When they were all settled, Master Varron beamed at all of them. "Welcome all," he said. "And a special welcome to our friends from Grey Holt. We're glad Leeston was able to reach you in time so that you could join us, for the teaching journeys begin tomorrow.

"Apprentices and journeymen, Wort Hunters and Beast Healers—you will go in small groups for your journeys so that you may have the fullest attention of your teachers. From this spot a variety of places can be reached on foot: old woods, marshlands, hills and valleys, pine forests—all places where useful and valuable herbs grow. You will learn as much as possible in each area, then return here so that you may have a day or so of rest, then be sent on to learn in a new place. So over time you will learn the herbs of each habitat.

"This is especially important for you young Beast Healers. Once we're past our apprenticeships, we Wort Hunters often choose to concentrate on plants from a certain area, be it woods or marsh or meadow. But you Beast Healers must go wherever your animal patients are. You need to know about the plants in many different areas.

"And now I shall ask Mistress Helda to give you your assignments." With that, Master Varron took a seat.

Pod sat up a bit straighter. She recognized the name from the conversation she'd overheard and wondered what such a fearsome woman would look like.

Mistress Helda proved to be an elderly woman with a face seamed with wrinkles. Despite her age, though, she strode briskly to take her place before the bonfire. She stood, scroll in hand, and surveyed them. "A fine-looking group," she said approvingly. "A fine-looking group you are, indeed. Luck and good learning to you all."

She snapped the scroll open and, holding it to the light, began reading in a clear, firm voice. Pod soon noticed that while the apprentice Wort Hunters might go in groups of two or three, the young Beast Healers were never two together. She listened carefully and finally heard her name.

"Pod of the Beast Healers, Kaeliss Ageslin of the Wort Hunters—you will both start with the woodland plants. Your instructor will be Fiarin Smithson."

Beside her Kaeliss gave a squeal of pleasure. The young Wort Hunter leaned over and whispered, "Hurrah! We're lucky—Fiarin is one of the most successful Wort Hunters—and I've heard that he's generous with what he knows, not like some others."

For a moment Pod didn't know what she meant, then remembered something Jeord had said on the journey here: "Gunnis told me that the Wort Hunters hunt not just for their Guild, but for themselves as well. They're paid by the Guild for what they find and the competition between them can be harsh."

The idea of such competition had seemed alien to Pod then, and she wasn't sure she understood it any better now, even after overhearing that earlier conversation. Still, she supposed she was lucky to get Fiarin rather than the mysterious Master Heron; she still hadn't figured out who he was. Perhaps tomorrow . . .

No, tomorrow they would be on their way shortly after dawn—or so Mistress Helda was saying to a chorus of groans.

"To bed with you all! To bed!" Mistress Helda said, shooing them all off.

Soon Pod was wrapped in a light blanket, one hand resting on the softly snoring Kiga. She fell asleep wondering what new plants she would learn about.

In the middle of the night something woke Pod. "Whaa?" she mumbled into the darkness.

"I drank too much wine," Risla whispered urgently. "I'll never make it until morning. Come with me? Please?"

"Guh. Give me a moment. Kiga—stay."

The woods dog snuffled and curled up again on his blanket. Pod hastily pulled on her clothes. She crawled to the tent's door and undid the tie holding it shut. "Ready?"

"Gods, yes!"

Pod led the way into the moonlit night. Risla motioned for Fleet, sleeping outside the tent, to stay when the stag made to rise. The two girls trotted through the camp and across the field to the woods. As Risla disappeared behind some bushes, Pod kept watch.

Something moved at the far end of the camp. Pod ducked beneath a bush, wishing she'd brought Kiga along. Then she recognized the tall figure of Fiarin.

Had he also had too much wine? Oh gods, if he began to unlace his breeches . . . Pod made ready to cover her eyes.

But Fiarin stopped at the edge of camp and turned, looking to the west, his back to her, hands at his sides.

He was still there when the girls slipped back into their tent.

Twelve

It was early yet to stop, but Leet was sore and tired. He was also alone on the road for once; he'd turned down numerous invitations from parties who thought that it would be a fine thing to have a minstrel entertain them every night. If any site looked even remotely appealing, he'd camp now.

Shading his eyes with a hand, he scanned the surrounding countryside. A tiny flash between far-off tree trunks caught his eye. A heartbeat or two later his tired mind said, *Water.* With a sigh of relief, he turned his horse's head to the left and slowly rode down a gentle slope and through a rocky meadow filled with wildflowers.

Bees thrummed as they bumbled from flower to flower in the warm sunlight and he could hear cicadas singing in the trees that surrounded the meadow. His leg brushed against a small shrub with fernlike leaves. A sweet odor tickled his nose for a moment, and then he was beyond it.

Wonder what that was, he thought without any real interest. He was sure there were those among his brethren who could name it—fools like Otter who enjoyed gallivanting about. He wished he was back in his comfortable quarters or sitting before Queen Aelynn in Bylith. He could still turn back. . . .

No; this was for Arnath. Arnath who had shown such promise; Arnath who would have followed in his footsteps with honor and acclaim.

He would endure anything for Arnath's sake—for the sake of revenge. It was Thomelin's fault, really, that he was driven to this. If the child's father hadn't been too much of a coward to Challenge that murdering bastard . . .

The sound of distant voices came to his ears, carried on a sultry breeze. Leet cursed and kicked his tired horse into a canter. The packhorse snorted a protest as the sudden change of gait caught it off guard. Could he make the trees by that hint of water before they saw him?

He could. Leet drew both horses behind a screen of underbrush just before a party of travelers passed by. He could hear their loud banter and the creaking axle of their small oxcart even from here. Peddlers on their way to the fair at Balyaranna, no doubt. He held his breath, fearful that they would somehow spot him and decide that they, too, would stop early.

But the group was soon out of sight. Leet sighed in relief and set about making camp.

The glint of water he'd seen proved to be a small, spring-fed pool. Leet picketed his horses out of sight of the road and relieved the packhorse of its burdens. Next he led each horse in turn to the pool and let it drink, then hobbled and fed them. As they munched contentedly in their nosebags, Leet set himself to gather wood, interrupting that task from time to time to arrange rocks to shield the glow from the fire he'd light for his meal or to pick berries he'd found.

Without conscious thought, Leet busied himself with a hundred little things, pushing himself even though his weary body cried out for rest. At last there was nothing else to do. The horses were settled for the night, his meager meal cooked and eaten, and he had enough firewood to feed a much larger fire than he'd built for the night.

Twilight was creeping over the land when Leet found himself sitting on a log before his little fire, his arms wrapped around his knees, rocking back and forth. There was nothing to do, nothing to distract him from . . .

He was imagining it, that sweet seductive humming at the back of his mind. He had to be imagining it. But it felt real. He *knew* the harp was calling him; the very special harp that he'd forced Thomelin to make for him. But it was just a harp. . . .

Yet if it was just a harp, then all he'd done, all his planning was for naught. With a start, Leet recognized the small voice that denied that the harp might have powers for what it was: fear. Fear that his wild guesses had been right. Fear that he would not be able to master . . .

"I am a bard," he growled to the gathering night. "By Auvrian's golden harp, I am a Master Bard, an elder of my guild. If it can be done, I will do this thing."

With that, Leet rose. A groan escaped his lips as his abused muscles protested; with ruthless determination, he pressed his lips closed against it. For a moment he stood, gathering his will, then walked stiffly to where the two crates with their harps inside rested. He ran his fingers over the V shape carved into the wood of one of them.

"Thomelin said that you would be held by the silk and the rowan wood," Leet whispered as he eased off the ropes holding the lid. "But I still can hear you calling, can't I, Gull?"

He slid the lid to one side and pulled the blood-colored silk away from the harp, then drew it into his arms. "So was I right, Gull? Was your spirit in that witch spruce as the old legends say? Or was it all just the fevered imaginings of an obsessed old man?" he said, remembering the books he'd read in the library of Dragonskeep, the volumes written by the now long-dead Lord Culwen who had been so fascinated by tales of death and evil.

A shimmer of notes drifted on the greying light. A sudden breeze through the strings? But not a leaf stirred. Was it . . .

Leet settled himself back on the log. "Let us see, Friend Gull. Let us see. . . ."

He began playing.

The camp always seemed so empty after all the Wort Hunters and the apprentices left, Mistress Helda thought as she sipped her tea in the main tent. She wondered what plants—and knowledge—they'd bring back with them and hoped no one would get hurt. It seemed that every year, at least one clumsy 'prentice would stumble into a nest of bees or wasps, wade through the biggest patch of poison ivy in the land, mistake moonseed for wild grapes, or—or *something*.

At least word of Currin's incredible find of King's Blood or the fire at White River hadn't gotten out before the groups left. She'd gotten to Baylor before he could spread the news. Readen and Fenris—the only two Baylor had told before she'd spoken to him—hadn't told anyone, either, they'd said. They'd just gone to Readen's tent to discuss it privately.

Mistress Helda closed her eyes for a moment to offer up a quick prayer of thanks. She'd have to find Varron and tell him, of course. But by the time everyone returned, it would be too late for a certain overly competitive Wort Hunter to try for the Haunted Wood.

She shivered. She hated being even this close to it.

The more Leet played, the more convinced he became that he'd been right. There was power here. Faint, so very faint, but unmistakable power—though it seemed reluctant to wake fully. It felt, he thought with grim amusement, like a lazy farm lad who didn't want to get up and was determined to stay asleep no matter how loudly the rooster crowed in his ear. He played with a delicate touch, improvising or coaxing old songs from the strings, songs that perhaps the one whose spirit he hoped dwelt within the harp would recognize. As he played his thoughts began to wander.

He remembered the first hint he'd had that the gods favored his plan; he'd thought he would faint when he found the map in a book at Dragonskeep—the map that showed where Gull was buried. It had been so easy to slice the page from the book when the Dragonskeep archivists' backs were turned.

It had not been as easy finding men desperate enough to enter the Haunted Wood, even for that much gold, even though they knew exactly where to go. If they had known what tree they were felling . . . But he'd paid them well; enough that they could leave and begin new lives elsewhere where their reputations would not follow them.

As for the others, it had been the luck of the gods themselves that had given him the means of coercing each man. And that, Leet believed, meant that the gods felt his cause was right. He savored the thought.

Suddenly the bard realized that his improvisations had subtly shifted from random patterns to the beginnings of a melody. There was only a hint of it so far, yet it was quite a pretty one, he thought. Though there was a sense of . . . longing? Desire? No, that wasn't quite right. So what—

He was suddenly aware of his horses' nervous whickerings and stamping of feet. Then a movement caught the corner of his eye. Startled, Leet gasped and looked up from the strings, fearing bandits.

It was only a deer—a fawn, really—that stared back at him, its brown eyes filled with bewilderment and fear. Even as he exhaled sharply in relief, Leet was seized with a desire to sink his teeth into the fawn's tender throat. To feel the hot, sweet blood run down his chin . . .

Leet retched at the thought, nearly dropping the harp. The song—if that's what it was—ended in a jangle of notes. As if released from a spell, the fawn bounded away.

It was only then that Leet recognized the feeling he'd tried to put a name to before: hunger.

A deep, dark, soul-wrenching hunger. Shaking, Leet laid the harp in its case and threw the silk cloth over it. He burrowed into his blankets and stared into the fire until sleep claimed him.

The sun in his face woke Leet. He lay still, trying to remember. . . .

Such strange dreams! Such strange, strange dreams!

His fingers twitched. He was suddenly aware of a desire to pick up the harp again. For he now realized there had been something more than just that frightening hunger last night; there had been something elusive woven through it like a shining gold thread in an acre of cloth.

Joy. He'd felt it, a feather's touch. Leet crawled out of his blankets and looked hungrily at the harp.

This time, before he began playing, he laid his knife on the log beside him.

Thirteen

Otter lay in bed, listening to the storm that had swept in from the west after dinner, glad to be somewhere warm and dry even if he couldn't sleep. Thunder boomed and rumbled, rattling the windows, even shaking the sturdy walls now and again. Lightning blazed across the sky, turning night into day. Almost worse was the wind: it howled around the eaves like a hungry ghost.

Yawning, he pulled the pillow around his head and turned his face to the wall. He then arranged a bit of blanket to shield his eyes from the sudden bursts of blinding light.

Mm—it was working, he thought sleepily after a bit, his thoughts turning honey-thick with fatigue. Teaching students was hard work. Kept him on his toes, they did. A fine lot they were, though; Charilon was doing a good job with 'em. . . . Could hardly hear anything, thank the gods for feather pillows. Storm was moving off, too, getting longer and longer between lightning and thunder. Oh, yes, slipping away. . . .

The clap of thunder was so loud he would have sworn on all he held dear that it went off just above his nose. He jumped, and half fell out of bed. Untangling himself from the blankets, Otter crawled from the bed and groped for the breeches and tunic he'd left hanging over the chair, grumbling all the while as he dressed once more. The storm raged overhead.

Bloody hell, a new storm must have moved in—and a nasty one to boot! Worst I've heard in years. Gah—I'll never get back to sleep with this racket; might as well take myself downstairs and see if there's a bit of bread and cheese left over from dinner.

Moving as quietly as he could, Otter slipped from his room and padded barefoot down the hall. No light from the celestial tantrum outside reached this inner hall, but it didn't matter. He knew these halls as well as—hell, even better than—the reflection of his own face. As he went down the staircase, he skipped the sixth step from the top without even thinking about it. He'd learned well as an apprentice that on a damp night it would let out a squeak that could wake the dead.

Not that anyone would hear it tonight. . . .

When he reached the main hall, Otter paused for a moment to listen and carefully look around. No, no one about; he hurried on into the passage to the kitchen.

Not that anyone would say anything to a senior bard on a midnight food raid. But he'd been caught enough times before he'd reached such an exalted rank that old habits died hard. Besides, it made him feel young again.

Otter grinned as he reached the kitchen undiscovered. He hadn't lost his touch. And there was just enough glow from the banked hearth fire for someone who knew his way around. If he were younger, he'd dance a jig.

Not long after, Otter had his plunder wrapped in a cloth napkin and was ready to leave. He paused in the doorway, turning around to look back into the kitchen. Bread and cheese alone would be dry eating; perhaps a bit of good brown ale that wasn't under lock and key . . .

"The keg's in a different place these days—we stuck it amongst the barrels of vinegar," a voice whispered from the blackness of the hall behind him. "Tap's still where it's always been, though."

Otter yelped in surprise. He spun around, swearing under his breath at the man standing behind him, candle in hand. The faint light turned the other's grin into a troll's leer.

"Damn it all, Geryd, don't *do* that! You nearly—" Otter paused as the other's words sank in. He laughed softly. "By all the gods—you mean that you and Bern—?"

"And Towhee are still sneaking a keg of the best stuff and hiding it? We certainly are. Shame to let a good tradition die, don't you think? Had to stop for a while when someone found the full keg amongst the empty ones, though; that's when we moved it.

"And it's bit harder these days. You and Olinia aren't here very often to help anymore. Naril, Jaida, and—" A pause as Geryd swallowed hard. "—and Sether are gone, and our backs aren't what they used to be. But we still manage—haven't had to ask one of the youngsters to help us yet," Geryd said smugly. He raised the candle; its bright light shone on his bald head. "Come along—I'll show you where it is now. And speaking of traditions, once you've gotten your ale, take yourself down to the old practice room in the north wing to see another one still going strong. They're even using that same beat-up old bench. Remember—don't let them see you. Might make 'em nervous."

The old practice room was never used anymore. Instead it had become a kind of a graveyard for harps. A cracked pillar? Put it in the old practice room until it could be fixed—*if* it could be fixed. Impossible to keep the tuning pegs from slipping all the time? Store it until someone could set it to rights. A harp had outlived its player? Tuck it away with the others until someone had the heart to make it sing once more.

For generations of fledgling bards, it had made a wonderful place to tell ghost stories.

Otter could hear the murmur of voices, muffled squeals, and nervous giggles that spoke of a gathering even before he reached the corner. Gods, things hadn't changed a bit since he'd last been down here, first as a nervous youngster getting the daylights scared out of him, then as an older 'prentice doing his best to give his younger cohorts nightmares. In his day, thunderstorms or winter nights with howling winds had been deemed the best time for a session of scary tales; it seemed these youngsters thought the same. The tradition was still alive and well.

He cat-footed down the hall and settled himself against the wall opposite the open door of the practice room. Here, in the deepest shadows, he could see into the room—at least a bit—but unless someone came to the door, he couldn't be seen by those within. This was a thing for the younglings.

Inside it was just as it had always been. A small fire burned on the hearth, making the shadows dance eerily, playing tricks on the eyes. Draped harps turned into hunched-over trolls, or a pair of young 'prentices huddled together beneath a blanket became a two-headed monster in the flickering glow. Here and there it glinted on eyes round with delicious fright. Judging by the number of mouths gaping open in fear and wonder, someone was telling a corker of a story. Otter pulled off a chunk of bread, bit off a mouthful of sharp cheese, and leaned back to enjoy himself.

Not bad at all, Otter thought, nodding from time to time as he listened. *Not bad at all and some are damned good; they're giving* me *a good case of the cold grues!*

He grinned. This was just what he needed; he hadn't had this much fun in a long time.

The curly-haired young man who currently held the floor finished his story to a round of muffled shrieks and nervous laughter. He stood up, bowed with a flourish, and relinquished the storyteller's "throne"—a battered bench that had seen much better days, held together now by glue, twine, and the goodwill of the gods—to another young man and a young woman working their way through the audience. Both were medium height, with dark brown hair and apple-cheeked faces.

Otter sat up a bit straighter. *These must be Elrin and Daralinia, the brother and sister from up north that Geryd told me about when he tapped the keg. Where were they from? It had something to do with why they're so good at this, Geryd said. Oh, that's right: Little Coppice. Same place as Daera. Surprising that such a small village has produced three bards. Little Coppice . . . Still don't see why that would make them so special. Ah, well—let's see if they're as good as Geryd says.*

They were. Both were uncanny mimics; they took turns telling their stories, and while one spoke, the other imitated sounds like wind moaning through tree branches or the eerie hooting of a killy owl with its unnerving screech of *k-k-killl, k-k-kiiillly!* at the end.

Oh, my—look at those faces. There's going to be some with nightmares to-night!

Otter rubbed his hands in delight; he might well be one of the victims. These two were *good,* and they had a seemingly inexhaustible fund of terrifying yarns. But from time to time as he listened to the duo, the question nagged at the back of his mind: What did their home village have to do with their tales?

He got his answer when, at the end of their turn, one of the youngsters asked, "How do you two know so many scary stories?"

The siblings looked at each other and laughed. Daralinia said, "How can we *not* know scary stories, spratling, considering what our village is near?"

"What's that?" several voices chorused.

"Why, the forest that holds the grave of Gull the Blood Drinker. Lost in the woods, it is now," Elrin said, his voice low and menacing. "But you can find it—if you're foolish enough. Go into the deepest, darkest part, until you can't walk anymore, until the trees are crowding around you, and where on even the brightest summer day the sunlight is sickly pale."

The wind sobbed and whistled outside the windows. Something—leaves? Twigs? Skeleton fingers?—tap-tapped against the glass.

Elrin whispered harshly, "Go on until you feel eyes boring into your back. Go on until you hear whispers just at the edge of your hearing, and something chitters soft and cold from the leaves above you. That's when you know your luck's run out. Say whatever prayers you know. You're in the heart of the Haunted Wood."

The window latch rattled as if something more than the wind wanted entry.

"And if you've been very unlucky indeed, you'll find yourself in front of a certain tree. It's the witch spruce they planted over that evil, evil soul to keep it from walking. . . . Oh, yes, it's still there, grown huge on the dark spirit feeding it, its branches waving even when there's no wind, for Gull . . . still . . . seeks . . ."

Here Elrin waved his arms and swayed like a tree in a storm while he made a sound so exactly like the creaking of a branch—or perhaps a branch stretching out—that Otter looked up and down the dark hall. Not that anything would be there . . .

The low, menacing voice whispered, "For Gull . . . still . . . seeks . . . BLOOD!"

As Elrin shrieked the last word, Dalarinia lunged at two girls sitting huddled together under a blanket and pulled it up over their heads just as a blast of thunder rattled the walls. The girls screamed; so did at least half the audience. A moment later, everyone burst into laughter, the two "victims" loudest of all.

"That was *fun,*" one said when she finally caught her breath. "Tell another story!"

"Yes! Yes!" demanded a chorus.

"Another night," Elrin said. "It's late, sprats, and time to sneak back to your beds."

That was Otter's signal to take himself off before he was seen. He grabbed his mug, stood up stiffly—*Owww, how long was I sitting there, anyway?*—and scuttled off, leaving behind the sounds of scraping chairs and lively chatter. It wouldn't do to let the younglings know that they'd had an unseen audience; let them think—as he and his friends had thought—that it was a cleverly kept secret only they enjoyed.

All his friends, that is, but Sether. *Poor Sether; never could stand those gatherings,* Otter thought, tired but content as he made his way back up the stairs to his room. *Wonder if there's anyone like him in this bunch—*

He stopped dead on the stairs. "By all the gods," he said aloud. "*Now* I remember what it was about Leet at Dragonskeep."

Otter looked quickly around before starting up the stairs once more. Gods, if anyone found him here at this hour, in the middle of a thunderstorm, talking to himself, they'd be certain he was going soft in the head.

But he'd finally dragged up the memories that had been teasing him since visiting Jaida's grave: seeing Leet in the library at Dragonskeep. Jenna, one of the Keep's archivists, later showing him the books that Leet had read during his only visit to the stronghold of the Dragonlords. His own astonishment at Leet's choice of reading matter: tales of hauntings, tales of blood and death and murder—especially tales about Gull the Blood Drinker.

Something hit the wall outside with a ear-shattering crack. After swallowing his heart once more, Otter told himself it was just a tree branch, likely from the old apple tree in the courtyard, poor thing. *There'll be trees down all over Bylith tomorrow, I'll wager!*

A cold shiver rippled down his spine. Another memory came back to him; he "heard" Linden say once more, "Let's hope that witch spruce they planted over his grave still keeps his soul pinned down."

Let's hope no storms like this ever hit those woods, Otter thought, listening to the wind outside shrieking like a mad thing as he let himself into his room once more.

He pulled off his clothes, shivering as he slipped back into his bed, then wrapped the blankets around himself like a cocoon. He shook his head at the thought of ever going into the woods that held the grave of one of the most evil men he'd ever heard of. He could easily imagine that witch spruce reaching for him.

Brrrr! Then, *Why anyone would found a village near there, the gods only know! And odd how many good young bards have come out of Little Coppice. . . .* With that, Otter slipped into an uneasy sleep as the thunderstorm snarled its way into the distance.

Fourteen

Pod shifted her pack slightly and wiped the sweat from her forehead. By all the gods, Fiarin could walk fast on those long legs of his! It was all she could do to keep up with him and Kaeliss.

At long last Fiarin stopped, motioning them to do the same. A few more paces, then he knelt and studied something on the ground. Some kind of mushrooms, Pod thought. She halted by Kaeliss's side, glad to see the other girl was breathing hard as well.

"Does he always walk this fast?" she whispered.

"Yes." Then the young Wort Hunter gave her a rueful grin. "Don't worry— you'll get used to it . . . eventually."

"Gah." Pod wondered if she could ask him to slow down for Kiga's sake— though the woods dog seemed happy with the pace.

Kaeliss giggled. "I know. Now you know why the others call him—"

"Come look at this, girls! Morels! We'll eat well tonight."

It had been, Pod thought as she walked behind Kaeliss, a few hectic but productive days. Fiarin was indeed a good teacher and he'd been pleased to discover that she was already well versed in all the basic and even some of the rarer herbs.

"Who taught you?" he'd asked.

"Conor of Red Dale, now of the chapterhouse of Grey Holt," she answered proudly. "He's a good friend and teaches me many things whenever he's at the chapterhouse. But he's in great demand among the nobility for he's very skilled at healing and with medicines, so he's not at Grey Holt very often."

"And he had a very attentive student when he was there," Fiarin said in approval. "The best teacher in the world can't teach someone who won't learn. You're doing very well."

Pod felt herself blush. Truth was, Conor was her hero. So whatever he'd taught her, she'd learned with fierce attention to detail. Since she wanted to make Conor proud, she listened to Fiarin as if his every word were carved in gold.

Oh, yes—she'd make Conor proud of her no matter what it took. She just wished that Fiarin didn't walk so fast! And was it her imagination—or was he spending less time showing them herbs than he had in the previous days?

Maybe he just wants to get somewhere special, Pod thought. *But I do wish his legs weren't so long!*

As they journeyed on, Pod noticed that Fiarin was searching for something—and not finding it. Day by day—indeed, almost candlemark by candlemark—he was growing more and more annoyed. At first Pod thought she was imagining it, but one evening as she and Kaeliss picked berries for the evening meal together, Kaeliss brought it up.

"So it's not just me imagining things," Pod said in relief.

"I don't think so," Kaeliss said. "True, I haven't known Fiarin all that long—I only came here from Pelnar last winter—but while he might be a bit of a stick-in-the-mud at times, he's usually not so, well, *cranky.*"

"Let's hope he finds what he's looking for—ow!" Sucking her thumb, Pod thought, *These bushes have thorns like sewing needles!*

They sat around the campfire, toasting strips of meat from the rabbit Kiga had caught earlier, washing them down with the last of the wine they'd brought with them.

They'd had a good day. Fiarin had been pleased with their progress and the questions they'd asked. It hadn't hurt that they'd found a few white mandrake plants. He'd laughed when Pod nervously asked him if it was true that a mandrake screamed when you pulled it out.

"Naught but an old wives' tale," he'd reassured her. And throughout the rest of the day they'd hear him chuckle now and again as if remembering.

Their good fortune had done much to restore Fiarin's usual pleasant humor and the food and wine had done the rest. Pod gazed contentedly into the fire.

"We did well finding those plants," Fiarin said, popping a berry into his mouth. "About the only thing rarer than white mandrake is King's Blood. Now *that's* a find. Very rare, it is, very rare."

"So that Wort Hunter was lucky, wasn't he?" Pod asked. "The one who found so many of 'em together. Fifty, wasn't it?"

Fiarin frowned at her. "What are you talking about? I've never heard of such a thing! Now *I* once—"

Kaeliss turned to Pod and said excitedly, "So that was it! Just before we left camp I overheard Baylor, Fenris, and Readen talking together. Something about a fire at a chapterhouse and about someone who'd made a big find—but they never said of what. Was it really fifty? I hope we're that fortunate!" She laughed. "As long as we're asking the gods for the impossible, let's ask for twice that! Who was it? They didn't say."

Fiarin abruptly held up a hand for silence. "A fire? Where?" he demanded. "Do you know?"

"At White River," Kaeliss answered. "It started in the storerooms, Baylor said."

"Gods, no!" Fiarin choked out. "That's where most of the King's Blood is kept. Fifty plants isn't enough—the lung sickness will be worse this winter. Oh gods— and Master Emberlin needs . . ."

The older Wort Hunter buried his face in his hands for a time. At last he looked up. "Who found the plants?"

"Someone name Curlew—no, that wasn't it. It wasn't a Yerrin na—" Pod began.

A sharp sound from Fiarin silenced her. Pod looked across the fire at him. The dancing flames cast strange shadows on his face; his eyes looked like black pits. Despite the warm night, a chill crept down her spine.

When he spoke, his voice was cold and hard. "Was the name . . . *Currin*?"

Pod had to swallow twice before she could answer. "Yes. That was the name. Currin."

Fifteen

Raven was up early, long before the rest of the inn's lodgers. He groomed Storm-wind and saw to it that the stallion had fresh grain, hay, and water before he went in to break his own fast. As he finished his meal he heard footsteps and voices upstairs.

For a moment he thought about waiting until Arisyn came down. He hadn't seen the boy last night; the Cassorin nobles had taken a private room for din-ing. He wondered if Arisyn had come up with any guesses yet. He'd love to hear them. But likely the boy's elders would take it ill that a commoner approached them.

No, he'd wait and see if the boy found him at the horse fair as he'd said he would. And it was high time he got on the road; he wanted to get Yarrow's mes-sage to Lord Sevrynel's Master of the Fair. He went off to the stable to saddle Stormwind.

Later, as Stormwind followed him out into the stable yard, Raven saw the two young men who were traveling with Arisyn come out of the inn. One jerked a thumb at Stormwind and sneered, "You're supposed to hitch a plow to it, you fool—not saddle it."

The other hooted with laughter.

Stormwind turned his head so that he could see the two men, and pinned his ears back. Raven laughed as the stallion snorted in disgust.

"Are you so certain of that, my lords?" he asked with a grin as Stormwind, with no signal from him, sank down on his haunches and pirouetted in place so that he faced the road.

Raven swung into the saddle and gathered up the reins. Stormwind, with a dismissive flick of his tail, paced regally down the lane before breaking into a high, floating trot.

Raven turned in the saddle and waved farewell. "I'll see you at the fair, my lords," he called to their astonished faces.

Now, why does that one fellow look familiar? Was he ever at Aunt Yarrow's holding?

But somehow that didn't feel right. After a while Raven gave it up and set himself to enjoy the ride.

As he topped the hill and looked down onto the fields below, Raven's first impression of the great horse fair he'd heard about all his life was of an anthill, an anthill that had been kicked open, no less. He'd listened to travelers' tales about the fair and knew from them that it was the largest in the Five Kingdoms, but he'd never expected anything like this! It was larger than many towns he'd been in.

He eased Stormwind onto the grass along the road and out of the way of traffic; then he sat and just stared. Dear gods, it was enough to take one's breath away.

After a time Raven realized that there was order to the seeming madness. In even this short time, horse lines had been set out and temporary roads delineated. Below him a rough "wagon wheel" was taking shape. The anthill had not been kicked; it knew exactly what it was about.

At the hub of the "wheel" was a large tent of yellow silk, just as Yarrow had described to him. It was surrounded by a circle of slender poles, many of which already had pennons fluttering from their tops.

That was where he had to go. Raven patted his belt pouch, feeling the stiff hide tube that held his aunt's letter through the leather. Suddenly he realized how great a responsibility Yarrow had laid upon him.

Not to hold her place, no. True, it was an important task. But any of her grooms and handlers could have done it—if not as quickly as he and Stormwind had.

No, it was up to him and Stormwind to make the first impression, to play the ambassadors for the future colts. For the future of Yarrow's holding.

Raven took a deep breath. "Let's go, boy," he said.

Stormwind tossed his head and started off once more.

At the great yellow tent, Raven dismounted. "Let's hope there aren't too many nobles' stewards ahead of us," he murmured to the Llysanyin, "or we'll be here all day."

As he crossed the threshold into the tent, Raven paused to let his eyes adjust. While the inside of the tent was not as dim as he'd first thought, it was a far cry from the blazing sunlight outside.

Trestle tables had been set up around the perimeter of the tent. Clerks sat at them, quill pens busily scratching in account books as they accepted fees from the men and women in line and deposited the coins in the iron-bound wooden boxes at their sides. Men and women in all manner of dress milled about, some in livery, some quite well dressed, many in plain but good clothes, and a good number in the shabby finery or motley of mummers, minstrels, jugglers, and acrobats.

Raven looked around in bewilderment. Which line should he get into? Or did it matter?

A small, wizened old man wearing blue-and-orange livery appeared at his side. "Horse trader, merchant, blacksmith, or entertainer, good sir?" the old man asked briskly.

"Horse trader," Raven answered, remembering that blue-and-orange were Lord Sevrynel's colors. This was no doubt one of the understewards who ran the fair.

The old man studied him. "I've never seen you here before, sir. How many horses have you to sell?"

"I'm here for Yarrow Whitethorndaughter. She's been delayed by bad weather and a blocked pass. She sent me ahead."

"Ah!" The old face broke into a gap-toothed grin. "Yarrow Whitethorndaughter is well known and much respected here. I must tell you, sir, that we were getting a bit worried whether she was coming this year. Usually she's here before this. You've a letter from her?"

Raven patted his belt pouch in answer.

"Excellent." The old man indicated a long line of fairly well-dressed men and women. "That's where you go, Master . . . ?" He tilted his head in question.

"Redhawkson. Raven Redhawkson, sir. Yarrow is my aunt." He almost added *And partner,* but the words still felt awkward on his tongue, as if he bragged.

Bushy grey eyebrows went up and the old steward stared at Raven for a long moment.

"We'd heard that Yarrow has taken a nephew as her partner," the old man said slowly, fingering his chin. There was an odd note in his voice. It was not, Raven thought, unfriendly; just . . . thoughtful.

"That would be me," Raven replied, unsure of just what was happening and surprised that word of Yarrow's new partner had spread this far.

"Indeed." Now the old man looked beatifically up at him and said, "Just take your place before that table, Master Redhawkson, and Elamry will see to everything." He tilted his head toward a table where sat a grey-haired woman, busily writing with a quill pen in the account book before her.

With another gap-toothed smile and a slight bow, and the old man turned away to assist someone else. Raven took his place at the end of the line, still wondering.

Though the clerk and her assistant were brisk and efficient, the line was long. And while many accepted the site in the horse lines allotted to them, others argued for a better position in the camp. Raven wondered how many prevailed; very few, he thought, judging by the sour expressions as the petitioners passed him.

At last there was only one person ahead of him, a portly man in a dull green tunic heavy with white and yellow ribbon trim. When he began protesting that he wanted a different spot, Raven sighed and let his thoughts wander once more.

Then the mention of his aunt's name cut through the mental debate of which food tent he'd passed had the most appetizing aromas wafting from it. At once Raven's attention was riveted on the conversation ahead of him.

"Well, then—if you won't give me Darsi Coper's place, what about Yarrow Whitethorndaughter's? You know as well as I do that she's never this late, she must have changed her mind about—"

Raven interrupted in alarm. "Yarrow's coming. She's just been delayed."

The man turned and glared at him. "And who are *you*?"

"Raven Redhawkson. Yarrow is my aunt." To the clerk, Elamry, he said in some alarm, "Truly, she's on her way."

As the man snorted "I don't believe—" the clerk held out her hand.

"Your proof, young sir," she said.

Raven fumbled his belt pouch open and tugged out the hide tube that held Yarrow's letter. He gave it to Elamry.

The clerk studied the wax seal on the ties over the end cap for a moment, then nodded. "That certainly looks like Yarrow's seal. I recognize that little chip in the rim," she said. "Let us just make certain. . . ."

She broke the seal at one end and pulled out the letter. "Mmmm, hrmmm, hrmmm," she hummed as she read it. "Oh, yes—this is from Yarrow. Ah! This young man, you might like to know, Master Rupern, is her partner and named in this letter as one who may speak for her. Now let us see what else . . ."

She read on. "I'm sorry, Master Rupern, but Yarrow Whitethorndaughter is indeed on her way. You may not have her place on the horse lines."

Raven thought he detected a note of satisfaction in the words. Master Rupern shot Raven a look of pure venom and stalked from the tent.

When he was gone, Elamry said cheerfully, "He's been trying to oust Yarrow from that spot for years—it's much better than his."

"So are her horses," muttered the assistant with a snicker.

"Jaster!" Elamry said sternly.

"Sorry, Mistress Elamry," the young man. "I know, I know—it's not my place—"

"To comment about any trader's horses . . . while on duty." She hrmmmed once more, then said to Raven, "Very well, then, young master, you just need to pay the fee and I'll have the men set up your aunt's tents on her site."

Once more Raven dug into his belt pouch. He pulled out five silver pennies. "Here you go," he said as he dropped them into Elamry's waiting hand. "Three for grain and hay and firewood and two for the camp, is that right?"

She nodded as she scribbled something on a quarter sheet of parchment, then handed it to him. "Show this to anyone wearing a blue-and-orange baldric—

they'll show you where to go if you're not familiar with the fair. Is there aught else, young sir, that we might help you with?"

"Aunt Yarrow said she'd pay for next year's storing of the tents at the end of the fair. We're to get one for me while we're here."

"Which will change the fee for that," the clerk said as she made a note in her book. "That's done, then." She looked shrewdly at him. "This is your first time here at Balyaranna, isn't it, young sir? I suggest that you visit the camps on either side of yours. It will be impossible for you to guard your camp by yourself until your aunt gets here, and I know that Skorrie Dunreid at least owes Yarrow a favor or two. He's the one selling the Mountain Lilies."

She was referring, Raven knew, not to flowers, but to a breed of highly prized palfreys from Kelneth known for their creamy white coats and wheat-gold manes, intelligence, and sweet tempers as well as to being uncannily surefooted. Yarrow was doing well to be in such company; but then, when the first of their Llysanyin half-breeds came to market, Skorrie Dunreid would count himself lucky to be *their* neighbor on the horse lines.

Elamry went on, "Ask them to lend you someone to keep an eye on things when you're not there. It doesn't happen often, thank the gods, because the penalties are so severe, but some fool may think your hay and grain stores to be easy pickings because no one's at the camp."

"Thank you for the suggestion," Raven said gratefully. He'd been wondering how to deal with that problem. Sitting in camp all day and night until his aunt came didn't appeal to him. And once he'd finished his travel rations, how would he eat if he couldn't leave? "I'll do that."

"Then allow me to wish you a good fair and a good profit."

"Thank you," Raven said with a slight bow and left the tent.

Once outside, he whistled for Stormwind. Then he picked one of the "roads" leading from the steward's tent at random. He intended to find one of the aides and get himself to Yarrow's site as quickly as he could to supervise the setting up of the camp and the storing of the grain and hay. He'd see that Stormwind had a good feed, then—if Yarrow's neighbors agreed to help—it was off for a bit of something for himself. And after that . . .

He smiled. After that, he would ride through the fair. Let any fools about think he rode a plow horse. Those with eyes to see would know. Oh yes, they would know.

Skorrie Dunreid proved to be a jolly-looking Kelnethi with the longest beard Raven had ever seen. The man wore it in two grey-streaked braids that hung down over his big barrel of a chest and past the wide leather belt snugged around a grey-and-black-checked tunic that strained over his stomach. When Raven led

Stormwind into his camp and introduced himself, Skorrie slapped him on the back and roared for ale.

He also stared and stared at Stormwind. As they waited for the ale, Skorrie sidled up to Raven and muttered, "Was that song true? Did you really . . . ?"

"I did."

Skorrie exhaled loudly and tugged on one of the braids, winding it around a fist. "As if I needed to ask—the proof's standin' in front of me," he said quietly. At Raven's quizzical look, he went on, "When I was a lad, Dragonlord Brock Hatussin halted at our holdin'. It was foul weather and he was lookin' for a place where he and his Llysanyin, Aedis, might wait out the storm. I spent every moment I could studyin' Aedis so that I would know it if I ever saw another Llysanyin. I'm lookin' at one now."

He held a hand out for Stormwind to sniff. "Oh, now—you're a bonny, bonny lad, aren't you?" Skorrie said softly, and rubbed the Llysanyin's nose for a moment. A voice calling "Here, Da!" made him turn.

He accepted two foaming mugs from an apple-cheeked girl who smiled shyly at Raven before scurrying off. "My youngest, Lia," Skorrie said proudly, gazing after her. "She rides the Lilies to show the customers. A fine, light hand on the reins she has, and a perfect seat. The horses'll do anything for her."

They raised their mugs in a toast to Lia and fine riding. Skorrie took a long draught, wiped the foam from his mustache, and said briskly, "So, then—what might old Skorrie do for you, lad?"

Raven explained his predicament and mentioned Elamry's suggestion, Skorrie chiming in every few words with "I see, I see."

When Raven was done, all Skorrie said was "First Balyaranna?"

Raven nodded, not daring to say anything.

Skorrie blinked, then roared, "Well, then, lad—we can't have you sittin' about on your arse your first time here, now can we?" He slapped Raven on the shoulder again, then said seriously, "Yarrow once saved some of my Lilies from thieves. Found themselves starin' at the tip of her sword and ran for it, they did. Don't worry, son. Me and mine will keep an eye on your things. You and that fine lad of yours go enjoy yourselves."

Raven thanked him profusely. "I'll just see to the setting up—" His stomach rumbled.

"Pfft!" Skorrie waved a hand in dismissal. "I know how Yarrow likes her camp arranged—I've been next to her for enough years, haven't I? While that's goin' on, I want you two to have your noonings here, then go off and see the sights—and I won't take no for an answer. It's a grand fair, it is, and there's nothing like your first one. So off with you."

Raven spent the rest of the day becoming familiar with the fair and getting the layout set in his mind. It amused him to watch people's reactions to Stormwind as they passed. Many clearly saw no further than the Llysanyin's sturdy legs, feathered feet, and round barrel. Others stared with puzzled intensity. Raven wondered if those had seen Shan when Linden was in Cassori to be a judge in the debate over the regency.

Raven chuckled, remembering Chailen's description of Shan's escape to go after his two-foot: "Knocked Varn and me head over heels early one morning and was off down the road like an arrow. We laughed our heads off imagining just how surprised Linden would be when Shan caught up with him—and how bruised. Lucky for Linden he had been ill. Shan took pity on him, I guess."

Linden sat before the evening fire, scratching in the dirt with a stick. Maurynna came up from behind and leaned against him, looking over his shoulder.

"Counting off the days?" she asked.

"I am. If we're to get to the Balyaranna Fair in enough time for Sevrynel to ask us to be marshals—and *not* have to risk giving offense to someone he's already asked—we need to leave the party tomorrow morning. And I think we should all go together."

"Poor Shima."

"Poor Shima," Linden agreed. "But we've given him as much time with Kare-linn as we could, and—"

"And he'll see her again when she gets to the fair," Maurynna finished for him. "Still, I'll let you break the bad news to him."

Sixteen

Leet pulled his horse to a halt at the crest of a hill. Before him the road marched on to Balyaranna; to the right of the road a small yet charming manor house and its grounds lay before him.

If Thomelin had not played him false, this was the manor of Ridler Barans, the Lord Portis of Portishome, and father to Tirael Barans. Leet clenched his jaw at the thought of that cursed name, then forced it from his mind.

Keep to the task at hand, he told himself sharply. *If Thomelin is right . . .* Woe to the luthier if he had lied or misled him, Leet thought balefully. *I'll not be made a mock of, especially by him.*

Damn the coward, anyway. It had been his duty to cry Challenge for his son's death. Instead the craven had swallowed the lie that "it was an unfortunate accident."

"You should have cried Challenge, you coward," Leet hissed. "Instead you left it to me."

He shifted in the saddle, trying to ease his cramped muscles. Pain lanced through his body. A groan broke from his lips despite his efforts to suppress it.

Auvrian help him, he was too old to ride this hard. Even the long journey to the far north and Dragonskeep hadn't been so bad. But if he was to have any chance at his revenge, he had to get here while Portis was away. He only hoped he was neither too early nor too late.

There was only one way to find out. Clenching his teeth against the pain he knew was coming, Leet urged on his tired horse. At the tug of its rope, the weary packhorse trailed obediently behind.

It seemed to take forever to reach the lane that turned off the road and led to the manor. As they turned onto it, Leet let the tired horses set the pace. To his exhausted body, it seemed the lane went on forever; to his mind, with its thoughts whirling in a mad rush, the end of it would come too soon.

What would he find at that end? Portis gone as Thomelin's news said he would be, or Portis at home awaiting his kinsman instead? If the former, Leet had a chance; to do exactly what, he didn't know. He had no real plan, for there were too many variables. But he knew what he wanted and he trusted his wits. If a chance came, he would seize it.

And now someone had seen him. He sat up straighter so that his shabby tunic of yellow and red might be seen more clearly.

"Ho, minstrel!" came the call. "Welcome!"

A short time later Leet forced himself to smile ingratiatingly at the man who studied him. This was not the stable hand who had been so pleased to see him. No, this was a man of some standing here, a man with responsibilities. Leet could read it in the stern expression and the confident set of the man's shoulders.

Leet knew well what the man saw—or thought he saw. A minstrel, sure enough; there was no mistaking the twisted-wire torc, the yellow and red tunic, and the two wooden cases for traveling harps on the packhorse.

But this was clearly not much of a minstrel; so much the shabby clothes and dusty horses proclaimed. Leet was satisfied that he should think so. Let this man take him for one of those who journeyed from place to place, grateful for a meal and a place out of the weather, a minstrel to whom a few copper pennies were a largesse rarely seen. Such men were quickly forgotten.

At last the man spoke. "Our lord is away for a few days, minstrel," he said.

The unspoken "Not that the likes of *you* would be good enough to play for him" hung in the air between them.

It was all Leet could do not to shout with joy. Instead he said humbly, "I'm sorry to hear that, sir. But would you have a place that I might rest myself and my horses for the night at least? I'm for the fair at Balyaranna and thought I'd make it today, but these old bones don't travel as well as they used to." Leet spoke in a slightly raspy voice that quavered, a voice long past its prime. A quick, hopeful smile flitted across his lips. "Anything, good sir—I don't expect to guest in the great house. But perhaps a bit of field to camp in . . . ?"

Relief that Leet wasn't going to insist on staying in the manor house made the man unbend a little. "I can do you better than that, minstrel. I'm sure you'll understand that no strangers are allowed near my lord's horses. But we've an old hay barn that's not used now that you may stay in. It's not much, but it's warm and dry and out of the morning dew."

This was better than he'd dared hope for. "Auvrian bless you, sir," said Leet, meaning it wholeheartedly. "That would be perfect."

Now the man smiled. "This is Lord Portis's holding, minstrel. I'm his assistant stablemaster, Blaine. Let's get you settled and your horses turned out, and I'll have my nephew Robie bring you a meal from the kitchen. It'll be plain fare but plenty of it, the same as what we get. And your name, minstrel?"

"Osric, good sir."

As Blaine led the way to the stables, he glanced back; Leet saw him studying both the animals and the burden the packhorse bore. "You've two harps?" the man asked genially.

But Leet's trained ear caught the hint of suspicion in the amiable tone: *How can a poor beggar like you afford two instruments—and two good horses?*

"Alas, good sir," he said with good-natured regret. "I wish both were mine. But one belongs to a bard who's supposed to be at the fair. I'm merely delivering it. The luthier was so grateful that he hired these two horses so that I could make the journey in time."

He gave Blaine a conspirator's wink. "I think the old scoundrel was desperate—he'd said the harp would be ready much earlier. And we all know that it doesn't pay to get on a bard's bad side, eh?"

Blaine nodded and chuckled, apparently satisfied. "And this should put you on his good side, shouldn't it?"

As he followed Blaine away from the stables, Leet saw two stone buildings ahead. These, then, must be the hay barns, set well away from the stables in case of fire. One was clearly newer; of the other, nearly half of its roof had collapsed. With a quick, wry grin, Leet thought he could guess which would be his lodging this night. A stablemaster this cautious would never allow a stranger to stay alone with the fodder for his charges.

As they entered the old hay barn, the assistant stablemaster waved a hand and said, "There you are, Minstrel Osric. Get yourself settled and Robie will be here soon."

As soon as he was alone, Leet straightened up, stretched and rolled his shoulders. Gods, who would have thought that walking slumped over could be so tiring! He fingered a greasy strand of hair and grimaced. Feh! He'd be glad when he could leave "Osric" behind. He tucked the strand behind his ear and promised himself a good soaking at the public bathhouse on the outskirts of Balyaranna. It would never do to show up at the castle looking like this. He'd not give his old student Daera a chance to gossip of how he'd turned up looking like something the cat dragged in.

Leet sat, looking around the old hay barn. True, half was falling down, but he couldn't complain. It was likely just as well he was a good distance from the stables; each time he'd played the Gull harp, his horses had become nervous. There was a still sturdy wall between him and the section that was giving way, and his part was warm and dry as promised, very well furnished with straw, and he was well fed indeed.

The last two were courtesy of Robie, the absent stablemaster's son. When the boy had found out his charge was a minstrel, nothing had been too good for "Osric."

Robie, it seemed, wanted more than to work in a stable all his life. He wanted to go to the Bards' School someday; he had a very good voice—everyone said he ought to be a bard, they did!

Leet had learned that and much, much more from the voluble Robie. The boy chattered endlessly at him in a quicksilver run of words while he ate his meal. Slightly bemused, Leet wondered how it was the boy didn't faint; it seemed he never stopped for breath.

"We're so excited, sir! Our lord's kinsman, Lord Lenslee from Kelneth, is coming for the fair! He's got a wonderful horse that will win the Queen's Chase hands down! Everyone says so! Do you think I could sing for you later? The horse's name? Oh, you *must* have heard of him, sir—it's Summer Lightning! Oh—you have heard of him! Good! Beautiful animal everyone says he is—coat like a new copper penny! Bless you, sir, no, the horse won't be tired from his journey! My father—he went with Lord Portis to go meet our lord's cousin—my father says they'll be taking it in easy stages and that they'll rest here before going the last bit to the fair—we're quite close, you know! Our lands border Lord Sevrynel's. He's the lord who hosts the fair on his lands. And Lord Portis is one of the few who has a *real* stable of wood and stone at the fairgrounds because he's helped Lord Sevrynel many times. And Father will be in charge of that stable and I'm going to help him because my older brother broke his collarbone and can't go now! It will be my first time at the fair. Will it be yours as well, sir?"

Before Leet could swallow and answer, Robie rushed on, "Lord Portis gave Father orders that Summer Lightning is to be given the best pasture for his own when he gets here—I can't wait to see him!—but we can't give him the very best one after all! Uncle Blaine found a patch of yellowfool in it today—can you imagine that? You know how dangerous that—"

As Robie rattled on and on, a memory from Leet's childhood struck him with the force of a blow. . . .

He was six, walking the boundary of the upper pasture with his father, slashing at the tall grass with an apple switch, laying low his "enemies."

Suddenly his father stopped and peered over the stile in the wattle fence. Leet jumped as a string of lurid curses filled the air; Papa never cursed! He stared round-eyed and frightened at his father. Was Papa angry with—

No. Papa was still looking over the fence. Now he was calling for Recik-the-Elder, who oversaw the horse pastures.

When Recik-the-Elder reached them, Papa pointed to something. The pasture steward began cursing, too. Curious, Leet climbed the steps of the stile and looked. All he saw was tall grass, some elderberry bushes, and a big patch of pretty yellow flowers that stretched like a hand toward the fence. The pointer finger almost touched it, he noted.

His father told Recik-the-Elder to get Recik-the-Younger and his men to "rip that foul stuff up and keep a close eye on this pasture!"

Recik-the-Elder puffed off as fast as he could.

Puzzled, Leet asked, "But why, Papa? It's pretty."

"It's vile, that's what it is. That's yellowfool, son. It can kill the animal that eats it. Oh, not as fresh grazing or fully dried in hay—but the poor animal that eats it half-dried and wilted will bleed to death inside. Not even the best Beast Healer in the world can save it then. If that stuff gets into a pasture and there's a bad dry spell—"

Leet swallowed hard. He didn't like the picture forming in his mind. No, he didn't like it at all. . . .

The bard sat as one stunned, almost forgetting to breathe. *I know now how to do it. I'm certain I can do it. I'm meant to do it. This is a gift from the gods.*

When he came back to himself, Leet found that Robie had gathered up the now-empty bowl and had passed on to another subject.

". . . You'll earn lots and lots at the fair, sir, I just know you will! Aaaaaand—will you play for me later, sir?"

The flood of words ended at last. Robie sat watching him, the bowl clutched to his chest, eyes wide, half hopeful, half afraid. He reminded Leet of a puppy that hoped for a pat but feared a blow.

Leet smiled kindly at him. His hand stole out and caressed one of the harp cases. "I would love to, lad. I would surely love to."

Robie bounced to his feet, grinning from ear to ear. "Would you truly, sir?" He was so excited that he tripped over his own feet. Putting out a hand to catch himself, he cut his forearm on a protruding nail. While not overly deep or long, it bled freely.

Struck by a sudden inspiration, Leet pulled a clean kerchief from his saddlebag. "Here, lad—stanch the blood with this." He watched avidly as the embarrassed boy pressed it against his wound.

When the bleeding was done, Robie thanked him, then looked ruefully at the bloodstained kerchief. "I'll ask my mam to wash it for—"

Leet twitched the square of cloth out of the boy's fingers. He knew just what to do with this. "Don't fret yourself about it, my boy. Just get that cut bandaged and take care of it—you don't want to miss the fair, now do you? Oh—and Robie? Believe me when I say that I want to play for you more than anything in this world."

It had worked. By all the gods, it had worked. Leet had to force himself to keep to his role of the beaten-down Osric. He never thought he'd be grateful for aching muscles, he thought with amusement. If he didn't have that reminder to move like a man well-nigh worn out with a lifetime of hard travel . . .

It had worked—though he'd almost wrecked his chance. Leet had reached for the other harp he carried—the one he thought of as Tern—intending to play that first. He wasn't certain why he hesitated to play the other instrument; he certainly hadn't hesitated to wipe the bloodstained cloth over the soundboard as soon as Robie had gone before. Leet told himself that the uneasiness he felt was merely imagination.

Then he realized that the sound of music might draw the other stablemen. He wasn't certain enough yet of his control of the harp and its power. No; best to get this done while there was but one mind to suborn.

So Leet laid his hand upon the harp his brother-in-law had so reluctantly made to his bidding and ruthlessly crushed the pang of conscience that said, *This is but a child!*

So was Arnath. And now he lies cold in the ground, he told his conscience fiercely. So he first traced the figure of the gull burned into the shoulder of the harp. "Are you there?" he whispered. Then he set his fingers upon the strings and began playing, soft as thistledown, soft as the touch of a mouse's whiskers.

Robie's eyes glazed as the music took him. Leet sang softly to him of what he must do. When he was done, Leet put that harp away. And just as he settled Tern into his arms, he heard other voices approaching. Dusk was eating the shadows; the stable hands were done with their chores and were coming to listen to the minstrel. The gods were with him.

Leet patted Robie's cheek gently. "Time to wake up, lad."

Robie blinked at him in mild confusion, then smiled as his uncle and the others settled themselves into the straw around him.

Leet smiled at the men benignly. "Good evening, gentlemen," he said in Osric's travel-roughened voice. "Let me thank you for the aid you've given me this night. You've no idea how grateful I am."

It was late before the stable hands and Robie left. Leet gratefully settled the harp in its case and massaged his throat. Forcing himself to sing in Osric's slightly hoarse tones had been more tiring than he'd thought it would be. Hopefully, he'd done no damage to his voice. He arranged his blankets and lay down, suddenly exhausted. He fell asleep almost as soon as his head touched the pack he used for a pillow.

During the night, he dreamed. A dream he'd had many times since Arnath's death, and always, always it was the same. He'd never seen the horse in life, but knew it when it entered his dreams.

Coat like a new copper penny, shining like a flame as the brute raced across the green field, scorning the figures that lined the fence watching him: two young men and, a short distance from them . . .

A boy. Arnath; beloved Arnath with his gift of song.

Then the stallion came up to the fence next to Arnath and began grazing. So enraptured was the boy that he never noticed the two young men stealing up behind him.

Each time Leet reached this point in the dream, he would desperately cry out a warning, his heart breaking, but there was no sound. It was as if he were but a wraith, doomed to watch the unfolding tragedy over and over, unable to stop it. Helpless, he was so helpless. . . .

Like a striking hawk, one of the men caught up Arnath and tossed him over the fence onto the horse's bare back, laughing all the while.

But over the laughter, Leet could hear the boy's terrified screams: "Father! Father! Help me!"

Then the stallion leapt away from the fence and bucked. Arnath flew from his back and landed heavily on the ground, too stunned to move. For one terrible moment, the stallion looked over his shoulder at the helpless boy as if considering, then deliberately turned, reared up, and—

Leet woke, gasping, as he always did at this point. He heaved himself up on one elbow, tears running down his face. He had not seen Arnath's death, had only been told of it, but each time the dream felt as real as if he stood there. He lay tossing and turning, unable to sleep, and thinking about his revenge.

Seventeen

The dawn found a tired Leet riding through a cow pasture. He had spent a fitful night, wondering if his plan would work, if he'd overreached himself, if someone would realize what Robie was up to.

A couple of candlemarks before, a sleepy, inquiring yip from one of the dogs had brought Leet to the door of the stable. He'd peered out, straining his eyes to make out anything in the near-darkness, wondering if his plan was afoot at last. He hadn't dared go outside lest the dogs catch his scent and raise the alarm.

But he'd known that drowsy yip should mean— Yes! A slight boy's form hurried across the yard, heading for the pastures, an empty sack flapping on his back as he ran. If someone were to follow Robie and find him at his task . . . Leet used the time to make ready to get out in a hurry if needed.

But his luck had held. Soon he'd seen Robie returning, more slowly this time, the full sack heavy on his back. The boy had come up to him, vacant gaze not truly seeing him, and handed over the sack.

"Good boy," Leet had whispered as he tied the sack into place on the pack-horse. Then, still whispering, he infused his voice with the note of command that had made many an apprentice jump to obey. "Now forget all this. Forget until I call you once more."

"Yes, sir," Robie said dully.

"You will answer that call."

"Yes, sir."

"And you'll do exactly what I tell you to do without question."

"Yes, sir."

"Good boy, Robie. Now keep the dogs quiet while I leave and then get you back to bed and forget all this."

The boy had dumbly done as he'd been bidden.

Now Leet rode with his means of revenge snugged down between the harp cases like so much innocent luggage.

He hoped he'd soon find the abandoned byre that Robie had told him about. Before the sun was much higher, he wanted to lay Osric to rest. It was time for Leet Welkin of Sansy, Master Bard of the Bards' School of Bylith, to rise again like a Jehangli phoenix from the ashes of its pyre.

The image made him snarl. Damn that bastard Heronson yet again. Though Leet wouldn't admit it even to himself, it still rankled that Otter had won such glory; first with the trip to the fabled kingdom of Jehanglan, and then—adding insult to injury—with the sweeping success of the song about the journey that he'd written soon after returning.

If I'm asked to sing that damned song one more time . . .

The sight of the half-ruined byre was a welcome distraction. It was a picturesque thing of flat grey stone, one wall a tumbled ruin, its stones scattered through a carpet of long grass and wildflowers, empty windows staring blindly out at the distant hills. The thatched roof was long gone; the sharply pointed gables reared up to the sky.

Like something from that old fairy tale, the one where the handsome young lord falls in love with the beautiful shepherd girl and meets her on moonlit nights in the old ruins. A part of his mind whispered, *Or the weaver girl . . .*

Leet shook his head, refusing to follow the memory. As he led the horses into the byre, he squinted up at the pale robin's-egg blue of the sky. Dawn was passing; he must hurry.

He worked quickly. The tunic, breeches, and cloak, all of minstrel yellow-and-red, and the mummer's powder went into a hole created by pulling out some of the fallen stones. Shivering in the morning chill, Leet washed himself with the cold water from his waterskin, wishing he dared light a fire. But it would take too long to heat the water and someone might see the smoke.

No, cold water, soap, and a good scrubbing would have to do until he reached the public bath near Balyaranna. He washed his hair again and again to get out the grey that had added years to his appearance. When he was satisfied that the worst traces of his rough journey were gone, and that he was as clean as he could be, Leet roughly toweled himself dry and dressed faster than ever he had in his life.

Ahh! It was good to be back in his proper garb once more! Leet smoothed the rich fabric of his red tunic and flicked a bit of straw from the black breeches. He settled his bard's torc around his neck, stretched, and stood tall, a Master Bard of Bylith once more.

He mounted his horse and rode down from the byre toward the road, the packhorse ambling behind. First that bath, then he'd find an inn to break his fast. Best have the ostler give both animals a good grooming, too.

He was bound for the royal castle near Balyaranna. Everything must be perfect.

Eighteen

As Raven rode slowly down the section reserved for saddlers and harness makers, he saw young Lord Arisyn come out of one of the tent booths and mount a seal-brown gelding that whickered gently to him. Raven whistled in appreciation; it was a handsome, well-bred animal and obviously fond of the boy. Once he would have given all he had for a horse like that. Once.

"Good day, my lord Arisyn," Raven called.

Arisyn looked around. His face lit up as Raven halted Stormwind next to him.

"Oh, good!" the boy said in delight. "I'm so glad to see you again!"

"And Stormwind and I are glad to see you again as well, my lord," Raven said, deliberately giving Arisyn another clue with the Llysanyin's name. Then he grinned. "Any more guesses?"

Arisyn looked sheepish. "No. I'm at my wits' end." Then he tilted his head; his lips quirked up in a sly smile. "Perhaps a wee bit of cheating . . ." Leaning over, he called out, "Coryn, I'm going home now."

A muffled voice answered from inside the tent, "Already? Your loss, pipsqueak."

"Hah! We'll see about that!" muttered Arisyn as he wheeled his gelding around and sent it trotting off. To Raven he said over his shoulder, "Come on! I want you to meet my foster father."

When he and Stormwind had caught up with Arisyn, Raven asked, "Cheating, my lord?"

Arisyn grinned. "Very well, then—perhaps not cheating. Not quite, that is. But I want to see if my foster father recognizes your horse's breed. If he doesn't, then I won't feel like such an idiot that I don't."

"And why should you feel like an idiot? I can assure you that many people have never seen horses like Stormwind." Raven remembered what he'd been told by Linden, Lleld, and Jekkanadar about traveling unheralded. He added, "And even fewer have known *what* it was they saw."

The boy groaned. "Is that supposed to be a hint? I'll freely admit I'm baffled. I'm enjoying the game, but I'm baffled. I'm just wondering if my foster father will be as well." After a moment, he blurted out, "I'll certainly feel better if he is!"

Raven had to laugh. "And your foster father is . . . ?"

"Lord Sevrynel, Earl of Rockfall," Arisyn replied. "I went to Kelneth to visit my parents. I came back with my aunt and uncle and cousin."

Raven was delighted; this was a stroke of luck! Yarrow spoke highly and with affection of Lord Sevrynel; Raven also knew that Linden thought well of the man and his knowledge of horses.

And he was the Lord Marshal of the Balyaranna horse fair. It was all Raven could do not to whoop with delight.

"Wait in there," Arisyn directed. He pointed to an opening in a hedge that bordered one side of a cobbled courtyard before a large stone stable. "I'll see if my foster father has a moment. Here—take Arrow, please." He tossed the reins to Raven.

"In there" proved to be a smaller courtyard, also cobbled, surrounded by a high hedge. The overhanging branches of a chestnut tree shaded the far end and the stone bench there.

Raven led Stormwind and Arrow within. He waited nervously, running his fingers through Stormwind's mane again and again to comb it, brushing any hint of dust from the Llysanyin's glossy coat. It wasn't long before he heard Arisyn's voice beyond the hedge.

"Now remember, foster father—if you know what breed his horse is, *don't* tell me. I want to guess it on my own. Coryn and Dunric said it's just a Shamreen draft horse, but I don't think so. I think they're idiots. I *know* that it's more than that." Arisyn came around the corner, a huge grin on his face.

Then Raven caught his first sight of the Earl of Rockfall. Lord Sevrynel, a short, slender man, was blinking owlishly in the sudden dimness. But short as he was—especially to a Yerrin—this man was a giant among horsemen and -women, the same world that Raven lived in. It was by his generosity that the great horse fair of Balyaranna lived and gave his aunt and a score of other breeders a chance to reach buyers that they would otherwise never have seen.

Lord Sevrynel came a few steps into the enclosure and stopped short. Then he stared from Stormwind to Raven to Stormwind and back again. But all he said was a soft and startled "Oh, *my!*"

"Well?" Arisyn demanded when his foster father showed no further sign of speech.

Indeed, Raven wondered if Sevrynel was even capable of speech at that moment. The man looked thunderstruck. Raven bowed to him. Lord Sevrynel nodded absently, still staring at Stormwind, humming a song softly to himself.

"Well?" Arisyn asked again. "Who's right—Coryn and Dunric or me?"

The Cassorin lord said in a dreamy voice, "Coryn and Dunric are idiots."

"I knew it!" crowed Arisyn. Then, with a trace of resignation, "You know what he is, don't you, foster father?"

"I certainly do. I even know his name, Stormwind." Lord Sevrynel looked down at his ward.

"How did you know? I only just found it out," Arisyn said.

Sevrynel chuckled. Even from where he stood Raven could see the twinkle in his eyes. "I saw another of this breed once—and it's not a thing you forget, my lad."

Arisyn sighed. "Why do I feel I'm missing something by a good league and more?"

The earl laughed. "I'll tell you this much, my boy—when you find out, you'll feel remarkably silly you didn't guess. Why, you've heard this very horse described."

"I have?" Arisyn gaped at him.

"You have. Think about it."

As Arisyn scratched his head, looking puzzled, Lord Sevrynel turned back to Raven. "Your name, sir?"

"Raven Redhawkson, my lord earl," Raven said respectfully, though he had to hide a grin. He knew where Sevrynel had learned of Stormwind: Great-uncle Otter's song of the journey to Jehanglan, "Dragon and Phoenix." It was the song Sevrynel had been humming.

He'd also heard from both Yarrow and Linden how horse-mad Sevrynel was; trust the man to remember a horse's name—but not a human's. "I'm nephew and partner to Yarrow Whitethorndaughter."

The smile that lit Lord Sevrynel's face warmed Raven's heart. "Excellent! Your aunt is well known here, young man, and well thought of, very well thought of. She has excellent horses."

"She'll have even better ones to bring here one day, my lord," Raven said boldly.

Sevrynel's eyes grew huge. "You mean—?"

"I do, my lord."

"Oh, my. Oh, *my!*"

From somewhere beyond the hedge a frazzled-sounding voice called for Lord Sevrynel. The Cassorin noble sighed and called back, "I'm coming, Answell." To Raven he said, "I would speak further with you, young man, rest assured of that." He turned to his foster son, whose face wore a grimace of puzzled frustration. "Don't worry, my boy, you'll get it soon enough. Do show Master Redhawkson the way to Sweetflag Pond tomorrow, there's a good lad. I'm certain he and his . . . horse will enjoy swimming there. And now, farewell all."

Suddenly Raven thought of something. "My lord earl, a moment more of your time, please? I may have some news for you."

Sevrynel stopped. "Oh?"

"Yes." Then, realizing that his tidings would end the game, he said to Arisyn, "My lord, would you mind?"

The boy studied him a moment, then said shrewdly, "It's something that would be a huge hint, wouldn't it?"

"It would. Do you want the game to end?"

"Oh, no!" Arisyn answered, and moved off.

Bending down so that he could whisper in Lord Sevrynel ear, Raven said quietly, "I don't know if you're aware of this, my lord, but Maurynna Kyrissaean, Linden Rathan, and Shima Ilyathan are coming to this year's fair."

The little earl reared back in surprise and stared up at Raven. "How do you know?"

"They visited my aunt's holding just after the turn of the year, my lord. Maurynna and Shima have never seen the fair, so Aunt Yarrow and I invited them. I imagine they'll get here within the next few days."

Sevrynel's eyes were still huge. "I thank you for this news, Raven Redhawkson. Oh, my . . ." Suddenly he grinned like a little boy who'd just found a pie cooling on a windowsill and no one around. "I wonder if—"

But Raven never found out what Lord Sevrynel was planning for there came a loud cough from the hidden Answell.

Once more Sevrynel sighed. "Master Redhawkson, I am in your debt. And as much as I would like to know more, I really must leave now. Farewell once again." He bowed, then hurried off, muttering, "Oh, my! Oh, *my*!"

Raven noticed he had included Stormwind in his bow and wondered what Arisyn, standing in the entrance to the enclosure, would make of it. But it seemed the boy hadn't noticed, he was so busy worrying his foster father's earlier words for clues. Lord Sevrynel stopped a moment and whispered something in his foster son's ear. The boy lingered in the enclosure for a moment.

At last Arisyn gave it up. "Shall we go to the pond?" he asked as he came back.

"If it would please you, my lord, I'd like to do just that," Raven replied. He hoped Yarrow got here soon. She'd be well pleased with this news.

"Thank you for showing me this, my lord," Raven said. He settled himself more comfortably in the lush grass that led down to the little pond. Save for this small stretch, the entire pond was ringed with the yellow-green, irislike leaves of sweetflag.

Stormwind swam back across the pond, coming to stand in knee-deep water next to Arisyn's gelding, Arrow. He shook his heavy mane, sending water flying. Arrow snorted at him as if in reprimand.

"It was my pleasure. I'm glad my foster father said that I could. And please, call me Ari—all of my friends do," Arisyn said. "I'd like us to be friends; I can tell that Lord Sevrynel thinks highly of you."

"My lor—Ari, I'm honored," Raven replied. "Thank you."

Then the boy sat up, a puzzled look on his face. "I almost forgot—as he left, my foster father said to tell you that you were 'to feel free to invite any friend of yours who came to the fair to go with you to the pond.'" The puzzled look deepened. "He had the *oddest* expression—as if he were trying not to laugh."

Raven could well imagine Lord Sevrynel had been trying not to. "Tell him I thank him. I know my friends will like this place as much as I do—and their . . . horses will appreciate it as much as Stormwind."

At the mention of his name, Stormwind half turned toward them. Seeing he wasn't being called, the big stallion lowered his head once more to drink.

Arisyn plucked a long blade of grass and chewed on it. "I've never seen a horse that knows his name as well as Stormwind seems to. He's clever, too. With a horse like that, you could pretend you were riding a Llysanyin."

Raven swallowed wrong and began coughing.

Not noticing, Arisyn went on shyly, "Did you ever pretend you were riding one? When you were younger, I mean?"

Raven got his voice under control and replied, "Who doesn't? There was one horse in particular, I remember. Rynna—a girl I grew up with in Thalnia and my best friend—came from a family of wealthy merchants. My father was also a merchant; well-to-do but not wealthy. But because Rynna and I were friends, I was allowed to take lessons with her from the riding master that they retained. Master Oberus said it was a kindness to his horses; Rynna's family were sailors. Ships they understood. Horses, now—the less said, the better.

"Anyway, he had one horse, old Pell, that had been there and back a dozen times, seen everything, and, as the saying goes, wrote a book about it. In his own way, Pell was as good a teacher as Oberus. Oberus would let me take Pell to exercise him on the days when there were no lessons. Then I'd give Rynna a riding lesson. Back then I wanted to be a riding master and she was the only one who would be my 'student.'

"One day Rynna didn't tighten Pell's girth enough when she saddled him. It began slipping. Pell was really very tolerant, but he *hated* having his girth tightened. When he was tacked up, you had to cross-tie him so that he couldn't reach around and bite your backside. It was the only time you couldn't trust him.

"This time, Pell was already annoyed because Rynna had been bouncing around on his back—I'd been teaching her to post—so I offered to tighten the girth for her. The instant I laid my hand on it, Pell turned his head and glared at me as if to say, 'Touch that thing, boy, and I'll take your head off.'

"Without thinking, I blurted out, 'Ah, have mercy, Pell!' And do you know, that horse just gave me a long, long look, then turned his head away and deliberately stared up at the clouds while I tightened the girth. I swear he was gritting his teeth the whole time. It was as if he'd understood me. Wasn't the only thing like that he did, either."

"Oh, my," Arisyn breathed. "How odd! D'you think he could have been part Llysanyin?"

"Not a chance, my lo—Ari," Raven said cheerfully. "Old Pell was pure Thalnian Beckford, rabbity ears and all."

"Did your friend Rynna ever learn to ride?"

Raven grinned, thinking of Rynna's newest teachers: Linden and her Llysanyin, Boreal. "You wouldn't believe how much she's improved, my lord, though she'd probably tell you that she's still a better sailor than rider. She's actually captained a ship for her family—and fought pirates."

Arisyn looked impressed. "I wish I could meet her someday."

"You will, my lord. She and her soul—her, ah, husband, that is, and a friend are coming to the fair." Raven paused a moment, then went on, "I think you'll enjoy meeting them very, very much."

Arisyn invited Raven to return to Lord Sevrnel's manor with him. "I've a feeling that my foster father would like to see more of you."

"Or of Stormwind?" Raven asked with a smile.

The boy grinned in return. "Um, well—yes. But you can't say I wasn't trying to be polite. Just wanted to spare your feelings and all that."

"Don't worry," said Raven dryly. "Wait until you meet my aunt."

When they returned to the manor, Arisyn's words were proved true. They found the little Cassorin earl still in the forecourt as he consulted with various fair marshals. Sevrynel was indeed delighted to see him once more. Calling his steward, the earl gave Raven the freedom of the manor and its grounds.

"Do come as often as you want, my lad," Sevrynel urged him. "I wish I could show you about myself, but the duke and duchess are here. I can't even leave you Arisyn as a guide." He rested a hand on the boy's shoulder. "My apologies, Ari, for I know you're not on duty this day, but . . ."

"It's fine, sir. I'll be happy to help," Arisyn said.

"Well enough, then. Answell, you know where to bring Raven."

The steward bowed as Lord Sevrynel and Arisyn entered the manor. Turning to Raven he said, "This way, if you please, good sir."

To Raven's surprise, Answell did not lead him to the stables as he'd expected. Was there some mistake? Then he remembered Sevrynel's mysterious order. Raven paused just inside the rose-covered arch. "The gardens? Why . . . is there some mistake?"

"Not at all, Master Redhawkson. If you will please follow me, I shall explain as we go."

Mystified, Raven had no choice but to follow.

"After you and Lord Arisyn left earlier, my lord sent word to the castle regarding your news about the Dragonlords. Knowing how busy Lord Sevrynel is with the fair, the duke and duchess kindly came here to consult with him. Lady Rosalea, the young daughter of one of my lord's guests, is a playmate of Prince Rann and his friend Kella Vanadin, so they brought them along. And when the prince heard who'd brought the news, he insisted that you be sent to him if you came back while he was here. It seems that the two of you have met before."

Raven gaped at the man. He couldn't help it. The prince of Cassori remembered him? Why, they'd only met a couple of times just before he, his great-uncle, Maurynna, Linden, Lleld, her soultwin Jekkanadar, and the traitor Taren Olmeins left for the first leg of their mission to Jehanglan. He'd been the least of that company and in a permanent sulk to boot in those days. "You're jesting," he said weakly. "Aren't you?"

"Not at all, Master Redhawkson," Answell said, the very picture of bland serenity—except for the mischievous twinkle in his eyes. As they came to an opening in one of the tall hedges, Answell repeated, "Not at all, Master Redhawkson—and here we are!"

They came upon two little girls sitting atop a pretty little pony; Raven recognized one as Maurynna's younger cousin Kella. She waved at him. The other little girl had golden curls cascading down her back and the biggest eyes he'd ever seen. Then Raven went down on one knee as a sturdy little boy with brick-red hair ran, whooping, to meet him, an enormous wolfhound cantering behind him.

Nineteen

Leet rode up to the castle gates. He waited; it was for the guard to approach him, not for him to petition the guard for entrance.

A tall woman in the scarlet of a royal guard briskly came up to him. "Your name and business, sir." She studied him, no doubt taking careful note of his clothing and torc of rank.

"I am Leet Welkin, a Master Bard of Bylith."

The guard nodded. "I see, sir." She turned and signaled to the guardhouse. One side of the great wrought-iron gate slowly opened. "Please wait inside while we send word to the steward, my lord."

Leet rode inside in time to see a youngster run off, bearing the news of his arrival. To his satisfaction, it was not long before the steward himself, the chain of his office swinging against his chest as he walked, came to greet him. Leet nodded as the man bowed to him.

"Welcome to Balyaranna Castle, my lord bard," the man said. "I am Steward Lewell."

Leet smiled at the steward, wielding the charm he rarely bothered to use; his rank was normally sufficient to get what he wanted. "My apologies, Steward Lewell, if I have arrived at an inopportune time. My journey has been long and wearying, and I thought I might break it and visit my old student, Bard Daera," Leet said, ignoring the little voice in the back of his mind wryly commenting on how surprised Daera would be. "And to provide entertainment should the duke and duchess wish it, of course."

The steward smiled in return. "I'm certain they shall," he said.

Leet knew they would. Daera was good, one of the best students he'd ever had—but she was not a Master. Not yet. And no one, not even a royal, would turn away a bard of his rank. Unless, of course, they wished to have their niggardly hospitality mocked in song throughout the Five Kingdoms.

No, Leet was certain of accommodation. Likely they would not be as luxurious as he might expect at another time; no doubt the small castle was full of guests for the fair. Even so, his room would be far from the worst the castle had to offer.

He was suddenly aware of an odd feeling in his fingertips, as if, as if . . . The next instant a craving burned through his body; Leet fought to stay erect in the saddle.

Suddenly feeling as if he couldn't breathe, he said, "If I might be shown my room? I've journeyed far and . . ." He forced himself to smile genially once more. "And alas, I'm not as young as I once was."

Something of what he felt must have shown in his face. The steward's eyebrows drew down in concern. "Of course, my lord bard. You must be weary."

A few snapped orders later, Leet was on his way to a comfortable room, servants trailing behind, their arms filled with his packs. It was all he could do not to turn and snatch one particular harp case from its bearer.

But that would cause gossip among the servants. Above all else, Leet wanted no wagging tongues, no cause for speculation.

By the time they finally reached his room, Leet felt as if his very bones ached. The steward struggled with the latch. "My apologies, bard," he said, "but this latch is stiff and hard to work."

Leet forced himself not to howl at the delay. At last the recalcitrant latch gave and they all went inside. He barely noticed what the room looked like. At that point, he would have consented to a cell in the dungeon as long as he was left alone.

"I'll send someone to fix the latch," the steward began.

A thought came out of nowhere. *No—it will give warning if someone tries to walk in on us.*

"Don't bother," Leet said, forcing himself to smile benignly. "I'm certain that you've much more important things to deal with than a mere latch."

"But—"

"I insist. Believe me, it's not as obstinate as some of the thickheaded students I've had over the years." He paused, waiting for the obligatory chuckle. "I don't mind it at all."

It took forever but he finally convinced the steward that he meant it. The moment the door closed behind the last servant, he collapsed on the bed. Then, his hands shaking, he scrambled for one of the traveling cases—the case bearing the V marking on one corner. He clawed it open and lifted the harp into his arms.

His fingers brushed the strings. Leet let out a breath he hadn't realized he'd been holding, closed his eyes, and ran his fingers along the cold strings.

After a second trip to the pond, Raven and Arisyn decided to go in search of a meal. At the young noble's suggestion, they took a different way back to the fair. "It will take us down to the road that goes between the fair proper and the exercise grounds," Arisyn explained. "While I've never eaten there, I've heard that there's a farmer and his family that sell bread and cheese by a big copper beech—they're supposed to have good cheese. I once heard someone tell my foster father that it tasted like Big Moreby—" He paused. "No, that's not right. Big Borley—something like that. Some Thalnian cheese."

Raven started in surprise. "Fat Gorly?"

With a snap of his fingers, Arisyn said, "That's it! Is that good?"

"Better than good—it will be nothing short of a miracle! If it really does taste like Fat Gorly, I'll have to bring Rynna here. It was a favorite of ours back in Thalnia. We never got enough of it save for one time."

As they trotted down the track, Raven told Arisyn how he and Maurynna had once stolen half a wheel of Fat Gorly from her family's larder; they'd been playing their usual game of pretend: they were Bram and Rani, the mercenary leaders in the Heirs' War of Kelneth, raiding for "war rations."

Raven chuckled, remembering. "Of course we got caught—though not before we'd eaten our way through a good portion of it. It was the better part of a tenday before either of us could sit down without hurting—the cheese had been meant for a feast that night!"

They rode quickly, Arisyn guiding them to a well-beaten path. Raven's stomach was growling by the time they reached the plank table where the farmer had set up his business.

Arisyn tied his horse's reins to a sturdy bush; Raven merely dropped his on Stormwind's neck.

The young noble frowned. "Aren't you going to tie him?"

Raven smiled. "No."

"Or hobble him?"

"No. Stormwind's not going anywhere without me."

Both boy and elderly farmer looked askance at him, but since Stormwind showed no signs of bolting, they let the matter drop.

When Arisyn and he had been served and sat down in the shade of an enormous copper beech, Raven found that the simple meal of bread and cheese was as good as he'd hoped it would be. As he chewed in bliss, he told himself that he'd have to remember to tell Maurynna about this. Aside from that one memorable occasion, neither one of them had ever gotten their fill of Fat Gorly. And this cheese was, he thought, even a tad better.

This was going to be a *good* fair.

As they ate, they talked about this and that and watched the passersby on the road. Some trudged along on foot along the edges of the road, talking excitedly about watching the nobles' horses exercising before the races. It was likely, Raven thought, the best view they'd have of the horses in action. Yarrow had told him that the best spots along the racecourses would be taken by the aristocracy.

The center of the road was reserved for riders. Most of these were gaily dressed nobles, though Raven spotted a few high-ranking priests and priestesses from various cults. There was even, Raven noted wryly, a pair from the temple of Duirin in Thalnia, mounted on sturdy Beckfords. He studied their blue-grey robes, wondering if the wool for them came from his family's sheep, the sheep that had been his stepbrother Honigan's brilliant idea to import from Yerrih. The sheep that were part of the wool business that Raven had wanted no part of and that Honigan had longed for.

I'm glad that Da's finally given Honigan his rightful place, Raven thought, watching the priests of Duirin disappear down the road. He truly was happy for his stepbrother, though Honigan's good fortune had come at the cost of Raven's alienation from his father. *But that's Da's problem, not mine,* Raven told himself firmly. *He's the one that pushed me away, not the other way around. I can't live his dreams for him.*

He took another bite of his bread and cheese, wondering if he would have been desperate enough to give in to his father's wishes if he'd had nowhere else to go. Or would he have had the courage to strike out on his own, to find his own place in the world?

His thoughts were interrupted by a happy shout from Arisyn.

"Hoy there, Javiel! Marus!" The boy waved madly at two riders.

As Raven watched, two boys a little older than Arisyn turned their horses and eased out of the traffic on the road. They dismounted and led their horses over. Arisyn performed the introductions with a flourish.

Javiel and Marus were, it seemed, pages in Lord Sevrynel's household; Javiel was the shorter of the two, a stocky lad with light brown hair pulled back with a silver clasp. Marus was black-haired with a thin, triangular face and eyes the color of jasper.

The two were puzzled by Arisyn's choice of companions, Raven thought, amused at their surreptitious glances from him to Stormwind to Arisyn and back again. *Likely wondering what on earth Arisyn's doing hanging about with a Yerrin commoner.*

Still, when Arisyn mentioned that Raven was Yarrow's nephew, their interest was clearly piqued.

"She's the Yerrin that has the site next to the Mountain Lilies in the southeast quarter, isn't she?" Marus asked. When Raven nodded, he went on, "My father bought a broodmare from her, oh, must be eight years ago now. Every foal she's dropped has been a grand animal. Father says that mare's one of the best choices he's ever made."

"I'm glad to hear it, my lord," Raven said with pride. "And one day we'll have even better for sale." He nodded at Stormwind. "That fine lad there is standing at stud now."

Marus and Javiel looked at Stormwind, shock and dismay writ large upon their faces.

"But he's just a—" Javiel began.

"I know what you're going to say, Jav," Arisyn interrupted. "He isn't—a Shamreen plow horse, that is. I don't know *what* he is, I'm still trying to guess. But I can tell you that Lord Sevrynel was very interested when Raven told him that bit of news. *Very* interested."

Astonishment, disbelief, consternation: the emotions flashed across the boys' faces. Raven managed not to laugh.

A weak "Is that so?" was all Javiel could manage, it seemed; Marus said nothing but looked skeptical. Saying that they were expected back, the two made their farewells and mounted their horses once more. As they rode away, they looked back a couple of times, shaking their heads.

"You know that they now think Lord Sevrynel's lost his wits," Raven said.

"Then they're fools," Arisyn replied tartly. "Are you done?"

"I am."

"Then let's be off. I want to find a gift for my mother."

As Arisyn went off to get his horse, Raven whistled Stormwind to him. He mounted and sat easily in the saddle, waiting for Arisyn.

When Arisyn was settled in his turn, he drew alongside and frowned at Stormwind. "It's not possible," he muttered under his breath, "but I'd almost swear . . ." He shook his head. "Not possible." He urged his horse on.

You'd be surprised at what's possible in this life, my young lord, Raven thought as he fell in alongside Arisyn. *You just have to reach for what you want—and be willing to fall flat on your face if you can't hold on.*

Twenty

Leet settled himself on a bench in a quiet corner of the gardens. It had taken him a while to find this spot, for he was not familiar with the gardens, but they seemed deserted. And that was just what he wanted.

He had to smile, if a bit ruefully. It was ironic that it was his rank that had "evicted" him from his quarters. He'd been all set to play the Gull harp when a knock had interrupted him.

Sharp on the heels of the knock came a bevy of servants led by an understeward. Some carried brooms and dusting cloths; others were laden with fresh bed linens. A trio bore a table and chair; they were followed by a lad carrying parchment sheets and writing tools.

"My lord bard," the understeward said with a bow. "Her Grace the Duchess Beryl has asked that we make this room fit for one of your rank. She apologizes that we cannot give you finer quarters, but begs your understanding that the castle is small and that all the best rooms have already been assigned." As the understeward finished, she looked anxiously at him.

He wanted to scream at them to get out. But he wished no undue attention, and long years of playing in the Kelnethi court had taught Leet how to dissemble. Hiding his anger, he bowed to the understeward. "If there is any fault, it is mine. This room is far above what I deserve, coming unannounced and unexpected as I did. Please thank the duchess for me for her extraordinary kindness and generosity. And if she or the duke have any desire to hear my humble talents, they've but to ask."

He stood and slipped Gull into the embroidered canvas case used to carry a harp short distances. "Ah . . . is there a place where I might practice in private? New song—not ready to be heard yet," he said with a self-deprecating smile.

And so he found himself in the gardens. Remembering the fawn, this might be a much better place to play, he realized. He had no idea how strongly the harp could "call." It would be most awkward if people found themselves drawn to his quarters for no reason—at least, no reason they could fathom. Eventually some-one would ask awkward questions.

No, this was not the inconvenience he'd first feared. This was the answer to a need he'd been unaware of; more proof that the gods looked kindly upon his quest. Therefore he would make it his habit to practice in the gardens away from all others. Here he would hone his new skills.

The sight of a squirrel dashing across the grass reminded him there were other benefits as well. Leet took a deep breath and slipped the ties that held the canvas case shut.

With Prince Rann and Bard Daera leading the way, the children laughed and giggled as they entered the little alcove in the garden for their music lesson. Before them were benches holding their harps. But it was the tables to the side that made the children clap their hands and cheer in delight: those were decked with flowers and laden with pitchers of sweet-sour honey drink and little sweetmeats and cakes for afterward.

"This is a lovely idea, Prince Rann. Thank you *so* much," Willena, Lord Morelby's ten-year-old daughter, simpered as she edged up alongside the prince.

He felt his face burn and mumbled something.

"I'm sorry, Your Highness?" Lady Willena said, tilting her head at Rann.

"It was Kella's idea because the day was so nice," Rann said. "I thought it was a good one, so I ordered it done."

Willena's mouth pursed for an instant. "Oh." She looked around, trying to hide a triumphant smirk. "Then what a pity that she's not here to enjoy it. I do hope she's not being punished."

Rann thought that it was a good thing Willena didn't have to make her living in a troupe of wandering players. She'd get rotten eggs thrown at her every time. He also truly hoped that his uncle the Lord Regent didn't betroth him to Willena; he knew Lord Morelby was making Uncle Beren's life miserable about it.

"Not at all," Bard Daera said pleasantly. "Duchess Beryl wished her to have some new gowns. Kella will come once Mistress Colwe's finished fitting them on her."

"Oh," Willena said again. "How . . . nice for her." She dropped back.

Good, Rann thought. *A music lesson's bad enough; I don't need Willena, too!*

Another little girl, Lady Rosalea, scampered up to take Willena's place. She grinned at him; Rann grinned back. Rosalea was fun and she liked Kella. He wished Rosalea were staying at the castle instead of Willena. But her mother was some kind of distant kinsman to Lord Sevrynel, so they stayed with him. Maybe he and Kella could stay with Lord Sevrynel, too, during the whole fair, not just go there to play. . . . They'd have such fun games all the time with Rosalea's pony and Raven.

"Did you remember to ask for lots of honey-spice cakes, Your Highness?" she asked.

"Of course I did, silly."

She stuck her tongue out at him. Rann returned the favor. He thought that if he had to marry someone someday, he wouldn't mind the pink-and-gold Rosie, even if she did give her pony a silly name like Buttercup.

As he and Daera passed under one of the many rose-covered arches in the gardens, Rann heard the sound of a harp being tuned somewhere. He looked up at his teacher in question.

"It must be Bard Leet, Your Highness," she said. "He was once one of my teachers. Steward Lewell told me he arrived yesterday."

From the tone of her voice, Rann guessed that this Leet had not been one of Daera's favorite teachers. And since Daera was so nice, it probably meant the older bard was mean.

He was glad he had Daera for a teacher and not that bard.

Leet froze at the sound of children's voices. *Not children! Not here—not now!* He damped the strings and waited, hardly daring to breathe. After far too long a time, it seemed, the young voices faded.

Even after they were gone, Leet sat without playing. Fatigue from his journey to Balyaranna still weighed heavily upon him; he'd never been fond of travel, and he wasn't as young as he'd been even during his journey to Dragonskeep.

And it was getting harder to bend this harp to his will. . . . Too often of late he'd found himself reaching for it without thinking. Leet closed his eyes.

The strings beneath his fingers vibrated slightly. Very well, then; time to match wills once more with the instrument he cradled in his arms like a lover.

Perhaps a candlemark later, Leet forced himself to set down the harp and put a hand to his forehead. Odd; it was a warm day, but he felt cold. And yet there was sweat on his brow.

He remembered how for one terrifying moment he'd thought he was falling into the harp's music like a man falling into a well. It was impossible, of course; he was the master here, not the harp. But the sensation was still enough to unnerve him.

He thought of the fountain that he'd passed on his way here. *I'll get a drink from it and splash water on my face. That should wake me up from these fancies.*

It was hard to stand; his knees felt wobbly. It was even harder to leave the harp behind. Leet kept looking back as if it might disappear, or, or . . .

It will be safe enough here for a few moments. There's no one about. You can't even hear those cursed children anymore! Pull yourself together, man!

* * *

The tables were bare and the castle servants were waiting to clean up. Bard Daera clapped her hands. The laughing children paused in their play and looked to her.

"Time to go back," she announced to a chorus of groans. "Both lesson and picnic are over."

Not, she admitted to herself, *that it was much of a lesson today.* Eyes and minds had been on the tables full of sweetmeats, not on strings and chord progressions. *Ah, well—a holiday once in a while is good for them.*

As she walked back with the children, Daera thought she heard Leet's harp again. She sighed; she'd have to greet him sometime. She might as well get it over with. Hopefully after this she could avoid him most of the time.

"Portran, Fane," she said to two of the servants, "please escort the children for me. I must see my old teacher."

The servants nodded. But before she could go off to find him, another servant approached. He held out a sealed note to her.

"This just came for you, bard."

She took it and studied the beeswax seal. Just a blob of wax, no sigil impressed in it—so whom was it from? Frowning, she broke it open and read. "Oh, no!" she gasped.

Kella stared at the flame burning down through yet another mark on the banded candle. She twitched impatiently, wanting to be done with this and off to her music lesson. Another twitch, and a pin jabbed her. "Ouch!"

"Hold still, girl, and it won't happen again," said Mistress Colwe pleasantly. "And we'll be done that much faster."

When Mistress Colwe was finally done, Kella raced outside as fast as she could. She ran through the mazelike garden, grumbling mightily. While she was thrilled to have new gowns, she'd missed the music lesson. Why, oh why had the duchess ordered so many gowns for her? And Mistress Colwe was so fussy and kept her there for three whole candlemarks making certain the fabrics fell just *so*! This was all her fault.

She tripped and fell hard, sliding in the grass. It was a moment before she got her breath back. "Ouch!" She clambered to her feet and ruefully inspected the grass stains on the knees of her skirt and the front of her tunic. And still so far to go! She'd better use the shortcut. She ducked through a spot in the hedge into the next path.

A thread of music came to her ears, a bare whisper of notes on the breeze. To her surprise, it came from her left and sounded quite close by.

Oh, good—they're not in the Queen's Retreat after all! Maybe I'll still have time to get a cake or two at least.

She turned and trotted off in search of the music that still floated on the air. It took longer than she'd thought it would, but a few twists and turns later she came upon a harp sitting by itself on one of the marble benches scattered throughout the gardens.

It wasn't a full-sized harp, but a small traveling harp. And it was exquisite. Kella stared and stared, enchanted beyond words.

Whose is it? she wondered. Then she clapped her hands. "It must be Daera's new one finally come."

She ran up and studied it. She thought she'd never seen anything so beautiful; the sweep of the neck was perfect. And what was that carved into the shoulder of the harp? Some kind of bird?

The strings seemed to be calling her; she stretched out her hand. *Daera won't mind,* Kella told herself. *She's already promised I could play it. . . .*

So caught up in her enchantment with the harp, Kella never wondered where Daera was and why she was in the garden alone after class was over. Her hand crept closer. She knew she should wait for renewed permission, but it was so beautiful!

Kella screamed as a man's hand viciously slapped hers aside. She jumped back, her eyes watering in pain.

"How dare you try to touch my harp!" roared a man wearing the red tunic of a bard as he towered over her. "I ought to have you whipped!"

Kella stared up at him in shock. Hot tears slid down her cheeks. She clutched her stinging hand to her chest. "I—I'm sorry, bard, I thought it was Daera's new one finally come—"

"*Bard* Daera, you guttersnipe! You, a mere servant girl—and a slattern of a servant at that," he said, his voice heavy with disgust as he looked at her grass-stained clothes. "How dare you address a bard so familiarly!" His hand rose once more.

Kella stumbled back to avoid the blow. To her relief and everlasting gratitude, she heard Daera call out from behind her. "Bard Leet! *No!*"

Bard Leet glared past her at Daera. Kella scurried to stand by the younger bard.

"She's not a servant, sir," Daera said quietly. "This is Kella Vanadin, the daughter of merchants from Casna. She's one of my best students in the royal classes. She's also—"

Bard Leet stared at her in patent disbelief. "A *merchant's* daughter? They allow a *merchant's* daughter to take lessons in the royal classes? No matter, how dare she try to touch my harp!"

Kella took a deep breath. "I'm sorry, sir, I didn't know it was yours. I never would touch a bard's harp without permission. I thought it was Da—Bard Daera's new one and she'd already said I could play it when it came."

"I did," Daera said. "It was an honest mistake, sir, she thought it was mine. And I should tell—"

"Never mind your excuses. You've noble students here—I hope you haven't been shorting them to give this common brat lessons. We'll speak of this later, Daera."

With that, Bard Leet caught up his harp and strode angrily off.

Kella wiped away her tears. She looked up at Daera. To her surprise, the young bard's eyes were red. Yet as she looked after her superior, her lips curved in an odd little smile.

"I *tried* to warn him," she said to the air. Then, shaking her head, she looked down at Kella. "I'm sorry about this, Kella. How's your hand? And look at those stains! Did you fall as well, sweetling?"

Nodding, Kella held out her hand. It was still an angry red and she knew there would be a bruise. "It doesn't hurt now," she lied. "Daera, *why* was he like that? Otter's never acted as if he's better than the rest of us."

"He's noble-born, sweetling, so it makes him proud."

"Like Lady Willena and some of the others?"

"Just so. And since he's one of my guild's elders, he's a Master Bard as well. But still . . ." After a moment, Daera said, "Shall we have Simpler Quirel look at your poor hand? He can put a poultice on it."

Kella shook her head; she wanted as few people as possible to know about what had happened. It was too humiliating. There were only a couple of people she'd trust with this news. And then . . .

She'd find a way to get back at him, she would. She'd show Master Stuck-Up Bard Leet he couldn't treat a Dragonlord's kin that way!

"No, I'd just like to go to Rann's quarters, please."

"He *hit* you?" Rosie asked in outrage. She and Rann bent over the hand that Kella held out. It was red and Kella knew that by tomorrow morning a bruise would show. "But you never even touched his stupid harp!"

Rann scowled. "I'll ask Uncle Beren to send him away. We don't need him. We have Daera to sing for us."

"But we won't. While she was walking me here, she told me she had to go away. She said she got a message but didn't say what it was about, just that she was going to ask permission to go home. She looked awfully upset."

"Oh, no!" Rann said after a moment. "Do you think we'll have to take lessons from *him*?"

"I won't," Kella said firmly. "He'll refuse to teach me. He was awful mad at Daera for teaching a 'common brat.' "

Rosie giggled. " 'Common brat'? He doesn't know about your cousin the Dragonlord, does he?"

"No," Kella answered, thinking. She *could* tell Maurynna or even Linden when next she saw them that the bard had hit her. But . . . "No. I don't want to tell her. Or anyone. Promise me you won't tell anyone about this."

The other children placed their hands over their hearts and solemnly swore, Rann grumbling all the while.

"And don't let on to Bard Leet that you know what he did to me, either. Promise that, too?"

Once more, hands went to hearts.

"Thank you."

Rann said, "I wish you would let me tell my uncle, though. He'd know how to pay back Bard Leet without him knowing it."

Kella shook her head. "I want to get back at Bard Leet myself."

"How?" Rosalea asked.

"I don't know," Kella said. She twirled a lock of hair around her finger. "But I will. I will."

Bard Leet hefted the flask of wine he'd ordered a servant to bring to his chamber upon his return from the gardens. It was nearly gone. But even that much wine had hardly steadied his nerves from the fright that brat had given him.

Gods above! If the girl had touched that harp, no telling what might have happened.

Likely nothing, he told himself. *So many of these brats are taking lessons only because it's expected. They've as much talent as a fly.*

Relief flooded him; everything would have been just fine, she would never have felt a thing. . . .

A memory clawed its way to the front of his mind: *She's one of my best students.*

Daera wouldn't say that lightly—especially not in front of a student. A sudden rush of fear froze the very marrow in his bones. Leet caught himself reaching for the flask again and stopped. No; he'd had enough. It wouldn't do to make this a habit.

But his hands now were shaking worse than ever. A little more wouldn't hurt. . . .

Twenty-one

The next morning Raven left Stormwind at the camp. "Arisyn and I will be going into the Gold Quarter," he told the Llysanyin as he brushed him. "And horses aren't allowed there, I'm told."

Stormwind snorted in disbelief—or disgust; Raven wasn't sure which.

"'Deed they're not," Woodbine, Yarrow's oldest groom, agreed as he tipped a bucket of water into a nearby trough. "And good reason for it."

"Oh? Why? This is a horse fair, after all."

"Thieves," said the old man with a smack of his lips. "I were just a younker then, a mere bit of a lad, and I saw it happen."

"Saw what? A robbery?"

"No, not the robbery itself. I was there with Mistress Yarrow's da and we saw those murdering scum ride down five innocent people who had the ill luck to be in their way. They'd killed the goldsmith they was robbin' and knew they had to get out of there in a hurry or be caught and hanged. So they just rode over whoever was in their way. Three people died, two was crippled for life, and nigh a score was hurt jumpin' out o' their cursed way. Damned bastards was never caught. Too much of a head start, they had.

"So ever since, no horses are allowed in the Gold Quarter where all the big gold- and silversmiths have their wares. Iffen you plan to rob someone there now, you'd best be the fastest runner in the Five Kingdoms—for once the hue and cry is raised, everyone and his cousin'll be after you!"

Raven nodded. It made sense now that he knew the reason. He finished and slapped Stormwind on the rump before putting the brushes away in their painted leather case. "Sorry, lad, but you'll have to stay. Arisyn wants to look there for a pin for his mother."

Once again Stormwind snorted as if to say *he* was no mere horse, *he* was a Llysanyin. Then he ambled off to stick his head in the main tent to see if there were any treats for him—as there usually were.

Laughing, Raven went off to meet Arisyn in front of the saddler's where they usually met. When the young noble arrived, he had a huge grin on his face.

"You're in a good mood," Raven said.

"I am! I think my foster father will give me permission to sleep in Lord and Lady Pearrin's encampment soon! Coryn, Marus, and Javriel have had permission for ages already. I think he was just about to say 'Yes' when Lord Huryn, the fair's High Marshal, came in."

"That will be something." The young Lord and Lady Pearrin of Cassori, he'd heard, were favorites with the younger nobles and an invitation to their encampment was a sought-after favor. They were famous for engaging the best puppet shows, mummers, and acrobats for each night's entertainment. "You'll have to tell me about it when you do go." He suspected that he'd not be welcome at the encampment himself. Perhaps one day, as Stormwind's get proved themselves, but not yet.

"I will," Arisyn promised. "Shall we head for the Gold Quarter now?"

"Lead on," Raven said cheerfully. "I haven't been to that part of the fair yet." He fell in alongside Arisyn as they set off.

It was a long way to the Gold Quarter, made longer by frequent stops to look at this or that. Raven and Arisyn ambled on, talking horses as they went. They had just worked their way single-file through a crowd gathered to watch a juggler when Arisyn stopped so abruptly that Raven almost ran into him.

"What are you doing here, Tirael? You were sent to Pelnar!"

Alert for trouble, Raven came up alongside the young lord. A glance at Arisyn told him a quarrel wasn't far off.

Gone was the affable youth he'd come to know. Arisyn stood with his fists clenched and face white with fury, glaring at the man standing in front of a pie man's booth, sharing a wineskin with Coryn and Dunric and sampling the small, crispy pies.

Tirael, Tirael . . . Why is that name familiar? Raven racked his brains but couldn't place it. Still, he had the feeling he wouldn't be pleased when he did remember.

Javiel and Marus, standing by them, started guiltily before scrunching down as if they could make themselves disappear. They stared down at their feet, at the booth, at the pile of firewood by it—anywhere where they didn't have to meet anyone's eyes for more than a moment or two. They were the very picture of two schoolboys caught with stolen sweets: half guilty, half defiant, and embarrassed down to the bone. The other youths about the booth just looked at one another.

But not one chose to leave. And when the man pressed a hand theatrically to his chest and said, "Oh dear, oh dear, Coryn—Ari doesn't like me," there were smiles of bravado and outright smirks. It was clear whose side they were on.

The cause of the discord took another long, lazy pull on the wineskin before passing it on. He stared a challenge into the very teeth of Arisyn's anger, a tiny, supercilious smile playing about his lips. One hand gestured as if brushing away an importunate insect; Raven could almost hear the drawled *Spare me.*

So, it was clear, could Arisyn. He shook with rage; Raven had a sudden mental image of a young war hound held back by a single thread. With one wrong word, the tenuous restraint would snap and the hound would leap for his enemy's throat. Arisyn took a step, fists raised.

Raven caught him by the shoulder. "Don't be stupid," he whispered in the boy's ear. "He's much bigger than you. Not to mention it'll be at least six of them to the two of us—if we're lucky. Look at them, Ari. They're his."

It was true. Whoever this Tirael was, Raven could see that for good or ill, he was one of those who drew others to him like moths to a flame. Never mind that they might burn themselves to a cinder while he remained unscathed; they would think themselves fortunate for the chance to circle his flame.

The man smiled broadly as Arisyn slumped under Raven's hand. His gaze flickered briefly to Raven, then away again, bored. Servants, that look seemed to say, were beneath his notice.

Then the narrow-eyed gaze returned. "Ah," Tirael said softly. "It's the plowboy from near Fern Crossing, isn't it?"

What is he talk— A sudden memory blazed in his mind: a dusty road and a pack of riders circling two children like the sharks that Maurynna had told him of. . . .

Oh, bloody hell, Raven thought in disgust. *Not him again.*

"You and that Beast Healer interrupted my fun."

Raven took a deep breath. "You find tormenting children fun . . . my lord?" The last two words were as close to a sneer as he dared in Cassori. *If only we were in Yerrih. . . .*

Tirael heard it; his eyes blazed, but Arisyn spoke before he could say anything. "Coryn—you know that Lord Sevrynel said that while you were with him you weren't to have anything to do with Tirael!"

Arisyn's voice cracked. Raven saw the boy's face go red, heard the gulp that was half a sob. Worse yet, the breeze chose that moment to shift; the smoke from the fire beneath the bubbling kettle of oil billowed over them, stinging their eyes. Now Arisyn looked as if he were crying.

"Go back to your nursery, little crybaby," Tirael sneered. "Or should I say, 'little tattletale?' Go ahead—prove you're nothing but a little snitch. It's just what I'd expect from you."

Raven's jaw clenched. Damn Tirael; he'd just made certain Arisyn would never tell his foster father about this. No one wanted to be known as a snitch— especially not a youth that age. That prickly age when one was no longer a child, but not yet a man, and all choices were still black and white, without the shades of grey that age and experience teach one to see. Though he was not really that much older than Coryn, Javiel, Marus, and, he guessed, Tirael, Raven suddenly felt as old as Morlen the Seer, the ancient truedragon he'd met at Dragonskeep.

"Never mind," he said quietly as he drew the boy away. "He's not worth the trouble. Let's go."

For a moment he thought Arisyn would pull free and go back to shove a fist down the laughing Tirael's throat; he knew *he* wanted to in the worst way. But thankfully Arisyn chose to be sensible—though he was walking so fast that Raven had to stretch his legs to keep up despite the difference in their sizes.

At long last Arisyn spoke. "What did Tirael mean that you and a Beast Healer spoiled his 'fun'?" The last word dripped contempt.

Raven told him how he and Beast Healer Gunnis had come across Tirael and his friends tormenting two children, Teasel and Speedwell, in the road.

"They'd best not let Reed Thornson see them for a long, long time," Raven finished. "He views his fosterlings as his own kin and—"

He stopped in midstride as a sudden realization hit him. *Oh dear gods . . .*

"Ari," he said slowly. "I think Dunric was one of those riders."

Arisyn groaned. "Oh, no! I like him—most of the time. When he's not treating me like a baby. It's that Tirael! I swear he could turn a high priest bad—I wish he'd drop dead!"

"Don't worry, Ari. One day it will all catch up to him," Raven said. "The gods will see to it. One way or another, they always do."

Arisyn merely grunted and shrugged as if to say *Perhaps.*

They turned onto the "road" leading to the Gold Quarter. An excited group of fairgoers clustered in the center of the lane, blocking most of it. As he and Arisyn edged around them, Raven caught part of their discussion.

"Have you heard?" one of them said. "Summer Lightning's here at last!"

Pod had lost count of the days. Then, one morning Fiarin shook them awake. Pod sat up, pulling her blankets around her against the predawn chill. She looked around in confusion. Why, it was still dark!

"Whaaa—" Kaeliss mumbled.

"Get up!" Fiarin snapped. "We've a long way to go."

Pod opened her mouth to ask where, then quailed before Fiarin's fierce scowl. Instead she made haste to roll up her blankets and pull on her boots.

"Eat this," Fiarin ordered, shoving a few strips of dried meat at her, "as we walk. Now let's go!"

The moment the young women were ready, the senior Wort Hunter set off. Pod caught Kaeliss's eye and mouthed "What's wrong with him?" But Kaeliss just shook her head and fell in behind Fiarin; she looked, Pod thought, a little frightened. Mystified—but not willing to be left alone—Pod hurried after her, Kiga loping alongside.

What on earth is happening? What is driving him? Yet Pod wasn't certain she really wanted to know.

There were no lessons that day, not even the pretense of one; no gathering of useful herbs, though Pod saw a number of them: goldthread, spikenard, heal-moss, and wild ginger among others, and once, high up in an oak tree, a glimpse of mistletoe. Whenever either she or Kaeliss tried to point them out, Fiarin would dismiss them with a contemptuous wave of his hand.

"You'll thank me for this," he snarled at them when they protested the unre-lenting pace. "You'll thank me for this, oh yes. Now *move!*"

He frightened Pod so much that for a moment she considered setting Kiga on him so that she and Kaeliss could escape. But she had no idea where they were or how to find her way back to *anywhere* with people.

At least Fiarin seemed to know where he was going. So Pod held her tongue and followed, her fear growing with every step. If she'd had the faintest idea of where she was or how to find her way out of these cursed woods, she would have left, training journey be damned. But she didn't. So she followed Kaeliss, who followed Fiarin, and tried to be brave.

Twenty-two

A village straddled the road ahead and spread along the banks of the small river beyond. The road continued over a wooden bridge that was barred by a gate. It was a pretty little place, Maurynna thought; many of the whitewashed homes had roses or ivy climbing over their walls and thatched roofs. Late-afternoon sun bathed the village in golden light and an air of quiet contentment hung over the town.

"Ah, good," Linden said as he halted Shan. "This must be Oakbridge. Fooled me at first—it's grown a bit since I last saw it. Most times I've approached Balyaranna from the north." He paused. "Hmm, the gate's new. Used to be just a wooden beam they raised and lowered. And the inn's new as well."

"And what's good about being in Oakbridge?" Maurynna asked.

"This inn has good food?" Shima asked hopefully.

"It means we're not far from Balyaranna," Linden said. "I've no idea about the food." There was a long silence, then a resigned sigh. "We should enter the fair wearing the traditional garb, I suppose."

Maurynna tried not to smile. Linden's dislike of the full, dagged sleeves of the Dragonlords' formal garb was legendary at Dragonskeep. Truth was, they *did* seem to have a talent for landing in the gravy.

She said, "I think it would be best. I wonder if we can get baths at the inn as well as a meal? I'm as dusty as this road."

Shima laughed and nodded. "As am I. I cast my vote for breaking our journey here."

"Very well, then," Linden said. "Even if we take our time, we can reach the fair by dusk."

Very well, then, he needed to go farther into the gardens. Leet cursed under his breath and hitched the carrying strap across his chest to a more comfortable position. Damn that stupid girl, anyway! He'd thought that little nook had been perfect, hidden away and with a fountain nearby in case he grew thirsty. Clearly, though, it hadn't been far enough from the castle.

At first he wandered aimlessly, taking good care to keep an eye on the sun and noting anything unusual; a striking topiary form here, another one there, a circle of dwarf apple trees whose branches were so cunningly grafted together that they made a "house," a fountain with a frieze of carved rabbits running around its rim—all were landmarks in his search for the perfect place.

From the signs around him he was now in a neglected part of the gardens. The roses were smaller here and all of a color, red, pink, or white; more like their wild cousins rather than the showy, many-petaled wonders now grown with their astonishing range of colors and streaked petals. Likely this part had fallen out of favor long ago. *This bodes well,* he thought. *Very well indeed.*

He turned down yet another path and saw before him a long tunnel of rose-covered arches stretching before him. Curious, he entered it. At its end was a lawn of chamomile. And across that lawn . . .

Leet bared his teeth in a fierce grin. "Perfect," he whispered. "Absolutely perfect."

Raven walked briskly to meet Arisyn. The boy hadn't found something for his mother during their first foray to the Gold Quarter, so they were going back. It was just as well; Yarrow had a few lords and ladies coming to the camp to see some horses and she wanted them to see Stormwind, too. But the last thing Raven wanted was to stay in camp tonight. For some reason he was restless and wanted to be out and about this evening.

Soon he and Ari were browsing the offerings in the quarter. Just as Raven was certain that they'd have no more luck this time, Ari spotted something.

It was a circular, domed brooch of silver delicately inlaid with swirling gold lines. Set in the center was a round piece of honey-colored amber.

"Just the thing for my mother's shawls!" Arisyn whispered in Raven's ear. "I hope it's not too much, though. . . ."

One look at the expression on Arisyn's face and Raven said, "Quick—the merchant's coming this way. How much do you have to spend? That should do it—now hand over your money and leave this to me."

A short while later they were leaving the Gold Quarter. Arisyn's belt pouch was lighter by a few coins—and heavier by a silver brooch.

"Where did you learn to bargain like that?" Arisyn asked in awe.

"That? That was nothing. If Rynna was here, we'd have done better," Raven said. "She was determined I wouldn't embarrass her when went to fairs in Thalnia, so she beat some skills into my head."

"I thought you said she was a sea captain, not a merchant," Arisyn said. By the tone of his voice, Raven could tell that Maurynna had lost status in his eyes.

"She was both. These days . . . These days she's doing other things," Raven said vaguely. "So—where are we bound to now?"

"Somewhere. Anywhere. I must be back before the bell for the last—"

"Ho! If it isn't little Ari and his pet plowboy! How's your plow horse, peasant?" a drunken voice caroled behind them. Laughter followed the gibe.

Raven sighed and turned around. Sure enough, it was Tirael, Dunric, Coryn, and a few more of Tirael's hangers-on. Tirael waved a wineskin and leered at them in mock fellowship. "I'd offer you a taste, plowboy, but it would be wasted on a peasant like you."

As Tirael and his group closed the distance between them, Raven noticed the crowd around them disappear with amazing speed.

"I'm not a plowboy, and Stormwind isn't a plow horse," Raven said, suddenly fed up with the insults. "As you'd find out if I could enter the great races here, my lord. But since I'm not noble . . ." He spread his hands.

"Since you're not noble, you'll never have to prove that boast, will you, plowboy?" Tirael said. He tipped the wineskin and took a long drink, then pointedly turned his back on them.

"It's not a boast!" Arisyn yelled. "You all think you're such good judges of horses—well, you're nothing but a pack of self-important idiots! None of you know a good horse from a spavined nag. You just look at the trappings on its back and judge from that. And you and Tirael are the biggest fools of the lot, Coryn!"

Coryn goggled drunkenly at the furious boy; it was plain that he never expected such fire from his young cousin. Tirael, though, spun around. He came swiftly toward them, moving with the deadly grace of a snowcat, his angry eyes fixed on Arisyn. His fist went back.

Raven hastily stepped between them, bracing himself to take the blow. He couldn't let Arisyn take a beating on his—and Stormwind's—account; certainly not from a full-grown man. The boy could be seriously hurt.

He just hoped he could leash his own temper and not retaliate. This was Cassori, not Yerrih or Thalnia. Tirael would be in the right no matter what provocation he offered.

Stopping barely a pace from Raven, Tirael glared at him; it certainly didn't appear to improve the other man's temper that he had to tilt his head back to do so. "Damned Yerrins think you're as good as anyone, isn't that right, plowboy? But just remember this: You're not noble. And that means you're nothing here in Cassori." He slapped Raven.

Raven bit his lip against the pain and said nothing, but his fists clenched. A slap was for an insolent slave, not a free man.

"Now get out of my—"

"What's going on here?" a gruff voice demanded.

Everyone jumped. Raven dared to turn his head, enough to see a small group of mail-clad men approaching. They wore the white shoulder sashes of the fair's peacekeepers. He recognized the stern-faced noble who led them as Lord Huryn, High Marshal of the fair, and breathed a tiny sigh of relief. Huryn was known to be a fair man—for a Cassorin.

"You two," the High Marshal said, pointing a gloved finger at Raven and Tirael. "Move away from each other."

Raven stepped back as Arisyn skittered out of his way.

"This peasant was insulting me," Tirael argued.

"I don't care, Tirael. Do as I say, then I'll hear your story."

After a long moment, Tirael stepped back as well.

Huryn scowled at them both from under heavy black eyebrows. "You!" he said, jabbing a finger at Raven. "What's your name and business at this fair? I've seen you riding through the fair the past few days but I've never seen you here before this year."

"My name is Raven Redhawkson, my lord. I'm here with my aunt, Yarrow Whitethorndaughter, a horse trader. I came ahead to hold her space for her. It's my first year at the fair."

Huryn nodded. "Be sure I'll make certain of your claim, young man. Yarrow Whitethorndaughter is well known here and well respected. I'll not have her name used by a rascal." He paused a moment, one gloved finger tracing the line of his bearded jaw, his eyes distant. Then a slight smile crooked his lips. "Raven Redhawkson, hmm? I believe I've heard that name before."

Abruptly he turned back to Tirael. "Very well then, Tirael. How did this Raven Redhawkson insult you?"

"He called me a fool," Tirael snapped. "This plowboy dared to call *me* a fool." He added sullenly, "My lord."

Huryn stared at him like a man who'd found a beetle in his bread. "Indeed?" To Raven he went on, "Did you?"

"No, my lord earl, I did not call my lord Tirael a fool." *Never mind what I was thinking.* "I merely said that Stormwind—my horse—is not a plow horse."

So softly that Raven almost didn't hear it, Lord Huryn said, "I can well imagine you did." The faint smile appeared once more, only to disappear an instant later, replaced by Huryn's customary scowl. "And that was all you said?"

Raven nodded. "Oh—and that I wasn't a plowboy."

"Hardly an insult, Tirael, unless you're even more sensitive than my lady wife during her moon time," Huryn said dryly.

Tirael's lips thinned to a pale line.

"My lord?" Arisyn said in a small, frightened voice. "I'm the one who called Tirael a fool."

"So I heard, Arisyn," Lord Huryn said. "Quite clearly. I don't like being lied to, Tirael. Remember that. I also saw you strike this man for no reason."

"He got in my way!" Tirael said in outrage. "You saw him!"

"I saw him protecting Arisyn from your fists. Which likely saved you from being banned from this fair and possibly every fair to come. Or had you forgotten that Arisyn is Lord Sevrynel's foster son, and all this," Huryn waved a hand to take in the cheerful uproar that was the fair, "is by Lord Sevrynel's goodwill?"

The soft, regretful "Damn!" slipped out before Raven could stop it. He instantly regretted it as Lord Huryn frowned at him.

Tirael leapt upon this sudden advantage. "I ought to have you whipped for that insolence, but I'm going to be generous," he said in a voice sweet as honey and sharp as a dagger. He smiled, a slow, vicious smile. "We race—your plow horse against my Brythian."

One of the young nobles guffawed. "Brythian will grind him into the dirt! This I must see!"

"Distance, my lord?" This was critical; Raven knew that Tirael's mount was a Waylshire. And a Waylshire was so fast over a short distance that Raven wasn't sure even a Llysanyin could beat one. He wished he could consult with Stormwind first, but to those unused to Llysanyins, it would seem a bizarre—if not downright mad—request. Worse, this lot would see it as a way to worm out of the challenge.

The smile widened. "From the Stone Witches to Radlyn's Ford."

Hellfire; that's perfect for a Wayl—

"Oh, no, Tir," one of his other friends objected. "It'll be over too quick! I want to see our little plowboy choking in your dust for a good deal longer than that. Come on now, Brythian's good for it."

"He's right! Make it there and back," another urged. "Hell, you'll be able to walk Bryth back and still win!"

Pleeeaaase . . .

For a long moment Raven feared Tirael wouldn't rise to the bait. At last he shrugged and said, "You're right. Bryth can do it easily. There and back, plowboy, the day before the Queen's Chase. Do you agree to the course?"

Thank you, thank you, thank you! "I do."

"Good. And the wager I propose is fifty gold crowns."

Gasps greeted this pronouncement. Raven blinked, momentarily stunned. By the gods, never mind just fixing the roof on the stable—he and Yarrow could build a whole new one! Still, a wager that size changed things. It was one thing if it had been for one gold piece. Even he could come up with that much, though he'd owe Yarrow for a long time; to a noble like Tirael, it would be nothing. So he wouldn't feel bad about taking the man for that much—indeed, it would barely cover the wergild that Raven considered the man owed Stormwind for the insults heaped upon the stallion.

But *fifty*? Oh, yes—that was another game altogether. He'd have to reveal what Stormwind was and give the man an honorable way out.

Damn; he would've enjoyed seeing the look on Tirael's oh-too-handsome face when he lost. Badly.

Raven took a deep breath like a man coming up from deep water and said, "You must know, my lord, that I don't have that kind of gold, so I can't match your wager. So what do you get if *you* win?" *Which you bloody well won't. . . .*

"You and that creature are mine, plowboy. You become my serf," Tirael said in a voice like a dagger slipping into its sheath. "And that nag will spend its days pulling a cart."

Dead silence now. To Raven it seemed even the crickets held their breath. "Even that much gold is a poor price for a man's freedom, my lord," he said quietly. "But I know I'll win, so I'm not afraid. You, though, will want to reconsider when you know what Stormwind is."

"I don't care what you claim that Shamreen nag is," Tirael snapped. "I'll race you no matter what! Do you think you can scare me off? Is this your way of trying to weasel out of a race you know you'll lose? Bah! I've seen mice with more courage than you!"

To Huryn he said, "I ask you to witness my word on this, my lord. I'll race this scum no matter what he claims that horse is! And now I've had enough of him— I'll see as much as I like when he's mine and I can school him well to respect his betters."

The High Marshal said mildly, "I suggest you listen, Tirael."

But Tirael shook his head. "I don't listen to serfs, my lord—even those who are not quite yet mine. You have witnessed, my lord, that I said that I would race him no matter what. Now also witness that should I win, he's mine and that he agrees to it—he hasn't done that yet."

"Before I agree, my lord, will you witness that Lord Tirael has refused to hear my warning?" Raven asked. "I'll not have it said that I tricked him to get my hands on his gold."

Lord Huryn nodded, his face grave. "I will bear witness to that, Raven Redhawkson, before any man or woman in the realm. You tried to warn Lord Tirael as an honorable man should do and he refused to hear your words as a reasonable man ought to. On his head be it."

Sudden doubt filled Tirael's eyes at Huryn's words. But it was too late; Tirael could not back down now, Raven knew, without being named craven.

"Now, Raven Redhawkson, do you agree to Lord Tirael's terms if you should lose?" the High Marshal asked.

"I agree," Raven said.

The old, cocky Tirael was back in an instant. He smiled like a wolf. "Then I look forward to whipping your back raw, plowboy—because I know that you're bluffing and I'm going to prove it."

The sound of a distant commotion brought Huryn around like a hound questing on a scent. Tirael hurried to say, "By your leave, my lord, I've had enough of this peasant."

He backed away and called his friends to him. "Let's be off, lads, where we don't have to breathe the stink of field muck. To Garron's!" He hastened off, followed a moment later by his surprised friends.

Wait a moment—something's not right. . . .

For a moment Raven thought Lord Huryn would call Tirael back, for the High Marshal looked like a man trying to remember something. The same thing, perhaps, Raven was trying to think of?

But a redoubling of the distant racket made the black-browed High Marshal swear. "I must leave now. But listen well, Tirael," he called after the other man where he had paused for a hurried conference with his friends, "if there's any trouble from either of you before the race, I'll have you up before my lord Sevrynel and request that he ban the troublemaker for five years—and rest assured I *will* find out who's responsible."

With that, Lord Huryn called his men to him and hurried off into the night. Raven put his hand on Arisyn's shoulder and said quietly, "Time for us to be off, Ari. Despite what Lord Huryn just said, I don't trust our dear Lord Tirael not to cause some kind of trouble if he can." He nodded at a face peering around the corner of a tent. It ducked back when it saw him watching.

Before it could return, Raven urged Arisyn into the darkness between two tents. They quickly walked away. After a time, Arisyn asked, "Where are we going?"

"I don't know," Raven admitted. "No place particular, I just wanted to get away from them."

"Shall we go see what all that noise was about?" Arisyn said. Before Raven could object that a brawl was the last place they'd want to be, Arisyn went on, "It was a happy sort of noise, don't you think? Like people cheering."

That made Raven stop. The boy was right; he hadn't really thought about it, but the clamor hadn't had the knife-edge feel of a fight about it. Curious now himself, he said, "Let's go see."

Arisyn grinned and set off like a hound on a scent. Raven groaned and ran after him. Soon they had come upon the edge of an excited crowd kept back by soldiers bearing torches to illuminate a lane.

"What's afoot, mistress?" Raven asked a matronly woman who was peering eagerly around those in front of her—though he thought he might know.

The woman turned and looked up at him. Despite the crow's-feet around her eyes and wisps of grey hair escaping from her head kerchief, she looked as excited as a young girl. "Eh? Haven't you heard yet, lad? A messenger rode in a bit earlier to say that there are Dragonlords coming tonight! Imagine that! I didn't get to see them when they were in Casna during the regency debate a while back, I had to go to my daughter in Oakbridge, her youngest was that ill. . . . But

Dragonlords came to Casna—you've heard of that? Wild times, it was, wild times, what with attacks on the Dragonlords, the young prince kidnaped, black magery, and the gods only know what else! Or so my second cousin Tarrant said—and he heard it straight from his niece who got it from her neighbor what has a lad as works in the tavern in their town and he heard it from a carter passing through." Here she drew another breath and went on, "And that carter said she once cussed out Linden Rathan himself before she knew who he was!"

Here the goodwife looked a little doubtful. "Don't know if that last was true, young Dar said she was an old woman and maybe a bit daft—but I'm sure as sure that all the rest was true!" With that, she turned back to her eager watch on the road.

"I wasn't there either," Arisyn said mournfully. "But my uncle said it was awful. He still hates to talk about it, it was that close to civil war and all."

"Rynna did say it was damned scary at times," Raven said absently as he looked over the heads of the crowd. Luckily there were relatively few Yerrins or Thalnians in this part of the crowd; he had a clear view of the lane.

"Your friend from Thalnia was there?" Arisyn asked, all puppy-eagerness. "Did she ever get to see the Dragonlords up close?"

"Indeed, yes, she was here. And I know for a fact that she's certainly seen Linden Rathan up close," Raven said, somehow keeping a straight face. He watched Maurynna's stock with Arisyn soar again.

"I *must* speak with her one day! Did she get to see his Llysanyin as well?"

Thank all the gods that Arisyn turned away then to watch the road once more; else Raven would have burst out laughing and given away the game.

Then suddenly, out of the blue, Raven knew what had seemed wrong before. Tirael had never sworn before Lord Huryn that he would pay the fifty gold pieces if he lost. Raven had put his freedom and Stormwind's hostage to chance. Tirael had risked nothing.

There was no way to get out of the race without damaging his reputation—and Yarrow's—irreparably.

You wretched, thieving cur, Raven thought in a cold fury. *You'll pay for this.*

Twenty-three

"Uncle Beren? May I speak to you, please?"

The regent of Cassori looked up in surprise from the reports he and Steward Lewell were going over. His nephew, Prince Rann, stood in the doorway, standing straight as a soldier. Bony little-boy ankles peeked out from beneath his linen nightshirt. His nurse hovered behind him.

"Of course, Rann," Beren said. "Is something bothering you?"

Rann considered. "Yes," he said at last. Then, with an endearing gravity far beyond his years, "But what I've really come for is to ask a boon, my lord regent."

Beren blinked at the formality. A slight cough made him glance at his steward. The man was hiding a smile behind his hand. A warning glance from his royal master and Lewell was serious again, though the twitch at the corner of his mouth told of the smile trying to break through. Beren couldn't blame him.

But he schooled his own expression to a gravity that matched Rann's. "Of course, Your Highness. Ask, and if it is within my power, I shall grant it." *And though I know Willena is a pest, I shan't risk offending her parents, my lad, so don't ask me to send her packing!*

"Thank you, my lord uncle." His eyes slid to Steward Lewell as he padded into the room. "Um—alone, please?"

Beren nodded. "Lewell?"

Lewell bowed to both of them and removed himself, hand still over his mouth as he muffled coughs that sounded suspiciously like chuckles. He closed the door behind him.

Rann climbed into the chair in front of the desk and settled himself, bare feet swinging. Beren said, "Your boon, Your Highness?"

Rann met his eyes squarely. "That until Bard Daera gets back, we don't have harp lessons," he said, his voice firm.

Hmm—didn't see that one coming! Beren thought with amusement. He knew that Rann was all thumbs when it came to playing the harp, but he hadn't realized that the boy hated lessons *that* mu— Wait; he'd said "until Bard Daera gets back." So it was not Daera that was the problem; it was something about this bard from Bylith. "Won't Kella miss them?" he probed. "I understood from Daera that this Leet was considered one of the finest bards and teachers at the Bards' School. I know Kella is hoping to enter the school one day. This could be a good opportunity for her."

"Kella won't miss them," Rann said. "Not with *him*."

Something in Rann's voice made Beren pause. He studied the boy. "Can you explain a bit more?"

Rann shook his head. "No, sir. I gave my word."

"I see." Beren considered Rann's request. At least it was an easy one; there didn't *seem* to be any pitfalls in it. But he wished he knew what lay behind it— especially Rann's certainty that Kella would not want lessons from this bard. He well knew that Kella had talent. Still, no doubt such a famous bard would consider it beneath him to teach beginners though he would do so if it was by royal request. And most of the children—if not Kella—would be overjoyed at the reprieve; more time for the fair!

"Your Highness," Beren said formally, "I hereby grant your boon. Music lessons will not resume until Bard Daera returns from visiting her ill mother."

He thought Rann would melt with relief. "Thank you, Uncle Beren!"

Rann hopped down from the chair, all happy-go-lucky little boy once more. "I promise to study twice as hard when Daera comes back! Good night." He threw his arms about Beren's neck and hugged him hard, then scampered out the door.

Beren watched him go, giving way to his own chuckles at last. Gods, but he loved that little imp like his own son!

Still, he wished he knew what was behind all this.

Kella lay in her bed, staring into the darkness, unable to sleep. She gently rubbed her still-aching hand and sniffled. If only Maylin were here! But she'd had to stay in Casna to look after their mother. *If only Mama hadn't hurt her leg.* She'd been sad when the message came, telling her the news, but now it was horrible. Kella just wanted to climb into her big sister's lap and cry while Maylin rocked her.

Maybe she should have asked Simpler Quirel to look at it. But someone might see her go to Quirel's rooms and ask why. And if certain of the other children found out she'd been slapped by a bard—a Master Bard at that—they'd laugh. *They* could be so mean, not like Rann and Rosalea and a few of the others. *They* would make fun of her forever and ever.

She knew *they* were jealous of her growing skill with the harp—the ones who cared about learning to play, anyway. And all of *them* were jealous of her friendship with Rann. She was Rann's best friend.

And she knew that some of their parents were afraid that she'd somehow marry Rann. That was silly. She wanted to go to Bylith and be a bard like Otter and Daera.

But not a bard like Leet. Oh, no—not like him, even if she became a Master Bard, one of the respected elders of the guild. She had to find a way to get back at him.

She shut her eyes, chanting to herself. *Have to find a way. Have to find a way. Have to find . . .*

When Kella woke the next morning, she discovered that Maurynna, Linden, and Shima had arrived the night before. She spent an ecstatic morning with them before court life claimed them for itself.

The only bad moment came after Linden and Shima left. Maurynna caught her hand and turned it back and forth, studying it. Kella snatched it away.

"Sweetling, what on earth did you do?" Maurynna asked with a frown. "That's an awful bruise you've got, and Maylin not here to help you. What happened?"

Kella froze. She'd never thought what excuse she could give to explain away the bruise. Then inspiration struck. *I'll have to remember to tell Rann and Rosalea.*

"I fell onto the stone hearth in my room, with my hand beneath me because I was holding my doll. I was running in my stocking feet and slipped."

She hung her head; lying to Rynna felt awful. But she couldn't tell her what had really happened. She knew her cousin's temper and was afraid she'd do something that would get a nasty song written about her; Daera had once talked about why it was not wise to anger a bard.

No, she wouldn't tell Rynna or Linden or Shima. She'd sort out Bard Leet by herself . . . somehow.

Twenty-four

The Dragonlords spent their first night in Balyaranna at the royal castle. But it was so crowded that when Duke Beren, the Regent of Cassori, mentioned the royal encampment by the start of the Queen's Chase racecourse, Linden asked if they might move there. He knew that the tents they'd be provided with would be as luxurious as any king or queen might desire. It might even be a little calmer—and certainly not as formal.

"You just don't want to have to wear the traditional garb again," Maurynna teased him when he told her about the move.

"Yes," he said smugly.

Still, their first couple of days were a whirlwind of court activity. Luckily, though, the first excitement wore off and the Dragonlords had more time to themselves. At Balyaranna, horses came before anything, even Dragonlords.

So, on their first free day, Linden went to Lord Sevrynel's manor to talk horses. Maurynna begged off; she spent the morning with Kella again and then went off to find Raven.

But Shima had the best day of all. For, by dint of hard riding, Lady Karelinn, Lady Merrilee, and their father rode into the courtyard of Balyaranna Castle along with Lord Eadain and a few others from the inn.

The dappled light of the arbor danced across the two large parchment sheets upon the table. They were covered with neat writing, the entries upon them spanning centuries.

Linden sipped his wine as he looked over the pedigrees Lord Sevrynel had brought to him. To his right was the pedigree of one of Sevrynel's best brood-mares, a bright blood bay named Fliss who was descended in a long line from Rani eo'Tsan's mare Mhari. To his left was the bloodline of a stallion also descended many generations back from the long-ago mare.

"What think you, Your Grace?" the little earl asked. "Both are of Mhari's blood, but not too closely related. And neither has Hornet in their ancestry."

Linden thought for a moment. "Ah—wasn't he the one with those absurdly small hooves? What on earth was anyone thinking to breed that into their blood-lines?"

He shook his head in disgust. No doubt there were some that thought such hooves looked elegant, but to him it was a useless—even cruel—vanity. He re-membered hearing how badly the poor horses so afflicted fared on journeys. They were only good for short distances about a holding.

"And there's worse, so the Beast Healers think," said Sevrynel. "It seems that—"

"My lord! My lord!" a young voice called in distress.

Both Linden and Sevrynel looked up at the sudden interruption. A boy—one of the stable hands by his dress, Linden thought—rushed up to them. Tears streaked his dusty face.

"My lord," he sobbed as he stumbled to a halt before the two men. "My lord, please come . . ." He stopped, panting for breath.

"Everrad, what means this ill-mannered—"

"My lord—it's Fliss. Someone let old Aster into the mare's pasture and she's gored Fliss badly," the boy gasped, so upset that he interrupted the earl without apology. "She's been brought to the mares' barn."

"Oh dear gods have mercy!" Sevrynel was so distraught he ran off without a word of apology.

Not that Linden could blame Sevrynel. The Earl of Rockfall loved all his horses, but he made no secret that Fliss was the jewel of his heart.

Linden turned his attention to the boy, patting him on the shoulder. "Easy, lad. Catch your breath now. Better?"

The boy nodded, hiccuping.

"Good. Well, then—who's this Aster? And has anyone sent for a Beast Healer?" *Thank the gods this happened during the horse fair—Beast Healers are nigh as thick as the flies around here. It shouldn't take long to find one.*

"Aster's one of the goats, m'lord, and a foul-tempered old nanny to boot. She once blinded one of the yearlings who stuck his head over the fence into her pen. She knows how to use her horns too well, that one—"

Here the boy paused and peered up into Linden's face, his gaze suddenly riv-eted on Linden's Marking. Linden thought he paled under the dirt on his face. "Your . . . Your Grace, couldn't you . . . ?"

"Change and Heal her with a dragon's Healing fire? Lad, think—what would the poor beast do when a dragon appeared in front of her?" Linden asked with a smile.

He could almost see the image take shape in the boy's imagination. "Oh" was all the stable boy said, shaking his head. "No. No, no, no."

"Indeed. And we won't even talk about the rest of the stable. Now—a Beast Healer?" Linden prompted.

The stable boy took a deep breath and answered, "We were in luck, Your Grace. One was already here to see another mare that's due to foal in a few days."

"Thank the gods for that, then. Now I'm off to see if I can help either the Beast Healer or Lord Sevrynel." *More likely than not, it will be poor Sevrynel—if only it wasn't* Fliss!

He ran after Sevrynel, managing to catch up with the little earl just as the man reached the broodmares' barn.

Linden followed a near-frantic Sevrynel through the broad open door. The Cassorin lord raced ahead and stopped before a roomy box stall; he peered over the stall door.

"How bad is it? Is she dying?" he asked anxiously. "Oh gods, her poor leg . . . Is it broken? Will she be well?"

A voice rich with the burr of the Kelnethi north country answered him from inside the stall. "Aye, she'll be fine, m'lord. Not to worry now, nothing's broken. And the cut, while bad, is nothing to fret yourself about. She'll bear many a foal yet, the gods willing."

Linden reached the stall and looked over the high partition in time to see a long, lanky figure in the leather breeches and brown-and-green hooded tunic of a Beast Healer straighten up from examining the injured horse's near hock, his back to the stall door. The hood of the tunic, Linden noticed idly, seemed rather bulgy.

Odd—I wonder what he keeps in there. Packets of herbs?

"Oh my poor Fliss," Sevrynel whimpered, his face pale. Nervous sweat beaded his forehead.

Two grooms hovered by the mare's head, casting nervous glances at their lord chewing his fingernails. The Beast Healer gestured for the leather satchel lying to one side. At once one of the grooms jumped to fetch it for him. The man rummaged through it and withdrew a flask and a cloth. Pouring some of the contents of the flask onto the cloth and the rest over the wound, he cleaned the gash carefully.

The man's movements were slow and deliberate, his touch gentle but firm. Linden nodded in silent approval; this was a man who knew his art well.

When the Beast Healer stepped aside to wipe his hands on a cloth one of the grooms offered him, Linden could see the long, deep gash the goat's horn had torn in the mare's leg. He winced in sympathy. Sevrynel muttered something—a prayer or curse—at the sight of the blood that still dripped sluggishly from the wound. Yet the mare had stood quietly as the wound was cleaned; her head hung down and her eyes were half shut. Linden knew she'd had a touch of the Sleep laid upon her.

The man must be a strong Healer—that mare hasn't even twitched!

The longer he watched, the more certain Linden was that he knew the man from somewhere. Yet he was also certain it wasn't one of the Beast Healers he'd met at Dragonskeep from time to time. So who . . .

Then a hint of a memory surfaced; Linden remembered joining forces with a gangly journeyman Beast Healer to rescue a young orphan. What was—

By the gods—could it be Conor? If only the fellow would turn so that Linden could see his face. It *looked* somewhat like . . . Linden watched and waited, still not certain, as the Beast Healer returned to examine the wound one more time.

Then the man turned his head enough so that Linden could see his profile. It *was* Conor; there was no mistaking that long, gaunt face with its crooked nose.

But now it was the face of a man, with the prominent bones settled into themselves, rather than the yet-unfinished features of the youth Linden remembered and still held in his memory's eye. Not surprising, he realized; it had been nigh ten years or more since he'd last seen the Beast Healer. Time enough to grow from boy to man.

And since it was Conor, Linden had a fair notion of *what* made the bulge inside the hood—he just didn't know *who* it was these days. He smiled at the thought, pleased to see Conor once more. He'd fulfilled the promise Linden had seen a decade ago. Not many Beast Healers could keep an animal with a wound like that so calm. When Sevrynel, unable to stand it any longer, fumbled at the latch of the stall door, Linden laid a hand on the Cassorin lord's shoulder to hold him back.

Sevrynel looked up at him in an agony of apprehension, but stayed put.

"Watch," Linden whispered. "All will be well."

Even as Linden spoke, Conor spread his big, bony hands over the wound and closed his eyes. An instant later a haze, akin to that of a Healer's, but greener, surrounded them. The sound of Conor's deep, steady breathing filled a stable suddenly gone quiet as if every creature in it knew a Healing was going on. Even Lord Sevrynel stopped twitching.

Then the haze melted away and Conor stood up again. Only a faint scar bore witness to the now-vanished wound. He moved to the mare's head and ran his fingers gently down her face, murmuring words under his breath. The mare's head came up, her eyes alert now, yet calm; she lipped at the palm Conor offered her.

"There, there, pretty one," he crooned, rubbing her nose. "That wasn't half so bad, now was it?"

"Well done, Conor," Linden said. "I know it's not easy to bring an animal that's been hurt and frightened out of the Sleep so gently."

"Eh?" the Beast Healer said, eyebrows raised in polite inquiry as he looked about to see who had addressed him. Then the craggy face broke into a wide grin. "Why, Your Grace! This is a wonderful surprise! I'd not thought to ever see you again. It was, what, a bit more than ten years ago?"

"Something like that," Linden said. "You were only a journeyman then, I remember. I'm glad to see—"

Unable to bear it any longer, Sevrynel burst out, "Fliss *is* well again, isn't she, Conor?"

Running his hand along the mare's back as he moved toward the stall door, Conor gave the mare a final pat on the rump. "Aside from a bit of stiffness for the next day or two and a faint scar, it will be as if naught happened to her, my lord."

As he let himself out of the stall, Conor said to the grooms, "Feed her lightly until this time tomorrow, but see that she has plenty of fresh water—as much as she'll drink. Is there a bit of pasture where she can spend the next day or two alone, with only an old, gentle mare that she trusts for company? There is? Good; I'm thinking it would be well for her if she can move around freely instead of standing in a stall. That will let her walk off that stiffness without the risk of a kick to that leg."

As Conor stepped into the aisle, Sevrynel slipped past him and into the stall. While the Cassorin lord petted and stroked the mare, Linden held out a hand to Conor, who grinned at it and shook his head. He held up his blood-streaked hands.

"Hmm—you're right." Linden turned to look at Sevrynel once more. The man still stood by his mare's head, petting her. Linden guessed that the little Cassorin lord had forgotten Dragonlord, Beast Healer, and likely the rest of the world. He'd never even notice they were gone. "Let's get you outside where you can wash up."

They left the barn. At Linden's request, a stable hand brought a bucket of clean water and a dry cloth.

Conor squatted by the bucket and rinsed his hands and forearms. "Hoy! That's cold," he said, laughing as he picked up the rough cloth. At last he was clean and dry.

"Well met," Linden said, grasping the hand now held out to him. "So—tell me how things have gone since we last saw each other. How's Pod?"

Conor beamed like a proud father. "Pod's doing well. A wonder with the animals, she is. She'll make journeywoman soon even though she's a bit young for it yet.

"The last bit of news I've had of our Pod is that she'll be journeying with one of the masters of the Healwort Guild, learning to recognize the wild-crafted herbs where they grow."

Linden shook his head, not understanding. "What journey is this? And I thought the Wort Hunters were part of the Healwort Guild, not the Beast Healers."

"They are. But not all the herbs we Healers—beast or human—use will thrive in a garden. Shy they are, or else they want their oak to grow beneath or their marsh to bide in. So during our training we're sent to the Worties to learn what we can. We go out into the wild with one of their masters and learn to find and prepare the herbs we use most often, as well as whatever else can be driven into our thick heads. Remember, we sometimes heal wild beasts as well as tame—and you can't find a Simpler's shop in the middle of the woods if you run out of slippery elm or healmoss.

"At least, that's for those of us with a taste for wandering. Those with the knack for gardening train with their Growers—which is not Pod. She's likely tramping through the woods even now."

"So your guild was the proper place for her after all?" Linden asked.

"It was indeed." There was no mistaking the heartfelt agreement behind the words.

"Thanks the gods for that. I'd always wondered." Linden heaved a sigh of relief; sending the young orphan away from the people who had treated her hardly better than one of their animals and giving her care to Conor's guild had been the right thing to do after all. He'd always wondered if he'd guessed right that she had a gift worth developing.

A small masked face appeared at Conor's shoulder. Then came a huge yawn and the ferret slid bonelessly back down into Conor's hood. A moment later it was back, nose twitching.

"Who's this?" Linden asked, holding out a hand for the ferret to sniff.

Conor grinned. "Oh, just a bit of Trouble," he said.

It took Linden a moment to get the joke. He groaned. "Trouble, eh? That sounds a bit safer than Havoc."

The ferret licked Linden's fingers. He rubbed it gently under the chin. It yawned again, but this time stayed put, enjoying the attention.

"My brother-in-law Fisher was always naming his ferrets things like that, too. Isn't that asking for problems, giving them names like Havoc, Disaster, or Mayhem?" Linden asked, giving the ferret a final chin rub.

"I think of it as just facing the truth," the Beast Healer said ruefully.

"Hunh—that's what Fisher always said. Had the same martyred expression, too. Are you free to grab a pint of ale, or have you another patient?"

Conor shook his head. "Not another patient as such—here now, I washed this morning, so stop licking my ear, young lady," he complained as Trouble set about her task with a will. "What was I—oh, right; Therinn Barans, Lord Lenslee, is here and sent word that he wishes me to stop in and have a look at the horses he'll be running in the big race." As he spoke, Conor eased the ferret from his shoulder—and away from his ear—then cuddled her in his arms.

"Is something wrong with his horses?" *That would be a nasty bit of luck, to come all this way and have your horses fall ill!* he thought.

"Not that I was told of—I think he's just being cautious. He's like Lord Sevrynel that way, I hear; nothing's too good for his horses."

Conor paused to sling the strap of his scrip over his head. Then he smiled wryly and went on, "And since Lord Lenslee's given the guild the land and monies to build a fine new chapterhouse in Lenslee, with plenty of prime pasture and good water for it, well . . ."

Linden whistled in appreciation. That was a princely gift; Lord Lenslee must do well wagering on his horses. "Your guild is willing to indulge him a bit. I don't blame you." He thought a moment. "I remember his great-grandfather; the man had an uncanny talent for breeding."

"Did he now?" said Conor. "Wonder if the great-grandson fancies he has the same knack? It would explain some of the things I've heard. Ah, well, I'd best be off to see him. He's staying with his kinsman, Lord Portis, so I was told."

"You're going to Portis's?" a voice demanded behind them.

They turned as Lord Sevrynel bustled up to them. The little Cassorin lord must have finally decided his "sweet lady" was indeed out of danger, Linden thought with amusement; he'd left the stable and was no longer pulling out bits of his beard. There was even a hint of color in the ashen face once more.

"That I am, my lord, unless there's something else wrong with Fliss," Conor said with some alarm. He slipped Trouble back into his hood. "Stay there," he ordered her.

Sevrynel waved his hands in extravagant negation. "No, no! Everything's well now, thanks to you, Conor," he exclaimed. "Fliss is even now going out to a pasture. No, no, what I meant was: you're going to see Lenslee's racers, not one of Portis's horses?" He stared intently at the Beast Healer as if trying to get an unspoken message across.

"Aye, that I am," Conor said cautiously. He frowned slightly.

Linden could understand his concern. What was Sevrynel getting at? Surely he wasn't going to ask a Beast Healer to harm another man's horses—especially not in front of a Dragonlord!

Please don't let Sevrynel say anything stupid . . . , Linden thought unhappily. He liked the little horse-mad Cassorin lord.

Sevrynel, completely oblivious of the sudden wariness of the other two men, went on in a worried tone, "I just wanted to warn you about that stallion of his, the one who's winning all the races for him these days. Big, beautiful animal, runs like the north wind, and . . ."

Here Sevrynel paused; then, with the expression of someone jumping off a bridge, went on in a rush, "Oh, hang it all! The damned horse is as chancy and foul-tempered as they come, Conor. Vicious, even. He's crippled a groom since Therinn got him, and two before that, I've heard. And there's worse."

Conor's eyebrows went up. "Would this be a chestnut stallion?" he asked. "Color 'like a new copper penny,' I was told."

Lord Sevrynel nodded. "That's the one—Summer Lightning by Stormcloud out of Sun Lady, and *her* dam was—oh, never mind."

"What else did the horse do?" Linden asked, remembering the grim tone of Sevrynel's "worse."

Sevrynel took a deep breath. "The brute killed a boy who tried to ride him."

For a moment Linden thought Sevrynel would elaborate, but it seemed that was as much as they would get. After a moment, the little earl said in a colorless tone, "Yet as ill luck would have it, Therinn's best jockey, another one of his grooms, and Therinn himself are among the few people the beast will tolerate. And since the horse wins and wins, Therinn doesn't give a fig what it does to anyone else. Myself, I don't care how many races it's won, I wouldn't have a horse like that in my stable," he ended in a final burst of vehemence.

It was clear from his expression what he felt should be done with such a vicious animal. Surprised, Linden glanced at Conor and saw the same thought in the Beast Healer's eyes as their gazes met: *If* Sevrynel *speaks ill of a horse . . .*

That was damnation indeed.

The little Cassorin lord went on, "But Therinn can be reckless, you know. Gods, he's even standing the creature at stud." Sevrynel put an imploring hand on the Beast Healer's arm. "So *do* be careful, Conor. You're too good a man to lose to an animal like that."

"Be sure I'll remember your warning, my lord," Conor said. "And my thanks for it. I'll keep my eyes open around him, be certain of that, my lord earl."

"Do that," Lord Sevrynel commanded. "And—oh, bother! Now what?" he said as a servant jogged up to them.

"Your Grace," the man said with a quick bow that included all of them, "my lord earl, Beast Healer. Lord Sevrynel, I'm sorry to interrupt you, but Lord Furney, Lord Havillar, Lord Portis, and Lady Donatalia arrived for the meeting—" Here he coughed discreetly. "—some time ago, my lord."

"Meeting? Meeting? What mee— Oh, bother it, bother it," Sevrynel complained under his breath. "I'd forgotten about it and them."

"They're the other marshals for the horse fair, aren't they?" Linden asked.

"Indeed they are, Your Grace. Fliss's accident drove it out of my head that I'd asked them to meet with me today. I was going to propose to them that we ask you Dragonlords to be among the marshals in the big race." He peered hopefully up at Linden.

Linden managed not to smile. "I can tell you now that Maurynna, Shima, and I would be honored."

Sevrynel beamed like a little boy with a sack of barley sugar treats. "Oh, wonderful, Your Grace! Could I ask you to come and meet my fellow marshals?"

Linden nodded. "Of course, my lord. Are they meeting you at the grape arbor? Good—I know how to get back there. I shall meet all of you there. I wish to speak a little longer with Conor first."

Sevrynel bowed, then turned and set off after the servant. But before he disappeared around the corner of the stable, he called back, "Mind you watch that animal, Conor!"

When they were alone, the Beast Healer undid the leather thong holding his long hair back and ran his fingers through it, picking out stray bits of hay. "Whew!" he said. "I was afraid there for a moment! Thought he was about to ask me to put Lenslee's horses out of the running. D'you think he's right, my lord? About that horse?"

Linden thought for a moment, then said slowly, "I'll tell you this: If I were you, until I found out otherwise, I'd take Sevrynel's opinion as the word of the gods. The man can be flighty and a bit daft, but from all I've seen, Sevrynel knows horses. And think about this—he didn't say 'it's *rumored* that the horse killed a boy.' "

"Eh—that's right. When he spoke of what the horse did to those two earlier grooms, he was careful to say then that it was something he'd only heard about."

"Just so," Linden said. "And if anyone will give a horse the benefit of the doubt, it's our horse-mad little earl."

"I'll not argue with that, Your Grace. You wouldn't believe some of the tales I've heard of the man."

Just so, Linden thought, remembering some of the tales *he'd* heard about Sevrynel; tales someone else had told him. . . . He shook his head, refusing to go where those memories led. "Sevrynel spoke as one who *knew* that the story about the lad's death was true."

"As if he knew the boy, you mean?" Conor said.

"Or knew someone who saw it happen. Someone whose word he trusted. I'd be damned careful if I were you, Conor."

"Your Grace, I'll take that as Dragonlord's orders," the Beast Healer said solemnly, though his eyes were twinkling as he bound his hair back again.

"You do that," Linden said with a grin. "My lady, Shima, and I are having dinner with Lady Gallianna this evening, but that's a few candlemarks yet. Shall I wait for you by that big red tent in the food merchants' row?"

"If you'll let me buy the first round," said Conor.

"Done," answered Linden.

Twenty-five

"Hoy! Raven!" Maurynna called to the rider ahead of her.

Raven looked back over his shoulder as Stormwind pirouetted in place. "Hoy there, Beanpole! I was wondering if I'd find you wandering about. This fine lad and I were on our way to a place we know. Want to come?"

Maurynna pressed her heels against Boreal's sides and urged him forward. Soon the former stablemates were walking side by side, walking swiftly through the fair as their riders talked.

As they reached the line of yellow banners that marked the edge of the grounds, Maurynna asked, "So how has the fair been for you so far? Aside from playing with Kella and Rann—she told me about it."

"And besides being challenged to a race that I know I'll win? By a cheating dog who has weaseled out of paying his wager before the race is even run, no less? Fairly uneventful. My only annoyance is all the people who won't believe Stormwind's a Llysanyin." He grinned. "But there are enough who know what he is—like Lord Sevrynel and a few other nobles."

"I'm surprised they haven't spread the word," Maurynna said.

Raven's smile grew even wider. "Spread the word? And you a merchant born and bred." He shook his head in mock dismay.

Maurynna looked blankly at him for a moment, then smacked her hand against her forehead. She said in disgust, "Oh, for pity's sake—of course they're not telling all and sundry. They want first go at the coming crop of foals, don't they? Before everyone finds out."

"And said foals become scarcer than teeth on a chicken. Glad to see you haven't forgotten everything you knew," Raven teased. "Just bits here and there."

She thumbed her nose at him. "Very funny."

"That's me—Jester Raven at your command. Come along now—this is where we turn off the main track. I want to show you something special."

She felt a familiar tickling in her mind and smiled, holding up her hand to stop Raven. "Wait—I might have to go back." She tapped her two middle fingers against her forehead, the Dragonlords' signal for mindspeech.

Raven obligingly halted.

Linden! Were the pedigrees interesting? she teased.

They were, actually—and there was a bit of excitement as well. I also met an old friend, Maurynna-love. Meet you at the encampment later? I want to catch up on things with Conor for a bit.

Conor, Maurynna thought, must be the old friend. *Enjoy, and I'll see you back at the tent.*

Until then. A gentle "kiss" against her mind and he was gone.

She said, "I'm to meet Linden later. Shall we ride on?"

"Yes—I've something to show you. I think you'll like it."

They rode on, turning twice onto smaller trails that twisted and turned around craggy little hills and through copses of birch and alder. Just as Maurynna was wondering how much farther it was, they came out of yet another copse and before them was a large pond fringed with sweetflag. It lay like a jewel in the green of the meadow with the blue sky and drifting clouds reflected in the clear water below.

"Oh—it's lovely!" she exclaimed. "How did you ever find it?"

"This is part of Lord Sevrynel's lands. He gave me—or rather Stormwind—permission to come here whenever we wanted."

The stallions snorted eagerly at the scent of the water and broke into a trot. They stopped a few feet from the water's edge and waited.

Maurynna pulled off Boreal's tack as quickly as she could. The instant he was free, the dapple grey stallion trotted into the water. He snorted in surprise when it reached his stomach.

"I forgot to warn you," Raven called. "It's *very* cold."

Boreal turned his head and stared at Raven for a long moment before wading in more slowly. Soon both horses were swimming.

"Let's bring everything over here," Raven suggested. "Then we can talk."

They spread out the saddle blankets and, after arranging their saddlebags as "pillows," lay down with their faces turned to the sun.

"So—tell me about the race and the cheating dog," Maurynna said.

After a time the Llysanyins heaved themselves out of the water. They wandered the meadow, grazing and rolling to their hearts' delight while their riders talked. Maurynna listened as Raven told her about playing with Kella, Prince Rann, and Lady Rosalea at Sevrynel's.

"Have you met Karelinn, Merrilee, and Eadain as well?" she asked. "They're staying with Sevrynel."

Raven nodded vigorously. "I have. My friend Arisyn introduced me to them.

Wonderful people, aren't they? Make you feel like a friend they haven't seen in a long time rather than a stranger they've just met."

"That sounds like them." Maurynna pointed at a cloud. "Look at that one! Doesn't it look like a seagull?" After that, they amused themselves with their childhood game of finding things in the clouds.

At last the stallions were done. They wandered back to their two-foots. Boreal came to stand over Maurynna where she lay nibbling on a sprig of lemon balm she'd found growing wild. She offered it to him and he took it daintily from her fingers, his head tilted to one side as he sampled it.

Gods, it was good to just lie here in the sun, to relax where no one but Raven knew who—or what—she was. She might even drift off to sleep. . . .

Then her stomach rumbled. Loudly. Boreal's ears twitched back and forth in surprise. Raven snickered.

"Bother," she said lazily, half inclined to ignore it. But she looked up at the sun and realized it would be at least another four candlemarks before Lady Gallianna's feast. "Is there somewhere that we can get a bit of something to eat before you have to go back to help Yarrow?"

"Mmm, yes. There's a booth at this end of the fair I've been meaning to tell you about. I'll not have time to go today, but no reason you can't go alone. The road the booth's on goes to the exercise field, but if you go east and take the first turning, that will meet the main road. You'll find your way from there—if you can tear yourself away from the booth.

"It's run by an old man, Cade, and his daughter-in-law, Raeli. Doesn't look like much, but she bakes some of the best wholemeal bread I've ever had. And if that's not enough to tempt you, the old man makes a cheese that I'd swear is Fat Gorly," Raven said. "Interested?"

"Fat Gorly? Really? I haven't had Fat Gorly in ages!" Maurynna threw off her languor and bounced to her feet. "I'm for it!" She gathered up Boreal's tack and began the task of saddling him.

Raven rose and did the same for Stormwind. As he worked, he said, "Good. I told them that my friend, another Thalnian, also likes Fat Gorly. They made me promise to bring you one day; they're very proud of their cheese." Raven gave her a leg up into the saddle, then mounted Stormwind. "Follow me. I'll set you on the track."

Their way took them through little patches of trees and sunlit meadow, sometimes past fields shimmering green and gold in the summer sun. Snatches of birdsong and the lazy drone of insects drifted on the thick, warm air which smelled of honey and sunshine. It looked, Maurynna saw with pleasure, to be a good harvest year. She mindcalled Linden to let him know where she was going.

Tastes like Fat Gorly? Really? Damn! I can't go—Sevrynel's dragged out more pedigrees to settle an argument. Oh, hellfire! Now they want me *to settle this for them!*

Maurynna nearly laughed aloud at the thwarted yearning in his mindvoice. "Linden has to negotiate a peace or I think he'd be on his way right now, pedigrees or no pedigrees," she told Raven. "I'll just have to tell him about how good it is."

"You're a cruel woman, Beanpole," Raven said, shaking his head in mock sadness.

As they cantered through one little pasture a brown and white cow lifted her head to watch them. At least, Maurynna thought it was brown and white; it was hard to tell beneath the riot of wildflowers that bedecked the placidly chewing animal.

"Gods help us," she said, laughing. "It's a cow made of flowers."

Even as she stopped Boreal to stare at the odd sight, a pair of small hands clutching a garland came into view from the far side of the cow and another tribute was laid upon the stolid "altar." A moment later the bovine bouquet ambled to another patch of grass, followed by a little girl picking more flowers as she went.

Raven rode back to her and said, "I'll wager that's old Cade's youngest granddaughter and the family cow. The old man said that the little girl was fair daft over the animal."

"Cade is the cheese maker?"

"Indeed he is. See that path? It'll take you down to the road by his booth," Raven said.

Maurynna followed his pointing finger. Sure enough, she could see a narrow path skirting the edge of the field. "I see it—sure you can't go with me?"

But he was turning Stormwind away. "I'm already late. We'll come back together another time. Tell them I sent you," he said and, with a wave of his hand, cantered away.

Maurynna waved back and urged Boreal on. The Llysanyin ambled through knee-high grass and wildflowers. Maurynna looked up at the blue sky, enjoying the ride. *What a perfect day,* she thought happily.

Less than a quarter of a candlemark later she passed through a thin belt of birch trees and saw the road—and Cade's "booth"—ahead.

In reality it was simply a low table made of boards laid across a couple of trestles. It sheltered in the shade of a huge copper beech set back from the road. At one end of the table sat a few wooden cups. A cloth covered the rest of the table; odd lumps hinted at the promised delectables. An old man weaving a cheese basket and a much younger woman busy with sewing sat on stools at the other end. Near them was a bench screened from road and sun by the trailing branches.

She urged Boreal into a trot.

As they reached the road, the old man shaded his eyes and studied her. Maurynna stopped before him, saying, "Are you Cade and Raeli? My friend told me about you."

Neither said anything for a long moment. A sudden thought struck her. *Oh no—what* else *did Raven tell them about me?* The last thing she wanted was to frighten these poor people with her rank.

Then, to her relief, the old man smiled. "Oh, aye—tha's Raven's friend, then? Welcome, lass."

Maurynna nearly melted with relief. Raven hadn't said anything to them. And it was unlikely they'd link one "Rynna," the friend of an obvious commoner, with Dragonlord Maurynna Kyrissaean. She could relax. *Thanks for not telling them, Raven,* she sent to him.

He answered, *What, that the friend is a Dragonlord? No, it tends to make folk skittish. They'd probably be so nervous they'd drop your bread and cheese in the dirt. Didn't think you'd appreciate that, Beanpole.*

Not if it's as good as you say, Maurynna replied as she dismounted. *Waste of good cheese and all.*

Boreal immediately wandered off to graze.

Cade scratched his chin. "Tha has the same sort o' horse that Raven does, doesn't tha? He does the same—just lets it wander about."

Maurynna nodded. Both Cade and Raeli eyed the stallion as if not quite certain what to make of a loose horse that didn't run away, but it was clear that they were used to Raven's "odd" behavior regarding his mount and accepted hers as more of the same. Just something Thalnians did, no doubt.

"Pleasure to meet tha, lass," Cade said, beaming up at Maurynna as the woman rose and flicked the cloth back from a golden loaf of bread and a wheel of herb-flecked cheese. "I'll just go on setting here if tha don't mind, got a bad leg, see." He slapped his leg; to Maurynna it looked as if it had been broken and badly set. A gnarled walking stick, its head shiny from long use, lay on the ground beside him. "But Raeli here will help tha. Just make thaself comfortable on the bench."

Maurynna did as he bade her. She watched as Boreal meandered near the road.

As Raeli handed her a thick slab of bread and cheese, she asked shyly, "Would tha care for summat to drink with that? The spring on the hillside is known around these parts for its fine water and m'boy is filling the jug again even now."

"Yes, thank you." Maurynna bit into the bread. "Oh my!" she exclaimed in surprise around a mouthful of bread and cheese. Remembering her manners, she finished chewing and swallowed. "This *is* as good as Fat Gorly. Maybe even better. And what's that flavor in the bread? It's delicious!"

Old Cade puffed up like a peacock. Raeli blushed and said, "Sage honey, young mistress. M'mam keeps bees in her herb garden."

"S'wonderful," Maurynna mumbled around another mouthful. Raeli ducked her head with a shy smile and went back to her sewing.

Maurynna leaned back against the tree, peeking between the hanging branches now and again. She ate her bread and cheese in contentment. This was bliss: a beautiful day laden with the scents of summer, a bit of shade, and good, simple food. She idly wondered if it would be possible to get Cade's cheese north. Fat Gorly didn't ship well, so it never made an appearance upon the tables of Dragonskeep. But from Cassori, now . . . Perhaps it could be sent north with the regular supply trains? She'd have to ask Cade before she left if he thought his cheeses could stand the journey.

And if not, well, now that she could Change at will, Cassori wasn't that bad a flight to indulge a whim now and again. She smiled, thinking, *I wonder what Cade and Raeli will think of a dragon or two landing on their doorstep?*

A cloud of dust down the road caught her attention. It was a group of perhaps eight or ten riders coming from the city.

Wonder if anyone I know is with them? But even with her sharp eyesight it was impossible to discern anyone in the thick dust. Ah, well; she'd see soon enough.

When they drew closer, though, Maurynna could see it was made up of young nobles, mostly men with a few women among them. They were laughing and talking as they rode in the summer sun, as cheerful a group as she'd ever seen, but none that she recognized. Dismissing them from her thoughts, she looked around in time to see a young boy coming through the tall grass, a clay jug clutched in his arms. Raeli went to meet him. Back at the table, she poured out two cups and brought one to Maurynna.

But before Maurynna could take the proffered mug, a scornful voice called out, "Will you look at that? There's another of those damned plow horses about! Someone else is riding these things!"

Maurynna slewed around on the bench and peered out between the branches once more. She saw that the riders had stopped and one had ridden up to point derisively at Boreal. He was a handsome young man—or would have been if not for the sneer. She was also less than inclined to be charitable to some ill-mannered oaf who had just insulted her Llysanyin. *Lout.*

The Llysanyin merely stared at the young lord a moment, then went back to his grazing.

"How fast do you think *this* one can waddle? Maybe I should see about getting myself another serf!"

Waddle? Maurynna felt her cheeks grow hot; how *dare* that gormless idiot insult Boreal? She stood up, so angry she nearly choked on a thousand sailor's curses all trying to get out at once. She made herself pause, counting to ten and beyond, knowing if she went out there this angry, she'd do something she'd regret later. Besides, she wanted to be sure she wouldn't trip over her tongue. Nothing took the edge off a tongue-lashing like mangling your words.

"Young mistress," Raeli said in trepidation. She put out a hand as if to restrain Maurynna, then withdrew it. "Please, he's a nasty one. We've seen him before. Best to just endure until he grows bored and takes himself off again."

"Raeli, I want you and Cade and your son to stay well back. Whatever happens, don't do anything. I don't want them to have an excuse to go after you, do you understand? All will be well."

"But—"

"Don't worry, Raeli," Maurynna said. "I'll not do anything foolish."

Not for a Dragonlord, she continued to herself as she stepped out from the sheltering branches. She could hear Raeli hustling her father-in-law and little boy away. *Bless her for listening.*

Maurynna stopped by Boreal's side. The stallion turned to lip her hair, then dropped his head once more.

Now the young men in the band crowded around their leader, laughing and egging him on. He continued, "You! Is this your horse?"

She nodded. *Let's see how deep he can dig this hole.*

"Where's your plow, peasant? Did you lose it?" He shook his head and glanced back over his shoulder to his friends. "Can you imagine that—another Yerrin like that dog Raven aping his betters, riding around as if those creatures are real horses!"

"Actually, I'm Thalnian," she said pleasantly. Too pleasantly; anyone who knew her would have been looking for a way out.

Oblivious to the edge in her voice, he patted his horse's neck as if to say *Now this is a horse.* To Maurynna, it looked like a rail next to Boreal. But considering his pride in it, the horse was likely some well-bred something or other; she openly acknowledged she was no judge of horseflesh. It seemed this fellow did not own up to the same; remembering his comment about serfs, she was suddenly certain of who this arrogant ninny might be.

This had to be Tirael Barans; far too good an opinion of himself and a terrible judge of horses, just as Raven had said. Even *she,* horse idiot that she was, had realized the first time she'd seen a Llysanyin that here was something special— and her without the faintest idea that there might be one within a hundred leagues. This idiot wouldn't have the same excuse; it was no secret that there were Dragon- lords and Llysanyins at this year's horse fair.

Boreal snorted in disgust and turned his back on the man. He flicked his tail high over his back and began eating again. If that cocksure young man could ever look uncertain, he looked it now. But no doubt his innate conceit told him it was naught but chance. The sneer returned.

Maurynna, on the other hand, knew exactly what was happening. She burst into laughter.

That brought the young man's attention back to her. Maurynna saw his fingers tighten around his riding crop. Pointing it at her, he said with a sneer, "You're a . . . *friend* . . . of that . . . dog Raven, aren't you?"

"I am indeed, my lord. And I'd leave now, if I were you," Maurynna said much too sweetly. "I've been told a time or two that I have a lovely temper—and I haven't even begun to lose it." *But if you call Raven a dog one more time . . .*

"How dare you speak to me that way!" the young lord snapped. His friends exclaimed in astonishment.

"I'll speak to you any damn way I please," Maurynna shot back. "And don't even think of using that riding crop."

The chiseled jaw dropped; he looked like a fish out of water. It was, Maurynna decided, a beautiful sight. From the corner of her eye she saw Boreal ready to come to her defense; she signaled him to stay put. By the gods, if she couldn't hand this spoiled brat's head to him on a platter, it was time to find a seat by the hearth at Dragonskeep and drowse in front of the fire all day.

She glared up at the well-dressed young man looking down his nose at her. The riding crop trembled in one white-knuckled fist. The image gave her the shivers inside; she remembered the fiery pain when another riding crop caught her across the eye, so long ago and yet no time past at all.

But this time she was ready with a Dragonlord's strength, speed—and rank. One move she didn't like and she'd dump him out of his saddle before he could react, and there wouldn't be a damned thing he could do about it.

But it seemed the brat had decided to change his tack. "Listen to her! She dares speak to me as if she's as good as I am! Is it something in the water here-abouts?" he asked his friends in mock consternation.

"Must be, Tirael," one of his friends called back, laughing. "I'd say she needs a lesson."

"Make an example of her," another urged. "Have her whipped for insolence, eh?"

"I know a better use for her." Tirael leered at her.

His friends whooped with laughter as Maurynna thought with grim satisfaction, *Oh, yes, fool—dig that hole a little deeper, why don't you?*

Tirael dug into the small leather pouch at his belt and held up a copper. "This should be more than enough for the likes of you, trull!"

Before she could say anything, a dappled-grey blur flashed past her. Boreal lunged at the rider, his strong white teeth snapping in the young noble's face. The man yelled, and his frightened horse squealed and fell back before the enraged Llysanyin's attack.

Maurynna stared in astonishment. By all the gods, she'd no idea her sweet-natured mount hid such a temper. "Boreal!"

At first she thought he didn't hear her—or chose not to. He snapped a second time at the man's face. Then Boreal wheeled around to stand by her side, his ears pinned back, still watching the man. She patted his neck and whispered, "Thank you, but I can take him if necessary. Honestly."

Boreal just snorted but she felt him relax under her hand.

"Did you see that?" Tirael cried to his friends. "That damned plow horse attacked me!"

"Oh, by the gods—how thick are you, anyway?" she asked in exasperation.

"You can thank whichever poor god has to look after fools like you that I don't have a belaying pin at hand—I'd be tempted to smack you alongside the head to let in some sense."

Tirael's face flushed an unbecoming brick red but he seemed too stunned to do anything. Maurynna suspected he'd never before been spoken to this way.

She went on, "And if Boreal had really attacked you, there'd be gobbets of you spread about by now. He's war-trained.

"How dare you speak to *me* that way, anyrate? Turnip or Tirael or whatever your name is, you have worse manners than a pig at feeding time."

Her last words seemed to be the cask that popped the ship's planking, as her aunt Maleid used to say. The riding crop came up.

"Tirael! What the hell do you think you're doing?" a man's frantic voice yelled. "Stop!"

Maurynna jumped in surprise; she hadn't noticed a new rider coming down the road from the exercise grounds. She looked to see Lord Eadain galloping toward them.

The crippled lord pulled his horse to a halt barely an ell from them. "Tirael," he said between clenched teeth. "Put. That. Whip. Down. *Now.*"

"And who the hell do you think you're ordering about, Crook-leg?" Tirael said viciously. "Get out of here before I give you a thrashing after I finish with this upstart peasant." He turned back to her.

Eadain's lips thinned at the taunt. Tireal's friends laughed as if at some clever joke.

That tore it. Insult her because he thought she was a peasant, fine; she knew that she'd have her revenge in the end, so it didn't matter very much to her. This odious wretch was not one whose opinion she gave a rotten fig about, anyway.

But he'd called Raven a dog. And worse yet, to mock Lord Eadain about his crippled leg like that . . . Enough was enough, and this was beyond that. Tirael had just popped *her* planking.

But before she could say anything, Eadain smiled coldly and said, "Remember those boys swimming in the stream, Tirael? They weren't the peasants you thought they were. And neither is she."

Maurynna had no idea what Eadain was talking about, but it stopped Tirael like a blow to the stomach. His face worked as he looked from her to Eadain and back again.

She smiled at him. It was not a kind smile.

Then Tirael wrenched his horse's head around and spurred it cruelly, leaving his followers gaping after him.

"I understand your dear friend is going to be in a match race," she said to the nearest one. "Tell him I am looking forward to it. I intend to lay a wager—a very *large* wager—"

She paused, holding her victim's gaze with her own, long enough that Tirael's hanger-on squirmed before continuing softly, "On the 'plow horse.' Now I suggest that you leave."

Tirael's followers looked at one another in consternation. Then, one after another, they turned their horses' heads and pelted off after their leader.

"Well and well, that was less than amusing," Maurynna said briskly. "Will you be at Lady Gallianna's gathering later, my lord?"

"I will, Dragonlord, as soon I finish with some business I'm helping Lord Romsley with."

"Then I shan't keep you any longer. I look forward to talking to you again, Lord Eadain."

Eadain bowed in his saddle. "Your Grace, and I look forward to seeing you again this evening under far more pleasant circumstances. Good day, my fine Llysanyin lord."

Boreal "bowed" in return. It was one of the tricks Lleld had taught all the Llysanyins before the journey to Jehanglan.

Lord Eadain raised a hand in farewell and urged his horse on. Maurynna went back to the table; she watched the three Cassorin peasants make their way back, Raeli and her son helping Cade along the path. They looked both relieved and baffled.

"You see?" Maurynna called to them as she picked up her food once more. "All's well."

Cade shook his head as he settled himself onto his seat. "I wouldna have believed it, Lord Tirael backin' down like that. He's got a bad name 'round here, that 'un. Good for tha, lass!"

"Thank Lord Eadain. Now, Cade—I've a very important question for you."

"Aye, lass?"

"How well does your cheese travel?"

Twenty-six

For all that Conor had spoken lightly when he'd told Linden Rathan he'd be careful, the Beast Healer intended to be on his guard when he looked over the notorious Summer Lightning. He'd been hearing about the horse's racing prowess for some time; but before this, he'd heard only the vaguest rumors of a temper to match the amazing speed and jumping ability.

Likely Lord Lenslee's kept most people away from him, he thought as he strode through the merchant's section of the fair. *It would be the only sane thing to do; if it ever attacked some noble . . .*

That the horse still lived told Conor that whoever the stallion's young victim had been, he had not been anyone of importance. *At least,* Conor thought with grim sarcasm, *of no importance to anyone who "mattered." Just his mam and da and anyone else who loved him.*

Lord Sevrynel was right. The horse should never have been put to stud; likely his get would inherit the temper, whether or not they got the speed as well. It was irresponsible as hell of Lenslee to breed such an animal. If he did indeed have his grandfather's knack, he was misusing it badly. Blowing through his lips, Conor shook his head to rid himself of his foul temper.

The humid air hung heavy and thick around him as he walked; it was, he thought, like pushing through a dirty, wet wool blanket. His feet stirred up dust with every stride; it would be long before the grass reclaimed the "roads" worn across the meadow by boot and hoof.

Everywhere around him swirled a tumult of sound and color and scents. Odors of every kind of cooked food seemed to grab at his stomach. Fairgoers called to one another, peddlers of every kind shouted the virtues of their wares, young apprentices tramped through the milling crowds, each one waving a colorful banner with the symbols of their master's trade and personal mark upon it. Some of the pennants were crude patchwork, others more skillfully done. A select few were of the finest embroidery. Conor noted with wry amusement that most of the banners in the last group belonged to betting masters. As they walked, the 'prentices sang out their masters' names and trades. A few rang out over the tumult.

"Master Orvis, saddler! Finest leather, finest stitching! The best in the Five Kingdoms!"

"Come one, come all! Mistress Phalarope has the hat to suit you! Straw hats, leather hats, hoods of good woolen cloth! Come one, come all!"

"Cure your palsy! Cure your ringing ears! Go see Master Isserlan, purveyor of the finest remedies from mysterious Jehanglan! Never suffer from the nightmare again!"

Likely just ground-up beetles from the garden with a bit of spice thrown in to make it taste exotic, Conor thought in disgust. He'd heard Bard Otter's song— who hadn't?—of the Dragonlords' great adventure in Jehanglan. Though the magic that had once shielded that faraway land was now gone, that didn't mean that the Jehangli were eager to deal with any but their old trading partners, House Whatever-it-was out of Assantik.

Gods, what herbs might they have for healing, he thought wistfully. *Things we've never even dreamed of, I'll wager.*

Herbs . . . Hmm—he needed more myrrh and witch hazel for his wound wash, come to think of it. He'd have to remember to stop at the Healwort Guild tent at some point and see if they had any at a decent price. Perhaps he'd even find someone who had news of Pod. He wondered how she was faring. Pod was bright, and she already knew most of the common plants. She'd do well and make their chapterhouse—and him—proud; he was certain of that.

The thought took him from the merchants' area into the beginning of the horse lines. He heaved a sigh of relief. Not that it was quieter here; in place of the proclamations of the merchants' "heralds," there were the shouts of owners, grooms, and stable hands as well as the ear-ringing hammering of the various blacksmiths scattered throughout.

He followed one of the makeshift lanes that cut through the horse lines like the spokes of a wheel. It took him to a large open area, the hub of the wheel. At the very center, hedged in by a forest of long poles bearing flags with the arms of some noble or even royal house, was a huge yellow circular tent. Men and women of all stations bustled in and out of it. This, Conor knew, was the heart of the great horse fair of Balyaranna.

He circled the tent, looking for the banner bearing the arms of Therinn Barans of Lenslee. It wasn't long before he saw it: a red horse within a wreath of golden oak leaves, all on field of white. Sitting beneath it was a well-dressed— and clearly bored—young man.

As Conor's shadow fell on him, he glanced up, then rose to his feet and bowed.

"Beast Healer Conor," he said. "Thank you for coming." He might have been saying "Thank you for the bag of dirt" for all the enthusiasm he put into his words.

Reminding himself of Lord Lenslee's gift, Conor made himself reply with far more cordiality than he felt. "My pleasure," he said, while thinking *As long as your master's horse doesn't rip my arm off.* "There was an emergency at Lord Sevrynel's stable. I hope you haven't had to wait long for me."

A haughty sniff was the thanks for his concern. "I'd expected you before this," the other answered with another sniff. "Lord Lenslee is a very busy man, Beast Healer. This way, please." He sauntered off with yet another disdainful sniff.

Conor fell in behind him, wondering if he could keep a straight face while suggesting mint-and-horehound tea for the other man's "cold." A pity Pod wasn't here; she'd have no trouble at all.

Trouble swarmed up onto his shoulder once more and draped herself around his neck like a furry scarf. It was a little too warm for it, but Conor let her bide; he knew she enjoyed watching the big world outside his hood from the safety of her favorite perch.

The way led through a confusion of horse lines that Conor hadn't seen before. *Gods, this is so much larger than the last Balyaranna fair I went to! I swear that it's doubled even in the last few da—*

"Kerras have mercy!" he exclaimed, invoking the Great Stag the Beast Healers followed. Without thinking, he put out a hand to stop his guide and stood in openmouthed astonishment at the horse being ridden in the cross lane a short distance ahead. He wasn't certain what had first caught his eye: the high, floating action of the slow trot, or the horse's unusual coloring, black with an iron grey mane and tail. Its rider sat easily, holding the reins in one hand. By his reddish blond hair and long clanbraid, the man was a Yerrin.

Conor watched, more baffled by the moment. "What is that?" he wondered aloud.

The man shrugged Conor's hand from his shoulder and glared at him in outrage that a mere Beast Healer should have dared lay a hand upon his exalted self. He barely deigned to glance over.

"Some kind of plow horse, a Shamreen most likely," he said waspishly. "I've seen it before. The peasant gives himself airs, but that will end soon enough," and finished with a sniff of dismissal. He waited with exaggerated patience, straightening the embroidered hem of his tunic, for Conor to come out of his reverie.

Conor shook his head in disgust. Yes, there was a passing resemblance to a Shamreen draft horse—a particularly fine one. The stallion was a big animal with a round, broad barrel, legs that looked as sturdy as young trees, and feathered feet; it might be understandable that a man might make that mistake—if the man in question had no eye for horses *and* the horse stood still.

For no plow horse moved like that. Nor had Conor ever seen a grown horse with that coloring. Foals, yes, but those had gone pure grey as they'd grown.

There was something familiar about the horse even though Conor was dead certain he'd never seen this animal before. Where had he seen something like it?

Then it came to him, and he almost left Lord Lenslee to wait in vain so that he might chase after it.

No, he'd never laid eyes on this particular animal, but had seen one like him: Linden Rathan's irascible stallion, Shan.

"By the gods," Conor whispered as horse and rider disappeared from view.

His mind raced. Linden had said there were two other Dragonlords here—one of which was his soultwin. That left only one other possibility; but there was no chance that the man he'd just seen was the newest Dragonlord, Shima Ilyathan from Jehanglan. Not with *that* hair. Conor remembered the songs he'd heard of late, and could guess who it was. "I must find him," he whispered.

His guide looked up from brushing imaginary specks of dust from his clothing. "Did you say something, Beast Healer?"

"No," Conor said. "Let's be off, shall we?"

A sniff was his only answer.

To his surprise, Conor's guide led him a short distance to where two horses were tied.

For pity's sakes, the fair isn't that *big.* "Aren't Lord Lenslee's horses kept within the fair?" he asked as he swung up into the saddle.

Sniff. "No—Lord Lenslee's kinsman, Lord Portis, has an estate near here and allows my lord to stable his horses there during the fair. It's much safer for the horses. They'll move to Lord Portis's stables at the fairgrounds in time for the races." *Sniff.*

Conor nodded and fell in behind his guide. It made sense; while it was uncommon, more than one horse had suddenly turned up lame the morning of a race. Lame—or worse.

They rode out of the fair and along a winding road that curved through woods and meadows and once over a cheerful stream. The horses hooves thudded hollowly as they crossed the wooden bridge. Since his guide showed no inclination to pass the time in conversation and the horse was a steady creature content to follow its stablemate, Conor let himself fall into a half doze. Trouble lay across his shoulders and snored softly in his ear.

Conor came awake when the horse ahead of him turned onto a well-traveled track only a little narrower than the road. It swept up the crest of a small hill. When they had followed it to the top, Conor saw a small manor house before them. He had no need to ask which of the buildings surrounding it was the stable; the hum of activity around it made it seem a giant beehive.

With a final, dismissive sniff, his guide left him in the yard before the stable. As the man turned away, Conor said cheerfully, "My thanks for guiding me, my lord—and you might want to try a bit of horehound-and-mint tea for that cold, I'm thinking." He dismounted.

Before the startled young lordling could say anything, Therinn Barans, lord of Lenslee, strode out of the stable. Conor recognized him from his visit to the Beast Healers' main chapterhouse the year before: a tall man, with brown hair springing back from his forehead and falling to either side of his face in waves. A neatly trimmed beard followed the line of his strong jaw and square chin. Lenslee bore himself like one who knew where he was going in life and would turn aside for no man.

Conor bowed. "My lord."

Lord Lenslee nodded. "Beast Healer Conor of Grey Holt? Good; I want you to have a look at Summer Lightning. Nothing wrong, mind you. I just want to be certain that he's fit for the big race."

The Kelnethi lord grinned fiercely. No doubt, Conor thought wryly, at the certainty of the gold and glory Summer Lightning would bring him.

"Robie!" Lord Lenslee bellowed at a youngster peering out of the stable door. "Tell Beckrum that the Beast Healer is here."

The boy ran off. Conor waited with Lord Lenslee; the Kelnethi lord rocked from heel to toe in anticipation.

"Have you ever seen Lightning, Beast Healer? No? Ah, you're in for a rare treat, then. There's nothing out there that can catch him. Ah—Gorith, a word with you."

An old man wearing a farrier's leather apron turned from whatever errand he'd been on and limped across the yard to them. "Aye, m'lord?"

"This is Beast Healer Conor. You and any other stable hand will render him any aid he needs, understand? Pass the word on to the others."

Gorith nodded to Conor; Conor returned it. The old farrier said, "I'll do that, m'lord."

The sound of hooves striking cobbles caught Conor's ear. While it could have been any horse being brought in, from the way the stable yard suddenly emptied, he was certain it could only be the notorious Summer Lightning approaching around the corner of the stable. Even Gorith with his limp was gone.

Conor, m'lad, this is not *good.* His mouth felt dry. He reached within himself for a powerful calming spell. Though if this horse was as fast as he'd heard . . .

Between one breath and the next the stable yard went from an empty expanse of grey cobblestones to a swirling cauldron of life and color too small to hold the stallion that suddenly spun and danced in it, glowing copper in the hot sunlight. For a moment Conor didn't even notice the handler at the other end of the lead rope as the chestnut stallion reared, bursting with life.

He was a beauty all right, Conor thought to himself. Yet he felt no warmth for the glorious animal. He'd seen the hard, cold look in its eye and knew that Summer Lightning was that blessedly rare thing: an animal with a heart as dark as night. Then that cold eye caught sight of him and Conor lost all doubt that this creature had deliberately hurt humans before.

As the horse's ears went back and it bared its strong white teeth at him, Conor gasped as the man holding the lead rope put out his hand. Certain that the fellow was about to lose fingers, Conor raised his own hands in warning.

But the instant the weathered hand touched the muscled neck, the horse calmed. Conor remembered what Lord Sevrynel had said: *Therinn's best jockey, Summer Lightning's groom, and Therinn himself are among the few people the beast will tolerate.*

Hoping whatever hold the man had over the vicious stallion didn't fail, Conor gingerly approached the horse that held both so much promise and so much darkness within him.

After leaving Lord Sevrynel and his fellow marshals still arguing details, Linden wandered afoot through the fair. Luckily the fair drew Yerrins to it like flies to honey; for once in Cassori he wasn't the only one standing head and shoulders above most of the crowd. And since he wasn't wearing the formal garb, he looked like any other of his countrymen strolling about. Hardly anyone gave him a second glance.

Since Sevrynel had told him that Lord Lenslee would keep his horse at his kinsman's nearby manor until the races, Linden knew he had time to wander before meeting Conor.

He considered going back to get Shan and seeing if he could find the cheese seller Maurynna had spoken of, then decided it would take too long. If the stuff *did* taste like Fat Gorly, he hoped Maurynna remembered to bring some back. Instead he bought a small fruit pasty from a booth and set off again, gingerly nibbling the hot pie. He wandered here and there, not looking for anything in particular, just seeing what the fair had to offer now; it had been a good twenty years or so since he last attended.

Considerably more than the last time I was here! It's also a damn sight larger. Sevrynel's done well now that the stewardship of the fair's fallen to him.

After a final squint at the sun, Linden decided it was time to find that tent. It took longer than expected. When he got there he was relieved to see that he'd arrived first; it would not have been fair to make the busy Beast Healer wait for him. Since it was past the nooning, it was not as busy as it usually was. Linden sat at the end of an empty trestle table under an awning.

Luckily he hadn't long to wait. Even as the young serving man came to ask what he wanted, Conor arrived, puffing.

"You've not been waiting long, I hope," he said as he settled himself opposite Linden.

Linden shook his head. "Just got here myself. Are you hungry?"

"That I am."

They ordered a platter of cheese and bread, and ale. When the tankards arrived, Linden took a deep draught and sighed with pleasure. Wiping the foam from his lips, he asked, "And how was Summer Lightning?"

Frowning, Conor leaned forward and said in a low voice, "Lord Sevrynel was right. There's a darkness in that horse, Your Grace. I just hope by Kerras's golden antlers that his get don't inherit it. That animal should never be allowed to breed—I don't care how fast he is."

Gods, this has Conor upset! "You don't want to talk about him, do you?"

"No."

"Then tell me more about Pod," Linden said.

The long, gaunt face brightened immediately. "Now, Pod I'm willing to talk about, Dragonlord," Conor said proudly.

"Linden—remember? Or do I have to throw some soap at you?" Linden smiled at a memory. If he'd had to listen to "Your Grace," "Linden Rathan," or "Dragonlord" all the while they were trying to give a certain four-year-old hellion a bath . . . It was hard to be formal when you, the walls, the floor, and everything else were soaking wet and you kept losing the soap to boot.

Conor smiled. "I didn't know if *you'd* remember that, Your—Linden."

The serving man set a laden wooden trencher between them and flipped back the napkin covering it, revealing a round loaf, a thick wedge of blue-veined cheese, and a knife. Linden took the knife and sawed the loaf in two, then cut a few thick slices from the cheese. The yeasty aroma of bread still warm from the oven filled the air.

As if the mouthwatering aroma were a piper's call, Conor's hood began moving; a moment later a small, masked face had popped out of it. After a huge yawn that displayed a fine set of needle-like fangs, Trouble oozed her way out of the hood and climbed backward down her master's arm to the table.

Conor gave her a bit pulled from the inside of his half of the loaf. "There you are, my pretty lady."

Trouble daintily ate her morsel, then darted forward, grabbed a slice of cheese, and, scrambling down Conor's leg, hid under the table with it.

"Thief!" Conor scolded as Linden chuckled.

"My long-ago brother-in-law's ferrets were just the same," Linden said. "If it wasn't tied down, off it went. One of 'em once decided he wanted my saddle. Actually managed to move it a good few handspans, too, before Fisher grabbed him. I always wondered what he would've done with it if I'd let him have it."

"Best not to ask," Conor said gloomily, tossing another bit of cheese down to Trouble. "My first ferret stole a belt of mine and hid it the gods only know where. Never did find it.

"But back to Pod—she's finally found her familiar and you'd never guess in a thousand years what it is."

From the twinkle in Conor's eye, Linden wasn't sure it was safe to know. But something he'd said . . . " 'Finally found?' There was a problem?"

"There was. At the time I left Grey Holt to study at the main chapterhouse of Stag Holt, Pod still hadn't found her brother-in-fur. We all knew she belonged there because she could heal, but we were getting worried. . . ."

Conor dug in his scrip and pulled out a small leather wallet. Undoing the ties, he said, "Here—read this. I keep it to cheer myself up when I'm tired and lonely." He handed Linden a much-handled sheet of parchment. And if you wouldn't mind reading it aloud? I rather need it."

Linden held it so the sunlight fell on the faded writing and read:

> *Well, Conor old lad,*
>
> *You've gone and done it now. I don't know whether Master Jern wants to kiss you or skin you alive and hang your hide on the wall.*
>
> *What's this about? Pod, of course. She disappeared the day you left. No one noticed until suppertime and it was near dark; guess everyone thought she was off somewhere crying. I know I did. We tore barn, stable, crofts, and house apart looking for her. No Pod.*
>
> *Then the acorn dropped. Everyone was kicking themselves that they hadn't guessed she'd try to follow you.*
>
> *At first we thought it would be a simple matter of riding down the road and catching up to her, so Jyulen and Tamar went after her at a gallop. How far could a child on foot get, anyway? When they returned two or three candlemarks later, they said that not only had they not found Pod, but that no one else had seen her, not the tinkers who remembered you passing in the morning, not the harvesters in the fields, not anyone.*
>
> *They were scared witless, let me tell you, and so were the rest of us, because we knew then she'd gone into the woods so as to make it harder to find her. Those are not good woods to be lost in, Conor. They are especially not good when you're a child alone. Master Jern turned dead white and ordered us out with torches.*
>
> *We searched through the night but couldn't find her. Come the dawn, we straggled back to the hold and Master Jern sent word to the neighboring farmers. We ate a bit and snatched what sleep we could until the farmers came.*
>
> *We were certain that, with so many people and Farmer Kerils's hounds, we'd find her that day. We didn't. We kept searching until full dark and still no sign. Then it started to rain, and that washed away any scent for the hounds.*
>
> *Master Jern called off the search lest someone break his or her leg in the dark and wet, what with everyone so tired. Jyulen, Tamar, Harebit, and I refused to go back; we didn't want to have to tell you that we'd lost your Pod. Master Jern ordered us back. I'm sorry,*

Conor, but we had to go, he was that angry. Everyone agreed to meet at dawn the next day.

Which we did, in a grey drizzle that got into everyone's hearts. We were certain by then we'd never find her alive, and fair certain we'd never find her at all.

So when, barely a candlemark later, Tamar screamed, "There she is!" I didn't believe her at first. No one did; we were so shocked that no one moved. But there was Pod, staggering across the meadow, wet and muddy and scratched all over, and with a prize of a black eye like she'd been in the best tavern brawl ever. And she was carrying something wrapped in her over tunic.

She went straight up to Master Jern and said, "I've found a wee beastie and he's hurt. May I keep him?"

("Wee beastie," my ass! Conor, we both know how strong Pod is, especially for a young girl. Whatever she had, it filled her arms and made her stagger with its weight.)

Master Jern asked, "What is it?" (Oh, Conor—I wish you could have seen his face. He knows your Pod, he does.)

"Just a wee beastie," she said again. "Please, sir—I want to get him inside where it's warm and dry. I laid the Sleep upon him, but I think he's waking up again."

Just then her "wee beastie" stuck its head out of the tunic. Conor, you son of a bitch, have you any idea what YOUR Pod brought home? It was a bloody half-grown GHULON, by the Goddess's paps! You know what I'm talking about, don't you? It's what you Kelnethi call a woods dog.

But whatever name you give them, they're nothing you want to get within a league of. This one looked around at us, snarling like a mad thing. I swear I thought we were dead. You know how vicious those things can be; remember the one we saw chase some wolves off of its kill? And this one wanted to rip our guts out. You could see it in its eyes.

So what does Pod do? Drop the thing and run like a sensible girl? Not YOUR Pod. She stuck her face right up to those big fangs, met it eye to eye, and snapped, "Stop that, Kiga!"

And it did. Damn me, Conor, if the thing didn't start licking her face and crooning to her like some big mekeera.

Poor Master Jern, he didn't say anything. He couldn't. His eyes were all funny-like. He just pointed back toward the chapterhouse. Pod said, "Thankee" and staggered off. I'm sure you'll forgive us that none of us offered to help.

So now, along with all the dogs and cats, and the few odd ferrets

*and birds and mekeera or two and suchlike, we now have a ghulon in
the hold. Something had clawed his back right fierce. If Pod hadn't
found him, he'd have died a miserable death. He's still healing, but
he can follow her around now. The other animals have learned to
stay out of his way—mostly. (Daken's idiot hound tried to go after
Kiga; that's what comes of his letting it chase the cats. Daken's damn
lucky Kiga was really quite gentle and just slapped Tipper aside.
Tipper didn't even need that much of a Healing.)*

*Kiga still won't let anyone else but Pod touch him yet, but he
doesn't try to attack anyone, either. She's teaching him proper manners, she is.*

I know you must be damn proud of her, Conor.

We all are—

Robin

Jyulen

Tamar

Harebit

Linden handed the letter back as he wiped tears of laughter from his eyes.
"Oh dear gods," was all he could say at first. Then, "A *ghulon*? Oh dear gods."
Finally he shook his head. "Why am I not more surprised? I only knew her as a
young child, so you'd think I would be—but I'm not."

"Know what you mean. I'd have never had thought of it, but when it happened, all I could think of was 'Of course! What else?'" Conor said.

"So was she looking for you that day?" Linden asked.

"She was. I got the story at my first visit. Thought she'd cut through the
woods—woods she'd never been through, mind you—and head me off near Fern
Crossing, the silly little turnip. Got herself properly lost and was getting scared,
she told me later, when she felt a 'pull' and had to follow it. She had no choice.
And that's how she found Kiga, jammed into a hollow 'twixt a log and the ground.
She dug him out and stayed with him, doing as much Healing as she could, then
set off for home."

"Luckily," Conor finished dryly, "she picked the more-or-less right way by
chance. Terrible sense of direction the girl has."

"How old is she now?"

Conor shrugged. "She was, what, three—perhaps four years old—when we
found her? She's something like thirteen or fourteen now, I'd be guessing. None
of us have ever been sure whether she's younger than we think or just a wee bit
of a thing."

"So, have you met this Kiga?" Linden asked. "And has he learned manners?"

"Yes, I've met him, and—" Here Conor held up both hands and wiggled his
fingers, "as you can see, since I've still got all my fingers, he's learned manners.

There are some people he won't let touch him, but he doesn't even snap or snarl at them. He just moves away. Trouble likes to sit on his head and groom him."

They talked for a while longer of various things. Then Conor said he had to get back to the Beast Healers' pavilion and Linden realized he'd best be on his way himself or he'd be late for the supper at Lady Gallianna's.

Their paths lay together for a short while. As they parted, Linden asked, "Have you any idea how long Pod will be away from Grey Holt? Perhaps Maurynna, Shima, and I could stop there on our way back to Dragonskeep. I should have gone to see her before this, but it seemed such a short time ago. . . ."

And it was—to him. Ten years—or twenty or thirty—were little more than the blink of an eye to the weredragons of Dragonskeep. But to a truehuman . . . "Maybe she's forgotten me."

"And maybe the sun will rise in the west tomorrow morning," Conor replied with a laugh. "No fear of that. The lass has picked my brains over the years for anything at all I can remember about you. I can tell you that Pod would be thrilled beyond words to see you again. Beside herself with joy, she'd be. Trust me on that, Linden. Trust me on that."

Twenty-seven

Kella had had another wonderful morning playing with Rynna before her cousin went off to find Raven.

"Tell him hello from us," Kella had said. "Me, Rann, and Rosie."

"I will. And what will you do now? Find Rann?"

Kella had said, "No, he's with one of his tutors. So I shall write a letter home to Mama and Maylin. I don't know whether to tell Maylin that Raven is here when she can't be."

Rynna then asked, "And why not?"

"Because she has plans for him. I heard her tell her friend Delina so one day. He'd better watch out."

Rynna had laughed and laughed. "Good for her! I don't think I'll warn him. Will she be able to come to the fair after all, do you think?"

"I don't know. Maylin wrote that if Mama's leg is better and Papa's sister can come to take care of her and it's not too late, she and Papa will come to the fair."

"Well now, I hope she can. The poor beggar won't know what hit him."

The letter was done and given over to a royal messenger. Now Kella sat on one of the deep windowsills in Rann's quarters. She peered through one of the diamond-shaped panes into the garden below. "What a bunch of sillies!"

Rann climbed up beside her and found another pane to look through. "He's being very patient with them, isn't he? Just sitting there talking to them—even though most of them just giggle, giggle, giggle. I hear them all the time when they're talking to the younger lords. They're the most awful gigglers."

"They are. Poor Shima. I think he likes Lady Karelinn 'cause I heard Rynna and Linden talking about it. Why won't those silly girls go away and leave the two of them alone?"

"I think they're hoping he'll like one of them better."

Kella tossed her head. "Hunh! None of them are as nice as Lady Karelinn and her sister."

She scooted to the edge and dropped to the floor. "Do you still want help learning those chords?"

Rann heaved a martyred sigh. "Not really."

"You don't want to forget everything Daera's taught you! That would make her so unhappy when she gets back. And what if that awful Bard Leet should ask you to show him something she's taught you? He wouldn't say anything mean to you if you make a mistake because you're the prince, but it will look bad for Daera. And I'll bet you a barley sugar stick that he'll say nasty things about her when he gets back to the Bards' School if he thinks she isn't teaching you right."

"Oh, very well. But can we go out into the garden? It's too nice to be inside. And Bramble wants to go outside, too."

The wolfhound's tail thumped at the mention of his name.

"That sounds nice. I missed the last lesson out . . ." Kella's voice trailed off as she rubbed her hand.

"I'll get my harp. It's in my sleeping chamber," Rann said, and went off, dragging his feet like a man heading to the gallows.

Kella waited, fuming inside. Just the thought of Bard Leet was enough to sour her temper. Hmph—she'd bet *five* barley sugar sticks that old nasty would say bad things about Daera back at the Bards' School! Bard Leet was mean all the way through. And she still hadn't had her revenge on him.

She *could* march up to him and ask him to bear a message to her cousin, Dragonlord Maurynna Kyrissaean—but it wouldn't be *her* revenge somehow.

No, she had to think of something she could do all on her own.

At last Rann appeared, harp under his arm. "I suppose we should go now," he said glumly, snapping his fingers at Bramble.

"It's not that bad," Kella said when she saw the misery in her friend's face. "Here—why don't I carry it? I don't trust Bramble not to trip you and it's a lovely little harp."

"Very well, here," Rann said as he handed her the harp. "Are you going to make me do those chord in, in, invertle things?"

"Chord inversions," Kella gently corrected. "And, yes, I will. You have to learn them, Rann."

"Why can't the wretched chords stay still? Why do they have to turn themselves inside out?" he complained as they went through the door. They stopped just short of colliding with one of the youngest serving girls, Aralie, who was coming in with a ewer of scented water in one hand and a wool duster in the other.

Aralie bobbed a courtesy. "Good day, Your Highness, Kella," the girl said with a smile.

Kella grinned back; Aralie was nice and always helped them when they wanted to hide from Willena. She was also one of the few servants their age.

"Good day, Aralie," Rann said. "If Lady Willena or her father come looking for me, we're in the stables."

Aralie nodded solemnly. "I'll remember that, m'lord." She winked.

They went on through the castle. As they crossed the great hall, Kella saw Bard Leet. For a moment her jaw clenched.

Then came the idea. It was a brilliant idea. All at once, she knew how she would get her revenge on Master Stuck-Up Bard Leet. She caught Rann's sleeve, dragging him to a halt.

"Look!" she whispered fiercely. "There's Bard Leet." Her chin jerked, indicating a spot beyond his shoulder.

Rann looked over his shoulder. "Um, yes, I see him. So?"

Kella nearly stamped a foot in annoyance. "Don't you see? He doesn't have his harp with him! This is a perfect opportunity for me to get into his room and touch his precious harp!"

The prince shook his head. "But Kella—you don't know how long he'll be away. What if he came back while—"

"He won't!" Kella nearly crowed. "Not if you help me! Remember how we saw Shima in the garden from your window? And remember the song he sang for us that first morning? I've got an idea. . . ."

She whispered in Rann's ear. He listened carefully. When she was done, he said reluctantly, "Very well, I'll do it. But I think you should run back to my rooms first and see if Aralie is still there."

For a moment Kella looked blank. "Why—?"

Rann tugged on the sleeve of her tunic, rubbing his thumb along the embroidered hem, and stared pointedly at her.

"Oh! Good thinking!" With that, Kella shoved the small harp into his arms and hurried off.

Kella found Aralie just as the young servant was leaving Rann's chambers. She caught the other girl's arm and dragged her back in.

"Rann and I need your help for a jest," Kella said, not quite lying. *She* thought it was a fine jest, even if Bard Leet wouldn't.

Alarie grinned. "What do tha need, young mistress?"

Kella explained; Aralie nodded. When they were done, Aralie pointed to the ewer of scented water it was her duty to refill throughout the day.

"Best take that and the towel," she said. "When tha are one of the lesser servants, it's best tha aren't seen empty-handed. Water's still hot, so mind tha hands."

"Good idea!" Kella pounced on the towel and wrapped it around the gently steaming ewer. She made for the door. "Thanks, Alarie! I'll meet you back here in a little while to switch back."

A moment later she was walking quickly down the hall, grinning from ear to ear.

She trotted through the halls of the castle. It was clever of Rann, she thought, to think of switching clothes with Aralie. No one *really* looked at servants, especially pages and maids. She shifted her grip on the ewer of steaming water; the heat was uncomfortable despite the folds of linen toweling that swathed the vessel. She stared straight ahead, with what she hoped was the proper expression on her face. Almost every servant she'd ever seen look bored; she suspected she looked more like a nervous rabbit.

La-la-la, I'm just bringing scented water for washing to some spoiled little lordling who drank too much wine last night or is too lazy to get out of bed at a decent candlemark, tra-la-la-la-la-la, she told herself over and over again. If she believed it, so would anyone else—she hoped.

It seemed to be working. No one stopped her as she passed by, no one grabbed her by the shoulder and demanded to know what she was doing. When one or two people did seem to take a second glance, with that puzzled expression that says "You look vaguely familiar, but something's not quite right . . . ," Kella just bowed her head a little so that the brim of her servant's cap hid her face a bit more and hurried past as if on some urgent errand.

Still, she felt as if every gaze drilled a hole between her shoulder blades. She didn't dare look around.

No one really looks at servants. . . .

The thought was her only comfort against her growing unease. This had all seemed such a lark when they'd planned it in the hallway: a game, nothing more, a way of thumbing their noses at the arrogant bard. He hadn't had to slap her hand and treat her like dirt because she was from a merchant family. He could have just said, "Don't touch it." Hmmph—she wouldn't have even *considered* touching it if she hadn't thought it was Daera's. She knew what was proper.

Her hand still hurt, too. *It will serve him right for being so mean,* she told herself, and held the thought as a shield against any prickings from her conscience.

But the closer she got to Bard Leet's room, the more uneasy she grew. Bards, like Healers and Dragonlords, were among the favored of the gods. If she dared touch Leet's harp against his wishes, would the ground open up beneath her? Would her fingers curl up with a palsy? She gnawed on her lower lip. Maybe this wasn't such a good idea after all. . . .

And if she turned around now and admitted she was too scared to go through with it? She could imagine what Rann would say, especially since it had been her idea. No, she'd not beg off and be named 'fraidy cat. She could be as brave as any boy, she told herself, even a prince. Kella squared her shoulders and walked on even though her mouth was suddenly dry. The ewer felt as heavy as lead in her hands.

Almost there, almost there, almost there, a frightened little voice in the back of her mind chanted. *Don't let anyone notice me!*

A servant bearing a towering armload of used bed linens looked over his burden at her as she approached. His nose twitched like a hunting dog's. "Hoy, there," he called sharply.

Certain she was discovered, Kella nearly threw down the ewer, ready to hike up her skirts and flee. But after a quick look at the bulbous red nose, she was certain she knew who he was: Griff, the laziest sack of bones in the castle according to Aralie. Griff, who'd grab any of the younger servants he could and make them do his work.

Griff didn't know who she was; Griff didn't *care* who she was. He just wanted to dump his chores on her. She swept past him with all the bravado she could scrape together.

"Sahrreh," she replied, mimicking the accent of a Casna wharf brat so broadly she could barely understand herself. "Baht eft His Lahdship's w'ter's caowld, hit'll be wurf moy hoide. Yeh knaow how hay is."

Kella dared a quick glance over her shoulder. The servant stood, flummoxed, mouthing her words, trying to make out just what she'd said to him. She couldn't blame him; she'd laid that accent on with a shovel. Kella nearly choked on a torrent of suppressed giggles as she scurried down the hall and around the corner.

There! She broke into a shuffling run. The scented water sloshed wildly in the ewer, threatening to spill over with every step. *Third door down is Bard Leet's.*

To her dismay, as she reached the door, she thought she heard Griff coming after all. She fumbled one-handed to open the heavy latch. It stuck. The footsteps came closer.

Open, open, open, you stupid thing!

The door swung open and she was through it like a racehorse at the drop of the starting rope. Kella shoved it with a foot; the thick door shut with a muffled thud. She stood, listening.

Nothing. No one called after her from the hall, demanding to know her business bringing water to a man long awake. No one jumped up from the bed, angry at her invasion. She was safe.

Kella let out a breath she hadn't known she was holding. "That was too close," she said to the air. After a moment she set the ewer on the small table next to the door. As she turned, she ran her shaking fingers through her hair. An image of her mother's calf's-foot jelly quivering in a bowl came to her mind; she decided that was just what she felt like.

"I've gone this far," she muttered to herself. "I'm not quitting now. Best get on with this."

She made herself take the time to examine the room; Rann would demand a description as proof. Almost the first thing she noticed was the extravagance of two clothes chests at the foot of the bed.

No, wait—only one was for clothes, she decided, after a quick look at the footboard and seeing that the carvings on both matched. The bigger chest was part of the room's furnishings. The other must belong to Bard Leet; it was a different kind of wood, uncarved, and the wrong size and shape entirely. Kella thumped her forehead with the heel of her hand. Of course; that one must be the wooden traveling case for his harp.

"The harp I'm not good enough to touch," she muttered angrily, all nervousness burned away by a hot wave of remembered humiliation. While she hoped the case wasn't locked, she didn't have the nerve to risk that disappointment just yet. *In a moment. . . .*

Instead she made herself walk around the room. It was much like any other guest chamber she'd seen in the castle while playing with Rann. Not as grand as some, true, but then Leet wasn't a visiting prince. Still, it was large enough—and well-furnished enough—to do him honor; no odds and ends of the castle's furniture for a master bard.

Even the carvings match, Kella thought as she prowled the room, *not like my things. I like these acorns and oak leaves—they're pretty.* A warm breeze from the open window brought in the scents of sunshine and the gardens. She looked with a touch of envy at the rich furnishings: a good-sized featherbed with thick curtains, now pulled back; a clothes cupboard; a washbowl and water pitcher with a pretty green-and-white glaze—neither one chipped—resting upon a little table by the window. By the head of the bed and half-hidden by the bed curtains was a second little table. And upon that table . . .

Kella blinked, then grinned. There was no mistaking the shape under the covering of red silk. It wasn't locked away where she couldn't get at it after all. With her hands on her hips, she tossed her head and said, "We'll see if I'm not good enough!"

She stalked across the room, muttering, "Keep him busy, Rann."

Telling her conscience to hush its yammering, she tugged at the covering. It slid to the table in a cascade of heavy silk, covering the leather music case lying on the table.

Before her stood Leet's harp.

Kella caught her breath at the beauty of it. The forepillar swept up, elegant as the neck of a swan; the harmonic curve rose from the soundbox of the instrument, dipped, and rose again to meet the forepillar, like "a salmon leaping," just as Daera had said of a fine harp. Would she ever be able to afford anything half as good as this?

"Oh, you *are* a beauty," Kella whispered. She peered at the design burned into the wood at the inside "shoulder" of the harp where neck met soundbox. It was a bird, long, narrow wings outstretched in flight inside a circle of flowers. She hadn't been able to see it clearly before. It was perfect in every tiny detail.

The flowers look rather like ruffly morning glories. And the bird . . . Oh, I see.

It's a seagull. Hunh—not what I would have picked, she thought, remembering how a seagull once dropped a clam on her head. The resulting gash had bled and bled, and she'd cried for candlemarks. Besides, seagulls couldn't sing worth a bent penny.

She traced the gull's outline with an outstretched finger. A roughness under her fingertip surprised her. Curious that the luthier would leave such a flaw, she bent closer, searching for the source. It was a few moments before she found it: a tiny gouge as if the artist's hand had slipped right at the end of one wing. It looked as if the gull were missing part of the leading feather, like a finger missing its first joint. Still, it was pretty design.

The breeze slipped through the window again and teased a haunting refrain from the strings as it blew over them. Kella stood enchanted as the harp "sang" for her. Then, unable to resist the temptation, she trailed a finger along the strings. The glissando hung shimmering in the air, calling to her.

"Oh, how lovely," she breathed. Still, she didn't quite dare play it; if she was caught in here . . .

If she was caught in here—even if she never touched the harp—she'd be lucky if she'd be able to sit down for a tenday.

Oh, hang it all, she thought, *just play the wretched thing. You might as well be hanged for a sheep as for a lamb. Just do the best you can with that hand.*

So she slipped around the little table and pulled the harp to nestle against her right shoulder. She placed her fingers on the strings, a touch light as a snowflake, then hesitated. What to play? "The Barley Boy"? "Autumn Dance"? She knew both songs well but both seemed too simple and rustic for such a fine instrument.

Still—with her hand still so sore, it wasn't as if she could play one of the more complicated pieces she'd been learning. She'd be lucky if she could play even scales without making a complete mess of it, let alone even something as easy as "The Barley Boy."

Then her fingers chose for her. As if directed by unseen hands over her own, they picked out a melody, at first slowly, then with growing confidence.

It was a pretty tune, yet strangely eerie, and made the back of her neck prickle. The more she played, the worse the prickling got, until she feared the skin would crawl off. And now there was another feeling, crawling up her fingers, slithering up her arms like a snake. Cold, so cold, and heavy, and . . . evil.

Her breath came short and fast. No more of this! She tried to pull her fingers away.

But the harp wouldn't let her go.

Twenty-eight

Rann watched Kella leave, then turned his attention to the bard. When the man finished his discussion with the steward, he started off again.

Rann followed at a discreet distance. He hoped the bard was leaving the castle; that would be safest. But if he showed signs of returning to the part of the castle where his chamber was, Rann would intercept him and put Kella's plan into play. She was right—it was something the vain master bard wouldn't be able to resist.

Rann stalked his prey here and there, pretending he was a snowcat on the hunt.

The mountain ram wandered through the valley, unaware of the great snowcat stealing along behind him. Step by slow, stealthy step the big cat crept up on his unwary prey, using every blade of grass, every tiny bush as cover, moving like a ghost. The doomed ram walked on—

Whoops! Bard Leet had finished whatever business he'd had in the great hall and was heading back to the one place he shouldn't go—not yet. Rann leaped into action, dodging around a countess and between two arguing lords, almost tripping over Bramble as the wolfhound cut in front of him.

"Bard Leet!"

As the lean figure of the master bard turned, Rann trotted up to him. He made himself smile at the man. "I wonder if you could help me."

Bard Leet bowed and looked pleased as a cat. "Yes, Your Highness?"

Rann launched into his appeal. "Shima Ilyathan sang a song from Jehanglan for Ke—" *Oh dear,* Rann thought, *I can't mention Kella and I don't want to lie and say Shima Ilyathan sang it just to me, it was really for Kella, oh dear. . . .*

He swallowed hard and rattled on. "Er, ah . . . It's a lullaby called 'Blanket of Stars' and it's very pretty. I'd like to play it for my great-aunt, Duchess Alinya, when we go back to Casna, because I think she'd like it, but I'm not good enough yet to figure it out by myself"—here he patted his harp and gave it a mournful look—"and Shima Ilyathan doesn't play, because they don't have harps in Jehanglan. And Bard Daera's gone to her family because her mother's so ill. . . ."

I hope her mother gets better. I don't want anyone else to lose their mother. . . .

Rann took a deep breath and gazed up at the bard, giving him the full treatment of what Healer Tasha called his "poor little lost puppy dog" look. Few adults could resist it, he'd found. "Could you help me? Please?"

"Why, of course, Your Highness. I'd be delighted to."

"Thank you!" Rann said brightly. "I'd be ever so grateful."

He thought the bard would purr. Rann, young as he was, had learned that many people thought mostly of the benefit to themselves when they did him any favor, even if that benefit was as intangible as prestige. Rann didn't care if Bard Leet asked for gold—not that he would, at least not openly—as long as he kept the man as far away from his chamber as possible. Switching from snowcat to sheepdog, Rann started for the gardens, knowing that Leet would follow. Which he did; but then—

"Hmm—a moment, Your Highness. It would be easiest with two harps, I think. As I learn the song, I'll begin teaching it to you. I'll get my harp, meet you here, and we'll go together to find Dragonlord Shima—"

Rann nearly dropped his own harp. His heart felt as if it hammered in his throat; it was hard to force words past it. "Oh, ah—no! No! You can't— You mustn't—"

At Leet's surprised look, Rann babbled, "When we—uh, I mean when I was in my room a little while ago, I saw Shima Ilyathan in the garden—" *Surrounded by all those silly girls.* "—but it looked like he might be leaving soon. If we hurry, I think we can get there before he goes. . . ." *Not that they're likely to let him get away.*

"Then let us go," Bard Leet said, "before he does leave. I'd like very much to hear this song." He held out his hands in an unspoken offer to carry the harp.

Rann handed it to him gladly. Kella was right; one of these days, Bramble was going to succeed in tripping him while he was carrying it, and that would be the end of the poor harp. Rann did *not* want it to be this day.

As he and the bard walked deeper into the fragrant heat of the gardens, Rann barely noticed various young noblewomen drifting past them in groups of two or three. Some pouted. Most had their heads together, whispering and giggling behind their hands, even as they made him quick courtesies.

Rann shook his head in disgust. The young women sounded like a flock of particularly foolish birds, all twitter, twitter, twitter. *Sillies, all of them—and Lady Niathea looks like she swallowed a wor—*

Niathea? Panic seized Rann. The last time he'd seen Lady Niathea, she'd been in the group surrounding Shima Ilyathan. He spun around, looking more closely at the young women already past him.

They had also been in the group around the newest Dragonlord.

Oh, no! Don't tell me— He broke into a run, leaving the sputtering bard behind. If Shima Ilyathan was gone, Rann had no reason to keep the bard by him— and away from his room.

Rann couldn't let that happen. He wasn't certain how long Kella needed, but he couldn't let her get caught.

He came around a bank of moss roses like a hound after a fox and stopped so short he nearly fell over. Thank all the gods, Shima Ilyathan *was* still there!

Though he was not alone. He sat with Lady Karelinn of Kelneth on one of the white marble benches near the fountain.

Oops. Rann had run in unannounced enough times on his uncle Beren and his aunt Beryl both before and right after they were married to know when his presence was, well, not as welcome as it might be another time. In embarrassment, he would take himself somewhere else as quickly as possible.

But not this time. He didn't care if Shima Ilyathan and Lady Karelinn were making calf-eyes at each other the way Uncle Beren and Aunt Beryl still did sometimes. He didn't care if they were *kissing*. Not even that would drive him away—not this time. He had Shima Ilyathan where he wanted him, and that would keep Bard Leet where he wanted *him*. Rann heaved a sigh of relief.

As he heard the bard come puffing around the bank of moss roses, Rann launched into his request, eyes as wide and appealing as he could make them. When he was done, Lady Karelinn smiled and gracefully withdrew. From the looks she and Shima Ilyathan exchanged, Rann knew that they meant to meet again later.

If he had anything to do with it, it would be much, much later. He flopped down in the grass as bard and Dragonlord greeted each other.

Conspiracies were hard work!

It was working. Despite his initial annoyance, Shima Ilyathan unbent under the bard's genuine interest and appreciation of his people's music. He sang the lullaby that Rann liked.

"I see why you like it, Your Highness," Leet said absently as he concentrated on teasing the melody out of the harp. "A lovely tune, simple, but sometimes those are the prettiest."

He played a phrase, at first tentatively, then with confidence. "There! I have it. I'll set that to parchment for you, Prince Rann, so that you may learn it later with Daera when she returns." Turning to Shima, he asked, "Could I impose upon you for more, Your Grace? The harmonic modes your people use are fascinating."

Shima Ilyathan smiled, all traces of irritation gone now. "I'd be happy to. This is a wedding song; the two parts are sung back and forth between the women and the men. It tells of the joy and wonder of beginning a life together, and calls the blessings of the Lady of Spirits upon the new couple. This is the men's part."

As Shima sang it, Rann sighed with pure happiness. This had been a good plan, a wonderful plan. Kella would have plenty of time. . . .

Then the first part of the song ended, and before Shima could begin the women's part, Bard Leet got to his feet, saying, "What a beautiful melody! I must ask your indulgence, Dragonlord. If you would be kind enough to wait, I'd like to get my music case for some parchment to write this out as you sing it. I'll be as quick as I can."

Shima Ilyathan nodded, and the bard was on his way at a respectable trot before a horrified Rann could say anything. All he could do was stare at Leet's back as the man disappeared around the moss roses.

"Oh, no," he whispered. "Oh, no." There was nothing he could do but wait—and pray.

"Prince Rann, is something wrong?" Shima Ilyathan asked.

Rann jumped, making Bramble yip in surprise, and dragged his attention back from his watch for Bard Leet. "Wh—what do you mean?" He looked every-where but at the newest Dragonlord.

"You're squirming as much as my little brother Tefira did when he sat on an anthill for all twenty-five verses of the Planting Song." Shima Ilyathan shook his head, smiling, a faraway look in his eyes. "I still can't believe he took that dare, the little ass." Then, coming back from his memories, he asked crisply, "*Is* something wrong? And is there anything I can do, Your Highness?"

Yes—you can run after Bard Leet and drag him back here, Rann wanted to say. He wished he could tell Shima Ilyathan what was afoot; he liked him almost as much as he liked Linden Rathan.

But could he trust him? He didn't dare. Shima Ilyathan was a Dragonlord. Rann couldn't take the chance that his sympathies might be with Bard Leet. Why, what if the Dragonlord considered this some kind of, of . . . *sacrilege?* Being a prince wouldn't help him escape punishment if a Dragonlord denounced him. It would only lessen the severity of that punishment.

But Kella had no rank of her own to protect her, just his friendship and her kinship to Maurynna. And she was the one actually trespassing in a senior bard's chamber; everyone's wrath would fall upon her. At the least she'd be banned from the castle. He'd never see her again.

Was it beginning already? Surely Bard Leet had been gone too long just to retrieve a music case. Rann's imagination presented image after horrible image: Leet catching Kella playing his harp; Leet hitting her, dragging her out into the hallway as he yelled for the guards; Kella being dragged away by the soldiers.

Worst of all, a weeping Kella lying on the filthy straw in a dungeon cell, to remain there until she died.

Despite the sunshine, Rann turned cold at the thought of the last image. But he didn't dare let any of his fears show.

"No, Dragonlord," he told Shima. "Nothing's amiss. Nothing at all." He pulled up a handful of grass and concentrated on the blades drifting through his fingers back to the earth so that he wouldn't have to meet Shima Ilyathan's worried gaze.

Twenty-nine

Against her will and despite the stiffness in her hand, Kella's fingers danced unerringly through the unknown song. Not once did she damp the wire strings; they rang on and on. Yet the sound never muddied as it should have. Instead each new note added its voice to the others, added another layer to wrap her in darkness. To catch and keep her. . . .

Her heart pounded; whatever was in the harp wanted to devour her. She *knew* it. She was terrified as she'd never been in all her eight years, yet could do no more than stare in horror as her fingers darted like mad swallows. Why hadn't Otter or Daera ever mentioned that there was a curse on a bard's harp to punish someone playing without permission?

She had to stop—she had to! Or else whatever was in the harp would eat her very soul. But her hands, burning with the unholy cold emanating from the strings, would not obey her. She played on and on.

Finally, in pure desperation, Kella swung her head sharply, smashing her cheek into the top edge of the soundbox. The instrument slewed in her arms, turning the run of notes into musical gibberish. Her cheek throbbed as if she'd been clubbed, but she was free. She clapped her hands together from either side of the harp, trapping some of the strings between her tight-pressed palms, silencing their deadly ringing. She slid her hands down the rest of the strings. Note by note, the sweet, poisonous sound died away.

Silence had never been so welcome. Kella's hands dropped heavily to her sides; they felt like lead weights—if lead weights could burn with cold. With an effort almost beyond her, she held them up before her face. *They way they feel, they should be bleeding or blistered,* she thought hazily. She felt strangely detached from the pain in her hands and what had just happened; her thoughts blundered through a fog, impossible to catch and shake into order. She fancied she could almost hear them whimpering like blind puppies lost from their mother.

Then the last sound she wanted to hear brought her back to herself: the rattling of the latch.

She was caught! For a moment that lasted beyond forever, she stood frozen with panic, listening to whoever was on the other side struggle with the stiff catch. Then, with a swift movement, Kella threw the heavy silk covering back over the harp. The next instant she dove under the bed—and smacked her head on the corner of something already there. Blinking back tears of pain, Kella squirmed around it, pushing aside a sack full of something that rustled and smelled faintly sweet, rather like honey. She settled herself so that she could peek into the room, but well back so that she couldn't be seen. It severely limited her range of vision, but she didn't dare risk moving closer to the edge of the bed.

It was only as the door swung open that Kella remembered the ewer and towel on the little table. Kella prayed as hard as she could that whoever it was wouldn't notice them beside the basin.

He—for the boots that were all she could see were definitely those of a man—didn't seem to, thank all the gods. Whoever he was walked across the floor, breathing heavily as if he'd been running.

Kella held her breath, staring at those boots. They were of too good quality for a servant. This was Bard Leet himself. Would he notice the cloth over the harp had been moved? Would he notice the ewer? Would he find *her*?

The boots crossed to the bed and turned. The bed ropes above Kella creaked as the mattress pushed down against them. She pressed herself against the floor. One foot disappeared from sight. She heard a soft grunt.

Kella stared in horror at the stockinged foot that reappeared within her range of vision. What was the bard doing?

"Gods—I haven't run that far in ages. Whew!"

She listened to him catch his breath. Then a horrible thought flashed into her mind. *Oh gods—what if he lies down for a nap?*

She nearly yelped from sheer nerves when a tiny pebble hit the floor and *tik-tik-tikked* across the tiles to rest bare inches from her nose. Kella pressed her hand over her mouth.

"Ah, that's better."

She remembered to breathe. *It was just a stone in his boot,* she thought. But her relief was short-lived.

The bed ropes creaked again as Leet lay across the bed. "Trying to get out again?" the bard asked. He sounded amused.

Kella was too stunned to answer right away. *How did he know? Did someone see me after all? Or did he see the ewer and towel?*

Then the bard plucked the lowest string of the harp. It sang, though muffled by the heavy silk.

That was cruel! He doesn't have to mock—

Had her hand not been over her mouth, Kella would have cried out as one all-important detail suddenly dawned on her: She could still see one of the bard's feet on the floor in front of her. Even lying across the bed, Bard Leet couldn't have plucked that string, not unless he'd wriggled all the way across the wide bed first—the harp was too far away on the other side. She doubted if even Linden could reach it, and he was the tallest person she knew. Yet Leet still had that one foot on *this* side of the bed. That meant . . .

That meant the harp had played by itself.

No, it can't be. That's impossible!

More strings joined, the lowest chord it could play. And now she heard a word in those notes: *Blood.*

BloodbloodbloodbloodBLOOOOOOD, the harp sang over and over.

Kella hoped she'd never hear anything like it again; it made her feel as if something cold and slimy and with far too many legs squirmed down her back. She closed her eyes, wondering if she'd gone mad, trying not to cry in sheer terror. Better to think about how much her cheek and forehead hurt. That was ordinary—and safe.

Yet if she had gone mad, so, it seemed, had Leet. For the bard chuckled and said, "No, no blood for you today, friend Gull."

Gull? Who's Gull? Then Kella remembered the mark burned into the harp.

Leet went on, "There are no fawns or rabbits or squirrels to charm in here."

The chord warped into angry dissonance.

The bard laughed softly, a sound that chilled Kella to the bone. "Well-a-well, perhaps someday we'll get that bastard alone, so don't lose hope. But today you shall remain here. It's safer—there are too many people wandering the gardens today. When I think back on how that child nearly . . ."

The strings thrummed so violently Kella thought they would snap. Above her, the ropes creaked again as Leet sat upright once more.

Kella lay sick and shaking, her eyes squeezed shut, hardly aware when Leet put his boot back on and got up, or when he walked around the bed to the harp on the table. When he spoke, his words barely penetrated the miasma of fear and shock that gripped her.

"You really must stop disarranging your cover, friend Gull," the bard said as if he spoke to another person—or the harp could understand him. "After all—it's not as if you could go anywhere by yourself, now is it?"

Dimly she heard the rustle of silk, and an eerie few chords that nearly made her scream; she knew those chords only too well. They were part of the diabolical tune with which the harp had almost trapped her.

But Leet only laughed again. "No, I haven't changed my mind. I want this music case and your sister, not you."

Next she heard him go to one of the chests at the foot of the bed, heard it open. Next came a rustling sound, followed by the lid slamming shut once more.

She listened to his boot heels cross the floor to the door, listened as the door swung shut once more.

Get up, get up, get up and get out of here, her mind whimpered desperately.

But she was as afraid to move as she was to stay. What if, when she crawled out from under the bed, she saw the harp moving under its cover? From what Bard Leet had said, it could! What if—may the gods forbid it—it played by itself once more, and called her?

What if she went to it?

Tears welled from beneath her eyelids. She had to leave, and leave *now.* Weeping, she scrabbled forward, determined to at least keep the width of the bed between her and the hellish thing on the table.

She burst from under the bed. Keeping her gaze upon the tiles before her, she half crawled, half stumbled as fast as she could to the door. Behind her she heard the first chords of the demon song, soft and mocking. Only instinct made her snatch up the ewer and towel before opening the door and running out into the hall.

The scented water, cool now, sloshed over her hands as she ran. She didn't care; all she wanted was to get as far away from that harp as she could.

Tears streaming down her face, she ran through the castle as if a nightmare chased her. And, still hearing the harp's song in her mind, she wondered if it was no more than the truth. What had just happened was so awful she wanted it to be a dream. The only thought in her mind was to reach her own room and hide there.

People called after her as she raced headlong down the halls. Some sounded concerned, others furious at the way she pushed by. She ignored them all, lord, lady, or servant. If she stopped, *it* would get her.

At last she reached the shelter of her little chamber. Kella burst into the room and, casting aside the ewer, threw herself onto her bed and burrowed headfirst beneath the blanket.

Despite the stifling heat, she lay shivering, the horrible tune still running through her mind as if it would never let her go. It didn't release her until she cried herself into an exhausted sleep.

By the time Bard Leet came back around the rose hedge, Bramble was snoring gently in the sun, and the patch of lawn around Rann was well on its way to looking as if a starving gopher had fallen upon it. When Rann saw the harp in the bard's arms, he felt sick to his stomach. Had Kella—? He was afraid to even complete the thought.

But . . . the bard was smiling. It was a moment before that realization penetrated the panic shrouding Rann's mind. The young prince heaved a huge sigh of relief.

If he'd caught Kella, he wouldn't look so happy. He'd still be furious. Hurrah!

She must have gotten away! he thought, nearly bouncing with delight. He could feel Shima Ilyathan's concerned—and suspicious—gaze on him, but kept his own on the Master Bard.

"I brought my own harp," Bard Leet announced, "because it has a larger range than yours, Your Highness." To Shima he explained, "It makes it easier to work out the accompaniment, Dragonlord."

Shima Ilyathan nodded. "I see."

It sounded as if he did, too; Rann wondered glumly if he was the only person in the world who couldn't understand music. Scales and modes and inversions and major and minor keys and chords and the gods only knew what else. The most frustrating part was that the wretched chords wouldn't stay decently in one shape, but turned themselves inside out on top of everything else—and not once, but twice! No wonder they kept falling out of his head. And Kella understood everything so easily. . . .

Rann sighed at the unfairness of it all. She'd better have a good tale to tell him when this was all over.

Bard Leet sat on the grass and arranged some parchment scores from his music case before him, then settled his traveling harp in his lap. "If you would kindly begin again, Your Grace."

Worn out with worrying, Rann lay on the grass alongside Bramble as Shima Ilyathan sang that song and others for Leet's benefit. He wanted nothing more than to run off and find Kella, but thought it best to stay and listen as if he had nothing better to do. Shima Ilyathan was already watching him too closely.

So Rann pillowed his head on the wolfhound's sturdy flank and watched the bard's clever fingers move along the strings, echoing Shima Ilyathan's song.

I wonder why he had the luthier put a seagull on the harp—they don't have pretty voices was the last thought to drift across his mind before he fell asleep in the warm sun.

Thirty

Leet wandered through the gardens, harp case on his back, the small oil lamp in his hand lighting the way. He hadn't meant to come out this evening, but he'd been driven to it. When he'd touched the harp's strings back in his room, he'd nearly recoiled at the intense feelings that had come through: hunger, anger, and . . . cheated?

The last made no sense, but the ravening hunger drove all speculation from his mind. Leet packed the harp and took himself outside. He thought of going to the place he'd found, but then considered it would be best to save that against some great need; it would be best not to wear a path to it.

So he found an isolated spot and stood, listening carefully. Not that it was likely anyone would be out at this candlemark but one never knew with couples in the first throes of a dalliance.

The only sounds that greeted him were those of crickets and other night singers, and frogs from some nearby pool. Leet nodded in satisfaction. This would do.

He settled himself on the ground and made himself ready. Then, harp nestled in his arms, lamp and well-honed knife by his side, Leet began to play.

Soon a rabbit peered at him from a stand of lilies. Leet smiled as, transfixed, it emerged from its shelter and lolloped slowly across the lawn, pausing now and again to study him.

Switching the melody to his left hand, Leet slowly took up the knife. "Come along, come along," he sang softly.

The rabbit obeyed.

Coryn looked over his shoulder. No, no one from Lord Sevrynel's was following him. He heaved a sigh of relief and shook his head. He *still* couldn't believe that Arisyn hadn't told their foster father that Tirael was here in Balyaranna. But, wonder of wonders, the little prig hadn't, thank all the gods.

He slipped inside Garron's tavern tent, wondering if Tirael would be here this early. Coryn hoped so; he didn't have time to go searching. He was on duty today and had to get back before the banquet started. Though if he couldn't find Tirael, he wouldn't have to tell him. . . .

But there sat Tirael in the midst of an admiring group of young nobles, many—like Tirael himself—heirs to rich holdings. Though proud to count himself among such company—for his parents had but one manor—Coryn reluctantly made his way to Tirael's side.

Once there, he laid a hand upon his hero's shoulder. Before Tirael could curse him for interrupting his story, Coryn quickly whispered a single word into his ear. "Merrilee."

Tirael stood up and followed him to the back of the tent. They stepped over the snoring drunks Garron's men had dragged here to sleep off their wine and ale.

"What news?" Tirael demanded. "Did she read my note?"

"She did," Coryn said slowly. He dug a folded sheet of parchment from his belt pouch. "Then she gave it back to me."

Tirael snatched the note from Coryn's fingers and examined it. He frowned. "She didn't write anything. Wasn't there a reply?"

Coryn desperately hoped that Tirael was not inclined to blame the messenger for bearing bad news—and worse news. "She asked me to tell you to . . . to stop."

" 'Stop'?" Tirael asked, incredulous. "What the hell do you mean?"

"Writing to her. Asking her to meet you, to run away with you, all that sort of thing."

Tirael gawped at him. "That's impossible."

Coryn squirmed. That was the bad news; now came the worse. "Tir—Eadain's courting her." He didn't have the nerve to add, "And I think she's listening." Not with that look on Tirael's face. Instead he mumbled, "I have to get back before they miss me," and fled.

It took a bit of doing, but Merrilee finally managed to elude her admirers long enough to escape to the terrace. Fond as she was of him, she wished Lord Sevrynel didn't have a banquet or other gathering every night! They lived quietly at home; life here was nigh overwhelming—at least during the fair. She supposed it was different the rest of the time.

She sat on a stone bench and fanned herself with a hand. While the summer night was warm, it was still cooler than the great hall, and the air much fresher. She inhaled deeply as a stray breeze brought her the rich scent of roses from the night-shrouded gardens. She closed her eyes and smiled, savoring it, and blessed whichever ancestors of Lord Sevrynel's had been at least as interested in roses as they had been in horses.

"So you still sneak out for a bit of air after banquets? Good," a voice whispered out of the darkness.

Merrilee jumped up and spun around, so frightened she could barely breathe. Her heart pounded; she knew that voice. She stared out into the darkness but could see nothing beyond the light of the torches that marked the stairs.

It went on, "You've been avoiding me, Merri, and I don't like that."

She fell back, one step at a time, as a man came slowly up the wide, shallow stairs that led to the gardens and into the torchlight. Tirael stopped at the top and frowned.

"I've sent you notes telling you where to meet me and you haven't come," he said, his voice low and angry now. "Why not? And what the hell do you mean, sending word by Coryn that I'm to stop?" He advanced upon her again, step by slow, menacing step, like a wolf stalking its prey.

She managed to say, "It's over, Tir. Though did it ever truly begin? You aren't the man you led me to believe you were. That man I could have—"

"Over? What do you mean, 'over'? It's not over unless *I* say it is," he snarled. "And it's not."

He began cursing her. She stood frozen, too shocked to speak, too stunned to move as with every hateful word Tirael destroyed the last hope she'd held in her heart. He hadn't even heard that *he* might be the one at fault; he'd heard only what was important to him. Her father had been right.

The cursing stopped. "You're coming with me or—"

She didn't know if he laid his hand on his belt knife deliberately or by chance. But the sight was enough to break her paralysis. She screamed and turned to run. Her foot caught in her long skirts and she fell. She twisted around to face him, terrified, as he loomed over her.

The door to the terrace opened. "Lady Merrilee? What's wrong?" Shima Ilyathan called as he ran outside.

But when Merrilee looked back, Tirael was already gone. She realized that he must have fled at the first glimpse of light escaping through the opening door. She didn't know whether to be sorry he'd escaped—Merrilee was certain he would have had no chance in a fight against the newest Dragonlord—or relieved that Tirael was gone.

Shima Ilyathan knelt by her, his brow wrinkled in concern. "Lady Merrilee, what happened?" he asked as he helped her up. "Karelinn asked me to find you out here, then I heard you scream."

She shook out her skirts and tried to collect herself, not sure of what to do. A small, traitorous part of her still cared about Tirael—or at least the Tirael she'd thought she knew. For the sake of *that* Tirael, she would tell no tales this one time.

"It was a bat," she said with a laugh. It sounded brittle even to her own ears.

"Just a bat. It swooped by my head and frightened me. And silly goose that I am, I screamed and tripped over my own skirts trying to run away."

She laid a hand on his arm and smiled. "Please don't tell my sister or father. I feel like such a fool to be both so clumsy and so easily frightened."

For a long moment she thought he would refuse. Then he nodded. "Very well, my lady," he said slowly. "Very well."

Shima Ilyathan escorted her inside. To her surprise, Lord Eadain was waiting just beyond the door. He leaned heavily on his crutches. The Dragonlord came to a stop before the crippled young lord.

"I must return to Karelinn and tell her that her sister is well," Shima Ilyathan said to Eadain. "Will you see to Lady Merrilee?" He smiled.

"Gladly," Eadain replied with an answering smile. "If she'll have me." He turned to look at her.

The kindness and . . . yes, love . . . in that gaze steadied her. "Of course," she said softly.

The Dragonlord bowed to both of them and slipped into the crowd. Wordlessly, Eadain made his way to one of the shadowed nooks that edged the large dance floor. They stood together, watching the dancers move in a stately pavane across the floor. She marveled at how safe being with him made her feel. She remembered her first sight of him, how gently he'd cradled the wet, miserable kitten he'd found in the rainstorm.

And would Tirael have held Soot so carefully? Would he even have stopped for a kitten?

She was certain she knew the answer, now. It saddened her.

As if he'd heard her thinking about the kitten, Eadain turned to her and asked, "How is Soot faring these days, my lady?"

"Very well indeed, my lord. He's made a slave of my maids. They'd roll balls of yarn across the floor for him by the candlemark if they could." She glanced at him.

He smiled at that. It always surprised her how young he looked when he smiled, how it lit up his warm brown eyes.

"And you, my lady? Are you well?" he asked, his voice gentle.

For a moment, she was silent. Then, looking steadily into that warm gaze, she smiled and said, "Yes, Eadain. I am well, and safe . . . now."

He held out his hand; it trembled slightly. She laid hers in his without hesitation. Together they turned to watch the dancers once more, their fingers intertwined.

Thirty-one

Fiarin pushed them hard, barely allowing them time to eat or rest until one day, as the sun was sinking, the woods ended abruptly. Before them lay two lakes, separated from each other by a brush-covered esker that snaked between them. They had emerged from the woods before the right-hand lake. The water looked dark and mysterious.

As if the sight of the lakes and the esker were some sort of signal, Fiarin stopped. He stood staring at them as if searching for some sign or omen. He stood for so long that the light faded from the sky. Behind him Pod and Kaeliss, not knowing what Fiarin's strange behavior portended but thankful for the respite, sank down to the ground and rested. Behind them they heard the last birds sleepily calling each other to bed.

Pod slapped at a mosquito that had landed on her arm. The noise cut sharply through the growing silence. All at once Fiarin shook himself like a man waking from a deep sleep. He turned to them.

"We'll make camp in the woods. Tomorrow . . ." He turned his back on the lakes and went back up the faint path they had made.

The two young women exchanged worried looks as they followed him back into the forest. What was all this about? And what were they to do tomorrow?

Pod shook her head. At least they didn't have to go far to get water, she thought gloomily. Leaving Kaeliss to break dried meat into the little pot, she set off to fetch water for their stew. On her way back to the lake she spotted some wild leeks and paused to dig up the bulbs to add to the pot. She was so tired she kept yawning as she washed them.

Hope I can stay awake long enough to eat.

She managed it—but barely. As soon as she could, Pod unrolled her blankets and settled down by the fire. Kaeliss did the same.

But Fiarin kept walking down to the edge of the lake and staring across it.

Then he'd walk back to sit and stare into the fire, muttering all the while to himself; it sounded oddly like an argument.

During one of his absences Pod asked softly, "What in the name of all the gods is the matter with him? And is this the usual way of a training journey?"

"I've no idea what's wrong with Fiarin," Kaeliss whispered back. "And I don't *think* this is how it's supposed to be. I talked to some of the older apprentices before I left. They said it was 'Look at this, learn that, what's this and what does it do' all day long, every day. Some teachers will even wake you up in the middle of the night and demand all the different names for hedgemaid before you're really awake. And I'd heard that Fiarin, for all that he was generous with his knowledge, was one of the worst for that sort of thing!"

Pod considered the other girl's words. Something was very, very wrong. At last she said, "Do you think he's gone mad?"

Kaeliss shivered despite the heat. "I don't know. All I know is that he's frightening me. He's never been like this before—not that I know him well, he's usually off on a trek, but . . . If he *is* mad, what can we do?"

"I don't know. Do you know where we are?"

"I've no idea. Remember, I'm from Pelnar. I haven't been here long enough to really learn all the towns and villages and what-have-you in Kelneth. What about you?"

"The same, save that I'm from the south of Yerrih, near the Kelnethi border. This is the first real journey I've ever taken. I haven't left Grey Holt—not really—since I was brought there."

They sat, gloomily staring into the dying fire. Then Kaeliss said, "Wait—I do remember someone talking about a village. Someone said we might stop there when the treks were done."

Hope blossomed in Pod's heart. "Oh?" She waited, hardly daring to breathe.

A long silence, then Kaeliss screwed up her face in disgust. "But can I remember the name? No—just that it's Little Something-or-other. And more importantly, I can't remember where it is. There was something about it, though. Some of the 'prentices didn't want to go there, but I didn't pay much attention."

Pod bit her tongue so that she wouldn't snap Kaeliss's head off. Why get her hopes up only to squash them the next moment? Yet it was no use taking it out on Kaeliss; the other girl was just as uneasy as she. Nor would giving way to her nerves help them. Still, all she wanted to do was dash off into the woods—anything to get away from Fiarin and his burning eyes.

Suddenly Kaeliss cocked her head to one side and held up a hand. "Shhh! He's coming back!"

An instant later they were wrapped up in their blankets, feigning sleep as Fiarin stalked into the camp.

For a long time he stared into the embers, then finally unrolled his blankets. Pod, watching through slitted eyes, thought he was going to sleep at last.

Thank the gods! All this coming and going was making Kiga restless—so of course I can't get to sleep either. And maybe when he wakes this fit will have passed.

But Fiarin stood up once more and walked down to the water. Ready to scream in exasperation, Pod squinched her eyes shut and told herself she didn't care what Fiarin did anymore, she wasn't going to pay attention, he could go soak his head for all it mattered to her.

But tomorrow . . . If this madness didn't cease by the morning, she'd, she'd . . . Pod wasn't certain *what* she'd do—after all, Fiarin was a master and apprentices obeyed masters without question. True, Fiarin wasn't a master in *her* guild, but she knew that for this training, she was supposed to accord him the same respect and obedience she'd give any master of the Beast Healers.

Still—*something* had to be done.

She was drifting off when he came back. As if from a great distance, she heard him get into his blankets; then, so softly that she wasn't certain her ears weren't playing her tricks, he whispered, "We can't lose Master Emberlin, nor will you best me, Currin."

What an odd thing to say, she thought dreamily. *How very, very . . .* Before she could finish the thought, Pod fell asleep.

Thirty-two

Therinn Barans, Lord Lenslee of Lenslee, put his hands in the small of his back and stretched. He took a deep breath of the cool early morning air.

"Ah, that feels good!" he said contentedly. "And even better to be *here*. It was good to reach your manor, coz, but it's best to be here at the fair proper at last. I've been *waiting* for this."

He stood with his kinsman, Ridler Barans, Lord Portis, as they watched his prize stallion, Summer Lightning, trot majestically around his paddock. The sun shone on the burnished copper of his coat.

"Mm" was all Ridler answered.

Therinn turned and studied his kinsman. A frown wrinkled the other man's forehead and he looked distracted. Nor would Ridler meet Therinn's eyes, keeping his gaze instead on the horse.

"What is it? You've had something on your mind ever since Lord Dunly left, old fellow. Out with it," Therinn said.

He was glad Dunly hadn't insisted on dragging him off for that "little meeting" as well. Dunly was a bore. Still, ever since the old meddler had pounced upon Ridler almost as soon as they'd ridden in to the fair, something had been preying upon his kinsman's mind. "Out with it," he repeated.

For a long moment he thought the older man would refuse to answer. *Oh gods—don't tell me Tirael's gotten himself into trouble yet again. It's a wonder Ridler isn't greyer than he is.* He resisted the urge to shake his head in disgust at the thought of his younger kinsman. The gods knew that Tirael had caused enough trouble for *him* once upon a time. . . .

"You've heard the rumor going about?" Ridler said abruptly.

"Eh? Rumor? What rumor?" *Whatever they're saying about Tirael, it's most likely true—if it isn't even worse,* he thought cynically as he watched Summer Lightning once more. *Gods, he is so beautiful. And he'll pay off that debt that Tirael—*

Ridler cleared his throat. He still wouldn't look at Therinn. "About—about a Llysanyin at the fair."

Hmm—that was an odd way of putting it. Ordinarily one would say "a Drag-onlord at the fair." Any listener would then assume that there was a good chance of a Llysanyin as well. Still, it was no rumor about Dragonlords; there were some here. Ridler had met one of them, Linden Rathan, at Sevrynel's.

He said as much to his cousin, adding, "I'd heard they rode in. So that means Llysanyins, yes?"

Another long silence; then, "Ye-e-ss. The three youngest Dragonlords are here and their Llysanyins with them. But that's not what I meant. I meant a Llysanyin . . . with a truehuman rider."

That made no sense. "That's impossible! No Llysanyin would—"

" 'Dragon and Phoenix.' " The words were barely more than a whisper. Ridler cleared this throat again. "You've heard the song, haven't you?"

Therinn nodded slowly. He'd heard it, yes, though he was not certain of all the details. He did seem to remember something about Llysanyins and truehumans. But surely that part of it was simply bardic embellishment. . . .

"It's said that the rider—a fellow named Raven Redhawkson—is the partner of one of the Yerrin horse breeders."

"*What?* Which one?" Therinn snapped.

"Yarrow Whitethorndaughter."

Therinn went cold at the name. Not only was that peasant Whitethorndaugh-ter a breeder of some renown, but she was also the bitch who'd gotten the best of Sansy's broodmares before he'd even heard that Sansy was breaking up the herd. By the time he'd gotten wind of it, only the dregs were left; he hadn't bothered with them. Not that it was likely Sansy would have sold him anything—let alone the best mares—after what happened to Sansy's nephew. . . .

But that Yerrin bitch with those mares and a Llysanyin stallion? "Wait—mare or stallion?"

"Stallion," Ridler said with a sigh.

Therinn cursed loud and long. He spun away from the fence, nearly trip-ping over a boy who bore a yoke and a pair of water buckets was passing behind him. "Get out of my way, brat!" he snapped, and aimed a slap at the boy.

The lad squeaked in surprise, ducked, and scurried off, sloshing water every-where.

"Robie!" Ridler called after him. "Get a broom and sweep the water off these cobblestones *now*!"

Still cursing, Therinn strode off to the house. He had to think about this. Be-sides, he had people coming to meet him, seeking his permission to breed their mares to Summer Lightning, ready to pay him gold for the privilege. Gold that he *needed,* damn it all.

"Ridler, tell me everything you know. Is it *certain* that the horse is really a Llysanyin? Could it be a cheat?"

Relief flooded him. That was it: It was a cheat. It had to be.

Maurynna rode hard for the castle. The guards must have been watching for her; the gates swung open as Boreal thundered up to them.

An instant later his hooves struck sparks from the cobbles as he clattered to a halt. Maurynna swung down from the saddle even before he stopped. She saw Duchess Beryl waiting for her.

Beryl rushed up to her, wringing her hands. "Thank the gods you could come so quickly, Maurynna Kyrissaean! Please—this way!"

The little duchess bustled ahead of Maurynna, who followed, worry making a cold ball of ice in the pit of her stomach.

"My lady, what's wrong with my cousin? Has Healer Tasha seen her yet?"

Beryl looked over her shoulder. "Healer Tasha stayed in Casna, Dragonlord. Duchess Alinya caught the lung sickness this past winter and has been doing poorly ever since, so we all deemed it best that Tasha stay with her. Since Rann's doing so well these days—quite a normal little boy—we thought little of it. Perhaps you remember Quirel? He's Tasha's apprentice."

"Yes—he's the Simpler, isn't he?"

"Just so. Tasha sent him with us so that we would not be quite unprepared. He's been to see Kella and cannot for the life of him figure out what's ailing her," the duchess said over her shoulder.

"Hold for a moment," Maurynna said, laying a hand on the duchess's shoulder. "Please, tell me what you know. The message said she wasn't ill or injured, but didn't say what was amiss. Did something happen? What brought this on?"

Beryl stopped in the middle of the hall. She waved everyone away from them and looked up at Maurynna. "We don't know," she said. "We just don't know.

"I apologize that you were not told sooner about this, Maurynna Kyrissaean, but truly, Beren and I only found out this morning ourselves! There's so much coming and going because of the fair. . . ."

She drew herself up. "It would seem that something happened yesterday that upset Kella greatly. She won't tell us what. She won't even tell Rann what it is— and they tell each other everything.

"This is what little we've been able to discover: Sometime yesterday afternoon, Rann and Kella went their separate ways. Rann asked Bard Leet to go with him to get a song from Shima Ilyathan, something he'd heard him sing."

Maurynna nodded. He'd been humming their first morning at the castle and Kella had asked what it was. "I remember. It was a lullaby he sang for all of us— Kella thought it was pretty."

"So did Rann. He wants to learn it to play for Alinya, bless the boy, though the poor song will never be the same. Anyway, we found him in the garden asleep, with Shima Ilyathan and Bard Leet talking about the songs of His Grace's land. There was a feast that required Rann's presence, so his governess and I quickly hustled him off to get ready."

The duchess sighed heavily. "I'm ashamed to say that none of us thought about Kella, Dragonlord. We all assumed that she would do what she usually does when Rann attends a court function: borrow Rann's harp and practice in her room. I don't know if you know this, Dragonlord, but Bard Daera—who teaches the children—says that Kella has real talent and should be tested at the Bards' School in Bylith."

"Her sister Maylin wrote and told me that." *Oh, Maylin—why aren't you here? You'd get to the bottom of this in no time!* Without thinking, she started walking again.

Beryl hastened to her side and went on, "One of the servants brought Kella's supper to her last night." Her mouth was set in a grim line that did not bode well for someone. "He didn't think it worth mentioning to anyone that she was abed when he brought it in. We didn't find out until this morning when the maid who brought her breakfast found her shivering under her blankets. *She,* thank the gods, had the sense to run for Quirel and Rann's governess, Lady Ralene. Ralene sent for me. And I sent for you."

They reached Kella's room just as Quirel came out, quietly shutting the door behind him. He saw them and bowed.

"What's wrong with my cousin?" Maurynna asked bluntly. "Is she ill?"

"No, my lady—at least with no illness I've ever seen or studied. Nor is there any injury to her aside from a bruise on her cheek as if she fell." He frowned. "If I didn't know better, I'd say she'd had some violent shock. Yet nothing untoward has happened that anyone has heard of. I must own myself baffled, Dragonlord. I wish Healer Tasha were here. She might make some sense of all this."

Maurynna considered his words, then said, "Is she well enough to see me?"

"I would say so. It might do her some good."

Maurynna went into Kella's room, leaving Beryl and Quirel to quietly continue the discussion. Just before she shut the door behind her, she heard Quirel ask, "Is there any way she could be sent back to Casna? I would feel better if Tasha could see her."

And she would be back with her family, thought Maurynna. It was something to consider.

One of Duchess Beryl's ladies sat by Kella's bed, knitting a new heel into a stocking. At Maurynna's gesture, she carefully tucked her knitting into a small basket, whispering, "I hope you're well soon, Kella." She made a courtesy to Maurynna and slipped out of the room.

"Sweetling," Maurynna said softly. "Kella—are you awake?"

A small head appeared from beneath the embroidered linen sheet. Maurynna flinched as she got a good look at her little cousin.

Dark circles under eyes heavy with exhaustion, skin pale and ashen; whatever was wrong, it had taken a toll on the child. Even her hair hung lank and lifeless about her face.

Struggling to hide her fear, Maurynna asked, "Kella, what on earth is the matter? Are you ill?"

A small shake of the head was her only answer.

"Did you hurt yourself?"

Another shake of the head.

"Then how did you get that bruise on your cheek?"

Once again, Kella shook her head.

"Did someone else hurt you?"

A moment of hesitation; Maurynna thought she had her answer and was silently vowing to hunt down whoever had harmed her youngest cousin when Kella whispered, "No. No one hurt me."

Maurynna sat down on the bed and took Kella's hand. "Beryl told me you haven't eaten. Would you like—"

"No."

Indeed, Kella looked as if the mere thought of food would make her vomit.

"Can you tell me what's wrong, sweetheart?"

Kella's shoulders shook and, if possible, she paled even more. "No."

Though her fear urged Maurynna to grab Kella by the shoulders and demand an answer, she made herself say calmly, "Do you want to see Rann? I'm sure he's worried about you. We all are."

Kella went very still. "Yes," she said slowly. "I would like to see Rann, please."

The prince was summoned. When he arrived, Maurynna led him in. Kella sat bolt upright.

"Just Rann," she said. "Only Rann."

Maurynna opened her mouth to protest, but stopped when she saw the feverish light in Kella's eyes. Whatever this was about, the last thing Kella needed was to spend what little strength she had in tearful argument. It was one of the hardest things she'd ever done, but Maurynna made herself leave. She would ask Rann about it when he came out.

Which turned out to be a remarkably short time later. He looked shaken; clearly the change in his friend had frightened him. He also looked puzzled.

Beryl pounced upon him. "Did Kella tell you what was wrong?"

"No, Aunt Beryl. She didn't."

Is that because you already know? I wonder. She dismissed the thought. Rann wouldn't look so puzzled if he knew—he'd look guilty. Maylin had once told her he couldn't hide anything from his aunt. She'd said the boy was utterly convinced his aunt could sniff out any wrongdoing of his from the other side of the castle.

"Very useful, that," Maylin had said, laughing. "Of course she can't, but as long as he *thinks* she can, anytime he's done something wrong, she finds him out in an instant because he looks guilty as sin."

But Rann didn't look guilty. He just looked as baffled as the rest of them felt.

Then the young prince turned to her. "She did say, Maurynna Kyrissaean, that she wanted to go home. Now."

The duchess frowned. "There's no one returning to Casna that we could send her with. I suppose I could ask Beren—"

"No need," Maurynna said, thinking quickly. "I can take her. I'll need some blankets—and tokens for the royal messengers so that Maylin can send me letters."

While she waited for the things she'd requested, she mindcalled Linden.

What in the name of the gods is going on? he asked worriedly. *I remember you getting up early and telling me to go back to sleep. The next thing I know is that something's amiss with Kella and that you'd gone to the castle. But no one can tell me anything, for they've no idea themselves. I didn't mindcall you, because I didn't want to risk interrupting something important. Maurynna-love, is the Kitten ill?*

Not that Quirel can discover. But he doesn't know what is *wrong with her. He was wishing that Tasha could see Kella. He's about to get that wish—Kella wants to go back to Casna. Now. I'm going to fly her home.*

With that, Maurynna broke the mindlink. She went back into Kella's room. "Kella, if you really want to go home, I can take you. But are you certain you really want to go?"

"Yes! Yes, yes, YES!"

"Look! Look up! Look up!"

Raven heard the cry and like Yarrow, and Lord Ashton, who'd come to look at the horses, and everyone else in the camp, looked up into the blue, cloudless sky. To his surprise, a dragon flew overhead. Its scales glittered peacock blue-and-green in the sunlight. It also seemed to be carrying something cradled in its front legs.

It took a moment for it to sink in, then he sputtered, "That's Maurynna! But where's she going?" *Not to Dragonskeep—she's flying south. And what's that in her arms? I could almost swear it looked like a person all bundled up—a child, even.*

Lord Ashton hissed in anger. "Young man—that's 'Maurynna Kyrissaean' to you! That or 'Dragonlord'!"

Raven turned to him. "My lord, I grew up with Maurynna Kyrissaean in Thalnia. We were best friends. We are *still* friends."

He spoke more sharply than he'd meant to; but he'd seen Maurynna in dragon form enough times now to read the tenseness in every line of her body. "My apologies, my lord, for speaking so sharply. But something's amiss—I just know it. I think that was a person she was carrying."

He shaded his eyes and looked after her as she rapidly dwindled from sight. "She's flying hard," he muttered to himself. "What's to the south?" *And if that was a child, who . . .*

Casna. Casna was to the south. A sharp whistle called Stormwind to him. He leapt up onto the broad, bare back. "Aunt Yarrow, would you mind if I go find Linden or Shima and ask them what's wrong? I think that was a person she was carrying and I've a bad feeling I might know him or her." He added the Yerrin word for "child" and hoped Lord Ashton wouldn't understand it.

If he was right, it was one of two children: Kella or Prince Rann. If it was the prince and he was taken ill, it might well cause a panic and break up the fair early—at the least. Yarrow would need to know. If it was Kella . . . damn, there was nothing he could do but find a temple of the Mother in Balyaranna town and leave some coins for prayers for the little girl.

"Go then," Yarrow said. "Set your mind at ease."

He rode off. But he could find neither Dragonlord, though he searched until late in the day. Discouraged, he rode into Balyaranna proper and finally found his way to the temple of the Mother.

Whoever it was, this was the least—and all—he could do.

Thirty-three

Lord Lenslee pushed aside the door flap of the tavern tent and looked around in distaste. The noise was deafening, a raucous mix of babbling voices, bawdy songs, and curses, all spiced with squeals and giggles. Worse yet, the air was thick with heat and the stale smells of sweat and sour ale and roasted meat.

It was, in Therinn's opinion, a sty. Why in the name of all the gods Garron's was the current favorite of the younger nobles, he could not fathom. Well and well, it didn't matter; he wasn't here for pleasure. Where was—?

Therinn sighed. He should have known he'd find Tirael with a girl. This one, though, didn't seem to be falling under his handsome cousin's spell. Indeed, she was trying to push him away, her eyes flashing angrily. The Kelnethi lord pursed his lips in sardonic amusement; how refreshing.

Therinn elbowed his way through the crowd and tapped Tirael on the shoulder. "A word with you, cousin."

Tirael kept one arm around the serving girl's waist as he turned to see who wanted him. "What is it?" he said sullenly. "Can't you see I'm busy?"

"Not as busy as you're going to be," Therinn said too sweetly.

Taking advantage of her captor's distraction, the girl stamped on Tirael's foot. He stumbled back, letting go of her in his surprise. She eeled off into the crowd that hooted with laughter at her erstwhile tormentor's discomfort.

Good for her, Therinn thought. He grabbed Tirael's arm before the other man could go after her. "Let her go. I've something important to discuss with you. Outside, where the air's fit to breathe." When his cousin balked, Therinn growled, *"Now."*

His face flushed with wine and pouting like a child, Tirael obeyed with no good grace. Therinn shook his head as he pushed back through the crowd. His parents had much to answer for in their raising of this spoiled puppy. How Tirael managed to charm almost everyone else was beyond him.

A pity his old tutor's eyes began to fail and he entered the temple of Rhoslin as one of their scholars. Luyens was the only person who could influence Tir for the better.

When they were finally outside, Therinn took a deep breath of the night air, grateful for its fresh sweetness, dusty as it was. He took the torch from the groom's hand and pulled Tirael well away from both tent and retainers.

"Are you sober enough to be worth talking to?" Therinn snapped.

"I'm not near as drunk as you think or as I want to be," Tirael retorted, wincing in the torchlight. He glared at his cousin. "What the hell do you want?"

"Keep a civil tongue in your head, or have you forgotten all you owe me, dear cousin?" Therinn said in a voice edged with steel.

Tirael dropped his gaze, mumbling something that Therinn didn't give a fig for. He had more important things to worry about.

"Have you seen a Yerrin here, a man with reddish blond hair, young? He rides a big stallion, black with a grey mane and tail," he said.

Tirael grimaced. "Him? Arisyn Darnhollis's pet Yerrin? Yes, I've seen him, the insolent dog. Needs a good whipping to teach him his place, he does. He'll get it soon enough." Tirael smirked. He went on, "What the hell's important about him?"

"He's not important. The horse may be," Therinn said tensely.

His cousin rubbed at his ears as if not trusting what they'd just told him. "The horse?" Tirael said in astonishment. "That bloody plow horse, important? It's naught but a Shamreen draft horse."

"According to the gossip running through the fair," Therinn grated, "that bloody plow horse may well be a Llysanyin." He couldn't be certain in the torch's flickering light, but he thought the other's face went pale.

Tirael's mouth opened and closed once, twice, thrice, but no words came out, just a strangled sound. Then, at last, "No, it can't be," he said, looking wildly around. "It *can't* be. He's no—he's just a commoner!"

There was a note of—panic?—in Tirael's voice that Therinn didn't understand; he knew why *he* feared that the horse was one of the fabled mounts of the Dragonlords, but why that should frighten Tirael . . .

No matter. Whatever bothered Tirael was of minor importance compared to what this would mean to him if it were true.

"It had better not be possible. Now tell me what you know about this fellow. Lord Dunly said that he's with a Yerrin horse breeder—Yarrow Whitethorndaughter. Is that true or have Dunly's brains turned to porridge at last? And what's *his* name?"

Not that he remembered that damned song that well, but perhaps if he heard the name it would jog his memory. . . . He grabbed Tirael's upper arm and was startled to find his cousin was trembling despite the heat.

Tirael jerked away. He rubbed his arm, his breath coming hard and fast. "*I* should bother remembering what some damned peasant's name is? Why do you care, anyway? You don't believe those lies, do you?"

"I don't believe or disbelieve. I don't know enough yet. But I *do* know that if enough people believe him, there's trouble ahead."

Tirael sneered. "You're afraid of a peasant?"

"Of a peasant, no. Of a peasant with a Llysanyin stallion who is also allied with a respected horse breeder—I'm terrified. As you should be."

"I don't believe what I'm hearing! You're afraid of a mere pe—"

Therinn cuffed his cousin sharply on the ear. "Need I explain it in words a child of three would understand, you horse's ass? It seems I must, so think upon these two: stud fees."

"Who'd want a plow—"

Therinn snarled in frustration. "And if it *is* a Llysanyin, who'd want to pay stud fees for anything less? By the Mother's left tit, Tirael, is there anything in that pretty head of yours?

"Until now, I've had every lord and lady who fancied themselves a breeder of racehorses throwing themselves at my feet, shoving their gold at me, begging me to accept their mares for Summer Lightning. I could pick and choose, name my own price, make whatever conditions I wanted, and they still begged me to take their money.

"Then came . . . this Yerrin and his horse. The horse that *you* call a plow horse, but that many say looks much like Linden Rathan's Llysanyin. The Llysanyin that journeyed from Dragonskeep on its own to find him—don't you remember hearing the story from Lady Niathea last winter solstice?"

At Tirael's nod, Therinn said sarcastically, "Good. I was beginning to think that too much wine had addled your wits permanently. Now—where was I? Oh, yes."

He went on relentlessly, "As I said, then came this Yerrin and his possible Llysanyin. And suddenly, no one wants to bring his mare to Summer Lightning. Men and women who were begging me to hold a place for them are now avoiding me. A bold few have even demanded their money back. I've spent the better part of this day arguing with Lord Ranklin over the money he's paid me.

"Money that I *need*, Tirael. I had to pay wergild to Lord Agon's sister for the death of her eldest child, Tirael, remember? And do you remember *why* I had to pay it, dear coz? Because of you, Tirael. Because of your arrogance, cruelty, and complete stupidity. Because it was either pay or let him take Summer Lightning—and I knew that Lightning could get that money back and more."

Therinn took a deep breath to calm himself. He'd offered a staggering sum for the wergild. Not because the family's rank demanded it; indeed, the boy's father—or, rather, stepfather, though that wasn't common knowledge—wasn't even noble. A craftsman of some sort, if his memory served him.

Hell, if Agon hadn't married his sister off to that fellow, the child would have been a bastard. Therinn knew what few others did: Agon's sister had been with child when she married her craftsman. She'd hoped to snare herself a high-ranking, rich husband and so got herself pregnant by the son of the noble family she was fostered with.

At least, she'd claimed he was the father; Therinn knew that there were two or three other possibilities, all heirs to great estates. What was her name again . . . Ah, yes: Romissa, whose plans for an estate of her own had come to naught when her foster mother guessed at her game and turned the trollop out. To save the family's name, Agon had wed her to some commoner who'd become besotted with her and paid Agon a hefty bride-price.

No, Therinn hadn't needed to pay Romissa or Agon so much; what he'd needed, though, was to close the matter before their elder half brother heard the news. By accepting the wergild, Agon, as Lord Sansy and therefore head of the family, had constrained all his kin to regard the matter as closed and done with. So he'd borrowed heavily and at usurious rates—and with Summer Lightning himself as the guarantee. He'd had to, to get the money in time.

And it *had* been just in time, too; mere candlemarks after the wergild was handed over, the half brother had shown up, furious and grieving. Therinn had never understood that. It wasn't as if the boy had been any true kin of his, after all. It was something of an open secret that someone other than the old Lord Sansy had fathered Agon and Romissa, but since the old man had never gotten around to disinheriting them before he died, Agon had inherited.

But the man had had to accept the agreement. Therinn still shuddered when he thought of how narrow an escape he'd had. Not only was the "half brother" a bard, he was an elder of that guild, one Leet by name. Thank the gods, it was only in his worst nightmares that Therinn became the butt of many a scathing song.

Songs. The thought brought him back to the matter at hand; what if this Yerrin was the one spoken of in that damned song, the one about some Dragonlords and their journey to Jehanglan? He'd not heard it for a while—he preferred ballads about old wars or rollicking ditties in praise of fast horses—but he seemed to recall that the bard who wrote the song and some kinsman were chosen by Llysanyins. If Tirael's "peasant" was the kinsman . . .

Pray all the gods he was not. But even if he was an impostor, it would still be no help. The gold for the all-important stud fees would go to him and by the time anyone was the wiser, he would be long gone, lost among the craggy hills and mountains of northern Yerrih.

Therinn took a deep breath. If he didn't get that money . . . Then inspiration hit. "Listen to me, Tir—listen well. There are some Shamreen draft horses here at the fair, aren't there? And you've already said you think that damned horse is a Shamreen, yes? So now I want you and your friends to spread it *everywhere* that you've heard the horse is nothing but a particularly fine Shamreen whose owner thought he'd separate some fools from their purses."

For a long moment Tirael didn't say anything. He licked his lips, then asked eagerly, "Do you think it really isn't one? A Llysanyin, I mean."

He sounded so like a frightened child asking to be reassured that Therinn frowned in surprise. This was so different from Tirael's usual arrogant manner that if he hadn't heard it with his own ears, he wouldn't have believed it.

"Of course the damned horse isn't," he snapped. He had to believe that; he had to, or else he might as well just give Summer Lightning over to that cursed Assantikkan princeling visiting the Kelnethi court. Yes, he'd been grateful that the man was willing to lend him that much gold on just his word and a single horse for surety; but he'd known he'd could get the money back.

Yet if this horse truly was a Llysanyin . . . Therinn slammed the door on the thought even as it tried to creep into his mind. The thing was a plow horse, nothing more; an uncommonly handsome plow horse if Dunly was to be believed, but no more than that.

"Now go," he said. "Get to work."

Maurynna slipped into the tent as quietly as she could. It was late and she didn't want to wake Linden.

She didn't. He was still awake, sitting in one of the camp chairs, a book open in his lap and a ball of coldfire hovering over the pages.

"How's Kella?" he asked as he shut the book and set it aside.

"I swear by the gods, the further we got from Balyaranna, the better she felt." Maurynna sat down on the edge of the bed and pulled her boots off with a sigh of relief. "It was the damndest thing and I *still* don't understand it."

"So she's not ill? And she never said if something had . . . happened to her?"

She saw his fists clench and knew what he was thinking. "No—and if someone had done anything to her, you would have had to get in line to hurt him. I'd claim kin-right by blood."

"I'd just make you promise to leave something for me," Linden said lightly, but his eyes were hard. "What could have happened, then?"

"I've no more idea of that than a fish has of reefing a sail." Elbows resting on knees, she frowned at her stocking feet planted squarely upon the Assantikkan rug by the side of the bed. "By the time I gave her into her mother's arms—and Aunt Elenna was over her fright and done fussing over Kella—she was her old self again."

A memory came back to her; a quick-caught glimpse of a shadowed look in Kella's eyes. . . . Maurynna amended her words. "Almost herself, that is."

"Almost?"

She looked up at her soultwin. "It's the oddest thing, Linden. It was as if Kella was running away from someone and was finally far enough away to feel safe— yet then she'd think she'd, I don't know, heard him."

Linden came over and sat beside her. "Why do you think she 'heard' someone?" He began rubbing the back of her neck.

"I don't know. It was just an impression I got. Likely it was just my imagination."

"Likely not. When I was a mercenary, I learned that impressions like that were more often than not right. It's as if your mind notices details and warns you of something, but doesn't tell you why."

"Like a bad storyteller, hmm?" Maurynna said with a little laugh. "Very well, then: say my impression was right and Kella did 'hear' something—or someone.

"The question, then, is . . . what did she hear?"

Thirty-four

But whatever Fiarin had planned for the next day, it didn't happen, though he woke them before it was barely light. Instead he repeated his odd behavior, walking down to the esker, staring across it, then returning to camp. He said not a word to the girls; it was as if he didn't see them.

Not knowing what else to do, Pod and Kaeliss busied themselves around the camp or made forays into the nearby woods to look for herbs on their own. Pod found a good-sized bed of healmoss and Kaeliss came upon a patch of wild ginger. The finds cheered them immensely. And when Kiga brought back a rabbit for supper, they could almost pretend that nothing was wrong. At least, as long as Fiarin stayed away. . . .

Pod remembered something she'd been meaning to ask Kaeliss when they were alone. As she skinned the rabbit, she said, "Kaeliss, who is Master Emberlin, and why does he need King's Blood? Flarin mentioned his name that one time, but I've no idea who he is."

Kaeliss looked up in surprise as she sliced a tiny bit of their wild ginger into the pot of water heating over the fire. "You don't—oh, of course you don't. I forget sometimes that you're not a Wortie like me." She finished her task and dusted her hands on her breeches. "Master Emberlin is one of our most accomplished Simplers, the men and women who blend various healing herbs. He's brilliant, really, and his medicines work wonders. I swear he must have a 'little magic' for it, he's so good at it even though he's but a young man.

"But even though he's so young, he's also very ill. Even the Healers can't help—or not very much. From what I've heard, the only thing keeping him alive is regular doses of—oh gods! The fire at White River chapterhouse! We might have lost most of our supply of King's Blood, and this winter is the third year of the lung sickness!"

Pod, confused, asked, "Third year?"

"Every winter there are always a few cases of the lung sickness. But now and again, it goes in a cycle: first year more serious cases and more deaths than usual; the second year, it gets worse. I've heard the masters saying that we're in another cycle, and this past winter was the second one. . . .

"Pod, if we don't have enough King's Blood, the lung sickness will be as a plague this year. It doesn't take much King's Blood to cure it, but if you don't have it to give to people . . ." She was near tears now. "I don't want to talk about it anymore."

They ate their meal in silence and tidied the camp, waiting for Fiarin to return.

Finally, Kaeliss shook her head. "I can't stay up any longer. I'm too tired."

With that, she climbed into her blankets. Pod pulled her own blankets around herself. They lay near the fire, not speaking and fell asleep waiting for Fiarin to return.

When she awoke the next morning, Pod was stiff and sore. She sat up slowly and massaged her calves and feet.

Owwwww—why does it always hurt worst the day after the day after? she complained to herself. Before, when they'd spent each day walking, her muscles hadn't had time to stiffen up. Now they had—with a vengeance.

Looking around, she saw Kaeliss was still asleep but Kiga was gone; hunting, no doubt. Pod hoped he brought back another rabbit. She was tired of dried meat; though last night's rabbit had been old and rather tough, it had made a welcome change.

The thought of the Wort Hunter made Pod realize something: It was full light. She squinted at the sky. It was, she guessed, some four or five candlemarks after dawn. Had Fiarin overslept as well? Thank the gods!

No—his blankets were empty. So he was awake—or had never gone to bed. But where was he? And why hadn't he gotten them up? He'd been an absolute bear about that. Was he hurt?

Pod staggered to her feet with a groan. She'd better find him as soon as she could. But where to look first?

Then she remembered his fascination with the esker that separated the two big lakes. She'd try there first. If he wasn't there, she'd call Kiga and see if he could follow Fiarin's scent.

There was no need to call her familiar. Fiarin stood at the edge of the esker, staring at the far end. Pod stayed within the shadow of the trees and watched him.

Every line of his body shouted of tension, of fear, of longing. He would step forward—then stop. His fists clenched and unclenched. It was as clear as the sun in the sky that though Fiarin wanted to cross the esker before him, something held him back.

Pod shook her head. She still had no idea what all this was about, but there was nothing she could do right now. It was back to the camp for her until the time was right. She also wanted to rest while she could before Fiarin dragged them off on another mad trek.

A long while later, Fiarin returned to camp. Kiga was back, Kaeliss was up, their packs and bedrolls were ready, and they'd broken their fast though Pod was disappointed that there was no fresh meat.

Which was just as well, for Fiarin knelt to roll up his blankets, saying, "We're moving on. Hurry—there's a swampy area I want to get through before dark."

"Where are we going?" Kaeliss asked, her voice shaking.

At first Pod thought he hadn't heard her as he worked. Then he said softly, "Never you mind where, girl. Never you mind. Just know that it will make your name in the Guild."

Something in his voice sent prickles of unease down Pod's back. Taking a deep breath, she said, "That's not good enough. What is all this about? You haven't shown us anything in days. And we're well past the time we should have gone back, aren't we?"

Fiarin surged to his feet, his face dull red with anger and his fists clenched. But before he could take a single step toward her, Kiga was between her and the furious Wort Hunter, just as she'd known would happen. The woods dog snarled, daring the tall man to strike his person.

Fiarin stopped short. He stared down at Kiga for a long moment, then slowly and carefully stepped back. He took first one deep breath, then another. Then came the last thing that Pod had expected: the Wort Hunter grinned wryly.

"Well played, young Pod. I suppose I have been, ah, rather mysterious of late, haven't I?"

Pod just nodded; it didn't seem to be right to add *And a damned bastard to boot*. Conor always said it wasn't fair to kick a man when he was beaten.

"Well and well, then, girls—this is the truth of it. According to some old, ah, records I've studied, somewhere near here is a patch of King's Blood. A very large patch."

Pod heard a gasp behind her; Kaeliss was beside her an instant later.

"Truly?" the apprentice Wort Hunter said avidly.

"Truly. And think of this, young Kaeliss: That description is years old. So all this time that patch had had time to spread . . . and spread."

He ran his hands through his hair. "Pod, you won't understand this, but Kaeliss will. As I said before, this will make your name—both your names, actually—in the guild. King's Blood is one of rarest and most valuable plants a Wort Hunter can find. It grows in so few places and helps so many illnesses, and . . ." He faltered to a stop.

Pod eyed him. There was more to this; there had to be. Surely a man so senior in his guild wouldn't risk his standing within it lightly. "This isn't just about gaining prestige within your guild, is it?" she asked. "Or beating out Currin?"

Fiarin actually laughed at that. "No, though the thought of Currin besting me at our game does rankle. Nor is it about prestige. Over the years I've already earned the respect of my fellows. Yes, I *do* risk my rank and will most certainly be punished, but I think my hope is worth it."

Kaeliss nodded. "You're thinking of Master Emberlin, aren't you?" she said softly.

"Just so. The guild can't afford to lose him, Kaeliss. Young as he is, he's already accomplished so much. Can you imagine what he could do if he has the years he *should* have ahead of him?"

"The King's Blood that Currin found—it's not enough?" Pod asked.

"No," Fiarin said. He sighed. "Not when we're certain that when the lung sickness returns, it will be even worse than it was this past winter. Our supply of King's Blood was low then. If what you heard about the fire destroying that storeroom is right, this winter . . . Oh gods, this winter will be devastating.

"Emberlin has always refused to take more King's Blood than is enough to keep the thing that's eating him at bay. He knows that many lives could be saved with the amount he'd need to cure him. Now he might refuse to take any at all. But if we had enough . . ."

He looked at Kaeliss. "You will *not* face punishment. When we get back, I'll tell the guild elders that neither of you had any idea of what I'd planned. It's naught but the truth, and when we find the King's Blood, it will be share and share alike."

Kaeliss said slowly, "You'd share equally with us?"

"I'd already been planning to—it would be the only fair thing after I've made such a mess of your training. The two of you will have missed most of your treks by the time we get back. But I promise you that it will be worth it. Are you with me?"

Kaeliss crowed "Yes!" and caught up her pack and bedroll.

Pod wasn't as certain, but what could she do? She had no idea how to find her way back. And if this plant was so useful, and next winter's lung sickness as bad as Kaeliss and Fiarin feared it would be, surely it was a good thing to find a lot of King's Blood, right? So she nodded and swung her own pack and blanket roll onto her back. She had no choice but to go on.

Thirty-five

As they were on their way to Yarrow and Raven's camp to share ale and news, Linden, Maurynna, and Shima crossed paths with Conor as he walked through the fair. The Beast Healer had his familiar cuddled upside down in his arms and tickled her stomach as he walked. Trouble "chuckled" when she saw Linden.

"Hoy there, Conor! Well met again," Linden called.

Conor grinned. "Well met indeed." He bowed carefully to Maurynna and Shima; Trouble scolded him anyway for bouncing her about.

After he made the introductions, Linden said, "You seem lighthearted. Any particular reason?"

Conor laughed. "Do I now? Well-a-well, I'm guessing that still having all my fingers and such would account for that."

"Ahhh. Been to see Summer Lightning again, have you?"

"That I have. He's in fine fettle if foul temper." Conor shook his head. "Sad, it is. Just sad."

I agree, Linden said in Conor's mind, using mindspeech because he didn't want the next part to be overhead by any fairgoers. *And I'm afraid I have to agree with Sevrynel. When it became clear he was that vicious, Summer Lightning should have been put down. At the very least, he should have been gelded.* Aloud he went on, "We're on our way to visit friends. Are you free?"

"I'm on duty now at the guild's tent. I was just on my way back."

"Then I hope we'll have a chance to see you again."

"The three of you are to marshal the Queen's Chase, yes? Then we'll likely cross paths there." He bowed once more. "A fine day to you, Dragonlords—and Linden," he added with a cheeky grin and a wave.

The Dragonlords set off once more. As the camp came into view, Maurynna asked, "Was that the old friend from the other day? I'd meant to ask you how you met him."

"It was. Let's get everyone settled with a tankard of ale and I'll tell you the tale of Conor and Pod."

The Llysanyins greeted each other happily and went off to one end of the horse lines where they stood in a circle, heads together.

"Look like a bunch of old grannies settling in for a good gossip, don't they?" Yarrow whispered as she led the way into the common tent. "Sit down, sit down." She waved a hand at the trestle table in the center. The grooms and handlers grinned at them and cleared the table of the remnants of their meal.

Tankards of ale and a platter of cold chicken and vegetables appeared like magic before them even before they'd seated themselves on the benches.

"Where's Raven?" Shima asked.

"With his friend Lord Ar—make a liar of me, lad!" she said as Raven ducked into the tent.

He grabbed a tankard of ale and joined them at the table. "Gods, but it's good to see friendly faces!" He took a long pull of his ale.

Yarrow asked sharply, "What's wrong?"

"What else? I ran into dear Lord Tirael."

Maurynna made a rude noise of dismissal. "That spoiled brat? My sympathies."

Linden nodded. Maurynna had told him of Raven's wager—a foolish one in his opinion; even a Llysanyin could go lame—her own encounter with Tirael, and finally of how that spoiled young lord managed to squirm out of paying if he lost the race with Raven. He rarely made judgments of someone before he met them; this Tirael would be an exception for which he would feel no guilt. "What happened?"

"Arisyn and I had just parted ways when I ran into Lord Tirael and a few of his hangers-on. Even for him he was in a foul temper and I think I know why. Gossip around the fair has it there's a young woman he'd decided was the one for him, but she had the good sense to send him packing, though no one seems to know just who she is—or else they're not saying. Now she's turned up at the fair and is being courted by someone else, someone who's succeeding where Tirael failed. And I get the feeling that her suitor is someone that would set Tirael off something fierce. It seems if there's one thing our dear Lord Tirael can't stand, it's losing."

"He'd best get used to it," Maurynna said sweetly.

Raven chuckled. "Too true. But could we talk about something else? Being told that there soon won't be two fingers' width of skin on your back tends to spoil your day."

Shima said, "We met a friend of Linden's on the way here and Linden said he'd tell us how the two of them met."

"Don't forget Pod," Maurynna added. To Linden she said, "That's an odd name even for a Yerrin, isn't it?"

Linden laughed. "It would be indeed. It's even odder for a Kelnethi, which is what we guessed Pod to be. We never knew for certain because she was an orphan.

At least, we think she is. It was a nickname Conor, who was just a journeyman Beast Healer then, gave her because of her hair—it's short for Milkweed Pod."

"How did you and a journeyman Beast Healer end up playing nanny to an orphan child, anyway?" Raven asked. "This sounds like one of my great-uncle's funny stories."

"It wasn't," Linden said, frowning. "But at least it had a happy ending."

He stretched out his legs. "The short version is that about, oh, ten years ago I got restless and went on a journey. Decided it was time to pay my respects once again at Bram and Rani's tombs. When I got to Waylshire in Kelneth I found the countryside at the end of horrible cattle plague. The Beast Healers had sent out everyone they had above the rank of apprentice trying to stop it before it spread throughout the country, so there were a number of young journeymen about that normally would not have been on their own for some time yet. One of them was Conor.

"When I came across him, he was sitting by the side of the road in the middle of nowhere. He was exhausted from working nonstop, hadn't eaten for three days, his horse had thrown a shoe, and he had a bad case of ague to top it all off. Oh, and there was a small pile of dead mice at his feet. His familiar then, a little ferret named Havoc, kept bringing them to him. She seemed quite put out that he wouldn't eat them; as I reined Shan up before him she was standing on his shoulder, a dead mouse under one paw, scolding him."

"Familiar?" Shima asked. "Are these Beast Healers witches, then?"

Linden shook his head. "No, but the bond is similar enough that most people call the animals that. Each Beast Healer seems to bond very strongly with one kind of animal, though they can care for any beast. In Yerrih we call the familiars *kal-enteya,* 'brothers-in-fur.' I think that's a closer description than 'familiar.'"

"And the bond does something to the animal that chooses to partner a Beast Healer," Raven said. "It somehow, I don't know, *enhances* them. You'd swear they could think sometimes. They're often much smarter than others of their kind, and they're utterly devoted to their person."

"Just so," Linden said. "Anyway, I found Conor—he was barely seventeen—almost done in. I gave him some of my food, cared for his horse, set him on Shan, and went with him to the last farm he was due to visit. It was a remote holding belonging to some lord or another, almost a four-day ride, and I was afraid he'd never make it alone. Poor lad was frantic to get there. He was certain they'd lost most of their cattle and was determined to save what he could for them even though he'd heard they were a hard, inhospitable lot."

When he paused to cut himself another slice of cold chicken and began eating, Maurynna prompted, "Were they?"

"Maurynna-love, you'll never have any idea how tempted I was to leave them to their troubles—and that was less than half a candlemark after meeting them," Linden said wryly. "Conor, though, was still resolved to do his duty. But even he wavered after we found the little girl—she was, perhaps, four years old?—living in the barn like another animal."

He shut his eyes and saw once again in his mind's eye his first view of the child he and Conor would name Pod. The farmer and his family called her Pig Girl or just Pig for short. Filthy rags hung from a skinny frame and half-healed cuts and sores covered the thin arms and legs. She was covered with mud and filth and her hair was a witch's nest of snarls and yet more filth. He hadn't even been able to tell what color it was then.

But it was the big hazel eyes that had angered him the most. No child's eyes should ever have that fearful, suspicious look in them, he thought, even at the sight of strangers. When he had the image fixed in his mind, he shared it with the others; shock, anger, and dismay came back to him.

"Oh dear gods," Yarrow whispered.

Yet when Conor knelt in the mud and spoke to her, she took the hand he offered her though it was plain she was terrified. The next thing we knew, she was hugging him like she'd never let go. It was as if she'd suddenly found her best friend in all the world. She knew *him. It wasn't until later that we realized the "why" of it.*

"Conor was the one who added everything up," he continued aloud. "After talking with one of the milkmaids—almost the only person who kind to the child—and watching Pig with the animals, he realized that she was a Beast Healer." He shook his head. "Gods, I hate calling her that, but it *was* her name then.

"The farm had lost nowhere near as many animals it might have—especially considering that their new bull calf was from the fair where the plague had first appeared. The lord had sent it there before everyone realized what was happening. That's what made that particular illness so deadly—it took a while to develop and by then it would have spread throughout a herd. But that calf was still alive even though it had been the first one stricken with the plague. When it was sick, Pig went to sleep in its stall with it. She told us that she 'wished' it better. She did that with any animal that was 'sad' and it usually felt better, she said. When we saw her playing between the front hooves of their old bull, that's when Conor was certain; that creature was downright *vicious,* yet it was clear that it doted on Pig.

"Anyway, when it was time to leave, we told them we were taking Pig with us. To put it mildly, they were reluctant to let her go. They knew what had kept their animals so healthy all that time and were loath to lose her even though they despised her as the by-blow of a 'strumpet'—as if her parentage was Pig's fault."

"They knew her parents?" Shima asked.

"No. Her mother had appeared on their doorstep in the middle of a snowstorm, newborn babe in arms, and died that night. Pig wasn't even kin of theirs. They had no right to her and, as the most senior Beast Healer around,

Conor did. I had to draw my sword to convince them that we meant business—I hadn't revealed myself as a Dragonlord at that time, not even to Conor.

"But when they tried to ambush us that night, I did. I'd felt certain they would try something like that, so when we camped, I made sure it was in an area large enough for me to Change. When Shan gave the alarm, that was just what I did."

He couldn't help smiling at the memory; it was one of the few times he took a wicked satisfaction in scaring the living daylights out of someone by Changing. "We had no trouble with them after that. We made our way to the nearest shepherd's cot. The shepherd was so appalled at Pod's condition he let us use the big wooden tub for washing the fleeces to give her a bath. She squalled and howled and thrashed until Conor and I were almost as wet as she was, but we got her clean in the end. And we kept losing the damned soap in the tub. I never," he said firmly, "ever want to do that again."

Maurynna burst out laughing. "Poor Linden," she said with not a bit of sympathy in her voice. "Not cut out for a nursie, were we?"

"Hmph." Linden threw a radish at her. She caught it and blew him a kiss. He went on, "Anyway, her hair was beyond us, it was so matted and snarled. So we borrowed the sheep shears and cut it about two fingers' width long. After that we were able to get it clean.

"And that's when we found out her hair is white; I suspect she's a throwback to the old Kelnethi royal line." He paused for a moment, reliving his shock, the feeling of his stomach dropping away, the leap of his heart. Not that the little girl had looked anything like Rani, but the sight of white hair around so young a face had brought back so many memories. . . .

Remembering? Maurynna asked him gently after a few moments.

Oh, yes, he replied. *There are so very many memories there. . . .* He rubbed his forehead as if he might push them back. "We gave her the nickname Pod because when she woke up the next day after falling asleep with wet hair, it stood up every which way. Conor burst out laughing when he saw her and said, 'You look just like a split milkweed pod! Hello, Pod!' So instead of Pig, we called her Pod after that. I suspect she accepted it because Conor came up with it. She adored him from the beginning."

"And she's a Beast Healer now, you said?"

Linden nodded. "She is—or rather, will be. She's still an apprentice."

Shima asked, "This talk of familiars intrigues me—what is hers?"

"Let us hope it's not a pig," Maurynna said devoutly.

Chuckling, Linden shook his head. "No, it isn't—though I've met more than one Beast Healer who's had one. No, that was the part of Conor's news that made my jaw drop when I saw him the other day.

"He told me that Pod had never found a familiar after she came to the Grey Holt chapterhouse. She—and a few others—were worried that it meant she wasn't really a Beast Healer after all. At the time he left the chapterhouse, she was about ten years old and *still* didn't have one.

"Then, about a month after he left Grey Holt, Conor got a letter from his friends there. Pod had finally found her familiar. That was three years ago. Conor still has the letter and let me read it." He refilled his tankard, looked around and asked, "Anyone care to take a guess what the familiar is?"

Raven, whose grin had been growing as he listened to the story, held up his hands and shook his head. "I abstain. I think I've heard about this young lady already from a Beast Healer named Gunnis."

Linden raised his tankard of ale to him. "To honorable men! Any guesses, then?"

"A ferret like Conor's?" Maurynna hazarded.

"A cow?" Yarrow guessed.

Linden shook his head. "Wrong, both wrong. Shima?"

"I would have guessed a ferret as well since she seems to be so attached to Conor. Um—a rabbit?"

"All wrong. It's a *ghulon*."

"Gods have mercy!" said Yarrow as Maurynna whistled her astonishment. "A little girl with a *ghulon*?"

To Shima's baffled look, Linden said, "An animal with long, thick fur, dark brown with a band of yellowish tan along each side. It looks something like a small bear with a long tail. They are *not* known for sweet dispositions. They are also extremely strong for an animal their size—astonishingly so. *Ghulon* is the Yerrin word for them. Other names are woods dog and wolvering."

Maurynna said, "It's hard to believe that a *ghulon* could be a brother-in-fur, but you have to say this for having one: that girl will be quite safe when she goes on her solo journeywoman's trek! Good for her.

"Now tell us more about your race, Raven. Do you really think Tirael will dare ooze out of paying when he loses?"

They talked for a while longer. Then Yarrow could no longer hide her yawns and went off to her tent. Linden and Maurynna took their leave as well. Only Shima stayed.

Raven raised an eyebrow at him. "Aren't you going to see Lady Karelinn this evening?"

Shima laughed. "She, Merrilee, and a number of the other ladies were going to help one of their friends choose the silks for that lady's wedding dress. Linden warned me to stay well away—it seems he remembers his own sisters' wedding preparations all too well, even after six hundred years!"

Laughing, Raven poured each of them more ale. "Then how about a game of *diyinesh*? Maurynna gave me a traveling set for a gift last Midwinter Eve. She showed Yarrow and me how to play, but I'd like to learn more." At Shima's nod, Raven went on, "I'll get it from my tent."

Soon the two men were engrossed in the game.

* * *

Therinn of Lenslee nearly turned and headed off in another direction as Lord Dunly bore down upon him. But that would have been too obvious, and he dared not risk offending the old bore. Not only was Dunly a powerful noble, but he was friends with, or kin to, many others. Therinn pasted a smile upon his face even as he mentally cursed Lady Ramissilen for inviting the old windbag to her gathering. Though, upon consideration, Dunly had likely invited himself.

Gods, wasn't it bad enough that he'd finally winkled an invitation to the castle—then had to turn around and leave almost as soon as he got there? What the bloody hell was that damned bard doing here? He'd understood that Leet rarely left the Bards' School in Bylith. It was likely the only reason he'd had enough time to settle the wergild with Agon for his nephew; not being a seasoned traveler, Leet had made poor time on the journey.

And now Dunly . . .

"Yes, my lord?" Therinn asked politely as the old man harrumphed to a halt in front of him, snorting and snuffling like an old dog sleeping by the fire as he caught his breath. Then he saw the malicious gleam in the other's eye and braced for—what? A duel with this old bag of bones?

"So, Lenslee—who are *you* wagering on tomorrow?" Dunly fairly cackled.

Therinn blinked. There were no races set for tomorrow; the next one was the Queen's Chase, but that was for the day after tomorrow. What was the old man blathering about? Had his wits finally deserted him? Therinn had always known it was going to happen one—

No. Everyone else within earshot looked as if they knew what Dunly was talking about. Indeed, they waited expectantly for his answer.

"I'm afraid I've no idea what race you mean, my lord," Therinn said stiffly.

Dunly cackled. "Need to get out and about the fair a bit more, man—not just sit like a spider in his web and wait for fools with money. Fools that aren't coming, that is. You mean you haven't heard?"

It was nothing short of a miracle, Therinn thought, that he didn't slap the old man silly. Instead he said with icy politeness, "Pray enlighten me, my lord. What race?"

The malicious gleam was a fire in the old man's eyes now. "Why, the match race between your cousin Tirael and that Waylshire of his—the one from *your* stable—and . . ."

Dunly paused and pulled a linen kerchief from his sleeve and coughed into it. A cough so patently false it was ludicrous.

It went on and on until Therinn, unable to bear it anymore, demanded desperately, "Yes? Go on, damn you!"

As if by magic, the cough disappeared. "Tch! Manners, manners! Why, that young Yerrin fellow, of course! You know—the one with the . . . Llysanyin?"

* * *

How he got back to Ridler's town house in Balyaranna, he didn't know. As soon as he got through the door, the steward rushed up to him.

"My lord! Is something amiss?" Tiniver asked in concern.

Therinn took a deep breath, waiting until he could speak without shouting. "Is Lord Portis back from—?"

"Lord and Lady Jalinet's gathering," Tiniver supplied. "No, my lord. I don't expect Lord or Lady Portis for some time yet."

Damnation, Therinn fumed silently. Then, cynically, *You fool—why bother with Ridler? Likely he doesn't even know what his precious brat's done. I'll have to find Tir—*

Like an answer from the gods came Tirael's voice from the top of the stairs. "Damn it, Tiniver—where the hell is my wine? I told you to get me more wine!" The slurred words were followed by an enormous belch. Then came the sound of retreating footsteps, a feminine giggle, and the slam of a door.

Tiniver cast a worried look up the stairway as he wrung his hands.

Therinn rested a hand on the steward's shoulder. "I'm afraid my young cousin has had a wee bit too much," he soothed. "And shouldn't have any more. Go on now, Tiniver, and don't worry. I'll be the one to tell Lord Tirael that there will be no more wine tonight."

He gave the man a smile and a gentle nudge when he hesitated. "Don't worry, Tiniver; you attend to your other duties. I'll attend to my cousin. You must have a thousand other things to see to."

Tiniver heaved a sigh of relief. "Thank you, my lord, I do. If you'll excuse me . . ." The steward hurried off as if afraid the Kelnethi lord would change his mind.

"Oh, Tiniver! A moment."

The steward turned, his face wary. "Yes, my lord?"

"Please have someone fetch Summer Lightning's groom, Beckrum. Tell him to wait for me in Lord Portis's study."

"I'll see to it at once, my lord. At once!" Relief made the normally reserved steward gush.

Therinn went up the stairs and down the hall to Tirael's room. A giggle made him hesitate at the door—but only for a moment. The next instant he shoved the door open so hard it crashed against the inside wall and bounced partway back. Slamming it behind him, Therinn stalked into his younger cousin's chamber.

Tirael lay sprawled on an Assantikkan rug before the cold fireplace, his head in a young woman's lap. She giggled drunkenly down at him as he batted at a squat bottle, cursing it for being empty. It clinked forlornly as it came to the end of the rug and rolled across the floor. A large red stain covered the rug.

No wonder the fool had needed more wine. He'd spilled the bottle across the costly rug. It was ruined and a fine wine wasted; Therinn recognized the bottle used by the Marlchand vineyard in Pelnar, one of the finest in a land known for its grapes.

A waste—just like Tirael.

"Tiniver? Is that you?" Tirael demanded.

"No," answered Therinn.

The girl goggled at him, her eyes bleary with wine. From her dress—what there was of it still on her—she was a serving wench from one of the many tavern tents in the fair.

"You," Therinn said in a voice filled with quiet menace as he pointed at her. "Get. Out. *Now!*"

She scrambled to her feet, letting Tirael's head thump to the floor, and grabbed for her clothes.

"Ow! You bitch, get back here!" Tirael struggled to roll over.

Wisely she paid him no heed. Therinn followed her with cold, hard eyes. She stumbled hastily to the door and fumbled the latch open, whimpering whenever she looked back and met that steely gaze.

When she was gone, Therinn looked back at his younger cousin who had finally managed to get, however unsteadily, to his feet. Tirael stared sullenly at him.

"What the hell do you want now, damn you?" he demanded. "You ruined—"

"Shut your filthy mouth," Therinn said with quiet fury. He went to the table that Tirael used as a desk and sat down. It was littered with empty bottles, broken quill pens, and papers. Therinn absently noticed that there was a letter from Tirael's old tutor in the one clear space; he recognized the old man's still beautiful script. "Now tell me—is it true that you're in a match race with that Yerrin?"

Tirael wouldn't meet his eyes. "Yes."

"Before or after I spoke to you about him?"

"Before."

"And you didn't tell me."

Tirael laughed, a laugh full of drunken bravado. "Stop being such an old woman, coz! My fifty gold pieces are safe. Brythian will beat that plow horse easily. And then that damned Yerrin and his horse are mine. He agreed to become my serf, did you know? Lord Huryn witnessed it."

That stopped Therinn cold. He hadn't known what the wager was. He closed his eyes at such stupidity—Tirael's, not the Yerrin's. The fury he'd felt before was nothing to what coursed through his veins now.

He surged to his feet and slammed his hands against the table. "Are you mad?" he roared. "Or just abysmally stupid, Tirael?" He swept the table clear in frustration. A few of the bottles shattered when they hit the floor. He didn't care.

"You idiot," he snarled. "You complete and total *idiot*! Didn't you understand what it meant that he was willing to make such a wager? Or have you drowned whatever wits you had in your pretty little head in too much wine?"

The look of drunken incomprehension on Tirael's face was too much for him. "It means the horse truly is a Llysanyin, you bucket of horse piss!" he shouted. "Only a man who knows he's guaranteed to win would risk a wager like that—unless he was either desperate or as stupid as you! And from all I've heard, this man is neither."

"A Llysanyin! The only thing that could make Brythian—one of the finest horses to come out of *my* stables and half brother to Summer Lightning—look like a snail! I'll tell you this now: Do not come looking to me for those fifty pieces of gold."

Tirael smirked. "Even if I lose, that gold's safe." He belched, then leaned over the table and confided, "Y'see, *I* never swore I'd pay. Never, ever gave my word to Huryn, and the silly asses never noticed, neither him nor that damned Yerrin up—upstart."

Therinn stared at him. Of all the things Tirael had done in his short and wasted life, this was somehow the worst. Arrogance, conceit, selfishness—all of these things Tirael had in abundance. That his cousin had a streak of meanness—even cruelty—Therinn knew well, else Tirael would never have put that boy up on Summer Lightning's back.

Yet he'd thought that Tirael had at least a spark of honor hidden somewhere. But that foolish hope had just shriveled and died.

Therinn knew what all this meant for him. The first was bad enough; a horse that everyone who mattered knew came from his stable would be made to look like a nag, thereby driving away more potential breeders.

But that his good name would be linked to a cheat's. . . . The thought sickened him. "You will not race. You will concede the victory to the Yerrin and pay him the gold."

Tirael gaped at him. "The hell I will! I don't have that much gold and you know it!"

"Then you shouldn't have made that wager, should you?" Therinn said coldly.

"Be damned to you," Tirael snarled. "I'm riding tomorrow. So what if I can't win? I want to see the bastard's face when he realizes that he won't get his gold and there's not a thing he can do about it."

One last try . . . "An honorable man's word is his bond," Therinn said with quiet regret. This was useless, but he had to try . . . for Brythian. "You shouldn't need Huryn's witnessing your pledge to pay. When you made that wager, you gave your word."

Tirael told him in no uncertain terms what he could do with his stupid, old-fashioned ideas about honor. Told him graphically and in language that would have made a mule driver blush.

So be it. Therinn walked out, not caring that Tirael would see it as an admission of defeat, hardly hearing the mocking laughter that followed him down the stairs.

There stood Beckrum, waiting. Therinn stopped before him and buried his face in his hands as he thought.

If only there weren't so damn many Beast Healers about! he thought with sad irony. Almost any other time and place, he could have Beckram simply lame Brythian—something that would heal on its own in a tenday or so—and that would be the end of it. Nor did he have the time for an elaborate plan. "My faithless cousin plans to run Brythian in a match race," he began, then faltered. "He also plans to renege on his wager. And Brythian is certain to be defeated—soundly. The race is tomorrow."

The groom studied his face and nodded.

Therinn drew a deep breath. "That must not happen, Beckrum. There must be no chance of it happening."

Once more the groom nodded. "Brythian goes out to pasture with the other horses at sunrise every morning," he observed.

"I leave it in your hands," said Therinn with a heavy heart. "Don't tell me how— Just don't tell me anything."

Thirty-six

It was time. The solstice was nearly here; the Queen's Chase was soon.

He should wait. His revenge would be so much more delicious if he snatched Lenslee's near-certain victory from him at the very last instant.

But the closer to the heart he cut this wound, the more chance that something would go wrong. No, he'd not take any more chances than he had to.

As had become his custom, Leet slipped out of the castle, harp under his cloak. But this time along with it he carried a small sack.

It was warm enough that they didn't really need the fire in their bedroom. But Merrilee had asked for it, so a servant laid a small one for them. She sat now, staring into it, night robe pulled tight around her as if she were cold. Her long fair hair, hanging loose down her back, looked almost white against the dark blue of the night robe. The sight of it gave Karelinn an idea.

Let's try this one last time, she told herself as she picked up Merrilee's hairbrush. "Will you please tell Father what happened?" she asked as she began brushing.

"No, Kare. Fighting a Challenge is forbidden during the fair and you know Father's temper. He won't be able to wait until it's over." She leaned into the brush.

Pity, Karelinn thought sourly. *That's likely the only reason the cowardly wretch dared approach Merri. If Father goes after that craven—and he will!— he'll be fined heavily. Fines we can't afford.* "You're right, of course."

It was their father's only real fault, that temper. And, Karelinn suspected, where the safety or happiness of his daughters was concerned, a snowcat would do well to back down from their father. "Then what about Shima? I told you what he said back at the Gyrfalcon's Nest."

"*Shima* is it now?" Merrilee teased. "Not Shima Ilyathan, Dragonlord, or His Grace?"

Curse it all, she could feel her cheeks burning. "Merri," she scolded, "stop trying to change the subject."

"I'm not—yes, I am." Merrilee's shoulders slumped. "Sorry, Kare. It's just . . ."

"What about Eadain?"

Merrilee twisted around on the stool so fast the brush caught in her hair and was yanked from Karelinn's hand. It hung for a moment, then fell to the floor with a thud.

"No! Not Eadain! Especially not Eadain!" Merrilee gasped.

"Merri! Calm down! Why 'especially not Eadain'?" Karelinn retrieved the brush and ran it lightly over the long hair. Just as she thought; that had made a snarl. She began to gently work it out.

It was a few moments before her sister could calm herself enough to reply. She said, "Because Eadain will ask Tirael to leave me alone. In his own way he's as protective as Father. He's just more rational about it. But I'm afraid of what Tirael would do if he found out that Eadain's courting me—and that I'm listening. I—I couldn't stand it if anything happened to him."

Oh, my, Karelinn thought with amusement. *You're falling in love with him, aren't you?* And she found that the thought of Eadain as brother-in-law was an appealing one.

But once again Merrilee was right. With his twisted leg, Eadain would stand no chance against the healthy, strong Tirael. If only Tirael would fall in a hole somewhere . . .

But now Merrilee was talking so softly that Karelinn had to stop brushing and bend close to hear.

"I just wish Tirael would go away. I've been listening, you know, when people talk about him. He's . . . been making himself known at the fair. And you know how Arisyn says that Tirael won't honor the wager if he loses the race? I think Ari's right. And remember that story he told us—about the first time Raven saw Tirael? What he and his friends were doing to those children? It's not the only tale like that, Merri. Nor is it the worst.

"And it's all making me feel like such an . . . an idiot! How could I have been so stupid as to be fooled by him? It makes me feel so . . . worthless."

Karelinn set the brush down and hugged her sister from behind. "You're not a fool, Merri, and you're certainly not worthless. You're just such a good person that you don't look for the badness in anyone else. And you're not the only one who was taken in by him, remember? Aunt Perrilinia thought he was wonderful as well—and if she isn't a shrewd old bat, I don't know who is! So dry your eyes, my girl. Think about the gem you've found this time and forget about that piece of . . . coal."

As she'd known it would, what came after that pregnant pause made Merri giggle. She was still giggling when Karelinn went to go answer the knock at their door.

It was Coryn. One look at his face and Karelinn knew why he was there. "At least you finally have the grace to look embarrassed at running errands for that bully," she snapped.

Coryn flushed a deep red. Wordlessly, he held out yet another note.

"Is that from Tirael?" Merrilee asked. Coryn nodded. "Kare, give it to me. And Coryn—you stay there and witness this," she ordered.

Marveling at her gentle sister's imperious tone, Karelinn brought her the note. Merrilee snatched it from her hand and flung it into the fire. Moments later it crumbled into ash.

"And that," Merrilee said clearly, "is all my answer."

Leet smiled like a cat as he watched that fool boy Robie go off, sack clutched in his arms. The calling had worked perfectly! He knew without a doubt that Robie would follow every instruction, take every care, so that he would not be discovered. And the foul stuff was at that perfect stage. . . . This would soon be over; he would have his revenge at last.

The gods were good.

Thirty-seven

Raven was filling nose bags with grain for the grooms to distribute when Arisyn raced into Yarrow's camp, pulling Arrow to a sliding halt before him.

"What in Gifnu's nine hells are you doing up this early?" Raven asked in amazement. It was just past dawn and Arisyn was rarely up before the eighth candlemark. Nor was the race to start for some time yet.

Part of his mind noted in amusement that it was a good thing Arisyn hadn't shown up even a quarter of a candlemark ago. If he'd seen Shima—who'd stayed the night after talking racing strategies until the stars were fading—departing from the camp, the game would have been over. Linden or even Maurynna he could explain away as fellow Yerrins to account for why their horses looked like Stormwind. One look at Shima and Je'nihahn, though, and Arisyn would have guessed everything in an instant.

Then Raven saw the look on the boy's face. Arisyn was not here for pleasure. "What's wrong?"

"You haven't heard the news?" Arisyn said grimly as he swung down from Arrow's saddle. "No—I can see you haven't."

Raven gestured for one of the grooms to take Arrow's reins. "Walk him," he ordered. Then, to Arisyn, "I've been working here since before sun up so I've had no chance to hear any gossip. What news is this?"

"You'll not be racing today," Arisyn said. "And likely not ever—racing Tirael, that is. Brythian and some of the other horses got out of their pasture this morning. Luckily, all the horses have been found—all save Brythian."

Raven felt a moment's regret that he wouldn't be able to demonstrate Stormwind's speed and endurance past all doubt. Ah, well—the less he had to do with Lord Tirael, the better. Still, it was a coward's way out.

His disgust must have been plain on his face, for Arisyn added, "I don't think it was Tirael. Coryn said that last night he was boasting how he was going to cheat you out of that fifty gold. Said he couldn't wait to see your face when you finally realized that he'd never sworn to pay you."

Raven made a rude noise. "Hate to disappoint him, but I'd realized it the night we made the wager. I was going to race anyway to show everyone what Stormwind can do."

"I know." Arisyn took a deep breath. "But there's worse."

The look of fear in the boy's eyes set the hair on the back of Raven's neck prickling. "What?"

"Summer Lightning's dead. And no one knows how."

Leet gave up trying to sleep. He had to know if fortune still favored him. So, as the light crept into the sky, he dressed and took himself down to the kitchens. He'd done this often enough that no one would remark upon it. Indeed, at the sight of him, Mistress Cook nodded at the table, then jerked her head at an underling.

Soon a cup of small ale and an egg cooked just the way Leet like them appeared before him. As he ate, he debated where might be the best place in the fair to listen for news.

He had no need to; the news came to him. As one of the farmers who supplied the castle carried in a basket of carrots, he called out, "Have tha all heard the news? Summer Lightning's dead as dead!"

For a moment Leet feared he would weep for joy. His revenge was complete! He rubbed the indentation under his lip. This—this was a moment to treasure for the rest of his life.

Then a hated memory reared its ugly head: the smug look on Therinn Barans's face as he told Leet that he was too late. That his brother, Agon, Lord Sansy, had accepted wergild only candlemarks before. That there would be no songs made of Arnath's death. That it was over, done with.

It was not over. Not until he saw another expression upon Therinn Barans's face.

"Look at him! Look at my poor Lightning! What killed him?" Lord Lenslee demanded. "There's not a mark on him and he was healthy just yesterday—you said so yourself!"

Conor stared down at the dead horse sprawled across the stall floor. One dull, sunken eye stared up at him in dumb accusation. The heavy buzz of flies droned in his ears as they crawled over the body.

He took a deep breath. Dear gods, he felt sick to his very soul. Had he somehow missed something? But the horse *had* looked well yesterday evening. Hellfire, "well" didn't even begin to describe the chestnut stallion—he'd been vibrantly alive, dancing at the end of his lead rope with the sheer joy of living, reveling in his speed and strength and beauty.

Now he was meat for the worms. So what had happened?

Conor passed his hands over his eyes. "My lord," he said bitterly, "I've no idea. As you said, there's not a mark on him."

A murmur went through the watching grooms and stable hands at his words. "Magic," it said. "Dark sorcery," it whispered. It filled his ears like the buzzing of the flies and sickened him even more.

Gods help him—what if they were right? He was no mage to fight a wizards' war. He was only a Beast Healer.

"My lord, is something . . . wrong?"

Conor looked up to see a man silhouetted against the opening of the stable. All he could make out was the red tunic of a bard. For a moment he wondered if this was Otter, the bard of whom Linden Rathan had spoken from time to time. Conor had always wanted to meet the man.

But then Lord Lenslee said, "Master Bard Leet!" so he knew this wasn't the Dragonlord's friend.

What was odd, though, was Lenslee's reaction to the bard's appearance. The man's jaw actually dropped. Conor wondered why the amazement; he'd met a good number of bards on his travels and had never known one to think he or she was too good to enter a stable—especially a lord's stable with its treasure of blue-blooded animals. Were Master Bards different? he wondered. *Perhaps they don't have to worry about keeping potential patrons happy. . . .*

After a moment, Lord Lenslee said softly, "There is indeed something wrong. So very, very wrong. . . ."

As Lenslee stared down at his lost hopes once more, biting his knuckles and whispering, "My poor, poor, beautiful Lightning . . ." over and over again, the Master Bard stepped inside, giving Conor his first good look at the man: medium height and build, with deep-set brown eyes, a cleft chin, and light brown hair gone silver at the temples. A very ordinary man, save for his almost lordly air of assurance and the gold trim on his tunic that proclaimed his as one of the elders of the Bards' Guild.

"What killed him?" the bard asked as he came down the aisle. When he reached the door of the stall, he looked over it at the animal lying within.

Conor thought the bard must either have the tightest rein on his emotions that he'd ever seen, or that the man was the most cold-blooded bastard he'd ever come across. There was no flicker of emotion on the man's face as he stared down into the stall, not even an eyebrow raised in surprise.

Since the distraught Lenslee seemed not to hear the question, Conor said shortly, "We don't know—yet." He wasn't sure what made him add the last word;

it sounded like a challenge. He hoped the bard wouldn't take offense—the last thing he needed right now was to be made the butt of a sarcastic tune. But something was not quite right here. . . .

Master Bard Leet glanced over at him. Conor saw the cool gaze quickly take in his brown-and-green tunic.

"Quite the mystery, Beast Healer . . . ?" Leet cocked his head in inquiry.

Reluctantly, Conor gave his name.

"Beast Healer Conor," the bard went on, "I don't envy you the task ahead." He shook his head. "Luck to you."

With that, the bard leaned close to Lord Lenslee and murmured something Conor didn't catch. But it must have been some kind of condolences, for Lenslee, his voice husky, said, "My thanks, Bard Leet. I appreciate—"

His voice broke; he turned away from the stall and stumbled to the door. The bard followed him. Conor looked away; it was not an easy thing, watching a man as proud as Therinn of Lenslee break down. True, the Kelnethi lord was not one of Conor's favorites; he was haughty and arrogant, and ofttimes cared little for those beneath his station. But by the gods, he loved his horses as if they were his children and treated them accordingly. That was more than many lords or ladies did for the beasts who won them gold and honor.

So out of respect Conor averted his gaze. But at the last instant, he looked up again in time to see the bard pause in the doorway and look back over his shoulder.

The bastard was *smiling*. Before Conor could react, the bard was gone and old Gorith, Lenslee's farrier, limped up to stand by his side. The old man scratched his head like one bemused. "Guess old quarrels are forgiven," he said. "Though I never thought *that* one would be."

"Oh? And what quarrel was that?" Conor asked. He didn't hold with gossip usually, but he'd give a great deal to know the why of that self-satisfied smirk.

"Not certain 'zackly what it were," Gorith said. "I weren't there, y'see—I were at home working with a colt that needed special shoes. Iffen I remember aright, it happened at the Bellford Fair races. Them's in south Kelneth, not far from Bylith. His Lordship always goes to those iffen he's got some good horses.

"Now, where was I? Oh, yes—heard summat about it afterward, I did, but it were a few years back. Now what . . ."

Gorith tugged at his earlobe as if he could pull out the elusive memory. Conor waited patiently.

At last the old farrier spat to one side, then said, "Think it were summat 'bout a young lad. . . . Killed, he was, when he were thrown. Tried to ride too much horse for himself and got thrown. Horse kicked him in the head, so m'brother Rumsy told me."

Gorith jerked his chin in the direction of Summer Lightning's stall. "That horse, and it were done real deliberate, Rumsy said."

Before Conor could ask what he meant, the rumble of a large cart across the cobblestones cut him off. It came to a halt before the wide stable door. Lord Portis's stablemaster Tuerin entered at the head of a crew of workmen. Gorith slipped away.

"You're taking him already?" Conor asked, seeing the ropes and pulleys the men carried.

"We must, Beast Healer," said the stablemaster. "Lord Lenslee cannot bear the thought of him feeding the flies. And in this heat . . ." He let the sentence trail off.

Conor ran his fingers through his hair. "I'd hoped to have one of my superiors look at him, but I understand. Still, leave his stall uncleaned, if you would. I'd like to come back to look it over with someone."

"That I'll do," Tuerin promised. He turned to his crew. "You know what to do" was all he said.

Conor left as the men entered the stall. He couldn't bear to watch.

Maurynna rode into Yarrow's encampment. She sat Boreal a moment in front of the common tent and looked around. No Stormwind; that meant Raven was somewhere else. She saw one of the grooms she knew from Yarrow's holding in Yerrih pitching hay to the line of horses in the center of the camp. "Alder! Is Yarrow about?"

"She's inside, Dragonlord," he called back. "And Raven should be back soon."

Maurynna waved a hand in thanks. She dropped the reins on Boreal's neck and swung down from his broad back as Yarrow pushed the tent door back.

"Welcome, Maurynna," Yarrow said. "Come in and have a bite to eat and some ale."

She spoke pleasantly enough but Maurynna could see signs of strain on her face. Boreal snorted and eyed her for a moment before ambling off to the water trough. Alder followed Boreal.

Maurynna ducked into the tent after Yarrow. "Is something amiss? You look worried."

"Gods, yes. Worried and upset."

"What is it?" Maurynna sat down at the trestle table as Yarrow uncovered some cheese and a half loaf of bread on a platter.

But Yarrow said nothing more until she'd drawn a pitcher of ale and set it down on the table along with two mugs. "You haven't heard about what happened to Lord Lenslee's prize horse?"

Maurynna shook her head as she cut bread for the two of them. "No, though I did notice that the fair was buzzing like a hive of bees as I rode through it. What horse—oh, is that the one who's so fast and so ill-tempered? Linden knows the Beast Healer who's been looking after Lenslee's stable."

"Summer Lightning and Conor, yes," Yarrow answered.

"So what happened?"

Yarrow tore her piece of bread into bits, her eyes staring at a point somewhere beyond Maurynna's shoulder. "Summer Lightning. Dead. In his stall. Not a mark on him."

"Dear gods! How?"

The Yerrin horse trader shook her head. "No one knows."

"Magic?" Maurynna asked, feeling a little sick. *Please—not another dark mage like Kas Althume. . . .*

"Looks like it, doesn't it?" Yarrow answered. "And that's certainly the rumor going around."

"Have you seen it? The horse, I mean," Maurynna asked.

Yarrow made a rude noise. "You're jesting, hmm? Think you the likes of me would be allowed into His Lordship's precious stables even at the best of times? He'd be certain I was a thief or a spy. And now the man's half-mad with fury and fear, I'll wager. If a mage struck down his best horse, no doubt he's wondering if he's next. *I* would be."

Maurynna suddenly knew what Yarrow truly feared. If there *was* a mage killing horses, where would he strike next? Here? Maurynna knew how Yarrow felt about her horses. No wonder she looked tense and worried.

"If it was magic," Maurynna said slowly, "someone must have hired him—I can't believe that some insane mage is wandering about killing horses at random. Does Lord Lenslee have enemies?"

"He *must* have some," Yarrow said with a harsh laugh. "The man treats damn near everyone who's not noble like they were lower than what gets mucked out of his stables. Of course, as long as you're useful to him, that's another tale." She shrugged.

Maurynna nibbled a bit of cheese. "So those who might have the most reason to strike at him likely haven't the means to hire a mage. Soooo—that would seem to leave a racing rival. Someone whose horse might have had a chance but for Summer Lightning." She poured them both more ale while Yarrow thought that over.

"Now that Lord Duriac's in prison," Yarrow said, "Lord Therinn of Lenslee is Lord Sevrynel's chief racing rival." She frowned at the foam threatening to spill over the top of her mug. "And now Lenslee's best horse—the only one in his stable that without question could win against all comers—is dead without a mark on him. Just dead in his stall."

The thought that Sevrynel might be behind the crime made Maurynna feel ill. She liked the Cassorin earl. "Don't seemingly healthy horses sometimes just drop dead? I remember that happened to my uncle's friend when I was a child in Thalnia."

"Oh, I've heard of it many a time—hell, it happened to *me* once—but not when a horse is resting in a stall. It happens when a horse is working."

Maurynna nodded. "My uncle's friend was riding at the time." She paused a moment to consider. "What if it wasn't magery? What if it was, oh, poison? Anyone could do that."

That set Yarrow thinking. "True," she allowed at last. "But from all I've heard, the way Lord Portis keeps his stables guarded during the fair—especially when his cousin Lenslee has his horses there—it's not likely it would be an outsider, some nobody who would have no business at the stable. So it would seem that it's one of his stable crew. Yet . . . yet from all I've heard—and horse-copers gossip worse than a bunch of old nannies, mind you—Lenslee's grooms and handlers are well paid and treated decently. So they're loyal to him; they know they'd be hard-pressed to find such a good place with anyone else. And it's not likely that one of Portis's people would kill a horse of Lenslee's, for their lord doesn't have a horse entered this year."

"Hmm." Maurynna set her elbows on the table and rested her chin in her hands. "So it's not very likely that a horse would just drop dead. . . ."

"Considering it had just been examined by a talented Beast Healer and pronounced healthy? I think I've a better chance of waking up tomorrow and finding out I'm the next heir to the High Chief of Yerrih. And since I'm in no way related to him, that would be a pretty trick."

Both fell silent, each woman retreating into her own thoughts.

Please, please, please let it not be a mage, Maurynna thought. *Or Sevrynel.*

Fiarin had them start too late, Pod thought wearily. This was taking far, far longer than they'd thought it would. The esker hadn't looked like bad walking from the shore, but it was thick with brambles and pricker-bushes and rambling vines right down to the water on either side. It was getting dark and they were not yet at the end.

For a time Fiarin had forced them to wade in the water alongside. With his long legs, he looked more than ever like some big wading bird, but Pod was too tired to be amused. While they made better time, slogging through the mud was exhausting.

But after Fiarin had slipped and fallen into a deep hole, they went back to forcing a way through the vicious thorns. In the end it had taken Kiga's enormous strength to pull the senior Wort Hunter back to dry land. Fiarin had been unable to find any purchase for his feet to help and he weighed more than Pod would have thought.

They stumbled into another of the few clearings they'd found during the day. A kind of rank, coarse grass with sharp edges held sway in them, somehow holding off their thorny cousins.

"I'm not going any further today," Pod heard herself say, astonished at her daring. She sank to her knees.

Fiarin gave her an evil look. So; the madness was back. For a moment Pod thought he would strike her—or try to. Kiga would never let the blow land.

Then, by the mercy of all the gods, Fiarin had a passing fit of common sense. "It's too late to enter the swamp today," he conceded, looking around as if just noticing the dying light. "We'll camp here for the night. We cross the swamp tomorrow. And then . . ."

He stopped and stared greedily at the distant tree-shrouded swamp fading into the darkness. "And then . . . the Woods."

Thirty-eight

Raven and Arisyn spent the day riding slowly through the somber fair. There was no speech between them. Instead they listened, eavesdropping shamelessly. Few spoke of the match race that was never to be. All the talk was of the mysterious death of the favorite of the Queen's Chase. "Summer Lightning's dead!" was all they heard. "Did you hear? Summer Lightning's dead!"

Everywhere they looked, fairgoers gathered in small groups, rank forgotten for once as nobles and commoners gathered together and discussed the little they knew. And because no one knew the truth, rumors flew faster than, well, lightning, Raven thought.

"Poison, it was!"

"Magic, *I* heard!"

"And I heard that his head was chopped off! Someone saw a man with a sword running from the stable!"

"Have to be a big man," the first gossiper scoffed.

"It were! A giant, I heard!"

Raven shook his head. He'd no more idea than the next man what had happened to the favorite, but a giant with a sword to match would likely have been noticed in the fair by now.

"How could someone do something like that?" Arisyn asked in a subdued voice.

"I don't know. Whatever it was, I just hope the poor animal didn't suffer. Is the Queen's Chase to go on?"

"Oh yes. It's always run on the solstice, no matter what. The Rockfalls have hosted the fair of Balyaranna for generations. And come what may, my foster father told me, the race is run to honor a vow the first earl made to the Mother. Every earl or countess since then has held to that. When Countess Beline was dying, she ordered that the race be run even if she died that day."

"What happened?" Raven asked. It seemed horse-madness ran in the Rockfall bloodline. "And did she? Die, that is."

"She did—the night before. They ran the race as she'd ordered," Arisyn said. "The legend is that she'd threatened to haunt her family if they didn't. Guess they didn't want to take the chance."

"Good for her." Raven chuckled. "She knew what was important."

Arisyn grinned impishly. "But they did draw the line at propping her up in the royal box as she'd also wanted, Lord Sevrynel told me. She was his great-grandmother and he remembers the day even though, as he says, he was but a wee little boy."

"There he is, Huryn! There's the thief!"

Raven recognized the voice—much to his annoyance. He glanced over his shoulder, hoping he was wrong.

No; no such luck. It was indeed Tirael. But why was he pointing at him?

Hold on there—did that bullying popinjay just call me "thief"?

It seemed he had, for Lord Huryn called out, "I require you to stop, Raven Redhawkson."

"As you wish, my lord." Raven dismounted and waited for the High Marshal and his men to reach him.

Arisyn snorted in derision. "Don't blame Raven if you were so drunk you lost your belt pouch again, Tirael. Go back to the last tavern tent you were at and start looking there instead of wasting our time."

"Be quiet, you miserable little pile of turds," Tirael said viciously. "You helped him steal Brythian, didn't you?" He lunged at Arisyn with the clear intent of hauling him off Arrow.

Lord Huryn was too fast for him. Somehow the black-haired High Marshal cut Tirael off. "None of that, Tirael!" Lord Huryn said sharply. "I suggest you—"

"They're both thieves!" Tirael shouted. "I demand you arrest them both!"

A gasp from Arisyn made Raven look up at him. The boy's face was pale—but not from fear as Raven first thought.

This was bone-deep, righteous fury. Sevrynel's foster son drew himself up and stared down at Tirael like a man looking down upon a maggot. "How dare you," he said, his voice full of barely controlled rage. "How *dare* you, sirrah! Who are you to name *me* thief—you who never had any intention of paying a wager you made! Trot out your witnesses, you sack of lies! Where's your proof that we stole your horse?"

Raven had to bite his lip to keep from cheering. A glance at Lord Huryn told him that the High Marshal—as well as his men—were hard put to keep smiles from their faces.

Arrow sidestepped until Arisyn was directly in front of their accuser. He leaned down until his face was a bare handspan from Tirael's. "The penalties for laying false charges against a fellow noble are severe, Tirael. Shall I cry Challenge and name my Champion? Have *you* a Champion? Mine will be Black Althur, my father's captain of the guard."

From the guardsmen's whistles and the way Tirael's face paled, Raven guessed that this Black Althur was known as a fell warrior. A little voice in the back of his mind snickered, *He'd likely wet himself if you named Linden.*

"You little—" Tirael sputtered. "You wouldn't da—"

"Lord Arisyn would be well within his rights," Lord Huryn said mildly. "That is, unless you have incontrovertible proof, Tirael—such as eyewitnesses?"

"I withdraw the charge against Lord Arisyn," Tirael said sullenly. He pointed at Raven. "But not against him! Arrest him, I say!"

Raven said quietly, "I was in my aunt's camp all night long with a friend of mine, my lord, playing a game from his native land, and talking over the race. He left not long before Lord Arisyn brought me the news about Brythian. And in that short amount of time I was within the view of the men and women of my own camp and the camps around me. Nor would there have been enough time for me to get to wherever you keep your horse, steal it, and hide it someplace it *still* hasn't been found—which is the last I heard. I'm sorry your horse is missing, my lord Tirael, for he seemed a fine animal indeed, and I was looking forward to our race even though I'd already known I'd never see my gold when I won. But I had nothing to do with it."

"Lies!" Tirael hissed. "And who cares for the word of a bunch of peasants!"

"One of my witnesses is no peasant." Raven turned to Arisyn. "My lord, would you ride aside, please?"

Arisyn chewed his lip. "Knowing who your visitor was would end the game, wouldn't it? As long as High Marshal Huryn has no objection, I'll wait for you by that leather worker's booth."

"The 'game'?" Lord Huryn asked.

"Lord Arisyn has been trying to guess what breed Stormwind is. Very honorable about it, as well. He won't listen if someone tries to talk to him about it."

Chuckling, Lord Huryn waved away the young lord.

When Arisyn was gone, Raven said to Tirael, "My lord, the friend with whom I talked all night long is Shima Ilyathan. I met him in Jehanglan. Would *his* word be enough for you?"

"Yet another lie! You dare claim friendship with—"

"Oh, give over, Tirael," Lord Huryn said in disgust. "He's not lying. Surely you've heard the song 'Dragon and Phoenix' at least once? Remember the part about some truehumans with Llysanyins? He tried to warn you when you challenged him to that race, but you wouldn't listen. Brythian would have lost, pure and simple. A lucky thing for you that he's gone, isn't it—not that you ever intended to honor your end of the wager, did you?"

The last was said in a tone of such disgust that Tirael's face flamed. He turned and stalked away, snarling over his shoulder, "If you come to your senses, Huryn, and arrest that serf, I'll be at Lord and Lady Pearrin's encampment."

When he heard where Tirael was staying that night, Arisyn said, "Oh, hang it all—I finally got permission to stay there tonight along with Coryn and Marus and Javriel!"

Raven studied the fuming boy and came to a decision. "Never mind him— we've somewhere else to go. I think it's time to let you know what Stormwind is, and I think you'll like this other campsite even more. Follow me." He led the way through the fair. Once outside the grounds, he set Stormwind to a slow canter through the growing dusk.

Soon they reached the royal encampment. Raven led the way to the gate Maurynna had shown him at the Dragonlords' end of the camp. A banner hung across the top of the gate: a silvery white dragon on a black background, the whole bordered in red. The guards at the gate eyed them.

"Here we are!" Raven said cheerfully.

Arisyn tugged at his sleeve. "This is where the Dragonlords are st-staying," he stuttered.

"Yes," Raven agreed. "They are."

"But we can't just barge in—"

"Ari—remember the best friend Rynna I told you about? The one I grew up with?"

Arisyn stared at him blankly for a moment. Then—well, Raven could tell the exact instant *that* acorn dropped. "Oh gods—you mean 'Rynna' is short for 'Maurynna'?"

"Guessed it in one. She's still my best friend even though she's Maurynna Kyrissaean now. But that hasn't made any difference, save that because of her, Linden Rathan, Shima Ilyathan, and a couple of other Dragonlords have also become good friends of mine."

Raven forbore to add that he and Linden had not started out as friends. Then common sense—his—had prevailed at last. He'd accepted that he and Rynna would never be more than friends now. He never knew when it had happened, only that it was after their adventure in Jehanglan. But one day, he'd realized that the knowledge that they'd never be together didn't hurt anymore. It was just something he knew as he knew that the hawthorn bush outside his window bore red berries. It just *was*.

Considering Rynna's temper, perhaps it was just as well, he thought, though he was fairly certain she wouldn't try to box his ears for him anymore. But most of all, he knew she was happier than she'd ever been and in the end that was what counted.

He glanced over at Arisyn and smiled. The boy's eyes were huge.

"Oh," said Arisyn weakly. "*You're* one of the truehumans mentioned in the song, aren't you? The two with Llysanyins . . ." He stared at Stormwind. "Oh, my." Then, with a big grin, "We're going to camp with the Dragonlords? Hah! Eat dirt, Tirael!"

The light of the standing torches flickered over the servants as they moved among the men and women gathered around the royal encampment. The dancing glow turned their faces into fantastic masks as they offered wine here, sweetmeats and savory tarts there, or finger bowls and scented towels to the lords and ladies relaxing at tables set beneath the gaily colored awnings.

Not that the awnings were needed anymore; the sun had gone down a candlemark or so ago, taking with it the day's wilting heat. The night was pleasantly cool. The fire that blazed merrily in the center of the encampment was more for show than for warmth.

There was something about being outside at night, Linden thought, that begged for a campfire, and not just for cooking, either. He watched the leaping flames, content for the moment to sit lazily at the table with Shima and Maurynna, listening to Bard Leet as he played.

A pity Otter couldn't be here. I prefer his version of "Mist on the Moor," though it would be damned sticky with both of them here, Linden thought. *Leet's a master, no question of that, but some songs—the old ones at least—are better without the fancy flourishes.*

Still, the harp's song flowed sweet as honeyed wine, a gentle counterpoint to the various conversations. Linden let it flow over him as he looked around.

The mood of the camp was subdued. A sense of unease, even fear, hung over the gathering due, no doubt, to the mysterious death of the favorite. Linden knew that each owner had doubled the guard on his or her racers. Yet there were also undercurrents of a kind of fierce . . . excitement.

Yes, that's what it was: excitement. Before—barring some accident—the only question was which horse would come in second. Now . . . Now others had a chance at gold and glory.

A leather ball rolled to his feet. He picked it up and tossed it back to Rann. The young prince grinned and waved in thanks, then went back to the serious business of a game of three-cornered toss with two other children that kept Bramble scrambling happily after the ball.

A pity Kella couldn't be here, he mindspoke Maurynna. *Have you have any more word of her?*

The last letter from Maylin said that she was back to her old self and that Aunt Elenna has stopped hovering over her like a worried hen. Oh, and Kella says to give her love to Rann and Rosalea. I think Rosalea's the little girl playing with Rann and that other boy.

The song ended with a rippling double run up the strings, a delicate filigree of sound that hung bell-like in the dusk. Then it slipped into something Linden didn't recognize, but liked right away.

Shima straightened in his chair. "I know that one!" he said in delight. "It's one of the songs I sang for him—though with a great deal added," he added, his brow furrowed.

Linden poured wine all around. "He does seem to like complex arrangements, doesn't he? Always has, Otter says—the more elaborate, the better, and never able to resist another bit of tinkering with a tune."

When the song ended and Leet stood up, Maurynna said, "You know, I can't help feeling that Leet looks vaguely familiar somehow, but I'm certain I've never met him. Are he and Otter friends?"

The bard wandered among the tables, talking and sometimes playing a snippet of a song, or drinking a cup of wine.

"Um—no," Linden said, remembering the long-ago rivalry between Leet and Otter for the love of Jaida, another bard. She'd chosen Otter; unfortunately, she'd died during the birth of their first child, and the child with her. Leet had never forgiven Otter.

But rather than revive old gossip, he left it at that, hoping that Maurynna would assume it was nothing more than the professional jealousy that happened all too often between bards.

"Ah." She flashed him a knowing grin. "I see."

"Dragonlords?" a hesitant voice asked behind them.

As one, they turned to see one of the guards who walked the perimeter of the royal encampment. He was young, and looked uncomfortable, likely at being so close to some of the "gentry," Linden thought.

"Yes?" he asked in amused sympathy. When he was a soldier, he hadn't liked disturbing nobles, either, especially when they were drinking. He wondered if this poor beggar had drawn the short straw.

The guard cleared his throat nervously and stood up a little straighter. "There are two men—er, one's a boy, really—asking to see you. The older one says he's Raven Redhawkson, Your Graces, and that you'll know him."

"So we do," Linden said with a smile. "He and any of his friends are welcome to join us anytime."

Said Maurynna, "He and I grew up together. And about time he showed up, too. I was expecting him before this."

As relief flooded his face, the guard saluted. "Thank you, Dragonlords. I'll escort them here at once." He turned on his heel and marched briskly off into the darkness. Shima called for two more chairs and goblets to be brought to their table.

A short while later, the guard was back with Raven and a boy of about thirteen or fourteen years. Raven smiled and waved at them. Once again the guard saluted and left, his task accomplished; he'd looked far happier this time.

Raven dropped into the empty chair by Maurynna's side. "Well met, Beanpole," he said, tugging a strand of her hair. "Fall off Boreal yet?" He laughed as she made a face at him, then reached across the table to clasp hands with Linden, then Shima. "Shima, remind me to tell you how glad I am that you came by last night."

Linden caught his eye and nodded in amusement at the openmouthed boy who stood a little behind Raven.

Raven waved the boy forward and pointed to the waiting chair. "This is Lord Arisyn. Ari, don't be shy—come here and sit down. They won't eat you."

The boy edged nervously toward the chair.

"Not without plenty of green sauce," Linden said with a straight face. While he hadn't recognized the boy himself, he recognized the name of Lord Sevrynel's foster son.

Arisyn stopped short. His eyes went very big.

"Horseradish," Maurynna countered. "Or perhaps just verjuice and salt?" She looked thoughtful.

"Gravy and pepper," Shima voted, all wide-eyed innocence.

Arisyn's throat apple bobbed visibly as he eyed the Dragonlords. Linden swore the poor boy turned at least two shades paler. It wasn't until Raven burst out laughing and asked, "What, no one for bread sauce?" that Arisyn finally realized he was being teased.

He ducked his head, grinned sheepishly, and slid into the empty seat. "Thank you, Dragonlords."

Before any introductions could be made, Bard Leet approached their table. Linden cursed under his breath; hopefully neither Leet nor Raven would remember seeing each other before. It was possible, he thought. It had been for only a few brief moments in the library at Dragonskeep two years before.

"Greetings, Your Graces, Lord Arisyn," the bard said, smiling graciously and bowing as well as he could with the harp in his arms. He went on, "And to you, my lord—?"

Raven said, "No one's lord, bard. I'm a freeman of Yerrih, a breeder of horses."

Leet's eyebrows went up. "I see." He glanced at Arisyn.

Good, Linden thought in relief. *He thinks Raven's here with Arisyn, not the other way around. Let's hope that cat stays in its bag.* To steer the conversation into safer channels, Linden went on, "Your harp has a lovely voice, Bard Leet. Who made it?" He admired the wood-burned ornamentation on the shoulder of the harp: a seagull within a circle of bluebells. Beautifully done, he thought.

Leet hesitated just long enough that Linden wondered if the question were somehow rude. "A luthier named Thomelin from Bylith," he said at last. "May I ask why you wish to know, Your Grace?"

"I was thinking of a new harp," Linden said vaguely. "I play and yours is particularly fine." *Am I imagining things or did the man just relax?*

"Ah. I will say this for Thomelin: He can make wood sing." The bard looked around the table once more and winked. "Who do you think will win tomorrow, my lords and lady?"

"We're judges," Shima said with a laugh. "I don't think we're supposed to have favorites."

"Raven would if he could race," Arisyn said proudly. "He has a Llysanyin."

Oh, no! Linden knew what was coming next and winced.

"May I ask how you—" the bard began.

Linden coughed loudly, like a man whose wine had gone down the wrong way. Maurynna slapped his back.

It worked, but only for a moment. Then Leet frowned and fingered the cleft in his chin as if he were trying to recall something. Linden prayed silently, hoping the bard wouldn't put two and two together—and that no one would say anything.

That hope promptly went to hell in a bit bucket. "A pity Otter's Llysanyin is a mare," Shima remarked thoughtfully. "It would have been nice to have another stallion in the family."

Linden nearly groaned; if that didn't let the cat—a whole *herd* of spitting, yowling cats with very sharp claws—out of the bag, nothing would.

The gracious smile vanished from Leet's face like dew beneath a desert sun. Despite the warm night, a sudden chill seemed to descend upon the little group; any colder, Linden thought, and there'd be a blizzard in his wine cup. He couldn't quite read the expression that flashed across the bard's face: annoyance, wariness, or . . .

Or perhaps it was merely a trick of the flickering torchlight, for when he spoke again, the bard was pleasant enough. "You're kin to Otter Heronson?"

"Grandnephew."

Leet nodded. Any remark he might have made was lost as Lord Sevrynel bustled up to their table. Linden caught a barely breathed, "Oh, no," from Arisyn, and looked at him curiously. He'd have hardly thought the mild-mannered Sevrynel would be such an ogre of a foster father.

"Your Graces, Master Bard Leet, please excuse this intrusion, but . . . Arisyn, what are you doing—I thought you were going— Oh, hello, Master Raven, I'm sorry, I didn't see you at first, eyes aren't what they used to be, and these wretched torches, you know. . . ." He blinked and looked around in mild apology, then began telling Leet all about the wonderful horses Raven would have.

The panicked look that had filled Arisyn's eyes when his foster father came up slipped away by degrees. That look piqued Linden's curiosity. Since no one could ever convince him that Lord Sevrynel was some kind of monster (Horsemad, yes. Absentminded, likely. But a bully? No.), there was something else going on here. Something the boy didn't want Sevrynel to know about. Some boy's mischief, perhaps, or an ill-considered bet on the race tomorrow?

Linden came back from his speculations in time to realize that Sevrynel was begging the Dragonlords' pardon, but there was someone he'd like Arisyn to meet, and could he borrow him for a while? And would Master Raven kindly consent to being one of the messengers for the Queen's Chase tomorrow?

"I'd be honored, my lord," Raven said in delight.

"Excellent!" said Sevrynel, leading Arisyn away. "Come along, my boy. I assume you've finally figured out what Stormwind is?"

After foster father and son had left, Maurynna said to Raven, "I hope you can stay awhile longer. Where are you camping this night? With Arisyn, wherever that might be?"

Raven grimaced. "Ah, well now, Beanpole, the reason Arisyn and I are here is to ask if we could camp with you. We ran into Lord Rudeness and *he's* camping where Ari was going to stay tonight.

"And from what Ari said once, Lord Sevrynel's other fosterlings aren't supposed to keep company with him, but they're all going to be there." He took a sip of his wine. "To tell you the truth, the more I see of this fellow, the more I understand why Lord Sevrynel wouldn't want any of his fosterlings hanging about him. Tonight he accused us of stealing his horse so that I wouldn't lose the race! I had to invoke your name, Shima, as my witness so that the fair guards wouldn't arrest me."

Linden sat up straighter. "Did the fool Challenge you or the boy? I'd be happy to act as Champion for either—or both—of you."

"Believe me, I thought of you," Raven said, laughing. "But he backed off accusing Arisyn when the boy threatened to cry Challenge on him and named his father's captain of the guards as his Champion. Looked downright ill, our fine little lord did, at that. If one of us had named *you,* no doubt he'd still be running."

"Hmph—typical bully. Big and bad—until someone bigger shows up. Could he have hidden the horse away himself?" Maurynna asked.

Linden had been thinking the same thing.

Raven shook his head. "No," he said slowly. "I will give him that. I don't think Tirael did. He seems honestly upset—and baffled—over Brythian's disappearance."

"Tirael?" the bard asked quietly. "Tirael Barans?"

Raven said, "I'm sorry, I've no idea what his second name is, Master Bard. If I ever heard it, I don't remember it. But . . . dark brown curly hair, slim, and a face like a maiden's dream?"

"That's him." The words were barely more than a whisper.

"Oh gods." A dark flush spread across Raven's cheeks. "Bard Leet, I hope I haven't insulted a fri—"

Leet shook his head, smiling tightly. "Pray don't worry, Master Redhawkson, I'm not insulted. Not at all. I'm well aware that Lord Tirael can be . . . difficult." His long fingers stroked the harp cradled in his arms like a child, playing over the design burned into the shoulder of the instrument. "I know him of old, you see."

The mellifluous voice trembled the tiniest bit. Leet drew a deep breath, then bowed abruptly and with a few courteous words took his leave of them. Someone called to him to settle an argument for them.

Maurynna smothered a laugh behind her hand as they watched Leet listen carefully as each party stated their case. "Oh, my—I'd say that this Tirael Whatever-his-name-is got Leet's back up once."

"Why am I not surprised?" said Raven. He rolled his eyes. "Arisyn said he's charming when he wants to be, but when he isn't . . . look out! Nasty, sarcastic tongue on him and a cruel streak a league wide."

"Sounds like a fool, then, if he turned it loose on a bard," Linden said. Seeing Shima's blank look, he explained, "It's not wise to annoy a bard—not unless you've a taste for winding up as the butt of a scathing song. And somehow, they always manage to come up with the catchiest tunes for those," he added dryly. "Spread like wildfire, they will. Everyone singing them wherever you go, and they hang around forever, it seems."

"Everyone knows who you are—and not the way you'd want them to," said Maurynna, smiling wickedly. She raised a hand to beckon the steward of the camp. "Let's see about getting you and Arisyn some shelter for tonight, Raven. There must be an extra tent somewhere."

As Maurynna explained their needs to the steward, Linden wondered what Tirael had done to annoy Leet so much. Still, it couldn't have been too bad; he hadn't heard of any mocking ditties with the young lord's name in them—at least, not from Otter. And Otter knew them all.

Dismissing the thought—rude young lordlings held *very* little interest for him—Linden asked Raven if Yarrow had yet seen that band of mares from Pelnar, the ones that came in yesterday afternoon.

Both she and Raven had, it turned out. That led to a spirited discussion of each mare's strengths and weaknesses and which ones—if any—might cross well with Stormwind if Yarrow could get them. Then the conversation turned to tentative plans to stay at Yarrow's holding for the autumn and winter.

At last, yawning hugely, Shima announced he was going to bed. "I didn't sleep much last night, nor did you. A fine pair of fools we'd look, falling asleep and tumbling off our Llysanyins just as everyone raced past."

That set off a round of yawns. "The only thing to spread faster than a rumor," Linden said, shaking his head as he finished his. "And since we need to be off before everyone else so that we can be in our places, we'd best get to sleep."

Groans greeted the reminder. "Who are the other judges?" Raven asked as they all rose.

Linden ticked the list off on the fingers of one hand as the small band walked through the camp. "Besides the three of us, there's Archpriest Urwin of the temple of Valerissen in Kelneth; Palani, the Head Priestess of the Grove of Mila; and, finally, Bard Leet. He's an elder of the Bards' Guild, hence the honor.

"Priestess Palani will be the judge at the start-and-finish line—she's too pregnant to ride far, especially over rough terrain—and the rest of us will be strung out along the loop that forms the route. Your job will be to patrol a section of the course, going between the judges at either end, looking for injured riders or to take messages."

A servant came up to them and bowed. "Good evening, Your Graces. Master Redhawkson? Your tent is this way, sir."

Raven waved as he went off with his guide. "See you in the morning. Let's hope for an exciting race, eh?"

As Raven disappeared into the darkness, Shima chuckled and said, "Let's hope it's not too exciting."

"Oh?" Linden said, pausing before turning off onto the little track that led to the pavilion that he and Maurynna shared.

"The Jehangli have a curse: 'May you live in interesting times.'"

Linden thought that over for a moment. "Eh, that *is* a nasty one, isn't it?"

Frowning and shaking her head, Maurynna said, "I must be more tired than I thought. Why would that be nasty?"

Shima said, "Consider what can be 'interesting': war, fire, floods, pestilence, drought—"

"Getting caught up in one of Lleld's schemes," Linden muttered under his breath.

"Say no more," Maurynna said, laughing. "May the gods spare us all of those."

"Especially the last," Shima added. He raised his hand in farewell and continued along the main track. "Sleep well," he called back to them.

"Mm," Linden said, slipping his arm around Maurynna's shoulders. Hers went around his waist as he led her down the faint path. As they reached their tent, he said, "So you're tired, love?"

A soft laugh. "Not *that* tired."

Linden smiled as he held the door flap aside for her. "Good. Because neither am I."

"I feel silly," Arisyn said as he accompanied his foster father on his final walk through the camp. "I cannot believe that I didn't figure it out."

Lord Sevrynel chuckled. "And after the hint I gave you, too."

"Hint?"

"The song I was humming. Couldn't help it, really."

"Song?" Arisyn thumped the heel of his hand against his forehead. "Oh gods, I remember now. You *were* humming something but I didn't really pay any attention at the time."

"That will teach you to pay more attention to your elders. And as for feeling foolish that you didn't recognize Stormwind for what he is, remember—I had an advantage over you. I saw Shan when Linden Rathan was here for the regency debate.

"Now, tell me what you think of Lord and Lady Inavriel. They've graciously agreed to host you for your year in Pelnar and they're very close to King— Oh! Bard Leet! A word with you, please."

The bard turned. Arisyn thought he looked annoyed, but perhaps he was tired and just wanted to get back to his tent. "My lord?"

"I'm having a small gathering for the victor of the race tomorrow—whoever that might be—and wonder if you would consent to play for it. Not the night of the race itself, mind you, but the evening after. The Dragonlords and the duke and duchess will attend and I saw how much they all enjoyed your music tonight."

Bard Leet smiled slightly. "I would be honored, of course."

Hmph, thought Arisyn, *he certainly doesn't sound it.* Then a horrible thought popped into his mind and out of his mouth before he could stop it. "Oh, no— Lord and Lady Portis will be coming, won't they?"

"Of course. He's one of the fair's marshals. Why?"

Arisyn took a deep breath. His foster father had to find out sometime. "Because . . . because Tirael's here."

Lord Sevrynel made a face like a man who'd just found half a worm in the apple he was eating. "Much as I'd rather not, I suppose I'll have to invite him as—"

"You can't!" Arisyn blurted. "Merrilee's afraid of him!" Oh gods—and he'd promised Merri he wouldn't tell anyone. He knew she was ashamed that she'd fallen for Tirael's lies. He hadn't even told Raven and here he was babbling about it in front of a complete stranger.

"Lady Merrilee of Romsley?" the bard asked, half a breath before Sevrynel's astonished "What? Why?"

Arisyn nodded to the bard, saying reluctantly, "When Merri and Kare were in Pelnar visiting their aunt, Tirael began courting Merri. She didn't know about him and from everything they've said, he took good care to show her only his best side. But she found out about him and sent him away."

Now he had to tread delicately. The next was not from the sisters, but overheard between Coryn and Dunric. "He's been sending her notes that she's refused to answer. I think he's demanding she run away with him." Then he was back to safer ground. "I know she's afraid of what will happen if he finds out about Lord Eadain courting her—and that she favors him."

Arisyn had never seen his foster father look so stern. "Then I will certainly see that there is no invitation for him. I shall be sorry if his parents are insulted, but there is nothing I can do about that. Lady Merrilee is my guest," Lord Sevrynel said, "as is Lord Eadain. Thank you for warning me, Arisyn. Now—if you'll both excuse me, I must see to this."

With that, Lord Sevrynel trotted off, no doubt to find someone to bear a message to his house steward, leaving Arisyn standing awkwardly with the bard. But when he turned to him, intending to bid the man good night, Bard Leet was already striding away.

How rude, Arisyn thought in surprise. *But perhaps you don't need manners when you're a Master Bard.* He shrugged. He was tired; time for bed.

Alone at last in his tent, Leet set his harp down on its stand. He stood staring at it. Each breath rasped in his throat; a red haze clouded his vision. He staggered to his camp bed and sat, one hand pressed to his chest. Gods—if his heart beat any harder, it would burst through his breastbone.

He forced himself to breathe, to inhale and exhale in a steady rhythm, slow and deep, working through the breathing exercises like a nervous journeyman facing an audience for the first time.

Breathe in, slowly, slowly, count to ten . . . exhale, slowly, slowly, again and again and again . . . It was working. The mad racing of his heart slowed under his hand, the red haze receded.

Then came the thought *How dare that filth come to Balyaranna!* and his fragile calm was shattered. Leet had to bury his face in his hands to keep from howling his rage to the gods.

To add insult to injury, the whelp who'd delivered the news—who had no idea what wounds his offhand comment had ripped open—that same whelp was Otter's grandnephew.

That . . . that was salt poured into the wound. He slumped in defeat. Thank the gods that this gathering was nearly over; he should still be out there, but he couldn't face anyone.

Leet decided to go to bed. There was nothing he could do; perhaps he would be able to escape into sleep. He blew out the lantern, undressed, and lay down. For a long time he stared into the darkness. The camp finally fell quiet around him.

He'd thought it would be revenge enough that Summer Lightning would never vent his unnatural rage on anyone else. Never take another life, never destroy another family. And the look on Lenslee's face as he stared at his dead horse! Ahhh—he would treasure that.

But to find out that Tirael Barans was here in Balyaranna . . . The last he'd heard of that demon's spawn was that he was in Pelnar and likely to stay there for some time. So he'd come back chasing a woman; how like him.

Gods, it was as if his revenge had been erased as a cloth would wipe clean a writing slate. For while it was a blow from Summer Lightning's hoof that crushed Arnath's skull, it was Tirael who had tossed the boy upon the stallion's back. Tossed him there and laughed about it. Now Tirael was here, and there was not a damned thing he could do about it, for Tirael would stay well away from him.

Even the proverbial village idiot could guess that Leet, while barred from referring to Tirael's part in Arnath's death, would be looking for any insult, any slight, anything at all that he could write a scathing song about.

So much work, so much planning to kill Summer Lightning . . . wasted, all wasted. Then the idea burst upon him like a bolt of lightning. He sat up. The sheer ruthlessness of it, the iron-cold nerve it would need, the absolute *rightness* of it took his breath away. Leet shivered, well-nigh overwhelmed at the odds against him.

Was it possible? With luck and a bit of time, yes. More importantly, *could* he do it? He had already strained the limits of his oath as a bard. This would break it.

That made him pause. Ever since his youth, that oath had shaped his thoughts, his behavior, his very life. He looked inside himself, saw the scars left by the deaths of the two people that he had loved almost more than life itself. Deaths that could have—should have!—been prevented.

Within his heart he set those deaths—those *murders*—on the scale against the weight of his oath. The memories made him close his eyes and sway like a reed in a wind. His oath was less than a feather to the two faces he saw within his mind's eye.

Besides—hadn't Otter already broken the oath years ago? He'd known Jaida was too small to safely bear a child sired by a man as big as him, Yerrin that he was. But had that stopped him from letting Jaida risk herself—and dying? No; no, it hadn't. Otter had broken the oath in spirit if not in fact.

For Jaida's sake, I will make him pay as he should *have paid.* So be it—he could do this thing. He *would* do this thing.

The decision banished all hesitation, all fear. Leet felt suddenly giddy, like a man deep in his cups. He smiled. By the lost songs of Satha, this was a gift of the gods. All he need do was stretch out his hand; his revenge was there for the taking. And not one revenge, but two!

He dressed once more, his hands shaking. A short while later he rode up to the guards at the entrance to the camp.

"Halt! Who—" The captain of the watch held a torch up. "Apologies, Bard Leet. I didn't recognize you at first. You're leaving us?" He sounded surprised.

"Just for a short while, I hope, Captain." Leet patted the case strapped to his back and went on, "I just found one of the tuning pegs on my harp is loose in its hole. And like a fool I left my kit to fix such things back at the castle. . . ." He shrugged and smiled ruefully.

The captain nodded in understanding. "And since you'll need it in the morning, sir—"

"It's without sleep a certain foolish bard must go." Leet sighed, shaking his head as if he couldn't believe he'd been so stupid.

Turning, the captain called back into the darkness, "Terk—mount up and escort Bard Leet to the castle and back."

"Yes, sir!"

This was *not* what Leet wanted. "Captain, I shall be perfectly safe, I'm cer—"

"Perhaps, sir, but it's dark, your cloak looks black rather than bard's red, and there have been footpads about. I'd rather not risk it, bard."

Leet knew from the captain's tone he would brook no argument. While they waited for Terk, he forced himself to maintain his pose of a man who'd rather be abed.

Still, when his escort appeared a short while later, Leet couldn't resist setting spurs to his mount. He heard exclamations of surprise behind him, heard Terk's horse scramble to catch up.

He didn't care. He had to get to the castle as soon as possible.

Raven snuggled down into the bed. Though he was certain it was plain compared to the ones that the nobles were used to, it was more comfortable than many an inn bed that he'd slept in, and pure bliss compared to a blanket on the ground. Amazing what could be done with boards and ropes . . . and a featherbed. If only he could carry one of these along when he and Yarrow journeyed to distant holdings! He shut his eyes and smiled.

The bed ropes across the tent creaked. "Psst!"

"Hmm? Yes, Ari?"

"Stormwind himself chose— And you really went to— Truly went?" The words tumbled over each other.

"He did and I did." Raven chuckled at the muffled squeak of delight from Arisyn's side of the tent. "But I'm not telling you about it now, so go to sleep, Ari."

He considered telling Arisyn that he'd ask Stormwind to let him ride, then decided against it. The boy would be bouncing around the tent all night in excitement. He certainly would have been.

No, he needed his sleep. Tomorrow was going to be an important day for him.

Thirty-nine

Pod pushed some branches out of her way and grimaced as the wet ground sucked at her boots. One foot caught in the mud; she pulled, careful not to yank her foot clean out of her boot. One soaking-wet foot was bad enough. Luckily, this time both foot and boot came out together, though with a rude sucking sound. She wrinkled her nose at the stink of rotting vegetation that followed. In front of her Kaeliss bent over, also trying to work foot and boot out together.

"It is always this wet here?" she asked, eyeing a mossy branch lying across the path—such as it was—a bit ahead of her. Hmm—was it too big a step to it? Behind her she could hear Kiga growling in disgust as each paw sank into the foul muck.

To her surprise, Fiarin answered pleasantly. It seemed that now that he was nearly to his mysterious goal, the senior Wort Hunter's mood had improved.

"Most of the year, yes, save in winter or when there's been a bad drought," Fiarin said. "You can't really tell at this time of the year—too many leaves blocking the view—but there's a long, gradual slope from the south to here where the land goes flat again. So it gets all the runoff from the melting snow and there are springs as—"

He broke off with a gasp. Pod stopped in surprise and looked past Kaeliss to see what was wrong. Much of her view was blocked, but she saw Fiarin try to jump backward, his arms flailing wildly. But one foot stuck in the treacherous mud; his action merely stretched his leg out invitingly as he fell onto his back in the ankle-deep water. His head just grazed the toe of Kaeliss's boot.

Pod gasped as *something* struck twice in quick succession at Fiarin's leg, almost faster than she could see. She barely had time to register an impression of a long, whiplike form when a raging Kiga shoved past and threw himself upon the sinuous body.

There was a brief but furious battle, punctuated by snarls and hisses. Then all was quiet again. Too quiet; to the stunned Pod it seemed that the whole swamp held its breath. Kiga stepped back from his foe, revealing a snake clad in mottled copper-and-brown scales. Its large triangular head was attached to its body only by a thread of skin, yet the jaws still snapped reflexively. A rough triangle of yellow scales just above the eyes caught her attention.

Pod stared at the dead snake like one caught in a spell; there was something about that yellow marking, something important, but her stunned mind refused to work. It was as if the world hung suspended in the unnatural silence and her mind spun in the center of the void.

The moment shattered. Fiarin sat up and clutched at his leg. "Oh gods, no," he whimpered over and over again, his voice high and frightened. Then, "Oh gods, please—not a crowned viper! Not one of those!"

Crowned viper! Pod gasped; there were very few poisonous snakes in Kelneth, particularly this far north, but the crowned viper was the most dangerous. The only good thing about them was their rarity—though clearly, a half-hysterical voice in the back of Pod's mind said, they were not rare enough.

A quick glance at Kiga told her that the woods dog was unscathed; had he been hurt, he would be trying to show her his injury as he'd been trained to do. Instead he stood snarling at his enemy's head as if daring it to another battle.

Kaeliss fell to her knees by Fiarin's side. Pulling her belt knife, she slashed the leg of his breeches open. "Lie back," she ordered. "Pod, support him."

Nodding, Pod knelt in the shallow, mucky water. Fiarin slumped against her, his eyes closed. To her alarm, Pod saw that his face was already a sickly grey. Was it the venom acting already—or fear that death waited for him? She prayed to all the gods that it was the latter. At a hiss from Kaeliss, Pod craned her neck, angling for a glimpse.

The marks of the fangs were clear on Fiarin's leg: two small, circular punctures, a knuckle's width apart. Already the skin around them was an ugly mottled color.

It must have missed once—oh gods, why couldn't it have missed both times!

"I could put a tourniquet on . . . ," Kaeliss began.

He must have heard the doubt in her voice, for Fiarin gasped, "No! That's tricky even for a Healer. Do it wrong and I lose the leg."

"But if I don't—"

"*No!* I won't lose the leg." He groaned in pain and spasmed in her arms. "Not worth . . ." The next words trailed off into another groan.

Pod could guess the rest: If he couldn't tramp his beloved forests, life was not worth the living for Fiarin. He would rather die doing what he loved, not spend the rest of his life hobbling on crutches around his chapterhouse.

She didn't know if she agreed; she was young and life was very sweet. But this was Fiarin's choice, not hers, not Kaeliss's. If only she was a Healer!

Well, she was—of a kind. It might not work—Beast Healer magic often didn't work on humans, just as a Healer's power usually had no effect upon a hurt animal—but she had to try.

"Snakebane . . . healmoss. Try . . ." His words were barely audible.

Pod held him tighter. If nothing else, she could try to lay the Sleep upon him to ease his passing if the herbs that Kaeliss was pulling from her pack didn't work. The thought made her want to cry, but she could not watch him suffer needlessly. She'd heard what the victims went through; Olbari, one of the senior Beast Healers, had come upon someone after a crowned viper bite.

He hadn't been able to help; Pod remembered the grief—even guilt—in his voice as he told the tale. She watched Kaeliss crush the herbs together into a thick, dripping wad that she pressed to the tiny but deadly wounds and bind it in place with her kerchief.

"Let's get him back to dry ground," Kaeliss said.

"I want to try a Healing first," Pod replied. "Switch places with me."

When she had taken Pod's place, Kaeliss asked tensely, "Will it work? You're a Beast Healer."

Pod studied Fiarin's face; his color—or lack of it—alarmed her. Nor did he seem to hear them; Pod wondered if it was because he was simply focusing inward, husbanding his strength, or if he was so far gone already he *couldn't* hear them.

That scared her. "I don't know," she said, more shortly than she meant to.

Resting Fiarin's leg upon her knees, Pod gently laid her hands atop the poultice, closed her eyes, and invoked her magic. When she felt the familiar tingling in her hands, she looked down at them.

Damn! Instead of the usual steady blue-tinged green, the misty haze surrounding her hands pulsed and eddied as if confused or even angry. Or was it her fear for Fiarin's mortal peril coming through? Pod drew a deep breath and let it out slowly, willing herself to calmness as best she could.

The agitated swirling eased; Pod reached out with her Healing magic. It fought her, recognizing that this was no creature of fur or feather. She bit her lip and "ordered" it to heal Fiarin.

It was one of the hardest things she'd ever done. Pod could feel that some healing was taking place, but the battle for every tiny bit of progress took a toll on her. Her stomach threatened to rebel; she clenched her jaw against it. Her last meal stayed down, though it was a close thing.

But when the world turned grey and swam before her eyes, she knew she had to stop. If she fainted, Kaeliss would have to keep both her head and Fiarin's above water. And a Healer—for beast or human—who pushed too hard might lie in a swoon for candlemarks.

Pod withdrew from the Healing. Her blood pounded in her ears. The haze that surrounded her hands lingered for a few moments; swirls of dark green twisted angrily in it, a thing she'd never seen before. A dazed voice in the back of her mind blathered that she'd have to ask Conor about it when next she saw him. She rubbed her face, then peeked under the poultice.

The edges of the two puncture marks looked less red and angry; she was sure of it. And the mottling of the surrounding skin *did* look better—if only a little. She shook her head to banish her fatigue. It didn't work.

"We've got to get him to dry land," she managed to say at last.

Kaeliss looked long and hard at her. "You take his legs," she said. "They're lighter."

It was a long, slow, torturous journey. And if it hadn't been for Kiga, they would not have made it. At Pod's command, the woods dog led them not back along the path they'd taken, but to the nearest dry land. By the time they reached it, Pod trembled like one palsied. And although she carried the lighter half of the load, by the time they pulled themselves out of the thick mud that dragged at their feet with every step, Fiarin felt as heavy as if he were made of lead.

At last they could lay Fiarin down. Kaeliss pulled the senior Wort Hunter's pack off and tossed it aside. It landed with a soggy *squish*.

"We need to keep him warm," Kaeliss said, letting her own pack slip off her back.

Pod nodded as she fumbled her pack off and pulled her blanket roll free. Kaeliss did the same. Soon they had stripped Fiarin of his wet clothes and settled him on Kaeliss's blankets with Pod's on top.

"I'm going to make a new poultice to try to draw out the poison," said Kaeliss. "As for you—get into dry clothes and get in with him. You need to rest and he needs the extra warmth."

Though a part of her felt she was somehow shirking her duty, Pod knew that Kaeliss was right. She peeled out of her wet tunic and breeches, then rolled them up and slipped them under Fiarin's leg. "I seem to remember hearing that you should elevate a snakebitten limb," she said to Kaeliss's puzzled frown. "And shouldn't we try to suck the venom from the wound? I thought I'd heard that as well."

"No—that's an old wives' tale. A Healer who stayed the night at my chapterhouse told us that the teachers at their college weren't advising it anymore. Seems one of their herbalists did that when he had a cut in his mouth. Both he and his patient died from that one snakebite."

Pod digested that as she slipped under the blankets and arranged herself along Fiarin's uninjured side. "Gods, that's a scary thought. When Kiga's dry, I'll have him lie down on Fiarin's other side."

"Good idea. Now try to sleep."

Pod didn't think she could; she was listening, waiting, for each breath of the man who lay so frighteningly still beside her. But between one raspy breath and the next, her body surrendered to the fatigue that she'd held off. Pod sank into the welcoming blackness like a stone in a lake.

She woke late in the night. At first she thought she was back at the chapterhouse. Why was her bed so hard, her pillow so lumpy and made of leather to boot?

Then came the realization that there was somebody in the bed with her. Panic gripped her. Who—

Memory flooded back and with it came a different fear, for she no longer heard the raspy breaths that had filled her ears as she'd fallen asleep. She fumbled her way to rest a hand on Fiarin's chest. After an eternity she felt the slow, shallow rise of his chest. Weak with relief, she closed her eyes for a moment, then sat up and looked around.

On the other side of Fiarin was a small fire, barely more than embers, and beyond it a lumpy shadow against the darker blackness of a tree.

"Kaeliss?" Pod whispered. Kiga's head appeared for a moment on the other side of Fiarin. "Stay. Keep him warm," she said.

Kiga's head dropped. The shadow beyond the fire stirred. "Unh?" a tired voice said. Then Kaeliss sat up, pushing back the hood of her cloak from her face. "Oh dear gods—I fell asleep, didn't I? I didn't mean to . . ." She knuckled her eyes. *"Fiarin!"* she gasped.

"Still alive," Pod said. Then, because she was honest, "Barely."

Kaeliss tried to rise but fell back, groaning. Pod scooted out from under the blankets. She wasn't fully recovered—she still felt light-headed—but she was fit enough to stand a watch. Kaeliss, on the other hand, was clearly done in.

"Take my place and get some sleep," she ordered crisply. "And I won't take no for an answer. Hurry before the blankets get cold."

The other girl hesitated, then gave in. From the sound of her breathing, Pod thought that she fell asleep as soon as her head touched the pack pillow. Pod knelt before the fire, Kaeliss's cloak wrapped around her, feeding it a few twigs from a little pile of wood by it.

As soon as it gets light I'll have to look for more wood. I want to make broth with some of our dried meat. She hoped they could get some of it down Fiarin; they couldn't let him get weak from hunger.

She sat through the rest of the night, feeding the fire an occasional twig or bit of branch, arranging rocks she found into a makeshift fireplace, making a thousand plans and finding fault with each one. Through the long, dark candlemarks her thoughts danced around what she knew had to be done. The sky was shading into pearly grey when at last she made herself face it.

She had to try to Heal Fiarin again. That he was still alive meant that her attempt hadn't been a complete waste. She didn't know how many candlemarks had passed since they'd reached this spot—for all she knew she'd slept straight through a full day—but from all she'd heard about the bite of a crowned viper, Fiarin should have been dead long ago.

But would *she* survive it? It was possible for either kind of Healer to spend so much of her own life force in a Healing that she died of exhaustion. And that was *before* adding the wrong kind of Healing into it.

Oh gods. Two of the earliest lessons drummed into the heads of all fledgling

Healers: Heal those the gods meant you to heal. And just as important: Know when to stop. You can't save everyone.

By breaking the first, she'd broken both. And she was planning to do it again. If she and Kaeliss could keep Fiarin alive long enough, perhaps his body could throw off the poison. No doubt she was a fool, but she had to try.

Pod pushed herself to her feet. Her head spun; she hugged a tree to save herself from falling into the fire. Yes, she'd have to try another Healing. But not now; if she tried now, she would kill herself.

She emptied her waterskin into the small cook pot, crumbled a few slices of dried meat into it, and set it across the fire. "Kiga," she said softly.

The woods dog's broad head came up. Dark eyes regarded her steadily.

"Water. Find water, boy."

The woods dog scrambled free of the blankets and turned slowly, nose held high, snuffling the clean, sweet air of dawn. Pod held her breath. Suddenly the woods dog grunted and set off at a lope. She followed as best she could.

The gods had mercy—finally. Kiga found a spring only a few hundred ells away. Still, Pod's legs were shaking by the time she pushed her way through the thick underbrush.

She knelt by the small stone-lined pool before the spring and splashed the cold, clear water on her face again and again. Then she drank long and deep before filling the waterskin.

It wasn't until she was back in the makeshift camp that she realized that nature had not set the stones in that pool. Only the hand of man—or of the Children of the Forest, though Pod shuddered at the thought—could have done that.

Pod stared at the gently simmering pot and wondered why would anyone take the trouble to do so much work on a spring in the middle of nowhere? There were no trails to it. Even the forest dwellers would leave a trail over time, wouldn't they?

So what had once been here?

She suddenly remembered that Fiarin had seemed not to hear when Kaeliss had dared ask him the name of these woods—and how he'd hesitated before leading them over the rocky esker that separated the first forest they'd traveled through from this one. Why? What did he know about this forest that neither she nor Kaeliss did?

Pod racked her tired brain for what she knew about this part of Kelneth and found precious little. She'd been content to follow Fiarin blindly. Hellfire—she hadn't even noticed which hand the sun had been on when they crossed the esker.

She glared angrily at Fiarin, watching the slow rise and fall of his chest as if she might find the answer there, and prayed that if he died, she and Kaeliss could find their way out again.

As if the thought of her had been a summons, Kaeliss sat up. She sniffed the air. "Stew?"

"Of sorts. Give me Fiarin's bowl—I want to put his share aside to cool while we eat."

Kiga sniffed at Fiarin's bowl as Pod set it down. He looked up at her and whined.

For a moment Pod couldn't think what was wrong. Then, "Oh gods, boy—I'm sorry. Go hunt, Kiga. Go."

The woods dog shook himself and loped off. Pod watched him disappear into the dappled light, the dark-and-buff stripes of his fur melting into the shadows.

Still staring at the last place she'd seen Kiga, she said, "Do you know where we are? Or—or how to get back?" She couldn't look at the other young woman; she knew she couldn't hide her fear—and she didn't want to see Kaeliss's. That path led to despair.

There was a long silence before Kaeliss answered. "No," she whispered at last. "I don't. What . . . what do we do now?"

Pod swung around. "Pray. I don't know which god or goddess you look to, but pray to him or her as you've never done before. Now let's see if we can get that broth into Fiarin."

Dawn was breaking again when something woke Pod. She lay against Fiarin, trying to figure out what the sound had been.

She didn't have long to wait. An agonized moan broke the silence. Frightened, she scrambled out from the blankets as Fiarin twitched violently; she saw Kaeliss hastily rise on the other side of him.

Pod cursed as tremor after tremor racked the senior Wort Hunter's body and his limbs jerked this way and that. All the while his moans grew more terrifying. Pod wanted to flee the terrible sounds.

Instead, she forced herself to undo the latest poultice from Fiarin's leg. Kaeliss, crying softly, looked over her shoulder. As the wrappings fell from Pod's shaking hands, they both gasped in horror.

While the small puncture wounds had not shown any signs of healing, neither had they looked worse last night when they'd changed the dressing. But now the flesh around the bite marks was blackened and withered; lurid red streaks ran from the twin holes.

But it was the stench that made them fall back retching. "Oh gods," Kaeliss moaned over and over again. Tears ran down her cheeks.

Oh gods indeed. Pod buried her face in her hands and breathed as shallowly as she could. She wasn't ready; she hadn't fully recovered, she knew that deep in her soul.

But she also knew she had to try. Screwing her eyes shut, Pod stretched her shaking hands out over Fiarin's leg and reached down inside herself, calling up the Healing energy.

At first it wouldn't answer, though she felt it hiding deep within, felt it trembling like a fawn. She insisted and it uncoiled, filling her with the familiar warmth. Pod opened her eyes enough to see the familiar haze forming around her hands.

Relief flooded her. But then came a shock that flung her back like a rag doll.

Pod picked herself up from the ground. Every bone, every muscle, every joint ached. Tears stung her eyes.

She had failed. Fiarin was dying—and dying in agony. Every rasping breath, every spasm and moan told her so.

Grant us this one grace, she begged the gods as she dragged herself back to his side.

For one long, terrible moment she thought they would turn a deaf ear to her plea. Then Pod felt her power flow once more, at first tentatively, then with growing strength. She cradled Fiarin's grey-hued face in her hands and willed the Sleep upon him.

At once the spasms ceased; his breathing came easier as he rested quietly. A little color even came back into his sunken cheeks.

Pod slumped back on her heels, exhausted yet at peace.

Kaeliss crawled to kneel by her. "Did you Heal him?" she asked in awe.

Pod shook her head.

"Then why does— Oh. It's the Sleep, isn't it?"

Pod just nodded; she didn't trust her voice.

"He's dying, isn't he?"

"Yes."

Then, so softly that Pod almost couldn't hear the words, "Thank you for easing his way."

They sat together, holding hands, keeping vigil through the long, hot morning. All around them the forest came awake: birds calling to each other, insects humming, squirrels rattling the leaves overhead as they jumped from tree to tree. Once a rabbit paused at the edge of their little clearing and sat up to watch them. It fled as Kiga pushed his way through the underbrush and lay down with his head on Pod's knee. She twined the fingers of her free hand in his thick, coarse fur.

Pod knew the moment Fiarin died. In the space of a heartbeat an undefinable *something* went out of his face. She bowed her head. Beside her Kaeliss broke into soft weeping.

We'll need to bury him soon in this heat, Pod thought, even as she realized that they had no shovel, not even a hoe to dig with. They would have to find rocks for a cairn or leave Fiarin to the animals. And that she would not do.

She let Kaeliss grieve for a while longer. Then she stood up. "We must build a cairn," she told Kaeliss gently. "Then I think we should find another place to camp. But first we need to eat."

Kaeliss wiped her eyes and nodded. They gulped down a few strips of dried meat and a handful of dried fruit each, washing down the paltry meal with water.

They then separated to search for rocks, calling to each other so that they might not wander too far apart and blazing the trees with their knives.

Just as Pod feared they would have to leave Fiarin after all, she heard Kaeliss calling excitedly to her. With Kiga leading the way, she pushed through the underbrush.

"Look! I walked and walked but found nothing useful. I was just about to give up—then I found this!" Kaeliss said with a sweep of her hand.

"This" proved to be a long, jumbled pile of stones perhaps an ell wide that stretched off into the woods in both directions. The stones were the right size, too; not too big for two strong young women, yet heavy enough that with enough of them, nothing would be able to get at Fiarin. Yet something about the pile made Pod uneasy; there was something familiar about it. . . .

The work was long and hard. Nor did it feel right, stacking rocks on top of Fiarin. Pod kept expecting him to open his eyes and demand angrily just what they thought they were doing. But a final look at the waxen pallor of his face before they drew his cloak over it convinced her. Only the dead had that look, she knew, as if the skin had turned to tallow.

At last they were done. Next they divided the contents of Fiarin's pack and his blanket roll between them. "I keep expecting someone to yell at me for this," Pod muttered.

"I know how you feel," Kaeliss replied. "But he would have wanted it this way. To do otherwise would be a waste."

They bade Fiarin a final farewell, and then the two young women set off. They chose to go east, for Kaeliss had kept somewhat better track of their journey. She was certain that the morning sun had been behind them when they left the main camp and, later, to their left as they had crossed the esker.

That meant that north was the swampy woods with its deadly snakes. They would not go there. But east might take them back to the Wort Hunters' encampment—they hoped.

Pod settled her pack on her back, sent a silent prayer up to the gods, and followed Kaeliss, with Kiga close behind.

Kaeliss stopped and looked back just before they lost sight of the cairn altogether. "Farewell, Master Heron," she said softly.

Pod froze. "Master Heron?" she managed to get out at last.

"Yes. It was what everyone called him—behind his back, of course. Didn't you ever notice how long his legs were? Just like a heron's."

Forty

It was well after midnight before one of the masters could accompany Conor back to the stable. Luckily Lord Lenslee—or someone less distraught—had remembered to leave word with the guards to expect the Beast Healers. They passed Conor and Master Edlunn through the gates with no trouble.

Conor carried the lantern one of the guards had given them at Master Edlunn's request. The soft light fell around them in a yellow pool. Somewhere nearby in the warm night he could hear a nightingale singing. Its lovely song just made Conor feel worse.

What did I not see? And how did I miss whatever was wrong with Summer Lightning?

"There's the stable given over to Lord Lenslee's use," he said hoarsely.

"So I see," Master Edlunn said, mild as mild. "Conor, stop flogging yourself. It may well have been something none of us could have foreseen whether apprentice, journeyman, healer, or master. Such things happen sometimes; it's the will of the gods."

They had reached the door. Conor held the lantern up. "Mind the sill, it's high. I know, sir, but—"

He stopped, for in the faint light that now penetrated the stable, he could see a shadow moving in Summer Lightning's stall.

"Hoy, there—you! What are you doing?" Conor shouted. "Didn't Stablemaster Tuerin tell you to leave that stall be?"

He thrust the lantern at Master Edlunn and ran into the stable. A young stable hand jumped and looked about like one just waking up.

"Wha—what? Oh, yes, of course he did," the boy said in confusion. "I'm no—" He looked down at the small hand broom he had been using to clean out Summer Lightning's manger and staggered backward. The little broom fell with a clatter. "By all the gods," he said in astonishment. "What was I doing?"

"That's what I'd like to know," Conor said grimly. "Now get out of there."

The boy shook his head in confusion as he came out. "I—I don't understand," he said as Conor gripped his shoulder roughly. His eyes filled with fear. "I was asleep and— Where did Osric go? I heard him playing. Or—did I dream that?" He looked around. "I was in bed. How am I here?" he begged.

Conor shook him. "Don't mock me, boy—you're in enough trouble as it is. Now what were you doing?"

The boy whimpered. "Beast Healer, please! I don't know. I was asleep, I tell you!" Tears welled up in his eyes. "Please—you're hurting me!"

Master Edlunn held up the lantern. "Easy, Conor. Look at him; he does have the look of someone just waking up. What's your name, lad?"

"Robie," the boy snuffled. "And I swear I don't—"

"What's going on here?"

Conor turned to see Lord Portis's stablemaster, Tuerin, clad only in his breeches, come down the ladder from the sleeping quarters upstairs.

The stablemaster came to a stop. "And what," he said with cold anger, "are you doing to my son, Beast Healer?" As he spoke, a few of the grooms appeared, their faces unfriendly. One reached for a hay fork.

"Your son?" Conor said in astonishment, letting go of the boy, who ran to his father's side. "Then why was he in Lightning's stall?"

"*In* the stall?" Tuerin asked. He looked at his son. "What were you doing *in* the stall? You were supposed to sleep in the empty stall next to Lightning's."

He looked at Conor. "As you asked, Beast Healer, no one's been allowed into Lightning's stall; we've even posted a stable hand by it to make certain it was left undisturbed. Robie begged to be allowed to watch at night. I thought it would do no harm."

Conor thought he knew what he meant by "no harm." No harm to the boy anyway; if it was illness or magery that had killed Summer Lightning, it had already done its work.

Tuerin went on, "Boy, that stall hasn't even been cleaned out. What were you thinking, sleeping in all that muck?"

"He wasn't sleeping, stablemaster," Master Edlunn said quietly. "He was sweeping out the manger."

"What!" Tuerin turned on his son, a hand lifted to box his ears.

"I was doing *what*?" Robie squeaked, dodging.

Conor stared at him and held up a hand to check Tuerin. *The boy truly doesn't remember.* Then, aloud, "Do you sleepwalk often, Robie?"

Tuerin's hand fell and he looked at his son in concern.

"No! Never—at least, I don't think so. . . ." Robie bit his lip in confusion.

"Hmm—you did this time, son," said Master Edlunn soothingly. He smiled at Robie. "Don't worry, lad; no one's going to hurt you, I promise."

Conor recognized the voice Edlunn used on frightened animals. It was sometimes effective on humans as well, particularly children. Robie was perhaps a bit old for it, but it seemed to be working, particularly when Master Edlunn went on in that same soft, soothing tone, "Now then, lad—you said you were dreaming? Can you remember about what?"

Robie visibly relaxed. He looked up at Master Edlunn. "I'm not certain, sir. I remember thinking that I had to clean Lightning's stall for him before he came back to it. It had to be perfect for him because . . ." He swiped at his eyes. "Be-because he'd won the Queen's . . ."

Here he broke down and buried his face against his father. Tuerin stroked his head.

Master Edlunn cleared his throat. "I think Robie can go back to sleep now—upstairs. Could we have a few more lanterns?"

Tuerin nodded and herded his son up into the loft as the grooms fetched lanterns for the Beast Healers.

They'd gone over the stall from one end to the other. Master Edlunn even scraped up some of Lightning's droppings into a small wooden box he pulled from his scrip.

"I've not seen anything amiss yet, have you? Didn't think so. I'd like to look at what was in the manger," he said, straightening up with a grunt. "Anything left?"

"Only a few bits," Conor replied. "If there was much there when Robie started, it's trodden into the straw and muck now."

"Worth looking at now?"

Conor shook his head. "Even with all these lanterns, the light's not very good here. I've another small box—shall we put the bits into that and take them with us?"

"Good idea."

When it was done, they blew out the lanterns and set off for the Beast Healers' encampment.

Forty-one

Raven trotted up the trail that ran alongside the racecourse. A few wisps of morning mist still lay across the path like gossamer ribbons and twined among the trees. Soon, he knew, they'd burn off, but for the moment they made the forest a magical place.

A pity there had been no way to get word to Yarrow about the honor Lord Sevrynel had done him this day; he'd forgotten to ask one of the Dragonlords to mindspeak her. True, he wasn't a course marshal—he couldn't hope for that—but to be one of the messengers for the Queen's Chase was considered a privilege.

He looked up at the sun. *The race must have started by now.* He was sorry he couldn't see it or the finish, but this part of the course was thick woods. He ticked off the route in his mind: first came a string of open meadows, then some woods, followed by fields with a series of fences to jump, another stretch of forest—this one—with twisting trails and streams and fallen trees to jump, and finally back to the meadow where the race began.

Until then, he would patrol his route, riding between the tall slabs of stone that marked his section, the downhill section of the last field and well into the woods. He pulled Stormwind to a halt as he heard the thunder of hoofbeats coming toward him. Moments later two horses came over the crest of the small hill and down the straightaway that led into the forest. The horses ran neck and neck, their riders jockeying for position as the track narrowed before it entered the woods.

Now a pack of horses surged around the turn in a tight bunch. He turned in the saddle to watch them and devoutly hoped they straightened themselves out before the trail narrowed.

They did—barely. Raven let out a breath he hadn't realized he'd been holding.

Now a single horse appeared: a chestnut with a blaze, Lord Sevrynel's Dawn Star. Raven nodded in approval as he silently cheered Dawn Star; the jockey was holding her back, saving her for the very end. When the frontrunners were exhausted, she'd still have strength and speed left.

He urged Stormwind on. "Come along, then, my lad. We'd best get back to the beginning of our stretch."

The sun was at the nooning when, after riding his part of the course a few more times, Raven saw Ormund, another messenger, waiting for him.

"Time to head back," Ormund said, pointing at the sun. "Everyone's past us, so it's safe to ride the course itself now. Tha knows what to do now, aye?"

"I do," answered Raven. "Linden explained it to me. See you back at the camp, Ormund."

"Come have a jack of ale with us when tha are done, lad," Ormund called as he turned his horse around and headed for the course.

"I'll do that," Raven called back as he cut across the intervening grassy sward.

A moment later he and Stormwind were alone on the track. Raven heaved a sigh and patted the stallion's neck. "A pity we couldn't have entered, my lad. *That* would certainly have shut a few mouths! But it wouldn't have been much of a contest then, would it?"

Stormwind shook his head.

"Ah, well—let's finish this final patrol and get ourselves back to camp and some food and drink."

They were deep into the woods when Raven heard a noise; it sounded suspiciously like a moan. Stormwind stopped at the same instant, looking around. Raven dismounted and studied the underbrush along the track.

There! It looked as if something had crashed through the brush. "Hellooo!" he called. "Anyone there?"

"Here," a weak voice answered.

Raven pushed through a patch of spicebush and brambles. He found a man—more a boy, in truth—lying on his back, hand pressed to his collarbone. He wore a particolored tunic of brown and green. Raven recognized him as one of the last two riders he'd seen pass.

The rider tried to sit up, but sank back with a groan. "My collarbone. I think it's broken."

"And I think you're right," Raven said as he gently pulled the tunic's neck to one side. "You did a hell of a job on it, too, I'd say. What happened? And what's your name?"

"Trevorn. We were going hell bent for leather when a fox ran under Oak's nose," the boy said. "Stupid horse panicked, went right off the course—and I went right off Oak when he stumbled. He ran off, don't know where."

"Stormwind—can you find the horse?" Raven called. He heard a snort and the sound of the Llysanyin moving away. "Let's see what we can do for you, Trevorn."

A short while later he had the rider strapped up as best he could to keep the bone ends immobile. As he helped the boy sit up, he could hear horses moving through the woods. He hoped it was help arriving, but a moment later he recognized Stormwind's whicker.

"I'll be right back." Raven pushed through the underbrush to the course.

Stormwind stood by the side of a blue roan whose head hung down. It stood with one forefoot barely touching the ground, its fetlock clearly swollen.

Raven groaned. He knew what *that* meant; the roan would have to be walked back—slowly. Even Stormwind's walking pace would be too fast. He'd have to do it on foot.

But the rider needed a Healer as soon as possible. Raven knew he hadn't a hope of "tickling" either Maurynna or Linden's minds at this distance. So that meant . . .

"The rider—Trevorn—is hurt. Will you carry him to the camp while I walk the horse back? He needs a Healer for that broken collarbone as soon as possible."

Stormwind nodded.

"Let's get him, then."

Even though Stormwind sank down on his haunches, it was a delicate job getting Trevorn onto Stormwind's back because of the Yerrin saddle's high pommel and cantle. The injured jockey was white with pain by the time it was done.

But seeing Trevorn slumping like a sack of meal made Raven glad of that same saddle. It would cradle the boy and once the straps meant to hold an injured rider were buckled, Trevorn would have to work to fall off—especially since Stormwind would do everything he could to keep that from happening.

When they reached the track, Raven said, "Well, then, Stormwind—off with you."

Trevorn said, "Wait—aren't you coming? I don't think I can hold the reins." Beads of sweat dotted his pinched, white face.

"Your horse needs to be walked back slowly and Stormwind walks too fast. And when I get to that stream that crosses the course, I want to soak that fetlock to get the swelling down if possible," Raven answered. "Don't worry about the reins or anything else. Just worry about yourself. Stormwind'll get you there."

Trevorn shut his eyes, clearly in too much pain to argue.

Raven affectionately slapped the stallion's rump. The big Llysanyin started off at a smooth, gentle walk that ate up the ground.

Raven turned to the roan standing nearby, its head hanging down miserably. He caught up its dangling reins. "Welladay, my boy—let's see what we can do for you."

It wasn't long before they came upon the stream Raven remembered seeing on the map of the course. He took off his boots and stockings, rolled up the legs of his breeches as high as he could, and led the roan into a little pool. Raven yipped in surprise at how cold the water was. "If this doesn't bring that swelling down, I don't know what will!" he told the roan.

Leet had kept careful count of the horses that passed him. When all but one were past, he turned his horse onto the racecourse—*away* from the finish line. He could wait no longer.

It was time for the first step of his new plan. If it worked he thought he knew how to achieve the rest.

But this . . . This was crucial. Everything depended upon what would happen in the next candlemark.

He kicked his horse into a trot.

When he was satisfied that the cold water had done all it could for the fetlock, Raven led the roan back onto the bank of the stream. He dried his feet and calves as best he could with a handful of spicy-scented ferns and pulled on stockings and boots. He caught up the reins once more and set off.

It was slow going in the sultry heat; the woods pressed close to the track, holding in the hot, humid air. Raven wiped the sweat from his face and thought of the pool with longing.

Like an oven in here, he thought, swatting at gnats.

But at last the track passed through a shady clearing before curving around yet another bend. It was marginally cooler there; at least the air had a chance to move.

Nor was it empty. To his surprise, Raven saw Bard Leet ride slowly around the bend. Though puzzled, he raised a hand in greeting and politely called out, "Well met, my lord bard."

Odd that he's riding this *way—it's the long way around to the camp.*

"Well met indeed, Raven Redhawkson, grandnephew of Bard Otter Heronson," Leet said.

Raven wondered if he'd just imagined that odd note—an almost *hungry* sound—in Bard Leet's curiously formal greeting. But before he could think anymore upon it, the Master Bard smiled at him.

"I saw Trevorn mounted upon your Llysanyin, Raven Redhawkson, as I rode here. He said you were seeing to his horse."

"Oh, yes—I soaked its fetlock in the stream back—"

"This looks like a good place to change a broken harp string, wouldn't you say, young master Raven?" Leet interrupted.

Raven just stared at him in confusion. *What on—*

"It's a very distinctive sound," Bard Leet went on. "And I'm quite certain I heard one go while I was waiting for the last of the stragglers to pass me. Would you please take this?" He unslung the harp case from over his shoulder and held it out.

Raven stepped forward and caught the broad leather strap of the case in his free hand. He waited politely—if impatiently—while the bard dismounted, then took it back.

Why in Gifnu's hells had he brought a harp with him? Had he thought to serenade the squirrels and birds? And couldn't this wait until the man returned to camp, for pity's sake? It wasn't as if Leet had to perform right now.

Then Raven remembered how fussy his great-uncle could be with *his* harp, and stifled a sigh. No doubt to a bard this did have to be taken care of right away. *Oh, bloody hell . . .*

"If you don't mind, my lord bard, I want to get—"

"Wait for me, lad, if you will and I'll ride back with you. That way I can ask you more about these horses you're breeding. And find out more of Otter's doings."

Remembering Linden's words regarding the foolhardiness of annoying a bard, Raven ground his teeth but waited.

Leet walked a few steps to a fallen log and sat on it. With a swiftness born of long practice, he undid the lacing of the stiff leather case. A moment later he cradled the small harp in his arms. The fingers of one hand caressed a design on the harp's shoulder.

From the brief glimpse Raven had of the harp as it came out of its case, all looked well; he said, "Looks like no harm done, my lord bard. I wonder what you heard." *And would you now pack up that thing again and let us be off?*

As if in answer, Leet smiled—an odd little smile that made the skin on the back of Raven's neck prickle—and said, "Are you so certain? Look closer. Listen."

For courtesy's sake, Raven dropped the reins and moved forward despite a faint sense of uneasiness at both smile and words. Leet ran his fingers along the strings. A shimmering curtain of sound filled the air like the chiming of tiny bells.

It was one of the prettiest things he'd ever heard. Captivated by the sweet notes, he went even closer, forgetting his earlier apprehension as the bard's fingers danced along the strings once more, expertly damping each note a bare heartbeat after it sounded. Raven recognized one of the exercises that Otter used to warm up his fingers. Somewhere off in the woods a bird sang as if in answer to the lilting melody.

Then Leet's fingers swept over the strings a third time. A tune emerged, a pretty song, though in an odd, minor key. The song filled Raven's mind. He stumbled back, shaking his head, as the music reached for him, twining itself deeper and deeper within his mind. The horse behind him snorted uneasily.

For a moment he thought he'd broken its hold. Then Leet began singing—

nonsense syllables, or in some unknown language—and Raven was caught once more. His blood coursed like fire along his veins, each beat of his heart sending fresh agony through him. Raven went to his knees and wrapped his arms around himself as if he could ward off the pain.

Leet's voice changed and now Raven could almost make out words. He looked up at the other man, trying to say, *Stop! Stop singing!*

But the bard's lips were still.

Raven's stomach lurched as he realized what was happening. It was the harp that sang, and now he understood the words. They were horrible, filled with a sickening lust made yet more terrible by the beauty of the pure, belling tones.

Blood. Sweet, sweet blood. Give me blood, over and over again.

Raven told himself that this couldn't be real, he was dreaming, if he tried hard enough, he could wake himself from this nightmare. This was even more frightening than being captured by soldiers when he was in Jehanglan; he could understand spears and swords. What happened now was beyond all sanity. He raked the nails of one hand along his forearm in the hope that even "dream pain" would deliver him.

It didn't. Instead he fell to the ground, kicking feebly. He thought he heard the voice laughing in his head, demanding, *Feed me. . . .*

Raven tumbled into the well of darkness that opened in his mind.

Forty-two

"There you are!"

Recognizing Maurynna's voice, Raven stopped and looked around. He spotted her standing with a woman who wore a deep green dress over a brown undergown. Behind him the patient roan limped to a halt. Maurynna bade the other woman farewell, then strode toward him, her forehead creased in a worried frown.

"Something amiss, Beanpole?" he asked.

"Not 'something,' you idiot—'someone.' You. You were *a-miss-ing*. Where on earth have you been?"

Raven shook his head in confusion. "What do you mean? I've been walking this horse back for—"

She slashed a hand through the air, cutting him off. "For Trevorn, Lady Deverith's rider," she snapped. "And that was Lady Deverith. She wanted to thank you for helping him.

"Bard Leet said he saw you soaking the horse's leg in a stream as he was returning. So we expected you to be a bit late. It's been so busy I didn't realize you *still* weren't back until Lady Deverith said something just now. Leet got back ages ago—did you get lost somehow?"

"I—I don't think so," Raven said. For the first time he was aware of a muddled feeling, as if his brain were wrapped in cobwebs. A memory drifted into his mind; he'd felt much the same way waking up from a dose of syrup of poppy after breaking his arm as a boy: distant and fuzzy.

Something told him he should be alarmed, this wasn't right, but it was too much trouble to sort it out. Easier by far to sink back into the cobwebs. . . . He rubbed his forehead with his free hand.

"Good gods—what happened to your arm?"

Raven followed Maurynna's shocked stare to look at his left forearm. His tunic sleeve had fallen back to reveal four long, angry red furrows running from inner elbow to wrist. Dried blood caked the end of one furrow.

Had he fallen into a thicket of brambles? No, the scratches didn't look right. "I've no idea," he said, examining his wounded forearm with detached interest.

"Raven, what is *wrong* with you? If I didn't know better, I'd say you were drunk. Did you fall and hit your head?" Maurynna asked. She peered into his face. "Your eyes look distant and unfocused." Maurynna's own gaze turned distant for a moment. Then, "I'm taking you to see Healer Tasha this instant. You're lucky—she arrived here this morning."

"But I've got to get this horse to a Beast—"

He broke off as Maurynna grabbed his clan braid and tugged.

"No, you're not. Linden or Shima will see to it—I've just mindcalled them both," Maurynna said. "*You're* coming with me. Now." She gave his clan braid a final tug before dropping it and setting off.

Not willing to risk her temper—he knew well from past experience that worry made her snappish—Raven dropped the reins and followed Maurynna. Besides, it was just too much trouble to argue. . . .

He shook his head. Since when had he backed down from an argument with Rynna because it was "too much trouble"? She was right; something was awry. He must have fallen and hit his head.

He gingerly ran his hands through his hair. So why didn't he have a lump, or even a sore spot?

Barely a quarter of a candlemark later, Healer Tasha's words echoed his own thoughts.

"I can't find anything wrong," the ginger-haired Healer admitted. "Nothing hurts when I press?"

She suited action to words, running her fingers through his hair, pressing with firm but gentle pressure along his skull.

"No," Raven answered. He was feeling more alert now—well, somewhat more alert, he thought as he yawned. "Pardon," he said when it was over. He tried not to grin as Healer and Rynna fought off yawns of their own, Maurynna unsuccessfully.

Tasha persisted, "And no headache, but you're sleepy, as if you could lie down right now and nap?"

"No, no headache, and not so much sleepy as feeling as if I just woke up from a dose of poppy juice. All logy and sluggish and with a tune I don't recognize stuck in my head."

"Ah!" said Maurynna. "Aunt Maleid calls those 'ear leeches.' She always said the worst ones were the songs you hated that got stuck there anyway."

Tasha said something that sounded like "H'rmph!" and stood glaring down at him as he sat on the low stool in her tent. Maurynna sat on the ground to one side, nibbling on a sprig of bee balm. Nearby a decoction simmered gently in a small pot on the brazier; the sweet scent of licorice root teased his nose. From outside came the faint sounds of the nearby camp: murmurs of conversation, the bright chatter of servants going everywhere at once, and the laughter of children. Weaving through the voices like a thread of gold in a tapestry came the hushed melody of a recorder playing somewhere nearby.

But above all else he heard the sound of horses. Horses stamping, horses calling to each other in challenge or recognition, the steady tramp of iron-shod feet on the hard-packed ground, the creaking of leather, and the jingle of harness. Raven let his mind drift with scents and sounds, coming more awake every instant.

At last the Healer threw her hands up into the air and turned away. "I can't find anything wrong with your head, young man."

An evil grin lit Maurynna's face, but to Raven's relief, she refrained from making a rude remark. Instead she said, "But there is something wrong with his arm."

"Oh? Let me see." *At last!* her eager expression said. *Something tangible!*

It was on the tip of his tongue to refuse; then Raven slowly pushed his tunic sleeve up. He was a little surprised at his reluctance to display his mysterious wounds.

Perhaps if he knew how he'd gotten them . . .

Healer Tasha winced when she saw the scratches. "Ouch! I can't do anything about 'ear leeches'—but I can certainly do something about those scratches, young man."

Linden unbelted his tunic as Maurynna settled herself on the side of the bed in their tent. "So what was this all about, anyway?" he asked. "Why couldn't Raven take that horse to the Beast Healer himself?"

He listened to Maurynna's description of Raven's arrival in camp—"Looked like his mind was a thousand miles away and he was half-drunk to boot"—and of their visit to the royal Healer.

Linden carefully pulled off his tunic and tossed it to one side. Sounded like a possible head injury, he thought, but nothing that Tasha couldn't put right with a Healing and an infusion. He rooted through the chest of clothes at the foot of the bed.

"How's the horse?" she asked.

"Fine now. Slobbered all over me while a Beast Healer cared for him. Thank the gods I was wearing an old tunic. Have you seen my green one?"

"I was wondering what that mess was all down your front. And your green tunic was at the bottom of the chest the last time I saw it."

"No it isn't. I just looked."

Hopping up, Maurynna came around to the foot of the bed. She nudged him aside, thrust her hand deep into the chest, and came up with the errant tunic. "Men," she said, rolling her eyes as she handed it to him.

"Hunh," he said as he pulled it on, "and who found your favorite sash when you'd lost it? The one Shima's younger sister made for you?"

"Not the same thing," Maurynna retorted as she settled back onto the bed. "*Someone* had tossed that across the room, he was in such a hurry one day. Not my fault I didn't see where it landed behind that chair."

Hmm—she had a point. He raised his hands in surrender. "I was talking to Lady Derwith's head groom while the Beast Healer worked on that gelding. The man was fretting that the delay might hurt the horse's chances for a full Healing. He was cursing Raven something wonderful for being so late. Before I could say anything, Leet, who was watching, said that he'd passed Raven soaking the gelding's foot in a stream as he rode back to camp. He wondered if Raven had slipped on wet moss or leaves and fell and hit his head on a rock.

"That shut the groom up right quick. He knew as well as the rest of us that if that's what happened, Raven's lucky he didn't land facedown in the stream. He'd've drowned." He glanced over at her as he wove the end of his belt through the two heavy metal rings of the buckle.

Maurynna was shaking her head. "Hmm—let me think. When Raven first came into camp, I grabbed his clan braid. It was dry. So was his tunic."

She screwed her eyes shut; Linden knew she was recalling the image of Raven's arrival. He waited, not moving, lest he disturb her chain of thought.

Her eyes opened again. "His breeches were dry as well, save for the very bottoms where they might well get damp from wading. Therefore he didn't slip while in the stream as Leet thought, thank the gods."

"How bad was the bump on Raven's head, anyway, love?" Linden asked.

To his surprise, she smacked her fists into the mattress on either side of her. "That's what is so *odd* about all this. There was no bump or lump that Tasha could find. Not even a sore spot. That surprised her—that, and the fact that Raven didn't have a headache. All that was wrong was that kind of daze he was in—oh, and those scratches on his arm."

Linden wondered what other stray facts would pop up. "What scratches?" he asked a little testily.

Maurynna made a motion of raking fingernails. "Like that—at least, that's what Tasha said they looked like."

This was getting stranger by the moment. "A fight?" he asked, even as he knew it wouldn't be so simple. Nothing ever was, it seemed.

"No one else has said anything about one."

And a fight would be news all over camp. "So what happened? Did Raven fall after all?" Linden asked, thinking aloud. He rubbed his chin. None of this was adding up. "Or—"

May the gods grant that Raven isn't seriously ill, he thought suddenly, remembering Maurynna's description of Raven's dazed state. Fear washed over him like a wave in a storm-driven sea. Despite a rocky beginning, Raven had become a good friend. It would hurt to lose him.

And for Maurynna it would be like losing a brother.

"You're wondering if it's something serious, too, aren't you?" she said darkly. "So is Tasha. I could see it in the set of her mouth when she turned away from Raven at one point." Fear—the same fear that chilled him—lurked in her eyes.

"I'm sorry, love," said Linden gently. He pushed a strand of hair behind her ear, then stroked her head as she threw her arms around his waist and buried her face against him.

He knew what she feared. She would have to face Raven's death eventually—his, and that of every other truehuman she now knew. But though this was a thing she knew, she didn't truly *understand* it yet, Linden thought. He hadn't—not until he'd buried the last person he'd known before his First Change. He'd heard his niece Moss Willow's birth cries and held her hand when death claimed her almost eighty years later.

He hoped it would be long indeed before Maurynna faced that pain.

The night was still. From somewhere far off in the distance, Leet heard the mournful hoot of an owl. He sat in the deep embrasure of the opened window to his room, arms around his knees, staring out at the stars. Comfortable—even luxurious—as his tent had been, give him four walls to sleep within any day.

Besides, if he'd been asked to play that damned song one more time, he likely would have broken a chair over someone's head. Curse the fool who'd realized that most of the players of "Dragon and Phoenix" were in the camp. Luckily he'd thought to plead an imaginary case of the rheumatics brought on by sleeping in the tent; it gave him both an excuse to stop playing and to return to the castle.

Gull was safer from a chance discovery here; it had been a risk bringing him to the camp, but one that had paid off handsomely. Leet smiled smugly at the memory, savoring it like a fine wine.

A star streaked across the night sky, its fiery tail cutting across the Badger forever chasing the North Star. The sight brought him out of his reverie. It was, he thought, time. Surely he'd waited long enough; surely Raven was asleep by now. . . .

With a grunt, Leet unfolded his now-stiff body and swung down from the windowsill. His knees protested at being suddenly made to work again and he squatted a few times to wake them up. When he could move without hobbling, he slipped the red silk cover from the harp on the little table by his bed and carried it back to his seat in the window. His joints protesting, he settled himself once more, Gull cradled in his arms.

He sat, thinking, as he absently traced a finger along the image burned into the harp's shoulder. It worried him a little that he couldn't bear the thought of leaving Gull hidden away in its case in his room. If he tried to, it preyed on his mind; sometimes it seemed hard to breathe and for a moment or two he'd even fancy that it was himself shut up in the case.

And now that he'd given it that tiny taste of Raven's blood—so kind of the boy to scratch himself like that!—the harp felt more . . . alive . . . than ever.

Leet shook his head. Bah! All those creepy tales from the old practice room had made a deeper impression upon his young mind than he'd thought. But he had no time for such 'prentice foolishness and moonshine *now*.

Now was life . . . and death. Leet began to play.

He didn't know when it began. He was riding Stormwind across the Jehangli plains as clouds like dragons—or dragons like clouds, he couldn't tell which— sped across the turquoise-blue sky above him. Then, faint as the whisper of an owl's wing, came a breath of music.

At first Raven didn't even notice, but then something familiar about it caught his attention. He turned his head to listen, and, in the way of dreams, he was suddenly standing alone on the vast green plain. As the music grew louder the cloud-dragons fled and the great blue bowl of the sky turned a leaden grey.

The skin along his spine crawled. He knew this music. He'd heard it before— and it had scared the living daylights out of him. If he could only remember where . . .

He struggled to remember, then realized it didn't matter. He could think about it later; right now he had to get away from the demonic tune. Fighting his rising panic, Raven whistled for Stormwind, but there was no response.

And all the while the music grew louder . . .

He ran. He had no idea where he was going; he only hoped that he could out- run whatever would follow the music. For he knew something was coming, some- thing was going to happen. And he knew full well that that something was vile beyond belief.

But he had no idea what, and that was the most frightening thing of all. So he ran and ran as one can only in dreams, not tiring, with no noisy pounding of feet or gasping for breath. Above him the sky grew darker.

For one blessed moment he thought he'd succeeded in escaping his night- mare; with the strange logic of dreams, he knew that if he could just crest the next rise, he'd find Stormwind again and then he'd be safe.

But with a heart-stopping roar the ground erupted in front of him and Raven found himself facing an enormous cliff. Panicking in earnest now, he threw him- self at it and managed to climb a good few ells high in his desperation. Then the next handhold crumbled under his clutching fingers and he fell from the cliff face like a stone cast from a tower.

Yet the fall did not hurt him as it would have in the waking world. Raven rolled onto his stomach and found himself facing a skull lying on a pile of what looked like moldering spruce needles. He could even smell them, though their scent was mixed with a reek of decay.

More blood, more blood, more blood, *the skull chanted in his mind.* Give me more blood.

Like one bewitched, Raven got to his knees and pulled out his belt knife, then set the sharp edge against the palm of his other hand. A tiny part of his mind whimpered in terror as the blade pressed down against the skin. But Raven had no more will than a puppet to stop himself from slicing his palm. Blood welled up, bright scarlet, the only color in the faded world of his dream. Though he struggled against it, Raven could not keep from holding his hand over the skull and letting his blood drip onto it. It immediately vanished, sucked into the bleached bone like water into parched earth.

The skull glowed with a sickly, yellowish light and tiny points of fire appeared in the eye holes. Yesss, *it hissed in his mind.* The first drink was good; this is better.

Raven stared in confusion at it. What first drink? When had he ever given this foul thing a taste—

Suddenly the skull shrieked, More! More! More! Get me more blood—a river of blood!

Raven clapped his hands over his ears against the shrill banshee wails, but the horrific sound pounded in his head, threatening to tear it apart. "Yes! Yes!" *he cried, desperate to silence the horrible thing.* "I'll get you—"

"—More blood," Raven whispered as he sat up. His head throbbed, his heart pounded, and his stomach churned so that he thought he would be sick. He scrubbed a hand across his face, wiping cold, sticky sweat from his brow, then cursed himself for an idiot.

"Fool!" he muttered. "You'll just open the cut again!"

Then he stopped and shook his head. What cut? He hadn't cut himself before going to bed—had he? Hadn't he? Raven looked down at his palms.

Both were whole. The skin was untouched and there wasn't a drop of—

Wait—didn't I say something about "blood" as I woke up? And that dream—wasn't there something in there about blood as well? But he couldn't remember for certain what he'd said as he awoke, and the dream was fading rapidly, spilling from his mind like water from a sieve.

He shivered. There was something important he should remember, *needed* to remember, and it was either the key to the dream or the dream was the key to it. But there was nothing to grasp hold of in the confused jumble of his thoughts, nothing that he could latch on to and follow into the maze to the memory he needed. Indeed, the effort made him feel queasy; Raven abruptly cast aside his blanket and staggered to his feet. He wanted fresh air, and he wanted it now.

Not caring if he woke Arisyn snoring gently in the other bed, Raven stumbled outside into the dark, predawn chill. He gulped in huge draughts of the cold air. Years ago, back in Thalnia, he and Maurynna had been swimming at a little cove they'd discovered. He'd dived too close to the rocks of the natural breakwater and the seaweed bed around it, and found himself tangled in the long, ropy growth. It had seemed like forever until he pulled free and found the air once more. He'd lain gasping on the surface for a long while; he'd never realized how sweet the air tasted. It felt oddly the same now, as if he had come but a finger's breadth from drowning somehow.

Had he dreamt about that? If so, he hadn't drowned then and he hadn't drowned in the dream, so that was one less worry, he told himself with forced cheer.

Yet something was still not right. . . .

He pulled the cord of his breeches tighter and went to find Stormwind.

Leet sagged in the window seat. His breath came short and quick, and every limb trembled. If he tried to stand, he knew he'd fall flat on his face. It was all he could do to keep the harp from tumbling to the floor.

Dear gods, he'd never imagined how much effort it would take. He felt like a wet rag left in the washtub for too many days.

But it was done. Leet shook his head in weary relief. He'd come so close to failing; he hadn't expected Raven to fight the harp's call so strongly. It had taken every ounce of his power as a Master Bard to hold the young fool in the summoning dream.

Or, said a tiny voice from somewhere deep inside the spark of fear growing in his soul, *was it Gull's power?*

It doesn't matter! Leet snapped back. *What matters is that it worked, that the apple of Otter's eye has bound himself to my will!*

Anger gave him strength. Cursing, Leet scrambled awkwardly from the deep windowsill, the small harp clutched in his arms. Pins and needles pricked his feet and legs; he staggered stiff-legged to the table by the bed and set the harp into its stand.

The strings thrummed gently at him. Worms of fear crawled down Leet's spine at the sound.

For in that delicate ripple of melody Leet heard a mocking *Come now*—your *will?*

He flung the heavy red silk cover back over the harp and crawled shaking and sweating into his bed.

Forty-three

Despite Raven and the Dragonlords' reassurances the next day, Yarrow would not believe that he hadn't hit his head. She stared at him when he showed up at their camp after breaking his fast with the Dragonlords, Arisyn, and a number of other lords and ladies. Word had gotten around that he was the Raven Redhawkson of "Dragon and Phoenix," and while not a lord, it seemed he was suddenly much more than the commoner most wouldn't have noticed the day before.

Yarrow turned to Shima. "My thanks once again to you for mindspeaking me last night. It was good to know what was happening." Then, catching Raven's chin in her hand, she turned his face from side to side. "Are you *certain* you feel well, boy? My old uncle Grey Mole used to look sharper after a three-day drinking bout than you do this instant," she said bluntly.

"Eh," said Raven, rubbing his forehead. If he could just get the cobwebs out of his head! "Just a bad night's sleep. Had one hell of a nightmare."

"A pity Zhantse, my old master, isn't here," Shima said. "He was always interested in dreams and nightmares. It's part of a shaman's duties to interpret them and decide which are significant—and which are indigestion. Can you remember any of it?"

As if he wanted to . . . Still, it was Shima asking; Raven shut his eyes a moment and thought. "A skull. It was resting on . . . oak leaves? No, that's not right—it was something like spruce needles. At least they looked like the needles that fall off if you leave the winter solstice decorations up too long. I remember I could even smell them, but they smelled of rot as well as pines. And the skull wanted blood. My blood."

Shima looked troubled as Yarrow and Maurynna made the sign against evil. "That's a nasty one. I wish Zhantse was here," he said.

"I know nothing of interpreting dreams and I've never met your old mentor, Shima, but I also wish he was here," Yarrow said. "Go lie down, Raven."

He started to protest, then reconsidered. Perhaps he should rest; the last time his mind was this foggy was when he and the others had stopped in Thalnia on their way back from Jehanglan. Since he knew he was leaving for good that time, he'd spent their last three days in Thalnia cramming in as much visiting of old friends and celebrating as he could, with a nap here and there.

Once on board the ship, he'd slept a day through and felt fine again. Maybe that's what he needed.

But why? I haven't been—ah, the hell with it! Raven was too muzzy to think about the "why" of it all. He just wanted to sleep. "I think I will."

"If you need to send a message to us, remember that we're moving back to the castle this day. The north tower, I think Beren said. But Steward Lewell will know for certain," Maurynna said. "Now go to sleep."

"We'll look after Stormwind for you," Yarrow said.

The stallion touched his nose to Raven's cheek, then lipped his hair, and ended by pushing Raven toward his tent.

"I can take a hint!" Raven said, laughing. When he was inside, a wave of weariness washed over him. He pulled off his boots and fairly keeled over onto his pallet.

His last thought before sleep claimed him was *Please don't let me dream. . . .*

Conor sat alone at one of the long trestle tables in the Beast Healers' tent, his hands wrapped around a steaming mug. He closed his eyes and inhaled the bracing vapor. Just what he needed: a strong-enough-to-wake-the-dead infusion of roasted chicory root, a bit of cream to take the edge off the bitterness, a healthy dollop of honey to sweeten it all, and Trouble, draped around his neck, sound asleep.

He relaxed, enjoying a moment of precious tranquility to make up for the day so far. He'd risen before the dawn to care for a nearby farmer's flock of sheep with the scours. At least they'd fed him when the nooning came so he wasn't hungry.

Nor had the farmer and his wife looked askance at him as so many did at the fair these days. Instead they had been delighted to see him and tearfully grateful when he was done. That was a good memory.

A little of the tension left his shoulders. *Now if I could just stay right here like this until the fair ends—*

"Hoy there, Conor!"

Krev—go away! Just go away and leave me alone, Conor silently begged. He slitted one eye open, hoping to see Krev turn and leave.

But it was not to be. The young apprentice—one of those brought along as messengers and errand runners—trotted between the tables up to him.

"Afternoon and all that, Conor! Master Edlunn would like to see you in his tent." Krev beamed down at him.

Conor gulped down his chicory drink, nearly scalding his tongue, wishing it had been anyone but Krev—at least until he'd finished his drink. How anyone could be that bouncy and cheerful all day long . . . The guild needed a rule against it, he decided morosely as he rose and followed the ebullient boy back through the tent.

Krev left him at the door to Master Edlunn's tent and raced off somewhere else, whistling jauntily. Conor glared after him, then rubbed his eyes; it had not been a good night and he had candlemarks of hard work behind him. His eyes felt gritty and his brain like overcooked porridge. And ten to one Lord Lenslee had sent around another complaint about his incompetence and a demand that he be booted from the guild. Ah, well—might as well get this over with.

Conor ducked inside the tent. Edlunn sat at a small table in the front part of the tent; a screen of painted canvas hid his sleeping quarters in the back.

On the table before him was the small wooden box that held the fragments from Summer Lightning's manger. Edlunn looked up from his study of them and smiled. "Come in and sit down, my boy. We're in luck this day."

"Oh?" Conor said cautiously as he sat down. Had Master Edlunn found something out?

"Indeed. From all you've said and all I've been told by Lord Lenslee and others, there was not a thing wrong with Summer Lightning when you saw him. Not a *thing*.

"A healthy animal doesn't just drop dead. I suspect the poor animal was helped along and I think the answer lies here." He tapped the lid of the box. "Now, while we Beast Healers make use of herbs, we're not the experts that the Worties are. So I decided to enlist their aid.

"I sent Krev to their tent first thing this morning to ask if anyone could help us identify these bits of grass and leaf—"

I hope the Worties were more awake than I was. At least he hadn't had to deal with Krev at the crack of dawn.

"—And he brought back good news. Because they buy a great deal of foreign herbs from the merchants here, one of their most knowledgeable people usually comes every year. It's said she can identify a thousand plants by scent alone."

Conor thought that unlikely, but to a drowning man, any straw looked like a rope. "She'll help us?"

"She'll try. One of their messengers came ahead to say she was on her way, so she should be here any—ah! That must be her now."

Indeed, now Conor heard a murmur of conversation outside the tent. A soft voice said, "Step to your left, Mistress Parmelle, there's a rope. Now straight ahead is the doorway tent pole . . ."

A hand pushed the canvas door flap aside, revealing a fat woman of middle years flanked by two girls, one older than the other. A pudgy white hand reached out, touched the pole, fingers like pale sausages running up and down it; then Mistress Parmelle advanced slowly as Conor and Master Edlunn stood up. The girl on her right caught up and steered the woman toward the chair that the other girl scooted ahead to pull out.

With a shock Conor realized that Mistress Parmelle was blind. She sat heavily, a soft, shapeless mass, her doughy white face turning from one man to the other. Her eyes, almost lost behind her fat cheeks, were filmed with grey.

"Greetings, Master Edlunn," she said in an unexpectedly sweet and childlike voice. "I understand that my small talents may be of use to you."

Master Edlunn rose and bowed. "Mistress Parmelle, we—Conor and I—hope you can solve a small mystery for us."

"Thank you for coming, Mistress Parmelle," Conor said, bowing. He and Master Edlunn sat once more.

She smiled at him. "I hear worry in your voice, young man. I hope I can ease it for you." She held out her hand.

Master Edlunn set the box in it. "Inside are some bits of leaves and such that we can't identify. Perhaps you . . . ?"

"I will try." She bent her head over the box and inhaled gently. "Hmm, hmm—there are a few different things here," she murmured. "Luce?"

The older girl produced a pair of copper tweezers and proceeded to pick up one fragment at a time and offer it to the older woman, who in turn sniffed it delicately before putting it aside.

"That's alfalfa. That's a bit of wheatgrass. And that's . . . hmmmm—ah, red top."

Conor's jaw nearly dropped. Mistress Parmelle had just named the grasses used in the hay at Lord Portis's stables. But while her skill was amazing, it didn't solve the mystery of what killed Summer Lightning.

Luce offered Mistress Parmelle another fragment; it looked to Conor like a bit of withered leaf. Once more she sniffed delicately, like someone enjoying the bouquet of a fine wine. Conor waited for her pronouncement.

She frowned. "Unusual," she murmured at last. "Unless I'm mistaken . . ." She took the tweezers from Luce and sniffed again. "From the other things, I would have guessed hay for horse or cow. But this—this is not what I would have expected. Am I wrong to think this is hay for an animal?" Once more she held the tweezers to her nose and concentrated.

Conor and Master Edlunn looked at each other, suddenly alert. "You are not wrong, Mistress Parmelle. It is—was—hay," Master Edlunn said.

What could it be? Conor thought. She'd confirmed Stablemaster Tuerin's information about the hay. What now?

Mistress Parmelle set box and tweezers down. "No, I was right," she stated. "That last was yellowfool. Wilted yellowfool. The scent is unmistakable. It's strongest and sweetest when half-rotted. Useful for certain conditions when administered by a skilled Simpler, but dangerous if used unwisely."

She "looked" at each of them with eerie accuracy. "While it is sometimes used for humans in this wilted state, I have never known it to be used for animals. Well-dried in fodder, yes, but not like this. Is this something new?"

Master Edlunn said, "No. This . . . this is something that should not have been there. But it . . . explains a great deal."

Mistress Parmelle cocked her head in a girlish manner that should have looked affected with her doughy bulk, but just seemed endearing. "Ahhh—I think I understand now. Girls," she rapped out, "not a word of this to anyone."

"Yes, Mistress Parmelle," they agreed as they helped her from her chair.

When she was gone, Master Edlunn said, "So—now we know the *how* of it. And I'm sure we can guess the *why*."

"To keep Summer Lightning from running," said Conor. "But most important now is: who?"

"That, thank the gods, is for others to find out. Let us go."

As Conor accompanied Master Edlunn to lay their discovery before Lord Sevrynel, he realized with a chill that the "who" was not the only pressing matter. *Oh gods—will he strike again?*

"Is tha Lord Tirael? Garron says tha is."

Tirael looked around from his mug of ale to find a grubby boy of twelve years or so eyeing him warily. "And if I am, you little worm, what's it to you?"

The boy flushed angrily but all he said was, "Then this is for tha," and flicked a well-folded piece of parchment at him.

It struck Tirael on the cheek. He cursed, but the brat was gone before he could cuff him for his insolence. Tirael settled back into his chair and studied the note.

Good parchment, sealed with scented wax, but no imprint in the wax. Had Merrilee come to her senses at last? Tirael opened it eagerly.

The hand, though educated, wasn't hers. It was clearly a man's handwriting, elegant, but not one he recognized. And it was unsigned. Tirael nearly tossed it aside after a glance when Merrilee's name seemed to jump out at him. Merrilee's— and Eadain's.

He read the note very carefully after that. Then he sat and thought for long, long while. This would explain some of the looks cast his way lately, the cryptic comments. Did everyone know but him? They must think him the veriest fool!

After a time, Tirael left.

When he reached home, Tirael called for the steward. As soon as Tiniver appeared, Tirael snarled at him, "I'll need one of the men to take a letter for me. Find one while I write it."

The steward bowed as Tirael ran up the stairs. Moments later, he sat at the table-desk in his room. He pulled a fresh quill pen and a new bottle of ink to him;

the others had been broken when his damned cousin knocked everything off the desk that night.

As he sharpened the quill, he thought long and hard about what he was going to write—and what he was going to do. Satisfied at last, he took a fresh sheet of parchment from the stack, dipped pen in ink, and began writing in his best hand:

Greetings, Master Luyens!

By the time you get this, I'll either be a married man or a hunted one.

He paused to study the words. He could still change his mind. . . . But no! She belonged to him, damn it! Why couldn't she see that?

He would see that she did. One way or another. Once more he set pen to parchment.

Linden had just finished saddling Shan when a messenger in Sevrynel's livery rode up to him.

"Your Grace," the young woman said, bowing slightly in the saddle as she held out a sealed tube. "I was to tell you that this is urgent. I'm also to wait for a reply, Dragonlord."

He sighed inwardly as he took it. "My thanks." In his mind he heard, *If this is more pedigrees . . .* He glanced over at Maurynna leaning against Boreal's neck and grinned.

The smile disappeared as he read Sevrynel's note. He swore softly in Yerrin.

I take it we're not going to old Cade's booth to get cheese and bread, are we?

No, love, we're not. Sevrynel says that they know how Summer Lightning died—he was poisoned. He requests that I be there when they inform Lord Lenslee. I don't know what he thinks I can do, but . . . Linden swung up onto Shan's back. "No need of a reply. I'll go there now. The manor house?"

"Yes, Dragonlord."

Turning to his soultwin, Linden asked, "Do you want to come along?"

Maurynna shook her head. *I think it would be too painful; from all I've heard, Lenslee loved that foul-tempered beast.* She continued aloud, "I think I'll go to the castle. I want to talk to Healer Tasha about Kella. She was so busy with the race I haven't had a chance yet."

Linden blew her a kiss and touched his heels to Shan's sides. The Llysanyin cantered off.

"Yellowfool? Someone put wilted *yellowfool* in Summer Lightning's hay?"

Linden winced at the raw pain in Lord Lenslee's voice. He'd seen a horse die from eating that stuff. The horse—one of his father's—had gotten into a field where cut hay lay in windrows. Drawn by the sweet smell, it had found a patch of almost pure yellowfool in the curing hay and eaten its fill. They'd found it just a short while later, but it was already too late. The horse spasmed, collapsed, and died before they reached the gate.

Ironically, had the horse gotten loose just a few days later, it would have lived. The hay would have been fully cured by then and whatever poison was in the yellowfool would have been driven off.

That, though tragic, had been an accident. This . . . this was deliberate cruelty. He looked at Lord Lenslee, face buried in his hands, with sympathy.

"There's no chance that it was in the hay by accident?" he asked gently.

"None," Lord Portis answered. His pale face looked stricken. "The hay came from my own fields. And while I know that yellowfool makes good fodder when it's dried and some esteem it highly, it's not a chance I'm willing to take. Whenever it's found on my lands, I have my people rip it out."

"Gods have mercy," Lord Sevrynel said. "That means . . ."

"That means that someone fed it to Summer Lightning deliberately." Master Edlunn shook his head. "Cruel—a cruel thing to do and a cruel way for an animal to die."

A muffled sob escaped from behind Lenslee's hands.

"May anyone enter the stables?" Linden asked, though he already knew the answer.

Portis shook his head; the last of the color drained from his face, leaving him as white as salt. He knew what Linden's question—and his answer—meant. "It must have been one of Therinn's people, or . . . or mine," he whispered. "But I would have sworn that . . ." He shivered though the room was warm.

The painful meeting ended soon after; it was clear that Lord Lenslee was close to collapse. The matter would be given over to High Marshal Huryn and his men for investigation.

"I know I said that horse should have been put down," Lord Sevrynel said softly as they watched Lenslee and Portis leave. "But not like that. Never like that. May the gods grant that Huryn soon finds the filth responsible. And now if you will all excuse me, I must see to the final plans for tonight's gathering."

Maurynna came out of Healer Tasha's quarters as confused as ever. Knowing that Maurynna would want the latest word on her cousin, Tasha had visited Kella at home the night before she left for Balyaranna.

And Kella had been, well, Kella. Just as every letter from Maylin and Aunt Elenna had assured her: *Kella is healthy and well and driving us mad. She sends her love and wants to know when you can take her flying again.*

The only odd note had come from one of Maylin's letters:

Abern Walbeck, one of the wealthiest members of Mother's guild, visited yesterday and brought a small harp with him. He told Mother that his son has no head for music. (In truth, I've heard that young Abern's teacher refused to have him as a student anymore. Something about mice in her music satchel . . .)

Anyway, it's a lovely thing, very sweet tone—and Kella won't touch it. Won't even look at it. This from the girl who was awake before the sun was up on the days of her lessons. Fickle child.

I could have sworn that Kella had a real gift, Maurynna mused. Enough of one to go to Bylith. Could this have something to do—no, how could it have anything to do with her illness? Likely she's just lost interest; after all, at one time she wanted nothing more than to be a tumbler!

As she made her way back through the castle, Maurynna wondered what new thing had driven music lessons from Kella's head. Each new theory was more outlandish than the last. By the time the castle steward intercepted her and asked if she would care to join Duchess Beryl for some small refreshments, Maurynna had nearly forgotten her unease.

Conor followed Linden and Master Edlunn as they left the manor. Emotions warred within his breast. First was righteous horror that anyone would treat an animal so. The second was less worthy, perhaps, but the more powerful.

Relief. Pure, blessed relief. It had not been his fault after all that Summer Lightning had died. He was not, as rumor had it—and he'd feared—incompetent, thank all the gods.

It must have shown on his face, for when he caught up with Edlunn and Linden, both smiled gently at him.

Master Edlunn stopped and rested a hand on his shoulder. "I, for one, never thought it was your fault, lad. I know you. I know how careful you are."

"So stop beating yourself about the head over it," Linden said. "And don't even think that if you had thought to look in on the horse that night you might have saved him. It happens too fast, Conor. I've seen it."

Conor nodded. He knew the Dragonlord spoke the truth, but there would always be a part of him that would wonder *if, if, if* . . .

He wanted to be alone for a bit. "If you've no immediate need of me, Master Edlunn, I'll have a look at Fliss. Just to make certain . . ."

The older Beast Healer looked at him shrewdly, then nodded. "Of course, lad, go on."

"I'm off to find my soultwin once more," Linden Rathan said. "And maybe even a bit of that cheese she keeps telling me about."

Conor watched until they had passed through the main gate; then, because his legs shook, walked slowly to Fliss's paddock. Reaction, he told himself, just reaction.

Fliss was well. Cantering around her pasture, even, her tail flying gaily in the air like a flag. Conor heaved a sigh of relief and leaned on the fence, letting all the fear and anxiety of the past days seep out of him.

He was still standing there when one of the stable boys pelted up to him. Conor listened to the boy's gasped explanation and started running.

He found his patient by a small stream that flowed sluggishly through the lower end of one of Lord Sevrynel's pastures: a small pony with a golden coat and flaxen mane and tail. It was being walked by Falk, one of Sevrynel's stable hands. Two other stable hands, Warin and Burwell, a white-haired gaffer, walked on either side of it. From time to time the pony would stop and snap at its sides or kick at its belly.

Standing nearby were two muddy children—a boy and a girl—as well as a young woman and a young man. The young woman had her arms wrapped around the little girl, plainly holding her back.

Thank the gods—Falk's kept the pony from rolling.

When he was close enough, Conor skidded to a halt. He walked the rest of the way so that he wouldn't spook the pony. Laying his hands upon its broad brow, Conor soothed it, easing the pain.

"What happened?" he asked.

"I'm going to rip her hair out!" the little girl shrieked. Tears poured down her dirty face. "I've *told* Willena a hundred times not to give Buttercup any apples!" She began sobbing.

Conor recognized her as Lady Rosalea, the daughter of one of Lord Sevrynel's guests; he'd seen her in the stable a few times when he'd come to look in on Fliss. "Apples and Buttercup don't agree?" he guessed. He'd seen more than one horse like that, the poor things.

"No," said the boy, a lad with brick-red hair. "They don't." He looked somewhat familiar, but Conor didn't have the time to think about it right now. He had a pony with colic.

He looked at the young woman. "Lady, if you would . . . ?"

She nodded. "Rosalea, please! You must come with me and let the Beast Healer work in peace."

Big brown eyes filled with tears. "But I want to stay, Lissa! Buttercup n-n-needs me!"

The boy rested a hand on her shoulder. "You have to go, Rosie. It's best. Besides, your mama will be angry if you're late to get ready for the gathering."

"And we'll be forever getting you cleaned up, Rosalea," the young woman added. She looked down at her charge's wet, muddy clothes and winced.

"Beast Healer Conor will take good care of Buttercup," the young man said.

"But, Ari . . ." Rosalea turned from him to look at the boy with the red-brown hair. He shook his head, then whispered something in her ear. "Oh—truly?" she asked. Then she turned to Conor. The biggest, brownest eyes he'd ever seen studied him for a long moment.

Ohhh, this one's going to be dangerous when she's older. He managed not to smile lest she misunderstand it.

"You have to make Buttercup better, Beast Healer Conor." The big brown eyes brimmed anew with tears.

"I will, my lady," Conor pledged.

Once more she studied him. What she saw must have reassured her, for she nodded and allowed her nurse and the boy to lead her away. The young man, who had spoken up for him, walked alongside the boy.

Conor turned back to the pony. "Falk, you stay to help walk him. Burwell, please see that Buttercup's stall is ready for him. Warin, I need you to fetch some things for me. . . ."

As the stable hands trotted off to do his bidding, Conor laid a hand on Buttercup's back. "Right, then—let's keep walking."

At last Buttercup was back in his stall. Falk went off to resume his usual duties. Conor leaned against the wall and heaved a weary sigh. He looked ruefully down at himself, then shut his eyes.

Trust a pony to pick the wettest, muddiest part of the pasture to fall ill in. They were, he swore to himself, the contrariest creatures the gods had ever created. He didn't care what anyone said. They were.

"Ah—there tha are, Beast Healer."

Conor warily opened an eye. He saw Burwell bearing down on him, face split in a nearly toothless grin. Warin was hot on his heels.

Why do I think I'm not going to like this?

Burwell planted himself in front of Conor. "Lady Rosalea insists upon seeing tha right away, Beast Healer. She's at the lord's gatherin', she is."

Conor boggled at him. "Now? Right now?"

Warin grinned and confirmed the unwelcome announcement. "That's right, Beast Healer—that's just what Her Little Ladyship said: as soon as tha was certain that her Buttercup was safe, to come and tell her thaself. Mad about that pony, she is."

"Not one to be put off, she bain't." Burwell's grin grew wider, wreathing his face in wrinkles.

Conor could imagine Lady Rosalea was one to get her way. She wouldn't need tantrums. All she had to do was just *look* at you. "And she's at this gathering of Lord Sevrynel's? You're certain of that?" Conor asked in resignation.

"Oh, that she is, Beast Healer, that she is," Burwell piped, his head bobbing up and down. "I told her tha wasn't dressed proper for a nobles' gathering, but the lass wouldna take 'no' for an answer." He sounded downright proud of her. Enchanted by those eyes, no doubt.

"No," Conor sighed, looking down at the grass stains on the knees of his breeches and the mud plastering his boots. "I daresay she wouldn't." He looked over the rest of his clothes. Oh gods—how did he tear that elbow? Damnation, but he was going to feel like a bumpkin. A very dirty bumpkin at that; as if to agree with him, Trouble crawled out of her bed in his hood, balanced herself on his shoulder, and proceeded to wash as much of his face as she could reach.

The old man went on enthusiastically, "Said that a Beast Healer's green-and-brown was worth any amount of silk and ribbons and lace and what-all even if it was dirty." Burwell favored him with a nearly toothless grin. "Couldna do aught but agree with her, I couldna. The lass was right, she was."

"Hunh, thank you." Conor slapped halfheartedly at the dusty front of his tunic. No, Lady Rosalea would brook no denial—not where Buttercup was concerned, he suspected. He considered just leaving, then dismissed the idea; from the stubborn look on Warin and Burwell's faces, he suspected they'd frog-march him to the gathering if he tried. Child though she was, Lady Rosalea already had her stalwart partisans. Besides, then he'd have to face those big brown eyes capable of making any male feel like an ogre with but a single mournful look.

May the gods help her suitors when she's older, Conor thought as he glumly picked stray bits of grass from his clothes. *They're going to need it.*

Warin must have guessed his concern. He said, "Tha could go the back way, Beast Healer, through the gardens until tha are nearly upon the gathering. From there tha can get one of the servants to tell Lady Rosalea that tha's come to see her."

Conor brightened. "Good idea, Warin. I'll do that." He looked up at the sky. It was nearing dusk; if he took his time, the fading light would hide a multitude of sins even if one of the gentry noticed him.

Lifting Trouble down from his shoulder and settling her into his arms, Conor bade farewell to the stable hands and set off to wend a leisurely way through the gardens.

It was the perfect ending to the day, Conor thought as he walked. One of those summer evenings that was neither too hot nor too cool, with an occasional breeze slipping past laden with the scent of roses and dame's rocket and rich, damp earth. He drew a deep breath and let it out with a happy sigh. Trouble's whiskers twitched as she sniffed the air.

Now the breeze brought with it a snatch of music, a fragment of a bell-like tune that haunted the twilight. He turned aside to find it without even thinking why. It would be only a little out of his way. . . .

He paused in midstep and shook his head like a man coming out of a dream. Lady Rosalea was waiting for him, worrying about her pony. Why in the world was he—

Once more the shimmering notes beckoned. He followed.

Forty-four

Leet arrived early at Lord Sevrynel's. When the harried understeward looked at him a bit curiously, Leet announced, "I require privacy and time to ready myself for my performance. I will do so in the gardens. When I am ready, I will join the gathering."

He glared at the understeward as if she were a student, the same withering glare that had made many a young upstart slink off, tail tucked between their legs.

For a moment he thought she would defy him. But then she bowed and stood aside. Leet nodded imperiously and swept past.

Now to see if the next step in his plan would work.

At last Leet found a place in the gardens that suited him, well away from the gathering, since he wasn't yet certain how many people might be affected by his "call." He settled himself in a likely spot.

Leet bent all his will to his summoning. Yet Gull refused to answer. Desperate, the bard bit his lower lip until he tasted blood, his fingers still running unerringly over the strings as the eerie yet beautiful tune poured forth like a bubbling spring.

Come! Come to me! he sang in his mind over and over again, calling the harp to answer. With his right hand keeping the tune, Leet touched the tip of his left forefinger to his bleeding lip, then brushed it against the soundboard. The bright red stain disappeared instantly. Leet held his breath; if this didn't work . . .

Nothing. Despair nearly claimed him, then he felt the spirit within grow restless, hungry as it woke once more. Now malignant lust vibrated through the strings. Gull wanted more than that paltry offering, much more: fresh blood, thick and hot, sweet and salty, all that was in a man's body.

Now Leet sang aloud, the merest breath of a whisper, sending his words aloft with the bell-like notes, cajoling, commanding those who heard his song to come to him.

The strings grew ice cold. For a moment Leet feared they would snap. He'd heard philosophers speak of the deadly cold that many said filled the space between the stars, a cold beyond any in the mortal world.

This, he thought, clenching his teeth against the ache that crawled up his arms, this was such a cold. He wondered that the wire strings did not shatter like glass. Yet they stayed whole; indeed, the sound became sweeter and more beguiling the colder they grew.

Otter's fool of a grand nephew was the first to arrive as Leet knew he would be, bound already by the magic of the harp. Raven stumbled into the clearing like a sleepwalker. When he shook his head as if trying to clear it, Leet commanded, "Wait you there, boy, wait you there without a sound, still as a statue. I'll have a use for you soon enough."

Raven halted, his eyelids drooping.

Leet smiled. Now for the other one . . . The bard redoubled his efforts; tears coursed down his cheeks as ache turned to pain, then to agony. But his voice held steady and his fingers did not fail him. This—this was his only chance. Leet squeezed his eyes shut against the burning cold and played on and on. He had no blood to call this prey. His hate would have to do.

He was so intent upon his playing that he almost missed the noise of someone crashing through the garden beds. A muffled exclamation of pain finally broke through his concentration; Leet opened his eyes in time to see Tirael jerk free from the rosebushes that caught him. The younger man's face and hands were badly scratched and his clothes torn. Leet smiled to see that perfect face crisscrossed with thin lines of blood.

Tirael stared listlessly at him, slack-faced like one devoid of wit. His lower lip trembled.

"Welcome, Tirael. Not so pretty now, are you, my fine lad?" he said softly. His hands continued their dance over the strings. "But you are still welcome, Tirael, very welcome indeed. I have someone here I'd like you to meet—and who wants to meet you so very, very much."

Tirael's dull gaze flickered toward Raven.

"No, no," Leet said with a laugh. "You already know Raven, don't you? And everyone knows that there's no love lost between the two of you. Even so, why don't I let him do the honors? He's met sweet Gull before—haven't you, Raven?"

Raven's eyes opened fully; a look of confused fear filled them as if Raven knew he should be afraid, but could not remember *why*. That look fed the blaze of vengeance in the bard's soul like oil upon a fire.

"Call Tirael a 'cheat,' Raven. Name him 'coward.' I order you to," Leet crooned.

And Raven did. Tirael was so cowed that he made not even the slightest sign of offense. But enough toying with these louts, Leet thought, no matter how amusing it was. Someone might come.

Ah! If only Otter were here to see his darling grandnephew's destruction. . . . Still, this was more—far, *far* more—than Leet had ever hoped for. He swept his fingers along the strings in a triumphant glissando before continuing to play. "You know what Gull wants, Raven," he said. "Give it to him. Give him Tirael's blood."

It all nearly came to nothing as both men fought his control. Leet swept his fingers across the strings once more, building upon the melody, but Raven staggered, shaking his head, fighting to cover his ears. Even Tirael, pampered brat that he was, tossed his head like a fractious horse. Leet knew that he would lose them in another moment.

Then the harp jerked in his arms. With an oath, Leet caught it just in time. But the harp kept twitching and Leet had to abandon any attempt to play. He clutched the soundbox so hard his knuckles turned white.

Frenzied thoughts tumbled over each other. *Must keep playing, damn it, I'll lose them both, what's going on, whatthehellishappening, MUST KEEP PLAY—*

But the music went on as if ghostly fingers plucked the strings. After one long, stunned moment, Leet realized that *the harp was playing by itself.*

His first instinct was to fling it away. Yes, a harp could "sing" when a breeze blew through its strings; that was common. But this—this was clearly a song. No vagary of the wind could play a song, damn it. This was more than he'd bargained—

Then he noticed that both Raven and Tirael had stopped struggling. Leet grimly forced his aching hands to keep their hold.

The tune changed, became a delicate, haunting melody that Leet had never heard before—a melody played with a subtlety unmatched by any human hand; a melody of heartbreaking beauty, graced rather than adorned by the simplest of harmonies, a melody that built upon itself, each repetition blending its bell-like notes into those that had come before. It should have sounded muddy. Instead it built a gossamer veil of sound, a shroud of notes that caught Raven and Tirael within its coils.

A cold chill gripped the bard's heart; he knew he now heard the song with which Gull the Blood Drinker had lulled his victims so long ago. Another heartbeat or two and Leet would understand the words. . . .

"No!" he gasped. Then, "Kill him! Kill him now!" *Lest I be caught in this web as well!*

A shiver of anticipation wove through the music and Leet clearly heard a single word drawn out like a wolf's howl: *blooood.*

Eyes blank, Raven drew his belt knife. He turned and marched stiffly to where Tirael stood, eyes equally blank. A fleeting regret passed through Leet's mind that Tirael wouldn't know the terror that Arnath had surely felt. Revenge would have to be enough.

The harp played wildly, passionately, like a lover who sees his beloved. Tirael's head tilted back; Raven's arm went back, back, then—

Leet closed his eyes, suddenly unable to watch. He heard a grunt, a noise like a sigh, and a dull thump. A crescendo of chords filled the air in sensual exultation and the harp quivered in his arms. Leet's stomach turned; it sounded too much like a man at the height of pleasure. *What kind of man was this, that death was to him what love is to other men?*

A wave of nausea swept over him and he found himself gasping as if he'd run a race. He swallowed hard and wondered if his legs would support him.

Gods help me, I—I hadn't expected anything like this. I must leave, must get—

A wave of cold shot up his arms, a cold so intense it was pure agony. He cried out, his eyes opening in reflex.

Raven stood before him, eyes empty; his knife was still in his hand. Blood dripped from it, drop by slow, thickening drop, and his hand and clothes were stained with the the horrible stuff.

Tirael lay on the ground at his feet. A dark pool spread around the young nobleman's head. By some trick of the dimming light Leet could see blood glistening along the edges of the gaping wound in his throat.

Leet's head spun at the ghastly sight and the world swam before his eyes. He knew he was on the verge of collapse.

Then, through no will of his own, the bard staggered to his feet. Still clutching the harp, he lumbered across the short distance, at first jerking and twitching like a mishandled puppet, then moving normally if somewhat stiffly.

He knelt by Tirael's side. One hand loosed its death grip on the harp and stretched forth, slowly, slowly toward the blood pooled around Tirael's head. Leet watched it from a place beyond terror; surely it belonged to someone else, this hand. . . . It wasn't his, it *couldn't* be his.

Oh gods, please, no. A squirrel or rabbit's blood is one thing. But a man's? Auvrian help me, I don't want to tou—

The hand scooped up as much blood as it could from the sluggish pool beneath Tirael's head. The feel of the warm, thick fluid nearly made Leet vomit. He desperately wanted to shake the stuff from his fingers, scrub them clean until the skin was raw, then scrub them again and again. But they didn't belong to him anymore; they were . . . They were going to . . . going to . . .

Leet stared at the thick smear of red that now ran down the harp's soundboard ending in a bloody palm print at the bottom. This was no mere streak of blood as before. How in Auvrian's name was he going to explain—

The blood disappeared, soaking into the soundboard like water into parched earth. Or was it the other way around? *Like a man dying of thirst would drink,* he realized.

The harp shivered in his arms; then a paean of unholy rapture burst forth from the strings, and the cold that had burned Leet vanished, replaced by a rush of ecstasy beyond anything he had ever imagined, ever dreamed of. He nearly swooned.

Shaking his head to clear it, Leet suddenly remembered that Raven stood over him, knife in hand. Cold fear shot through him. But to his surprise when he dared look, the Yerrin still stood rock-steady and blank of face.

How could he not feel that? the bard marveled. *It was like, like—I don't know; drinking sunlight, riding a thunderbolt, wrapping a cloak of fire around oneself! All of those, none of those, something even better!*

From deep inside—himself? the harp?—a soft voice whispered enticingly, *And you can have it again. . . .*

The sweet words echoing in his mind, Leet greedily scooped up more blood and slathered it on the keyboard. Let Raven stand there in a trance until he rotted; it was clear nothing would wake him until Leet released him, and Leet had better things to think about. He watched the soundboard, panting like a man after a long race.

Once more the blood disappeared, and once more the rapture took Leet. He moaned. This was like nothing else he'd ever felt, pleasure so intense it danced on the edge of pain. It was almost more than he could stand; indeed, he wasn't certain he could bear it again, yet he had to have more, so much more. . . .

But his shaking fingers had just touched the pool of blood when a voice startled him. He jerked his hand back, blood cooling on his fingertips.

No! a voice inside his mind shrieked in thwarted rage. *No! I want more!*

Somehow Leet managed to keep his head and not scream curses at the interloper. With a moan of frustration, he slewed around to see who had interrupted him. A grey haze rode the edges of his vision and his head swam, but Leet could just make out the figure of a man. It was someone familiar; he'd seen that craggy, almost ugly face before—hadn't he?

Go away, Leet begged him mentally. *Go away; I must—*

Without realizing it, he brushed his wet fingertips against the soundboard. Once more the rapture overtook him. It was not as powerful this time, but it was still more than his overwhelmed senses could bear. The world slid away. . . .

As he spiraled down into darkness, the man's identity came to him: Conor of Red Dale. Beast Healer.

The last thing he heard was a voice laughing in his mind.

And perfect witness, it said.

At first Conor couldn't understand the scene before him; he stopped, squinting against the failing light, trying to make out what had happened. He came forward slowly, reluctant to interrupt a private meeting. Some of these nobles were so damned touchy. . . .

Wait; that was Linden's friend Raven, he was certain of it. But why was

Raven staring so stiffly into the distance? And who was the kneeling man? *Why does he seem misshapen and what's that he's kneeling by,* Conor wondered. The skin prickled on the back of his neck. Fighting the urge to walk away and say that none of this was his concern, the Beast Healer walked on step by slow, cautious step. With a shock he realized that the thing on the ground was a man.

Someone's ill or hurt! Forgetting his earlier apprehension, Conor cried out, "What happened?" He set Trouble on the ground and ran to help.

The kneeling figure turned and Conor recognized the Master Bard. That explained the oddness of the figure, then; the bard was clutching his small traveling harp to himself. Then, to Conor's horror, Bard Leet fell to one side like a dead man.

Only then did Raven move. He shook his head, looking around with the air of a man who found himself in a place quite different from where he'd fallen asleep. But Conor had no time to spare for him; all his attention was for the two men sprawled upon the ground. If Raven could stand, he would do well enough for now.

The bard moaned and to Conor's relief, shakily pushed himself up onto one elbow. Thank the gods, then; the man hadn't dropped dead of apoplexy or something like as Conor had first feared. The Beast Healer skidded to a halt at the downed man's side and steadied him against the shuddering breaths that shook the spare frame. Satisfied that Leet wouldn't keel over dead for the moment, Conor was finally able to look at the fallen man. While his gift was with animals, not humans, he knew as much as any first-year Healer.

But one glance told him this man was beyond any aid he could give; not even a truedragon's Healing fire could save this one—not with that great, gaping wound across the throat.

That same glance told Conor that the man was a noble. Someone would hang for this. He swore aloud and looked up at Raven, saying, "Raven, what in the name of the Great Stag hap—"

For the first time he saw the knife in Raven's hand. Conor gaped at it, stared dumbfounded as that hand came up and Raven gazed blankly down at the dripping blade. The Yerrin's eyes blazed with sudden anger.

"The music," Raven said in a harsh whisper. His gaze shifted to Leet. "*His* music." The knife twitched in his hand.

"Raven—*no!*" Conor threw himself at Raven, one arm snaking behind the Yerrin's knees. Raven went down like a sack of wet meal. Before he could get up, Conor half fell, half jumped on him. Raven pushed at him and kicked, trying to throw him off.

Conor grabbed Raven's knife hand and hung on for dear life. He landed a crashing blow to the other man's jaw. Raven's eyes rolled back in his head and he went limp.

Panting, Conor pulled back and turned to Leet. "Are you hurt?" he asked. "No?

Then thank the gods—I came in time." He glanced at the thing that had once been a handsome young man. "At least in time for you." He looked back at Leet.

He found the bard staring at him with a madman's eyes. For a moment Conor wondered if the bard would attack him. Then, with a visible effort, Leet pulled himself together; to Conor's relief he turned that burning gaze elsewhere.

"Well done, Beast Healer," Leet said, half-turning away and cradling his harp to his breast. "You've caught His Lordship's killer. Justice shall be served."

To Conor it seemed that other words hung unspoken in the grey twilight. And there was something odd about Leet's manner, but he couldn't put a finger on that oddity. The bard seemed . . . he had no words for it. An angry hiss from the ground near his feet distracted Conor. He looked down.

Trouble had caught up with him; she stood facing Bard Leet. To Conor's surprise, her back was hunched and her tail fluffed as large as he'd ever seen it. Her mouth was open, showing her long canines, and she hissed again and again; Conor thought he'd never seen her so angry.

Angry—or frightened? For when Bard Leet turned his gaze upon her, she whipped around and in the blink of an eye scrambled up Conor and dove into his hood. He could feel her trembling against his back.

Conor craned his head around. "Trouble? Troublesome-weasel? What's wrong, girl?"

A soft, frightened hissing was his only answer. Then came the last sound Conor wanted to hear.

"I *know* I heard Beast Healer Conor, Lissa. I *must* find out if Buttercup's well," a high, clear voice declared.

"But my lady, perhaps he's busy. And are you certain you heard him? I didn't, Lady Rosalea. And your mother won't like it that you've left the gathering *again*. Please come back."

Lissa, Conor prayed silently, *get the child out of here. . . .*

The piping voice said, "Not until I find out about Buttercup. I *know* I heard him—right over there!"

"Oh gods—not now!" But Conor had no choice. Loath as he was to leave the bard unprotected should Raven regain his senses, he had to keep Rosalea from this. He jumped to his feet and ran to the opening in the hedge. Careening around the corner, he intercepted Lady Rosalea and her exasperated nurse just in time.

Leet watched the Beast Healer race away to head off Lady Athalea's daughter. A firestorm of emotions warred in his breast. Uppermost was fury, plain and simple. How dare that great, ugly lump of a pig leech interrupt him? Leet longed beyond anything to taste that rapture one more time. His thoughts tumbled over each other like a fever dream gone mad. Once more his trembling fingers stretched out.

Before the blood gets cold . . .

But one part of his mind remained detached. It knew he didn't dare feast one more time; soon there would be guards and gawkers. He mustn't risk becoming so lost in ecstasy that he was seen feeding the harp. No one must know about sweet Gull. . . . The fingers curled tightly into his palm.

And with cold calculation that same part of his mind also knew that Conor's arrival might have been the best thing that could have happened. A thing he hadn't foreseen wanting, but which was the crowning touch: a witness of unimpeachable character.

The Beast Healer was well known and, Leet knew, well thought of among the nobles here at the horse fair. He was also known to be honest and conscientious; his word would be accepted in any court of justice. And he had seen Raven, a dripping knife in his bloodstained hand, standing over a still warm corpse.

Leet hugged the harp and laughed softly.

"There you are!" Lady Rosalea exclaimed. "I was waiting and *waiting* but you didn't come! Didn't Warin and Burwell *tell* you?" She ran to him and put her hands into his. "Is Buttercup well now?"

Before Conor could speak, she looked beyond him as if something—some noise?—had caught her attention. "Oooo—did you bring him, Beast Healer? Is he in there?" she squealed in delight and tried to slip past.

Conor grabbed her. "No!" he yelled. Tucking her under one arm, he carried her away from the opening in the hedge. Lissa stared at him in astonishment as he strode past, but he had no time—and less inclination—to explain.

Conor set Rosalea down again and knelt before her; her mouth made a round O of surprise and her big brown eyes gazed in confusion at him. Then she giggled and, no doubt thinking it all some new game, tried to dodge by him. He caught her and set her in front of him again, this time gripping her arms.

Rosalea's lower lip began trembling. The game, it seemed, was no fun anymore.

"Now listen to me, my lady," he said roughly. "I swear to you that Buttercup is safe and well in his own stall in the—"

He'd been so worried about Rosalea, he'd forgotten about Lissa. A shriek from beyond the hedge reminded him all too clearly. Rosalea clung to him in fright as her sobbing nurse ran past, pale as moonlight. She disappeared into the darkening garden.

"What happened?" Rosalea asked in a tiny voice.

Conor resisted the urge to curse the curious Lissa from here to Assantik and back. "There's been an . . . an accident, my lady," he said in the voice he used for frightened younglings of any kind. "I don't want you to go there—will you promise me that? But I need to go back and see if—if Bard Leet needs help. Can you be brave and stay here by yourself?"

"No," she said promptly. Then, looking beyond his shoulder, she screamed and buried her face against him.

"Don't worry, Beast Healer Conor," a melodious voice said.

Conor looked around.

"I'm . . . quite well," the bard continued. He smiled.

But Conor saw the look in his eyes and somehow couldn't agree.

Maurynna rubbed the back of her neck, surprised at the tingling she felt. It had come on gradually, become almost painful, then suddenly stopped. *What was that about?* she wondered as she eyed her goblet of spiced wine. *Something in the—*

"Lord Sevrynel! Lord Sevrynel!"

The shriek tore through the gathering. The happy babble wavered as guests looked at each other in mingled astonishment and annoyance at such an unseemly disturbance.

Taller than most of the crowd about the laden tables, Maurynna could see a young woman running from the direction of the gardens. Even from here she could see the girl's face was chalk-white and her eyes huge. Maurynna set down her goblet and started for the edge of the crowd; she didn't know what was wrong, but from the look on the girl's face, it was something dire.

A cold pit opened in her stomach. *By the gods—isn't that the girl who looks after Lady Athalea's daughter?*

She began pushing her way through the stunned throng to where the girl had stopped, looking wildly around for Lord Sevrynel. A crowd immediately clustered so thick and deep around the frantic messenger that Maurynna was forced to stop lest she knock someone over. At least her height enabled her to see what was going on.

"Has something happened to Lady Rosalea?" Duchess Beryl demanded.

The girl jumped. Relief flooded her face as she recognized the duchess. "No, Your Grace, she's well, I left her with Beast Healer Conor," she babbled as she made the regent a sketchy courtesy.

"Then what's wrong? What's the meaning of this unseemly interruption?" snapped a nobleman.

Lissa looked at him with the frightened eyes of a hunted doe. "I—I'm sorry, Lord Oriss, but, but—" She took a deep breath and, breaking into hysterical tears, wailed, "There's been murder done, my lord! Lord Tirael's been murdered!"

Stunned silence greeted her words. Before anyone could so much as breathe, Lissa cried out, "It was that Yerrin fellow! The one that has the Dragonlord horse! Bard Leet said so—he saw him do it!"

The girl's words went through Maurynna like a dagger.

Forty-five

Linden! Linden, get back here! *For the love of all the gods, get back here* now*!*

Linden staggered under the force of Maurynna's mindvoice. *Maurynna— what's wrong? Are you hurt? Maurynna?*

When she didn't answer him, he stretched his senses to the utmost. But her mind was in such turmoil that try as he might, Linden could sense nothing more from his soultwin.

"Your Grace? Dragonlord?"

Linden opened eyes he didn't realize he'd squeezed shut while trying to sort out Maurynna's chaotic emotions. He found himself leaning against a stall door and looked down to find a worried Lord Sevrynel tugging at his sleeve.

"Linden Rathan? Are you ill, my lord?" the little Cassorin lord asked as he peered anxiously at him.

Lady Athalea asked, "Shall we send for Healer Tasha, Your Grace?"

Linden pushed himself away from the stall and told the group of worried faces around him, "I'm well, thank you. But my soultwin, Maurynna . . . Something's wrong. I must go."

With that he ran from the stable and across the courtyard. He heard the others running after him but paid them no mind. It seemed to take forever to find his way through the gardens; worse, he still could not make out what might be wrong with Maurynna—just that she was on the edge of hysteria. And *that* scared him, for panic was not like Maurynna at all.

Gifnu's hells—she's faced pirate raids and an attack by a mad truedragon! What could have happened at a summer gathering?

When he reached the site of the gathering, he found it almost empty. Only Lord Eadain and Lady Merrilee were there, holding hands and looking about them in puzzled apprehension. "What happened?" Linden asked.

They shook their heads. "We don't know," Lord Eadain said. "We heard someone screaming and then a great deal of shouting, so we came. We were . . . in another part of the garden."

From the northern path that led into this nook came a frantic buzz of voices and a glow that he was certain was coldfire. Linden ran up it only to find his way blocked by a crowd of nobles craning to see what was going on in front. As Linden began easing a way through the crowd, one voice rose above the rest.

"Tirael! Oh gods, Tirael!" the voice keened like a lost spirit. "He killed my son, my baby, my bonny, bonny boy!" Wail turned to hellcat shriek: "Kill him! Kill him as he killed my heart's own! Guard, I order you to kill that peasant!"

Murder? Here? And by the sound of it there might well be another if the guard forgot that even a peasant had a right to justice—at least if a Dragonlord was around. Linden dove into the crowd and pushed people aside in earnest as the voices in the front joined in the blood hunt.

An explosion of coldfire lit the garden like a noonday sun. Linden paused for a moment, eyes dazzled, as those around him cried out and cowered in fear and surprise.

"Run him through and I will hunt you down."

The menace in Maurynna's voice cut through the babble; silence spread out from it like blood flowing from a wound.

That menace shocked Linden. What the hell was going on? Gods knew he'd seen Maurynna angry enough times; she'd flare up, then be laughing again an instant later. But this . . . This was as far beyond anger as a forest fire was beyond a candle flame. This was a fury that would hound a man to the end of time. Linden prayed that the guard was a man of sense.

Now the only sound was a woman's voice thick with tears, sobbing over and over again, "Kill him. Please kill him. He killed my bonny boy, my poor bonny boy."

At last Linden reached the center of all the turmoil. He stared at the scene revealed by a large globe of coldfire. It cast a light like a winter moon, cold and hard with knife-edged shadows.

The sharp, sickly-sweet smell of blood lay over everything. Linden saw a body to one side of the little garden bay; in the icy white glow it was easy to see the gaping wound in the throat. An older woman knelt by the corpse's side, weeping bitterly over it. Only the firm grip of another noblewoman—Linden recognized Lady Jorusha, owner of one of the favorites in the cross-country races—kept her from throwing herself upon the victim.

Guards surrounded a kneeling man, twisting his arms behind his back and forcing his head down from the little Linden could see of him. A small belt dagger lay on the grass before the clot of figures. Even from this distance the blood upon it was plain to see. One guard held a drawn sword; he and Maurynna faced each other over it, their gazes locked upon each other.

Before Linden could react to the sight of that threatening blade, the contest of wills ended; the sword disappeared into its sheath. A moment later Maurynna turned away and went to the prisoner and his guards.

One, clearly their leader, said to her, "The bard saw him do it, Your Grace."

"That doesn't matter."

An ominous rumble of muttered rebellion greeted her words.

"There will be no more killing this night, do you all understand? You have laws; you will obey them."

Linden just watched and listened, puzzled. Maurynna seemed in complete control of both herself and the situation; true, no one looked happy, but it was clear none would disobey her command. So what had prompted the panic that he'd felt?

She said, "You will bring Ra—" Her voice came close to breaking for a moment. She took a deep breath and went on, "You will bring this man to a prison cell where he will await trial."

For the space of three heartbeats it seemed there might be a mutiny after all. Then the leader saluted, saying, "As you command, Dragonlord."

The barely hidden hostility in his voice roused Linden's anger. As the guards dragged the prisoner to his feet, he started forward.

Only to stop in shock at the deathly white face revealed by the coldfire's merciless glow. Now he understood Maurynna's fear. For herself, she'd react to a threat with anger. But for her heart-brother, yes, that would terrify her.

Yet . . . Raven? A killer? Linden looked again at the corpse; no sign of a weapon. Not just a killer then, but a cold-blooded murderer. He understood the guard's feelings.

As the guards hustled a dazed-looking Raven past him, Linden prayed that there would be some explanation for all this. But to save his life, he couldn't see one.

Nor, worse yet, did he see one that would save Raven's life.

"So what the hell happened?" Linden asked the air when they were back in their rooms in the castle's north tower. With them were Shima and Conor.

No one answered. Maurynna sat staring out the window at the night, her back to everyone, forehead pressed against the glass; Linden wondered if she was crying. She had not said a word since they left the ruins of Sevrynel's gathering, but walked like one ensorcelled. All had made way before her white, set face and burning eyes. She'd said nothing to Linden; there was not even a word of greeting for Boreal when he was led to her. Linden had not intruded beyond reaching out once with his mind, letting his love and trust brush feather-light against the turmoil of her thoughts. She'd smiled at him for that, a strained, grateful smile that disappeared an instant later. After that he'd left her alone, guessing how thin that armor of frozen calm really was.

Shima, who had come from watching a mummer's play with Karelinn in answer to Linden's mindcall, shook his head. "I can't understand it," he said, sitting cross-legged on the floor; in private Shima followed his people's ways more often than not. "The man was unarmed, you said? That is what I truly don't understand. Defending himself or another, yes, Raven—or anyone, for that matter—could kill someone. But an unarmed man? That is not the Raven I know. It's so hard to believe. . . ."

"Well, I don't believe it. Not one bit. He didn't do it." The muffled words came in a hard, flat voice; Maurynna still hadn't turned around. "He *couldn't* have done it. That's not Raven, not at all, and I would know better than anyone."

Conor opened his mouth, eyed Maurynna's rigid back, shut it again. He bit his lip and looked away.

"Maurynna-love," Linden said gently, "but what of Leet's testimony? He saw Raven cut the man's throat."

"Then he's lying, hallucinating, I don't know. But Raven would never kill someone in cold blood and for no reason." She turned around in her seat before he could get the next words out. He didn't even try in the face of that wild-eyed gaze. He was not, thank the gods, a stupid man—or at least not that stupid.

"And don't try to tell me that he had a reason because Tirael had oozed out of their wager, the slime.

"On the contrary, it was Tirael who would have had a reason to harm Raven. When he claimed his horse was stolen, he looked the world's worst coward and cheat—you know that most people are certain he knew where his horse really is. Then, when word got around that he'd never had any intention of paying the wager if he lost, he destroyed any respect that anyone—anyone decent, that is—had for him. You heard people talking about it. You saw them flocking to Raven. By the gods—you could even say Tirael did Raven a favor!"

Her voice breaking, she declared, "Even if Leet saw true, even if it was Raven's hand that wielded the knife—it wasn't Raven's heart!" Then she fled the room.

Forty-six

Something scrabbled busily in the straw at the far end of the room—if six paces away could be called far. A rat, no doubt. Raven huddled tighter into the corner as if he could push himself through the damp stone wall. He wished he was anywhere but here.

Then the heavy oak door swung open, creaking on the black iron of its massive hinges. Two burly soldiers entered. Before he could say or do anything, they caught him under his arms and dragged him out of his dungeon cell.

They hurried him down one hall after another. At last they pushed him into a long room with tiers of seats—with one section roped off—facing a raised dais. On it stood a low table before a lectern, and three chairs. One looked like any other chair in the room: that was for witnesses, Raven knew. In the center, on a small dais behind the lectern, was a more ornate one befitting the dignity of the Justice who would preside. The last chair . . . The last chair looked heavy enough to hold a bull. Thick-framed, it was, and dark with age. Leather straps dangled from its arms and legs.

The soldiers pushed him down into it and buckled the straps tightly over his forearms and ankles. Raven tugged. No, he wasn't escaping from here any time soon. He doubted even Linden could tear leather this thick.

Somehow it all felt unreal. Despite the things on the dais, he wasn't really in a Justice Hall. He couldn't be. Raven looked up at the balcony that ran along three sides of the room. The sections to his left and before him flowed together and were open to the room. But the balcony to his right was separated from them and screened. Stairs led down from this section to the dais.

Somehow the sight of that balcony brought home to Raven where he was even as the straps cutting into his wrists did not. This balcony, he knew, was where the witnesses sat hidden from sight until they went down those stairs to testify. From there they would go to the roped-off seats.

This cannot be happening.

The doors at the end of the room and the open balcony opened and in filed rank after rank of Cassorin nobility. Many he knew; they had been glad enough to treat him almost as one of their own when they heard that he was the Raven of song. Now they looked at him as if at a particularly noxious insect. He could feel their hate beating at him and wished he were back in his cell. The rats would be better company.

But worst of all was when Linden, Maurynna, and Shima entered. Maurynna's eyes were red and puffy from weeping. *Oh, Beanpole,* he thought sorrowfully. *I'm so sorry. . . .*

Last of all came Lord Asiah, the Justice of Balyaranna. Asiah was a lean man, grey of hair and beard, with piercing, ice-blue eyes. Silence followed him as he paced slowly down the center aisle, imposing in his ermine-trimmed black robes, his long staff of office tapping the floor with every other stride. It was said of Asiah that he was known to be a fair man, a man who loved the law but loved justice even more.

All this and more Raven had heard since he'd come to Balyaranna. Would Asiah be able to find justice for one Raven Redhawkson? Would he believe that Raven still had no idea of what had happened? That it could *not* have . . .

Whom was he trying to fool? It had happened. Tirael was dead. Raven closed his eyes, feeling sick, barely listening as Lord Asiah took his place at the lectern and recounted the occurrences of the night before.

Lord Asiah ended by calling one Leet, a Master Bard of Bylith. The door leading to the witnesses' balcony opened and Bard Leet slowly descended the curving stair. Lord Asiah motioned him to the witness's chair. Leet settled himself, his face grave and sad.

The Justice of Balyaranna studied him for a moment before saying, "As a bard, you owe fealty to Auvrian, do you not, Leet Welkin, once of Sansydale?"

"I do."

"Then do you swear by his name that what you say will be truth?"

Leet cleared his throat. "I do so swear."

"Then tell us what happened last night, Bard Leet."

Raven tried to remember what *had* happened. He remembered cutting through the gardens to get to the gathering, and then . . . what?

He heard Bard Leet say, "Lord Sevrynel had asked me to play for his gathering. I came early and found a spot in the garden where I could sit in private before going on to it." Though the bard did not raise his voice, his words carried throughout the room.

"Why is that?"

"The tuning of a harp is not the most entertaining of performances. Nor are vocal exercises," said Leet wryly. "I prefer a bit of privacy for it."

The Justice said, "I see. Please continue, bard. Then what?"

Yes—then what? If only I could remember! Raven bit his lip. *You were in the garden on your way to the gathering,* he told himself. *What happened—*

"Finished with that, I played a song or two to limber up my fingers."

Yes . . . yes! I remember a song! Raven thought with excitement. *I remember hearing music—and then . . .* It was as if he'd run into a wall. Yet the music was important. He *knew* it was important. But why couldn't he remember more? In despair he missed most of Bard Leet's next words.

". . . Then Tirael came into the garden alcove. As for what happened next . . . I was sitting in the bower—perhaps they didn't see me? Be that as it may, Raven Redhawkson called Lord Tirael a coward and a cheat." Bard Leet's voice faltered to a stop.

Gasps filled the room. Gasps and muttered imprecations. Raven squeezed his eyes shut even harder. By all the gods—he'd never say a thing like that to a Cassorin noble! Not even to Tirael, who had deserved worse.

But he had. Now that Leet mentioned it, he could remember saying it. Barely. The vaguest ghost of a memory, but it was there. Oh dear gods—if he did that, what else did he do?

Lord Asiah spoke over the angry rumble. "Silence! Silence! The witness is not yet done with his testimony." When the room was still once more, he said, "Please continue, Bard Leet."

"Raven Redhawkson is the grandnephew of one of my colleagues, Otter Heronson," Leet said softly, almost as if he spoke to himself. Then, louder, "I was afraid there was going to be a fight. I turned away to put my harp down. I was going to try to intervene—I am a bard, after all, such is my duty—but when I looked back . . . Oh gods, when I looked back . . ."

Bard Leet's voice cracked in a dry sob. "At first I thought they'd both gone. Then I realized that Raven had but stepped back a pace or two.

"I didn't see Lord Tirael. My first thought was that he'd left. Then I saw him lying on the ground. I assumed that Raven Redhawkson had struck him and knocked him unconscious. I hurried then to render what aid I could."

Though the bard's voice was scarcely louder than a whisper, it seemed to ring through the council chamber, so quiet was his audience. "I knelt by Lord Tirael, called to him, to see if I could wake him," Leet said. "I couldn't." He stopped, as if what came next was too painful to remember.

It *was* too painful. Whatever came next, Raven didn't want to hear it, though he finally opened his eyes and stared dully at the floor.

At last the bard took a deep breath and said, "Frightened, I put my fingers to Lord Tirael's throat to feel for a pulse. But what I had taken for shadow in the dim light was blood. I looked closer and realized his throat had been slashed. I was so shocked that I couldn't think what to do at first—I just kept kneeling. That was when Beast Healer Conor came upon us. I thank the gods that he did, for Raven Redhawkson might well have cut my throat next."

"What do you mean?" Lord Asiah asked.

"I hadn't realized it at first because of the poor light. My eyes aren't what they once were." There came a small, brave attempt at a laugh that ended in something like a sob. The audience murmured in sympathy.

"He still had the knife in his hand," Leet said. He sounded ill now. "Still in his hand, and both were covered in blood. Even his tunic was soaked in it."

At last Raven turned his head and looked at the bard. Their eyes met for a heartbeat.

The bard turned his face aside. "I—I had thought it was all shadows." The bard shivered as might any man who'd felt Death's cold robes brush past him.

"But it was not," Lord Asiah said.

"No. It was not. Blood—so much blood . . ."

Conor of Red Dale was called to witness next. Raven watched dully as the tall Beast Healer took the witness's chair, his long, craggy face unhappy. When he swore by the Great Stag to tell the truth, Lord Asiah had to ask him to speak up.

The Justice said, "Tell us your tale, Beast Healer."

Conor cleared his throat, then began with obvious reluctance, "I was on my way to Lord Sevrynel's gathering to find Lady Rosalea of Thennian."

"Why?"

"Her pony had been ill. She'd left word that as soon as he was back in his stall and safe, I was to come and tell her."

"I see. Pray continue."

So Conor went on with his damning evidence. When he was done, the Justice said, "It seems quite clear to me what happened last night: murder. Beast Healer Conor, you may step down."

"A moment, Justice," a deep voice interrupted.

Raven looked to where the Dragonlords sat for the first time since they'd come in. He'd not had the courage before; the sight of Maurynna's red eyes had come close to unmanning him.

But now Linden stood up, frowning slightly. "Something puzzles me, my Lord Justice. I would like to ask Beast Healer Conor a question or two if I may."

The Justice hesitated and glanced up into the balcony. Raven looked up as well. For the first time Raven realized that the regents of Cassori were here. He saw Duke Beren nod curtly.

"Of course, Dragonlord," the Justice said. He sat in his own chair as Linden came up onto the dais.

"Beast Healer Conor," Linden said, "since my fellow Dragonlords and I arrived at Balyaranna, I've spent a fair bit of time at Lord Sevrynel's manor of Rockfall."

There were smothered laughs throughout the council chamber; Raven heard someone loudly whisper "Pedigrees!" which brought on another spate of muffled laughter. Lord Asiah cleared his throat loudly and frowned at the assembly.

Linden went on as if nothing had happened, though the corner of his mouth twitched. "I've been through the gardens many times now and am quite familiar with them. I was under the impression you also knew your way around the gardens."

Conor nodded. "I do, Your Grace. From visiting Fliss and then reporting to Lord Sevrynel."

"The small alcove where Lord Tirael died is not on the most direct route from the stables to the place where gathers are held in the garden. Did you get lost?"

Conor frowned. It was some moments before he replied. "No, I wasn't lost," he said slowly. He sounded puzzled. "But you're right, Dragonlord, I shouldn't have been anywhere near—wait! I remember now. I heard music."

Music again! For the first time there came a chink in the despair that walled Raven in. He sat up a bit straighter and looked keenly at the Beast Healer.

Conor shook his head. "For some reason I went to see where it came from. Why on earth would . . . ," he muttered.

Lord Asiah rose. "Your Grace, with all due respect, may I remind you that, according to his testimony, Bard Leet was practicing in that alcove before performing? That must have been the music that Beast Healer Conor heard."

Linden looked steadily at the man. "I had not forgotten, my Lord Justice. I had not forgotten that at all."

And that was all he said, the only question he asked. That any of the Dragonlords asked. Linden sat down once again and Raven sank back into his despair.

Silence fell over the room. It seemed forever until Lord Asiah coughed slightly. "Very well then—let us hear what the accused has to say."

The Justice of Balyaranna turned a look upon him that seemed to pry into every corner of his soul. Raven felt colder than he ever had before.

Yes, he was named Raven Redhawkson. Yes, from Thalnia, now living in Yerrih with his aunt. Yes, this was his first fair at Balyaranna.

"What were you doing in Lord Sevrynel's gardens?" Lord Asiah asked.

"I was on my way to the gathering." To Lord Asiah's raised eyebrow, Raven insisted, "I was an invited guest."

The Justice looked over his shoulder. "Lord Sevrynel?"

The little Cassorin lord stood up, flustered. "True, my Lord Justice."

"Hmm." The Justice of Balyaranna turned back. "And then what happened?"

I don't know! Raven wanted to cry out. *I don't* . . . "It was the music," he said dully. "I felt the song in my head." He paused; even to him, the words sounded mad. "It was like it crawled into my brain and set it on fire. I think I remember seeing Tirael in the garden, but that's the last thing I remember. . . ." He looked around the court, silently begging them to understand, to believe him.

No one did. He read it in their faces. Not even Rynna—else why would she look so close to tears?

He *had* to make them understand. "Th—it was the music! I know it was!" he cried, struggling to get to his feet, forgetting about the stout straps that restrained him. It was hard to breathe now, as if the noose were already choking away his life.

The Cassorins shrank from him as if they thought he might get loose and cut all their throats as well. The only gaze that met his was Leet's.

The bard smiled as he rubbed the indentation beneath his lower lip. A tiny, mocking smile, gone an instant before Raven was certain he'd seen it.

As the soldiers hauled him out of the chair and out the door, Raven heard Lord Asiah announce, "My lords and ladies, the Judges' will now retire to discuss this matter. We will meet here again tomorrow at the thirteenth candlemark."

The rest was lost as his guards marched him down the hall. All the way back to his cell in the dungeon, Raven wondered if his eyes had played tricks on him.

Duke Beren made a small but comfortable chamber over to the use of the Dragonlords so that they would not have to go all the way back to the north tower. A tray of sweets, savories, and tartlets sat unheeded on a richly carved table. No one had any appetite.

But all felt the need for the Pelnaran wine also provided. Linden handed around goblets filled to the brim with the rich vintage.

For a long time nothing was said. Then, pouring herself a little more wine, Maurynna said, "It doesn't look good, does it?" Her voice trembled.

"No, it doesn't," Shima said gently. "It doesn't. But somehow, this just isn't right. I just can*not* see Raven cutting an unarmed man's throat over a race that never happened."

"I'll tell you what else isn't right," Linden said, frowning into the ruby liquid in his goblet. "What Conor said."

"Conor?" Maurynna and Shima asked together. The looks on both their faces said they thought he was mad.

"Yes, Conor. He was on his way to relieve a little girl's fears for her beloved pony—and he detoured to listen to some music?" Linden scowled at the reflection of his eye in the wine. "There's something wrong there—very wrong. But I don't know what it is. . . ."

Then a thought came to him and he shut his eyes for a moment in pain. "Oh gods have mercy—we need to get word to Otter. And this is not a thing you can tell someone at a distance." He tossed back the rest of his wine. "And since neither of you has ever been to Bylith—"

"How soon can you leave?" Maurynna asked.

"As soon as I can find an open space big enough to Change," Linden answered grimly.

Forty-seven

Linden flew steadily. He was making better time than he'd expected; earlier he'd found a current of air flowing westward and used it to speed himself along.

Still, it was long candlemarks before he spied Bylith below him. But not long enough. He hated being the bearer of bad news. He circled above the city, looking for landmarks that his dragon eyes could see in the dark.

Damn! Bylith had certainly grown since he was last here. Ah—there was the main building of the Bards' School; it was the only one with that distinctive cross shape.

And over there was the big courtyard where the journeymen and younger students gave performances for the townsfolk as part of their training.

He arrowed straight down for it. Even before he'd touched the ground, Linden let himself flow into Change. He fell from a little more than his height and landed like a cat. Then he set off at a run for the wing where Otter had his quarters.

"Drink this," Linden ordered as he thrust a goblet at Otter. The grey hue of the bard's face scared him, as did the blank-eyed stare.

Otter took it. The wine brought a little color back into his cheeks, but not enough for Linden's comfort. Still, he'd take whatever improvement he could get from the corpselike pallor of a moment ago.

"I simply cannot believe it," Otter whispered as he stared at the flickering oil lamp. "It's just not possible. Raven isn't the sort . . ." The goblet crashed to the floor. Otter buried his face in his hands and wept.

When the worst of the storm was past, Linden said quietly, "We need you in Balyaranna."

Otter wiped his wet cheeks. "Do you think I'll be able to get there in time? Before he's— I mean, Nightsong is fast, but I can't ride the way I used to, Linden. And I'm teaching Charilon's class until he returns." He sounded defeated.

"Someone else can take Charilon's classes or Belwynn can damn well give them a holiday," Linden said roughly. "And you won't be riding. I need to rest, so we won't leave until the morning, but I'll be carrying you. So pull yourself together, old friend, pack what you'll need and gather some warm blankets for the trip. We're leaving at dawn. Dragonlord's orders."

Shortly after breaking her fast the next morning, Maurynna went down to visit Raven. At first the guards didn't want to let her in.

"And why not? Do you think that I'll Change, scoop up the prisoner, and burn my way out?" she asked coldly.

The chief jailer squirmed under her withering stare. " 'Course not, Your Grace, even if he is a friend of yours. It's—it's just that a cell isn't a fitting place for—"

Maurynna stabbed a finger at the door. The jailer jumped to open it.

The stink that met her nearly made her gag. It smelled like the filthiest barn she could imagine. Gritting her teeth, she stalked inside.

An instant later, she hurled her mindvoice at Duke Beren.

Raven's being moved to a different cell? Why? Shima asked as they settled into their seats once more. There was still a bit to go before the flame burned down to the band of black wax that marked the thirteenth candlemark, but they wanted to watch faces as the others came in. Because there were a few Cassorins already ahead of them, they used mindspeech.

Because I demanded it, Maurynna replied grimly. *I've seen—and smelled— cleaner midden heaps.* And *there were rats in there that you could slap saddles on. While I can't demand that they ignore their laws and set Raven free, I damn well will use my rank to insist on better quarters for him. If anyone squawks, Beren will just tell them that I insist on visiting Raven and it was not a fitting place for a Dragonlord. End of argument.*

Shima considered that. As far as "abuses" of power went, it seemed a harmless one. *So where will he be?*

A cell in the tower opposite ours. It's called the Black Tower and is where they keep prisoners of royal blood if needed. Now I need to get them to let Yarrow visit him. Damn all stiff Cassorin necks!

More people were filing in, whispering eagerly to each other as they jockeyed for the best seats. Shima wondered what this day would bring for Raven.

Nothing good. No sooner had Raven been strapped into his chair once more than Lord Asiah rose and faced the assembly.

"My lords and ladies, Your Graces, the Judges' Council of Balyaranna has come to a decision." He turned his head to look at Raven a moment, then at his eager audience once more. "At dawn tomorrow, the man known as Raven Redhawkson shall be hanged by the neck until dead," the Justice of Balyaranna intoned.

Maurynna gasped. She swayed in her seat; Shima slipped an arm around her shoulders, afraid she would faint.

Shima, she begged. *Do something, say something! If I try to talk, I'll just, just—* Her mindvoice "gulped." *Please—there's something here we're not seeing.*

But what? Shima asked, racking his brains in desperation.

I don't— Wait! Remember what Linden said about Conor? There's got *to be something to explain this!*

It was the thinnest of threads, but Shima grasped at it. He rose. "If I may address this assembly, my lord Justice?"

From the way the man's lips thinned, Shima knew he was not happy. Shima counted on the reluctance he'd noticed to refuse a Dragonlord anything outright.

"Of course, Dragonlord," the Justice said stiffly.

Shima went to the front of the room. "I ask that you delay the sentence for a few days at least, my lords and ladies."

"But this man has taken a life," Lord Asiah replied. "And there is no evidence that it was otherwise."

"But once he also—at the risk of his own—saved a life," Shima countered.

"Whose?" someone called. "A pigherd's?" Laughter greeted the sally.

Shima glanced over in the direction the voice had come from. "Mine," he said grimly. Into the sudden, surprised hush, he went on, "During my First Change, a soldier—part of a Jehangli patrol—was about to throw a spear at me. I had no idea what was happening to me and I was helpless. Raven saw the danger I was in. He used the only weapon he had—a rock. A rock against a well-armed patrol. Had the soldier succeeded in killing me, Raven and my little brother would have fallen victims to the wrath of that same patrol. I can assure you, my lords and ladies, the Jehangli soldiers would not have been kind. Raven and Tefira had escaped them once. The soldiers would have made certain that it didn't happen a second time. *Very* certain." Shima looked around to make sure that all understood his last words.

He continued, "Luckily, Raven's aim was true. He knocked the spear out of the soldier's hands and saved my life. Until now, I've had no chance to repay him. Therefore I ask this boon: We need time. We feel there is something not quite right in the accounts concerning what happened. Please give us the time to make certain that there is no mistake."

He paused a moment, and once more studied the faces before him. He read denial in many—too many—of those faces.

So did Raven. He caught Shima's eye, then looked down at one hand. Shima followed his gaze and saw Raven raise the two middle fingers and tap the chair arm.

Shima understood; it was the closest Raven could come to the Dragonlord sign for mindspeech. He reached out to touch Raven's mind with his own.

Thank you for trying.

The Yerrin's mindvoice was exhausted. But worse was the feel in it of defeat, guilt, worthlessness, and, above all, giving up.

Shima swore under his breath. Were he playing *diyinesh,* now it would be the time to throw down his Luck piece, the Sun Eagle.

And he had one. *I'm not done yet,* he told Raven. He cast his Luck—Raven's last chance—before these people who held his friend's life in their hands.

Taking a deep breath, Shima said, "I ask it also in the name of the Lady of Dragonskeep and of the truedragon Morlen the Seer. I ask it in token of the services that Raven Redhawkson has rendered both Dragonskeep and the truedragons in the past."

May that prove to be the Sun Eagle, my friend, he thought, fighting to keep his fear from showing.

A lightning bolt couldn't have surprised the council more. Shima suspected that they had never dreamed he would invoke those names. He watched, amused, as the members of the Judges' Council turned in dismay to one another. The buzz of their hurried consultations filled the chamber. Shima's unnaturally sharp hearing caught snatches here and there.

"But he's only a commoner!" "How long must Lord Tirael wait for vengeance?" "Oh, dear! Oh, *dear*—it wouldn't be wise to anger the Lady." "Why did the damned horse breeder have to have Dragonlord friends, anyway?" "He was caught red-handed—literally! I say we hang him and have done with it!" "Bloody idiot—do you want an angry truedragon sitting on *your* manor house and rampaging through your fields because we didn't delay a few days? I don't! I say we wait—he'll be just as dead in a tenday as he would be tomorrow morning."

The last was courtesy of the irascible Lord Corvy, and everyone had heard it. Corvy's idea of a "discreet whisper" was a muted bellow. He sat back in his chair, whuffling in annoyance through his bristly grey mustache, glaring at the other members of the Judges' Council.

Shima watched as the mental image Corvy had evoked spread among the old lord's fellow nobles. Its path was easy to follow; first, eyes went wide, then face after face blanched and lips moved in soundless prayers—or curses. He was never certain afterward how he kept a straight face. Indeed, had it not been life or death, he would have laughed aloud.

Lord Oriss, one of the judges, stood up. He coughed delicately and said, "The Lady of Dragonskeep and Lord Truedragon Morlen might not appreciate such a request. Would you truly risk annoying them for the sake of a mere commoner?"

This was an attitude Shima had never faced among his own people, the Tah'nehsieh, though he'd heard of it among the Jehangli. He hadn't liked the thought of it then, and he despised the reality of it now. Shima stared at the Cassorin noble until the man squirmed. "Did you forget that I was also born a 'mere commoner,' my lord?" he said coldly.

Before the man could answer, Maurynna stood up and faced Lord Oriss. She said, "As was I, my lord." Her voice was quiet and controlled, but all the more dangerous for that. Even Shima flinched from the steely edge in it.

Lord Oriss looked as frightened as if he'd suddenly found a naked blade at his throat. "I—I m-meant no . . ." He trailed off.

A deep voice said pleasantly—too pleasantly, Shima thought; there was as much danger in that mild tone as in Maurynna's barely contained fury—"Until she reached First Change, the Lady of Dragonskeep was a weaver's apprentice. I don't think there will be a problem there."

Everyone looked to the door in surprise. Linden stood, leaning against the jamb. He looked, thought Shima, very tired.

Linden pushed off from the jamb and walked into the room. He went on, still in that deceptively mild voice, "And the greatest of the truedragons, Morlen the Seer, doesn't give a damn for what he sees as truehuman pretensions, my lords and ladies. He also holds Raven in high regard, for it was Raven's idea of using Llysanyins as performing horses that gave us the key to enter Jehanglan. Because of him, we were able to end the truedragon Pirakos's horrible suffering."

"I . . . see," Lord Oriss managed to say.

"But getting word to them and then returning would take days, wouldn't it, Your Graces?" someone asked.

The voice came from the back of the room. It was one Shima hadn't heard before, nor could he even tell whether it was male or female. What he *did* know was that he didn't like the sly note under the apparent concern. He suspected he knew just what plans the owner of that voice contemplated.

It was lovely to foil them. "Not at all," Shima replied. "All of us are strong fliers." *Though this one would be on Maurynna or me.*

From the looks on the faces before him, it was plain they'd forgotten for the moment that Dragonlords weren't bound to the earth as they were. Shima guessed they'd agreed with the unknown voice: *Hang the bastard while they're riding north. Not a damn thing they can do then.* Shima smiled sweetly at them.

"Nor do we even need as much time as flying would take, my lords and ladies," said Linden. "It's possible that even from this distance, I could mindspeak the Lady of Dragonskeep on my own. If Maurynna or Shima let me draw upon their strength, I *know* I can reach the Lady. Then a message out of Dragonskeep to Morlen the Seer and his kinswyrms as the Lady wings south . . ." He shrugged. "I understand many of the truedragons hold Raven in very high regard. Likely they'd come as well."

Dismay, consternation, fear; even a few devout prayers. It was plain this was *not* a thing the nobles of Cassori wished to see.

Folding his arms across his chest, Linden looked from side to side. "And all for the thing we ask you now. My lords and ladies—do we have our extra time?"

Lord Corvy said, "By all the gods, give it to 'em. We don't want a bunch of angry truedragons hanging about, now do we? So we wait a tenday or even two."

They had a tenday; the Judges' Council had recessed and then sent word of their decision. Now the question was, how could they prove a man caught red-handed was innocent? Linden hadn't the faintest idea. Neither, he suspected, did either of the others. By unspoken agreement, they headed for the tranquil seclusion of the castle gardens after the closing of the Judges' meeting.

"Otter?" Maurynna asked.

"Here," Linden said. "I asked Lord Asiah that he be allowed to visit Raven. As soon as he realized that it was *that* Otter Heronson, he agreed. The rest of the Judges' Council is still balking at letting Yarrow visit, however. I'll talk to Beren about it."

Walking aimlessly, they came upon a small grove of cherry trees. Centered in the grove was a little pool lined with white marble; benches made of the same stone faced each other across the water. Maurynna and Shima wandered off to see if any of the cherries were ripe. Linden stayed behind. He knelt on one of the marble slabs around the pool's rim and looked into the water.

It was so clear that he could see to the bottom where the center stone had a hole carved into it where the spring below entered. The excess water flowed over a channel carved in one of the rim stones and ran down a channel lined with more of the glossy white stone. After a few feet, the channel disappeared underground. Linden wondered halfheartedly where it went to before looking back into the water once more.

If only our course was as clear as this, he thought, dipping a hand into the water. It was icy cold. He scooped up a double handful and splashed it over his face, then took a seat on a bench. He watched as the other two came to join him, their hands empty.

They sat down, Maurynna next to him and Shima across from them. Linden couldn't help observing, "So, your search was . . . fruitless?"

Shima groaned. Maurynna smiled sweetly—*much* too sweetly—and said, "I ought to shove you in the pool for that. Headfirst."

"And I wouldn't blame you a bit. Thank Otter for that one. He used it on me once."

"Otter . . . Oh dear gods, Linden—how did he take it?" Maurynna asked. "If Raven is hanged it will break his heart."

"It was bad, Maurynna-love. Very bad."

"Do you think Otter can help us?"

"If there's a way Raven can be helped," Shima said, gazing morosely into the water.

"Aye," Linden muttered. "If there is a way."

A depressed silence fell over them. Time crawled past; Linden racked his brains trying to find a place to start. He saw none. Discouraged, he watched the water bubbling gently over the lip of the pool and listened to the breeze rustle the leaves around them.

"Linden—could you truly reach Dragonskeep from here?" Shima asked at last.

Linden answered, "If, as I said, you or Maurynna helped me, the answer is, yes, I can. Some of the older and more powerful Dragonlords wouldn't need help, but I often do. I once reached even further with the unknowing help of a band of merlings."

"When was that?" Maurynna asked, turning on the bench to face him. "I thought you'd rarely been to sea before we met, and you certainly never mentioned seeing merlings. They're not that common."

Linden smiled. "I wasn't at sea, but at Dragonskeep. It was the night I mind-spoke Otter when you and he were sailing to Cassori."

She gazed past him for a moment, lost in thought. "That's right—I remember now! I'd had the oddest dreams one night, and came out of my cabin the next morning trying to remember them. Then Otter began teasing me—he knew all kinds of things that he couldn't have found out before we sailed. Said he'd heard it all from a friend. The wretch wouldn't tell me who; all I guessed was that it wasn't one of my crew. Nearly drove me to distraction, trying to puzzle out who else he could have been talking to in the middle of the sea.

"Once I found out more about mindspeech, I'd wondered how you were able to reach so far. I know I couldn't. Then I decided it was because you'd been a Dragonlord so much longer than I. So you did it by tapping the magic of a pod of mer—?" She stopped short, staring at him in puzzlement.

"What's wrong, love?"

"Linden—where were those merlings?"

Now it was his turn to be puzzled. "They must have been right by your ship, else I couldn't have made use of their magic."

"But there weren't any merlings on that voyage. You don't see them very often; most of my kin have never seen any. I did, on one voyage, but that was when I was second mate on my aunt's ship. When they do come around, they'll follow a ship for days. They like ship's biscuits—the gods only know why, no one else does—and know that sailors will usually toss them some for luck. I would have seen them if they'd been there, Linden."

"There must have been some," Linden argued. "I remember straining to hold the link after finding Otter. Then, just as I thought it would snap, there was a surge of power. I realized there must have been merlings nearby. What else could it have been—"

The answer hit him with the force of mule's kick. "Oh, bloody hell," he said softly.

There had never been any merlings. He'd simply assumed there were because Otter was on a ship, and what other magic would be nearby? What else could have been the wellspring of the power he'd felt, used—

And woke before its proper time. Linden felt ill. It was on his head that the dragon half of Maurynna's soul, Kyrissaean, had been woken too early and faced dark magic before she was ready. All the problems Maurynna had faced were his fault. Thank the gods that Miune Kihn, the young Jehangli waterdragon, had been able to soothe Maurynna's dragonsoul during the journey to Jehanglan; would she have ever been able to Change at will if not for that? He decided he never wanted to know the answer.

"Linden?"

She'd put all the pieces together as well; he could see it in her eyes. "Oh gods, love—I'm sorry," he whispered. "If I'd known . . ."

They stared at each other without speaking. Finally Shima cleared his throat and said, "Would someone like to tell me what's going on?"

"No," they both snapped, still watching each other.

Shima threw his hands up in surrender.

Finally Maurynna said, "It's all right, Linden—you didn't know. No one knew."

"I should have. . . ."

She sighed in exasperation. "How? I asked you once before: Are you one of the gods to know everything? Or just a Dragonlord? Stop heaping ashes upon your head, or I'll, I'll—" She crossed her arms. "Let's just say you won't like whatever I think of when I do think of it."

But she was fighting a smile as she said it, and Linden knew he was forgiven—if she'd even truly blamed him. Perhaps she'd guessed—rightly—that he'd blame himself enough for the both of them, and would for a very long time.

"So," he said, "what do we know?"

"We know that Conor heard music and did something that you—and I will bow to your knowledge of the man—think was not in character," Shima said.

"Now what?" Maurynna asked.

"I can't help feeling we're missing something," Linden muttered, rubbing his chin. "Some little thing we've overlooked. . . ."

"But what?" Maurynna whispered. "And can we find it in time?"

Forty-eight

"The food's running low," Kaeliss said as she peered into her pack. "Even with Fiarin's share, we've only a bit of the dried meat left and not much more dried fruit." She looked up, fear writ large in her eyes. "What are we to do? I've not seen any berry bushes or anything else, have you?"

"No." Pod frowned; worse yet, Kiga hadn't been able to find any prey lately. She suspected the woods dog was keeping himself from starving by eating grubs from under logs, but she was a good way from being hungry enough to share *that* meal. Odd, though, that he hadn't found anything. Come to think of it, it had been some time since she'd seen even a squirrel in these woods. She was just about to mention it when Kaeliss stood up.

"We'd better push on," the Wort Hunter said, driving the thought from Pod's mind.

They walked on, pausing throughout the day to search for whatever edible berries or mushrooms they might find. It was late morning when they made a couple of welcome discoveries.

The first was a small stream. Pod silently thanked the gods; there were only a few mouthfuls left in her waterskin. They hurried to ease their parched mouths and fill their waterskins once more. As they knelt, wiping their faces, both became aware of a sweet scent in the air.

Pod sniffed and sniffed; she'd smelled this before. It brought back a welter of emotions, some good, some bad. What was—

She toddled after Old Simmy as the grunting matriarch of the pigsty pushed through the bushes. Something smelled nice. With a squeal of rapturous pleasure, the black-and-white sow began rooting at the base of some vines. Many of the tubers she unearthed disappeared down her gullet like magic; others she pushed to Pod, who gathered them up in her tunic. She didn't dare eat them; if they found out, they'd beat her. But maybe they would give her some. . . .

Pod scrambled to her feet and sniffed the air like a hound, tracing the delicious scent back to its source: a tangle of vines with purple-brown flowers. She followed the nearest to where it sprang up from the ground and began digging. A few moments later she held a string of small tubers in her hand. "Groundnuts!" she cried in delight.

Soon they had enough to fill their small pot. As the tubers cooked, they discussed what to do next. In the end, they decided to gather as many groundnuts as they could and press on as long as the light held, then make camp and send Kiga to hunt. If the gods were willing, perhaps he'd find a nice fat rabbit. After stuffing themselves with groundnuts, they crossed the stream and forged on, Pod in the lead.

After a time, Pod noticed that Kiga seemed uneasy. The woods dog kept stopping, looking this way and that. Now and again, he'd snarl, a soft, puzzled, uneasy snarl that prickled the hair on the back of Pod's neck. Each time she stopped and peered around as well, her heart pounding. What was out there? Surely no animal in its right mind would confront a woods dog. Hellfire—she'd seen a *bear* back down before Kiga!

But there was never anything that she could see, or even hear. Still, her uneasiness grew throughout the day. She kept telling herself it was just because she was still tired from the failed Healing, yet it didn't help when Kaeliss cursed behind her. She jumped "halfway to the moon," as Conor would say.

"What's wrong?" she asked anxiously, spinning around.

Kaeliss was on the ground, tugging at her boot. "I think I've got a blister," came the terse—and annoyed—reply. "Damn it all—just what we didn't need!"

Pod watched as Kaeliss examined her heel. "I had to be right, curse it," the other young woman muttered. She dabbed some ointment from a small jar on the blister. Pod recognized the jar as one they'd taken from Fiarin's pack. With another curse, Kaeliss pulled her linen stocking and boot back on and rose.

"You'd best lead now to set the pace," Pod said. Kaeliss nodded; they set off once more, Kaeliss limping slightly.

In the late afternoon they came upon another long pile of rocks like the one they had robbed to build Fiarin's cairn. As they clambered over, Kaeliss paused, then pointed.

"Those are apple trees!" she cried.

It took Pod a moment to recognize them; unlike the trees in the chapterhouse's orchard, these were wildly overgrown. But as her eye grew used to the tangle, she saw that Kaeliss was right.

She could also see that despite their wildness, they were arranged in neat rows. "This was an orchard," she said slowly.

And with that she realized what the stone piles were: the remains of old stone walls. "There must have been a village around here once," she told Kaeliss as they hopped down. "No one would plant an orchard in the middle of the woods."

Which explained why the woods had seemed so odd: unlike the other forests she'd been in, these were young trees, trees that had sprung up in abandoned fields and pastures.

And with that realization, her uneasiness grew. Why had this place been abandoned? She kicked at the grass, scuffing up a clod of crumbly black soil teeming with earthworms. Rich dirt, this; the people of this village hadn't left because the soil was worn out.

She narrowed her eyes and looked around. So why . . .

Kiga's whine made her turn. He stood on the old wall, scrabbling at the rocks with his powerful claws, head turning this way and that, now whining, now snarling.

"Kiga! Kiga come!"

But the woods dog ignored her. Pod whistled sharply and called, "Kiga! Come here *now*!"

At last Kiga clambered down from his rocky perch and trotted to her side. Pod scratched behind his ears. "All's well, boy, don't worry," she told him—and herself.

A call from Kaeliss made her look up again. The other young woman had gotten well ahead of her. She was alternately waving and pointing to something at her feet. As the skin between her shoulder blades prickled, Pod trotted to join her.

"Look!" Kaeliss said when Pod joined her in a small clearing. "Another spring!" She pivoted and pointed to a huge clump of tall orange flowers shaped like trumpets. "And those are daylilies—fancy their surviving all this time since the village was abandoned. You can eat the buds, the flowers themselves, and the tubers beneath. I think we should rest here a day or two. I don't want that blister to break open and get infected—and you haven't fully recovered from trying to Heal Fiarin, have you? You still look pale."

It was true, though she'd tried to hide it. To rest for more than a candlemark, to stay in one place for a whole day—perhaps even two! The thought made Pod giddy with delight. Besides, if Kaeliss's foot became infected . . . Pod's stomach turned over at the idea.

"I think it's a good plan," she answered, stubbornly ignoring Kiga's soft whines and her own uneasiness. "Let's cut some branches and make a shelter with the extra blanket."

"Good idea. Then I want to put more ointment on that blister."

When everything was ready, Pod turned to Kiga. The woods dog had stayed so close to her that she'd almost tripped over him twice. "Kiga—go hunt, boy."

But instead of loping off, the woods dog just hunkered down. Pod frowned at him and again ordered him to hunt. Kiga refused to go.

Kaeliss looked up from re-bandaging her foot. "Why bother? He hasn't been much use at it lately, has he?"

Really angry now—at herself, Kiga, or Kaeliss, she wasn't sure which—Pod did something she rarely did: she lost her temper with her brother-in-fur. "Bad

Kiga!" she shouted angrily. "Bad! Go hunt!" And she "pushed" at him with all her will.

Kiga jumped up as if she'd struck him. He stared at her for a long moment, a rumbling, singsong snarl deep in his throat. Then, the instant before Pod was sure he'd snap at her, Kiga turned and loped off. A mix of fright and anger made Pod yell after him, "And don't come back until you've caught something!"

As the woods dog trotted across the clearing, tears pricked Pod's eyes. She tried to call him back but the words caught in her throat. Then it was too late; Kiga disappeared into the shadowy woods.

Blinking back tears, Pod busied herself with gathering downed branches and twigs for the fire. By the time she stopped, it was full dark and she was exhausted and well-nigh sick with hunger and worry. When she finally sat down before the fire, Kaeliss wisely said nothing, just handed her a bowl of stew made from day-lily tubers, groundnuts, and the last shreds of their dried meat. Pod forced herself to eat, straining her ears for the sound of Kiga's return.

He still hadn't returned by the time she admitted defeat and rolled herself in her blankets.

And it was the first rays of the sun, not the tickle of Kiga's whiskers, that woke her the next morning.

Forty-nine

The noon meal—such as it was—sat on the table. It was not, Maurynna thought as she pushed the overcooked peas around her plate, particularly inspiring. "Is this what all your meals are like?"

Raven smiled wanly and nodded. "I'd guess that while they have to house me like a prisoner of rank—thank you again for that!—they refuse to feed me like one. If you let them know you're coming here to share a meal, I'm sure the fare will improve immensely. They might not even burn the bread next time."

Maurynna snorted in disgust. "I just might do that—for every meal."

Silence fell as they contemplated the pathetic meal. *The meat is grey and gristly, the peas are mush, the bread is burned, and the wine is barely this side of vinegar. Yes, I think I'll put them on notice that I might well be sharing Raven's table without warning.*

"Maybe this is how the gods are punishing me," Raven said suddenly.

"For what?" Maurynna asked in surprise.

"Taren."

For a moment she didn't know what he meant. Then she understood. She exhaled slowly and said, "Because he was a kinslayer and you helped him, you mean." She shook her head. "Raven, the gods wouldn't be so cruel. It's not as if you knew what he was. . . ." Her voice trailed off at the look in his eyes.

"As if the gods care whether I knew or not," he said bitterly. "Don't you remember the story you told me after we returned from Jehanglan—what Shima's mother, Lark, told you? How, because the captain of the ship she was the cook on gave Taren a berth on the crew, they were shipwrecked on the coast of Jehanglan, and all hands were lost save Lark, some other woman—and Taren. They didn't know, either, and the gods certainly punished them."

She couldn't deny his words. Still . . . "Dragonskeep gave Taren hearth-room, and nothing's happened there in all this time," Maurynna pointed out.

"You're among the favored of the gods, remember?" Raven snapped. "Dragon-lords and Bards and Healers. No doubt the gods will forgive the lot of you what they'd crush us ordinary mortals for. Or maybe they're just waiting. Maybe—"

The bitter tumble of words ended in something like a sob. Raven seemed to shrink in on himself like an old, old man. Alarmed, Maurynna reached out to him; the hands that caught hers across the little table trembled.

"I'm scared, Beanpole. More scared than I've ever been in my life," he whis-pered. "I killed Tirael—I must have. Who else? I don't remember doing it, or even know *why* I would do it. But they'll hang me nevertheless. And, may the gods help me, they'll be right to do it. I must be mad, or there's some evil in me I never knew about. . . ."

He squeezed his eyes shut and turned his face away, but not before Maurynna saw the glint of tears on his cheeks. "I deserve to die. But I—I don't want to, Rynna. I don't want to. Help me—please," he begged.

He squeezed her hands; Maurynna caught her breath at the sudden pain but said nothing. She'd not add to the burden he carried.

A sudden image formed in her mind of those same hands plunging a dagger into Tirael's throat; those same hands dripping with blood. . . . A chill crept down her spine. She fought the urge to pull her hands away.

Somehow Raven sensed her revulsion. He jerked his hands away as if hers had suddenly turned into red-hot coals.

Then his hands twisted and rubbed each other again and again and again. Raven seemed completely unaware of it. It was a moment before Maurynna rec-ognized the gesture for what it was.

But guilt can never be washed away, she thought sadly.

After a time, Raven met her eyes again. He said softly, "Will you please visit Stormwind for me? He must be wondering what's going on if no one's had the heart to tell him. Give him my love and tell him . . ." Raven wiped tears from his eyes. "Tell him I'll understand if he wants to go back to Dragonskeep."

A gentle smile curved Maurynna's lips. "I think you'll find him a truer heart than that, Raven. He'll wait for you no matter what."

Leet stared at the harp on the small table by the bed. His hands clenched in fists at his side as he fought to keep from touching the strings again. He'd only just put it down. . . .

It sat in its stand, mocking him with its beauty, its sweet voice, with its power.

Leet closed his eyes. *There is no one else's death I need seek. Tirael has paid the price for Arnath's death. Otter's grandnephew will pay the price for Jaida's life that Otter should have paid years ago. Curse the Dragonlords for the delay, but in the end it won't matter. His idiot grandnephew's death will destroy Otter.*

I will put Gull away now. I won't, I won't, I won't play him. I am stronger than any harp. He opened his eyes in triumph only to see that his fingertips were a bare handsbreadth from the strings. He fought to pull them back. But his fingers crept closer and closer and he remembered the ecstasy he'd found. . . .

A knock at the door ended the battle. He jumped, startled, and the spell was broken. "Who is it?" he called harshly.

"Daera," came the response.

Panic surged through him. What was she doing here? She was supposed to be— "Wait! Wait! I—I'm not yet dressed!"

The bard seized the harp and set it into its traveling case, too overwrought to feel its call. He pushed it under the bed and sat down on the mattress. He rubbed his hands over his face and took a deep breath to calm himself.

"Come in, then. Push hard—the latch sticks."

The door swung open after a moment and Daera slipped in. "Bard Leet," she said. "I am ready to resume my classes. My thanks for taking them. I hope they went well while I was gone."

Classes? He'd never been asked to take Daera's cla— "Ah, Duchess Beryl must have decided that while you were gone the children could have a holiday so that I might work on—on a new composition of some importance," Leet blustered.

A tiny frown appeared between Daera's brows. "Most of them must have rejoiced at that, sir, but poor Kella . . ."

Kella? Who the hell was Kella?

Then a memory rose before his mind's eye: a little girl in a grass-stained skirt, hand outstretched to Gull. "The merchant's brat who dared try to touch my harp? She would have been a waste of my time." He glared at her, the glare that had made many a student squirm. To his annoyance, she merely gazed back at him.

"She would not have been."

Irritated by her cool tone, he rose to his feet and said, "Is that so? I require you to explain why—and your insolence, as well."

Daera stood up a bit straighter. For a moment he thought she would refuse to answer. It would be her right; she was no longer his student. She was no longer even a journeywoman bard. Nor was it forbidden to take on a merchant's child as a student, but it rankled him that she'd set the brat on a level with her noble students!

But she answered calmly enough, "As I said, her name is Kella Vanadin, a merchant's daughter. And she has talent, Bard Leet. It is a pleasure to teach her—she's good enough to go on to Bylith one day."

The breath nearly froze in Leet's chest. The child had *that* much talent? Oh dear gods—if she'd touched the strings . . .

He refused to think about it. Instead he snapped, "That doesn't give her the right to take lessons with the children of nobles. Young as you are, you've been given a post many an older bard envies. You're the royal bard and teacher to the young prince and many of the highborn children of Cassori. How dare you make them share your time and attention with her? I always knew you weren't fit for this position—rest assured I shall report this gross neglect of your duty to Guild Master Belwynn!"

Her eyes blazed at his words. Then, to his surprise, something like a smile ghosted across her mouth.

"I'm sure you will, Bard Leet," she said smoothly. "But I'll not waste any more of your time—I'm sure you want to work on your composition once more. So if you'll excuse me, I really should send messages to all my students that lessons will resume tomorrow."

And with that she smiled in truth, an enigmatic smile that made him uneasy. She nodded to him and was out the door before he could call her back.

Of all the insolent—! Yet . . . there was something there, something he should know. . . . He took the harp out once again, set it on the table, and stood looking out of the window.

Behind him Gull's strings vibrated softly. He turned and brushed his fingers across them. He cradled the harp in his arms and forgot all about insolent young bards and merchant's brats.

Two gardeners plodded through the castle gardens, sweat running down their faces as they pushed along wheelbarrows full of rosebushes to be planted. The lead gardener, an old man with a straggly beard and a squint, halted so suddenly that his companion, following closely behind, all but ran him down.

"Ferdy, tha horse's ass, why did tha stop like that?" the second man demanded. "Nearly squashed tha like a bug, I did, *and* tha almost made me dump m'barrow." Then, seeing his companion sniffing the air, he went on in annoyance, "Oh, by the Great Consort's balls, not again! I tell tha, Ferdy, whatever it is these days that tha and Crispin think tha're smelling, it's all in tha empty heads, tha foo—" He broke off, almost gagging, as a foul stench reached his nose.

Ferdy turned to him, grinning toothlessly. "Ah—tha smells it at last, does tha, Ebler? Tha should—that's the wust yet. Or mayhap it's all in tha head, too? Nah, nah—it's real enough. Always has been. Has tha noticed how few squirrels and rabbits and moles there are in the gardens these days?"

"Some guest's cat or badger hound or something," Ebler grunted as he picked up his barrow again and pushed it along as fast as he could. "Doing us a favor getting rid of the vermin. Now let's get out of here. I'll be all day getting that stink out of m'nose." He forged ahead.

They hadn't gotten far when Ferdy said, "Whatever it is as does it, it's getting deeper and deeper into the gardens, Eb."

"Shut tha damned mouth, Ferdy."

A dozen more steps and Ferdy called out over the growing distance, "Did tha know that Crispin found a dead rabbit afore it were too far gone? Looked like its throat was cut, he said. Now what cat would cut—"

"Shut tha damned and ill-omened mouth, Ferdy!"

Fifty

Three days gone now. Raven looked out of the tower window at the eastern sky. The sun was just coming up; tattered banners of cloud glowed red and gold in the growing light. From the roof above him he heard the busy chattering of a flock of birds. A breeze slipped through the window. This far above the castle midden, it was fresh and sweet and brisk on his face as he pressed against the bars. It brought the scent of new-cut hay with it from somewhere; if he closed his eyes, he would be back in the meadows of Yarrow's holding, riding bareback through the long, dew-laden grass as a song sparrow greeted the new day from a nearby tree. Stormwind would be warm beneath him; he could almost feel the powerful muscles moving, the long, coarse mane in his hand as the big Llysanyin cantered down to the pond as they did almost every morning.

That was what was real; not this, not this. . . .

It was no good. Raven opened his eyes to the walls of his prison. At least it was worlds better than the foul cell they'd first thrown him into. He had Maurynna to thank for that—and for the fact that he was even still alive. Raven had little doubt that if it hadn't been for her, one of the guards would have run him through then and there in the garden.

And maybe it would have been for the best, he thought in despair. He still couldn't believe this nightmare was real. How could he have killed Tirael and have no memory of it? *Why* would he murder Tirael, anyway? He'd already had the best revenge he could possibly have against such a man.

Yet he must have killed the spoiled young noble. How else did he come to be spattered with Tirael's blood? And the bloodstained knife in his hand, *his* knife—even he could not deny that.

But why couldn't he remember anything? Why, why, *why*?

Raven flung himself from the hard bench and paced rapidly back and forth. His stomach churned; for a moment he feared he would be ill. He stopped, leaning against the wall, its cold stone rough against his cheek, then shut his eyes and concentrated on breathing deeply. He would not be sick. He would not, he would not, he would not . . .

But three days were gone and the Dragonlords were no closer to a solution.

Great-uncle Otter and Aunt Yarrow were gone. They were only allowed to visit for two candlemarks a day. Part of Raven wished that they didn't have to come together, but the guards wouldn't let Yarrow visit by herself. She was just a commoner to them. Hell, from what Yarrow had said, she wouldn't have been able to visit at all if it hadn't been for Linden. It would be nice, he thought wistfully, if they could come one after the other; then his day wouldn't seem so empty.

But another part wept at the sight of their stricken faces, their brave, sad attempts to pretend that everything would be well. He didn't think it would be even though Maurynna, Linden, and Shima were searching everywhere for a solution.

But at least he got news of Stormwind from Yarrow. He almost wished she hadn't let it slip that the Llysanyin was barely eating these days. Perhaps he'd ask Maurynna to have Boreal bully Stormwind into eating more if that was what was needed.

The door opened and shut. Raven turned his head just enough to catch a glimpse of a young servant bearing a covered platter that was almost bigger than he was. Indeed, at first glance it looked like something out of an old granny's tale; but instead of a magic table, it was a tray with legs, bearing food. He could barely see the top of a page's cap above the domed cover.

At least the food is better these days. "Put it down on the table," Raven said listlessly as he stared out the window once more, watching the activity in the courtyard far below. It was his one amusement—if one could call it that. From so high up, the people looked like ants scurrying around on their mysterious errands. To while away the long candlemarks, he made up stories about their comings and goings. Many involved mysterious benefactors and daring rescues. None came true.

He leaned one elbow on the ledge and sighed, chin in hand. If only he could be one of those people . . . Ah, well; at least this was better than the dungeon.

Or so he told himself again and again. It didn't really help. He heard the serving boy set the tray down with a grunt.

"Hsst."

Raven ignored the boy.

"Hssst!"

Raven ground his teeth. Another nosy little bastard who wanted to know what it was like to kill someone, eh? He pointedly turned his back.

Another whisper, this time exasperated. "Raven!"

Raven grabbed the rough iron bars as hard as he could, staring outside with grim determination. The slight coating of scaling rust gritted under his hands, digging into his skin. *I will* not *kick the little bastard's ass through the door. I will not kick—*

Next came the sound of a stamping foot. "Oh, don't be such a ninny! Raven, I order you to look at me!"

Raven blinked. "I order"—from a *servant*? Turning, he said, "Who on— Oh, by Gifnu's hells!" His knees suddenly weak, Raven nearly slid down the wall at the sight of the boy's brick-red hair.

Prince Rann, dressed in servant's livery, stood beaming at him, floppy cap in hand. Raven thought that if the boy had a tail, he'd be wagging it like a puppy with a stolen bone.

Stunned, Raven went down on one knee before the young Cassorin prince. "Your Highness!" He knew his mouth was hanging open and that he must look like the village idiot, but he didn't care. He was too busy trying to decide whether he was surprised, baffled, or just plain terrified. If the guard chose this moment to walk in and realized his young sovereign was within easy reach of a murderer, he'd kill Raven first and ask questions afterward.

"What in the name of all the gods are you doing here, my lord?" Raven sputtered. *Please,* please *don't let the guard come in now. . . .*

"I got the idea from something Kella did. Look what I brought you!" Rann reached into the front of his tunic. After a few fumbling moments, he pulled out a chisel. "I know you didn't kill Tirael, so I had Aralie's brother steal this from one of the stonemasons working on the new solar. You can use it to dig out the bars from the window and escape!" The boy fairly danced in excitement, he was so delighted with his idea.

Beyond words now, Raven numbly accepted the tool. He refrained from asking how he'd get down from such a height since he wasn't a fly to crawl down the walls. He'd not dash Rann's pleasure that way. The child was plainly thrilled to help him.

Never mind it was of bloody little use; Rann believed in him. That was what was important.

"Thank you, Your Highness," Raven managed to get out past the lump in his throat. "You've no idea how much your faith and trust mean to me."

Nothing else would do but that Raven must start immediately on the Great Plan. "I shan't be able to stay much longer and I want to make certain it will work."

So, as Rann watched, Raven began digging diffidently at the mortar at the base of an iron bar.

At least falling would be a cleaner death than strangling at the end of a rope.

He set to the task with a will.

The sun was low in the west as Leet strode eagerly through the castle halls on his way to the gardens, Gull riding in its case on his back. He twitched the carrying strap across his chest to a more comfortable position; he would have to venture farther into the gardens today. Squirrels and such were becoming scarce again. He turned the corner to the great hall. To his dismay, he saw Daera talking with Prince Rann and Otter.

Leet walked quickly for the archway leading to the garden door, praying that neither of them would see him. Ever since the day of their confrontation in his room, it seemed that Daera's blue eyes mocked him whenever she saw him. It took the pleasure right out of looking at Otter's pinched face, somehow. The other man seemed to have aged a good twenty years since coming to Balyaranna.

Almost there. . . . Then his luck deserted him. Otter had seen him. The other bard's trained voice cut easily through the noise in the great hall.

"Leet! Wait!"

He gripped the leather strap with both hands, as Otter worked his way through the ever-present crowd to him. "Yes?" he snapped.

To his surprise, Otter looked embarrassed. "I apologize for not telling you sooner, Leet. I guess I thought a messenger had reached you with the news—this whole thing with Raven has . . ." The Yerrin bard took a deep breath. "I mentioned it to Daera and she hadn't heard about Sether, so I daresay you haven't either."

"Sether?" Panic, pure and simple. "Did he say any— I mean, heard what about Sether?"

Otter gave him a queer look. "He's dead."

Thank the gods—that damned ladder got him at last! Leet crowed inwardly. A weak link gone, then—good! He managed to inject just the right amount of sorrow into his voice. "Accident in the wood barn?"

"No." A long pause. "He hanged himself."

Leet felt the blood drain from his face. "W-why?"

"No one knows. Just that something had been bothering him for a couple of years or so. But he never told anyone what." Once more an odd look filled the other man's eyes. "Have you any idea why?"

"Wha-what?" Leet stared at Otter, nearly frantic now. "What the hell do you mean by that? Why would I know?"

"Because I'd heard that you and Sether had spent a great deal of time talking together these past couple of years or so. I thought that he might have confided in you. You seemed to have become close friends."

"You're wrong!" Leet shrilled. "He wasn't a friend! And anyone who says I 'spent a great deal of time' with him lies!" With that, he spun around and hurried back to his room, past astonished faces that turned to look at him. Gull would have to wait.

Rann waited with Daera, watching the two older bards talking. He thought he could tell just when Bard Otter told Bard Leet the news that had made Daera so unhappy. Bard Leet's face went white and he looked like his eyes would pop out of his head.

He decided it was time to ask the question that had been bothering him ever since Kella came back from Bard Leet's room that day. That day she'd stopped being herself. He hadn't been able to find out before now; Bard Leet certainly wasn't the one to ask.

"Daera? Is a bard's harp, well, enchanted?"

"Do you mean does the harp play itself rather than the bard playing it?"

"No. Can a harp do things to people?"

That startled Daera out of her sad mood, he could see. She looked down at him, puzzled. "What do you mean, Your Highness? How so?"

Rann chewed on his lip, not quite certain how to put it without giving everything away. "If you didn't want me to touch your harp and I did anyway because you weren't there to stop me, would something bad happen to me?"

The question, as Kella would say, clearly "fair boggled" the young bard. "Of course not, Your Highness! A harp is just a harp even if we bards talk about the 'soul' of one. Wood and wire and tuning pegs—that's all a harp is. Um—why do you ask?"

"Oh," Rann said vaguely. "No reason. . . . There's one of my tutors. I have to go now." And he scurried off in the opposite direction.

When Otter rejoined Daera, he found her standing arms akimbo, staring after the rapidly retreating prince, a look of complete bafflement on her face.

"That," she said, "was one of the *oddest* questions I've ever been asked!"

"And what was that?" inquired Otter.

"Can a harp hurt someone who isn't supposed to play it," she answered, shaking her head. "Magically hurt someone, that is."

That *was* an odd question. "Must be the day for strange things," he murmured. "What do you mean?"

"Leet had the oddest reaction when I told him about Sether."

She snickered. "Speaking of reactions, I wish you could have seen his face when I told him Kella is talented. He was still whining about the 'merchant's brat' who'd nearly touched his harp. I'm just surprised Maurynna Kyrissaean has never ripped into him for what he did, the pompous ass."

"And what was that? Refusing to teach Kella because she's a commoner?"

"Worse."

And Otter listened, appalled, as Daera told him about the encounter in the garden.

He couldn't believe it. Sether had *hanged* himself? Why? Had Widow Theras thrown him over for another man?

Leet paced his room, wringing his hands. He glanced at the silk-shrouded figure of Gull on the small table by the bed. Or was it because of . . .

He twisted his fingers into his hair. He had no idea why Sether had killed himself and no way to find out. Had he pushed Sether too hard? Had the Wood Master finally snapped under his threats?

He couldn't very well go to Otter now, pretending to be concerned about Sether, and fish for whatever information the other bard might not even know he had. He'd closed off that route. Leet cursed his earlier panic. What should he do?

Leave. Go back to Bylith. Yes, that's what he'd do. He'd begin packing right now and set off in the morning.

As he reached for Gull, the harp rocked. The silk covering rippled and slid down. Without meaning to, Leet grabbed the harp's pillar, clutching it like a lifeline.

The strings hummed. Words formed in his mind. *Leave now? We haven't seen that whelp of Otter's blood hanged yet! Think of the look on Otter's cursed face as his grandnephew jerks and twitches on the end of a rope, fighting to breathe. The cursed face that Jaida preferred to yours . . . Make him pay.*

Calm washed over Leet. Calm, and . . . desire. Nay, a craving. No, that would not be a thing to miss. Not at all. He would stay. Leet smiled and stroked the harp's pillar.

Only a few more days . . . And now I want my blood.

Moving like one bemused, Leet slipped the harp once more into its leather case and slung it over his shoulder. Time to go to the garden, he thought dreamily.

And perhaps we should get rid of the boy—the one who knows Osric.

Fifty-one

Where in the name of the gods had all their time gone? Maurynna wondered in despair. They now had only four days left. "Has anyone found out anything that might help?" she pleaded as she looked around at the others seated at the table.

Linden, Shima, and Otter all shook their heads. They looked as hopeless as she felt.

"Shall we go over what we know once again?" asked Shima. "There must be *something* that we're missing."

Linden sighed. "To bed, everyone. We're too tired to think straight. We'd likely not notice a clue if it was chewing on our ankles. Maybe the morning will bring better news."

Ever since the death of Summer Lightning, Stablemaster Tuerin had slept fitfully. Now he woke—the gods only knew why—and stared into the darkness above. At least the cursed fair would be over in a few days! He wondered what ill fate had brought down so much disaster upon—

What was that? Tuerin listened intently. Something at the far end of the loft where the boys slept . . . He raised his head cautiously to look.

Though the shutters were open to the night air, only a little moonlight shone through the window. But there was enough to show him a dark silhouette; it pulled something from under its pallet and crept to the opening for the ladder.

There was something about the way the stealthy figure moved. . . . Frightened, Tuerin surged up from his own pallet and threw himself at the dark form. His hand closed on a handful of breeches just as the dark figure let itself fall headfirst into the opening.

"Robie, you fool boy!" he yelled, terrified for his son. "What are you doing?"

Tuerin hung grimly on to his son with one hand. He jammed the fingers of the other into a gap in the floorboards to anchor himself; Robie's weight threatened to pull him over. Pandemonium broke out in the darkness around him as the stable hands awoke. At last someone had the wits to find flint and steel and light the oil lamp.

Hands reached out, grabbed Robie, hauled him up. Tuerin yanked his fingers from between the floorboards, cursing at the crop of slivers he reaped.

By all the gods, he'd take a belt to that fool boy's backside. Tuerin opened his mouth to blister his son's ears for him.

Then Robie rolled limply onto his back. A sack fell from his fingers. And Tuerin's heart turned to ice at the emptiness in his son's eyes.

"Conor! Conor! Wake up!"

Conor struggled out of a deep sleep. "Wha-what? Whassmatter?" he croaked, peering blearily around the dimly lit tent.

Light flared, searing his eyes. Conor cursed and squinched them shut. When he opened them again, he saw Krev standing before him holding up a lantern.

"Sorry," Krev apologized. "Should have warned you I was going to turn the wick up."

Conor looked through the open door of the tent. It was still dark out! What the hell was Krev doing waking him up now? He wasn't on duty tonight.

Before he could rip into Krev—who looked annoyingly wide-eyed and alert, much to Conor's disgust—the young apprentice said, "Master Edlunn wants to see you right now! They know who poisoned Summer Lightning!"

Blanket wrapped around his shoulders against the dawn's chill, Raven scraped patiently at the mortar around the base of one of the iron bars of the window. He hummed as he worked. The last chunk of mortar broke away. He caught it before it fell out the window. Jiggling the bar to make certain that, yes, he could get it out any time he wanted, Raven replaced the chunk he'd caught and all the others he'd saved. From a distance the two bars he'd loosened looked secure.

One more, and there would be enough room for him to squeeze out. New fantasies of daring rescues filled his mind. He began humming again as he set to work once more.

Then, with a curse, he threw down the chisel. Damn it all, there was that cursed tune again! The one that filled his nightmares. The one that wouldn't let him sleep.

The one that he was certain that he'd heard the night he killed Lord Tirael. Raven clutched the blanket around himself, shuddering at the fragments of memory the song brought back.

Red streaked the eastern sky before he could bring himself to pick up the chisel once more. It was a fool's task, but it gave him something to do. There might not be a rescue, but he'd cheat the hangman's noose one way or another.

Conor presented himself at the castle as early as he dared. The guards at the gate eyed the brown-and-green of his tunic with respect, and Trouble, who popped her head out of his hood, with amusement.

Still, they crossed their pikes to bar his entrance. "Your name and business, sir?" one asked politely.

"I am Conor of Red Dale, a Beast Healer from the chapterhouse of Grey Holt. I've come to see Linden Rathan if he is awake. It may be of great importance to him."

For a moment he feared they would send him on his way. Then one turned and called one of the messenger lads to him. Moments later the boy sprinted away.

Conor waited in an agony of apprehension. What if they weren't awake yet? Worse, what if Linden refused to see him? His soultwin certainly couldn't be happy with a certain Beast Healer for his testimony against her best friend.

He well-nigh melted with relief when the boy ran back with word that the Dragonlords would see him.

"A *boy* poisoned Summer Lightning?" Linden asked with equal amounts of dismay and astonishment. "The stablemaster's own son? Conor—are you certain of this?"

The thought chilled Linden. Not only that a boy would do such a cruel thing, but that no allowance would be made for his age. He knew the boy Robie would be punished as severely as an adult. Shaking his head, he went to the window and looked out onto the new day. That a boy would do such a thing . . .

Behind him Maurynna said, "But that's awful! Why did the boy do it? Did he hate the horse or have some grudge against Lord Lenslee?"

"No. Quite the opposite. From all I've heard the boy thought Summer Lightning was the sun and the moon and the stars. He wept bitterly when the horse died, his father said."

Shima shook his head sadly. "The man must be brokenhearted."

"He is. But he's a man of honor. I think that even if the rest of the stable hands hadn't been there when Robie was found with the sack of yellowfool, he would have come to us to have his suspicions confirmed. But that's not why I came here. It was something that I remembered."

Linden turned at the rising excitement in Conor's voice. "Go on."

"When Summer Lightning died, Master Edlunn and I went to examine his stall that night. We found Robie there, cleaning it despite orders to leave it untouched. It seemed then, in his anguish over the horse's death, he sleepwalked. Or so I and everyone else thought at the time.

"Especially since he said something that made no sense at the time. Indeed, it seemed so useless that I forgot it until now. As he came out of his 'dream,' Robie muttered something about 'Where did Osric go? I heard him playing.'"

That caught Linden's attention. "'Playing'? As in an instrument?"

Now Maurynna sat up straight, all trace of antagonism gone. "Music?"

"Music," Conor confirmed triumphantly.

"That's three times now," Maurynna said, ticking the count off on her fingers. "Raven heard music—and killed Tirael. Conor heard music—and turned aside for it. Young Robie heard music—and disobeyed orders."

"Once is chance," Linden said softly, drawing on long-ago memories. "Twice is coincidence. Three times—look to your sword."

Maurynna tapped a fourth finger. "I wonder if Tirael heard music the night he died," she said quietly. "But who is this Osric? Was he at Sevrynel's that night? If so, I don't remember seeing him."

"Robie said he was a minstrel who stayed one night in a stable at Lord Portis's manor before coming to the fair," Conor offered. "An older man, he said."

Trembling with excitement, Maurynna said, "We need to find him!"

But Linden was already striding for the door to the antechamber. Throwing it open, he said curtly to the page cooling his heels there, "Aelfar, go to Bard Otter's room. Tell him we need him here *now*."

The lad jumped down from his chair. "At once, Your Grace!" he said, and was through the outer door as if shot from a catapult.

A short while later, Aelfar was back. "I'm sorry, Your Grace, but he's not there. His servant said that he went early to break his fast with his grandnephew."

Damnation, but he wouldn't cut short their time together. He could ask about Osric as soon as Otter returned. "Then send someone to Lord Portis's stable and have the boy Robie brought to us."

Aelfar bowed and ran from the suite again.

"There are some things here I don't understand," said Shima, frowning. "I've heard it said that true bards like Leet or Otter have a certain magic. It's how they can capture their listeners' imaginations, their hearts, how they make the songs 'real' to their audiences.

"This is a thing I can understand; it makes me think of the singing magic known by all the peoples of my land. It is said humans learned it from the water-dragons in the long ago, the time before history, the time before even the oldest stories. But you don't have waterdragons here in the north, and I'd always understood bards' magic to be different from—and not as powerful as—the magic I grew up with.

"Was I wrong? I know a dark shaman or a powerful Phoenix priest can take over a man's mind by spellsongs and make him do anything, no matter how vile, no matter how much against his true nature it is. Is this a thing your northern bards can also do?"

Linden shook his head. "Not that way. A bard isn't a mage. A song might give someone ideas—witness every ballad against a tyrant that inspired people to revolt—but control them? No. Bards don't use their voices to create magic; if they're so blessed by the gods, their voices *are* their magic. Does that make sense?"

"Yes. No. Almost," said Shima, scratching his head.

Linden raked his fingers through his hair, sighing in exasperation. How to best explain this?

Before he could speak, Maurynna said, "It makes sense to me. But then, I've grown up listening to Otter, who does have that magic. Whenever I listen to him sing, it's as if I'm transported elsewhere, that I'm living in his song.

"And sometimes, when everything is just right, Otter can make you see images in the flames on the hearth or the smoke from a campfire. He did that for Raven and me many times when we were children. Nor is Otter the only one; there are other bards who can do the same.

"But no matter how much Raven and I let the music take us someplace else, our minds were our own. Had we wanted to, we could have walked away, leaving song and visions behind," Maurynna said. "Otter never took—*couldn't* take— our free will from us. And if a bard could, he'd face Iryniel the Punisher for it."

"Who is that? Some royal court's executioner?" Shima asked.

Linden shook his head. "Bards look to Auvrian as their patron god. Iryniel is his wolf-headed servant. Remember the constellation of the Wolf that I showed you at Dragonskeep? Some say that's Iryniel.

"Bards who break their oath are 'given' to Iryniel. The torment of their punishment is as meat and drink to him—and woe to the man or woman who kills one given to Iryniel and ends that bard's sufferings."

Shima grimaced. "Not a pleasant thought. But what you said before . . . I still don't fully understand—it's too different from what I know—but I'll accept that a northern bard can't take over another person's mind. Both of you would know better than I. But if that kind of control isn't possible, then that means Raven's a cold-blooded killer who's either hearing things or is lying. And I don't think either of you believe that any more than I do."

"No more than I'd believe Morlen or any other truedragon to eat a truehuman, no matter what some of the old tales say," Linden replied.

"Just so," Maurynna's eyes blazed with a barely contained inner fire. "I know Raven. He can be a stubborn pain in the ass, but he's no murderer. Hell, I'd have said he's *far* more likely to be the victim, he can be such a pain." Her sudden wry expression said that Raven had more than once come close to an untimely demise—or at least the threat of one.

"All of which leaves us right where we started. And that," the Tah'nehsieh Dragonlord sighed, "is nowhere."

"Not so," said Conor suddenly. "You forget—if Raven's hearing things or lying, then so is Robie. So am I, for that matter. And I know I'm not lying. Nor, I suspect, are the others."

Robie stood in the center of the room, staring at the tiled floor and shaking so hard it was only the hard hand of Lord Portis's man-at-arms on his shoulder that held him up. It was bad enough that his own lord and Lord Lenslee were demanding he be thrown in prison, and his father suddenly looked like he'd aged years and years, but to have the Dragonlords furious with him as well! Though he fought it, a tear trickled down his cheek. He bit his lip, thinking, *I won't be a baby! I won't be . . .* It was no use. More tears followed.

He was so frightened he almost didn't hear Linden Rathan say softly, "Don't be so afraid, Robie. We want to help you if we can, but we need your help to do so. Do you think you can answer some questions for us? Could you tell us about the minstrel Osric?"

Robie dared to look up at him. This was the last thing he'd expected. Dark grey eyes looked kindly back at him. Robie instinctively felt he could trust those eyes.

"Yes, Dragonlord," he whispered. "My father and Lord Portis were away when Osric the Minstrel came to the manor, my lord. He had a fine harp with him. . . ."

When Robie was done with his story, silence filled the room. Linden rubbed his chin, considering. He had one last question.

"Robie, am I right in thinking that you've had a bit of time to wander the fair now and again? You have? Good. Now—did you ever see Minstrel Osric again?"

Robie hesitated, then spoke in a faint whisper. "I—I thought I did, Your Grace. My father sent me for the men who . . . the wagon for Summer . . ." His face crumpled and he pressed his fists into his eyes. After a moment, he continued, "As I came back, I saw a man come out of Lord Portis's compound. I thought it was Osric at first because there was something familiar about the way he moved. Then I wasn't sure. But they both did this—"

Robie stroked the indentation under his lower lip with a forefinger.

"When I saw that, I thought maybe it was Osric after all. But I wasn't certain so I didn't go up to him. Then I realized it couldn't be him. The clothes were wrong. His hair wasn't grey, and he didn't stoop. Osric stooped."

Linden nodded, thinking. "Thank you, Robie. I think that will be all for now. Conor, please go with Robie and wait with him in the hall. I'd like a word with his guard and I'm sure he has orders not to leave him alone."

The man relaxed perceptibly. When the boy and Conor were gone, Linden stood up. He towered over Robie's guard. The man looked up at him with seeming calm, but the color drained from his face.

"I charge you to tell Lord Portis and Lord Lenslee that they are not to punish the boy in any way. He may not have been responsible for his actions. We'll know more soon. Until then, I do not want Robie mistreated."

The man seemed to hear the unspoken *Or I shall be very angry* quite clearly. Hand over heart in salute, he said, "Yes, Your Grace." Then he bowed and left.

When Conor returned, he asked, "Now what?"

"Now we find out about this Osric." Linden closed his eyes and reached out with his mind. *Otter, we need you back here. We may have a light in the darkness at last.*

Fifty-two

"A minstrel named Osric? An older man with grey hair?" Otter said. He shook his head. "There is no such man."

Maurynna and Conor stared at him, dismay writ large on their faces.

"Are you certain?" Linden asked.

"I know all the minstrels, especially the older ones. And none bears that name. Why?"

Linden rubbed the back of his neck and sighed. "Because Robie said that a minstrel named Osric stopped at Lord Portis's manor on his way to the fair. And when Conor and Master Edlunn found him in Summer Lightning's stall after the horse's death, the boy muttered something about hearing Osric's music. But if there's no minstrel named Osric, then— Wait! Otter, do you know of *any* minstrel who has a habit of doing this—" He rubbed under his lower lip.

Otter frowned; Linden held his breath, waiting. Just when he was certain his old friend would say, "I've no idea," Otter's jaw dropped.

"Not a minstrel—a bard!" he blurted out. "Leet always does that when he's feeling particularly pleased with himself."

They all stared at each other in confusion.

"What have Leet and a minstrel who doesn't exist to do with each other?" Maurynna said.

"I don't know, but let us see what we have," Linden replied grimly. "There seems to be a common thread through all this: music. Robie said he heard music that 'Osric' played. Could Leet have been traveling in disguise?"

"Not like him," Otter muttered. "Especially as a lowly minstrel. But 'stranger things do happen' as my granddam used to say."

"Raven said he heard music. It called him to the garden where . . ." Maurynna bit her lip.

"And I heard it as well," Conor said. "That was why I turned aside."

"Which was unlike you," said Linden. "I always wondered about that. A pity we'll never know if Tirael also heard music that called him."

They sat in silence, considering what they had. It was, Linden thought, the thinnest of threads. But there was another one to add to it now. And no matter how thin the thread, twist enough of them together and you had a rope.

He went on, "But there's another thing we do know: who both Conor and Raven found at the other end of the music that night."

"Leet," Maurynna said. Suddenly her eyes widened and she bounced in her chair. "Linden! Remember the day of the Queen's Chase? When Raven was all befuddled? He said he heard music!"

"And Leet was there as one of the marshals." He leaned back in his chair and swore softly as he remembered something. "It was Leet who said that Raven was cooling that horse's leg in the stream." Another thread for the rope. . . .

"So he was the last one to see Raven that day until Raven showed up in camp with the lamed horse," Shima said. "At least—as far as we know."

Conor said flatly, "The race that Summer Lightning was the favorite to win. Leet was at Portis's stable the day of Summer Lightning's death—the day Robie saw him leaving it. Full of false sympathy, he was—I would lay any wager on it. And if I remember correctly, Lord Lenslee was surprised—hellfire, *astonished*—to see him. As if Leet was the last person he expected.

"But—gah!" Conor slapped the table. A chitter of protest came from his hood. "But why in the name of all the gods would Leet want Summer Lightning dead? As a marshal, he couldn't bet on the race."

Linden glanced over at Otter. The bard had a strange, faraway look on his face. "Otter, what is—"

"'Odd, how it's back to Leet,'" Otter said softly. His unfocused eyes stared past them to something only he saw. He went on in the same dreamy tone, "That's what Charilon said, you know, that day by Jaida's grave."

Linden stared at Otter, startled. The bard looked as if he had forgotten where he was. *And what was that about Jaida? She died years—*

All at once Otter was back in the room, his eyes hard and cold as he looked at each of them in turn. "The same day Sether, Wood Master of the Bards' School in Bylith, was laid in his own grave after hanging himself. For no reason that anyone could fathom—just built a bonfire of some wood that was not part of the barn's tallied holdings and then hanged himself.

"Sether, who for the last few years was frequently visited by one Leet as if they were friends—a thing that same Leet has vehemently denied to my face."

The only sound was the droning of a bee that bumbled in through the open window, flew lazily around the room, then back out the window for more bountiful pastures.

"I think," Linden said at last, "that part of the key to saving Raven lies in the past. I'm going back to Bylith."

"Dragonlord—I'm sorry to bother you, but may I speak with you a moment?"

Maurynna turned, one arm still over Boreal's back. The last thing she wanted was to talk to anyone save Linden and he was gone again. She needed to be *doing* something; every nerve in her body cried for action, yet she also did not want to leave Balyaranna and Raven. So she'd come to the stables for the comfort of her Llysanyin. His stolid presence helped as she pressed her cheek against him, listening to the strong beat of his heart.

She still didn't want to talk to anyone.

But the young woman standing at the paddock fence and looking apprehensively at her wore a bard's torc. Maurynna thought she could guess who she was.

"It's no bother," she lied. "You're my cousin Kella's harp teacher, Bard Daera, yes? Please come in. Boreal won't mind."

"Thank you, Your Grace." To Maurynna's amusement, instead of going to the gate, Daera scrambled over the fence as nimbly as a sailor and dropped cat-footed to the ground.

"You look worried, Bard Daera. Is it something I can help you with?"

Daera nodded. "It's about Kella, Dragonlord. Do you know when she's coming back for lessons? It's a pleasure teaching her. She makes up for the, um, less enthusiastic students."

Maurynna remembered the letter from Maylin and sighed. "I'm afraid she won't be coming back. She's given up the harp."

She thought she'd rarely seen anyone so surprised—and dismayed—as the bard.

"What?" Daera gasped. "But Dragonlord—Kella has a real gift! I truly believe she'd get into the School eas— Oh gods . . . is it because of what happened with Bard Leet? Is that why she went home?"

Maurynna stiffened. *Leet again!* " 'What happened with Bard Leet'?" she repeated, standing away from Boreal. "What do you mean? *What* happened with Bard Leet?"

For a moment Maurynna thought Daera might turn and run; she had the sick expression of someone realizing she'd just kicked over a bucket of worms.

"He—he slapped her hand one day. Hard. Too hard," she said weakly. She rushed on, "She saw his harp in the garden and thought it was mine, you see, and he thought she was a servant trying to touch his harp. He didn't know she's your . . ."

Maurynna remembered the bruise on Kella's hand with cold fury. "She told me she'd fallen on it."

"She was humiliated. She didn't want anyone to know. He . . . yelled at her." Daera looked up at her nervously. "I thought you already knew, that she'd tell *you* at least."

Maurynna seethed inwardly. Striking a child hard enough to leave a bruise like that—and her cousin, no less! Leet was damned lucky he was a—

"Wait—this happened before Linden, Shima, and I arrived, didn't it?"

Daera nodded. "Yes. That was the day I got word that my mother was gravely ill. You came after I left."

Maurynna tugged at a lock of her hair, thinking furiously. Aside from the bruised hand, Kella had been well at the time of their arrival; Maurynna was certain her later illness was not because of that. Besides—she knew her little cousin. Kella would have been plotting revenge, not taking to her bed with a delayed case of the vapors!

And she knew just the person to talk to: Kella's partner in mischief, Prince Rann.

"But I promised Kella I wouldn't tell," Rann said weakly. He looked from one stern face to another and sighed. If only it wasn't Maurynna Kyrissaean and Bard Daera. At least Aunt Beryl and Uncle Beren weren't here as well.

"Your Highness," the Dragonlord said with a sad smile. "Keeping someone's secret is a good thing—but not when it hurts that person."

"Prince Rann, *please* tell us what you know," Daera said. "You know that Kella is truly talented, don't you? We need to know if what made her so ill is why she gave up the harp."

Startled, Rann blurted, "Gave up the harp? But she can't! It's all Kella dreams about—going to the Bards' School someday!"

"She's refused to play since her mysterious 'illness,' " Maurynna Kyrissaean said. "She even refused the gift of a harp back home in Casna."

Rann twisted his fingers together in an agony of indecision. Kella would never forgive him. But something had happened that day she'd gone to play Bard Leet's harp. He knew it. Something bad . . .

Then Maurynna Kyrissaean spoke the words that freed him from his oath.

"Rann, dear," she said gently, "would it help if I said 'Dragonlord's orders'?"

Fifty-three

Ever since they'd left the main Wort Hunters' encampment, they'd had good luck with the weather if nothing else, Pod thought wryly. But now even that was ending. The day had started with the sun rising in a clear sky. Now grey, threatening clouds were moving in. She hoped the rain would hold off.

They had spent the morning and early afternoon exploring and calling Kiga. Pod blamed herself for the woods dog's continued absence. Her last words to her familiar echoed in her mind: "And don't come back until you've caught something!"

Hadn't every apprentice at Grey Holt been warned again and again to be careful what they asked their familiars to do? Faithful hearts that they were, the animals would try to walk through fire if their persons asked it of them. Worse yet, she'd "pushed" at Kiga, reinforcing her order with her power as a Beast Healer. She could only hope that he'd come back soon.

As they passed quietly through woods now turned gloomy—even frightening—Kaeliss stopped with a gasp.

"By the Lord and Lady of the Forests!" she cried, and fell to her knees by a patch of red flowers that covered the ground between the trees. "Fiarin wasn't lying!"

"What are they?" Pod asked as she knelt beside the other young woman. Whatever these were, Kaeliss was well-nigh weeping with joy. Pod studied them.

They were pretty things and looked, she thought, rather like morning glories, but much smaller and with deeply ruffled edges. They were also growing singly, not on a vine. She looked around. "Look—there's an even bigger patch!" she said, pointing to where the ground was literally carpeted with dark red as far as she could see in the dim woods.

Kaeliss looked. "Oh dear gods—it's just as Fiarin said! King's Blood is incredibly rare—the conditions have to be just perfect for it or it won't grow!

344

You're lucky if you find a patch of three or four plants, and the chosen of the gods if you find more! I've only heard of one place where—"

As Pod stared in astonishment, the color drained from Kaeliss's face, leaving her a sickly grey. She looked as if she might be ill any moment.

"No," Kaeliss whispered at last, still staring at the flowers. "No—Fiarin wouldn't have been planning to bring us there. I know he was jealous of Currin, but we've lost so many people here. Fiarin knows—knew . . ."

"What?" Pod asked roughly after a long silence. "Fiarin knew what? Where are we?"

"Fiarin knew these woods are forbidden. There's an old evil here. As for where . . . this was Worton. All this—the old stone walls, the abandoned orchards, the collapsing foundations—all this was . . . Worton."

The last word came out in a frightened whisper that Pod barely heard. It also meant nothing to her. "I've never heard of it."

Kaeliss turned slowly to look at her, eyes dull, defeated. "You've heard of Gull the Blood Drinker, haven't you?"

"But that's just a story . . . isn't it?" she asked in a tiny voice. Kaeliss shook her head. Now it was Pod's turn to feel sick with fright. "Oh gods—you mean this is where . . ."

"Yes." Kaeliss began crying. "We're in the most cursed place in all the Five Kingdoms," she sobbed, "and I don't know how to get out!"

Pod had heard the stories of Gull the Blood Drinker. Usually late at night around a bonfire when ghost stories were scariest. And now she remembered from the stories that the town that Gull had lived in had been abandoned. For not even Gull's death had ended the terror; it was as if the evil in him seeped into the forest even though he'd been buried under a witch spruce. In the end, the few remaining townsfolk had fled their once prosperous village.

How long ago it had happened, she didn't know. But long enough that the forest had reclaimed the fields. And by all she'd ever heard, a darkness still held these woods. Weighed down by the oppressive heat and thick air, the tales were all too easy to believe.

And Kiga? What had happened to her brother-in-fur? Had whatever haunted these woods taken him? If so, it was her fault. Tears pricked her eyes.

She fought them. Tears wouldn't help them; they had to get out of here as quickly as they could. She closed her eyes and sent up a silent prayer to Kerras of the Golden Antlers.

Please don't let anything happen to Kiga. And please help him to find us again—I can't wait for him. We must leave this cursed place as fast as we can!

She wiped away the tears on her lashes and shook Kaeliss's shoulder. "We need to get out of here. *Now.*"

Kaeliss sniffled and wiped her own eyes. "You're right. We'll keep walking east. It's our best chance." She started to rise, then paused. "But I need to get as much of this as I can. It's so valuable for so many ailments! And . . . it will make my name in the Guild, just as Fiarin said . . ."

She threw herself down and clawed at the dirt, dragging up the flowers and their precious tuberous roots, stuffing them into her sack any which way. "Pod, help me! Master Emberlin needs this!"

When Pod hesitated, Kaeliss pleaded, "Imagine all the lives that could be saved with this much King's Blood!"

Pod swore, and despite her fear, fell to her knees and dug up the plants as fast as she could. They worked in silence.

A fat root broke and red juice oozed over Kaeliss's fingers. It looked like blood. "I'll sort 'em out later," she muttered under her breath as she worked furiously. "I'll never see anything like this again."

A shiver went down Pod's spine at the ill-chosen words. *Avert!* she thought, making the sign to ward off evil. She could stand it no longer. After packing a last few roots into her pack, she grabbed the back of Kaeliss's tunic and heaved the young woman to her feet.

"Come *on,*" she said. "We've got to find shelter. It looks like a storm coming on and I want to get as far away from here as we can before it breaks."

"But—," Kaeliss protested. She looked longingly at the remaining flowers.

"No! You said yourself, this place is cursed. We're getting out of here." Pod caught Kaeliss's wrist and started walking as fast as she could, nearly dragging the Wort Hunter off her feet before Kaeliss broke her grip and fell in behind her.

She thought she heard something in the woods behind them. She prayed she was wrong.

Snap.

She walked faster.

Impossible as it seemed, the air grew yet more still and close as they marched on and on. By the time they came to the collapsed remains of yet another stone wall, they were nearly done in; the air was so thick and muggy it was hard to breathe. And so dark. . . . They clambered over it, then stopped, trying to catch their breath.

"You took the blood of the forest," a soft voice said behind them.

Both Pod and Kaeliss screamed and spun around.

A man stood before them. His clothes were ragged, his hair and long, straggly beard matted with dirt, twigs, and leaves. His hands were tucked under his armpits and he rocked gently from side to side as if listening to some music only he could hear.

But it was none of these things that filled Pod with fear. No, it was his eyes, set deep in his gaunt face, that frightened her; eyes filled with the madness of a fanatic, their burning gaze locked upon them. Then he smiled, revealing a mouth full of brown, rotting teeth.

It was the kind of smile that a snowcat might smile if it found a helpless mountain sheep, said a scared little voice in the back of Pod's mind. Her knees shook. *Kiga, where* are *you?*

"You took the blood of the forest," he repeated. His voice was gentle—oh, so gentle!—and all the more frightening for it. "The King's Blood. And blood must pay for blood."

"Arlim?" whispered Kaeliss. "Arlim—is that truly you?"

For the first time Pod realized that his tunic was green and yellow under all the dirt; this man was a member of Kaeliss's guild.

Kaeliss said, her voice shaking, "Arlim—we thought you were dead."

With that Arlim giggled and dropped his hands; one held a long knife. He turned it this way and that as if admiring the razor edge. Pod sank down, whimpering. Her hands clutched at the ground.

The ragged man looked down at Pod. The smile widened. He cocked his head to one side as if listening to someone. "That is good, isn't it?" he said softly. His head tilted the other way. "Oh yes, yess, Arlim—not so much blood lost th—"

Pod sprang up and flung a handful of dirt straight into those hateful eyes. The man fell back from them, howling in fury. He rubbed furiously at his eyes. Pod kicked the knife-wielding hand as hard as she could.

The gods were good; the knife flew through the air and landed in a patch of brambles. Then she took a deep breath and slammed the heel of her hand so hard into the man's chest that he fell backward.

Pod grabbed Kaeliss's wrist once more. "Run!" she screamed, yanking as hard as she could. *"Run!"*

Fifty-four

For the second time in less than a tenday Linden landed in the large courtyard at the Bards' School. This time, though, it was daylight and he had an audience. As he Changed back to his human form, Linden singled out a young man in a journeyman's tunic from the crowd watching from a respectful distance.

"Where would I find Bard Charilon?" he asked.

"In the infirmary, Your Grace, with the Healer from the palace. He fell and twisted his knee badly a short time ago."

Damnation—Charilon was likely sleeping off the Healing. "I see." Very well, then; he'd find his other quarry instead. He said, "Leave word for him that Linden Rathan would speak with him later."

"At once, Dragonlord." The journeyman turned and jogged off.

It took Linden a wrong turn or two before he reached his goal. Like much else, the Bards' School had changed since the days he'd spent time here when Otter was a journeyman. But he found it at last, and now stood before the well-remembered tall oak doors that had welcomed generations of bards and apprentices. One stood slightly ajar; he pushed it open.

The cool dimness of the wood barn was a welcome change from the muggy heat. Linden paused on the threshold to let his eyes adjust, then looked around at the wood arranged neatly in the array of large "cubbyholes" that lined the walls on either side of the wide center aisle that stretched in front of him.

Boards a handspan or so wide and perhaps a thumb width thick filled some of them; those were meant, he knew, for the sides and backs. Other bins held thicker lengths for the pillars and necks of the harps. He saw cherry and maple and walnut, even purpleheart from Assantik, and many woods that he didn't recognize.

A few of the wall bins held the spruce for the soundboards. There were even logs of willow for the most tradition-bound; Linden remembered his earliest harps, made at a time when the entire soundbox save the back was carved from a single willow log. Personally, he thought the newer method of joined boards an improvement. He liked the variety of voices the different woods gave the harps. But all the woods he saw as he gazed down the aisle were beautiful, each in their own way, and all held the promise of song in their hearts.

The bards had added on to the building; it was bigger than he remembered. He'd picked out the wood for an earlier harp from here only—

Hmm . . . Almost eighty years would be considered a long time ago to truehumans. There were no bards alive now who remembered the building he'd known. Even Otter was much too young.

He walked down the aisle, past the tall, thick wooden posts that lined it like trees along a path in the woods. Sawdust and shavings covered the floor and muffled his footsteps.

He called, "Hello—anyone about?"

"Back here," a muffled voice replied, followed by a series of little thumping noises.

Linden followed the sounds. In the far corner he found a young woman and a boy of perhaps fourteen years in the process of emptying out one of the large wall bins. Judging by the pile of mixed woods at their feet, this was where all the odds and ends of years past had been consigned. Near them sat a girl about the same age as the boy; she had a tally board on her lap.

Both the boy and the girl wore the grey tunics and red armbands of apprentice bards. The woman, although her own tunic matched theirs, also wore the red belt of a journeywoman.

"You're Rose of Littleford?" Linden asked the woman.

She straightened and dusted her hands on the seat of her breeches as she studied him covertly; Linden surmised she was trying to guess his possible rank and how to address him.

It seemed she decided to play it safe, for she answered, "I am, my lord." Her head tilted in inquiry.

"I'm a friend of Otter's," Linden said, pleased to see the younger two faces brighten at the bard's name. Rose, though, suddenly looked as if something niggled at the back of her mind. Linden could guess what it was and went on to distract her. "I wonder—while I'm sorry to disturb your work, Journeywoman Rose, may I speak with you alone? I've come on private business from Otter."

She frowned a little at that, then seemed to decide that if he'd gotten this far into the grounds of the School, he had legitimate business. She waved a hand at the two apprentices. "Off with you both. It's nearly time for your lessons, anyway."

They didn't have to be told twice. Like apprentices anywhere, these two were glad of a little free time to themselves. The girl set down her slate and jumped up, sprinting after the boy, who was already halfway down the aisle.

"Thank you!" they chorused as they disappeared through the door.

"I hope I'm not interrupting anything important," Linden said in apology as Rose frowned at the boards still in the bin.

"No, no. Just sorting through odds and ends. My master—" Her voice caught. "My . . . late master had a bad habit of stowing away boards that didn't meet his standards even for teaching the 'prentices how to work wood. I used to tease him that they weren't wine to improve with age. But he couldn't stand to part with any wood that came his way—the stuff fascinated him. He always said he might find a use for it someday." Her eyes, now bright with unshed tears, seemed to say, *But that day never came. . . .*

Blinking quickly, Rose waved her hand at the wood. "As you can see, they're not very useful."

Linden leaned closer to look. No, those boards with the big knots wouldn't be good for making instruments; that one to the right might make a good boat, it was so cupped, and the rest of the stuff seemed little better. Good for rough carpentry, perhaps, or to carve into toys, but not for fine instruments.

"And what will *you* do with it?" he asked, knowing from Otter that Rose had the same "little magic" of curing wood as the late Sether.

Her mouth turned up in a half-wry, half-sad smile. "Likely stuff it back in there once I know what's what. Maybe I'll even find that elusive use for it one day. I had thought at first that this was what went into that bonfire, but—"

She tossed her head as if shaking off sad memories and ran her fingers through her mousy brown hair. "Now, my lord, what are these questions?" she asked, all brisk practicality now.

"I spoke with Otter before I came here. He told me that something had been bothering your late master for some time. Is that so?"

She hesitated for so long that Linden thought she would refuse to answer. Then she nodded, the barest jerk of her head, so quick that if Linden hadn't been watching her closely, he might have missed it.

"Do you know what it was?" he continued.

She suddenly looked uncomfortable. Was she reluctant to be thought speaking ill of poor Sether? Or, as a mere journeywoman, was she afraid to bring up a certain name?

Linden was not. "Let's see if this helps: Some time ago, Bard Leet came back from the second of two journeys he'd made, didn't he? Journeys that I've been told were unusual for him—especially the first. I've also been told that he then went to see Sether, and it was shortly afterwards that Sether became . . . upset, shall we say?"

She stared at him, blank-faced, but made no sound or gesture of agreement or denial. Then her expression shifted to anger. "Who are you to ask me such questions?" she demanded, fists clenched. "And *why* do you ask them?"

"My name is Linden Rathan."

Her face paled and she steadied herself with a hand on the edge of the wall bin. "Oh gods, I should have guessed . . . ," she muttered. "A friend of Otter's with a birthmark—I should have been able to figure it out, I've heard talk . . ."

She bobbed a rough courtesy. "Your Grace, forgive me, I shouldn't have spoken to you like that." She babbled on in apology.

Linden held up a hand to stop her. "Journeywoman, I certainly don't fault you for your anger. Even as a Dragonlord, those questions would be impertinent if I didn't have a very good reason for asking them."

"May I ask that reason, Your Grace?"

"A man's life. A man I—and others—believe to be innocent at heart. A friend."

Rose stared at the floor; Linden waited, watching her silent struggle as she weighed what she should do—and what she dared do. Would she be named "traitor" by the others in the Bards' Guild? And if she dared speak—she, no master, only a mere journeywoman—might it recoil upon her if Leet found out who'd set the hounds on his trail? That is, if Leet was innocent . . .

Almost to herself, she whispered. "I've no proof. . . ."

He all but heard the unspoken, *But I have suspicions.* Her eyes begged him for something.

But what? He gazed at her, puzzled; she stared back with frightening intensity. Then, all at once, he knew.

Linden smiled. Clever girl; if this all came to naught, and anyone found out who'd told tales and made trouble for her, she could blame him. "Dragonlord's orders," he said with a wink.

A flash of a smile told him he'd guessed correctly. "Since you give me no choice, Dragonlord," she said, looking as innocent as a newborn lamb, "I must—"

She hesitated; for a moment he thought she would burst into tears. Then the words gushed forth like a dam breaking. "I'll tell you what I know, and may it help you and your friend. At least one life's wasted already; I won't have another one taken.

"Now mind you, I don't know where Leet went for the first journey," Rose began.

"Dragonskeep," Linden supplied.

The look she gave him was full of speculation. "Did he now? I wonder why. We all knew he wouldn't go there because Otter did so frequently. We used to laugh about it, how it must have galled him not to play before such an audience."

"I know part of why he went," Linden said, remembering seeing Leet in the library at Dragonskeep. "But not all. Go on, please."

"When he came back, I know he spoke to Sether at least once. I went to talk to my master one evening; we had a shipment of spruce for soundboards from Megara that was late and I wanted to know if he wanted me to ride out there and find out what had happened. But when I got to his office—"

Rose gestured to the back of the building; looking, Linden could make out a door in the thick shadows.

"—I heard voices. I recognized Sether's right away, of course, but it was a moment or two before I recognized Leet's, he spoke so softly. I almost went in anyway, because I didn't like Leet's tone, but . . . I stopped. I just knew something was very wrong."

She studied her boot toes for a moment, then looked up at Linden in appeal. "You know how sometimes you can tell—not from the words, because you can't really hear them, but from the voices themselves—that you'd best not interrupt? Or that it's something you'd just rather not know about? I felt that, that night, standing there in the darkness outside the office, listening to those voices murmuring like a distant stream. What I heard in Leet's voice scared me."

Linden nodded. He could well imagine how Rose had felt. Many times over the years that they'd been friends, he'd heard the power in Otter's voice; it was part of the magic that made a true Bard. Leet would have it as well.

And if you were only a journeywoman, and the two you'd interrupt were your master and a bard known for his hot temper and sharp tongue . . . He didn't blame Rose one bit.

"I don't mind saying that I turned and slunk off nice and quiet-like. I like my head on my shoulders. Almost forgot about it all, too, because late the next day that wood we'd been waiting for came in. At first it seemed the same as any other shipment."

She paused, frowning, lost in her memories. After a time, Linden said, "And what was different that time?"

Rose jumped a little. "I almost didn't see it, you know, or them. They waited until dusk was falling to unload that particular wagon. But by chance I looked around just as Leet, my master, and another man that I'm certain I recognized unloaded a good-sized wooden box from the wagon and hurried off with it."

"Did you ever see what was in it?"

Shaking her head, Rose said, "No. Nor did Master Sether ever mention it. Indeed, I never saw it again after that night; I suspect it was taken away straight off. And there was another puzzle on that wagon: boards of rowan wood that I never saw again, either. I think they went wherever the box went."

Rowan? Now that was odd. Linden rubbed his chin, thinking. He'd never heard of rowan used for a harp, but then he was certainly no expert; he liked walnut or cherry for an instrument himself and had never considered anything else. But someone else certainly might have.

But when he put the question to Rose, she shook her head. "I've never heard of anyone having a harp made from it, either. I'm not certain if it would work well."

So what does *one use rowan—*

Linden swore aloud. What was rowan used for? Protection against magic. Or, to turn it around, to shield magic from leaking. Mages often kept magical items such as amulets in boxes of rowan, he knew.

But what on earth would a bard need with something like that? Or was— "How big were those boards? Only enough for a small box or big enough for, say, a chest?"

Rose's eyes went wide and she raked her fingers through her hair. "They were narrow boards—rowan's not a large tree like maple or oak. But there were a lot of them. More than enough for a small box—more like something the size of a case for a small harp." She smiled wryly. "My apologies. That's how I think. Everything is about harps."

An idea began to niggle at the back of Linden's mind, nebulous as a wisp of fog. "A small harp . . . As, say, a traveling harp?"

Rose nodded. "Just so, Your Grace."

Linden stood silent, mulling over all that Rose had told him. Nothing that he could point to and say, "This! This proves Raven's innocence." All he had were hints.

But hints of exactly *what*? He needed hard, solid *proof.* And where the hell he was supposed to find that, he didn't know.

At last he said, "You've given me much to think about, Journeywoman Rose. I thank you."

She made him another courtesy. "May what I've told you help save that poor man's life."

Linden smiled a little ruefully. "I don't have enough yet. I need more, but I don't know where I might find it." With that, he left her to finish her work.

But when he was halfway to the door, the young woman called out, "Dragonlord!"

"Yes?"

"The third man who helped unload the wagon . . . He's a luthier, a well-known one, named Thomelin. He trained here. He's made harps for a number of the bards."

"I thank you again, Mistress Rose. And where might I find this luthier named Thomelin?"

"In the artisans' quarter here in Bylith, my lord—it's a large house and workshop on Carver's Lane. He makes wonderful instruments; he can make wood sing."

He can make wood sing. . . . Even as he wondered where else he'd heard that of Thomelin the luthier, an image answered it: *Leet standing in the encampment, the flickering torchlight dancing over the harp cradled in his arms.*

What else can this Thomelin make wood do? Linden wondered grimly.

After asking directions a few times, Linden finally found the luthier's dwelling. When the hell had Pig Lane disappeared and that big embroiderers' guild house taken its place? He'd had to go a way he didn't know and gotten lost.

At least Nightsong had agreed to bear him. He left her by the low fence that separated the shop and home from the street, and let himself in through the gate.

Thomelin does well for himself, Linden thought as he studied the luthier's home. The combination house and workshop was large and airy, with the lower floor devoted to the luthery and the living quarters above.

Linden entered a side door that had been left open to catch the fresh air and light. A few boys darted to and fro. Two were hanging up tools; another placed parchment seals over jars and deftly tied them down. Yet another swept the floor with a besom, gathering the long, curled shavings that littered the floor into a pile that he then scooped up and put into a large wooden bucket. All worked under the supervision of a big, rough-looking man; evidently the luthier and his apprentices were finishing for the day.

Or so Linden thought. "You are Thomelin?" he asked.

His answer was a growled, "No. I'm his journeyman, Cotler. What do you want? Can't you see we're closing up?"

Linden raised his eyebrows at the unnecessary rudeness but held his temper. "Then where might I find Master Thomelin?"

"He's away."

Linden swore to himself, then asked, "And when do you expect him back?"

"A tenday, maybe more," came the snarled reply. "What's it to you?"

"Then perhaps you could answer some questions for me."

"And perhaps I won't. Who d'you think you are, coming around like this? I don't have to answer—"

Just then the boy with the besom stopped his sweeping to stare at Linden. A big smile spread across his face and he stepped closer, his hand outstretched. A look at the boy's face and Linden knew he was simple.

With a curse, Cotler turned. "Get back to work, Brin, you lazy lackwit." His fist came up.

Without his even thinking about it, Linden's hand shot out and caught the man's wrist. He stared hard into the journeyman's surprised eyes. It must have been a shock to the man, big as he was, that someone could hold him immobile.

"Don't" was all Linden said at last. Then he released the man.

All the apprentices but Brin hastened to put one of the worktables between themselves and the two men. The young simpleton just stood looking from one man to the other, his brown eyes filled with confusion and dismay.

Cotler rubbed his wrist, his lips pressed together. Linden watched the fury building in his face. He didn't need a map to tell him where this was going.

He held up a hand. "Don't even think about hitting me," he said pleasantly. "You don't want to know what would happen."

A sly smile crept across Cotler's face and the look in his eyes went from angry to crafty. The boys sniggered together. That told Linden that the journeyman was either such a skilled fighter that the boys expected him to best someone larger than himself—or else he was one hell of a dirty fighter.

Linden wasn't interested in finding out which Cotler was. Sighing, he pulled his torc of rank from beneath the neck of his tunic just as the journeyman's weight shifted to his back foot.

Dirty fighter, Linden thought contemptuously. He'd recognized the start of a kick to the groin.

One of the boys squeaked in surprise. The sight of the torc with its ruby-eyed dragons' heads seemed to paralyze Cotler. He teetered for a moment before falling back a step to catch his balance. His face went fish-belly white and the watching boys went very still.

Only Brin moved. Smiling again now that the tension was past, the boy came to Linden and leaned against him, puppylike, the besom dangling forgotten from one hand. Cotler's hand jerked as if to knock the boy away, then fell to his side.

Linden rested a hand on the child's hair. "I trust there will be no problem with answering my questions now." It was statement, not question.

"N-not at all, Your G-Grace," Cotler stammered.

"I'm pleased to hear that, Cotler. Now—shall we step into that corner and talk?"

Once he'd had the fear of the gods and of Dragonlords put into him, Cotler couldn't answer Linden's questions fast enough. Indeed, at times the answers came so quickly it was almost impossible to make sense of the words spilling forth like a waterfall.

In a short time Linden found out from Cotler that yes, his master had taken a journey almost two years ago; that a journey wasn't unusual, but from something Thomelin had let slip, he'd gone back to his old village and that was odd. Why odd, my lord? He used to go there often, but he since he'd brought Brin back with him from the village a few years back, he'd never gone back until that trip two years ago. Cotler had gone in his place all the other times and glad to do it even though Little Coppice is the back of nowhere.

Your Grace wishes to know if he brought anything back with him that time? Just the usual spruce for soundboards. Everyone knows the best spruce comes from Megara near Little— Wait! There was also a good-sized box on the wagon and boards of rowan wood. Anything unusual about the box—why, yes. It was also of rowan.

Linden paused to think again, Why rowan? From Rose's description, and now Cotler's confirmation, the box was much too large to hold an amulet. So what *was* in it that needed rowan?

The sharp rustle of cloth behind him cut Linden off before he could ask. He half turned to find a woman flanked by two boys somewhat older than Brin and a younger girl. The children were well dressed; they watched with mild curiosity. Their mother—for the kinship was plain to see in their cleft chins—frowned.

"What is the meaning of all this?" the woman asked imperiously. Despite her short stature, she somehow managed to look down her nose at Linden. But her next words were to the journeyman: "Cotler, you know better than to stand about gossiping. If the boys don't eat now there won't be time for them to do so before the service. And I'll not have them go to the temple hungry; they squirm and don't pay attention. Priest Amas was quite sharp about it a few days ago. He said it was but a small step from inattention to outright evil and I agree."

No doubt this was why Cotler was so glad to travel in his master's place. He saw the small gold talisman hanging from a chain from the woman's neck: a pair of crossed flails, the symbol of the god Sarushun. But even before he'd seen it, Linden guessed what god she'd followed. Only Sarushun demanded daily devotion at his temple; every other god he knew of seemed content to wait for whatever holy days they had. If their followers had a small altar at home, well and good. If not, come to the temple when you could, and get on with living other times.

Sarushun, on the other hand, dictated every instant of his devotees' lives. His was not a worship that attracted Linden; to him it saw wickedness in everyone and everything, while displaying precious little tolerance or forgiveness for all-too-human weaknesses.

Still, this woman had the right to worship where and how she chose, and to order her household as she saw fit. For he was certain this was her household; her manner and her fine clothes proclaimed her Thomelin's wife.

"Mistress—?" he began, belatedly realizing he didn't know Thomelin's second name, or if the man even used one.

"*Lady* Romissa," she quickly corrected, her nose inching even higher.

Ah, a noblewoman from an impoverished family, no doubt, forced by circumstances to marry a well-off artisan—and resenting the hell out of it. That explained much in her manner, and perhaps even her choice of religion.

Before Linden could speak, Cotler said, "I was merely answering some questions—"

Lady Romissa turned her dark eyes on Linden and demanded, "Questions? How dare you! You will tell me the meaning of this impertinence. Questions indeed!"

"I'm afraid that I may not reveal my reasons, Lady Romissa," he said as pleasantly as he could bring himself to do. Though as a Dragonlord he was pledged to honor anyone's choice of god or goddess—indeed, it had always been his natural inclination, anyway—he had little patience for the haughty attitude many of Sarushun's votaries displayed. And the Lady Romissa seemed worse than most.

He forestalled an outburst of self-righteous indignation by turning to fully face her, his fingers touching one of the silver dragons' heads of his torc. "I am

Dragonlord Linden Rathan, my lady. May I continue? I promise I'll not keep Cotler any longer than necessary."

She recovered quickly from her surprise at finding one of the great weredragons of Dragonskeep in her little domain. Oh, she wanted to order him out; he could see it in the way her lips worked, the quiver in her delicately cleft chin, in her suddenly rigid stance. But she did not have quite enough nerve for it, did the good Lady Romissa.

"Boys, come with me," she snapped. "Else we shall be late for the service."

Linden guessed it was not by choice they went to the temple of Sarushun, but by Lady Romissa's edict; he'd rarely seen such sullen expressions. The apprentices slouched from behind the table and passed Lady Romissa single-file. More than one shot a look of pure venom at her back as they gathered by the workroom door.

Linden suddenly remembered a comment of Lleld's about Sarushun: "Such a sanctimonious prig, it's a wonder his fellow gods and goddesses don't dunk him in a rain barrel." He barely kept the grin from his face at the sudden memory.

Brin, the simpleton, dropped the broom and started to follow. Lady Romissa rounded on him.

"Not you!" she snapped. "You're not fit to stand before Sarushun, you who are but a badge of your mother's disgrace!"

The boy retreated in hurt confusion. Furious, Linden beckoned him; Brin ran to the shelter of his arm and buried his face against Linden's tunic.

"That will be all, Lady Romissa," Linden said coldly.

She spared him a look of pure hatred, then gathered up her children and the apprentices, pointedly herding them from the pollution of his presence.

When they were gone, Cotler sighed and said, "You had more questions, Your Grace?"

"Just one. That box of rowan—what became of it?"

"I don't know—truly, Dragonlord, I don't. I don't know what was in it, either. My master never told me, and it wasn't my place to ask." The journeyman hesitated a moment, then asked, "Is that all you wish to know, my lord? If it is, I'd best get to the temple."

"You're also a follower of Sarushun?" It surprised Linden; Cotler had the look of a roisterer about him.

The journeyman made a sour face. "No, my lord, none of us are, not even my master. We go because we're made to. At least when he's here we only have to go to the morning service, not the later ones. Plays hell with getting anything useful done in a day. Might I go now? The later I am, the more I'll hear about it—and she's already in a rare high dudgeon even for her."

"My apologies for that—I'm afraid that's because of me. Go, then." He looked down at Brin and ruffled the boy's hair. "I must go now, lad." To Cotler, he said, "Will the boy be safe on his own?"

"Cook watches after him while we're all away, Dragonlord; she and Master Thomelin are the only ones Lady Romissa's not been able to force her will upon. Master refuses to and Cook threatens to go elsewhere."

So Lady Romissa's efforts at conversion had their practical limits. Linden had to hide a smile; a good cook was hard to come by. "Very well," he said.

But when Linden made to follow Cotler out the door, Brin caught the hem of his tunic and held him back. The boy pointed urgently at a line of baskets under one of the worktables.

"He wants to show you his carvings, Your Grace," Cotler said. "I'll take him to Cook—"

"No, go on. I'll have a look at these carvings and then bring him to the kitchen myself," Linden said.

Cotler looked half grateful, half as if he would argue, then hurried away. As soon as they were alone, Brin scuttled under the table like a crab and began shoving the baskets out to slide along the wooden floor. Linden crouched down and raised the lid of the first one. But instead of the carvings he expected to see, this was filled with packets of hide glue. So was the next he looked into; the third contained boxes whose labels declared them to be dried pigments.

Puzzled, he turned to Brin. "Where are your carvings, lad?"

Brin pointed to yet another basket. But when Linden put out a hand for it, Brin caught his wrist for a moment and tugged, then pointed to the floor.

It looked like any other plank floor Linden had ever seen. Guessing, he asked, "You want me to crawl under the table with you?" The thought was not appealing; it wouldn't be easy to fit his height under the worktable.

Brin beamed and nodded. Then he pointed to the floor near one end of the table and caught Linden's wrist again, trying to guide his hand there. Then he made a strange gesture with his hands.

Like a dog dig—

Realization came like a thunderclap. With growing excitement, Linden tried to push the table aside, but it was bolted to the floor. So down he went on all fours to join Brin beneath the table after all.

The boy's fingers brushed aside a coating of sawdust and tiny wood chips and shavings, revealing a knot—or, at least, what looked like a knot at first glance. There was something not quite right about it. Linden twisted his hand in the air and brought forth a ball of coldfire.

At that, Brin made the first sound Linden had yet heard, a soft, startled grunt. His eyes were huge as he shrank back from the glowing ball.

"Don't worry, Brin," Linden said. "It won't hurt you. Though it looks like fire, it's cold. Touch it if you like."

After a long, long look deep into Linden's eyes, Brin stretched out a trembling forefinger and gingerly poked the coldfire. Finding that Linden's words were true, he cooed in delight and caught the coldfire, turning it over and over in his hands. Linden conjured another ball up and held it so that its light bathed the "knot."

Someone—Thomelin?—had removed the original knot and replaced it with one of blackened iron. It had been cleverly wrought; even if the worktable was moved, it looked so real that a casual glance would never see it. Linden wondered if the table was bolted to the floor to help insure it remained concealed.

Now Brin held out one hand, thumb down. Next he made a motion as if pressing something down. Linden held his breath, and, his own thumb resting on the false knot, mimicked the boy's action.

The knot sank slowly under his finger. Brin nodded and made a twisting motion. Linden did the same. As he turned the knot, something clicked. He removed his thumb; the knot remained depressed. Linden hooked his forefinger into the hole and lifted. A section of floor three boards wide and a little more than an ell long came up. He set it carefully to one side.

Brin, who had been smiling and nodding at Linden for all the world like a tutor with a clever student, lost interest in the proceedings and scooted away on his bottom. He sat turning the coldfire over and over in his hands, cooing happily to it.

Linden peered into the hidden compartment. It was longer and wider than its lid, extending under the floor on all sides, though not beyond the wide workbench.

It was, he thought, cleverly done; as long as the table remained in its place, no footstep would reveal the hollow area beneath. He sent the coldfire into the hole and saw that what he had taken for the floor in the dimness was in fact a dark length of cloth tossed over something. Linden reached down and pulled it up.

Silk! And heavy, too. Who'd waste such costly stuff by putting it in a hole? Wait—what's this? He called the coldfire back from the hole. By its light he studied the fabric spilled across his lap, looking for the slight roughness that had caught his fingertips.

The silk was not black as he'd first thought, but a blood red so dark it seemed to drink the light shining upon it. And what he'd thought were snags he now saw was embroidery. Embroidery done in a thread that matched the silk's deep hue—but why go through such trouble?

Someone must have gone well-nigh blind stitching this.

Nor was it the work of an expert. It was clumsy and uneven; it took a few moments of studying it to realize that the ragged stitching formed patterns. He recognized one, a symbol of protection used by mages to keep out—or contain—evil repeated over and over again.

Silk and mage sigils—someone wasn't taking any chances, was he? Let us see what needs such protections.

Leaning over the hole in the floor once more, Linden sent the coldfire back down. He found himself staring at a long, narrow box.

Fifty-five

Linden looked at it for a long, long moment. He was no expert on wood, but he would wager everything he owned that here lay the mysterious box of rowan.

Silk, mage sigils, and *rowan—what in Gifnu's hells is in here?*

The crate was girded with bands of iron, though there were no locks in the hasps. Instead a rope wound several times around the box served to both secure the lid, and, with loops at either end, as handles. Mentally cursing the cramped quarters—if he could stand up straight after this it would be a miracle—Linden dragged the long, low crate out of its hiding place and pushed it across the floor to an open area. He crawled out after it and knelt before his prize.

Now he would see what was so special that it needed to be both warded and hidden. Linden untied the knots as quickly as he could, wondering what he would find. At last the final knot was undone and Linden threw back the lid to find—

Boards. Thin boards about two handspans wide resting within a silk-lined box—silk the same color as the embroidered cover. Some were short, perhaps half their width, while others were much longer.

What the— Hardly believing what he saw, Linden pawed through the boards. He finished by picking up one of the smaller pieces and staring in bewilderment at it. No bones, no hidden weapons, no tomes of black magic with bloodstained covers of human skin. Just *boards,* for pity's sake. So why all the secrecy? Why a box of rowan wood lined with silk? And a cover of more silk embroidered with magical symbols? Why hide it all so elaborately?

He wasn't sure *what* he'd been expecting, but it certainly wasn't these, these . . . whatever they were. Or, more likely, were meant to be; the thin boards had an unfinished look about them. They reminded him of something, but what? He ground his teeth in frustration and swore under his breath.

So great was his annoyance that at first he didn't notice the coldness creeping up his fingers until it flared into icy pain. He flung the wood back into the box with an oath and cradled his hand against his chest. It ached as if he'd held it in an icy pond for a candlemark or more.

Worse yet was the feeling that had come with the cold.

What in every single one of Gifnu's hells was going on? Though the thought of opening himself to whatever was in the wood sickened him, Linden knew he had to find out more about them. He took a deep breath to settle both his nerves and his stomach; then he closed his eyes and reached out with the magic that bound the two halves of his soul.

Joy in causing pain. Even more joy in killing. Evil. A sick, twisted thirst for—

Linden slammed the lid down. At once the vile sensations ended. He sat back on his heels, feeling sick and dizzy, and wondering if his skin really would crawl off his body. He didn't know what he'd found, but now he understood the elaborate precautions. He only hoped they were enough.

While he waited for his stomach to stop its roiling, he debated what he should do with the vile thing he'd found. In the end, he decided to leave it where it was; at least there it was no danger to the general populace. When all this was over, he would come back and destroy it. Whatever it was.

He had to force himself to touch the box again. But there was no other way to get it back to its hiding place. So he did what he had to do, and as quickly as possible. He was replacing the baskets when a small hand moved into his range of vision and pushed one aside and moved another into its place.

Startled, Linden nearly swore aloud; he'd been so intent on his discovery, he'd forgotten Brin. Now the boy pushed past him to arrange the baskets under the table to his liking. Linden left him to it; though he lacked all his wits, the boy seemed to know where each basket belonged. Brin worked one-handed, the coldfire clutched to his chest with the other.

Linden concentrated on regaining whatever composure he could. It wasn't much—hell, it could be carried in a thimble—but he didn't want to upset the boy. This was not a problem for a child.

When Brin got to the last basket—the one that held his carvings, Linden remembered—he rooted around in it and came up with something clutched in his fist. He offered it to Linden.

It was a horse, and done well for a boy his age. It even looked a bit like Shan. *How did he know?* Linden wondered. True, it was somewhat crude, but there was talent there; Brin had skillfully used both the grain and curves of the original wood. When Linden tried to return it, thinking Brin was only showing it to him, the boy put his free hand behind his back and shook his head while holding up the coldfire.

"So," Linden said, "a trade, then." He forced a smile to hide the queasiness he still felt. "But it's not really a fair one, Brin. After a day or two, the coldfire will fade, then disappear. Do you understand?"

Brin studied the glowing ball in his hand. He nodded.

"Do you want your horse back, then? You can still keep the coldfire."

Brin shook his head so hard his hair whipped back and forth.

"Then I thank you, Brin, for the gift of this horse and for all of your help. While I don't yet understand what it is I've found, you may have given me the key to save a friend's life."

The boy gave him a brilliant smile, then rubbed his stomach.

"Ah, that's right. It's time to visit Cook, isn't it?"

Relieved to be gone from this place, Linden held out his hand and let Brin lead him from the room.

After leaving Brin with a very startled Cook, Linden rode through Bylith, letting the last dregs of uneasiness dissipate. His wanderings took him through the various sections of the city until he came out upon Mally's Hill in an area of houses and little shops that had been old when he first saw them more than six hundred years before. No wagons ever came this way, for the slope was so steep that the street rose in a series of wide, shallow steps. But if he remembered rightly, there had been a fine view of the city from the top, and a place to sit and think. He set Nightsong to the gentle steps that led to the overlook. The gods knew he needed to do some thinking.

Miracle of miracles, the overlook was still there: a few scrubby trees, a bench of grey stone, and an open area perched on the very edge of a precipitous drop. Someone had planted herbs or flowers, dead now in the fierce summer heat. The breeze that always blew here rattled through the brown stems and brought a sharp, resinous scent with it. Linden dismounted. Nightsong wandered off a few paces, snuffling the ground.

He stood on the edge and looked out over Bylith. From here he could see the castle, much larger now than the first time he'd seen it. Not so surprising; Rani had taken her place upon the Kelnethi throne more than six hundred years ago. Other kings and queens had added on to it since then. He let his gaze roam over the city, seeing without truly seeing the different quarters and the streets running like veins through it all, letting his thoughts go where they would. He'd often found that what he needed rose to the surface then.

But not this time; this time his mind shied like a nervous colt from what he'd found. He pulled Brin's horse from his belt pouch and rubbed a thumb along its back, idly wondering how the boy had come to be in Thomelin's household. It was plain Lady Romissa had little affection for him, poor lad.

After a time he noticed that his attention—such as it was—had paused at the docks. He smiled a little; funny how, ever since he'd met Maurynna, boats and docks and such like kept cropping up. He'd never thought much about sailing before a certain young sea captain came into his life and made him whole.

His interest caught, he spared a moment to watch the activity around one of the ships. From here the workers looked like ants scurrying about as they loaded her. The memory of his first meeting with Maurynna came back to him: the hot sun on their backs as they'd worked to empty her ship, the shouts and songs of the sailors and dockhands, the smells of river mud and tar, while overhead the gulls wheeled across the sky and screeched at each other, and the ship bobbed at—

Gulls. As if the word were a key in a lock, all at once he realized what the wood in the box was.

Soundboards. The cursed stuff was for soundboards, both entire and pieced together. And the best soundboards were made from . . . spruce.

But why would thinking of seagulls and Leet . . . There's something there, I can just feel it. Something I need to remember . . . Something to do with seagulls and Leet. But what is *it?*

He turned abruptly and went to the bench. He settled himself comfortably on it, then took a deep breath and closed his eyes, forcing himself to relax. *Leet . . . Leet . . . There's something about Leet and seagulls. . . .* The warmth made him drowsy and set his thoughts drifting.

An image floated to the top of his mind like a bubble: Otter sitting by a hearth at Dragonskeep, looking perplexed. Then came another, this one of Leet at a table in the library, a book open before him. What had been so interesting to bring Leet all that way?

As if from a long way off, Linden "heard" Otter's voice once again. *You know the kind of tales I mean—the ghost wolf of Lachlan forest, Grey Carra, the Creeping Hand—all those "scare small children into nightmares" kind of tales. Culwen seemed especially fond of the stories about Gull the Blood Drinker.*

And what was it he'd said to Otter just a few moments after that? Something about hoping that the witch spruce they'd planted over his grave still kept Gull's soul pinned down.

Not seagulls and Leet. *Gull* and Leet. Linden's eyes flew open. "Gods, no—he couldn't have," he whispered, horrified. "Not from *that* spruce—"

The idea so sickened him that he wanted to vomit. Despite the heat, he shivered. Elbows on knees, Linden hunched over and rested his forehead in his hands.

No one could do such a vile, evil thing, he thought over and over again. *No one—especially not a bard, dear gods. It would violate* everything *a bard is.*

For a wild moment he thought that he had the answer: for whatever reason— some private revenge, perhaps—Thomelin had tricked Leet by making a harp with that cursed wood and foisting it off—

No. That wouldn't work. Leet would have known the instant he touched the strings that what he held was tainted. Besides, from what Rose said, he'd been with Thomelin on that trip. Linden rubbed his face, wiping cold sweat away.

He had to find out where Thomelin was, and have a long, *long* talk with him.

* * *

Linden neared the gate of the luthier's house just as Lady Romissa and her little retinue of children and apprentices passed through it on their way back from Sarushun's temple. She didn't see him until one of her sons tugged her sleeve, making her look around. The face she turned upon Linden made her look as if she had just quaffed a goodly dose of vinegar.

"Get the children into the house," she snapped at Cotler.

As Linden came nigh to the gate, she shut it with a resounding clang. With that thin barrier between them, Lady Romissa drew herself up, and stared in haughty silence at him, daring him to invade her domain once more. Her little cleft chin quivered with rage.

Linden said nothing, merely sat easily on Nightsong and returned her stare, one eyebrow raised. Moments passed in the silent war.

Lady Romissa broke first. She looked away, then back to him. "Yes, Dragonlord?" she said.

"I would speak with your husband," Linden began. "Wh—"

"He is not here," came the quick interruption.

"I know that, my lady," Linden said as patiently as he could. "I want to know where he's journeyed to this time."

For a long moment Linden thought she would refuse to answer. Then with a sullen expression more befitting a five-year-old than a mother of three, she told him, "Parra, I think. For gemstones."

That made sense; many nobles liked their harps ornately decorated. "More money than taste," he'd heard Otter sniff more than once. And Parra in the northwest of Kelneth was one of the best markets for gems. He smothered a sigh of annoyance.

Lady Romissa went on, "Or perhaps Corrieton. My husband likes to choose his own gems for the harps."

Linden caught the faint note of derision on the word "husband." Suddenly fed up with Lady Romissa and her self-importance, he said curtly, "My thanks, lady. Now I bid you good day."

Without waiting for a reply—or, more likely, a thinly veiled dismissal—Linden wheeled Nightsong away. "Back to the Bards' School, my grey-maned lady."

She snorted and set off at a ground-eating walk. Linden let the reins rest on her neck and thought.

Gull and Leet. It could explain a great many things, but as yet it was naught but speculation. What they needed was proof, hard and cold as iron. But Thomelin wasn't here to give it—even if he would talk.

Very well, then. He'd do this the hard way: find out whether Gull's witch spruce was standing or not. And of the three Dragonlords, only he had been alive when Worton, the village Gull had terrorized, still thrived. It was not a place he'd ever visited, but he knew roughly where it had once stood. He was also the closest since he was already in Kelneth.

What else must be done? A trip to the library of Dragonskeep for— He couldn't do it all. There wasn't time. He must reach Maurynna, and soon. Thank the gods he was riding a Llysanyin and not an ordinary horse. Closing his eyes, he "cast his call on the wind" and sent his thoughts winging toward his soultwin.

At first he thought it was too far for him to reach her without some other source of magic to draw upon. But his fear for Raven lent him the strength he needed, it seemed, for he "heard" her astonished *Linden?*

It was faint, but it was real. *Maurynna, listen well,* he said, putting all the urgency he could into his mindvoice. *I can't hold this for very long. I know you'll want to stay with Raven, so send Shima to Dragonskeep. Tell him to get there as fast as he can and go to Lukai and Jenna. Tell him to find out from them the books Leet was reading when he was there—especially those by Lord Culwen— and to bring them back to Balyaranna. Understood?*

He remembered belatedly that she hadn't been present at the conversation two years ago with Lleld and Otter about Leet's odd reading habits, and prayed that she wouldn't ask for explanations now.

Yes, she replied. He could feel her puzzlement, even at this distance, but she wasted no time demanding to know what this was all about, or what the chief archivists of Dragonskeep had to do with their plight. For a moment he felt her mind turn away from his; then she was back, saying, *Shima's off as soon as he can find a place large enough to Change.*

Good. If I'm right, we'll save Raven from that gallows yet, Maurynna-love, he said. *Now I've a journey to—*

The contact was slipping from him. He had time only for a farewell and it was gone.

"Dragonlord? Are you well?"

Startled, Linden opened his eyes and looked wildly around. Before him stood the sturdy timber-and-stone stable of the school. A worried groom was looking up at him.

"Yes, I'm well. I was just mindspeaking my soultwin," he said. The groom's mouth made an O of surprise.

Linden swung down. To the Llysanyin, he said, "Thank you, Nightsong." She lipped his hair in reply. To the groom, "Please see to her."

As Nightsong followed the groom, Linden stood thinking furiously. Otter had named Charilon as one of the two people he needed to speak with at the school. He'd already spoken with Rose, and the bard should be awake by now.

But he needed to find lost Worton and the secret its forest held as soon as possible. Night was coming but he didn't want to wait until the morning. There was too little time left. No; Charilon could wait. If necessary, Linden knew he would have no compunction against rousting the bard out in the middle of the night.

His mind made up, Linden strode through the grounds of the school.

* * *

Oh, curse it all! Maurynna fumed silently. She'd been just about to tell Linden her suspicions about Leet's harp when the contact between them faded. She kicked herself mentally; between her surprise at "hearing" Linden and astonishment at his request, she'd never thought to try to help him hold the contact. "Idiot," she growled at herself.

She jumped up from her chair and began pacing their sleeping chamber. And what in the name of all that was holy did *books* have to do with any of this, anyway? Books didn't make music.

Harps did. Maurynna stopped short and dug her fingers into her long black hair, tugging it this way and that. She was the only Dragonlord left now in Balyaranna. She feared that if she left, something might happen to Raven. But ever since the conversation with Rann, a small voice inside her had been clamoring that what had happened to Kella would unlock this mystery.

Fifty-six

Pod had no idea how long they ran for. All she knew was that it seemed forever, a nightmare scramble through briers and brambles, over fallen trees and old stone walls. They'd long since lost all trace of direction. And now and again they could hear Arlim behind them, sometimes close by, sometimes far off as they twisted and turned like fleeing rabbits.

She knew that Arlim would find them; part of her suspected that he was toying with them, drawing the chase out deliberately. Sooner or later they had to face him.

Should they turn at bay and face him? Her greatest fear was that they would be too tired to fight when the chase finally ended. But they had no weapons save their small belt knives, nor had she seen any place that was easily defensible.

And night was coming. Soon it would be too dark to see. They had to find someplace to rest. The thought of stopping chilled her. At least Arlim wouldn't be able to see any better than they could in this poor light.

She pushed through a stand of tall weeds. Her heel came down on solid earth, but her toe . . . Pod staggered and swayed, her arms windmilling for balance, suddenly aware that she stood on the edge of nothing. It was only by the grace of the gods that she didn't scream aloud and give their position away to Arlim.

And it was Kaeliss who kept her from falling. The young Wort Hunter grabbed the back of Pod's tunic and yanked. They fell in a tangled heap. "Thanks!" Pod gasped. Together they crawled to the edge and looked down.

It was a gully, a little deeper than she was tall, Pod guessed, with a trickle of water running through it. She peered through the fading light.

"Look," she whispered, pointing. "See that fallen tree? Let's see if there's a place to hide under it—it's big enough."

They scrambled down and slipped and slid their way over mossy rocks to the tree. By the time they reached the tree, they were both soaked to the knees.

But it was worth it, every scrape and bruise. When the tree had fallen from its place on the edge of the gully, its roots held the bank at that spot, while the dirt below had eroded. The undercut formed a "cave" whose entrance was hidden from above by the huge trunk. They crawled inside and collapsed.

Pod lay with her eyes closed, gasping. She could go no farther. If Arlim found them, they would make their stand here.

She levered herself up onto her elbow, to tell Kaeliss that she at least was spent, when she heard twigs breaking in the woods above. She froze.

Footsteps came closer and closer to the edge. She clawed at her knife. Then came a startled curse and the footsteps retreated at a crashing run, fading into the distance.

They sat without speaking until full dark fell and the only noises were the normal sounds of a forest at night. Pod slumped against the back wall of their shelter; as her terror ebbed, she realized just how exhausted she was. Every limb trembled with weariness.

"We have to eat," Kaeliss said at last. Her voice sounded leaden with fatigue. Knowing she was right, Pod fumbled through her pack, finding her waterskin and a handful of cold cooked day lily tubers by feel. She could barely see her hand in front of her face.

After the pitiful meal, Pod unrolled her blankets. "He's gone—at least for the night. I think it's safe for both of us to sleep at the same time," she said. "Besides . . ."

"If we did try to take watches, we'd just fall asleep anyway," Kaeliss finished wearily.

Pod pulled her blanket over herself. "Just so. May the gods watch over us."

Fifty-seven

Shima landed heavily on the large flat cliff the Dragonlords often used when flying to or from Dragonskeep. He sank to his belly, letting his wings fall to either side. By all the Spirits, he hadn't flown this far this fast since his desperate first flight back in Jehanglan when he and Maurynna chased the mad truedragon Pirakos! His flanks heaved as he tried to catch his breath.

After a moment, he Changed. The cold of the mountain night washed over him. It felt good. Lying sprawled upon the rock, he made a decision; he was too exhausted to move, but from the urgency he'd felt in Maurynna's mindvoice when she'd laid this task upon him, there was no time to lose. Jenna and Lukai must begin looking for the needed books as soon as possible.

Yet he didn't want to be the one to roust the archivists from their beds. But there was someone who would happily do just that if her curiosity was aroused enough.

Luckily that was no great task. *Lleld?* he said. *Are you asleep?*

After a moment, a sleepy mindvoice grumbled, *Not anymore, thank you very much. Shima, it's* candlemarks *yet until dawn. What is so bloody—*

He felt her snap fully awake.

What are you doing here? You're supposed to be in Cassori with Linden and Maurynna! Is something wrong? And why do you sound so tired?

Because I flew here with hardly any rests, he snapped. Then, before she could say anything else, *I hope this will make more sense to you than it did to either Maurynna or me; I'm just passing on a message. From what Maurynna said when she sent me off, Linden seems to think that there's a clue in some books Master Bard Leet read when he—*

At last! Lleld crowed in his mind. *At last I'll find out why he was reading those horrid tales!*

Shima clutched his head and groaned. That had *hurt*.

Apologies, Shima, Lleld said, though her mindvoice held more glee than regret. Shima would have wagered she rubbed her hands in happy anticipation. *I know some of the books he studied while he was at Dragonskeep and I'll get Lukai and Jenna to make certain of the rest. Meet you in the library.*

Shima rolled onto his back and stared up at the stars fading in the sky, counting to himself. *One, two, thr—*

Lleld's mindvoice filled his head once more. *"Clue"? Clue to what? Uh, Shima—what's this about?*

Tell you when I get there.

Frustration; a brief image/feeling of Lleld, fists wound in his long, black hair, yanking as hard as she could. Then, *Damn it all! You'd bloody well better hurry!*

The next instant she was gone. Shima could picture the little Dragonlord leaping from her bed, dressing at breakneck speed, and running like a madwoman through the halls of the Keep.

At least he hoped she remembered to dress first. And why was he not more surprised that Lady Mayhem would know which books the Master Bard had read while he was here? He stood up and dusted himself off. He was curious to see those "horrid tales" for himself.

It was no use going any farther tonight, Linden decided. Yes, he could easily reach the general area of Worton. But he didn't know just where it had been. And even if he found it by luck it would still be dark when he got there. Dragonlord or not, it would be impossible to search the forest in human form.

He swooped lower, searching the ground for an open area. Spotting a large clearing by a river, he landed on the bank and drank deeply. He stretched his wings and settled himself, his wings rattling against his scales as he tucked his feet under and curled his tail around them like a cat. Then he stared into the darkness as he waited for the dawn.

Fifty-eight

When she awoke the next morning, Pod panicked. For a moment she thought she'd been buried alive; all she saw around her in the dim light was dirt. Then she remembered where they were.

She rolled over. Kaeliss was still asleep. Even in this poor light Pod could see how pinched and wan her face was under streaks of dirt. She guessed her own looked just as bad. As quietly as she could, Pod crawled out of their shelter, scrambled to the top of the gully, and looked around, trying to get her bearings.

There—where the sky glowed blood-red with the rising sun—that was east. The old rhyme came back to her: "Red sky at night, shepherd's delight. Red sky at morning, shepherds take warning."

She climbed back down to awaken Kaeliss. It was time to enter the nightmare again.

Linden? Linden, can you hear me?

Linden roused himself from the waking dream that dragons often fell into while resting. He recognized that mindvoice—nor was he surprised to hear it, he realized. What did surprise him was its unwonted seriousness. *I hear you, Lleld. Did Shima tell you what's at stake?*

Yes. Lleld couldn't quite hide her distress. *We have the books by Lord Culwen that Leet read the most, Jenna says. What do you need from them?*

The location of Worton and if at all possible, the whereabouts of the witch spruce. I never visited Worton, so I'm not certain just where it is.

More distress and a deep sadness. *I know where it was. I . . . I had friends there.* She then told him what to look for, finishing with, *The twin lakes and the esker between them are your best landmarks, I think, to find Worton. But some-one—we think it was Leet—has cut a page from one of the books.*

Linden closed his eyes, trying not to lose his temper. Damn Leet! *Let me guess—you suspect the location of the witch spruce was on that page.*

We do.

Have you any idea? Do you remember it?

He heard her "sigh" in his mind. *No, I don't. By the time I returned from Assantikkan, Gull had been dead for a few years already. I . . . I never went back there,* Lleld whispered.

I'm sorry to make you remember, Lleld, Linden said gently. *But have you any guesses whereabouts the tree might be?*

Silence followed. Then Lleld said, *I would think they would have buried that filth as far from the village as they could, even if they had to travel a few days by wagon or packhorse to do it.*

I suspect you're right. Who would want him nearby? Thank you, Linden said. *And I'm sorry about your friends.*

If I hadn't been in Assantik then . . .

The contact cut off abruptly. The guilt he'd felt in Lleld's mindvoice made him bow his head. He knew it was a guilt she didn't deserve, but could never escape.

There was no use waiting here. He might as well take to the air; he knew he was still too far south. Unfolding his wings, Linden crouched on his haunches, then sprang into the air with a mighty leap, spiraling up to meet the leaden sky.

He tasted the air. Just as he'd feared: a storm was coming.

Linden flew over the forest, slipping through the air from one side of the woods to the other. The witch spruce that held down Gull the Blood Drinker's soul should be in these woods. But if he was correct that the tree had been chopped down, he wasn't certain if he'd be able to sense anything, even while in dragon form. To make matters worse, this forest was much larger than he'd thought it would be. It was with relief that he saw the landmark of the twin lakes divided by a narrow esker in the distance.

The rain found him then; the drops came down hard and fast, rattling against his scales. Shaking his head, Linden saw what he'd been looking for—a long foundation of stone.

If he was right, this was the pride of Worton-that-once-was: the big stone barn for drying the rare herbs that had given the village its name and the people their living.

Or so it had been before a human demon had used it for his own twisted ends. Now barn and village were abandoned, forgotten by man; in another decade or two, even this much would be gone. Remembering the conclusion both he and Lleld had come to—that Gull was likely buried well away from the village— Linden quickly spiraled out from the ruins to begin his search.

He let his mind empty, seeking with the magic that bound the human and dragon halves of his soul for a trace of the spell that had bound Gull the Blood Drinker's spirit to the earth. The wind buffeted him, at one point almost flipping him. He fought to remain upright.

He thought he felt *something,* a sense of . . . wrongness, of a seething darkness. But he wasn't certain; nor could he afford to give the search the undivided attention it needed. The wind was at a dangerous level now, and the worst of the storm was almost upon him. For a moment he considered relinquishing control to his dragon half, Rathan, as he'd done a few years before, but discarded that idea even as it occurred to him. This time, he feared, Rathan might not subside into sleep again.

Linden swung his head from side to side, craning the long neck of his dragon form as he searched for the wellspring, the source of the darkness. But his quest was in vain: the entire forest below felt shrouded in evil.

And he would not be able to stay aloft much longer, anyway. He turned his long neck to look back over his shoulder. Yes, those storm clouds were closer and moving fast. They would be upon him in less than half a candlemark, he guessed.

He didn't dare fly through a thunderstorm. More than one Dragonlord had met their end by lightning. He had no intention of adding himself to that grim list.

On the heels of that thought, lightning flashed, followed immediately by a booming peal of thunder that made his ears ring. He would have to land, and the only place large enough was the abandoned village; there wasn't time to find somewhere else, somewhere clean of the taint he felt below him.

But as Linden came around to make for the clearing, a sudden, violent gust of wind tossed him like a leaf, wrenching at his wings as if it would rip them off. Knowing that if his wings were injured, he would crash into the trees below—a thing even a Dragonlord might not survive—Linden turned and fled before the storm. He'd have to find somewhere else to land, and quickly. The lightning was getting closer.

He flew desperately, seeking a place free of the malevolence that tainted the woods. For a moment he thought he'd found it, but then realized that what he felt was something alive, a pinprick of "light" in the foul darkness below. Before he could spare more than a moment's thought for it, he was beyond it.

He caught sight of another clearing ahead. It was much smaller, dangerously so, but he had no choice. He glanced back in time to see a jagged bolt of lightning blast a tree not far behind him. With a quick prayer to whatever gods watched over reckless Dragonlords, he spiraled in to land so hastily he brushed the branches of the surrounding trees with the tips of his wings.

He Changed even before he touched the ground. The soaked earth squelched under his boots as he dropped the last few feet in human form. His hands up to shield his eyes, Linden peered around the gloomy clearing for something that could serve as a refuge from the storm.

There was a shelter of sorts, built under the trees at one edge of the clearing. A charcoal burner's hut? Or did it belong to someone brave enough—or fool enough—to dare the haunted forest for the rare herbs it still held?

Linden didn't care. As the rain pelted down, he ran through the clearing. All around him the wind tossed the branches together with a sound like clicking bones.

As he pushed open the rickety door of lashed branches, a foul odor from the dimness within drove him back. Only the *crack!* of another lightning strike nearby convinced him to go in.

Breathing as shallowly as he could, he ducked inside the hut, leaving the door open behind him; let the wind clean this place as much as it could. He called up a ball of coldfire and looked around.

The hut was empty save for a sorry-looking bench near the back wall, two rickety stools, and a pile of rags in one corner. *Someone's bedding?* Linden wondered how anyone could sleep in such a stench.

Another corner held dried droppings—horse, or, more likely, donkey—so old they were crumbling into earth. Rain dripped through holes in the roof in a couple of places and the wind whistled through gaps in the wattle and daub walls like a mad piper.

But worse than the smell in the hut was the feeling that hung in the foul air like an invisible fog. He'd felt it while flying over the forest, as if the earth itself was ill. Confined in the dark squalor of the hut, it was worse, much worse. Cold crept down his spine.

Linden moved as carefully as a spy in an enemy camp as he searched the hut. The only two places to hide anything were behind the bench and in the pile of rags.

There was nothing behind the bench; that left . . .

Linden stopped. For the first time, he really looked at the pile in the corner, then crouched in front of it. Catching a fold of cloth, he pulled it free.

It proved to be a tunic; a tunic with a long tear in the front and a large, dark stain. Linden cursed softly, and seized another strip of fabric and pulled it clear. It took him a moment to realize that this, too, had once been a tunic, one that had been slashed nearly to ribbons. The shreds moved stiffly in the wind blowing through the open door; they bore the same dark stain as the other tunic.

Sickened, Linden sorted through the pile, finding more tunics, breeches, and once the tattered remains of a skirt. Three of the tunics caught his attention; it was hard to tell from the half-rotted fabric, but he thought they were the green and yellow favored by the members of the Healwort Guild. He made himself look closer at one of them—yes, there was the narrow yellow piping along the hems and neck that marked one of their journeymen. The only comfort he had— and it was a paltry comfort, indeed—was that none of the clothing seemed small enough for a child.

As he reached the bottom of the pitiful heap, Linden noticed that the foul smell that had pervaded the hut was stronger. He gingerly dragged the last remnants aside and saw that the ground below had been disturbed. With a prayer that he knew was futile, Linden caught up a stick from the floor and scratched in the dirt.

What he found sent him out of the door in a rush. He'd take his chances with the lightning. Linden crouched beneath a small pine tree to wait out the storm. He'd been a soldier, but what was in the hut . . .

Linden breathed a prayer for the souls that had died here.

Fifty-nine

"It's getting lighter ahead. *I* think it's a clearing," Kaeliss whispered over her shoulder.

They paused at the edge of it and huddled together, looking carefully around. The clearing was big, much larger than any other they'd come across with what looked like a tumbledown hut at one end. The thought of crossing that much open space made Pod's skin crawl.

A crow's harsh "Caw!" made her whip around. To her horror, she saw Arlim perhaps a hundred paces away, trying to push his way through a brier tangle to get at them. The long blade of his knife gleamed dully in the grey light.

"He's back!" Pod shrieked.

The girls ran as hard as they could across the clearing, the madman's curses following. As they plunged into the forest on the other side, the skies opened and rain pelted down. Half-blinded by the pouring rain and frantic to put as much distance as possible between themselves and Arlim, they ran heedlessly. And as they ran, Pod noticed that the underbrush grew thicker and thicker. Luckily there always seemed to be a way open; if they'd had to push through the thickets they might well have gotten caught in a bramble patch as Arlim had. They were soaking wet, shivering with cold and exhaustion, when the path they followed led them to another clearing.

While not as large as the one with the small hut, it was unnaturally even, an open circle in the middle of the forest. And where there should have been grass or cloudberry or *something* green growing there, the ground was instead covered by small, evil-looking mushrooms of a leprous grey.

But even the mushrooms kept their distance from the large stump that squatted in the center. Aside from piles of sawdust here and there, the ground was bare; nothing grew there, not even the tiniest patch of moss.

As if they're afraid to get too close. . . . Pod shook her head at the odd thought.

She knew one thing: she was not going to enter that clearing. Nothing could make her.

"Now why in the name of all the gods would someone cut down a single tree in the middle of a forest?" Kaeliss muttered. "That's not how timber is—"

A flash of lightning split the sky and a massive thunderclap drowned out the rest of her words. A sudden strong wind set the trees around them swaying, their leaves rustling with a sound like far-off whispers.

Prickles of fear snaked down Pod's spine. Then came a sound like stones rattling the branches overhead.

She looked up. Something smacked her cheek just below one eye. "Ow!" she cried. Tears filled her eyes. "Get down!"

They huddled together while the storm raged overhead and the rain pelted down, holding their packs over their heads to protect themselves as much as possible from the stinging rain.

In a momentary lull in the thunder, they heard something crashing into the bushes behind them. Kaeliss screamed and ran into the clearing, shrieking, "It's him! It's him!

Pod followed Kaeliss across the stump's clearing without thinking. She cast a look behind her, fearing to see Arlim. Instead, she saw a big, freshly broken branch dangling from a tree. As she watched, the last shreds of bark holding it on gave way and the branch fell with a noise like a horse crashing through the undergrowth.

Before she could call out to Kaeliss to stop, the other girl slipped on the wet, slimy mushrooms and slammed to the ground. Her pack burst open when it hit the ground, scattering the blossoms and roots of King's Blood everywhere. The red flowers looked like drops of blood against the mushrooms.

"Oh no! I've got to—" Kaeliss's words died in a moan of pain. She clutched her arm, then gasped, "Where's Arlim?"

"It was just a branch falling." Pod knelt and gently examined the arm. "This might be broken or just badly sprained. I can't tell. Either way we need to splint it, but we can't do anything about it just now," she said. "You must have landed on it just wrong. I'll help you up."

"Get the King's Blood first. Too many lives depend on it." Kaeliss moaned again.

It was the last thing Pod wanted to do. But the other girl was right, and Fiarin had died for the sake of these plants. She scooped them up and packed them away again as fast as she could. Every fiber of her being screamed at her to get away from this place *now*!

At last she was done. With Kaeliss leaning heavily against her, Pod led the way across the clearing. Something about the stump frightened her and she gave it as wide a berth as she could.

It seemed to take forever but at last they were into the woods on the other side. Pod needed all her strength to force a way through the underbrush. It was as if the woods were determined to keep them in the clearing. Whichever way she turned there were thickets of brambles whose thorns caught at them, snagged deep into their clothing, held them back. They had to fight desperately for every finger-length of progress. Their only reprieve was that the rain ended at some point in their nightmare journey.

At last they had to stop. Kaeliss sank down, her face grey with exhaustion and pain, cradling her arm. Looking at her, Pod knew they'd gone as far as they could. If the madman was still after them, it was here they would make their stand.

But until then, she would do what she could for Kaeliss. Drawing her knife, Pod cut some sticks and smoothed them as much as she could. Using strips cut from the spare tunic from Fiarin's pack, she quickly fashioned a rough splint and a sling. Then she found two long, sturdy sticks and began whittling one to a point.

"If he comes here, jab at him as best you can," Pod said. "Until then, rest as much as you can. I'll take first watch."

Kaeliss silently nodded. Moving carefully, she lay down, head pillowed on her pack. Soon she was fast asleep.

Pod dropped the first stick next to Kaeliss and began work on the second. Pathetic as these "spears" were, at least they were weapons of a sort.

And something—anything!—is better than nothing, she grimly told herself. *If only Kiga was here. . . .* Hot tears filled her eyes. She wiped them away; the last thing they needed was for her to slice her hand open because she couldn't see straight.

With each stroke of the knife, with each sliver that fell away, Pod thought over and over, *Kiga, stop hunting and find me! Stop hunting and find me!*

When she was done, she set the spear down next to her, then pulled up her knees, rested her head against them, and cried. Even as she realized that sitting still was a mistake, exhaustion swept over her and she fell asleep.

It was the rattle of leaves that woke her some time later. Pod lifted her head and rubbed her bleary eyes. "Kiga?" she whispered.

Kaeliss sat up. "Oh, thank the gods he's back!"

"Yes, I am," a soft voice said. Arlim's face leered at them through the branches and he laughed, low and chilling.

Sixty

It seemed a lifetime, but was likely less than a candlemark later that the worst of the storm passed. He listened as the thunder retreated, then slipped out from beneath the pine tree.

It was still raining, but he was running out of time. Remembering the "brightness" he'd felt earlier, Linden stretched out his senses. Everything else in this forest was tainted, but not that. Who could it be? Was it someone that could help him?

But to his disappointment, he felt nothing but the evil that seemed to permeate everything here. Sighing, he walked quickly to the center of the clearing. Turning his face up to the rain, he let himself flow into Change.

Moments later, a large, red dragon crouched in the clearing, hind legs tensed. A mighty leap, and Linden beat the air with his wings, fighting to clear the treetops. With the rain streaming from his wings, Linden once more began to search.

Candlemarks passed as Linden flew over a new part of the forest. It was far larger than he'd thought it would be and try as he might, he could not pinpoint the source of the evil. He was desperate now; he *had* to find that witch spruce. If his theory about the wood in Leet's harp was correct, Raven had a chance. But without that proof, the younger Yerrin would hang, and time was running out.

And still nothing. Linden cursed and dug deeper—dangerously so—into the magic that bound the two halves of his soul together. Any more and he feared he would wake Rathan, the dragon half of his soul.

Just as he feared it was all for naught, he felt that elusive spark again. It came and went, first flaring brightly, then dwindling so that he feared to lose it. Whoever it was, it burned bright and pure, and like nothing he'd ever touched before.

Not knowing what else to do, Linden waited for one of the "flares" and sideslipped through the air toward it. To his frustration, it died down once more as he neared it. Then he found it again, but in a different place, as if whoever made it was moving through the forest. Once more he followed, losing it, finding it, losing it again as it zigged and zagged seemingly at random.

The sun slipped lower in the sky. He peered through breaks in the trees, but could see nothing of his quarry, and whoever it was avoided the few clearings below.

Once more it disappeared. Linden cursed long and hard in his mind; he wanted to howl his frustration, but didn't want to terrify whoever was below. The roar of an angry dragon was a fearful thing to hear.

Then, just as he thought he'd lost it for good, the spark returned.

Who are you? Linden asked, seeking the other's mind.

What he found astonished him: no thoughts, no words, just a welter of swirling emotions and fierce, driving instincts.

An animal? The realization so shocked him that for a moment he forgot he was supposed to be flying. An instant later he spread his wings once more, catching himself just in time. *What in Gifnu's hells kind of animal could it be?*

There was no sort of animal he'd ever heard of that felt so . . . intelligent, was the best he could think of. *So very aware of itself.* Linden made one last effort to reach it, extending his magic to the limit, opening his mind as far as he could.

He touched the mind below him and held the contact; at the same time, he "heard" in his mind faint words, as if of a far-off echo.

Stop hunting! Come to me! The fear and longing and desolation behind those words tore at him.

Once more the spark below flared, this time so bright that Linden caught his breath at it. A love so pure that it could put many a truehuman to shame, a desperation to stand once more by the side of . . .

Of its person, Linden realized. *Gods have mercy, I think that's a brother-in-fur down there.*

At once the spark ceased its random wanderings and raced, arrow-straight, through the forest. Somehow, when he'd stretched his mind to the animal below, he must have acted as a link between a familiar and its Beast Healer.

What, by all the gods, is a Beast Healer doing here? he wondered. *And why is his familiar so far away that he couldn't call it back?* All Linden could think was that the Beast Healer was injured or ill.

He turned in the air to follow. As much as he needed to help Raven, this might be a matter of life or death to another. Perhaps the Beast Healer was no more than lost, but he would not leave someone in this forest of evil.

The trees were still too thick for him to see what he followed, but he had no difficulty now, the spark burned so steadily and bright. Whatever it was, judging by the speed it made, it was certainly larger than a cat. It wasn't, he thought, a horse. There was too much underbrush for something so large to move so quickly, and he was certain that if it had been near that size, he would have seen it through gaps in the branches.

Then he remembered the fierceness of the mind he'd touched. No, this was no eater of grass. A dog or a wolf was his best guess.

From his vantage point, Linden saw that his invisible guide was leading him toward the ruins of Worton and the section of the forest he'd deemed unlikely to hold Gull's remains. *Once this is done, I'll work out from there to continue searching,* he thought with resignation, certain now that he'd never find the witch spruce in time, but refusing to give in to despair. He'd search until the last moment.

Ahead of him he could see two small clearings; although they weren't close to each other, they lay in a line along the course his guide was running. Unless his quarry changed its course, it would pass through the first clearing in a few moments. Linden winged ahead so that he could see the animal when it broke from the cover of the trees.

Linden caught the barest glimpse of a brown shape as it burst from the trees, hurtled across the little glade, and disappeared once more. He snorted in surprise, smoke curling from his nostrils. What on earth had *that* been?

No dog or wolf; that he was certain of. Its shape and long fur, and the way it moved, were wrong. He would have said small bear, but not with a tail that long.

He cursed when he finally identified the creature: a *ghulon,* one of the fierce, solitary predators that made their home in deep woods. He hadn't been chasing a brother-in-fur; he'd been wasting time following a wild animal.

You fool. You're so desperate to help someone, anyone, your mind's playing tricks on you. There's no Beast Healer out here.

He tilted on the breeze and turned away from the futile chase.

Sixty-one

The two young women jumped up and ran, Kaeliss grunting with pain at every step as she cradled her arm against herself. They grabbed their packs, but only Pod thought to grab her sharpened stick.

This time the branches and thorns let them pass, but only along one path. *Like a giant funnel spider's web.* Pod knew they were being herded, yet they had no choice. Ahead lay hope, however faint it might be. Behind them . . .

They came out into the clearing with the wide stump once more. Pod pushed Kaeliss around to the other side of it. Arlim sauntered out of the underbrush like a man who had all the time in the world.

"Should we try to run through the woods?" Kaeliss whispered.

"No. I'm certain the woods will hold us here," Pod whispered back. "Then he'd catch us for certain. This way . . . maybe he'll make a mistake."

She wished he would try to jump up onto the stump; perhaps she could stab him with her spear as he scrambled across.

Instead he sidled around. Pod and Kaeliss matched him step for step, always keeping the stump between themselves and the madman.

Arlim tittered. "Such a charming dance, pretty girls. How long can you keep it up?" He held up his knife and turned it this way and that, making the light flash on the blade. "It would be easier, so much easier, to come to me now. So, so much easier . . ."

His voice was soothing as he droned on and on. Pod blinked; to her horror, it was akin to the "voice" that Beast Healers used to calm fractious animals. And now she thought she could hear a melody in it.

Beside her, Kaeliss came to a stop. Pod told herself she had to fight whatever Arlim was doing. Instead the spear drooped in her hand, then fell from her nerveless fingers.

With a triumphant howl, Arlim leaped onto the face of the stump, his knife held high. Pod screamed, knowing she'd never reach her spear in time.

But before Arlim could take that final step and fall upon her, a tremendous roar split the sky above the clearing. She fell to her knees, as did Kaeliss and Arlim, covered her ears, and looked up.

A red dragon glared down at them, its wings beating furiously to hold it in place. Its head turned so that one glittering eye was fixed on Arlim. It roared once more and Pod cowered from the fury in its voice. Then the dragon tucked in its neck and tail and, to her amazement, folded its wings. It dropped straight down like a stone.

A red mist enveloped the falling dragon, shrank, and became a man. Pod clapped a hand to her mouth; could even a Dragonlord survive a fall from that height without harm?

He landed heavily, close to the stump, falling to his hands and knees and shaking his head as if dazed. A long, blond Yerrin clan braid slipped over his shoulder.

Arlim launched himself from the stump, landing on the Dragonlord before he could stand. They went down together in a tangle, rolling over and over. Pod saw Arlim's knife flash as he struck at the Dragonlord.

A moment later Arlim flew through the air as the Dragonlord heaved him off. He fled into the woods.

The Dragonlord staggered to his feet and turned to where she stood wide-eyed with Kaeliss. She saw that he favored one leg and that a sleeve of his tunic was slashed.

As soon as she saw the wine-colored birthmark that spread across his right temple to his eyelid, Pod knew who he was. "Linden Rathan," she cried out in joy.

"Pod, you and your friend need to stay here while—" He broke off, staring at the stump. "Oh dear gods—the one place you *can't* stay."

He cursed under his breath. "Stay here, but as far away from that thing as you can while I hunt—"

A shrill scream from the woods cut him off. A second scream died in a torrent of snarls. In their turn, the snarls faded into an awful silence.

Linden Rathan ran a hand through his hair. "It's over," he said wearily. "Kiga found him."

"Kiga?" Pod asked, hardly daring to believe him.

"Yes, Kiga. You have him to thank for leading me here. I remembered at the last moment what Conor had told me about your brother-in-fur. I'd thought I'd wasted time following a wild animal."

A movement in the underbrush caught Pod's eye. The branches parted to reveal wild, fury-filled eyes above a snarling, bloodstained muzzle. But the instant that terrifying gaze fell upon her, the rage vanished. Kiga burst from the undergrowth and threw himself at her feet.

She fell to her knees beside him and hugged him. Burying her face in his filthy, matted fur, she cried with joy. For his part, Kiga whuffled and whimpered as he tried to fit his bulk into her lap.

At last she looked up at Linden Rathan. "Did Conor send you to look for us, Your Grace? How did he know we were in trouble?"

Linden Rathan shook his head. "I had no idea you were here or in danger. That I found you was a gift from the gods. I came searching for this," he said, and pointed to the stump.

Kaeliss joined them now. "A stump? But why, Your Grace? What is it?"

"It was," Linden Rathan answered slowly, "a witch spruce." He passed his hand over his eyes. "The witch spruce that was planted over Gull the Blood Drinker to trap his soul."

Sixty-two

Suddenly weary beyond belief, Linden looked around the glade. A splash of color caught his eye: red flowers scattered across a trail of crushed mushrooms.

Kiga squirmed off of Pod's lap and loped across to him. Then the *ghulon* rolled over onto his foot, begging to have its stomach rubbed. Without thinking, Linden bent to indulge it. The movement made his arm throb.

"We need to leave here. Now," he said as he stood up. "There's another clearing, a large one near here. We'll go there."

He led the way, grimacing at the pain in his right ankle. From the feel of it, it was sprained. If Maurynna ever found out he'd let himself drop from so high up, she'd be furious. He was lucky he hadn't broken a leg or worse.

Linden glanced over his shoulder. The young woman with the splinted arm walked behind him, with Pod following her, and Kiga as rear guard. "And what is your name, young Wort Hunter?" he asked.

"Kaeliss, Dragonlord," came the shy answer. "Kaeliss Ageslin."

"Well and well, Kaeliss Ageslin, the place we're making for is large enough for me to Change, as this is not. And even if it were, I'll not have the evil here touch my own magic.

"Once I've Changed, I can use a dragon's Healing fire on that arm."

The girl's eyes lit with excitement.

He examined his own arm. The sleeve was slashed open and blood oozed sluggishly from a cut on his arm. He'd taken worse when he was a mercenary, he decided. When they were away from this foul place, he'd ask Pod to bandage it.

While they walked, Pod and Kaeliss took turns telling him their tale until they reached the ruins of Worton.

Linden shook his head. *Even if he meant well, it was damned irresponsible of that Fiarin, taking two young women—hellfire; Pod's still a girl—into such a place.* But the gods had already levied punishment upon him; Linden would think no more ill of the man.

Now his arm throbbed painfully and he cursed under his breath in Yerrin. Curious, he looked at the cut; it hadn't seemed deep enough to hurt so much.

The flesh looked red and inflamed. *Odd; I've had worse. So why—damnation! Could the bastard have had poison on the blade?*

"What is it?" Pod asked. "What's wrong?"

"I'm wondering if the blade was tainted," Linden said.

Kaeliss bit her lip. "It might well be. Arlim was an expert on herbs and could concoct many medicines as well as a Simpler." She tugged one-handed at a pack. "I could make a poultice of—"

"Not yet. After I've Changed back into human form." He sent the two girls to wait by the edge of the forest, warning Pod to keep a good hold on Kiga.

He loped to the center of the clearing, wondering if he'd get back to Balyaranna in time. Tomorrow was the last day of grace for Raven.

Linden shook his head. Time to worry later; first he had to get Pod and her friend to safety. So he stood quietly, letting go of the evil he'd seen, putting aside his pain, the fear of poison, reaching within himself and finding the peace he needed. When it filled him, he let himself flow into Change.

Kaeliss squealed in surprise. Pod made no sound, but her eyes were huge and so was her smile.

A heartbeat later, he stretched his long neck around. *Kaeliss,* he said, *come stand before me. Pod, we might as well do something about all those scratches, so get yourself over here as well.*

The two young women came to stand before him. "I'd always wondered if I'd dreamed seeing you in dragon form," Pod said. "I was so young. . . ."

So you were, yet you weren't afraid then, either. Now off with that splint. . . . Good—now hold fast, brave hearts, and don't be afraid.

With that Linden opened his mouth and let the blue-green flames of a dragon's Healing fire wash over Pod and Kaeliss. A heartbeat later it was over; Kaeliss moved her arm this way and that as if she couldn't believe it was healed and Pod looked at her arms and patted her face, then whooped in delight.

"Thank you! I hadn't realized how much they stung until we stopped."

Good. Now if you'll both move back once more, I—

"No," Pod said firmly. "It's my turn." And she held her hands above the scratch that looked so insignificant on a dragon's foreleg.

Pod—no! After what happened to you trying to Heal Fiarin, I forbid it!

She grinned impudently up at him as the Healing haze blossomed around her hands. "But you're not human *now,* are you?"

There was a burst of warmth, the haze disappeared, and Pod pulled her hands back. The scratch was gone.

Linden laughed, a deep *hough!* that sent smoke curling from his nostrils. *Who would have guessed?*

"Now that ankle," Pod ordered.

Amused at her stern tone, Linden meekly stretched his hind leg out. Once more a green haze flowed from Pod's hands, and a welcome burst of warmth erased the pain in his leg.

She stepped back and set her hands on her hips. "There! That's done."

My thanks, Pod of Grey Holt. Now I must return as quickly as I can first to Bylith, then to Balyaranna. A friend there is in grave danger and what I've learned here might save him.

Two alarmed faces looked up at him. Kiga, who had come to join his person, sensed Pod's fright and whined.

Linden went on, *But I can't leave you two here; one evil is gone, but these woods are still tainted. So—Pod, can you pick up Kiga and hold tight to him? Good. I'm taking you two directly to the nearest Healwort chapterhouse. I know where that is. Very well—let us be off!*

With that, he carefully caught up the two apprentices and the *ghulon,* cradling them in his forelegs. Then he reared up and with a massive leap, launched himself into the air.

Shrieks of excitement and glee filled his ears as he spiraled up into the sky. He listened with amusement as Pod and Kaeliss excitedly pointed things out to each other as he flew. Kiga seemed content to be cradled in his person's arms. For that Linden silently thanked the gods. He didn't think even a *ghulon*'s claws could cut through his scales, but it was not a thing he wished to test right now.

Dawn was breaking when Linden spotted the chapterhouse. He circled the compound to the excitement of the early risers below. Then, at Kaeliss's direction, he landed in an empty pasture. He set Pod and Kaeliss down; Kiga wriggled free and thumped to the ground with a relieved *whuff!*

You're safe now, Linden said. *And I must go. Run!*

They ran. Linden waited, begrudging every moment, but he wanted them well away; the blast of air from his wings could well knock them over. *No sense Healing them just to hurt them again,* he told himself.

At the edge of the pasture, Pod stopped. Hands to mouth, she shouted, "Give Conor my love!" Then she hopped the fence.

Linden roared in reply and leapt back into the air as the first astonished Worties reached the two young women. An instant later he was racing through the sky to Bylith.

As he flew, he considered all that he'd learned. He'd been right: the witch spruce planted over one of the most heinous killers he'd ever heard of was gone, may the gods help them all. That dark soul roamed the earth once more, to live— and kill—again. For the tree of warding had been cut down not by mistake, but to become the dark, twisted soul of a harp; a harp used to snare others within its evil.

Arlim had been as much a victim as those he'd killed. And in the end, he'd paid with his life as well.

But Leet . . . He had set all this in motion without regard for anyone or anything. Yet . . . *why* had he done this?

In the end, it didn't matter. *He'll pay for this,* Linden vowed as he flew. *No matter what it takes—Leet will pay.*

He needed to speak with Charilon as soon as he reached Bylith. Then it was time for another visit to the house of Thomelin the luthier.

Once more Linden found himself riding Nightsong through the streets of Bylith. But this time he rode with a picked group of the city guards, their captain at his side.

They rode in silence. Linden turned over in his mind the things Charilon had told him about Leet, the tales and rumors still whispered in the village they had both come from.

None of it excused what Leet had done; it merely added cowardice to his already foul deeds.

They reached the luthier's house. "Clear everyone from the workroom," Linden ordered. He watched the men enter the workshop.

He waited outside until one of the men gave him a sign. Once inside, he stared at the table over the hiding place. Suddenly the image of the pile of bloodstained clothing in Arlim's hut filled his mind. With a blistering curse, Linden did what he seldom allowed himself to do: become enraged.

He grabbed the edge of the table and heaved. The bolts ripped out of the floor with a shriek. He tossed the heavy oaken table easily across the room. More than one of the soldiers watching muttered something between a curse and a prayer.

Now it was time to face what was left of Gull the Blood Drinker's soul.

Sixty-three

"What do you mean, 'Maurynna's gone'?" Raven demanded. "She said she would stay while Linden and Shima went on their missions!" He sank down onto his narrow bed, his knees weak with terror. "It's the last day," he whispered. "To-morrow they'll, they'll—"

"I'm sorry, lad," his great-uncle said gently. It was clear from Otter's voice that he was just as baffled by Maurynna's seeming desertion—and just as afraid. "The servants said that she left in the middle of the night."

Raven buried his head in his hands. Had she abandoned him? Did she know his cause was hopeless and fled because she couldn't stand to see her best friend hang? He rocked back and forth, feeling sick, hardly hearing his great-uncle's words of comfort.

"Perhaps Linden mindcalled her and sent her off to lo—aauuggghhh!"

Apologies, Otter—I didn't mean to scare you like that. I didn't even know you were in there. I just wanted to make certain that Raven hadn't . . . gone some-where.

Raven slowly looked up and stared at the window. He was dreaming. He had to be. It was simply not possible that a dragon was looking in at one of the cell's windows, fiery red scales glittering in the early sunlight. Not possible at—

Then he recognized the dragon. It was possible. "Lleld!"

Hello! Lleld said cheerfully. *Shima will be here soon—he's still tired and fly-ing more slowly than is his wont. I came ahead just to make certain no one here got any . . . ideas.*

He still couldn't believe it. Surely his eyes and mind were playing tricks on him. He'd dreamed of a rescue like this. No, he wasn't really seeing a dragon's head in that window, with what he could see of the neck going up and up to—

"Are you sitting on the *roof*?"

As best I can. At least it's one of those rounded ones. They're not too bad. The pointy ones poke you in the stomach. Now that I know you're safe, I'm going to

*land. The books are slipping and I'm getting the most gods-rotted kink in my
neck stretching down to look in at you.*

With that, Lleld's head disappeared. Raven ran to the window, barely beating
his great-uncle to it, in time to see her glide to the castle courtyard. He caught a
glimpse of a couple of small bundles clutched in one foreleg as she spiraled down.

Raven turned to Otter as the first stirrings of hope rose again. A huge smile
spread across his face.

But his great-uncle was still watching Lleld. "What I want to know," he said,
"is *how* she knows the 'pointy ones poke you in the stomach.' "

The courtroom was filled nigh to bursting. Even the balcony was packed. They
would be fortunate if someone didn't fall off before the day was through, Raven
thought. He clasped his hands in his lap. *At least this time they didn't strap me
down.*

To his partial relief, Otter, Lleld, and a very tired-looking Shima sat right in
the front. Conor sat behind them. Lleld held a large book on her lap, now and
again running her thumb across the leather cover.

The only two empty seats in the room were to Shima's left. *So where are
Maurynna and Linden? Especially Maurynna?* Raven searched the crowd for
them. They were not in the room—but someone else was. Once again Bard Leet
smiled at him, a tiny smile of cold amusement, gone an instant later.

Why does he hate me? What have I ever done to him?

Then Lord Asiah, the Justice of Balyaranna, entered the room. He went straight
to the podium and rapped his staff against the floor. "I call Priestess Aelwitha to
the witness's chair."

Shuffling sounds came from the witnesses' balcony. Coming slowly down the
stairs was an old woman dressed in the black robes of a priestess of the Crone,
her face wrinkled as a winter apple beneath the distinctive gable hood of her
calling. She carried something wrapped in cloth. Around her waist was a belt of
links. Links that were small silver skulls. . . .

Raven stared at her in horror. What was a lich priestess doing here? By all the
gods, weren't they at least going to let the Dragonlords present their case for
him? Were they planning to just pass sentence, hang him, and give his body
straight to her?

Calm down! Lleld said in his mind. *Gods—with a face that easy to read, I
hope you leave the horse trading to your aunt. The priestess isn't here for you.*

How do you know?

*Because executed murderers don't go to the Crone for the ritual washing and
anointing, remember? They're cast straight into a pit of quicklime. Now get hold
of yourself. Linden is on his way. He's flying as fast as he can, he said,* Lleld said
confidently.

But where's Rynna? he asked in despair.

The cheerful confidence wavered. *I don't know,* Lleld said softly. *No one knows.*

Lord Asiah assisted the priestess to the chair and handed her into it. Once more he thumped the floor with his staff. Silence fell upon the room.

"Something of interest has been brought to my attention. While I do not be-lieve it has any bearing upon this case, it is seems to contradict certain facts that had been presented to this court before. Priestess?"

The priestess sat up straight, her wrinkled face serene. "I am ready, my lord," she answered in a thin, reedy voice.

Lord Asiah said, "Your name, priestess?"

"I am Aelwitha, a lich priestess of the Crone at her temple here in Balyaranna."

"You were one of those who prepared Lord Tirael for his burial, are you not?"

Lady Portis buried her face in her hands. "My boy. My poor bonny boy . . ." She wept softly.

Priestess Aelwitha looked at her sympathetically and sketched a sign of bless-ing. The air shimmered for a moment. "I am. A younger priestess and three aco-lytes assist me, but I am the one who anoints the dead with holy oils and speaks the prayers. It is under my guidance that the others undress and bathe the de-parted one."

The Justice of Balyaranna nodded. "Will you tell us what you found that struck you as unusual?"

"My lord, even in the deepest sanctuary in the temple, we had heard of what happened to Lord Tirael, how he'd been struck down, and him unarmed. Not even a knife for eating on his belt. That's why we were so surprised when we found this."

She carefully unwrapped the bundle in her lap, folding each layer of cloth back like the petals of a flower opening. There was a gasp of surprise as she held up a long, narrow-bladed dagger, its hilt wrapped in wire. No fashionable young lord's ornament, this; this was a soldier's weapon, a blade meant for killing.

Lord Asiah's voice rang out over the buzz of speculation. "Where did you find it, Priestess Aelwitha?"

The priestess waited until the whispers subsided. "Hidden in Lord Tirael's right boot."

The Justice took the dagger from her. "Thank you, priestess. That will be all."

Priestess Aelwitha bowed her head slightly, then took her leave, her robes rus-tling as she paced slowly down the aisle.

When the door closed once more behind her, Lord Asiah brought the dagger to Tirael's parents sitting in the front row. "Do either of you recognize this weapon, my lord, my lady?"

They bent over it, studying the deadly weapon. Both shook their heads.

"Have you any idea what Lord Tirael was doing in Lord Sevrynel's gardens that night? I understand that he was . . . not invited," Lord Asiah said delicately.

Both Lord and Lady Portis blushed before shaking their heads again. Portis said, "But what difference does this make, Lord Justice? It was in his boot, not his hand."

"It only means that he was not unarmed, my lord. The record must be changed, that is all," Lord Asiah replied soothingly, inclining his head toward the scribe. She glanced up and nodded, her stylus gliding across the wax tablet on the table before her.

And I'm still as guilty as ever, Raven thought, watching her. He felt sick.

Lord Asiah turned the dagger over and over in his hands, studying it. "My lord and lady, one last question—have you any idea *why* your son was carrying such a weapon?"

"No doubt because he was afraid of him!" Lord Portis stabbed a finger at Raven.

"If so, it seems odd that he didn't draw it when he came upon his enemy in the dark," the Justice observed as he lay the dagger upon the table.

Suddenly both Lleld and Shima sat up straighter, their eyes unfocused. Surprise, even shock flitted across their faces.

What's that about? Raven wondered.

Then Lleld nodded. She stood up, the book clasped to her breast. "Lord Asiah—I would like to present the first part of *our* evidence," the little Dragonlord announced.

Sixty-four

Raven watched, baffled, as Lleld set the large, heavy book down on the lectern and turned the pages. He glanced over to see if Shima knew what she was up to and caught sight of Leet once more.

But this time there was no cruel smile on the bard's face. Instead he stared at the little red-haired Dragonlord with frightening intensity.

"Here we are," Lleld murmured. She rested her hand upon the page and looked up. Her light, clear voice rang through the room. "My lords and ladies, I have here a history from the library of Dragonskeep. A history written by one Lord Culwen of Cassori—one of your own."

Raven looked at Leet once more. Was it his imagination or did the bard look alarmed? As Lleld began reading, Raven watched Leet.

"Know all that there is one who surpasses all other killers for foulness and cruelty," Lleld read. "For reasons I do not pretend to understand, while all murder is foul, it is somehow much worse when a murderer perverts a thing of beauty for his vile purposes.

"Such a one was Gullanin Wortman of the village of Worton, known to all now as Gull the Blood Drinker. Here I shall set down a shortened account of his history. I will follow it with the full tales told me by those still living near where the village of Worton once stood. Some háve been proven true, some, no doubt, are made up. All are terrifying.

"Worton was famous for the rare and useful herbs in the nearby forests, especially the herb known as King's Blood. All the village prospered from the trade, but the most successful was the family called Wortman, though all their names have been lost but one. They had an uncanny ability to find that most rare and virtuous of herbs, King's Blood, and built their good fortune upon it."

Lord Asiah interrupted. "Dragonlord, with the utmost respect, what has this to do with this trial? It's just a scary story for a stormy night."

Lleld said levelly, "My lord Justice, it has everything to do with why we're

here today. Nor was it merely a 'scary story,' my lord. I remember Worton. I . . .
I had friends there. They died by Gull the Blood Drinker's hand."

When the uneasy murmuring died down, she continued reading. "They alone
in Worton had a secret method of preparing King's Blood so that there was no
loss of its virtue. So successful were they that they built a long stone barn for
their work, for that herb needs darkness.

"The family's fortunes rose. But then the gods turned their faces from them.
The oldest son, Gullanin, a man known for his fair voice, lost the first joint of one
forefinger and his brother lost a hand when the heavy blade of a root chopper
slipped. It is thought that was when Gullanin first tasted blood, a taste that woke
a raging darkness inside him, when his brother's blood sprayed upon him."

Raven heard the door quietly open and shut, but like everyone else, his attention was on the smallest Dragonlord. She didn't even glance up at the faint noise.

"Not long after, disaster struck again. The mother disappeared while searching
for herbs. Her body was never found. The same happened to the father, another
brother, the two married sisters, and their husbands and children.

"Soon only Gull and the one-handed brother remained. The village elders
pressed Gull to reveal his family's secret of treating the herbs lest the knowledge
be lost. Their pleas fell upon deaf ears. The one-handed brother disappeared and
Gull became more secretive than ever. The villagers heard his muffled singing
from inside the stone barn as he worked late into the night.

"Then the villagers began to disappear one after another. They grew fearful
and haggard as they went about their work in the forest, wondering what evil
spirit they had angered. Only Gull seemed unaffected.

"Some blamed the Children of the Forest. Others blamed demons and ghosts.
In time, they feared the forest that had nurtured them too much to enter it anymore. Instead they huddled around their hearths and prayed. Yet all too often
they would wake in the morning and find another bed empty. And all they knew
was that every one of them had 'heard' a wordless song of haunting beauty in
their dreams the night before.

"So it went until a family of tinkers came to the village."

Lleld looked up from the book. "You all know the rest of the story, I'm sure.
How the tinker's son Norrim awoke to see his sister rise from her pallet and go to
the stone barn. How he followed and found Gull waiting for her—Gull and a
knife with an edge that could cut moonlight, as the tales say. How Norrim fought
Gull and won, though Gull tried desperately to ensnare him with the song that
had caught so many in its web.

"He won, my lords and ladies, because Norrim was one of those unfortunate
few whom Auvrian, the god of music, turns his face from. To Norrim, all music
sounded like cacophony."

She closed the book firmly. "My lord Portis—was your son one of those un-
fortunates?"

Portis shook his head.

"Does anyone know if the stable boy Robie is?" Lleld asked.

"He is not," said Conor over the surprised murmur that arose at her question. For once Raven agreed with the audience; what had the stable boy to do with this? Conor went on, "His father has mentioned that the boy loves music."

"As does Raven," said Lleld. "Moreover, I've heard Raven sing, and sing well."

Lord Asiah shook his head. He looked confused. "Dragonlord, I'm not certain what you intend to prove with this. True, Raven Redhawkson *has* made a claim that some kind of music possessed him. Are you trying to say that since Gull the Blood Drinker found a way to do it, someone might have as well?"

"No," said a deep—and tired—voice from the back of the room. "What she's saying is that Gull the Blood Drinker walks again."

Sixty-five

As Linden leaned against the wall, gathering his strength and waiting for the clamor to subside, he felt Maurynna's startled mindtouch.

Your tunic is torn! What *happened to you? Were you attacked?*

Yes, but no lasting harm done, love. I'll tell you later, he promised. He glanced around but didn't see her. Odd; she had to be where she could see *him,* so why couldn't he see her? *Where are you?*

Later—for both of us, she said enigmatically.

He didn't have time to sort out what she meant by that. He needed to concentrate on what he was about to do. Gods, he was so tired. . . .

He walked slowly down the aisle to the lectern. Charilon had told him so many things that, exhausted as he was, he desperately hoped he'd kept it all straight as he'd strung together all the bits and pieces he knew—or guessed—like beads on a necklace as he flew back to Balyaranna. It had all made sense to him at the time; may the gods grant that he was right.

Still, there was one thing that *didn't* fit in. Worse, there was no way that he could see around it, either. And that worried him. But this was all he had.

He reached the front of the room and turned to face the assembled lords and ladies. They stared and muttered to each other at his appearance. "My apologies for appearing before you like this, but I have just returned from a journey—" He looked for a certain face in the crowd; surely the man would be here if he had guessed right . . . ah, there! "—to the north of Kelneth."

Though drops of sweat started on Leet's forehead, his expression never changed: polite interest, nothing more. Looking straight into the bard's eyes, Linden went on, "I found where once Worton had stood. I found the remains of the old stone barn, where Gull the Blood Drinker lured his victims with his song. Where he cut their throats, drank their blood, and then buried them under its dirt floor.

"I also found in Worton-that-was a man possessed by the evil lingering in the forest. He, too, had killed and buried victims. His name was Arlim. He was hunting two young women when I got there."

Linden kept his gaze locked on Leet's. Now the sweat dripped down the bard's face; yet still there was only that mask of polite interest.

Linden said softly into the uneasy silence, "But worst of all, I found that the witch spruce that had been planted over Gull the Blood Drinker's grave to trap his soul had been cut down, freeing his evil once again. The stump was there—but the tree itself was gone." He paused. "But I know what was done with the wood."

The color drained from Leet's face, leaving two spots of red high on his cheeks, like a man with a fever. Still, not a muscle twitched in that impassive countenance.

Once again a tumult of voices rang out. Swaying on his feet, Linden let it wash over him. Two nights without sleep and the long distances he'd flown so quickly had drained him. He shut his eyes for a moment as Lord Asiah thumped the heel of his staff on the floor again and again, shouting for quiet.

Lord Portis stood up. "Do you expect me to believe this man Arlim somehow forced Raven Redhawkson to kill my son all the way from northern Kelneth?" he asked in disgust.

"No. Do you remember that I said Arlim was hunting two young women? He died at the fangs of one girl's brother-in-fur, a *ghulon,* known to most of you as a woods dog or wolvering," Linden told him.

Conor's strangled gasp sounded like thunder in the quiet room.

Asiah frowned. "Then who do you think is responsible? And why would he or she do such a thing?"

Linden rubbed the back of his neck. He hoped Charilon knew what he was talking about or else he was about to slander a man and make a prize fool of himself. He took a deep breath. "I will answer the second question first, my lord.

"Like most things, my lord, the answer begins in the past. On the estate of one Rade Welkin, Lord Sansy of Sansy, now sleeping peacefully in his grave.

"He married twice. Much to his family's dismay, his second wife was a beautiful young girl from the weavers' hall in the village. She bore him a son and a daughter who were the delight of his old age. But then the whispers started: the children were not his. Did Lord Sansy believe those whispers? No one knows, for he died soon after they started. If the rumors were true, no one knew for certain who the man was—but some in the village suspected. Didn't they, Leet?"

"Lies!" Leet hissed. "How dare you? This is nothing but vile lies!"

"Is it, Leet? Then look in your mirror. That doesn't lie. While I've not met your son, Agon, I *have* met your daughter, Romissa. She has the same cleft in her chin that you have—the same chin that your mother had, Leet. Your *mother*—not your father. Charilon remembers her well, you know. It was seeing *her* chin on Rade's supposed 'children' that set the village gossips' tongues wagging, he said."

"Dear gods!" Lord Lenslee blurted out. He turned to gape at Leet. "So that's why you were so upset when that boy Arnath died—he was your grandson! I couldn't understand it at the time. Why should you care so much about a bastard? When you refused to visit your old home while your stepmother lived, that seemed to confirm that her children were sired not by your father, but rather by some other man. I remember my parents wagging their heads over it. Your *grandson*! . . . "

"And that was the reason Summer Lightning was poisoned. It was also why your son had to die, my lord and lady Portis. For it was Tirael who set Arnath on Summer Lightning's back, was it not, when the boy and his father broke the journey they were on so that they might see that fair? Well, my lord?" Linden asked harshly.

Portis would not meet his eyes. Linden went on relentlessly, "You know full well it was, my lord. Just as Tirael knew that Summer Lightning was vicious, had even killed a groom. He tossed Arnath onto Summer Lightning's bare back. But Tirael was often cruel to those he thought beneath him—such as a boy who had only one noble parent—if that parent was even truly noble at all.

"Of course Arnath fell off at the first buck—and Summer Lightning crushed his skull with a single blow." *Poor child—victim of two vicious creatures,* Linden thought in disgust. *The horse should have been put down long before. And as for Tirael . . .* He thought over the stories he'd heard of the cruel young lordling. *His parents have much to answer for, turning a blind eye to their son's true nature all those years.*

Once more Linden caught Leet's gaze with his own. "But you didn't dare take your own revenge, did you, Leet? First, it would mean you'd have to give up being a bard. Besides, your son, Agon, had accepted wergild for his nephew's life. So you ensorcelled an innocent boy to poison Summer Lightning, and Raven to kill Tirael."

Leet stood up, hands clenched at his sides, shaking. His face was white and pinched. "I never thought I'd hear such a pack of foul, disgusting lies from a Dragonlord!"

A buzz of agreement greeted the bard's accusation. Linden flinched from the righteous fury in the bard's voice. By the gods—had he guessed wrong? For one long, horrible moment he feared he had. Then he remembered the power in a bard's voice, what he'd found in the hut—and what waited in a room nearby, guarded by magic and swords.

"I stand by my words, Leet," he said, his voice edged in steel.

"Then you are a fool, Dragonlord," Leet replied venomously. "And I will make you pay for those lies."

Sixty-six

Maurynna peered through the screen shrouding the witness balcony as her soultwin and Leet glared at each other like two wolves over a kill. But then, to her surprise, Leet smiled. It was a cold smile that chilled one's soul like a howling northern gale; a smile that mocked. She wanted to slap it off his face.

"And how did I supposedly accomplish these fell deeds, Dragonlord? Can you tell me—nay, tell these good lords and ladies—how?"

"Your harp's sound—"

"My *harp*?" Leet interrupted in astonishment. "My harp is—what? Haunted? Like the music the prisoner *claims* he heard?" Leet pressed the back of one hand to his forehead with an exaggerated flourish. "Oh, oh!"

The hand dropped and Leet grew serious once more. "While a fine notion for a journeyman bard scaring apprentices, Your Grace, it is nothing but a fantasy."

Once more his face changed; now he looked grave, even sad. If she didn't know better, Maurynna thought sourly, she would have thought that there stood a man, who, though unjustly accused, felt only sorrow at a Dragonlord's folly. She didn't know exactly what proof Linden had found, but if her soultwin said Leet was guilty, he must know what he was doing . . . she hoped.

Leet went on, "And fantasies, I am sorry to say, Your Grace, have no place in a court of law." Now the bard turned in place, surveying the room, gathering all eyes to him before turning back to face the front of the room again. His voice rang out. "My lord Justice—while I am not the one on trial here, I find myself accused of a heinous crime. I beg an indulgence of you to prove my innocence. Will you grant it?"

Maurynna saw Linden tense. *Leet's up to something and it has Linden worried.* She held her breath in an agony of anticipation.

Lord Asiah said, "And what might that be, bard?"

"I ask you to send someone to my room to fetch my poor, maligned harp. It is sitting on a table by my bed, covered in a silk cloth to keep the dust off."

Small fingers dug into Maurynna's leg. "All will be well, sweetling," she whispered, slipping her arm around her cousin's shoulders and pulling her close. "All will be well."

A tiny, tiny whisper. "I can feel it again, Rynna. I've been feeling it ever since we got here. It's . . . it's calling me. So far away, but it's calling me. I don't want it any closer."

"Be strong, love, I won't let it hurt you again. I promise."

It seemed an eternity before the servant Lord Asiah had called for returned with the harp. Maurynna pulled the shaking child closer.

Leet took the harp and settled into the witness's chair. "Shall I play for you, Dragonlord?" he asked with overblown courtesy as he ran a finger mockingly down the strings.

Maurynna tensed as the rippling notes belled through the room.

Nothing. Nothing at all. Linden wasn't certain what he'd expected, but this was what he'd feared. Leet played on, a merry tune dancing under his fingers, smiling and nodding to this or that lord or lady in the audience. His color was back to normal; he might have been playing at a gathering. The harp was no more "haunted" than the chair Leet sat upon.

It was the one thing Linden had not been able to fit into his theory of what had happened. He'd seen this harp, heard Leet play it the night before the Queen's Chase. There was no magic in it. Had he been wrong? Terribly, terribly wrong in his desperation to find a way out for Raven?

At last the cheerful tune ended. Leet sat back, rubbing the indentation under his lip with a forefinger. "And now, Dragonlord? Do you still claim that my harp is—"

A child's voice cut across Leet's words. "It's not the same harp!"

Sixty-seven

Linden looked around, astonished. That was Kella! But where was she? And what in the name of Gifnu's nine hells was Kella doing *here,* anyway? The last he knew she was home in Casna.

Racing footsteps clattered down the curving stairs. It was Kella, closely followed by Maurynna. *Oh—the witnesses' balcony. Of course.*

Kella came around to face Leet. Though she trembled, she stood defiant.

"You!" Leet roared. "You're the one who tried to touch my harp that day in the garden, aren't you, you little guttersnipe? What the hell are you talking about, anyway? You saw my harp for only a few mo—"

"This isn't the same harp and you know it!" Kella yelled back. "There's nothing in this one. It's not the one I played in your room. *That* one was evil!"

The change her words wrought in Leet was shocking. In an instant, he looked decades older and shook like a man with the ague. He whispered, "Oh dear gods, you pla—" Panic crossed his face and he bit his lip. He tried to speak again but nothing came out.

Maurynna stood watching from the side, arms folded.

Leet finally found his voice. He took a deep breath and drew himself up. "You lying little—" Then, to Lord Asiah, "My lord, what place does this gutter trash have—"

"My cousin is not 'gutter trash,' Leet," Maurynna said coldly. "I have heard her story and it is one that this court needs to hear, my lord Justice."

Linden stood as if turned to stone as Kella's words sank in. So that was the answer! He took a quick look at the "shoulder" of Leet's harp. Yes, it was the one he'd seen before. And he would wager good money that his guess was right.

But what had she been doing in Leet's room? asked a confused voice in the back of his mind. He'd find out soon enough, he suspected.

"My lord Justice," he said, "with your permission, I would like to ask my kinswoman Kella a question."

Asiah frowned at him but nodded. "Very well, Dragonlord," he said reluctantly.

Linden knelt so that he looked Kella in the eye. "I need you to be certain, Kitten, whether or not this is the same harp. Did you notice a design wood-burned into the one you played? You did? Good. I don't think you can see it from here, but the one on the harp Bard Leet is holding is a seagull in a circle of bluebells."

Kella shook her head. "There was a seagull, and a circle of flowers, but they weren't bluebells, Linden. I know what bluebells look like because they grow under the apple tree in the yard. The flowers on the harp I played were something like the morning glories on the wattle fence around the yard but they had deep ruffles on the edges."

Just like flowers he had so recently seen scattered in a haunted glade. . . .

Leet made a small, strangled sound.

Linden, still kneeling by Kella, spoke so that his words carried through the room. "And while there is no color in a woodburning, I would ask you, my lords and ladies, to imagine this ruffled 'morning glory–like' flower in a deep, deep red. Can anyone identify this plant for me?"

A puzzled silence filled the room; then Conor said tightly, "King's Blood. That can only be King's Blood."

Lord Asiah turned to Leet. "Bard, I now ask you to step down from the witness's chair." He paused, then added, "But you are not to leave this room."

Once again the Justice called for servants to go to Bard Leet's room. But this time they had orders to search it down to the walls and floorboards.

Lord Asiah looked long and hard at Kella. Then he said, "Kella Vanadin, I call you to the witness's chair."

Kella was long done with her story when the servants, headed this time by Steward Lewell, came back to the room.

"And?" Lord Asiah asked.

"Nothing, my lord Justice," Steward Lewell said. "There was no other harp."

Leet stood up. "So much for your wild tale, Your Grace. Now—I would have all here witness that I claim wergild from Dragonlord Linden Rathan for his lies against me."

Linden gritted his teeth. "I'm not done yet, Leet. There is one more thing this court needs to see." In mindspeech, he said, *Now.*

Leet rolled his eyes. "More disappearing evidence, Your Grace?" he asked as the door opened and shut again. With an exaggerated sigh, he turned to look along with everyone else.

Two of the castle guards came in, carrying a box by handles formed from the ropes binding it.

"No!" Leet screamed. "No! How did you—" He clutched his chest and collapsed.

"Guards—set that thing down and take this man to Healer Tasha immediately!" Lord Asiah ordered. "Remain there to keep watch. No one but Healer Tasha or her assistants are allowed to enter—or leave."

When the ashen-faced Leet was borne away, Linden carried the box the rest of the way to the front of the room. He set it on the table and called Lord Asiah and Otter to him. "I don't know where the harp Kella played is, my lord Justice," he said grimly as he untied the knots and opened the lid, "but in this box—"

Kella screamed. "Rynna, Rynna—it's there! I don't want to see it! Please!"

Linden slammed the lid shut again. Damn it all—what had he been thinking? He'd heard Kella's story. "There's no harp there, Kella. Truly. My word as a Dragonlord on it. Is it better now? Can you still feel it?"

"Just a tiny bit now," Kella quavered bravely. Then in a tearful rush, "But I still want to get away from it!"

"Lord Asiah," Maurynna said, "do you still need Kella here to testify? I will see that she remains on the castle grounds. If you need her again, Linden, Shima, or Lleld can reach me."

Lord Asiah nodded; Maurynna scooped up Kella and hurried from the room. After the door shut behind them, Lord Asiah wiped his forehead. "By all the gods, never have I seen such commotion in my courtroom. And if the gods are good, I never will again! Now what in the name of those same gods do you have here, Linden Rathan?"

"Otter, suppose you tell Lord Asiah?" Linden said.

The bard leaned over to look. "Hunh—looks like soundboards for a harp. But why in Auvrian's name are they in a lined box like this? It's not as if they were powerful amulets or a mage's tools to need rowan and silk."

Before Linden could stop him, Otter picked up a piece and turned it this way and that. "No, no amulet here. It's just a piece of spruce for—" The color drained from his face. He flung the wood down with an oath and fell back, cradling his hand against his chest. "That's from Gull's witch spruce, isn't it?" he asked, his voice shaking. "Dear gods, how could Leet have had a harp made with such as this? You can feel the darkness in them!"

Lord Portis rose. "Have I your leave to speak, Lord Justice? Thank you. I don't believe these pieces of wood are haunted. As you yourself said, Bard Otter, 'It's just a piece of spruce.' Nor do I believe there's a haunted harp. All here know that this murderer is kin to you. Of course you'll say anything to save his neck from the rope."

Otter stood tall, though he still clutched his hand to his chest as if it hurt him. "My word as a bard on it, my lord. This wood is tainted with great evil."

"Prove it, then. You're a bard like Leet. Use them to make me do something,"

Portis demanded. Then, when Otter didn't speak, he taunted softly, "You can't, can you?"

"No," Otter said. "Because like this they can't sing."

"'Sing'? Oh, please, bard. This is nothing but moonshine."

"Was Leet's reaction when he saw the box 'moonshine'?" Linden countered.

Portis shrugged. "Perhaps the man is as mad as you seem to hope the rest of us are. Once more I say: prove it. And once more I say: you can't."

Maurynna walked down the hall, Kella by her side. She wasn't certain where to go, but anywhere away from the courtroom was fine with her. She turned at the sound of hurried footsteps.

It was Prince Rann, Bard Daera, and Raven's friend Arisyn. "Kella, wait!" Rann called. Kella ran back to him. The children hugged.

"You were so brave, Kella!" Rann said. "Both today and when . . . um, the other time. We were all watching from up in the balcony. But why didn't you tell me what happened?" he scolded. "I'd have told Uncle Beren to make Leet and his haunted harp leave."

"The haunted harp that nobody but us believes in," Arisyn said glumly.

Kella started to say something, then stopped. An odd look came over her face; half puzzlement, half . . . fear.

Alarmed, Maurynna said, "Sweetling? Are you well? What's wrong?"

Fear turned to excitement. Kella turned in a slow circle. Suddenly she stopped and went back half a step. "There!" she said triumphantly, and pointed.

"There what?" Maurynna asked, thoroughly confused now.

"Rynna, do you remember me saying I could still feel the harp calling me, but that it was far away? When the guards brought the box into the room, it didn't feel any stronger until Linden opened the box. Then it was awful. It went away again when he shut it, to just that little tugging. But it's getting stronger now!"

Maurynna stared down at her cousin. "You're feeling the other harp and not the—the whatever was in the box, aren't you, Kella? It's out there. . . ." She closed her eyes, murmuring softly, "If we could find it, then Raven is saved. . . ." Hope leapt up in her heart; the first real hope she'd let herself feel in far too long.

She knelt and looked deep into her cousin's eyes. "Kella, I know how frightened you are of this thing, but you're the only one who can find it. You're the only one who can save Raven."

Kella nodded, her face pale. "I want to help Raven," she said in a tiny voice. "But I'm so afraid of it, Rynna. . . ."

"I'll hold your hand," Rann offered. He caught her hand and smiled at her.

"And I'll hold the other," Maurynna said. "You won't have to touch it, sweetling. Just find it for me."

Soon their strange little parade was jogging through the castle and out a door to the gardens.

The Justice of Balyaranna looked from one man to the other. "We seem to have reached a stalemate, my lords. But I, for one, am curious. My lord Portis, please take your seat again. Dragonlord, if you would take the witness's chair, I am curious as to all that led you to these 'pieces of spruce' and where you found them."

Truth be told, Linden was glad enough to sit down. "It began, my lord Justice, before my soultwin, Lleld and her soultwin, Jekkanadar, Otter, Raven, and I left for Jehanglan. One day we came upon Bard Leet in the library at Dragonskeep. He had, it seemed, rather odd tastes in reading. . . ."

"I've never been here before," Rann said, looking around. He pulled Kella to a halt. "This is the oldest part of the gardens. There are . . . there are stories about it."

Kella squeaked in fright. Maurynna started to ask "What stories?" but thought better of it. "Another time, Rann," she said firmly.

"Yes, please, Your Highness," Arisyn said. To Maurynna's surprise, he reached out and snapped a branch on a bush, then propped it carefully against another. "One scary thing at a time if you would."

"I've heard those stories. There is nothing here that will hurt us," Daera said with quiet certainty.

Kella looked over her shoulder and searched the bard's face.

Daera smiled down at her. "I'm not just saying that, Kella. It's true."

A sharp nod, then Kella tugged Maurynna and Rann along again.

The small band went deeper into the garden. Though it was not neglected enough to be called "wild," Maurynna thought that the gardeners spent as little time here as possible. Yet the feeling of the place was not hostile or frightening; rather, a gentle melancholy pervaded the atmosphere, a kind of wistful sadness.

At last Kella led them to an arched "tunnel" of the roses that the Cassorins loved so well. It was the longest one Maurynna had ever seen; she peered down its length. There seemed to be an open area behind it and what appeared be a building of some sort beyond. And what was that stench? It smelled like something had died here. Then she realized that she'd caught similar whiffs from time to time as they'd walked through the gardens; she just hadn't paid attention at the time. At least it didn't seem to bother any of the truehumans.

"It's there," Kella said flatly, shaking like an aspen leaf. She pointed into the tunnel. "Somewhere in there. And I'm not going any closer!"

Maurynna nodded. "I won't ask you to, sweetling. You've done wonders already, Kella. I don't know if I could have been as brave. The rest of you can go back—"

"Raven's my friend," Arisyn said in a do-not-argue tone. "I'm going with you, Dragonlord."

"Very well. Daera, please take Rann and Kella back to Rann's rooms. I want Kella as far away from this thing as possible."

Daera hesitated. "I'm not certain I can find my way back, Dragonlord. We came through parts of the garden that I've never seen before and it all might as well be a maze with those tall hedges."

"Just look for the dangling branches," Arisyn said. "If there wasn't anything unusual there, every time we came to a choice of ways, I broke one and pointed it back the way we had come from. When you reach the apple tree 'house,' go down the path marked by the white rosebushes. At the rabbit fountain, go north. Oh— and when you get to the topiary bear, take the path that his right paw points to."

Maurynna clapped him on the shoulder. "Smart lad!" she said with a grin. "Now—off with you."

Daera led the children away at a trot. About a quarter of a candlemark or so later, Maurynna decided they'd given the others enough of a head start. "Let's get this over with." She led the way inside.

The tunnel closed over them and the scent of roses wrapped around them as they walked on and on. Save for the muffled sound of their own footsteps, the silence was absolute. No bird sang, no insect chirped. It seemed forever before they reached the glade at the end.

By some chance or a brave gardener—or magic—it was not overgrown with weeds. The lawn was of chamomile; it led up to the ruins of a large building of quarried stone, its empty windows staring blindly at them. A gaping archway led into its shadowed depths.

The smell was worse here. Maurynna breathed through her mouth as much as possible.

"Who would put a building here?" Arisyn wondered. "And what died here?" He wrinkled his nose.

So it was strong enough for a truehuman to smell now, too. That mystery would have to wait for another time. She stared at the building; something about it was familiar. . . .

"It's a folly!" Maurynna said. "One of my great-great-something-grandfathers built one on our country estate in Thalnia. He liked to go there and work on his book." She pointed to the dark opening. "I'll wager anything that's where we go."

At the edge of the entrance Maurynna paused and sent several globes of cold-fire ahead to light their way into the grotto. Dead leaves crunched under their boots as they walked. The sound bounced back from the walls, running ahead of them. Then, in an echo of the tunnel of roses outside, this tunnel opened into a room of stone.

And on a table made from one of the massive rectangular blocks that formed the walls lay a pale box of a shape that Maurynna easily recognized. How many times as a girl in Thalnia had she seen Otter take such a box down from the wagon that had brought him from the docks to Raven's house? Then she had danced with excitement at the sight. Now her skin crawled; she could feel the dark magic within calling to her own magic. It was like the dull throb of a toothache. *But at least a toothache doesn't make you feel . . . unclean.*

"You took an oath, Leet," she said softly. "One of the most sacred oaths in the Five Kingdoms and you chose to break it. I'll see you given to Iryniel the Punisher yet, you bastard."

Sixty-eight

When he got back to their chamber, Linden was surprised that neither Maurynna nor Kella was there. He considered mindcalling his soultwin, but if she was comforting Kella, he didn't want to disturb her.

He called for wine and left Otter, Lleld, Shima, and Conor in the outer room. Raven was back in his tower cell, true, but at least Linden had the satisfaction of knowing that Leet was under guard as well.

Once in the sleeping chamber, he stripped, heatspelled the water in the stone basin, and washed off the worst of the dirt and grime. Oh, for a proper bath and a good, long soak. . . . As he dressed once more, he felt Maurynna touch his mind. Moments later he burst into the small sitting room. Surprised faces turned to him.

"Maurynna's found the haunted harp," he announced grimly.

It seemed to take forever and a day before the door opened. To Linden's surprise, it was Sevrynel's foster son, Arisyn, who carried the traveling case. Maurynna followed him, pale and sweating.

"I couldn't carry it anymore," she said. "For some reason I could feel it even through the rowan. It wasn't like that with the soundboards. Those I couldn't feel at all, just a little when you opened the box. But this—this is horrible."

Arisyn set the case down on the hastily cleared table. "While I can't feel a thing from it," he said cheerfully. "And I think I'm quite glad, too."

They circled the table, staring down at the wooden harp case that lay there, its rowan boards pale against the dark chestnut table.

"I can feel it," Lleld whispered.

"As can I," Shima said.

"And I," Linden said thoughtfully. "But Arisyn can't. But why . . . Wait. Arisyn—can you sing?"

"Not a note, Your Grace."

"Neither can I," Maurynna pointed out.

"I know," Linden said dryly. "But you can feel it nevertheless. It must be calling to our Dragonlord magic." He glanced at Conor; the Beast Healer shook his head.

Otter said slowly, "Are you certain you can feel something from this, boyo? Because I can sing and yet I don't feel anything from it."

"Truly? Odd, I would have thought . . . Ah well—I suppose we might as well get this over with." Linden opened the box and set the harp onto the table, touching it as lightly as possible. "Hmm—no silk lining to this box. Maybe that's why it 'leaks.' "

It was a beautiful thing, he thought, just like the harp Leet had played the night before the Queen's Chase. As far as he could tell, the two were identical save for—yes, Kella had been right. The flowers around the seagull on this harp were *not* bluebells. He stared at the circlet of King's Blood and shook his head. "Save for the flowers, it might be the same harp we heard at the encampment."

"By Auvrian!" Otter said suddenly, bending closer to study the harp. "That's ash! He had harps made with *ash* wood?"

"What's wrong with that?" Shima asked. "It sounded very nice when he played it."

Otter snorted. "It might very well sound nice, but most bards wouldn't have a harp made of ash even if they could find a luthier to make it for them. Ash is considered unlucky because it's a wood of war; spear shafts are made from it."

"How appropriate for a harp meant to kill," Lleld murmured. "Brrrr! That thing makes my skin crawl."

Otter studied the harp. It truly was a beautiful thing; Thomelin the luthier had outdone himself. Still, as far as he could tell, it was just a harp like any other.

Then Shima ran a finger down the strings. He snatched his hand back with a curse in his own tongue.

Yet Otter barely noticed. With the first bell-like tone, he was in a different world. There was only himself—and the harp. Himself and the harp . . . Himselfandtheharp . . . He sat in one of the chairs, pulled the harp to him, and began to play.

Dearest gods, he'd never felt anything like this. Like a fine wine, there were different "flavors" to it. An undertone of fear, bewilderment, even a touch of revulsion—all from him, he realized—but lost in a rush of power, of standing like a god over all others. And now the last nuance was coming through. . . . He had it now. Hunger. So much hunger . . .

Powerful hands clamped over his wrists. He yelped in pain and surprise. Otter tried to free himself but to no avail. A deep voice ordered, "Get the damned thing away from him!"

Other hands snatched the harp away. "No!" he cried, struggling to get to the harp that called so sweetly to him. He wept, a lover wrenched from his darling.

There came a ripping sound, then—peace. It was over. The harp no longer called to him. Otter fell back in his chair. He felt like a man who had escaped from the jaws of a ravening shark and now lay gasping on the beach, trying to make sense of what had happened.

He stared dull-witted at Maurynna as she laid a cloth-wrapped bundle in the traveling case. As she tucked the last bits of embroidered fabric into the rowan box, she muttered, "Beryl will never forgive me for ruining that bed hanging"—here she slapped the lid on the box and pushed down to make it all fit—"but I daresay a bolt or three of Neiranal silk from Dragonskeep will help."

Whaaat? Otter's mind asked blearily. Then he saw one of the bed curtains was ripped straight across. The thought of the strength required to rip silk that heavy sobered him.

So did the pain in his wrists. He looked down at them as Linden, standing behind him, released his grip. The marks of the Dragonlord's big hands were plain to see.

"That will raise a fine crop of bruises," he said with forced lightness.

"My apologies, Otter," Linden said, coming around to face him. "But I had to stop you. Yours was not a truehuman's strength just then." A pause, then a wary "I didn't break anything, did I?"

Otter twisted his hands this way and that. "No, you didn't—but I still would have thanked you if it had taken that to free me from that, that . . . *thing*!" he said.

"It was horrible," Arisyn said. His voice shook.

"You felt it when Otter was playing?" Linden asked.

"I did. It was . . . *horrible*!" the boy repeated.

"It was," Otter agreed. He rubbed his forehead; all of a sudden he felt exhausted. "How could Leet do such a thing? Yet I can also understand why. You can't imagine the feeling. . . . It must be like rich wine to a drunkard. You can't stop; you always want more—and more and more."

"Now what do we do?" Maurynna asked. "This is the last grace day we had. Tomorrow they'll . . ." Her voice broke.

"We invoke our rank and privileges as Dragonlords," Linden said, "and we call the court back into session right now to show them this thing. I don't care what candlemark it is."

A terrifying thought froze Otter's blood. He said, "If—if Portis or someone insists I play it, all of you please promise me you'll do whatever is needed to stop me if it . . . if it takes me over again. *Whatever* is needed. Please."

"We shall, old friend," Linden said softly. "We shall." The others—even Arisyn, though it was plain the boy was frightened—nodded.

Otter rose. "Good enough, then. Let's get this over with."

Sixty-nine

It was late before the court could be reconvened. Many of the lords and ladies of the Judges' Council had gone off and had to be tracked down. And Maurynna insisted that Kella leave the castle entirely.

"We'll need to have that thing out of its box the entire time," she pointed out, "sitting next to the other harp so that the judges can come up and see the difference between them. Kella could feel it when it was far off in the gardens because there was no silk helping the rowan wood to shroud its magic. Can you imagine what she'll feel when it's out for that long? I'm already kicking myself that I didn't think of sending her farther away before we looked at it earlier."

So Kella was sent off—along with Prince Rann who refused to leave her—to Lord Sevrynel's manor, despite dark predictions from Duchess Beryl that the two would join up with Rosalea and drive their nurses to distraction. "At least the children will have a wonderful time," the duchess finished with a wry laugh.

The last of the judges had just settled themselves when word came that Kella was safely away. Linden looked over the room, surprised to see that so many spectators had also heard of the unusual session. Raven was brought in, looking half hopeful, half terrified. Linden couldn't blame him.

Lord Asiah, his face stern, came up to where Linden stood by the table. On it was the harp that he thought of as Leet's "bluebell" harp. Next to it was the box holding the tainted one, still wrapped in silk.

The Justice studied him. "I trust that this 'new evidence' is important, Your Grace," Lord Asiah said quietly. "Or else I shall dismiss this court. For, as I said earlier, you have not proven your case."

"It is important, my lord," Linden answered just as quietly. He rested one hand on the box, the rowan smooth and cool under his palm. "In here is the 'haunted' harp that holds what is left of Gull the Blood Drinker."

Lord Asiah inhaled sharply. "Can you prove this?"

"If necessary, yes," Linden said, though his stomach roiled at the thought of

411

playing it. He silently prayed to all the gods he could think of that Maurynna's testimony of how they found the cursed thing would be enough.

It wasn't. Oh, the judges came up one by one to examine both harps and all agreed that the harp from the box did indeed have different flowers around the seagull. Daera was called in to give her opinion as a bard that, yes, these two harps were indeed made from ash which was well-nigh unheard of in bardic tradition, and that they were clearly from the same maker—she could even identify who just from their appearance if they were so interested. Even Conor was brought forward to verify that the flowers around the purported "haunted" harp were in fact King's Blood.

Then Maurynna told the fascinated audience how she, Kella, Prince Rann, Bard Daera, and Arisyn Darnhollis searched for the harp, and how she and Arisyn found it hidden in the folly. All who were present in the room when Otter played it testified to the terrible experience.

It was not enough. The doubter, of course, was Lord Portis. "All you have shown us," he said, "is that there are indeed two harps. You have proven nothing." His voice was ragged with grief. "Nothing," he whispered. "And my son's killer still lives."

Maurynna said, "Lord Portis, Bard Otter has sworn that the harp holds evil within it. He played it in Linden's and my quarters. And Linden, Shima, Lleld, and I have sensed that same evil. You will not accept any of our words of honor on this?"

"No. You are Redhawkson's kin or friends. At least one of you owes him a life debt. I do not accept your sworn words."

A gasp ran through the room at Portis's audacity. He glared at Raven, his face twisted with grief. "That man killed my son. You claim he was forced to by this harp. Even if that were true—and I do not believe it for one instant—he could have resisted. He didn't, and because of that, my only child is dead."

Lady Portis wept. Portis laid a hand upon her shoulder.

"I tell you, my lord, that no one could have resisted that harp," Otter snapped.

"And I don't believe you," Portis retorted. He pointed at the harp on the table before them all. "I don't believe you. How could a—a *harp* make a man kill? Prove it to me, bard! Prove it! Play the thing! Control *me*!"

The blood drained from Otter's face. Linden knew what he feared: to touch the harp again, to succumb to the lure of its power once more—and not be able to break the bond this time.

"My lord," Shima said. "You don't know what you ask. This is not like the magics you have heard of all your life. It is much more akin to the magics of my land. For a bard like Otter—for any true bard—this thing is vileness, an unspeakable vileness. I touched it, I felt the darkness in it, and I am no bard to call forth its full magic. I merely ran a finger across its strings and it answered to the magic in me. It was dark and foul. Please don't ask a bard to risk his gift of music by playing it."

Lord Portis sneered at him and folded his arms across his broad chest. "Then I will not believe it can control a man."

A chair scraped across the floor in the back of the room. Everyone turned to look as Lord Eadain struggled to his feet.

"My lords and ladies, my lord Justice, Your Graces, while I am certainly no bard, I do play the harp for my own amusement," the young lord said. "And I am willing to attempt this thing that Lord Portis asks."

Linden frowned. "My lord Eadain, believe me when I say that we appreciate your offer. Yet from what I've seen of the effects of playing this harp, I'm loath to let anyone else be tainted by it. It should—"

A harsh bark of laughter cut him off. "So you won't let anyone else play the thing lest they be 'tainted'? We're just to take your word that this thing is haunted by an evil dead for—what? Two centuries or so?

"So we take *your* word for it that"—here Lord Portis clutched his hands to his chest and went on in wide-eyed innocence—"the harp is a bad, horrible thing and can make people do bad, horrible things, so they shouldn't be held accountable for them because it's not really their fault. We should let the poor man it took over go free—"

It was a deadly accurate imitation of the stock character of the not-very-bright, all-sweetness-and-light priest in a bad mummer's play. Linden pressed his lips together; he didn't trust himself.

The act ended. Portis snarled, "Even if he's a cold-blooded killer. How convenient that would be for you, Dragonlord. How *very* convenient for your friend." Portis's harsh, heavy breathing filled the room. "No, Dragonlord, no. Unless you can prove your claim to me beyond all doubt, I ask this court to see that this murderer pays."

Asiah said mildly, "I'm afraid that Lord Portis is right, Dragonlords. We must have incontrovertible proof that the harp can do what you say."

Lord Eadain's light tenor broke the silence. "Dragonlord, I thank you for your fear for me, but this is a risk I am willing to take. I count Raven as a friend, and—and there is more.

"And I can understand Lord Portis's feelings. I agree with him that this must be proven beyond all doubt—for everyone's sake. Please, Lord Justice, Your Graces, Lord and Lady Portis—let me try."

The thought of touching that harp was enough to turn Linden's stomach. How could he let anyone else do what he feared to try himself? "Lord Eadain—"

Eadain drew himself up. "Dragonlord, I claim this task as my right."

Linden bowed his head. He could not refuse Eadain now without making it seem he considered the young lord as less than a man; no doubt a thing too many people did when they saw the crutches—and only the crutches. So it must be.

It was up to Lord Portis now. Linden turned to Tirael's father. Bloodshot eyes, their rims red from weeping, met his with implacable fury. At long last, Lord Portis nodded. "Very well," he rasped.

"Thank you, my lord," Eadain said. He deftly maneuvered his crutches between the people sitting around him and slowly came down the aisle. When he was settled in the witness's chair, Linden gestured for a guard to bring the harp to him.

Eadain rested the harp against his shoulder and lightly ran a finger down the strings, testing to see if it was in tune.

Then Raven cried out, "Stop! Stop! It wants me, I can feel it. . . . If you must play it, then please bind me again or send me away—I'm afraid of what I'll do if I hear it again. Please!" he begged.

"You missed your calling, boy," Portis sneered. "You should have been a mummer."

"And a fine one he would have been, too," Lleld snapped. "The best in the land to turn white and break out in a sweat just for the wishing! Have you no eyes, Portis? This is no act." Lleld shook her head in disgust. "Bind him," she ordered the guards.

Portis darted a glance at Raven; Linden saw him waver. For a moment he thought the man might see the sense in Lleld's words. Then Portis shook his head and the moment slipped away.

"There's another thing we must consider," the little Dragonlord went on as the guards strapped Raven's arms and ankles down again. "What if magic is needed to call magic? It might not work for Lord Eadain."

Linden blinked. He hadn't considered that. *Good point, Lleld.*

Of course it is, Lleld shot back. *I thought of it.* Then, grudgingly, *You would have too if you weren't half-dead on your feet.*

"But it worked for the child—if her tale is true." Portis lifted his chin in challenge.

Seeing Maurynna's face darken, Linden quickly said, "But Kella has a touch of bardic magic, my lord. Bard Daera can confirm that the child shows a true gift for music and has said that her family should send her to Bylith for testing when she's older." He held up his hand against the buzz of speech that greeted his words. "I'm not saying that she could do what we say Bard Leet did. For one thing, *if* she does have the magic of a bard, it is yet weak and untrained. I suspect she has enough to awaken Gull, but not enough to control him. And I will *not* ask her to go through that again."

"Then let Lord Eadain play."

Softly at first, then with more confidence, Eadain played. He was no bard,

Linden thought, but the man played very well indeed. But while it was pleasant listening, there was no . . . magic to it, no quickening of the pulse as when a true bard played.

After the third song—an old, old one that was rarely played anymore—Lord Eadain stopped, an odd expression on his face. "For a moment I felt something," he said. "But then . . . nothing." He shook his head. "To me it's just a harp," he said apologetically. He held the harp out to the guard who jumped to take it, picked up his crutches and limped back to his place.

"As I said before, magic might be needed to call forth magic," Lleld said.

"Then we are stalemated, are we not, Dragonlords?" Lord Portis said coldly. "For you won't let a bard play it, and—let me guess—none of you can play?"

Maurynna, Shima, and Lleld all shook their heads.

"I thought not," said Portis. "How . . . convenient."

"As it happens, my lord, I can," Linden said mildly enough, even though he seethed with anger. Not only were they named liars by this man, but now he forced him to do a thing that he would give much to avoid. Ever since he'd felt that sick, twisted evil in the forest he'd felt tainted, as if part of his very soul was befouled.

Before he could change his mind, Linden took up the harp and sat down. He rested it against his shoulder and began playing. Without thinking he chose a song he had learned centuries ago—from Rani eo'Tsan, who had learned it in a dream from the undead harper Satha.

Whether it was his own magic, or a magic in the song itself—for like Otter, Linden believed some songs held an enchantment of their own; how else did they endure for centuries?—he soon felt his fingers moving in a pattern not of his choosing. And as the new tune flowed from the old, a burning cold crept up his fingers.

"Dear gods," he whispered. Is this what Kella had endured? He cursed Leet anew.

He wanted to cast the harp from him, break it into slivers. But that would prove nothing to Portis. Only one thing would convince the man, he knew. So Linden clenched his teeth and set his magic against the evil within the harp.

At first it fought him; his magic was not that of a bard. Then all at once it seemed to sense what he wanted and responded eagerly. The surge of unholy joy that burned coldly up his arms nearly made him retch.

But it was working. Linden could see Portis's hands twitch as his eyes glazed and his breathing turned rapid and shallow. The man lurched upright like a puppet whose strings were tugged first one way, then another. Lady Portis looked up at him, a worried frown creasing her brow.

An uneasy murmur ran through the courtroom as the spectators looked around at each other. More than a few made the sign against evil.

Would that was all one needed to banish this! Linden thought. Though it sat ill with him—he'd no wish to make a mock of Portis and his pain despite the man's thirst for revenge upon Raven—Linden wanted to be certain that everyone saw that Portis was not his own master.

"My lord Portis," he sang quietly, "flap your arms like a bird—and remember. Remember all this."

For a moment nothing happened. He wondered if it was because he was no bard. Then . . .

Eyes still glazed, Portis did as he was bidden. It should have been amusing in a nasty way, watching the dignified lord's wide sleeves flailing the air as Portis lurched about the open floor before the seats, but it was not. Indeed, from the frightened faces staring wide-eyed at the spectacle before him, everyone else found it as horrifying as he did.

Tears flowed down Lady Portis's cheeks. "Ridler! Ridler!" she cried. "What is wrong? You act as one possessed!"

At her words, Linden said, "He is indeed, my lady. Just as Raven was. Just . . . as . . ."

He gave Portis a silent command by mindvoice to lunge at Lady Portis. Portis spun jerkily around and flung himself at his wife. As his hands closed upon her throat, Linden shouted "Enough!" and tried to take his fingers from the strings.

But the harp would not let him go. Fear surged through him as he watched Portis's fingers tighten their deadly grip on his wife's throat. This was not what he had intended! And still his fingers danced upon the strings of the cursed harp as he struggled to break free.

A hand clamped his shoulder like a vise. Fresh strength flared through him from the touch. Wielding it like a sword, Linden slashed at the flow of blood magic from the harp. For a moment he feared it would not be enough. . . .

Then the harp fell from his hands. Maurynna let go of him and caught it. She spun around with inhuman speed and thumped the harp onto the table hard enough to make the strings ring. An unholy chord belled angrily through the room, leaving pale and ashen faces in its wake. With an angry curse, she muffled it with the torn bed curtain and shoved it back in the rowan case.

Portis released his wife's throat and stumbled back, staring at his hands in horror. Lady Portis fell back in her chair, gasping; she touched her throat gingerly.

For a long moment the only sound in the room was that of Lady Portis's harsh breathing. Then someone whispered, "Dear gods—what was that?"

Linden shook his head, unable to answer.

"Blood magic, my lord," Lleld said. "Dark magery of the worst—and the tool of a coward who would not shed blood himself, but used others to kill."

Linden forced himself to stand. "My lord Portis, my lady Portis," he began. He felt sick at how close he'd come to getting Lady Portis killed. He cleared his throat. "My lord and lady, I can never apologize enough to you. That is *not* what

I'd wanted you to do, Lord Portis. I thought I could control it, but it wanted to kill so badly. . . ."

"I felt it," Lady Portis rasped. "That urge to kill." Other voices murmured agreement. "It was in the song you played."

"It was." Portis stared at his hands once more. "It filled me, took control of me. A small part of me *knew* it was wrong, *knew* I didn't want to do this thing, but the, the . . . *other* was too strong."

He looked around the room. "I love my wife," he said, nearly weeping. "All of you who know me well, know that."

As heads nodded, he went on, "And I would have choked the life out of my beloved. . . ." His voice broke as he knelt before his wife. He laid his head in her lap. "Mariela, my lady, I'm so sorry, so very sorry. . . ."

Lady Portis stroked his head. "It wasn't you, Ridler. It was—someone else."

"It was Gull," Linden said softly. "Not you, my lord. Not Raven. Not Robie. It was Gull the Blood Drinker—and Leet."

Seventy

The Black Tower had a new tenant. Once it was certain that he was not ill, Leet was taken to Raven's old cell. From their tower rooms across the yard, Linden and Maurynna could hear him from time to time, screaming for his harp, his beautiful, beautiful harp, and promising the direst of punishments for those that kept it from him.

Yet Raven, even though it was now accepted that he'd been but a pawn, did not escape unscathed. He stood now in Linden and Maurynna's small common room, weary, haggard, and dressed for travel.

"I cannot believe they're doing this to you," Maurynna fumed as she tugged on her own riding boots. "Banned from Cassori for five years? They might as well punish your knife! It would make as much sense. After all, it wasn't your idea to kill Tirael."

Raven shrugged his saddlebag higher onto his shoulder. "No, but Lord Portis will never truly forgive me for killing his son. Nor will many of the other nobles here. I'm just thankful that it's not forever and especially thankful that they're not extending it to Yarrow. If you hadn't proved so powerfully to one and all just how compelling that cursed harp is, I doubt I'd ever be able to come back—and they might well have taken it out on Yarrow as well."

"What I'd still like to know, though, is why Tirael was even in Sevrynel's gardens," Maurynna said, standing. "I clearly remember Sevrynel wondering about it at the time."

"He certainly wasn't an invited guest," Raven said. "At least not by Lord Sevrynel. He'd forbidden all his foster children to associate with Tirael." He paused, then went on softly, "I wish to the gods that he hadn't been there that night."

"As well wish he'd never set that poor boy on Summer Lightning's back," Linden said. "That's what really started all this: Arnath's death. It was Tirael who set his foot on the road he chose to follow, a road that one way or another would lead to retribution from the gods."

"Couldn't they have just tripped him over a cliff or something and left me out of it?" Raven said with a wan smile. "Come on, Beanpole—if you're still planning to ride with me the first part of the way home, we need to leave now. The decree of banishment said that I have to be on my way before the noon candlemark."

"I'm ready." Maurynna caught Linden in a fierce embrace. "You—get some sleep. It's been what, three days or so? And flying all over half the Five Kingdoms to boot."

Linden returned the hug with equal fierceness and a kiss. "And you hurry back. There's a very important task ahead of us."

The sound of furious cursing came faintly through the open window. As one, they looked over to the Black Tower.

"Leet's at it again, I see," Raven said. His voice held no sympathy. "Wonder if he'll ever find that chisel."

"Chisel?" Linden and Maurynna asked together.

Raven grinned. "That's right. A certain little, ah, *adventurer* who shall remain nameless brought one to me with my dinner one day. I'm not certain how he thought I'd escape once I'd loosened the bars—the sheets would never have reached the ground even if I could have torn them into strips—but I knew how I'd escape the hangman," he finished grimly.

Linden cursed softly as he understood what Raven hadn't said. Maurynna paled and gripped his hand hard enough to hurt.

It was a horrible thought, but Linden could understand why Raven had even contemplated it. It would have been a kinder death.

Raven continued, "Wonder what they'll do to Leet? They can't hang him, because he's a bard. I guess that's up to the gods and the Guild Master. Me, I just want to put as much distance as I can between myself and that murdering filth."

Linden saw them to the door, then went to the window for a final look down into the courtyard. Leet continued to rant and rave in his cell. Linden ignored him; and after Maurynna, Raven, and an escort of guards rode away, he pulled the shutters closed and collapsed onto the bed. He fell asleep between one breath and the next.

Linden waited as the guard unlocked the door to the cell. As he swung it open, the guard announced, "You've a visitor, bard."

Linden went in. The door shut firmly behind him again. His quarry sat on a stool by the window, staring out between the bars.

Leet turned. Gone was the self-possessed, dignified, and immaculate bard. Facing him was a haggard man who looked years older, disheveled, a patchy beard stubbling his chin. Puffy eyes stared listlessly at him.

"To what do I owe this honor, Dragonlord?" Even the voice had changed, a hoarse, raspy travesty of the honeyed tones for which Leet had been famous. The words, meant to mock, fell flat.

"I've questions, Leet. Things that I'm curious about."

A spark of the old fire came back into Leet's eye and the bard drew himself up. Then, like a pricked bladder, he sagged once more. "What?"

If he were a better man, Linden thought wryly, he'd find a bit of sympathy for Leet within himself. This was one time he was content to be his flawed self. "Did Sether know where the spruce for the soundboards came from?"

Leet shook his head. "No. He just knew something wasn't right about it."

"So why did he help you?"

Leet stared past him, then began talking. Quietly, dully, a man talking to himself. "I made him, of course. You've been to Thomelin's, haven't you? You must have; you had the—you had . . . The boy Brin, the simpleton—he's Sether's bastard by a cousin of Thomelin's. She died a year after Brin was born. Thomelin was all the kin she had."

A ghost of a sneer twisted his mouth. "What a fool Sether was to be so besotted with that cow, Theras. If she'd had any notion the brat was his, she'd have run to her priest bleating for him to tell her what to do—and that would have been to cast Sether aside. He wouldn't risk that, so I had him. He had to use his 'little magic' to season the wood for me, perfectly and quickly." He rubbed a finger along the indentation between lip and chin. "I had him. But . . . he must have guessed. Else why would he have h-h . . ." Leet twined his fingers together and began rocking back and forth, hands between his knees.

After a time, Linden asked, "And Thomelin? Did he know?"

This time the spark of fire stayed lit. Leet snorted. "Does it matter? This is all his fault. If he'd been a man he'd have Challenged Tirael before Arnath's body grew cold. By the gods, I'll take him with me, the cowardly wretch. He wanted my daughter to love him—as if she'd ever lower herself to love a commoner like him!—so do you know what he did? His sister's late husband was a minor mage. He convinced the man to cast a glamour upon bits of colored glass. Then he set them into some of his harps, passing them off as costly gems. I overheard him talking about it once with his sister and I had *him* as well! He claims he stopped long ago and threw the rest of the glass 'jewels' into a river, but I'll wager anything—"

To Linden's disgust, Leet cackled gleefully. "Once I expose him, they'll cut off his hands as a thief and that will be the end of him!"

"You know damn well that Thomelin would have died had he Challenged Tirael," Linden retorted. "He's a luthier, not trained with a sword as Tirael and every nobleman is from birth. As you were." He paused, then went on with quiet contempt, "And you'd exact revenge upon him for that? A revenge as pathetic as all the rest has been?"

Leet's face twisted with hatred. He glared at Linden. "Pathetic?" he snarled. Spittle flew from his lips.

"Pathetic. Revenge upon a dumb—if vicious—animal, and *after* wergild was paid for its 'crime.' You didn't even poison the wretched horse yourself—you made a child do it! Then you saw a chance to revenge yourself upon your old rival by turning his innocent kinsman into a murderer. You never forgave Otter that Jaida chose him instead of you, did you?"

Leet's mouth worked; tiny bubbles of froth appeared on his lips but he was beyond speech.

"Had you renounced your oath as a bard and Challenged Tirael yourself, no one would have faulted you. But you would have had even less chance than Thomelin, wouldn't you? So you chose to hide behind your oath even while you drowned it in blood.

"And now you want to destroy a man because you can't stand going down alone. Go ahead, Leet. Destroy Thomelin—and destroy the blood of your blood with him."

"What do you mean?"

"You're so blinded by your selfish desires that you haven't even considered the consequences to others, have you? If Thomelin loses his hands, how will he earn a living? What will happen to your daughter and your remaining grandchildren? Will you turn them out onto the street to starve?"

"Damn you," Leet whispered. "Damn you all. Everything I've ever wanted I've lost. Jaida, Linny Weaver, my children, my first grandchild—the only one who had music in his soul—and now my revenge. All gone. All because of you."

"No, Leet—the blame for all of this rests at your feet." Linden got up to leave, then paused at the door. "You know, if you'd left this at the poisoning of Summer Lightning, no one would have ever found out." *But you've always liked adding embellishments, haven't you, Leet? Just like your music . . . ,* he finished to himself.

Leet waved a hand in dismissal. "What now? They can do nothing to me. I am a Master Bard, an elder of my guild. Only my guild can punish me. Tell them to bring my harp to me. It is an ill thing to keep his harp from a bard. Give it back—or I shall write such scathing songs of all of you that your names will still be a jest when the great-grandchild of the baby born tomorrow is old," he half chanted, his old power rising in his voice.

Said Linden, "You'll never see that cursed thing again, Leet." He left, closing the door against the bard's curses.

Three dragons rode the skies above the Haunted Wood. One dark red and larger than the other two, one black, one the iridescent blues and greens of a peacock's tail. They circled endlessly against the blue above them. The red and black dragons carried wooden boxes cradled in their forelegs.

Then came a small dragon winging up from the south; this one was also red, though a brighter shade. Next to the others, she looked like a dragon-child.

How went it? Linden asked, shifting the box yet again. Bound in silk and rowan though it was, he would swear he could feel the foul thing within.

They were appalled when they read Otter's letter and the copy of the court scribe's record that Lord Asiah insisted on sending along. A wise man, that. Guild Master Belwynn and the other elders decided they didn't need to see the Gull harp. Indeed, after reading everything, I think they feared to be too close to it. They've agreed that it needs to be destroyed as soon as possible, Lleld reported. *They'll be ready to leave for Cassori whenever we get there.*

Good. Now—let us end this. With that, Linden swooped down, the others following. Below him was the all-too-familiar clearing in the Haunted Forest that held Arlim's hut with its deadly secret. They would come back here shortly and cleanse it with dragon fire. Using it as a guide, Linden veered to the east, searching for the other, even deadlier clearing.

This time he knew just what he was looking for and there was no storm to distract him. Bare heartbeats later, he hovered over the place where a witch spruce had once stood guard over a grave, beating his wings to hold his place. The others joined him, quartering the circle below them.

Nothing had changed. The trail of broken mushrooms and scattered King's Blood flowers that the girls had left was still visible.

Shima—now.

The black dragon veered in and dropped his burden into the center of the clearing, then returned to the outer edge of the circle. The long box holding the extra soundboards shattered when it hit the ground.

Linden glided in and opened his forelegs. The rowan box fell, tumbling end over end. Its lid flew off and the shrouded harp fell out. Then the silk covering came free, wafting here and there as it drifted down.

But by some trick of the gods or because like called to like, the harp plummeted straight toward the stump. It smashed into it with a hideous jangling of strings. And though it lay splintered upon the broad surface of the stump, the harp's last cry rang on and on and on, filling the forest.

Linden slid away. *Go on, love,* he said. *Raven was your friend first.* This would be the end of it; the guilt-stricken Sether had done for the rest—he hoped.

Maurynna dropped down and spread her jaws wide. A gout of fire burst forth. The ringing became a shriek as flames leapt up from the dead wood of the stump, towering toward the sky.

Then came silence. Blessed silence, broken only by the crackling of the fire. Gull the Blood Drinker was gone at last.

Seventy-one

Otter came into their chambers; his face was grey, and he moved as slowly and heavily as if each of his years weighed upon him like an anvil. He sat down without a word and pointed at the goblets on the table.

Linden took the hint and poured out some wine for him. "Are you well?" he asked as he handed it to the bard. It was plain that whatever news Otter bore had stricken him to his very soul. "What was the Guild Master's decision?"

Without a word, Otter drained the goblet and held it out for more. After he'd drained that one as well and set the goblet to one side, a little color came back into his cheeks. Still, the bard shivered like a man with the ague. "A moment," he said in a ragged whisper. Then he gripped the arms of his chair until his knuckles stood out stark and white. He stared down at his hands as if he'd never seen them before.

Or would never see them again. Linden now knew what Leet's punishment was to be. The mere thought made him queasy and he was no bard; he merely played the harp as a pastime. Between the two of them, only Otter could fully appreciate the horror of Leet's coming fate. To a bard—especially a Master Bard—this was worse than death. No wonder Otter looked ill.

Yet what was coming was no less than Leet deserved for all he'd done and tried to do, Linden thought.

But the thought still sickened him; Linden left the sitting room and entered the sleeping chamber as the others clustered around Otter. Once there, he went to the open window and looked across the courtyard to the Black Tower. He sat on the wide ledge and stared at the shuttered window of Leet's cell. The window stared blindly back at him.

He wondered when they'd give Leet the news. Surely it would come as no surprise to the renegade bard. He'd broken his oath, trampled his sworn word into the dust. The oath that said never do harm, but rather help; never to kill—

save in the last extremity of defending oneself or another—and certainly never to kill for revenge.

Leet had done just that and, worse yet, used an innocent man as his tool. A man he would have let die when he could have saved him with a word.

It was that oath that kept bards safe, gave them free passage even between warring armies, kept them from harm while traveling. More than once, while journeying with Otter, Linden had seen a band of robbers turn aside when they realized their intended prey included a bard; even men that desperate didn't risk the wrath of the gods.

Leet's actions had jeopardized that protection for all bards. He had to be punished. But as Linden studied the heavy wooden shutters, he thought death would be kinder.

It was quiet this high up. The gentle breeze flowed like silk over his skin, and the honey-colored shimmer of the bright sunlight spoke of tranquil summer days riding through the mountains around Dragonskeep, of dallying in flower-strewn meadows. So peaceful on the surface, so serene . . .

He only heard the anguished scream because he'd been listening for it. Muffled behind the shutters, it was so faint it might almost have been imagination. He knew it wasn't.

Despite the heat, a shiver went down his spine. Linden glanced through the doorway to where the others still clustered around Otter and almost went to join them. Instead, something made him stay at his post. So he waited and watched—though for what, he wasn't certain.

After a time, something happened. The guards who had escorted Leet back to his prison chamber must have left, for the heavy shutters opened slowly. Pale hands thrust between the black iron bars of the windows; the long, agile fingers that once had danced skillfully upon harp strings clawed at the air, graceful no longer.

Linden wondered if anyone had had a chance to thoroughly examine the room since Leet had replaced Raven as its occupant so quickly. He knew he should have no pity for the man. Yet he understood why Leet had sought Tirael's death in revenge for his grandson's. The part of him that was still Yerrin—and a mountain Yerrin at that—sympathized with the need to see a blood debt paid.

Not that I can now. I'm a Dragonlord. But what would I do if someone killed Maurynna? Could I hold to my own oath?

But there was also the matter of *how* Leet had taken his revenge. By freeing Gull's spirit, Leet had driven one man into dark evil and cost his victims their lives as surely as if he himself had cut their throats.

Then he had used a child for a foul deed, and made Raven into a murderer, a tool to be destroyed in turn because Leet had always been jealous of his great-uncle. No, all that was more than Linden could forgive anyone, oathbound bard or not.

But he'd seen Otter's stricken face, knew what Otter—if faced with a choice between losing the first two joints of each finger and his thumbs, or death—would pick.

Leet would have no choice. Because he'd abused both oath and gift, his fingers would be amputated and he would be turned out to make a way in a world that would now regard him as a thing of vileness, a living blasphemy to be driven away with curses and blows. The only thing forbidden would be killing him and ending his punishment. Nor could he take his own life and end his misery. Linden knew a temple mage would lay a geas upon Leet to prevent it.

Oh, yes—Leet knew what he faced. Linden could see it in the way the renegade bard threw himself against the iron bars again and again, trying to force his way through the narrow gap, seeking the mercy of death.

Linden mindspoke Otter. *Do you hate him?*

As he waited for a response, he could see Leet slamming against the bars; Linden winced as the bard staggered back, then flung himself headfirst at the barred window.

The weary answer came back at last: *Believe it or not, I can't bring myself to hate him. I did before, because of what he's done to Raven, and I still loathe him for what he did to those other people, of how he perverted our calling. Yet now that I know for certain what will happen to him, part of me feels sorry for him. Can you believe that?*

Bright red ribbons of blood dripped down Leet's face. He threw himself at the bars once more.

Yes, Linden replied. *I can.* And he could. For him, it would be as if his wings were to be cut off. He'd be only half alive then. And as he soared through the sky on his wings, a bard's spirit soared in his music.

But you can't play the harp without fingers, Linden thought.

Leet collapsed against the bars. The sound of his weeping came thin and ghostlike across the gulf between the towers.

His mindvoice shaking, Otter went on, *Leet is to spend half the year wandering, and half the year at the luthier's home so that all folk will know Thomelin's part in this. By the gods, I wish they'd chosen to hang the man. It would be kinder, though I'm not certain Leet deserves any mercy for all he's done. But then I look at my own hands, and wonder if that had been* my *grandchild . . .*

You would never have chosen a coward's way of striking back, Linden retorted. *You would have openly Challenged Tirael even though it would have meant your expulsion from the guild.*

Would I, though? And let the world know why it mattered so much to me? Left my daughter to bear the shame of old scandal as Romissa will? No, I'm not certain I can point that finger, boyo.

Having met Romissa, Linden had somewhat less sympathy on that count than Otter. It was her surviving children whom he pitied. Not because they were the children of a bastard; to him, that was no shame. In the oldest Yerrin law—the law that Linden grew up with—there was no such thing as a bastard child, only degrees of legitimacy.

But an oathbreaker and murderer in the family was an ill thing for anyone. And Leet would likely live for years yet, a constant reminder for his grandchildren of the tainted blood they bore. Because of their grandfather's sins, they would be tormented endlessly, and shunned by all.

He felt no sympathy for Leet. He had precious little for Romissa. As for Thomelin, he was unsure. Had the luthier known where the wood came from? But the children . . . They were innocent.

Otter "sighed." *How odd—when I was young, someone once told me there were worse things than death. In all these years I never believed it. Now I do.*

I wish you'd never learned otherwise, Linden said. Then, *Have they given him to Iryniel yet?*

Linden couldn't remember the last time a bard was given to Iryniel; the Punisher must be hungry indeed these days. He would not easily let go of Leet, and woe to anyone who cut that cursed life short before Iryniel was moved to grant the final mercy.

But until that time . . .

No—that will be done at the dark of the moon, in the cusp of time between one day and the next.

Linden nodded; yes, that would be the proper time. And it meant half a tenday's grace.

He let the contact with Otter's mind fade. *I wonder if Leet's strong enough,* he thought. Then he reached out with his mind, letting an image of the other window flicker across it like a flash of lightning. The other window—and a chisel.

There; it's done. Now it's up to the gods—and Leet—whether he pays for all those lives with his own and his grandchildren live free of his shadow.

And if Iryniel didn't like it, Linden thought, the Punisher could bloody well take it up with him when he died in his turn. Too many children had already suffered.

Epilogue

"What in the world—?" Raven said as a shadow slid over him. Shading his eyes, he looked up in time to see Maurynna, in her dragon form, wheel in the sky to pass over him once more before spiraling down to land and Change.

"Well met, Beanpole!" he called as he rode to meet her. Stormwind neighed a greeting.

"Where are you bound for?" she asked.

"Nowhere in particular. Want to come with us?"

She laughed. "How can I refuse?"

He held out his hand and an instant later she was up behind him. Stormwind ambled on. "So what brings you here?"

"This and that. I've news for you. The first is . . . Leet was never given to Iryniel. He found the chisel."

Raven inhaled sharply. "And the loosened bars?"

"Yes."

"Ah." Raven thought about that, unsure how he felt. It seemed too easy a death for all the pain Leet had caused. "And the luthier who made the harps? Will he be punished?"

"No, there's no proof he knew just what the wood was. Besides, he's Kelnethi. Cassorin law doesn't reach that far."

They rode on in silence for a time. "Do you still blame yourself for Tirael's death?" Maurynna asked him at last.

Raven laughed bitterly. "You already know the answer: Of course I do." And he always would. It was like a wound that wouldn't heal, a sick burning in his stomach. It would never go away, he thought. Never.

"Thought so. This might make you feel a little better."

With that, her hand appeared in front of him, offering him a folded parchment. It had a seal on it, but the wax was already broken. She waggled the letter—for that was what it seemed to be—at him.

427

He took it, puzzled. "What is it about?" he asked as he turned it over in his hand.

"Just read it."

Raven sighed. As he unfolded the parchment, a small voice in the back of his mind complained that this was a waste of time. He thought of refusing, but no doubt Rynna would tell Stormwind not to bring him home until he did, and it was one hell of a long walk. Even so, he'd half a mind to refuse. . . .

As he glanced at it, certain words and phrases seemed to leap out at him. Raven held his breath and read.

> *Greetings, Master Luyens!*
>
> *By the time you get this, I shall be either a married man or a hunted one.*
>
> *Remember the girl I told you about? She's here, I've seen her, and I'm more in love with her than ever. I must have her.*
>
> *But she refuses to see me or to speak with me. She won't even read my notes! My messenger told me that he saw her cast the last one he gave her unopened upon the fire.*
>
> *Can you believe this, my dear old tutor, my friend? I, the heir to a rich holding, I who have women aplenty casting themselves at my feet, begging me for a dalliance—I am being scorned by the daughter of a lord with but a single manor! By the gods, who does she think she is, to spurn me so?*
>
> *Word has been brought to me that she will attend Lord Sevrynel's gathering this night. I'm going now to find her, and I will ask her one more time to marry me. If she refuses, and I find out that it's true she betrays me by listening to that cripple's suit, I—*
>
> *I must remember to take off my belt knife. I was rather foolish the last time I saw her, I'm afraid. If she sees that I'm armed, she'll call for the guards immediately—not that she need fear me if she's sensible. And if she isn't, it will be her own fault, won't it?*
>
> *Your affectionate student,*
> *Tirael*

Raven looked up. His hands were shaking so badly he could barely read the signature. "Rynna," he whispered. "Just what is this?"

Maurynna's hand appeared again and plucked the parchment from his nerveless fingers. "It means you saved two lives that night, Raven," she said quietly. "Remember the dagger Tirael had hidden in his boot? He wasn't carrying it because he was afraid of you. In his conceited view of the world, no doubt he was certain you, a mere commoner, would never dare lay a finger on him.

"It's far worse. We're certain Tirael was planning to kill Merrilee if she wouldn't come away with him. If he couldn't have her, no one would."

"Dear gods," Raven said. He shook his head, unable to make sense of the logic in the letter—if there was any. What made Tirael think Merrilee belonged to him? That because he wanted her, she had to want him—or suffer for it? "I can't believe it. It's—it's just too fantastic. . . . I mean, you hear of it in stories, but it's not real, it's just made up." Raven couldn't fathom the mind that reckoned like that, especially when the intended victim was as sweet and gentle as Lady Merrilee.

How could he even say she "betrayed" him? It wasn't as if they were married, handfasted, or even in the midst of a dalliance! "He would have actually *killed* her?"

"Yes."

"Gods." Raven ran a hand through his hair, still unable to understand a mind so warped. "Wait—you said 'two lives.' "

Maurynna said gently, "Eadain was with her in the garden that night."

An image of Lord Eadain leaning on his crutches sprang into Raven's mind. No, there was no way the frail lord could have fought off a man of Tirael's strength. But for Merrilee's sake he would have tried, and died for it.

She went on. "Eadain had just asked Merrilee to marry him—and she agreed."

Dear gods . . . That it should be the crippled Eadain who won Merrilee's hand rather than the "perfect" Tirael . . . Oh, yes, that would have driven the mind that could write that letter beyond any rational thought. To murder, even. And Tirael would have thought it no more than his right.

Raven shuddered at the warped reasoning. "Then if Leet hadn't—"

He couldn't finish; yet behind the deep reluctance to speak of what had been done to him, behind the shame of being used, there was now an unexpected sense of . . . relief? Comfort?

Or, even, pride? Both Lady Merrilee and Lord Eadain were people he admired, decent people, good and kindhearted. Not like that—

A sudden realization that Maurynna had slipped down from Stormwind's back and was walking away brought him out of the tangle of his thoughts. "Where are you going, Beanpole?"

She stopped, looked over her shoulder at him, and grinned. "I need room to Change, silly—remember? I only came to show that letter to you. I thought you needed to see it."

"I did," Raven said softly. "Thank you. But how did you—"

"Come by it? Conor. Lord Eadain gave it to him when he heard that Conor was coming north. Eadain got it from Master Luyens, Tirael's old tutor. It seems they were friends, too. And now I must go—oh, I almost forgot. Lord Sevrynel sent word by Conor asking if we thought you would be willing to run Stormwind in a match race at next year's fair."

"The fair? But I've been banned from—"

She shook her head, still smiling. "It's been lifted. When that letter came to light, it explained the dagger they found in Tirael's boot. Have no doubt of it, Raven—he went to Sevrynel's gathering intending to kill Merrilee at least.

"When he read the letter, Sevrynel begged leave of the duke and duchess to lift the ban. He's quite fond of both Eadain and Merrilee. If they had died at his gathering . . ." She shivered. "Lord and Lady Portis have also agreed. It's as if now that Tirael's not there to dazzle them, their eyes have finally been opened to the kind of man their son really was. Give Yarrow our love, please. Now I must go."

With that, Maurynna spun around and ran through the field, long grass rippling like waves against her legs. As she ran, her form faded into a red mist that spread, then took the shape of a ghostly dragon.

Then, in the blink of an eye, the mist solidified and a long, slender dragon the iridescent blues and greens of a peacock's tail leapt into the sky, her scales glittering like jewels in the bright sunlight. The great wings swept out and down, and Maurynna was aloft.

Raven tilted his head back and watched her as she spiraled up and up. When he got home he'd have to remember to tell Yarrow how incredible Maurynna looked flying against the pure blue sky.

A peal of laughter rang in his mind, and then Maurynna said, *Maybe Boreal and I should enter that match race, too. I wonder what we'll win.*

As he stood staring at her in openmouthed indignation, Maurynna rolled in the air, then flew due north. Laughter still echoed faintly in his mind.

"Of all the cheek!" Raven sputtered at her retreating form. "As if you have a chance in—"

He paused and thought for a long, long moment. Maurynna was a *much* better rider these days. Then he grinned.

This was going to be fun.

About the Author

Joanne Bertin is the author of two previous novels, *The Last Dragonlord* and *Dragon and Phoenix*. She lives in Connecticut with her husband and young son. Learn more at www.sffworld.com/author/44.html.